Brenna could feel his hot lips against her skin where the nightgown tied at the bodice. She could feel his warm, wet kisses on her flesh, evoking sensations that reminded her of another time, another place. She didn't know when he let go of her hands and reached up to slide the gown off her shoulders. She didn't know when he laid her gently back in the curve of his arm and began kissing her mouth, those slow, hot kisses that melted her soul and made her pliable and warm beneath him.

Oh, how the memories flooded back over her and seemed to intensify as he pushed the nightgown impatiently down past her hips, until she was naked on the bed with nothing between them but his own clothing.

Her breath came in a long sigh and she cared for nothing, no one, but him. Surely, this was her heaven, her destiny—with this man, for there was no other to whom her body seemed so perfectly attuned. No one had ever made her feel so complete, so fulfilled as a woman. She groaned with the intensity of the passion that was overwhelming her and closed her eyes . . .

PALOMA

Theresa Conway

BALLANTINE BOOKS • NEW YORK

Library of Congress Catalog Card Number: 80-69251

ISBN 0-345-28706-1

Manufactured in the United States of America

First Edition: April 1981

For My Daughters, Amy and Katie
With All My Love

PART ONE

Ireland

1865–1873

Chapter One

THE May breeze blew warm and soft through the valley of the Slaney River in County Wexford. Atop a grassy knoll to the east, Tyrone Kildare sat astride a fine, black steed and surveyed the part of the valley that was his. He smiled to himself, his blue gaze fiery with pride as it lit upon the grand, whitewashed brick house he had built with his own strong hands. It was surely the finest house in all the county—excepting, of course, Sir William Markham's, manor house, eight miles up the road.

Kildare's seventy-five acres had spread to a hundred when two of Markham's rood farmers had sold out and moved to America ". . . to find peace and freedom," they had said. Kildare shook his head. There was no true peace and freedom anywhere in the world if one was poor and Irish.

Ah, but he'd done well, he thought to himself. He took off his hat to brush it against his strongly muscled thigh, and his smile broadened. He'd done damn well, although, as much as he did not like to admit it, with a little help from Sir William. The Englishman had arranged the loans and guaranteed them with his own money, when Kildare, returning from exile in France, had come to him for help.

It had taken nearly seven years to bring this day about, Kildare reflected, leaning forward in his saddle. Now he could kneel before his parents' graves with a free heart and pride of accomplishment. He had done well, not only with the land, but with the age-old business of his ancestors—horse breeding. Kildare's Farm was renowned throughout Ireland, aye, and even into England, for the fine quality of its horseflesh. Kildare was a man of his word, 'twas said, and he wouldn't ever be selling you a bad horse.

He put his hat back on his head—his hair had no gray in it despite his forty-five years—and he urged his horse into a gallop, thrilling as he always did to the feel of the strong equine flesh beneath him. How he loved the horses! But then his face lost its good humor, and a frown creased wrinkles around his eyes. Aye, he loved the horses, but it was the scourge of his heart that his only son, Dermot, did not love them as well.

Dermot was an odd boy, Kildare reflected, one not given to the loud, raucous outbursts of laughter or boiling explosions of anger that marked his father's stormy temperament. He was more like his mother—and yet, he was not even much like her. Had there ever been a time when Dermot had done something wild and heathenish— something that might have made his father whip him soundly, but would have brought them closer together? Kildare shook his head. Dermot was not the wild sort— certainly not like that young devil, Rory Adair, whose antics ranged from boyish teasing to serious breaches of good conduct.

Kildare shrugged and sighed. Had it been within his power, he would have shaped, molded, and pounded Dermot into an exact replica of himself, but it was no use. Dermot was a dreamer, a boy with his head in the clouds.

Kildare wondered briefly if it had been Father Kinahan who had put such idealism in the boy's mind. For five years, Father Kinahan had tutored Dermot and his two sisters, for, like many other Catholics, Kildare would not tolerate sending his children to the nondenominational public schools that comprised the school system in Ireland, a system set up by the British Parliament. Could the priest have instilled his own ideals into the boy's young mind? Kinahan was a zealous advocate of the priesthood, it was true, but Kildare didn't think, somehow, that Dermot wanted to be a priest. If he had expressed such a desire, wouldn't Nora have been just that proud, he thought fondly.

Dearest Nora, what would I have done without you? he asked himself in a rare moment of humility. Could I have survived the first year of bad crops and little money to pay the rent to Markham? He shook his head. Nora had, just by her presence, given him the courage to return from France to build his farm. She was a good woman, his little half-French wife, he thought. And his daughter, Deirdre, would one day be an exact replica of her. Prim, delicate Deirdre had very little of her father in her. She wasn't dreamy like her brother, but neither was she willing to soil her new satin slippers in the mud and manure of the horse barn.

Ah, not so, his own little Brenna. Kildare urged his horse down off the rolling knoll and back to his house, his chest puffing with pride at the thought of his middle child. Would to God she'd been firstborn and a boy— then his happiness would have been complete. For in Brenna were mixed the best qualities of both parents: tough, Irish stubbornness, pride, and a love of horses all of which her father had bequeathed her, and intelligence, spirit, and winning ways, which were her gifts from her mother. She was, Kildare thought, his best hope to continue the business he loved so well.

As he galloped closer to home, he could see the brick and stone barn—he had insisted on this construction to prevent the catastrophe of a fire—which housed both the horse stables and the living quarters of the groomsmen and stablehands. Those groomsmen who had families were given two-room cottages away from the main house. Kildare was a generous man with his employees.

From his vantage point as he rounded the corner of the barn, he could take in with one sweep of his eyes the out-buildings, and the house, a long, rectangular shaped, two-storied building of white-washed brick. In the foaling pasture, across from the yard, two new foals were standing on steadily stronger legs. With them was young Kevin Ryan, a smart lad of fifteen years, who had a sure way with horses. The other stablehands said he had the gift of a gentle hand with the fiercest of horses—"*cogar i gcluais an chapaill*" they would say in their native Gaelic when Kevin broke in a new horse. He was an orphan lad, and his kindness and gentle manners had won him the hearts of everyone at the house—including Brenna's Kildare noticed with a stir of anxiety as he spied the shining black hair of his middle child, bound in thick braids.

Brenna was leaning over the fence post, her cheeks with a rosy flush, as she begged Kevin to bring one of the foals closer so that she could pet its nose. "Oh, Kevin, do bring that smallest one over," she pleaded prettily, her long-fingered hands stretching out to touch it.

Kevin, who was as smitten by her wiles as her father, complied, leading the horse to stand quite docilely by the corral post.

"Oh, do you think Papa will be letting me name him?" she asked breathlessly, her slender, twelve-year-old body draped carelessly over the fence.

"Aye," Kevin said, laughing at her earnestness. "But 'tis a girl's name you'll be picking."

Brenna wrinkled her nose in agitation. "You'd not be teasing me, would you, Kevin? For if it's a girl, Papa said she'd be mine!" She stroked the velvety nose. "Oh, I would be ever so gentle with her, Kevin, and I already know how to ride well enough."

"Brenna!" Her father's voice made her turn her head quickly, then wave at his arrival.

"Papa! Oh, Papa, she's mine, isn't she? You said she'd be mine!"

"What now? What did I say?" Kildare blustered, glancing at the boy who flushed and dropped his eyes, then turned the filly around to join the other foal.

"Papa, Kevin already told me she was a girl, and you said . . ."

"Kevin told you that, did he now?" Kildare felt like glowering at the lad but caught himself, grinding down the sudden disappointment that he had not been the first to break the surprise to his daughter. He ruffled her hair in his usual gruff manner, waiting for the first rush of irritation to leave his voice.

"Oh, Papa, is she mine—can I be naming her?"

Kildare waited a moment longer to draw out her breathless anticipation, then nodded. "Aye, she's yours, Brenna, and a more likely-looking filly I've not seen in a long while. You'll do right by her, for in all truth, I shouldn't be giving her to you, but keeping her for a good brood mare. She's got good markings and her way looks gentle."

"Papa, don't tease me," the girl said softly, knowing her father's moods. "You know I'll do right by her." She clapped her hands as she looked back toward the small, black filly. "She's mine! I'll name her—I'll name her—" Her forehead wrinkled with her frown.

Kildare laughed and patted her shoulder. "You have all day and tomorrow to be naming her, minx."

"Minx! I'll name her Minx!" Brenna chortled, her deep-blue eyes, so like her father's, except for the purplish blue that bordered the irises, meeting his in triumph.

"Minx, it is then. But now I shall have to be finding another name for you, hoyden!" he laughed.

Brenna laughed too, tickled at her father's gay mood. She felt him wrap his strong arm about her, and, for the moment, both Minx and Kevin were forgotten as she luxuriated in this rare outward show of affection from her father. He walked with her to the side of the house where she could see her mother in conversation over the half-door with Mrs. Adair, the matron of the next farm. With quiet dread, Brenna let her eyes dart about in search of young Rory Adair, for if he had half a chance, he'd sneak up behind her and pull her braids. She clung to her father, her bastion of defense, but he pulled her hands gently from his coat as he went to greet the ladies.

"Good morning to you, Mrs. Adair," Kildare said politely, sweeping his hat off in a show of good humored bravura.

Maud Adair bridled and dimpled in like humor as she bobbed him a mock curtsey. *"Dia Dhuit,"* she said in Gaelic, then in English, "God be with you. And how is your health this fine day, Mr. Kildare?"

"Never better, ma'm. Nora, are we going to invite our neighbor in, or are you going to gossip all morning over the door?" His smile softened his words.

"Maud's about to be off, Tyrone. We were just making plans for the trip to the fair tomorrow."

"Fair?"

"The May Fair in Wexford," Nora continued. " 'Tis only fifteen miles distant, and you did promise the children they could go. Maud's offered to take us in her wagon, since her son, Rory, will be hiring himself out for work for the summer." She looked down at the top of the pine door. "I knew you wouldn't be going 'til the fall to be selling the horses."

"Aye, you're right." He turned to Maud Adair. " 'Tis very kind of you to be offering to take my family for me."

"Ach, you know Conor and I don't mind. We love to take the children with us, and Nora'll be good company for me while Conor's dickering at the stalls." She turned to pat Nora's hand companionably. "We'll be bringing the wagon over a little after dawn, seven of the clock, if you'll be ready by then."

Nora nodded. She waved as Maud Adair drove off in her two-wheeled cart, then turned to her husband. "Maud's a mite anxious about Rory's hiring himself out."

" 'Twill be good for the lad," Kildare murmured thoughtfully. "Maybe 'twill take some of the wildness out of him."

"He's not a bad boy," Nora replied. " 'Tis just that he's their only child and they spoil him a bit, that's all."

"Aye, I'm thinking 'twould do our Dermot some good to hire himself out at the fair." He rubbed his jawline.

6

" 'Tis no dishonor for people like us to let our children work—not for the money, of a certain, but for experience."

"Tyrone, you know that Dermot couldn't. . . ." Nora stopped herself as a dour look crossed her husband's face.

"Aye, damnit!" In a sudden burst of frustration, Kildare pounded his fist against the door. "Dermot is good for nothing—he doesn't even do his share of work around this farm, though God knows, 'tis little enough I ask of him." He glared at his wife as though daring her to refute his words. Then, with a snort of derision, he calmed his temper, and in a gentler tone asked her, "Do you deny that the lad's too soft?"

Nora shook her head. "He just cannot care for the horses as you do."

" 'Tis no excuse. He would care well enough if the food the horses put in his belly and the roof they put over his head were to disappear tomorrow. Aye, that he would." His large hand pulled carelessly through the thickness of his hair. "Do you think we've done a poor job in raising the lad, Nora?" Then, in answer to his own question, "By God, I've given him everything he could want—education, soft living, more than most boys his age have got in this country."

"Aye, 'tis true, you've given him—you've given all of us—more than we could possibly have wanted or needed."

"And this is how my only son repays me?" He glanced behind Nora into the large kitchen, whence came the smell of newly baked oaten bread. "Where is he now, Nora?"

Nora blanched and shook her head. "He left this morning after breakfast."

"Bah! Off on one of his dreamy walks again with his head in the clouds and only the growling of his belly to bring him home." He turned away in disgust and his stormy countenance lit upon Brenna's small, oval face staring up at him with confusion and concern.

Immediately, his eyes cleared, and he placed an unsteady hand on her head. "Aye, Brenna, you shouldn't be listening to your mother and me discussing your brother. 'Tis not seemly for your young ears to hear our arguments."

"But, Papa, Dermot can't help the way he is," she said softly, her blue eyes large and worried in her pale face. "He told me he was afraid of the horses—that he'd rather be walking on his own two legs than to rely on an animal for transpor—transpor—"

"Transportation," Nora interjected softly, watching the play of emotions on her husband's face.

"If he said that, then he shall have no mount to carry him to the fair tomorrow—nor will he be riding in the cart," Kildare said to his wife. "We'll see how his own two legs bide the fifteen miles to Wexford."

He pushed his way between the two females and into the kitchen, seating himself abruptly at the table. "I'll be wanting no talk of it now, but a taste of that oaten bread before lunch would be to my liking, Nora. My appetite's come over me with a vengeance."

Nora hurried to take the bread out of the pan, while Brenna skipped away from the house, back to the foaling pasture to see her new filly. She was aware of the tension between her father and her brother, and knew of the sorrow it caused her mother; but she couldn't understand why Dermot didn't love the horses as she and her papa did—or why he couldn't at least pretend to love them to keep her father from bursting into his rages. No, she did not understand her brother at all.

Her brooding thoughts of Dermot quickly evaporated when she saw Kevin Ryan leading her little Minx back into the barn for a currying. She skipped along the pasture fence and darted swiftly around the barn into the side door to meet him in the stall.

Before she had gone three steps inside, she tripped on a rake handle and fell face first into a mound of hay, which had been cleaned from the stalls only that morning. The smell of manure and horseflesh hit her full in the face and she coughed hysterically for a moment as she tried to regain her footing on the tamped mud of the barn floor.

"Ha! What's this, blackbird, did you not watch where you were going?" came a laughing voice from above her.

Brenna pushed herself up by her hands and stood for a moment, regaining her balance as she brushed pieces of straw and dirt out of her face and hair. She knew that hateful voice, and she turned her gaze upward to spy a boy of fourteen laughing down at her ignominy.

"Rory Adair—I hate you!" she gasped. "No doubt you put that rake there in my path."

"No doubt I did." His laughter rained down on her.

She looked around for something to toss up at him, and made a wish that he would fall down off the bale of straw and bash his head in. Her fingers trembling with anger, Brenna shook out her skirt and brushed at her blouse, deliberately ignoring Rory as he jumped down off the hay, swinging his hand around to catch one of her braids and jerking it painfully.

"Ohh!" Tears came to her eyes, but she twisted her head and her sharp fingernails scratched a long gash down his browned forearm, causing him to let go of her.

"Damn you, blackbird!" he cursed, making her start in surprise. She had never before heard anyone curse but her father, who, she always supposed, had a right to. "I'll hang you by your braids from the barn rafters, I will!"

With a squeal of terror, Brenna took to her heels, careening past the horses' stalls and bales of new hay, putting as much distance between herself and her tormentor as she could. She prayed to God that He would save her from Rory Adair's wrath.

Gasping with fear and short of breath, she made for Kevin Ryan, a few yards away, who watched her with surprise as he combed the new filly. Flinging her arms wide, she threw herself at him, huddling close as Rory drew up behind her.

"What's going on, Adair?" Kevin asked protectively, holding the sobbing Brenna against his chest.

Rory spat in derision, then wiped the back of his hand

across his mouth. "Aww, she's just a baby!" he said belligerently, his blue eyes twinkling at the thought of a scuffle with the other boy.

Kevin kept his arm around Brenna, ignoring Rory. "What did he do to you, little one?" he asked softly.

When Brenna sniffed and told him haltingly how Rory had deliberately made her trip, Adair sniggered derisively.

"Leave her alone, Adair, or I'll see you answer to Mr. Kildare for your tormenting of the lass," Kevin warned. "She's only a little girl, after all. You're much bigger than she is."

"Hah! She's a crybaby, that's what she is. I don't know why I bother with her. Blackbird, crybaby!" he taunted her.

Brenna held on tighter to Kevin's shirt, ignoring the other boy's bait as she kept her eyes screwed shut and pressed deeply into Kevin's chest. I'll not answer him, she thought desperately. Maybe he will go away. Please make him go away, she prayed.

Kevin could feel her shaking and all his protective instincts rose up to shelter her from the young bully. "Get out, Adair," he said slowly. "You've done your devil's work."

"Aww. Why methinks Mr. Ryan has a soft spot for the little blackbird," Rory jeered, seeing a surer target and a more satisfying one for his taunting. "Hah! You're sweet on the little miss prissy, I swear." He threw back his head and guffawed. "Why, you're a bigger baby than she is."

Kevin stiffened, but found himself held tightly by Brenna's slender arms. He glared at the other boy, who was taller and more muscular than himself. "I told you to be on your way," he repeated.

For a moment, the two boys sized each other up; the only sound in the barn was Brenna's sobbing. Then, with a shrug, Rory walked toward the big barn door. "Hell, 'tis not worth bruising my fists on the likes of you," he threw back. "Protecting a girl! Like as not, you don't know how to fight with your fists."

"Why, you big-mouthed—"

Kevin would have pushed Brenna aside and gone after the other boy, but she held him with all her strength. Rory was a strong fighter, tough and cocky, and she didn't want Kevin to get hurt because of her. She hated Rory Adair, hated him for his meanness and his arrogance. But her hatred for Rory was outweighed by her concern for Kevin—Kevin, who was one of her best friends, who didn't treat her like just a little girl, but talked to her about the horses as if she were grown-up.

"Kevin, can—can I watch you comb out the filly?" she asked quickly, hoping to divert the boy's interest from the other lad. "Will you show me how?"

Kevin, still smarting from Rory's accusations, turned to the girl with impatience. "I haven't the time to show you today. Have you nothing better to do than bother me while I work?"

He was sorry instantly as Brenna's large, blue eyes filled with tears. "Aw, I'm that sorry," he whispered, putting his rough hands on her shoulders. "Forgive me my cursed tongue, Brenna. That Rory Adair could take the sweetness out of a saint."

She sniffled and gazed up at him. "I'm sorry too, Kevin, for—everything," she said lamely, not sure why she should feel sorry, for she had done nothing wrong to Kevin, but she could see the hurt look in his brown eyes and wished she could erase it.

He grinned suddenly. "Why, it's forgotten already, my lady," he said in a cheery voice. He patted her shoulders awkwardly and turned back to combing the satiny smooth coat of the little foal. "You've got to be most careful when they're young like this," he instructed her quietly, working the curry comb through the hairs with sure, gentle strokes. "Here now, do you think you could do that?"

"I'll try, Kevin," Brenna answered seriously. Taking the comb as though she had just been given a precious gift, she began to work it over the foal's coat as he had shown her. After a few moments, she stopped. The horse was becoming fretful, and Brenna looked up at Kevin worried. "Have I hurt her?"

He laughed. "Not at all, but I do think that perhaps it's time to give her back to her mother for a feeding."

"She's just hungry then," Brenna breathed in relief.

"Aye, and so am I," Kevin said, his warm brown eyes crinkling with a smile beneath his thatch of auburn hair. "And you must be too. Go on with you now, for I'm sure 'tis time for your dinner."

"Oh, but I'm not hungry, Kevin," she protested. "Can't I stay and watch my filly?"

"Now, you can't be bothering her while she's feeding, she might not eat, if you do," Kevin warned her. "You wouldn't want her to get skinny, would you, lass?"

Brenna shook her head. "No."

"Aye, that's right, now." Kevin watched her slender figure as she skipped slowly out the barn door. Her thick black braids swayed behind her, bits of hay and straw still clinging to them. He felt a twinge of some feeling he couldn't name as she looked about quickly for sign of Rory Adair, for he might be waiting outside the barn to torment her.

After assuring herself that her tormentor was nowhere about, Brenna turned and waved to Kevin, catching his odd look as he watched her. She smiled, thinking that he too was worried about Rory lurking somewhere about.

"I don't see him," she called back to reassure him. "And thank you."

She scurried out quickly and skipped back to the kitchen, where smells of lunch wafted deliciously through the open half-door. She stopped a moment by the steps to rinse her hands in the barrel of water that was changed every day—one of the few chores her brother was given —before going in to seat herself at the table with her mother and father and younger sister. Deirdre.

"You're late," Deirdre announced. Her eleven-year-old face was a small replica of her mother's. She was dressed primly in a red skirt and blouse with a pristine white pinafore. Brenna had a devilish longing to rub her muddy feet against it to see if she could make her sister cry in one of her tempers, but she caught herself. That was just the sort of thing Rory Adair would do. She lowered her eyes, ashamed of her wicked thoughts.

"Brenna Kildare, there's straw and dirt and—something else—in your hair," her mother declared in amazement. "What in the world have you been about?"

"I was in the barn, currying the new filly Papa gave me."

"And do we curry our horses lying in the mud now, Brenna?" her father interrupted. His thick, black brows nearly touched in the middle of his forehead as he frowned at her.

"No, Papa. I—I fell into a bale of dirty straw." Brenna bit her lip nervously. She couldn't tell on Rory no matter how much she hated him, for tomorrow she would accompany him and his family to the fair, and if Rory found out that she'd tattled on him . . .

"Brenna, you'll go upstairs and wash up before you sit at this table with the rest of us," Nora put in quickly. Her nose wrinkled at the offensive odor beginning to permeate the room.

"You can eat with your brother, for I'll not be waiting another moment for the lad," Kildare said as he reached toward the middle of the table, where a basket, called a "kish," sat steaming over a pot of water to keep the potatoes within hot and juicy.

Nora placed bowls of hot, salted milk before him and Deirdre, in which they could dip their potatoes. Brenna's stomach grumbled suddenly, and with a burst of energy, she climbed up the stairs to the second floor, which had been divided into three bedrooms, one of which she shared with Deirdre.

The smell of the horses lingered in her nostrils as she stripped off her clothes and dumped them in a woven basket bound for the laundry. She stood in her underclothing, which consisted of a short-sleeved cotton vest and a pair of long drawers. Pouring water from a pitcher into a washpan, she scrubbed her arms and face vigorously. Then she unbraided her hair and washed it too, for the aroma was too strong for her mother not to notice.

Finally, she dressed in clean clothing and rebraided her hair, still wet and dripping down her back from her long pigtails, then put on her clean shoes, and hurried downstairs to find her brother, Dermot, awaiting her at the table.

"Heard you had a nasty fall," he commented, eyeing her nervously.

She nodded. "Aye, 'twas clumsy of me."

He shrugged. "I saw Rory Adair on the road back to the house."

She blushed and leaned towards him. "He told you?"

"Aye."

"Did you—did you thrash him for me?" she demanded, still in a whisper.

He looked at her as though she had just asked him to jump off a roof. "Rory's a fighter, Brenna. He'd have decked me in an instant."

Brenna frowned. "Aye!" she said emphatically and turned away in indignation.

Nora served them each a potato and a bowl of milk, along with a buttered farl of dippity, which was a bread made out of the ever-abundant potato. A cup of hot tea sweetened with honey made up the rest of their midday meal, for, although they were wealthy enough to eat as well as their English overlords, the Kildares stuck to the Old Irish tradition of a simple luncheon.

Brenna ate hungrily, despite her disgust at her brother's cowardice. She knew she was being unfair, for Rory was a born fighter, quick on his feet and sure with his fists, but Dermot was just too much of a dreamer. Her father said he walked with his head in the clouds, and Brenna found that an apt description. Dermot was so filled with poems and stories and ideas and goodness knew what else that there was no room left for knowing about fisticuffs.

"What were you doing this morning, Dermot?" Nora suddenly inquired. "Your father was looking for you." There was always a softness, a curious protectiveness when Nora talked to her son, as though to shield him from a world that thought him dull and odd.

He shrugged. "Nothing important, Mama."

"Well, then, if it wasn't important, why do it?" Brenna asked curiously.

"I mean, nothing important to anyone but me," he answered with a laugh.

"Well, I'd like to know," Nora continued, her eyes fixed on her son.

"I took a book of poems and sat down by the stream to memorize them," he sighed, then I tried to name the different kinds of butterflies I saw flitting about in the sunlight. I watched a colony of ants spend hours building a tiny fortress, then a great black beetle came along and destroyed all their work.

"How sad," Brenna commented, her chin in her hands.

"As soon as he'd left, they started building again," Dermot said.

"Is that all they do then, build and rebuild their fortresses?"

"Aye, that's all they do."

Brenna sighed. "Perhaps you should have been born an ant, Dermot."

He laughed uproariously at her suggestion "I could never have built a fortress," he chuckled.

"Oh, Dermot, what would you like to do?" Nora asked, seating herself next to him.

"I don't know yet, Mama. I'd like to write poetry, I think, or perhaps books." He shook his head. "Papa would disown me if I became a writer, now wouldn't he?"

Nora shook her head. "There's a place for everyone in this world," she said firmly. "No one can make you be something you're not, Dermot."

Chapter Two

BRENNA was already washed, dressed, and eager for breakfast. "You'd best be hurrying up, lazybones, or you'll find yourself left behind when the Adairs get here!" she cautioned her sister, who was still wiping the sleep from her eyes.

"Oh, I don't care if I go or not," Deirdre returned grumpily. "Who wants to sit in that broken-down old wagon anyway?—especially with the likes of Rory Adair!"

Brenna's feelings mirrored her sister's, but she was determined that Rory, wouldn't get the best of her today. After all, her mother would be there, and so would his parents. She jabbed her sister in the ribs with her forefinger as the latter turned around to go back to sleep.

"Get up, Deirdre, or you'll miss the fair! Think of all the shops filled with beautiful laces and gloves and trinkets!" That would rouse her sister, she thought, for Deirdre was overly fond of feminine trinkets; Brenna sometimes thought her prissy because of it.

Scrambling to her feet, Deirdre stomped over to the washbasin and splashed cold water over her face. Brenna helped her into a clean dress. The plain, serviceable braids that adorned Brenna's head would never do for Deirdre. She insisted on one long tail braided with a brightly colored ribbon to match her frock. The two hurried downstairs. Their father and mother were already up and about, as was Dermot, who seemed even more subdued than usual.

For breakfast they had fresh milk over oatmeal stirabout and hot tea to warm out the brisk chill of the May dawn. Nora poured some of the brew into a covered kettle, which would keep the liquid cool enough to provide refreshment for the hot, dusty journey home. Into a large canvas bag, she put sweet oaten bread made with ground almonds, raisins, and honey, and added a generous portion of fresh carrots, crabapples, and raspberries, which Brenna and she had gathered the previous afternoon in the meadow.

As Brenna quietly sipped her tea, her eyes went from her father's face to her brother's. She knew that the silence between them was forced and bitter. Perhaps they had quarreled after she and Deirdre had gone to bed last night. She couldn't help feeling sorry for Dermot; yet at the same time, she sympathized with her father, for she could understand his bitter disappointment that his own son would not follow in his footsteps.

For Brenna the most important thing in the world was horses. She would be content to spend the rest of her life raising little foals and helping to break in new riding mounts on the farm.

When all had breakfasted, the family put on their best shoes with sturdy leather soles and crossed themselves in front of the picture of the Holy Family, which was always positioned over the hearth.

The creaking wheels of the Adairs' wagon could be heard outside.

"I'll not sit next to Rory," Deirdre declared loudly as she picked up the skirt of her yellow frock to follow her mother outside.

Brenna followed, noticing with a quick sweep of her long-lashed eyes that Rory was seated behind his father—a good omen for Mr. Adair would surely be keeping a keen eye on his mischievous son. Brenna hitched up her vivid green muslin skirts and felt her father lift her high onto the straw-covered wagon bed. Returning Deirdre's grimace by saucily sticking out her tongue, she quickly, took the seat behind Mrs. Adair. Dermot sat between Rory and their mother, however, so Deirdre was free to join Brenna on her seat. The two sisters scowled at each other.

"Well, you'll not be starting out with such faces," their father boomed at them heartily. "I want to see you both smiling as you leave, or I'll make you stay."

Their lips formed into reluctant smiles, which were immediately replaced by sullen frowns when their father turned away. "You were just hoping I'd have to sit next to that horrible boy," Deirdre hissed.

"I was just hoping I wouldn't have to sit next to him," Brenna hissed back.

"Hush, girls. You'll be greeting Mr. and Mrs. Adair properly," Nora broke in.

"Good morning, Mrs. Adair, Mr. Adair," the girls spoke dutifully. And, at another nod from their mother, "Good morning, Rory."

Rory answered with a preoccupied mumble, and the older Adairs gushed warmly. As they got underway, Brenna relaxed and watched the pink and gray sky lighten slowly into vivid hues of lavender, blue, and yellow. The monotonous rocking of the wagon caused Deirdre to drift into a light sleep. Rory and Dermot exchanged a few stilted phrases, for they were so unalike in temperament that they had almost nothing to say to one another. It remained for Maud Adair and Nora to converse brightly about shopping lists and things to do at the fair.

Mr. Adair kept watch for superstitious dangers of the road: many were mentioned in Irish folklore, and Conor Adair knew them all. For instance, if they met a funeral on the way, he would get out and take three steps backwards to avoid bad luck. He had obviously sprinkled himself with holy water before setting out, for tiny pinpoints of wetness on the shoulders of his coat were still slowly drying in the morning sun. If he saw a red-haired woman on the road, he would turn the wagon toward home, for she would be a bad-luck omen. But if he saw a white button or a weasel, he could continue in good faith, for those were the luckiest signs for a journey.

Brenna searched among the trees and bushes for a weasel to lay Mr. Adair's fears to rest. As her eyes skimmed the earth, they came to rest on the wagon bed. To her surprise, she saw a walking stick laid out beneath Rory's feet—a stout blackthorn cane, which could be used in fights. She glanced up at Rory's face, wondering if he reckoned on walking home: then she remembered that he might not come home today at all. This was a hiring fair, and Rory would be hiring himself out to the highest bidder to make money for the summer.

Rory noticed Brenna's interest in the stick. "I plan to use it in the fights today," he boasted proudly flexing the broad muscles of his arms and shoulders. He was tall for his fourteen years, as tall as most eighteen-year-olds; and his shoulders were broader than many. He would, Brenna realized, make someone a fine hired hand, if he could curb his Irish temper and his insufferable arrogance.

"You're going to fight today?" Dermot asked politely. He was a little in awe of this lad who was so different than himself, who boasted those qualities which his own father prized.

"Sure," Rory responded cockily. "There'll be cudgels today at the fair, and the winners will receive a purse, a quite generous one, I'm sure."

"But you won't be needing the money, if you're hiring yourself out anyway," Deirdre said spitefully.

"Don't be a chippie. Money's money, and too much is never enough, eh, Dad?"

His father snorted. "Don't you be thinking about the fights. Your ma will have my hide if you go and get your nose broken."

Brenna sat back and studied Rory's face with interest. He might be called *handsome* with his twinkling blue eyes and thick brown hair, but for a moment it intrigued her to imagine him with a broken nose. Would it ruin his face forever, she wondered? He might not be so cocky with a broken nose.

"There'll be horse racing and hurling too, I hear," Rory went on enthusiastically. "Money for the winners all around!" He clapped Dermot hard on the back. "Do you think you'll be trying your luck?" he asked sarcastically.

Dermot turned bright red. "I might just be doing that," he said, shrugging off Rory's arm.

Nora patted her son's shoulder with a soothing hand. "Now, Dermot, you'll not be needing to prove yourself." She admonished Rory with a stern look. "This is a fair. It's to be enjoyed."

"Aye, that it is," Maud agreed, giving her own son a warning glance.

Brenna hated the patronizing look in Mrs. Adair's expression—as though there was something not quite right with Dermot Kildare, as though he was a boy who had to be handled gingerly. Why, the Adairs had not one fourth the prestige and power their own father had, she thought with growing irritation.

"If girls could enter, I'd beat anybody at the horse racing," she suddenly shot out, disregarding her mother's astonished look. "I could win easily over you, Rory Adair!" Her pale cheeks flushed rosy with anger.

"You're just a baby, blackbird," he laughed "You'd fall off and scrape your bottom—" He stopped at the horrified look he got from his mother.

"Hey now, lad," Mr. Adair interrupted quickly, "you'll be stopping that way of talking. That lass is a good rider —better than most. She'd leave most of them at the post, I'll warrant."

Risking a glance at his mother, Rory saw that she had calmed down visibly at her husband's words, so he refrained from voicing an opinion. Meanwhile, Nora, who had flushed scarlet at the boy's boldness, gave Brenna a stern look of reproach. The rest of the journey passed in silence.

Nearly two hours later, they could see the gay red flag waving atop a wide circus tent, set in the middle of a large, mown field that was used for the fairgrounds every year. Deirdre clapped her hands gleefully. "Mama, look at the stalls and shops! May I buy something pretty, Mama?" Her gray eyes entreated her mother guilefully; she was quite aware that she was the only one in good grace at the moment, and she fully expected to take advantage of it.

"Of course, sweeting," Nora agreed, relaxing at the triviality of the child's demands. "And, Brenna, you may buy something too."

"Thank you, Mama," Brenna murmured, wishing she could stomp on her sister's foot without being detected.

The grown-ups looked forward to the fair as an opportunity to gossip with friends and to browse through the merchants' canvas-covered stalls. Even from here, the tantalizing aroma of food wafted through the warming air. As they neared the *booreens,* out-of-the-way lanes that led through the maze of stalls, they could see white sheets spread over counters full of apples, gooseberries, plums, meat pies, oysters, and boiled periwinkles. Other counters carried fineries for the ladies—velvet gloves, lengths of bright ribbon, tinkling bells, laces, hand mirrors, and tortoise-shell hair combs—all of which drew an excited breath of delight from Deirdre.

Set back from the stalls were multicolored tents, where one could pause and drink a cup of tea while perusing wicker baskets and butter churns.

"Oh, Mama, look! A real merry-go-round!" Brenna gasped, watching the gay, wooden horses go round and round as a man pulled laboriously at a turning crank attached to the bottom of the wheel.

"Aye, I think I'll take a turn myself!" Maud Adair laughed delightedly.

Brenna could see, set apart from the main activities of the fair, a broad platform on which was a raised dais shaded by a canvas awning. The hiring platform, she guessed.

Rory had spotted it too. There was a belligerent look about him as though he might use the blackthorn stick to bash anyone over the head who might try to hire him.

Conor Adair pulled their wagon into a nearby pasture and tethered the horses where they could graze comfortably during the long day. The children jumped out and waited impatiently for their elders to come along. Rory, holding his stick tightly in one hand, soon disappeared into the crowd. Deirdre pulled her mother toward the nearest stall displaying bright little baubles, and the Adairs wandered off down one of the booreens to look over a display of household articles. Brenna smiled at Dermot and offered him her hand.

"Where shall we go first?" she asked.

He shrugged. "I'd like to take a little walk to stretch my legs after the long ride."

Brenna gazed longingly at the stalls, but she tempered her desire and offered to go along with her brother. Hand-in-hand they walked into the adjoining meadow where fields of daisies and violets dotted the verdant grass in a riotous quilt of color. Brenna stooped to gather some of the fragrant blossoms into the apron of her dress.

Dermot chased her, and she threw handfuls of daisies back at him. They collapsed laughing on the ground together. Brenna was surprised: she had never played so freely with her brother—had never really enjoyed being alone with him.

Dermot sat up in the grass, hugging his knees against his chest, biting absently at the stem of a violet. "You know, Brenna, it's hard not knowing what you want to be in life."

"I know what I want to be," she replied stoutly, making a daisy chain to put around her neck.

"What?" he asked her.

She started a little at the directness of his question. "Why, I want to live on the farm and raise horses—to be like Papa, I suppose."

"Do you think you can do that? I mean, do you think other people would deal with you as seriously in business matters as they do Papa?"

She shrugged. "You mean because I'm not a man?"

He nodded.

"I'll raise the best horses in Ireland. They'll have to accept me."

"How easy you make it sound." Dermot sighed. "But the world is not really so easy, Brenna."

"What do you mean? You don't want to raise horses and neither does Deirdre. So who is left to do it? I must carry on Papa's work, mustn't I?" The trusting expression in her blue eyes made her brother wince.

"Yes, you're right," he said finally. A twelve-year-old girl, he decided, was really too young to be told about the ugly harshness of the business world.

"I am glad you agree with me, Dermot," she sighed in relief. "If I didn't have the horses to think about, what else would there be?"

"Oh, there'd be history and geography and writing and reading and—"

"You sound like Father Kinahan," she accused, setting the daisies about her neck and working on another garland for her hair. "Ugh, let's not talk about him until after the summer is over, and he comes back to teach us our letters."

"Don't you want to be an educated young lady, Brenna?" he asked.

"What difference does it make whether or not I can speak French and Spanish and English and Gaelic? What difference does it make if I can write beautifully and know the seven continents and do sums? Why do I need to know these things, Dermot?" she asked softly. She dropped the daisies as she looked earnestly at her brother.

"Because—because you can become a woman of quality," he replied, uncertainly.

"Is that so very necessary, Dermot?"

"I don't know, Brenna. But I think that when you're older you may be glad you had Father Kinahan to teach you all those things that many other little girls your age will never have the chance to learn."

"Do you mean when I decide to marry?"

He laughed and pinched the tip of her tilted nose. "When *you* decide, is it?"

"Of course," she replied. "I shan't marry just anyone. He will have to be someone who likes horses, someone who is gentle, fair, and kind."

"Noble attributes," he said.

Brenna thought for a moment. "You're like that, Dermot," she pointed out, "except for liking horses."

"Oh, I could never measure up to the husband you've got picked out for yourself," he assured her with a smile. "Anyway, I don't think that you will pick your husband for those particular qualities, little sister."

"Oh, bother this talk of husbands anyway!" she cried in sudden exasperation. "Let's not talk about something so far away!"

"I'm fifteen and you're twelve. Some families betroth their children at eleven, you know."

"How awful," Brenna shivered. She could hardly imagine being promised to someone like Rory because of her parents' decision. "I'm glad Papa and Mama didn't do that to us, aren't you?"

"Yes," he agreed thoughtfully. At fifteen, Dermot had already begun to think a great deal about girls. He was restless and in need of a companion with whom he could talk and share his dreams.

This rare moment of comforting conversation with his sister would not likely be repeated. It would be nice, he conceded, to have someone to sit in a meadow like this with him and share his love for poetry and reading more often.

He could already sense the restlessness in his sister, the need to see and experience things she could taste, smell, and feel. He smiled at her with genuine understanding. "Why don't you go on and see what you can find for yourself at the stalls?" he suggested. "You'd better hurry, or Deirdre will have spent all your money as well as her own."

Brenna looked longingly at the fairgrounds, then back to her brother. She sensed that she couldn't fully understand him, and that saddened her. "I'll be glad to stay here with you, Dermot, if you want company," she offered.

He waved his hand. "No, you go on now and enjoy yourself. I'll be along in a moment or two. I want to walk a little further by myself."

She nodded and on a sudden impulse jumped up and threw her arms about her brother's neck to kiss him lightly on the cheek. "Don't be long," she admonished with a crooked smile. She skipped down the path they had made in the long meadow grass.

Dermot watched her braids swinging against the vivid green of her dress, then he stood up to walk and think and wonder why he wasn't as certain of his own future as his little sister was of hers.

The garland of daisies fell from Brenna's neck as she ran toward the stalls, searching through the crowds for her mother and sister. Perhaps, when she was older, she would remember those lazy moments in the field and her odd conversation with her brother, but now her head was filled with girlish, delightful things.

Her eyes caught a group of children laughing shrilly as they threw mudpies at wooden effigies set up in a tent. She stayed for a moment, laughing with them when a strong-armed lad hit one of the dolls smack in the middle of its grinning red mouth.

When she grew tired of watching, she turned and entered a long booreen searching for her sister and mother. Her mouth watered at the succulent smell of meat pies and boiled oysters. Catching a glimpse of Deirdre's bright yellow braided pigtail, she caught up with them breathlessly.

"Well. So here you are!" Nora exclaimed, brushing a fond hand across the girl's brow. "Where've you been?"

"With Dermot in the meadow," she answered, licking her lips as she spied the juicy pie that Deirdre was trying to stuff whole into her mouth. "May I have one, Mama? I'm ever so hungry."

Nora gave her a penny. "Go on and get you one, but don't wander off too far. I promised Deirdre I'd let her watch the magician at the green and blue tent. You come back that way and meet us."

Brenna nodded, cupped the penny in her palm, and started off. As she rounded the corner of the meat pie stall, she nearly tripped over a young girl seated on the ground, crying dismally. Brenna halted for a moment to inquire if the girl was lost. The girl glanced up. She looked older than Brenna had at first thought—perhaps Dermot's age.

"I'm not lost," the girl replied, a little embarrassed.

"But you were crying," Brenna pointed out.

"I wasn't really," the girl said as she quickly wiped her hands across her face.

Brenna decided that her help wasn't wanted and started to go on.

"You're off for something to eat then?" the girl asked with less impatience.

"Aye, to the pie stall."

"Oh—I wondered. They're very good pies, I'll warrant. I—I should like one myself. That is, if you've a penny to spare."

The request must have cost her dearly, Brenna thought, for all the girl's feigned indifference.

"I've only one penny, but if you're very hungry, I suppose I could give you half of my pie. My mama would give me another if I got hungry later." Brenna hesitated. "But where is your mother? Has she no penny for you?"

"My ma isn't here," the girl said in a low voice.

"You're alone, then?"

"Aye. I've come to be hired out for the summer. My ma's bad sick, and my dad left us without a word as to where he's gone." She cast an awkward glance at the younger girl. "I'm scared witless about the hiring, I don't mind telling you."

"I'm sorry. Come. Let's get a pie before they're all sold out," Brenna said quickly, wanting to be away from her. She didn't mind helping someone, but she hated to hear sad tidings when there was nothing to be done.

"You said your ma was here," the girl went on, after they had eaten. "Do you think you'd be needing a good serving wench? My name's Bernadette Kavanagh."

"No," Brenna shook her head, "I doubt it."

"Ach, now I didn't think so, you know." Bernadette said. She seemed loathe to part with Brenna's company. "I thank you for your kindness," she murmured in embarrassment.

A horn sounded at the other end of the fairgrounds, and the girl started. "I suppose that be the horn for the hiring," she said to herself. She gave Brenna a tired smile, then walked steadily through the milling crowd until she was out of sight.

Despite Brenna's youth, she was touched by the girl's lonely plight. If only she could have done something more for her. She hurried to find her mother and caught up with her at the magician's tent.

"Mama, the hiring is about to begin," she said.

"Aye, but we've no need to be watching that," Nora

replied, recalling the threat her husband had made about Dermot the day before.

"Rory will be hiring himself out."

"True enough, but you've no liking for the lad, I'm bound."

"Mama, could we be using some help on the farm?"

Nora looked at her daughter in surprise. "You'd be wanting me to hire out Rory when you know he'd be tormenting you all summer? I'd think you'd be glad to see him gone for a while."

"I don't mean Rory, Mama—but maybe a serving girl to help you in the kitchen?"

"With two healthy daughters of my own? Now, don't let me think you'll be wanting to get out of your share of the work this summer so you can go galloping off on your horse," she said quickly, as she turned to slap Deirdre's hand away from a sticky bonbon that someone had dropped on the ground.

"No, Mama, it's just that it seems sort of cruel some-how . . ."

"Brenna, there's no shame to it." Nora reddened at her own hypocrisy.

"All right, then, but you won't mind if I watch?"

Nora hesitated. "Go on, but don't you be coming back to me with sad eyes brimming tears onto those rosy cheeks." She patted both of them maternally, then turned her attention back to Deirdre.

Brenna dashed back toward the other end of the fair-grounds. The booming voice of the auctioneer reached her even over the din of the crowd as she neared the hiring platform. Trying to get as close as possible, she wiggled her way through the gathering crowd, until she stood just below the dais. She looked up to where the auctioneer was blaring out rules of the hiring and explaining group-ings.

Her blue eyes gazed at the small group of boys and girls until she spied the face of the girl she had seen cry-ing earlier. Between the delicate corn-colored braids, the girl's eyes remained stoic, and her mouth tightened into a thin line.

"Ah, now, here we have a likely looking scullery maid or kitchen helper," the auctioneer began, beckoning to the girl to step closer to him. "Bernadette Kavanagh, age fifteen, hiring herself out for the summer, so it is. May we start the bidding at five shillings wages a month, gentlemen?"

Someone behind Brenna granted the five shillings, then another voice called six. Suddenly, a hush went over the crowd as a third bid went up: eight shillings a month.

Brenna craned her neck to see from whence this last bid had come, and she gasped as she recognized the silver gray mutton chops and black silk hat of Sir William Markham. She knew now why the crowd was hushed, for it was seldom that a member of the British gentry deigned to stop at an Irish county fair. Even more seldom did one push into a crowd of commoners to bid for a servant. More usually they brought their own servants from England.

Brenna's eyes looked up to the small knoll where Sir William had left his carriage parked beneath a large tree. She gasped in awe at the fine trappings and the four horses—sleek, black beauties—that pulled it. A face in the window of the carriage caught her attention for a moment. She waved, thinking it was Markham's son, Benjamin, but when the solemnly interested face did not wave back in friendly recognition, she knew she had been wrong. As she quickly turned her eyes back to the hiring platform, her face blushed pink with embarrassment.

"That was eight shillings a month," the auctioneer said, lengthening the pause, before adding, "—sir."

Markham nodded, not at all perturbed by the suddenly hostile atmosphere in the crowd. But then, Brenna reflected, Sir William was not like most of the English "ton." Her father used to visit him on business, and she could remember the English gentleman seating her on his knee while his cook handed out hot gingerbread cookies. She had always liked Sir William and his son Benjamin, as did all of her family. In fact, her own mother had often remarked how sad it was that Sir William's wife had

29

died so young, for now Sir William was denied the comfort he was entitled to in his later years.

"Yes, that was correct—eight shillings a month wages for Mistress Kavanagh." Sir William smiled at no one in particular, while Bernadette dared to peep out at him through her lashes.

The auctioneer looked for other prospects, shrugged, and smote the board with his gavel. "You've hired yourself a first-class kitchen wench, then," he barked out. He jerked his head to the side. "You'll be paying the cashier and signing the papers there. She's not indentured to you, you know." This last remark was delivered under his breath.

Moving slowly with the aid of his elegant, gold-engraved walking cane, Markham tipped his hat politely to the women in the crowd. Despite his courtliness, the crowd gave him little courtesy. Some of the more belligerent lads even refused to move out of his path. To Brenna it seemed that time stood still for a moment. She held her breath. Surely they wouldn't start a row, she thought painfully as she watched Sir William wait quietly with a patient look written on his face.

"You've no right to hire the girl," one of the men said in a low, threatening voice.

"The auctioneer accepted my bid of wages," Sir William reminded him.

"You've no right," muttered the man again, determined to make something of the incident.

Brenna thought they would remain like that forever, a frozen tableau set in time without end, but a whoosh of air breezed past her ear, and in a blurring instant, she was surprised to see Rory Adair jumping down from the platform, brandishing his blackthorn stick.

"Eh, now, leave the old gentleman alone. He's a good one, is Sir William," Rory growled in the same belligerent tone as the other man.

The latter spat on the ground in a show of bravado. "Perhaps you'd be willing to fight to prove those words?" he threatened, winking at his comrades.

"Aye." Rory grinned, so that Brenna got the impres-

sion he had brought the blackthorn stick for that very
purpose. Perhaps he'd been hoping for a good fight all
day to relieve the tension inside of him because of this
hiring out business. For whatever reason, Rory Adair was
not one to back out of a fight.

Brenna watched anxiously as the crowd parted. They
were used to such goings-on among their menfolk, for
there were plenty of rowdy brawlers among them. The
hiring was forgotten as a small space was cleared, and the
two young men stripped off their shirts, spread their legs
apart, and balanced on the balls of their feet. Rory had
the advantage of height, but the other man was older,
perhaps twenty, and Brenna was surprised to feel concern for the headstrong boy who was forever teasing her.

Someone handed Rory's opponent a walking stick and
the two squared off, both grinning from ear to ear. They
were unconcerned with the reason for the fight, feeling
only exhilaration as they took each other's measure.

Brenna thought of running for Rory's father, but as she
turned her head to look for a way out of the crowd, she
caught sight of Conor Adair looking on with an air of
serious calm, which somehow irritated her. Didn't he
care that his son might come away from the fight with a
broken arm? Or at the very least a good ration of
bruises? She jerked her head back swiftly as the sound
of the two sticks cracking together rang through the air.
In a few minutes, the assailants were being cheered
lustily by the crowd, and the Englishman was forgotten.

Markham took advantage of their distraction to make
his way to the cashier and complete the transaction for
the serving girl. Then he turned to watch the two oppo-
nents; his graceful white hands were folded, one on top
of the other over the head of his walking cane.

He looked back casually toward his carriage and
waved his hand as though beckoning to someone. Brenna
sneaked a glance and saw that the face in Sir William's
carriage belonged to a boy of about fifteen years, who
was just now reaching the knoll. He clasped his hands
behind his back and leaned forward intently to watch
the fight.

Brenna let her eyes follow the boy covertly as he walked jauntily down the hill to join Sir William. He was a tall boy and muscular, like Rory, although his strength seemed more implied by the cool, dark, watchful eyes in his tanned face, than by bulging muscles. His superbly cut kerseymere coat fitted smoothly over a green, satin-striped waistcoat and dark trousers.

Brenna was instantly fascinated by the foreign good looks of the lad, although she did not consciously think of him as handsome. She still separated all boys into only two categories—brotherly friends or teasing bullies. Still, something in his aristocractic poise excited her.

As though he sensed Brenna's eyes on him, the stranger turned his elegant head and pierced her with a look of curiosity. She felt oddly ill-at-ease as her blue eyes locked with his. Then her gaze fell away in a resurgence of embarrassment that irritated her.

Who was the boy? she wondered, turning away from him. He must be a guest of Sir William's, for the nobleman entertained a constant flow of visitors from England and the Continent. For a moment she lost herself in her curiosity.

Meanwhile, Rory was getting the worst of it from his opponent, for Rory's stamina and youthful eagerness were outmatched by the other man's experience and cunning. Twice, he caught Rory from the blind side and cracked him hard on the shoulder. The second time, the skin split and blood dripped down Rory's arm. The sight caused a stir among the crowd.

"Now, see here, there's no good done in spilling blood," the auctioneer shouted, trying to be heard over the hubbub of cat calls and cheers.

Brenna covered her eyes as the older man's stick cracked Rory behind the knees, causing him to fall to the ground in a dazed instant of pain. She bit her lip, then turned to see Conor Adair watching painfully, but making no move to help his son. Finally, the other man stepped back and allowed Rory to get to his feet.

"So, have you had enough now?"

In answer, Rory leaped forward, swinging his staff high

and downward in a move that was so sudden and lightning quick that the other man was ill-prepared to stave off the attack. He barely got his arm up to take the brunt of the blow, and there was a sickening crack as the hard stick met bone. The man's arm fell limply at a grotesque angle, and a cry of pain issued from his open mouth.

" 'Tis enough I've had—now." Rory's chest heaved in labored breath as he watched the other man, cradling the injured arm, sink slowly to his knees. Rory turned towards the crowd, holding his stick high and grinning devilishly.

The auctioneer wiped his brow with a sodden handkerchief and called down to Rory to come back up on the platform and have his wounds attended to so he could be the next one hired.

Somehow Brenna wasn't surprised to see Sir William make his way over to the auctioneer and speak privately with him for a moment. He nodded towards the beaming Rory, who had caught sight of his father and was standing tall and proud despite his bruised and bleeding shoulder and legs. The auctioneer called him over, and the three of them—Rory, Sir William, and the auctioneer—huddled together and spoke in hushed tones.

Brenna watched Sir William lead Rory off the platform to stand beside the girl he had just hired. Curiously, she made her way to where they stood; Conor Adair also came up to join them.

"Your son has extraordinary strength and courage," Sir William said to Rory's father. "By God, he'll do well in the Queen's Army someday!" The Englishman beamed with nearly as much pride as Rory did.

Conor Adair looked anxiously from his son to Sir William. "Aye, sir, Rory is a headstrong lad. I'm always afraid he'll be getting himself into big trouble one day." Then he added with a timid gesture, "Are you hiring him, then, to work on your estate?"

"Yes, by God! I wouldn't miss the chance of having him in my employ. I think—aren't you the neighbor of Tyrone Kildare?"

"Aye, that I am, sir."

"Good, good! Kildare is a good man. I wager that any

neighbor of his is of the same stamp. I'll take your boy for the summer, Adair. We'll see if we can turn him into a soldier—or at least give him a start. He could study with my son, Benjamin—the perfect thing for him too. Young Ben needs a fencing partner, and he's but two or three years older than your lad." Markham almost rubbed his hands together in his excitement.

"You're being too kind," Conor Adair murmured, punching his hat nervously. He did not even look at his son, who was grimacing from the pain of his wounds.

Brenna, who was standing behind Conor Adair, took the opportunity to glance shyly at the strange boy who stood silently a few feet from Sir William. He and Rory had at first eyed each other with a mutual unease, but the foreigner had smiled graciously and bowed as though to show his appreciation of Rory's courage and stamina. When the boy's black eyes lit on Brenna's wide-eyed expression, she quickly looked down.

The crowd had tired of the brawling and now turned its attention back to the platform where another wench was drawing high bids. As Brenna turned to watch, she felt a hand on her shoulder and looked back at Conor Adair.

"Will you be going now, Brenna, and find Mrs. Adair for me and bring her back here? We'll be needing her to tend to Rory." His eyes were kindly, almost relieved, Brenna thought. "I'm thinking she'll be over by the jelly stand with your ma."

Brenna hurried away, glancing about for her mother and sister as she went up and down the booreens. She came to the jelly booth at last and found Mrs. Adair sharing a sample of strawberry preserves with her mother.

Nervously, Brenna told her story, clasping her hands in the pockets of her skirt as she did so.

"Ach, now, Rory's been fighting, and you say he's hurt bad?" Maud was pulling Brenna behind her as she barked out anxious questions about her son's well-being.

They arrived at the hiring area, with Nora and Deirdre following close behind, to find Rory standing cockily next to the serving girl, Bernadette Kavanagh. His blue eyes twinkled with familiar devilishness.

"Aye, now, we're to be hirelings together, so 'tis only right—" Brenna heard him saying just as Maud Adair puffed up beside him and threw her arms around him.

"Rory, son, thank the good Lord you're all right!" she sobbed. "Brenna talked as though you were nearly killed up here!"

Rory favored Brenna with a scowl. "Ach, she's naught but a baby, Ma!" He tried to shrug off his mother's protective arms, uncomfortably aware of Bernadette watching with a faint look of amusement. "I was only—"

"Mistress Adair, your son gave us all a fine show of vigor and courage," Sir William interrupted, stepping up quickly.

Maud Adair gaped at the Englishman before stammering an inaudible reply. Her eyes slid quickly over the tall, foreign-looking boy standing with him. She gave a quick, secretive look to her husband, who shrugged his shoulders and took to punching his battered hat again.

The silence thickened, and Brenna sidled unobtrusively next to her mother. Markham noticed her, and a smile broke out on his face.

"Mistress Kildare, it's good to see you, madam," he beamed, offering his hand as he made his way over to her. "These two are your daughters, of course." He winked conspiratorially at Brenna. "I thought I recognized you, lass."

Brenna smiled shyly as her mother curtseyed with a spritely show. Deirdre followed her mother's example with a childishly haughty glance that made the old gentleman smile.

" 'Tis a fine day for the fair," Nora said awkwardly.

"Yes, a fine day for me too," Markham answered, ignoring the discomfort of the other adults. "I've hired myself two worthy employees." He lifted his hand to signal his carriage. "Forgive my leaving so quickly, but I have other business to attend to before returning home. My respects to your husband, Mistress Kildare."

"You mean Rory Adair gets to ride in a real carriage!" Deirdre burst out petulantly.

"Hush!" Nora hissed, catching the girl by her shoulder.

35

Markham hustled his two charges ahead of him. He clasped one hand around the shoulders of the black-haired boy and promised Mrs. Adair that he would have his own personal physician see to Rory's wounds.

When the carriage had rolled away, Maud sighed. "Do you think my Rory'll be happy working for the Englishman?"

"Aye," Nora replied brusquely. "Rory will be treated fairly by him. You have no need to worry on that score. You might even see a change in the lad when he returns at the end of the summer." She looked around distractedly. "Now, I wonder where Dermot has gotten himself to?"

Brenna watched the carriage until it rolled out of view down the twisting turns of the narrow ribbon of road. She wondered again who the strange boy was and if she might see him again. Odd, how he had so impressed her, she thought. But he was, after all, a foreigner, and that made him fascinating. It relieved her, somehow, to have come up with a solution.

Chapter Three

BRENNA caught her lower lip between her teeth as she watched Kevin lead her little Minx slowly around the corral. The filly promised to be a beauty with her dark, satiny coat and proud bearing. Brenna was certain her father had secretly regretted many times that he had promised Minx to his daughter: how he would have loved such a horse for himself.

Brenna tossed her thick black braids carelessly. She was, after all, all of twelve years old, and she knew how to ride a horse better than anyone else on the farm, excepting Papa, of course. She would see that Minx was treated like the queen she was; and maybe, someday, she would let Papa breed her with one of the big, terrifying stallions.

Restlessly, she pulled away from the fence and scuffed her riding boots in the summer dust. September was almost here—six more days, she counted, only six. Father Kinahan had already returned from the seminary and was moving his belongings back into his old room off the kitchen. She sighed unconsciously. The summer had gone by too quickly.

"Hey, there!"

Brenna turned quickly to see a young girl of about her own age waving to her from the front of the house. The glare of the sun prevented her from discerning who it was, but eager for any new diversion on this hot, lazy day, she gamboled quickly towards the visitor.

"Maureen Derry!" she exclaimed when she had reached the shade of the porch. "What brings you here?" She wiped the sweat from her forehead and scratched at the itchy broadcloth of her riding coat.

"Brenna, for heaven's sake, aren't you ready to die in that thing?" Maureen asked, her hazel eyes looking the other girl up and down in disbelief.

"Aye, but Papa likes me to ride in the proper habit," she shrugged in explanation.

"Well, come upstairs and change. I've come over to invite you to a *mihul!*" she laughed merrily. "We're all going on a picnic to the bog bank, and you don't want to ruin your riding clothes."

"A *mihul!* It sounds heavenly!" Brenna clapped her hands gleefully. Neighbors usually went on a *mihul,* or picnic, when someone needed more turf for their hearth fire. It was a time for sharing duties as well as sharing food and diversion and might prove fun on a slow day like today.

"Mama! I'm going with Maureen to help cut the turf," she exclaimed breathlessly as she rounded the corner of the kitchen. She found her mother already packing a good supply of pantry items.

"I know, I know," Nora returned, laughing. "Deirdre wants to go too, so I'm charging you to be watching her."

"Oh, Mama, must I watch Deirdre?" Brenna said crossly. Tending to her sister meant that she would have little time herself.

"Aye, you'll watch her, or you'll not go, missy," Nora replied, her brows knitting in a frown. "It will give me time to catch up on my sewing. Your father's been grumbling at me these past few days to patch up that rent in his riding trousers." She gave her daughter a sideways glance. "Unless you'd rather be staying here to do my work so that I can accompany your sister to the *mihul.*"

Brenna shook her head quickly. "I'll watch her then," she said, "but just tell her to listen to me."

"That she will, or she'll not be going again," Nora promised.

Brenna, followed by Maureen, climbed upstairs to slip into the old brown cotton frock that she had always worn for turf-cutting. They found Deirdre already dressed in an impeccably clean pinafore, and both girls grinned conspiratorially.

"That should do nicely in the dirt," Maureen whispered to Brenna as they skipped downstairs.

The three girls hurried down the road towards the

Derry's farm, where neighbors and friends were going along to help cut the turf from the bog banks near Wexford harbor. It would be a merry afternoon. Brenna loved the coolness in the salty sea wind blowing in off the shore. She glanced up at the cloudless sky and picked up her skirts to run alongside Maureen until they had to wait for a tearful Deirdre who could not keep up with them.

"I'll tell Mama if you're mean to me," Deirdre called out.

"Tattler!" Brenna threw back at her, but she slowed to allow the smaller girl to catch up.

At the Derry farm, they bundled themselves into a little crowd of people in a wide wagon. Everyone was chattering and laughing, and someone started a song which was taken up by the rest of the group. Before long they came to the long strip of boggy marshland, which was checkered like a patchwork quilt from other turf cuttings.

The girls clambered out of the wagon. The men cut sods of turf, and the women brought them up to higher ground to be molded into irregular brick-like shapes and dried by sun and wind.

Someone called out to come to eat and everyone dropped what they were doing to hurry over to the cooking fire. Hot potatoes and corn cobs steamed in a kettle. Strips of salted meat were laid out on a small table, and pitchers of milk stood ready.

After lunch, Brenna looked about restlessly. She knew that if she and Maureen didn't do any more work on the turf today, they would not be chided. Children weren't forced to help carry the sod unless they wanted to, and generally, after the first few hours of work, they were allowed to wander off and play.

"What's to do now?" Brenna asked her friend as they sat on their haunches, playing idly with strands of wet grass.

Maureen stood up, stretched, and pointed to a hillock some yards away. "Yon' lies the cabin of a *pishogue*—a wise woman—named Siobhan. Many of the young girls visit her for charms and such. Would you like to go there?"

"Is she a witch, then?" Deirdre asked, her eyes growing round.

Maureen shrugged. "Are you afraid of witches?"

Deirdre shivered and nodded.

"Well, then, you'd best be staying here while Brenna and I venture over. We'll not be gone long."

Deirdre's face screwed up in a practiced pout. "You cannot leave me—"

"Then come along with us," Brenna said impatiently.

Deirdre held back. "No, if you're going to see a witch, I'd sooner be staying here."

The older girls sighed, then hurried over the rolling marshland towards the hillock beyond which lay the wise woman's cabin. As they topped the hill, Brenna spotted the small sod hut and was tempted to turn around and go back.

"'Tis really a cabin," she said in surprise. "I thought you were saying that only to keep Deirdre from coming with us."

Maureen laughed and shook her auburn curls. "You're scared, Brenna Kildare!" she taunted.

"Aye, of witches and ghosties, I am."

"Oh, pooh on that! Siobhan isn't a ghost. My own sister went to that cabin a few weeks ago to buy something for her pregnancy. She's been having terrible pains, and Siobhan gave her a potion to chase them away." Maureen nudged her friend with an elbow. "Come along with me, for I cannot go alone."

Brenna nodded weakly, though her knees suddenly felt weak, and she held Maureen's hand tightly as they ventured nearer to the cabin.

"Ought we to come up like this, so sudden," she asked.

"My sister says Siobhan's always at home. So many come to her that she makes her living selling charms and such." Maureen seemed confident enough, although her hand was sweating in Brenna's.

"What shall we ask her when we get there?"

"We'll ask her for potions to make us the loveliest girls in all of Ireland," Maureen answered dramatically. "And then we'll ask her for a love philter to give to some handsome young man when we're older so that he will marry us, and we will live happily ever after!"

Brenna looked skeptical, but she was determined to see this out bravely. "Shall we just up and knock on the door then?"

"Aye, though Mary says Siobhan always knows when someone's about outside her cabin."

As they came closer, the two girls could hear a strange and lovely singing accompanied by the strings of a zither. They ventured closer, their eyes locked on the door of the cabin. The singing stopped abruptly as Maureen tentatively raised her hand to knock.

"And what would you be wanting," a voice called out. It was sweet and melodious, not at all the ominous croak that Brenna had expected.

Maureen jabbed her in the ribs, and she spoke up quickly. "Only some conversation. We are Brenna Kildare and Maureen Derry up for the turf cutting."

"Aye, then, why aren't you about your work."

"We're tired," she answered truthfully.

"My sister, Mary Reynolds, came to you some weeks ago to get a medicine for the pains in her belly," Maureen added in explanation.

The door opened slowly to reveal a middle-aged woman with long, dark hair hanging down straight around her pale, oval face. Her eyes seemed dark and bright at the same time. She beckoned the girls in with a quirk of her long fingers.

"Come in then, children, and refresh yourselves for a moment. I am alone right now and am glad of your company."

Brenna followed Maureen inside, glancing around nervously as though she expected something to pop out at her from behind the door. The interior of the woman's hut was brightened by the sunlight streaming through two curtained windows. Brenna could see, half-hidden behind a cloth screen, shelves along the whole of one wall, holding all sorts of jars and crockery within which, she surmised, were the *pishogue*'s medicines. Beneath the shelves was a narrow wooden table and chairs, to which the woman was directing them.

At the opposite end of the one-room cottage was a bed and washstand. Brenna's gaze touched on the neatly swept floor of hard-packed clay, covered by a hearth rug close to the stone fireplace in the very center of the back wall, directly opposite the door. When they were seated at the low table, Brenna and Maureen watched silently as the *pishogue* poured tea into fragile china cups.

"Drink, children. It is a special herbal tea that renews one's strength and clears the mind of frustrations," Siobhan offered, smiling kindly at the girls' tight faces.

Brenna sipped experimentally; the brew was deliciously tart, like fresh mint. She drank the rest of it quickly, then sat back in her chair. She wondered what words of wisdom the woman might have for them. Her earlier nervousness had calmed, and now she felt more excited than frightened.

Siobhan watched her with a smile. "Are you aware, my child, of the six maidenly gifts?" she suddenly asked.

Brenna shook her head.

"Do not frown so," Siobhan reproved her. "The six maidenly gifts are these: beauty of person, beauty of voice, the gift of music, knowledge of fine needle work, the gift of wisdom and a virtuous chastity. So they have been handed down to our people from long ago. Do you possess all of these, and you will have your heart's desire."

Brenna was bewildered. "I have no heart's desire," she answered.

"I would like to marry a handsome man and live in a fine cottage when I grow up," Maureen blurted quickly.

"So you shall, my dear," Siobhan answered her, then turned once more to Brenna. "But have you nothing close to your heart?"

"I do love the horses," she said slowly.

Siobhan laughed in delight. "Ah, I loved them too before—" She lifted her skirt to show them a twisted foot. " 'Twas the result of an accident in my youth," she explained with an air of fragile sadness. She fixed her gaze intently on Brenna. "You cannot put all your love to the horses," the woman advised.

Brenna reddened. "I—I think of nothing else."

"The time will come," Siobhan said.

She sat down at the table and took up her zither. She stroked the strings absently, humming softly to herself until the two girls grew restless in their chairs.

"Why do they call you a *pishogue?*" Maureen asked curiously.

Siobhan shrugged. "Do you not think me so wise, then?" she asked with a bit of mirth tugging at her smile.

Maureen blushed.

"We should be getting back," Brenna interjected diplomatically, raising her brows at her friend. Then to the woman, "You have been very kind to offer us tea and conversation."

"Oh, but you have hardly stayed," the woman responded graciously. "Only a moment or two, and already you have better things to do than to keep company with a loose-tongued old woman."

There was an air of loneliness about Siobhan, and Brenna wondered why the woman was not married. "We cannot be away too long from the others," she said gently.

"You will come again?" Siobhan looked sharply at her.

Brenna started. "Perhaps."

"When we find the ones we shall choose for husbands," Maureen said, "we shall come back for love charms and childbirth potions."

Siobhan's laugh was sad. She began to play sweet, sad music, and her voice rose gracefully with the notes, lulling the two girls like a whispering breeze. Brenna thought it was the most beautiful singing she had ever heard and wished they could stay longer, but Deirdre would be waiting, and the others would be wanting to leave soon.

"Thank you, once again," she said as they stood to take their leave.

Siobhan nodded, but continued her song. After a moment's hesitation, the two girls walked quietly to the door to let themselves out.

"God grant you be happy as the flowers in May,"

Siobhan called out suddenly. "Health and long life to you!"

The girls closed the door behind them as she began to sing again.

"What a strange old woman," Maureen said as they made their way back to the picnic area.

"She wasn't as old as I would have thought," Brenna returned thoughtfully. "Do you think she's really a witch?"

"Aye. She seemed so kind but strange and—and distant."

"Lonely," Brenna agreed.

"Well, at the least, she told us we'd be having health and happiness and our heart's desire!"

"She only wished it for us, Maureen."

"Then we shall have to come back someday when we're married and pay her another visit," Maureen said matter-of-factly. " 'Tis always nice to be on the good side of a *pishogue*, you know. Mary says the fairies and the wee folk are always about trying to do mischief. One can't be too careful."

Brenna laughed and skipped ahead. "I see Deirdre waving to us. We'd best be hurrying."

"Did the witch cast a spell on you?" Deirdre wanted to know as they rode home in the jolting cart. "Did she try to put the evil eye upon you?"

Brenna laughed. "Mama will put the evil eye on you, Deirdre, when she sees how badly you've soiled your frock. You've streaked mud on your cheek too." She spit on a piece of her skirt and rubbed at her sister's face. "There now. You're not too much the worse for an afternoon's work."

Deirdre pouted. "Mama will make us wash before supper tonight."

"Aye, and it will be doing us both good." Brenna returned absently, thinking of the long walk home from the Derry farm. Perhaps they could persuade Maureen's father to bring them home in the cart. Otherwise they'd both be in bad tempers by the time they arrived home.

Unfortunately, the Derry prize cow was calving when

they returned, and the evening was beginning to close in.

"We'd best be off then," Brenna said to Deirdre. "Mama'll be wondering if we're not home before dark."

"Take the shortcut through the willows," Maureen advised. "It'll get you home twice as fast as the road." She giggled. "But watch out for the wee folk, Brenna, for they've been on our minds this day."

The reminder made Brenna uneasy, but she set out determinedly with a protesting Deirdre in tow. They followed the road until it turned southward, and began to cross the back meadow where a thick tangle of willows formed a natural windbreak for the crops. Twilight quickened and Brenna hurried her gait. They still had to cross their father's fields before their own farm would be in sight. The encounter with the wise woman had nurtured her superstitious nature, and she strained for the sound of wee footsteps behind them.

"Hurry up!" she hissed to her sister, who was lagging.

"I'm so tired already," Deirdre protested strongly. "We should have stayed the night with the Derry family."

Brenna didn't answer, for she thought she had heard sounds somewhere close by. Instinctively, she motioned for her sister to be quiet. The road lay to the left—was that horses' hoofs she had heard?

She swerved stealthily to the cover of some gooseberry bushes. God only knew what highwaymen were about. She wished she had thought to ask Dermot to come with them to the *mihul*, but he had been off somewhere as usual.

The two girls emerged from the willows and the cover of the bushes. This time Brenna was certain she heard horses. Her heart thumped faster. These were the sounds of flesh-and-blood, not the stuff that inhabited one's fantasies. She held tighter to Deirdre's hand and kept close to cover along the road and away from the flatness of her father's fields.

"Ho! Who goes about?"

The gruff voice startled her so that Brenna thought for a moment she would surely die of fright. She and Deirdre froze, both too frightened to move.

"Who goes there?" came another voice with a slight Dubliner's lilt.

Brenna screwed up her courage. "We be on our way back to the Kildare farm beyond the fields," she shouted back firmly. "We're in a terrible hurry as our father is awaiting us this very minute."

The bushes parted suddenly as a horseman made his way through. Despite the hot weather, his face was muffled, and his hat was pulled low over his eyes. "You say you're for the Kildare farm—well, then, so are we. Come and we'll give you a ride."

Brenna backed up and shook her head. "No, 'tis not necessary. We've come a way already."

"I insist," the man said in a commanding voice. "Twilight comes early, and 'tis no time for two children to be about by themselves."

Brenna could see that there was nothing for them to do but obey the man's orders. He could easily overpower them if he chose, and she didn't want him to see how frightened she was. If she could but keep him from sensing her fear, she felt the danger would be alayed.

"Then, we must thank you, sir," she answered stoutly, and jerked a trembling Deirdre forward. "But we must ask you to hurry, for our father will be very worried."

"Aye," the man answered. He whistled low, and another horseman came up behind him. "We'll take these two to Kildare's farm as we have business there anyway," he said softly. He reached down to scoop Brenna up into the saddle in front of him. Deirdre let out a wail of terror as the other man snatched her up.

"Hush, ninny!" Brenna scolded her. "These gentlemen will be taking us to Papa." Despite her brave words, she could only hope that the Kildare farm was their destination.

They joined three more horsemen on the road, and they were off at a lazy trot. Silence reigned among the group until Brenna could see the lights in her farmhouse.

"There it is!" she proclaimed loudly, holding her breath until they turned towards the house. She let out her breath in a huge explosion that caused the man behind her to laugh.

" 'Tis difficult to tame the proud," he said enigmatically. "We can only be hoping that your father will not be *too* difficult."

Brenna slipped off the horse as soon as the nameless rider brought it to a halt. Tyrone Kildare, who had heard the approaching horses, stepped out of the house to meet them.

"Children, your mother is awaiting you inside," he said sternly, watching as the horsemen dismounted. *"Dia's Muire dhuit,"* he greeted them in the Gaelic, which meant "God and Mary be with you."

"Dia's Muire agus Padraig dhuit," replied the leader, who stepped closer.

Kildare gazed at the other man. "Do you have need of shelter?"

The man shook his head slowly. "Tyrone Kildare, do you not remember me?" He pulled off his hat and pushed the scarf from his mouth.

Kildare stared at him in the weakening light. "No, I cannot recall ever knowing you," he said slowly.

"I remember when the two of us hobbled into the same leaky boat bound for France some seventeen years ago," the other replied evenly. "You were a patriot then, Kildare, and proud of it. You risked much to free our country from tyranny."

"James Stephens!"

"Aye, 'tis the same," the man said, pleased at the recognition. "I'm back from France, Kildare, for our work is not done. Ireland is not yet free." He hesitated and looked back at the other four riders. "Can we talk?"

"My family is just sitting down to eat," Kildare said uncertainly.

James Stephens sensed the uneasiness in the man and shook his head. "We must talk, Kildare, for we have important business with every Irishman who calls himself a patriot!"

Kildare sighed. "Come then, and bring your men inside. We've soup and blood pudding on the table. You're welcome to refresh yourselves." He called to one of the stable boys to take their horses, then led the men inside.

Nora, who had already heard a quick account of what had happened from her daughters, blanched when she saw her husband bringing in these menacing strangers. Kildare gave her a wary look to keep her silent.

"Set the table for five more, Nora," he said quickly. "We've company this night."

"Aye," she answered and went to the cupboard. Brenna and Deirdre watched round-eyed as the five men took stools around the table. Dermot stared at them curiously.

"You've a handsome family," Stephens said as he assessed the boy.

"Aye."

These were the only words spoken through dinner. The men were noisy, ravenous eaters, slurping their soup like cattle at a trough, but they made no conversation. After supper Nora ushered her daughters upstairs. Brenna squatted down behind the balustrade to listen.

"So, it's been seventeen long years," Stephens was saying conversationally. He looked around the kitchen. "You've done well for yourself, Kildare."

Kildare nodded shortly.

"Better than many," Stephens went on, lighting his pipe and leaning back to puff his smoke thoughtfully.

"Come, Stephens, get to the business that brought you here." Brenna could sense the impatience boiling within her father and feared that he might lose his temper.

"Our business is this," the man stated, leaning over the table. "The Young Irelanders are no longer active, but we've begun a new brotherhood. The Irish Republican Brotherhood." His words became more heated. "For too long, we've waited for action. Now the society of the Fenian brotherhood has decided to move!"

"The Fenians? I've heard of them," Kildare replied quietly, "and I want no part of them."

A temporary hush filled the kitchen as Kildare and Stephens stared at each other. "We favor the good of Ireland," Stephens finally said. "We want to make you proud to be an Irishman."

"I am proud of it," Kildare replied.

"Dammit, man! How can you say that when you're nothing more than a serf here!" Stephens pounded his fist on the table. "Join up with us, and you'll be part of the new revolution!"

Brenna heard the sudden squeal of a chair pushed back angrily as her father jumped to his feet. "I want no part of your revolution!" Kildare answered savagely. "I joined your last so-called revolution, and look where it got me—exiled from my own country, and afraid even to set foot in Ireland for ten long years!"

"You don't seem to be starving now," Stephens commented dryly, tapping his pipe on the table.

"Aye, that I'm not, and it's not because I put my faith in brotherhoods such as yours, James Stephens. I put my faith in the land and my horses, and no one can say I'm not proud to be an Irishman! No, I'll not join up again, when I have so much to lose. I have my family and my farm to think of, and I'll not be throwing it all away!"

The two men eyed each other warily. After a moment, Stephens signaled to his men, causing Kildare to stiffen in defense.

"I'll not force you to do anything against your will," Stephens said tightly. "But I'm warning you, Kildare: when the Fenians break the tyrant's hold on us, you'll not be sharing in the glories. Then you'd best think about your family and your precious horses—for you'll all be refugees again!"

"If you're threatening me—" Kildare began angrily.

Stephens shook his head. "'Tis no threat, Kildare. Call it a warning. We'll not tolerate a British toady—"

For a big man Tyrone Kildare was amazingly agile as he leapt over the table and caught the other man around the throat. "You'll choke back those words, Stephens, or you'll not be uttering another sound!" He looked up at the four men who had begun to inch forward menacingly. "Call off your dogs, Stephens, or I swear I'll break your goddamned neck!"

Stephens waved away the men as he looked up into the fierce blue of Kildare's eyes. "Jesus, man, you've gone crazy," he choked. "For God's sake, we're all Irishmen!"

Kildare released his hold on the man and glared at him. "I'll let no man call me a toady. I've worked honestly and hard to get this farm and to keep it!"

Stephens rubbed his throat, then held up his hand in a gesture of peace. "Aye, you're right, Kildare. 'Twas my disappointment that got the better of my tongue, man, but we need all the help we can get! Can you not remember how it was during the famine? It's still like that with many of our lads and their families." He could see the memories cross the other's face. "Some of them are still starving. The few that can leave are going in leaky boats to New York, but they're fools, the lot of them. The same fate awaits them there!"

Kildare heaved a sigh and crossed his arms. "I cannot join you, Stephens, in good faith," he finally said, causing the other man to drop his shoulders in defeat. "But I can promise you a portion of horses to help you in your cause."

Stephens looked up hopefully.

" 'Twill help your cause to have a supply of horses on hand, and 'tis the least I can do," he ended slowly, glancing at his son who had been following the conversation with unusual animation.

Stephens followed his gaze and his eyes, too, lit upon the boy. "Your son—would he be willing to join us?" he asked in one last attempt.

Kildare looked surprised at the idea, then shook his head with a touch of scorn. "You'll not have your rebel patriot in Dermot," he said. "He knows nothing of fighting. Only about reading and poetry does he care. He has no feel even for horse breeding."

"We have other poets and writers in our ranks," Stephens began in a needling tone. "Charles Kickham, Thomas Luby, John O'Leary all work on our new sheet, *The Irish People*. Good men they are too. No, Kildare, 'tis not only the fighter we need, but the dreamer and the talker as well!" His brightening eyes took in the boy. "What say you, lad?"

Kildare shook his head even more forcefully. "I say no, for the boy's too young."

Stephens shrugged. "Well, then, I'll be taking your offer of the horses, Kildare, and be glad of that. If the lad happens to be changing his mind, we'll be staying at Liam Flaherty's inn a few miles down the road." He gave a meaningful look to the boy, then shook Kildare's hand and signaled his men to follow him outside.

Kildare shook his head after the men had taken their leave. He glanced at his wife who had remained on a stool by the turf fire throughout the conversation.

"Go to bed, Dermot," Kildare said gruffly to his son. "Forget about the Fenians. No good will come of their revolution."

The boy looked up with tears in his eyes. "You're ashamed of me, aren't you, Papa?" he asked in a small voice.

Kildare started at the accusation, then flustered. " 'Tis not that I'm ashamed of you, lad," he said quickly. "You and I both know you'd make no rebel. Dear God, you'd get your fool head shot off while you were daydreaming—"

"Tyrone, you're shaming the lad even worse," Nora broke in, coming to her feet. She glanced at her son, but he would not meet his mother's eyes. "You go on up to bed, Dermot."

"Mama, I—"

"Do as your mother says, son!" Tyrone growled. "Jesus, what a night!" he sputtered to himself as he watched Dermot slowly take the stairs. Then he glanced at his wife. "Did you ask Brenna how they happened to meet up with those men?"

She shook her head, her eyes on Dermot's back. "You've been hard on that boy," she said.

"I didn't mean to hurt him."

"I know you didn't, Tyrone, but hurt he is. I can see it in the way he drags his feet."

"He's a good lad," Tyrone Kildare said uncertainly.

"He'll feel better in the morning."

Chapter Four

"It's been a week!" Nora cried, wringing her hands as she tried to keep the tears from spilling down her cheeks. "I know he's run after those men—I know it! You shamed him, Tyrone!" She turned to her husband who was seated morosely at the table. "You shamed a lad of fifteen. Now he's gone away to get himself killed!"

"Dammit, Nora," Kildare got up from the table. "You're blaming me for speaking the truth! The lad's probably just wandered off to sulk for a few days. He'll be back when his belly can't find anything to fill it."

Nora gave her husband a withering look. "If he doesn't come back, Tyrone Kildare, I'll never forgive you," she vowed.

Brenna had listened for nearly an hour to her parents' argument. Finally, she decided it was safe to come downstairs. She took the steps quietly. Deirdre followed.

"Brenna, Deirdre, you'd best be getting something to eat before you start your lessons. You'll not get out of them today!" Nora said as she caught her daughters trying to sneak out the door. She had brought her anger under control and was mixing the oatmeal with a furious stroke.

Both girls turned and sat obediently at the table. This was no time to confront or contradict their mother. Tyrone frowned at their quiet faces.

"I suppose now you two will be blaming me for sending your brother out to his death," he challenged them.

Brenna looked candidly at her father. "No, Papa," she answered. " 'Twas his own choice to go, wasn't it?"

Kildare sat back, a pleased smile on his face. "Aye, 'twas his choice, though your mother seems to be forgetting that."

"But, Papa, I can't imagine quiet Dermot as a soldier," Brenna went on, encouraged by her father's smile.

That smile quickly disappeared, and he shrugged wearily. "Aye, lass," he agreed heavily. "But we'll wait to see if he comes home when he's had enough of rebel politics."

"I cannot be thinking of Dermot now," he continued, more to himself than to anyone else at the table. "Sir William has asked that I meet with him here, today— why, I've no idea, except that he'll be bringing a young lad with him, a guest of his who's been summering with him at Bath." He shook his head. "A young dandy from London, no doubt, who'll want to see how a real Irish horse farm is run. Damn!" he growled in exasperation, then silently ate his breakfast.

Brenna's interest had been pricked by her father's words. She recalled the young man she had seen with Sir William at the hiring fair in May. Could it be the same boy? No, she thought, 'twould be too much a coincidence.

After breakfast, Brenna went outside. The day promised to be a scorcher. Father Kinahan would not be giving them their lessons this morning. He had been called away the previous night to administer last rites and keep vigil by the bed of a dying man a few miles away. Her mother had forgotten, and Brenna had thought it best not to enlighten her. She hadn't the heart to go and visit Minx or Kevin, so she scuffled aimlessly down the path that led to the stream. It was cool beneath the arch of trees that sheltered the dirt and gravel path. Close to the farm, the trees were well-spaced and the grass kept clipped, but as Brenna walked farther down the path toward the stream, the trees grew thicker with tangled underbrush in between. She continued carelessly down the path, thinking she might decide to take a quick swim when the sun climbed higher during mid-morning.

She hated to see her parents arguing. It would ruin the entire day. Papa would shout, and Mama would weep or accuse; supper would be late and she would have to tuck herself in bed. She blamed Dermot for causing it all. If only the silly lad had not gone off like that, thinking to be a soldier. Really, he was no more a soldier than she was! Now, Papa would have made a fine soldier, she thought, or perhaps Sir William or his son, Benjamin, or Rory Adair . . .

As though her thoughts had the power to conjure him up, she was suddenly tripped in her aimless path and almost fell flat on her face in the dusty earth. Catching her footing, she turned sideways to spy Rory, himself, laughing at her from behind a tree.

"Hey, there, blackbird, you'll be watching where you're going next time," he advised.

"No thanks to you, Rory Adair!" she sputtered angrily. "Now, go away and leave me alone!"

"Hah! 'Twould be my pleasure, blackbird, but I've nothing else to do with my time right now."

"I thought you'd be at Sir William's still," she put in wrathfully, "or did he kick you out when he returned from Bath?"

He laughed. "I see you're up on Sir William's whereabouts," he sneered. "But for your information, miss prissy, Old William and I have become great friends, now don't you know. And his son, Benji, and I likewise. I'm to be going the eight miles every day to learn along with Benjamin. Sir William's even promised me a horse, so I won't have to walk!"

Brenna wrinkled her nose at him. "I'll not be believing you, Rory. Why would Sir William do that for you?"

He shrugged. "'Tis not my nature to be worrying about the why," he answered disdainfully. "But I've heard old William telling his friends how happy he'd be to turn one of us heathen Irish into a regular fighting soldier for the Queen. Just think of it! Fighting in far-off places like India and Turkey."

"You talk too much!" Brenna huffed. "What about your own country. What about Ireland, then? You'll not be fighting for her?" This talk of fighting and war had reminded her sharply of the reason for her brother's disappearance.

Rory skipped along beside her, taking the opportunity to catch one of her braids and bring her around smartly. "Brenna Kildare, someday you'll be weeping your heart out over brave Rory Adair, who lost his life fighting in some faraway place you can't even pronounce." He tweaked her braid. "Ah, then you'll be regretting the way you treated me."

She tugged her braid out of his hand. "Go away!" She stuck her tongue out. "I'll be regretting nothing, Rory. You talk about courage and soldiering as though you know all about it, but my own brother—he—he—"

Rory leaned against a tree and watched the girl's face turn red, then white. "Eh? What's this about your brother. That milksop wouldn't know the right end of a gun, much less how to be a soldier."

"That's how much you know! He's gone off to join the Irish army!" she claimed with mixed feelings of pride and guilt.

"The *what!*" Rory laughed, holding his sides. "The Irish have no army, you little ninny. Just a pack of rascals, who, like children, play at rebelling against their English cousins—that's what Benjamin says!"

"Benjamin talks like an Englishman because he's one of them," Brenna said reasonably.

"But he's not the only one. Aye, you should hear the foreigner talk of soldiering and rebellions and fighting," Rory said. Excitement lit his eyes. "Why, in the land he's from, there's a whole passel of big-headed fools who sound like they've nothing better to do than to go at each other day after day to see which one will head up the government."

"It sounds barbaric!" Brenna shuddered. She eyed Rory sharply. "What foreigner is this."

"Sir William's guest, the one he took to Bath with him. Hah, I thought you were so up and up on what Sir William did this summer," he teased her. "I guess I've caught you there!"

"Oh, Rory," she began, then stopped herself. If she wanted to see if Rory's foreigner and the boy from last summer were one and the same, all she had to do was return to the farm, for hadn't her father said Sir William was to be along this morning. Impatiently, she turned around to make her way back.

"Where are you off to?"

"None of your business!" she snapped and ran along the path, leaving Rory to watch her in bewilderment.

She emerged from the shade of the thick trees on the far side of the corral in time to see Sir William's carriage drive up. Eagerly she dashed toward the farmhouse, as she saw her father come out from the shadow of the porch to greet the Englishman and his guest. Her excitement caused her to misjudge one of the rocks she had to jump over, and her toe caught in a crevice, bringing her down ignominiously to earth. Frantically, she tried to stop the tears of pain that welled up in her eyes.

A strong hand circled her arm and helped her to rise. "The senorita is all right?" a deep, resonant voice asked with a lilting foreign accent.

Brenna got to her feet, her face several shades of red as she stared up into the eyes of the boy she remembered from the hiring fair. She wished, at that moment, that she could suddenly turn into stone. She caught her breath in a loud, gasping sob and wrenched her arm from his grasp. Running as fast as she could to the safety of the house, she ignored her mother's startled face and went straight up to her own room.

Brenna threw herself on her bed and sobbed into the covers; she had been so embarrassed, so mortified to look ridiculous to the very person before whom she would have given anything to appear poised and calm. What a stupid little child he must think her! After nearly half an hour, her crying tapered to hiccoughing sobs, and finally to a silent staring at the wall, though now and then she shuddered with humiliation. Dear God, let him be gone soon, she prayed.

Nora climbed the stairs and stood at the entrance to her daughter's room, watching her anxiously. "What is it, child?" she asked gently.

Brenna started, then relaxed at sight of her mother's calm face. "Oh, Mama, I—I made such a fool of myself in front of Papa and Sir William and that other boy!"

Nora smiled. "Aye, that you did, daughter, but not because you fell down. You embarrassed yourself by shooting off like that and coming up here to hide yourself like a mouse in its hole." Nora sat on the edge of the bed, took her daughter's hand, surprised to feel the warmth of it. Anxiously, she put a cool palm on her forehead and found it hot to the touch with a light film of perspiration on it. "Perhaps there's more to it than that," she said to herself.

Brenna looked up at her mother listlessly. "Oh, Mama, when will I be a young lady?" she asked.

Nora nodded her head. "More than likely, you'll be one before you know it, and when you least expect it," she advised, searching her daughter's pale face. "There now, don't be thinking of it anymore," she went on. "You rest up here a little longer, and I'll call you down for lunch. Your papa is out riding with Sir William and his guest, Steven Castanedo. They won't be back for a long time, so you've no need to worry on that account any longer." Her mother left her alone.

Brenna lay quietly on the bed, her head beginning to ache horribly. In fact, after an hour, she felt as though at any moment she might vomit. Nausea made her insides churn, and a dull ache began in the pit of her stomach, which confused and frightened her. Dear Lord, was she going to die because of a little fall outside?

By the time her mother called up to her for lunch, Brenna was thoroughly convinced that she was the victim of some dread disease. Her whole body ached, especially her abdomen and lower back. She curled herself up into a ball and tightened convulsively at each cramping spasm. Her mother found her in that position a few minutes later.

"Merciful heavens, child! What's the matter!" Nora cried, alarmed at her daughter's white face and the pinched look of pain about her mouth as she clutched at her middle.

"I hurt, ach, I do hurt!" Brenna complained breathlessly.

Nora hurried downstairs to bring up cool water. "Now, you'd best be taking your clothes off and getting into bed.

I'll sponge you down. You look to be catching some fever."

Brenna undressed slowly down to her underclothing. Her mother gasped as though she had seen some diabolical pox creeping over her daughter's flesh.

After the first gasp of surprise, Nora relaxed enough to smile wanly. "Aye, Brenna, my darling, you've become a woman sooner than you thought."

"Mama?"

" 'Tis the shame of Eve you'll be having now—the monthly flow I've told you about. You've flowered, child," Nora went on awkwardly, recalling how her own mother had just as awkwardly made her aware of the changes in her body.

"Is—is there shame in it, Mama, truly?" Brenna asked, bewildered.

"Ach, no," Nora said stoutly, busily making a pad out of a clean white rag as she took out clean underclothing from the chest. " 'Tis only a saying among the womenfolk. It's said 'twas because of Eve's sin in tempting Adam that we're like unto having it." She sighed. Her daughter's face began to tremble. "Darling, there's no need to worry so."

"But, does this mean I can't run about and play and swim in the stream and fish with Dermot and ride the horses?" she uttered forlornly.

Nora laughed to set her fears at rest. "Why, no, sweeting, except on those days when you have your monthly time, you can be just the same little hoyden, as your papa calls you." She put her arm about the girl's frail shoulders. "This makes you—ah, it makes you special. It means you're coming to be a woman grown soon. And it—it means you'll be able to have children when you're wed."

"Will it happen to Deirdre then?" Brenna demanded jealously.

"Aye, and to your own daughter someday, and to your daughter's daughter," Nora said quietly. " 'Tis the lot of women." She looked sternly at Brenna and wagged her finger. "Now, 'tis no cause to be thinking you're truly ill because of this, but for today you'll be staying in bed, and I'll bring you up your supper on a tray." She indicated the water and fresh clothing. "Now, you'll be washing yourself, and I'll be up in a moment with something for you to eat."

"But tonight, when Papa returns, won't he wonder why?"

"I'll be speaking to your father this evening," Nora said lightly.

Brenna gasped. "Oh, no, Mama, you can't tell him!" she agonized. " 'Twould be shameful for him to know!" This new thing that had happened to her would be separating her from her childhood—would be changing her from the little girl her father had always loved. Would he look at her with new eyes, with an expression that said she wouldn't be his pet anymore? She closed her eyes and gulped loudly. She did not wish to see such a look on his face.

"He'll be knowing soon enough," Nora said, gazing with understanding at her. " 'Twill make him love you all the more," she promised, "knowing that his little girl is growing up. He'll be proud of you."

Brenna bit her lip in perplexity. Why was life so complicated? Why did growing up have to do such things to your body? It was true, she had begun to notice the soft tissue of her breasts forming small hillocks on her chest, but that discovery hadn't been nearly as drastic as this! Still, Mama seemed not to be overly worried. Perhaps she was right. Perhaps it wouldn't matter to Papa. Besides, she had said that Papa would be knowing it anyway.

Brenna gasped. If Papa knew, if it was apparent through some reasoning unclear to her, could Sir William know? And the foreign boy? Mama had called him Steven Castaneda—would he know why she didn't come downstairs from her bedroom? Once again, hot shame washed over her, and she nearly dissolved into tears.

"I'll be up shortly with a tray," Nora said as she left the room. "I'll expect you to be cleaned up and dressed in those clothes." She was brisk, efficient. It would be easier on the girl, in the long run, if her self-pity was not indulged. Treating such things sensibly was the only way.

Brenna dried away her fresh tears with a corner of her

sheet and did as her mother told her. She changed and crawled achingly into bed with the cover over her. Despite the heat of the day, her mother returned with hot soup and a buttered farl and water. She eyed the sheen of sweat on Brenna's face.

"I'd be advising you to go without the cover on a day like today," she said sensibly. " 'Twill only make you feel worse."

Brenna shook her head, clinging to the muslin sheet with determined hands. Nora sighed and shrugged, kissed her daughter on the forehead and left the tray for her.

It didn't make matters any better when Deirdre skipped into the room and watched her from a somber distance.

"Why are you staring so?" Brenna demanded harshly.

"Mama says you'll be keeping to your bed today," Deirdre answered. Curiosity strained from every pore. "She said you weren't really sick."

"That's right!" Brenna snapped, throwing off the covers with a sudden flurry. "Lord, but 'tis hot in here!"

"Aye, that's because it's hot outside," Deirdre said reasonably, unsure how to handle her sister's lying abed when she wasn't sick.

"I know that, silly."

Deirdre straightened. "Don't you be calling *me* silly," she advised in ruffled tones. "I saw you fall down this morning in front of everyone—"

Brenna gave her a dark look. "Aye, so I did, because I tripped on a rock. 'Twas an accident!"

"Mayhap, but you had the silliest look on your face when that boy helped you up. You looked like the Christmas goose when she knows she's about to get her head chopped off!" Deirdre laughed behind her hand.

Brenna reddened. "So, I looked like a goose, did I?" she said fiercely. "Well, you'll be the one who gets her head chopped off when I get out of bed!"

"Don't make such a row, Brenna. We've company downstairs," Deirdre warned and abruptly stopped her laughing.

"You mean Sir William and his guest?" Brenna asked in a hushed tone.

"Aye. Papa is speaking with Sir William about letting the boy stay at the farm to learn the horse breeding."

"What!"

"Aye," Deirdre nodded vigorously. "I shall hate it if he stays here."

Brenna swallowed and strained her ears for sounds of conversation from downstairs. Voices drifted up from the porch outside. "You say that that boy is to stay here on our farm!"

"Didn't I just say that very thing?" Deirdre asked in disgust. "Brenna, your sickness has addled your head."

Brenna disregarded her and hurried over to the window, her cramps forgotten as she leaned forward to catch some of the conversation. She could hear the tinkling of glasses as the three males drank—probably some of Papa's good Irish whiskey—as they talked.

"Well, I'd be pleased to have you, Steven, and that's the truth without a touch of the blarney," Kildare was saying pleasantly. "I'd like to hear more about this proposal of your father's. 'Twould be a good source of business for me, although I'd have to be working out the details of shipping the animals."

"Yes, sir," the boy answered politely. "My father would be most anxious that we come to mutually agreeable terms as soon as possible. When Sir William mentioned your re-knowned horse breeding, I felt it would be in my father's best interests to ally himself with you. Paloma, our estate in Argentina, needs good breeding lines to establish her stock. Most of the horses of the pampas are rangy and tough. There are no thoroughbreds." He laughed richly and Brenna felt an odd thrill go up her spine.

"We have the finest horses here on the farm," Kildare said proudly. " 'Tis glad I am that you'll be finding that out firsthand."

"The length of his stay will depend on the desires of Steven's father, Miguel Castaneda de la Cruz, and yourself, Kildare," Sir William broke in. "But a good year —or even two—would prove most beneficial, for that would give Steven the experience of two foaling seasons, and he could also learn from the selling end of it." Sir

William coughed delicately. "Naturally, I would like for Benjamin to learn something of it too."

"Aye, and glad I would be of having him," Kildare assured him.

Their voices drifted off as they moved down toward the barn, and Brenna had a chance to watch them walk away. The sun gleamed richly on the black hair of the boy as he moved with an agile grace alongside her father. It was hard to imagine that he was the same age as her brother. He spoke with an intelligence and ease that must have come from much travel and experience on the Continent and elsewhere. Brenna suddenly felt insignificant, and she moved back to her bed dispiritedly.

"Where will he sleep? In Dermot's bed, I wonder?" Deirdre asked in a complaining tone. "Will we have to be on our best behavior?"

Brenna shook her head. "I expect he won't be sleeping here all the time," she said thoughtfully. "His father and Sir William must be friends."

"Aye. Then let him stay with Sir William!" Deirdre said spitefully.

"Ach, you'll be bringing back my headache," Brenna said, eyeing her sister disagreeably.

Deirdre tossed her head back. "All right then, I shall leave you to it," she said tartly.

After she had gone, Brenna lay back on the pillow, the covers off her now. She silently mulled over this new diversion in her life and wrinkled her nose in mingled distaste and humor as she thought that Steven Castaneda de la Cruz and her "flowering," as her mother called it, had both come into her life at the same time.

Chapter Five

A month later, Brenna and Deirdre were ensconced in their chairs, their open writing tablets in front of them on polished tables. Father Kinahan droned on interminably about the geographical locations of the Western European countries.

Dermot had not been heard from yet, so the household had sunk into a state of bleak anxiety; but Tyrone had determined to continue on as before, still insisting they would hear from the prodigal son as soon as he tired of the haphazard conditions of a rebel's life. Thus, Father Kinahan would promptly begin the girls' lessons at eight o'clock every morning, finishing by lunchtime.

Deirdre yawned without restraint, and her face slumped in her hand as she fiddled her pen in boredom. She glanced over to her sister, who was staring out the window of the priest's small, bare room (which was divided by a screen to hide his personal living quarters from the small schoolroom) to the corral beyond.

"Brenna!" The priest looked at his charge with a slight frown and began to tap the end of his ruler against the polished oak of his desk. "Brenna, we would like your attention, if you please!" he said loudly. This was the fourth time today he had caught the girl staring out the window.

Brenna looked around guiltily, her cheeks stained with embarrassment. "I'm sorry," she murmured, gathering her fingers together in a tightly laced knot.

"What *is* so interesting outside, child?" the priest demanded.

"Nothing, Father," Brenna answered quickly—a bit too quickly for the priest, who had a most lively curiosity.

"Nonsense, child. Something has grabbed your attention by the ear throughout the entire morning." He sighed and moved his thin sixty-year-old body toward the window. "Come now, I should like to see what has taken you away from the richness of the Pyrenees, the grandeur of Paris and the serenity of Vienna." He chuckled to himself, then adjusted his spectacles to peer out the window.

What he saw was a black-haired, fifteen-year-old boy standing inside the corral, speaking with Kevin Ryan. Both boys were inspecting a nervous, dark foal that now and then shook its head in protest. The stranger spoke animatedly, drawing out the more reticent Kevin. It was hard to resist, Father Kinahan thought, the dazzling, white smile and the liveliness of those snapping, black eyes that seemed to flit about with ceaseless energy.

"Brenna," the priest spoke softly, gazing back to the girl who was eyeing her notebook with flaming cheeks.

"Father, I— I was not being rude," she answered with a swift rush of breath. "It was just that—well—Minx is my horse and I—I'm not liking those two handling her so!"

"I see," the priest returned thoughtfully. "But they wouldn't hurt her, child, you know that."

She hesitated a moment, then nodded. "Aye, Father."

"Is it sure you are 'tis the horse you're so interested in, child?" the priest probed with an anxious look.

Her deep blue eyes flicked upward, startled. "Aye, Father. She's mine," she ended fiercely.

The priest let out another small sigh. "Aye, she's yours, child, but it does no harm to let her flaunt her beauty before the lads," he said in a teasingly cajoling tone. "Now don't you be worrying about her. Let's be getting back to our lessons."

Despite the priest's admonition, Brenna could not help feeling an odd mixture of jealousy, anger, and admiration, which caused her to glance out one more time to the corral where the two boys were running their hands over the horse's satiny coat. She couldn't hear what they were saying, but she could easily guess that their remarks would be flattering about her Minx. She wished with a sudden thought that she could be out of the school-room, stifling and airless, and with the two lads. Even better, she thought, to be astride one of the older mares, riding swiftly along the road that circled her father's fields. She closed her eyes and began to daydream again.

"What is the capital of Portugal, Brenna?"

The girl opened her eyes, horrified at being caught in deliberate misconduct. She had not really heard the question and glanced toward her sister for help, but Deirdre looked at her blankly. Her sibling had not been listening either.

"Pardon me, Father?"

"Brenna, you were not listening!" the priest accused her impatiently. Heaven knew he could be doing his sick rounds and not standing here with all the impact of a statue on these two. He quickly crushed out the unpriestly thought and sighed once again, wiping his hand over his forehead. Perhaps, he thought, he would soon be granted his wish to do missionary work in Africa. " 'Tis going on midday," he said in a gentler voice. "Tomorrow, children, I will expect you to pay more attention. Otherwise . . ." He allowed the unspoken threat to linger in the air before dismissing them with a wave of his thin hand.

Both girls hurried from the room and upstairs to their own bedroom—Deirdre to add a white pinafore to the plain gray tabby that Father Kinahan preferred they wear to class as a uniform, and Brenna to change completely into her riding habit. Her reverie had whetted her fancy for a good, hard ride. Perhaps she would catch her father somewhere in the pastures. It would be nice to have a few moments alone with him, for it seemed that during these past few weeks Tyrone Kildare had been most taken up with all the questions and demands the "foreign" boy made on him: demands, it had to be admitted, that Kildare was most eager to address.

At twelve, Brenna could not understand the mixed emotions that seemed to overwhelm her at the sight of Steven Cruz. (They had shortened his name for their own ease.) He was, she admitted, much more polite than Rory Adair or any of the other boys she knew. In fact, he was quite reserved around her and kept his distance. Because she couldn't understand the reason for this reticence Brenna found herself resenting him. She was used to people who expressed themselves openly. She did not like the way the foreign boy seemed to want to exclude her. Though she didn't realize it, she was also jealous of her father's attachment to the boy. Her father had found in Steven the son he had always wanted—a boy who was eager to learn about horses, who admired the same things he did, who held promise of becoming the kind of man a father could be proud of.

While his affection for Steven increased, Brenna found herself being left out of her father's daily routine and she resented it deeply.

"Mama will be wanting you to help with the bread baking after lunch," Deirdre put in slyly, noting Brenna's change of costume.

Brenna shrugged. "You can help her, Deirdre. 'Tis nothing else you've got to do!"

"Ach! Now listen to you! I wonder that—"

But Brenna was already skipping downstairs, ignoring her sister with a determined air. She certainly didn't feel like baking bread in this heat! Aye, Mama'll let me be off for an hour or two, she thought hopefully.

"Ah, Brenna, I'm glad you're already in your riding clothes, sweetheart, for I've a mind to have you help me make some bread for Sir William today. You'll be riding it over for me now, won't you?"

Brenna's heart sank. No careless gallop in the fields today, but rather a slow canter over to Sir William's, where she would no doubt be invited to stay a "moment or two" and wind up wasting the whole of the day. Lord, and she didn't feel like meeting up with the likes of Rory Adair today!

"Mama, I thought that I might—"

"Aye?" Her mother looked at her questioningly, and Brenna could see the redness in her eyes. She had wept over Dermot this morning, as she had every morning since he had gone.

"Nothing, Mama," she sighed.

"That's my girl. Now take this apron and put it on as soon as you've eaten. I thought some nice, sweet oaten bread would be good and perhaps a little dippity, though I'm not sure Sir William is that partial to it, you know."

Avoiding Deirdre's sly look of victory, Brenna swallowed the lentil soup her mother had made, following it with a cool cup of milk and fresh gooseberries in cream. The gooseberries were for Steven Cruz's benefit, she knew, for rarely did her family eat dessert except on special occasions.

Brenna watched the boy from beneath her long, dark eyelashes, noting the way he used his utensils, his accomplished table conversation, the polite thank you he gave to her mother. He even used a square of linen to wipe his mouth after eating. She wished she could jump over the table and pour her soup down his collar when he suggested to her father that they ride over the south pasture lands that day.

"Aye, we've got three good mares close to birthing. Off-season births are usually harder than the spring ones," he commented, looking at the boy fondly. " 'Tis best if we bring the mares in now to keep an eye on them." The two of them stood up and strode out the door.

"Your father likes that boy," Nora said with a quiver of anxiety in her voice.

"Nasty lad!" Deirdre exclaimed. "He treats me like a baby most of the time."

"You are a baby!" Brenna interjected.

"Now, girls, you're both to be helping me today to get this bread baked," Nora said to avoid a quarrel. "There's no need to make the day hotter with angry words. The oven will heat up the air quite enough, thank you."

"We should be baking 'India bread' for that boy!" Brenna said angrily. India bread was the symbol of poverty, a reminder of the old days of the famine. It was a simple bread without the sweetness of the oaten bread and much harder, so hard that the poorer boys who took it to school used it to pelt any who would tease them on their way home.

"Brenna! You don't like Steven?" Nora's voice was stern, perhaps because she harbored the same jealousy herself.

"Mama, he will go home someday, won't he?" Brenna asked worriedly.

"Aye, he has his own father, you know," Nora answered. "But I can't help wondering what kind of man could let his own son go off for years like that to a far-away country." She seemed to be relieved to get her thoughts out in the open. She briskly set about making the dough for Brenna and Deirdre to knead with their strong, young fingers. They worked silently, so absorbed in their own thoughts that Deirdre stole as many of the raisins as she wanted from the oaten bread dough. After several hours, they had made a half dozen sweet loaves as well as some of the Boxty bread which could be divided into farls and dipped in salted milk.

" 'Tis getting on toward dinner, Brenna, so you'll not be dawdling at Sir William's. I don't want to find you've gotten stranded again in the darkness," Nora warned, remembering the last time Brenna had come home in the dark and whom she had brought with her.

Brenna could see the look of pain that crossed her mother's face. "I'll be most careful, Mama," she promised.

Nora wrapped the warm, sweet-smelling loaves in cloth and tied them in a bundle for Brenna to tie to her horse's saddle. She patted her daughter's shoulder, and Brenna hurried out to the stables to ask Kevin to saddle one of the mares for her. Her father and Steven were just coming in.

"Brenna, lass!" Her father picked her up and jovially swung her around. "Where are you off to, sweetheart?"

Ordinarily, Brenna would have enjoyed her father's attention, but she was too aware of the foreign boy standing close by to feel any real joy. "We've been baking bread, Papa," she said soberly. "I'm to take a few loaves to Sir William's house."

"Aye, that's good of your mother. But don't you think it's a mite late to be starting out, lass?"

She shook her head. "No, Papa. I can take care of myself," she said. Her sullenness was lost on her father.

"Aye, that you can, daughter, but still—"

"I would be most happy to escort Miss Kildare, sir," Steven said formally.

Both father and daughter stared at him. Then Tyrone let out a booming laugh. "Miss Kildare, is it now! My boy, you'll be calling her Brenna, or we'll not know who you're meaning, eh, daughter?"

"Aye, Papa," Brenna said with as much of a sneer as she could get away with.

The boy flushed, but he stood his ground. "The senorita should not be riding alone, sir."

Tyrone's laughter died away. "Brenna's as good as you are in the saddle, boy, mayhap a little better. She's been riding since before she could walk. You'll find it hard to keep up with her, lad."

Steven waited.

Finally, Kildare shrugged. "All right then, but don't say you weren't warned," he laughed and waved them off.

Brenna couldn't wait for Kevin to saddle her horse and give her a leg up. She had the most dreadful scowl on her face she could make. She was determined to leave the unwanted stranger as far behind as she could.

"Senorita—Brenna, wait!"

Brenna pretended not to hear and tossed her black braids willfully. She urged her horse out of the barn, down the lane leading to the main road, and then flicked the mare into a gallop. Let him try to keep up with me, she thought angrily. Just let him try! I'll show him—I'll show Papa! She realized there were tears on her cheeks, and she wiped them away in disgust. Why? Why couldn't she have been born a boy? Why couldn't she have been the son that her father wanted?

The doubts and fears and self-questioning of puberty crashed in on Brenna, and they seemed intensified with Dermot's disappearance and this stranger's theft of her father's trust and affection.

"Brenna!"

She heard him calling again, but disregarded his cry and narrowly missed sending herself and the mare toppling head over heels into a ditch. Badly shaken, she pulled the mare up and sprang down to check its fore-legs. Had she injured the horse, she would never have forgiven herself, for it was Minx's mother.

Steven reined up a few feet away, but Brenna refused to look up.

"Are you all right?" Steven asked, even now perfectly polite.

"Aye," she said shortly.

"You forgot the bread," he went on, showing her the sack he held.

She flushed at her own stupidity. How I hate him! she thought, snatching the bundle from him.

"Brenna, wait." His demeanor was calm, poised. "I'm sorry you don't like me."

Avoiding his eyes, she stood up to leave.

"Listen just a moment, please," he went on. "I know that you don't care for me. Neither does your sister—or your mother. If it were in my power, I would leave now, but my father wished for me to learn everything there is to know about horse breeding, and your father is the best teacher there is."

"It's getting dark. We'd best be off," she mumbled sullenly.

"I am not trying to set your father against you," he said, "though I know you think I am. I do not understand what has come between your brother and your father. I am not even told where your brother is—but wait . . ." He held up his hand to keep her from interrupting. "I do not care to know. It is not my business. All that I am here for is the horses. Your lives will go on after I have gone back to my own country. But can we not make my stay here more pleasant for all of us? You make it so hard for me to like you—"

"I don't want you to like me!" Brenna flung at him.

The boy bristled, and Brenna could see, to her secret amusement, that it was becoming more and more difficult for him to remain calm. It pleased her to know he had a temper.

"But it would be easier for everyone," he said, "if you and I could . . ."

"I don't want to make it easier," she shot back. "It was easier before you ever came here."

"All right then!" he exclaimed, vexed beyond politeness. "You may have it your way, senorita! You are obviously a child, and for a child, I do not even dismount my horse," he snorted sarcastically.

She wanted to jump at him, to scratch at his eyes, but something in those eyes stopped her, and suddenly, for no reason she could fathom, she wanted to weep.

Hastily, she turned to remount, struggling into the saddle alone. She would not ask for assistance, and he would not offer it. In silence, they rode down the dark road at a steady canter, wishing that somehow the words they had spoken in thoughtless anger could be taken back.

Chapter Six

MID-OCTOBER finally brought relief from the stifling temperatures of late summer. The trees turned color almost overnight, splashing bright reds, yellows and oranges among the evergreens. The creek water became too cold for swimming, and the evenings became chilly. Nora had the girls bring out the winter clothing and bedding from the great cedar chests in the attic.

Tyrone Kildare kept himself busy mending the roof and supervising repairs of outbuildings. New straw had to be baled and stored for the winter feedings, and grass seed was sown in the pastures to ensure that there would be enough fodder in the spring. Nora salted down meat that had been butchered by Conor Adair, and laid aside dried vegetables and bottled fruits, while Brenna and Deirdre gathered the last of the potatoes and placed them in large bins in the root cellar.

One cool day in late October, the family received news of Dermot.

"Mrs. Kildare." Sir William tipped his hat politely.

"Sir William," Nora returned, looking up from her basket of freshly laundered bedding, "I think Tyrone and Steven rode out early this morning towards the—"

"Excuse me, ma'm," Sir William broke in hastily, "I have had word of your son, Dermot."

Brenna, who was helping her mother, saw Nora's face whiten and her hands begin to tremble.

"You have news about Dermot? But—how?"

Sir William's face was grave; the faint scowl wrinkling his eyes frightened Brenna. She had never seen Sir William look so stern. Was Dermot dead, then? She shivered and moved closer to her mother.

"He's alive and in good health, madam, but it is my grave duty to inform you that he has been arrested by the British government for treasonous activities against

75

Her Majesty, Queen Victoria. Your son was involved with a Fenian newssheet, *The Irish People*, by name, madam. Have you knowledge of this?"

Nora shook her head sadly, bringing up the hem of her apron to wipe away the tears from her eyes. "No, no! I—we haven't heard from our son since early September, Sir William. I cannot believe that Dermot had treason in mind, if indeed he wrote for this newssheet."

Kindness replaced the stern look on Sir William's face. "Mrs. Kildare, I know that you and your husband are loyal patriots of your country." He held up his hand when she would have interrupted. "Yes, and I'm glad that you are, as long as your loyalty doesn't exceed the bounds of our laws. But I'm afraid your son, by allying himself with this disreputable gang of hooligans, has placed himself in grave danger."

"Sir William, please believe me. This all came about because his father shamed him in front of—"

The clatter of approaching horses made all three turn in the direction of the field. Kildare and Steven Cruz galloped toward them. Brenna felt a deep and sudden shame that the foreigner might learn all about this most private family matter. She wished desperately that Sir William would not speak of it until Steven had been dismissed.

"Sir William! Aye, and it's good to be seeing you this fine, crisp day!" Kildare shouted out in greeting. He sprang down from his horse and hurried to clasp the older man's hand, beckoning to Steven to follow him.

"Sir William, I didn't expect to see you today," Steven said warmly, extending his own hand. His dark eyes slipped briefly over the faces of Brenna and her mother. He could see Mrs. Kildare's grief and the curious resentment in Brenna's blue eyes as she glared at him.

"Kildare, I have some bad news for you," Sir William began in a sober tone.

Kildare glanced at his wife and daughter, then back to the Englishman. "It's about Dermot."

Sir William nodded. "Yes. He's been arrested, Kildare. The authorities in London got word of a Fenian conspiracy to launch a rebellion. The government immediately seized the Fenian newspaper, it's editors, and leading members of the Fenian party."

"But you don't imagine that Dermot—"

"He was in the building that housed the printing presses for the newssheet, Kildare. Circumstantial evidence, perhaps, but in the confusion and panic, he was arrested along with everyone else."

"My God, he's but fifteen years old!" Nora put in tearfully. "What harm can a boy of that age do?"

Kildare turned to his wife and gave her a quelling stare. "Nora, 'tis not good for you to question Sir William thus. I'm sure he's doing all that he can for our son." He turned back to the dour Englishman. "Is there anything that I can do?"

Sir William shook his head. "I must warn you that this whole Fenian brotherhood has made the English government rather nervous, Kildare. Anyone even remotely connected with it is dealt with most severely."

Nora let out a sorrowful wail, and sobbing wildly, threw her apron over her head. Kildare put an arm about her shoulders and turned a bleak face to Sir William.

" 'Tis all my fault, sir. The Fenians came here in September to enlist my aid in their cause. I refused to cooperate with them, and when they suggested that I send Dermot along, I—well, I shamed the boy in front of them. He was gone the next morning. 'Tis the truth, sir, as sure as I'm standing here!"

Sir William rubbed his forehead, scratched his mutton chops, then rubbed his forehead again. "God, Kildare, you know I don't like this anymore than you do. I'm not even sure I can lift your son out of prison."

"You've got to try, Sir William. You *know* Dermot isn't the kind of lad to be making himself a hero." Kildare was pleading now, and Brenna felt tears gathering in her eyes, as much for her father's humbling himself as for her brother's plight.

"I'll go to Dublin tomorrow morning and see what there is to be done," Sir William said wearily.

Nora took the apron from her head and stared imploringly at the man. "Tomorrow?" she echoed on a sob. "Our boy will be in that filthy hole another night?" She shuddered and looked to her husband.

"There's nothing for it, Nora," Kildare comforted her with an arm about her shoulders. "We've got to trust Sir William in this."

Sir William mounted his horse and shook his head as he looked down at the distraught family. His gaze fell on Steven Cruz, whose dark eyes burned with anger at this story of injustice. "Come with me, boy. I will show you the workings of English jurisprudence."

"Yes, sir," the boy replied and hurried to follow the older man.

Kildare watched the pair until they were out of sight, his shoulders sagging with the burden of guilt. " 'Tis my doing," he murmured to himself. " 'Tis because of me that Dermot was driven to do what he did. Ach, that I could take back that night!"

Nora, who was crying softly still, shook her head. "My son, my son," she whispered in a trembling voice.

Chapter Seven

THE dewy mists of early December had given way to light snow, and on Christmas Eve, the countryside around Wexford was blanketed in frosty white. The cold was brisk but not numbing, and Brenna and Deirdre were outside drawing pictures in the snow with long, trimmed sticks. Tonight, as the youngest daughter in the family, Deirdre had the important traditional duty of lighting the festive candles and placing one in the window to "light the path of the Holy Family," a task which made her feel very important.

In a little while, Mama would serve up a huge repast of roast chicken, ham, and gravies. Brenna could feel her mouth watering as she recalled the little tarts she had helped her mother bake from sweetened flour and blackberries. There would be plum pudding and all sorts of breads and vegetables too. Father Kinahan and the Adairs would all be there, and it would be a merry affair, to be sure, if only . . .

Brenna looked toward the road, her eyes squinting hard to see if any rider was approaching in the distance. Sir William had sent a message that on the strength of his word and a written promise that he would assume responsibility, he had at long last gotten Dermot released from jail. The Kildares had wanted to travel to Dublin to fetch their son home, but Sir William had insisted that they allow him to do so, as he would be returning to his estate for Christmas festivities.

It was nearly five o'clock now, and Brenna scanned the horizon anxiously, as she knew her mother must also be doing from the sitting room window.

"Do you really think that Dermot will come home?" Deirdre asked without concern as she drew the image of an angel in the snow.

"Of course he will come home, ninny!" Brenna said

79

with impatience. She eyed her sister with thinly disguised irritation. "Don't you want Dermot to come home, Deirdre?"

"Aye, I suppose 'twould be all right if it would make Mama stop crying in the mornings." She did not like to talk about her brother, so she quickly changed the subject to the thing nearest her heart. "Have you made me something pretty for a Christmas present, Brenna?"

Brenna shook her head. " 'Tis not for me to say. You'll be knowing soon enough!" Her bad humor fled as she winked at her sister.

Deirdre shrugged nonchalantly, although her gray eyes were eager. "Aye, 'twill be pretty—Mama said so." Then she pouted. "I don't see why we should have to make presents for Sir William and Benjamin and Steven."

Brenna sighed. She had thought the same thing. "Mama says it will be our way of thanking Sir William for everything he's done for Dermot."

"Shall we be going to their house then, tomorrow?"

"I suppose, although Sir William will most likely make us stay in the kitchen," Brenna giggled. She had never seen the whole of the inside of Sir William's magnificent manor house. Mama had always told her it wouldn't be right for them to be going in the front door. Brenna had never understood why this was so, but she had not bothered herself about it. It was probably a silly custom of the English.

"Oh, *m'anam le Dhia!*" Nora suddenly shouted, running out of the house, her face pink with excitement and joy. "My soul to God! Dermot! Dermot!"

Brenna and Deirdre turned to look at the road and saw a coach, with the Markham crest on its side, turning in to the farm. Nora didn't even take the time to look for her cloak, but her husband, who came right behind her, swirled it quickly around her shoulders. His own face was lightened with gladness.

The family gathered expectantly by the coach block as the driver reined up the horses, and the footman sprang down from the back of the coach to open the door. The steps were brought out, and Sir William stepped down, his creased face lined even more by a huge smile.

"A Christmas package for the Kildares!" he announced, stepping aside.

Dermot's brown hair, escaping from a knitted cap, and his gray eyes in a painfully thin and white face, peeked out. He was bundled up warmly, no doubt in one of Benjamin's coats, and looked nearly lost in the thick woolen outergarment.

Nora Kildare stifled a sob and held out her arms to her son. He nodded to her almost shyly, as though he were a stranger to them, then turned to his father, who was standing back from the others and manfully keeping the mistiness in his eyes from streaking his face. A painful moment followed as silence descended on the group.

"Welcome home, son!" Kildare finally got out and opened his big, strong arms.

The prodigal son had returned home at last.

Christmas Eve dinner was determinedly gay, despite the appalling change in Dermot's appearance. He was much thinner, and his face was haggard. He refused to speak of his experiences but there was a new maturity in the lines around his eyes and mouth that kept Nora in a state near tears.

The girls were quieter than the season warranted. Deirdre did not even fight over the last of the pudding, but offered it silently to her brother. The Adairs were subdued, and Rory left immediately after dinner as he had promised Benjamin Markham that they would go hunting in the wee hours of Christmas morning, despite his parents' displeasure at such an undertaking on the holiest day of the year.

When the presents were opened Dermot found himself with three woollen scarves, which drew a tired chuckle from him. "Thank you all," he said, his gray eyes on his mother and sisters. "I'm sorry that I've no presents for you."

" 'Tis nothing to be sorry about, Dermot," Nora assured him quickly. "We understand."

"Dermot, you're tired, son. You go on up to bed now, and we'll have a talk in the morning, if you're up to it," Tyrone said heavily as he patted his son on the shoulder.

Dermot breathed a relieved sigh and trudged upstairs.

"What's the matter with him?" Deirdre wanted to know, licking jelly from her fingers. "Why is he acting so odd, Papa?"

"You'll be remembering, Deirdre, that your brother has not had the most comfortable situation over the last few months," Tyrone said sternly. "He's been through a great deal, so we'll have to be patient with him."

"Will he ever be like he used to be, Papa?" Brenna asked.

Her father stared at her. "I cannot answer that, my girl," he said finally.

That night, the Adairs left earlier than usual, and the Kildares retired almost immediately, despite Deirdre's protests. Long groans and fervent denials could be heard coming from Dermot's room as he tossed and turned in his sleep; it was all Nora could do to keep from running to him.

"Leave the lad alone, Nora," Tyrone advised her softly. "He's suddenly become a man, I think, and he must deal with his memories alone."

Nora hung her head. She had truly lost her little boy, and in his place was a man with whom she was not yet familiar. "Aye, you're right; but be patient with me, husband, for 'twill be hard for me to hear his anguish."

" 'Twill be hard for us all," he answered back.

It was not easy for Brenna to fall asleep, listening to Dermot's cries, and when dawn came into her window, she heard the click of a door latch, then her brother's footsteps padding quietly downstairs. Curious, she quietly rose from her bed, threw a cloak around her nightgown, and softly descended the stairs. Her brother was sitting at the kitchen table, crying.

He looked up from his folded hands as he heard her

footsteps in the room. His eyes were reddened, and his face was distorted with weeping. "Brenna! What are you about, girl?" He said in a harsh, sobbing voice.

"I was worried about you, Dermot," she answered.

He laughed bitterly, "Aye, perhaps you should be," he answered, "for I'm not knowing what to do with myself."

Brenna took the chair nearest him. "Have you changed so very much, Dermot?" she asked earnestly.

"Aye, little sister. The prisons are not a pretty place to be cooling your heels. There's no air and no clean water to wash with—none even to drink. The food wouldnt be thrown to the dogs on a farm like ours. And the stink of it! Aye, I'll be smelling that foul odor in my nostrils for a long time to come." He looked at her warily. "But you'll not be finding it easy to understand, will you?"

Brenna, whose expression mirrored her distress, shook her head. "I'm sorry, Dermot. 'Tis sorry we all are. Papa blamed himself, and Mama blamed herself, and—"

"Did they cry over me?" Dermot demanded.

"Aye, buckets and buckets, especially Mama. But Papa was fair worried too. He was sorry he shamed you that night, truly sorry."

" 'Twould be grand to hear him say it," Dermot said bitterly.

"But you knew Papa didn't mean what he said."

Dermot shook his head. "Ah, now there be the crux of the matter, Brenna, for he did mean it. He's always been ashamed of me and unhappy because I've not taken to the horses. I still feel no warmth for the bloody animals." His hands closed into impotent fists. "If only I could make him understand and accept me for what I am!"

"Aye, then and what are you, Dermot Kildare?" Tyrone asked harshly from the doorway. His black hair was still mussed and his face unshaven.

Brother and sister swung around in surprise.

"Papa, I couldn't sleep, and I heard . . ." Brenna began.

"Go back to bed, Brenna. I'll be having a talk with your brother now."

Brenna obeyed, and a feeling of panic rose in her: they were sure to argue after she left the two alone. She listened for a moment at the top of the stairs; after awhile, she heard them open the door and go outside. Shivering and praying that Dermot wouldn't be made to leave again, she hurried into the room and the warmth of her bed.

Much later, she was awakened by Deirdre's noisy bustling around the room. Brenna hadn't even been aware when she had fallen asleep.

"What time is it?" she asked wearily through a huge yawn.

"Nearly ten o'clock. We're to be over to Sir William's before noon. Mama said to stir yourself."

"Where's Papa and—and Dermot?"

"Around somewhere," was the noncommittal reply. "Now hurry." She smoothed the candy-striped ribbon on a package. "Oh dear, do you think Sir William will like the stockings we've knitted for him?"

"Yes, I'm sure he will," Brenna answered absently. She struggled into a clean camisole and drawers, then searched under the chair for her stockings. Mama had said she could wear her good white silk ones instead of those tiresome dark woolens that she was used to. When she put them on, their soft slipperiness against her skin thrilled her.

She ducked her head into her Christmas dress, made of dark red linsey-woolsey. Of course, she wore only one petticoat beneath the full, round skirt—nothing like the highborn English ladies who would be visiting Sir William; they would dress in layers of frothy silk and taffeta, beneath which six or seven starched petticoats would cause a delicious rustling sound . . . Brenna caught herself up abruptly. What did she care about such furbelows and gewgaws. Lord, she was beginning to think like her frivolous little sister!

In recompense, she brushed her black hair very hard,

then divided it into two tight braids, which trailed over her shoulders and effectively ruined the grown-up look of her new dress.

Deirdre gave her sister a critical frown. "Ugh, you look horrid with those braids!" She patted her own thick tail of chestnut brown which had been looped cunningly around both ears and fastened with twin bows of mulberry red. "Why must you insist on looking so homely, Brenna?"

"Don't you be worrying about me, Deirdre," Brenna returned airily, although now she wished she hadn't been quite so severe with herself.

When Nora came in to check on them, she took one look at her eldest daughter and shook her head purposefully. "No, Brenna, you'll not be wearing braids today. 'Tis a holiday, and you should be looking festive!" She sat down on the chair, and with the help of Deirdre's box of pins, wound the braids in a double coronet and placed two gaily colored bows over Brenna's ears. She would have preferred arranging the silky thickness into spiral curls like those she herself was wearing on this special occasion, but there was no time to heat the iron again. She glanced critically once more at her daughters. They looked proper enough.

"Now, we'll just be waiting on your brother, then we'll be off," she said as they descended the stairs.

"Mama, I saw Papa and Dermot go out this morning—" Brenna began uncertainly. She did not want to bring her mother to tears.

"Aye, and returned a few moments ago," Nora replied, smiling tiredly. "They've been talking and I think—I hope —that our Dermot will be trying to forget all that he's been through and will be thinking about living normally again."

"'Tis proper in the Christmas Spirit," Brenna said softly and caught the warmth in her mother's eyes.

Dermot appeared shortly, dressed in the new clothes that his mother had steadily worked on all the weeks he had been gone. The trousers were made of fine brown wool and matched the long coat, which was only a little bit big in the shoulders. There was still an anxious look about him, but he managed to smile at his family, nodding to his father and kissing his mother and sisters.

They bundled into the wagon with its makeshift canvas cover. " 'Tis a coach you'll be having this time next year, Nora," Tyrone promised his wife tenderly, as he helped her in.

The eight-mile drive to Sir William's estate, Markham Hall, took nearly an hour on the snowy roads, and all the Kildares were glad when they finally came within sight of the manorhouse. As always, when she saw the magnificent three-storied house linked by curved colonnades to additional wings that housed servants' quarters and storage areas on either side, Brenna sighed with awe. The pink-bricked house, built in 1725 by an Italian architect who had embellished the colonnades with Italian marble columns, was breathtaking with the light frosting of snow to add to its beauty. The family could see the billowing smoke coming from the manor's chimneys and knew there would be roaring fires within the great house. Brenna rubbed her cold hands and blew into her cupped fingers, aware that her ears must be red as well as her nose, despite the woolen hood of her cloak. She wondered what the English ladies might wear to travel on such a day— perhaps a fox-lined satin cape, or a fine, strong broadcloth with a muff of squirrel or rabbit. She sighed and her breath escaped her lips in a cloud of vapor in the frosty air.

"Down we go," Kildare said as he helped each one out of the wagon. "Straight around to the back, for I've no idea how many guests Sir William might be entertaining."

"But didn't he invite us, Papa?" Brenna asked. She gazed at the polished oak front doors longingly.

"Aye, that he did, but we're still to be remembering our place," he chided her.

Carrying their packages in their arms the family trudged over the swept brick walk that circled around to the back of the sprawling pink brick country house. The warmth of the kitchens blasted them full in the face as they opened the door.

"Well, now, 'tis the Kildares!" cried Mrs. Longstreet, the Markham's cook. "Come in, come in, poor little chicks; your dear faces must be numb with the cold!" She ushered them inside the kitchen and made them sit down while she poured a generous portion of buttered rum for Tyrone and Nora and gave the children each a cup of hot chocolate.

"Aye, that's good, Mrs. Longstreet," Tyrone said, winking at the woman.

She blushed, for she privately thought Mr. Kildare one of the finest-looking men she'd ever seen—although the thought followed quickly, if somewhat guiltily, that Mrs. Kildare was a handsome woman too.

"Is Sir William entertaining?" he asked.

"Yes, he's in the front parlor with his guests now." She sat down, obviously in a gossipy mood. "He's having his nephew over, Sir Oliver Markham, and his family—a wife who's the biggest bag o'wind you're likely to meet, and four little ones, who could use a good switching each and every one! Then there's Sir William's brother Theodore, Oliver's father with his wife, Mary, and Mr. Quigley from London, and his dear mother. Of course, Benjamin's here with an acquaintance from Dublin. And there's Steven Cruz, poor lad; I can see he's homesick for his own family." She clucked sympathetically, then poured more rum into the Kildares' empty cups. "Sir William don't mind on the holidays," she said when Tyrone would have protested.

Brenna, who had been listening to the portly, iron-haired cook with a good deal of interest, grew sullen at the sympathetic remarks about Steven Cruz. 'Twas his own fault that he wasn't at home with his own family, she thought. Would that he were there instead of here!

"Oh, do let's sneak out through the hall and catch a peek at the visitors!" Deirdre whispered excitedly. She eyed the two kitchen maids dubiously. "Do you think they'll be watching us now?"

"We're not prisoners in the kitchen!" Brenna hissed back, but she was unsure of the wisdom in leaving their non-prison.

"Oh, we can't just sit here and listen to old Mrs. Longstreet all day. It's Christmas," Deirdre exclaimed grumpily. "Please, do let's go."

Brenna was about to shake her head when she caught the eye of one of the kitchen maids. The servant's corngolden hair and light blue eyes struck a memory in Brenna, and she frowned as she tried to puzzle out the identity. Then she had it! At the hiring fair, last May!

"Hello!" she called out from the table.

The girl started, then smiled shyly. "Why it's—it's—"

"Brenna Kildare," Brenna supplied helpfully. "And you're Bernadette."

"Bernadette Kavanagh," the girl said as she came forward shyly. "It's good to be seeing you again."

"But weren't you only to be here for the summer?" Brenna asked.

"Aye, but my ma died in August, and Sir William let me stay on with proper wages and room and board. 'Twas too good an offer for me to turn down."

"I'm sorry about your mother," Brenna replied soberly. She glanced at her sister, who was tugging at her sleeve. "Hush now, Deirdre, we can't be walking in as bold as you please!"

"What's this, what's this!" Mrs. Longstreet wanted to know, seeing the altercation beginning between the two sisters. "What's the matter, my lambs? Is it the pretty gowns you'll be wanting to see, Brenna, lass?"

Brenna flushed. "No, 'tis my sister who likes to gawk, Mrs. Longstreet," she said with irritation.

"Please, may we just go down as far as the hall and peek in the doorway?" Deirdre begged, looking her most innocent. "Just for a moment or two?"

Her pretty pleading melted the heart of the cook. "Why, of course, you can, sweeting. Bernadette will take you, eh, girl?" She looked at the kitchen maid with upraised brows.

"Aye, Mrs. Longstreet," she answered dutifully.

"And you go along too, Dermot, lad," Mrs. Longstreet went on, taking charge with her usual aplomb. She noticed the flush about the boy's cheeks and the way he had been staring at the gilt of Bernadette's hair. She smiled secretly, catching Nora's eye. " 'Twill do the boy good to be with the young people on such a caper," she said.

Nora laughed and nodded helplessly.

"Now, you go on—and if you're caught—" she paused for emphasis, "—why then, you just tell Sir William 'twas the cook who sent you to see if the food had run out!"

"Thank you, Mrs. Longstreet!" Deirdre whispered, catching her sister's hand. She wanted to be gone before the cantankerous cook changed her mind.

Dermot had opened his mouth to protest his going, then caught Bernadette's shy smile and was lost. He followed the girl and his sisters without a word.

Once in the long, dark hall that led from the kitchens to the main part of the house, Bernadette advised the others how to proceed.

"This leads into the dining room, then across the main foyer to the parlor on the other side. I'm hoping they've left the main doors open, or you'll not be seeing much," she whispered. She glanced at Dermot. "You're Brenna's brother, then?" She must have heard, through the servant's gossip, about his escapade.

"Aye," Dermot said tightly.

"Ah, it's a hero you are, then!" she said with awe in her voice. "I'm that proud to be meeting you."

Dermot, who had not expected such worship, had the grace to soften. "I—I'm glad to meet you, Bernadette Kavanagh," he answered.

She laughed softly. "Ach, but I didn't know how handsome you'd be—and so tall!" Bernadette was not an accomplished flirt, but there was an innate goodness in her, which had sensed the hurt in Dermot's withdrawn, temperament, and she sought to bring him out. Besides, she liked the look of him, if the truth be known.

Deirdre laughed at her brother's flushed cheeks. "You'll be embarrassing him, Bernadette," she confided. "He's such an old sourpuss!"

Dermot gave his sister a severe look. She chuckled, caught Brenna's hand, and hurried down the hall, leaving the young boy and girl to look shyly at each other. Brenna looked back once. She was surprised—and disturbed—to see her brother catch Bernadette's hand in his own.

"Ought we to be leaving them alone?" she questioned Deirdre.

The latter laughed. "Aye, for mayhap he'll be kissing her when we get back!"

Brenna was astonished. "How do you know that?"

Deirdre looked wise. "I've talked with Lucy Gallagher. She's told me all about such things."

"Deirdre! You'll not be thinking I'll believe that. What would Lucy know about it?"

Deirdre shrugged. "Oh, she knows—and has told me a lot more than you might guess. Of course, all you know is horses," she snorted in disgust, but at her sister's stricken look, she relented. "Well," she conceded, "maybe he won't be kissing her today, but it's plain to see he likes her. Don't you think it might be good for him?"

"Deirdre—I am astounded at you!"

"Oh, do let's go on, you slowpoke!" She was practically pulling her sister's dragging body along. "I simply must see the gowns and the jewels. Oh, wouldn't it be lovely if we were English and entitled to wear such things."

She would have chattered on, but they had reached the end of the hall. The dining room had already been cleared of the remains of a huge luncheon. It wouldn't be used again until supper, so they had no worries of being discovered by one of the guests. Only a few candles remained lit and the frosty sunshine outside streamed through the French windows.

"It looks like a bloody church!" Deirdre exclaimed, noting the stained glass panes in some of the windows and the rich deep brown of the banquet table. Even the walls were hung with portraits solemn-looking enough to be religious.

"Deirdre, for goodness sake! Must you speak so!" Brenna reprimanded her.

"Oh, hush. Don't be so prudish, Brenna!" Deirdre fumed impatiently. "Here's the door, let's slip out into the foyer. Ah, here we are! Aye look there! We can slip beneath the staircase and look out the other side right into the front parlor! Oh, Lord, can you hear that heavenly music!"

Brenna could hear it distinctly. A quintet of musicians was playing Christmas carols, and the room was vibrant with voices singing old songs. The girls scurried out of the dining room onto the richly-veined marble floor and slipped under the double staircase. The bannister was decorated with live evergreen boughs which filled the air with the scent of pine. Merry red bows had been placed in the boughs, and there was mistletoe hanging everywhere.

"Look! Oh, do look!" Deirdre squealed, for she had spotted in the center of the parlor an enormous fir tree decorated with sweetmeats, cookies, tiny white candles, red bows, and silvery ornaments. "What is it?"

" 'Tis a tree, of course," Brenna whispered calmly, although her eyes were round with delight. "Ach, and how beautiful it is!"

Everything in the room seemed to glow with warmth and joy, and Brenna tried hard not to compare it with the drabness of their own sitting room. After all, who ever heard of putting up a real tree right in the middle of your house and decorating it so! What foreign custom was this? They had always lit candles and laid pine boughs around the door, but nothing like this! It was all so very beautiful!

They could see people moving back and forth around the tree, exchanging gifts and pleasant banter. Sir William was seated across from their hiding place. Deirdre immediately pointed out the elegance of his starched linen jabot, and the luxury of his velvet coat, which seemed to be buttoned with real diamonds.

"Oh, look, Brenna! That must be his nephew! But, oh,

what a disagreeable-looking wife! Her hair is just much too—too—" Deirdre, the sophisticate, searched for words.

"There is a girl who looks to be about our age," Brenna pointed out as a porcelain doll skipped gaily around the room, back and forth in front of the door, trailing pieces of paper and ribbon behind her with careless abandon. She looked very fragile with moon silver hair and pale white skin. Brenna fingered a stray wisp of her own black hair, looked down at her own ivory skin —and sighed.

"She looks so—so clean!" Deirdre said, dismissing her abruptly. They couldn't see the other children, but they heard yells and cries and shouts, so the others must be younger than the girl they had seen.

Brenna looked behind her, out the other side of the staircase and through the open dining room doors. "I cannot see Dermot. Do you suppose that he has gotten himself lost?"

Deirdre shrugged. "He doesn't care about such things anyway. Our brother will probably never aspire to be anything more than he is."

Brenna thought her sister was being a bit unkind, but before she could make a tart comment, she saw Steven Cruz walk up to Sir William. The somber look in his dark eyes caused her to remember the cook's words about his homesickness. He did, indeed, look as though he weren't quite as jolly for the season as he should have been, she thought, but she suppressed the twinge of pity that welled up in her.

Both sisters cringed back against the staircase as Benjamin Markham swept out of the parlor, dragging a laughing girl behind him. Her laughter was as bright as a bell, and her cheeks flushed becomingly. Brenna thought her quite attractive.

Apparently, Benjamin did too, for as soon as they were out in the foyer, he whisked her to the side of the open door, and searching for a kiss, proceeded to press her up against the wall. The girl laughed low in her throat and pushed her hands up against his chest playfully.

"Benjamin Markham! Shame on you, you forward gentleman!" she breathed, still eluding his lips. "What should my dear mama think if you returned me to my home tomorrow a compromised woman?"

"Sheila," he said through a smile, "I don't give a damn what your dear mama might think tomorrow. Now come here, you tease, or I shall drag you underneath the mistletoe." He laughed boyishly. "Better yet, I might drag you beneath the staircase and—" He had turned to make good his threat, when his laughing blue eyes caught the movement of two frightened bodies.

"Good Lord! I say, Sheila, I think we have two little eavesdroppers here. I daresay your honor is quite compromised now, my dear." He was still in good humor but determined to find out who his unwelcome guests were. Leaving the girl's side for a moment, he bent down and dragged the two out by their arms.

"What's all this?" he asked, frowning.

"Oh, sir, we didn't mean any harm by watching. We —we only came to—to—" Brenna sputtered, gazing into the face of the seventeen-year-old with utter embarrassment.

"We came to see if the food had run out—the cook wanted to know!" Deirdre supplied.

Brenna gazed at her with relief.

"But you're the Kildare girls, aren't you?" Benjamin said. "Where are your parents?"

Brenna had recovered herself by now and faced him with a semblance of composure. "They are in the kitchen," she answered. "We have come to give Sir William our Christmas gifts. We've been waiting . . ." Her dark eyebrows arched upwards.

"By God, cheeky wenches, aren't you?" Benjamin laughed again. He gestured to his companion. "Sheila, dearest, come here and meet the daughters of one of my father's best tenants."

"Irish brats—Benjamin, love, you are picking them rather young, aren't you?" the girl said. Brenna was surprised by the meanness in the young woman.

"Sheila, watch that tongue and be civil, will you? These two have no claims on me—" he put a hand under each of their chins, "—yet!" he finished merrily. Brenna could smell a trace of whiskey on his breath. She recalled the day after the fair when he had been so drunk that he had been sick out in the yard. The thought made her giggle.

"Something funny?" Benjamin asked her, smiling broadly.

"Aye," Brenna laughed, not at all frightened now. "I was recalling the day you brought up your cud in the yard of our farm!" Deirdre joined in her laughter.

For a moment, Benjamin looked nonplussed, then his smile returned. "I suppose I should get your parents and have you in to see my father before you humiliate me any further in this lady's eyes," he said, glancing at Sheila. "Come on then. We're off to the kitchens to get the rest of the family."

"I'll be waiting in the parlor," his companion told him abruptly and swung her rustling taffeta skirt in a huff.

A few minutes later, a protesting Tyrone and Nora Kildare were hurried from the kitchens to the front parlor. When they came upon Dermot talking quietly and earnestly with Bernadette in the farthest corner of the dining room, Tyrone whispered in his wife's ear. "Ah, now, he seems to be enjoying himself," he said. "Leave him be."

So the Kildares were brought in to join the family gathering in the opulence of the front drawing room. Deirdre nearly fainted from the beauty of the rose and gold papered walls and the intricate plasterwork that decorated the ceiling. She had never seen anything so elegant as this room with its Oriental rugs and marble fireplace. Gold-framed oil paintings hung on the walls and velvet-cushioned furniture invited one to sink down into it. Her eyes shone at the splendor of the decorated tree and the mountain of packages beneath it. The Kildares placed their own small gifts with the others at Sir William's request.

"And how about a glass of mulled wine, Kildare, to celebrate the coming new year?" Sir William asked as he genially offered seats to the two adults. He was well aware of the stares from all his other guests. Only the Quigleys, mother and son, were considerate enough to introduce themselves. "Hang them all!" Sir William whispered to Kildare, and winked.

Whereupon, the Irishman accepted the wine and relaxed for a moment in the splendor of his overlord. Brenna and Deirdre seated themselves on stools, as close to the tree as they dared, gazing at it with awe. Deirdre even forgot to sigh over the beauty of the women's gowns; neither did she notice the bad manners of a prissy little girl about her own age who had stuck out her tongue when Deirdre's gaze passed over her.

"Have you never seen a Christmas tree?"

Brenna looked up to see Steven Cruz bending down beside her. Much to her discomfort, he sat cross-legged on the carpet next to her.

"No," she admitted. Her eagerness to know more must have shone on her face.

"It is a custom brought over from Germany," he explained as he watched her slender fingers laying quietly in her lap. "The Queen's consort, Prince Albert."

"You mean her husband," Deirdre interrupted.

"Yes, pardon me, senorita. Prince Albert brought the custom to England when he married Queen Victoria. The royal family set the fashion for Christmas trees, and now everyone in England has them. The English have brought the custom to your country, and I'm certain it will eventually become popular with the Irish." He laughed to himself. "Though they are a stubborn people!"

Brenna did not miss the slight dart, but she refrained from retorting. It was pleasant sitting here in this cheery, colorful room, gazing at the beautiful tree, and listening to this rich, vibrant voice talking; she did not want to ruin it all with sarcasm. There was barely a hint of an accent in Steven's speech, and she supposed it had been carefully erased during his travels on the Continent.

She was aware, suddenly, that he was looking at her,

not with the brotherly casualness she was used to from boys, but more intently, his eyes noting the different way her mother had fixed her hair, the way her gown fit her, noticing everything about her. There was a tingling feeling in her chest, and she wanted to smile, widely and openly, even to laugh. The feeling scared her for a moment, but the tingling left her to be replaced by an unreasoning anger at this foreign boy who could mix her up so. She wished she could tell him to move away from her. Why had she even bothered to make him embroidered handkerchiefs for Christmas? She hated him.

Sir William was thanking the Kildares for the stockings and the plum pudding Nora had made. He gave each of the girls a box of sweetmeats, wickedly luscious confections, which made them drool with anticipation. To Nora and Tyrone he handed a leather pouch, inside which one could hear the chink of heavy coins. After everyone had exchanged gifts, it was time to leave.

Brenna was surprised at her sharp disappointment as they left the house. She only half-listened to Deirdre's prattling about how stuffy Sir William's relatives had been and how wicked Benjamin had been for his behavior with his naughty companion.

Dermot was quiet and reflective; it was not hard to guess of whom he was thinking. Nora looked at her son and was thankful that he found someone to confide in. With two mugs of buttered rum and a cup of mulled wine in her, she felt sleepy and contented.

Brenna and Deirdre stayed awake in bed for hours, talking about the wonderful things they had seen at Sir William's. Deirdre clapped her hands and giggled, remembering how they had upset Benjamin's plans with his lady friend, although precisely what those plans might have been neither of the sisters was completely sure.

"Ah, what snooties those females were—all of them!" she complained. "Hah! Someday we'll be showing them something, eh, Brenna!"

"Aye, that we will," Brenna laughed, but she was remembering that tingling in her chest and how Steven Cruz had thanked her so gravely for his embroidered handkerchiefs. He had given both her and Deirdre lengths of ribbon for their hair—ribbon which Brenna swore to herself she would never wear.

"Ach, but that Benjamin is a handsome lad," Deirdre sighed. "I do think, Brenna, that someday I'll be marrying someone just like him." She yawned sleepily.

Brenna laughed indulgently and told her sister to go to sleep.

Chapter Eight

AFTER the Christmas holidays, the household settled down into the regular winter routine.

Besides their morning lessons with Father Kinahan, Deirdre and Brenna were instructed in the arts of the spindle and loom, while from their mother they learned informally how to sew up torn hems and sleeves, how to bake bread, and how to cook. Father Kinahan, trying to help Dermot catch up, took a special delight in the lad's eagerness to read anything he could get his hands on. It was a busy time.

Benjamin Markham had returned to school in England, taking Steven Cruz with him, and Sir William had closed up his estate until spring, when he would return from his wintering quarters in London.

Brenna passed her thirteenth birthday in late February, and three weeks later, Deirdre turned twelve. In mid-April Dermot would be sixteen. Nora would sometimes sigh and hold back motherly tears as she wondered and hoped and prayed for her children as she watched them all sitting together in the kitchen—Dermot, straining his eyes over his lessons from the light of the paraffin wall lamp; Brenna, wiping dry the gleaming blue-willow-patterned dishes after dinner, and Deirdre, disinterestedly pounding the beetle into the corn meal to make muffins for the next morning.

By mid-March the weather was already warming up considerably. On St. Patrick's Day Tyrone organized the sowing of the grain, as it was considered most lucky to do so on that feast day. Afterwards, he and all of the older men of the district celebrated by gathering together in the public house to drink *pota Phadraic* or St. Patrick's pot.

When he returned home, he took a charred stick and marked the arm of each member of his family with a cross. This was an old custom among the Irish, and as he made the mark, he intoned the solemn words: "In the name of the Father, and of the Son, and of the Holy Ghost." The girls had already made crosses out of colored ribbon and had distributed them for others to wear on their breasts.

The day was a solemn reminder of their ancient and holy heritage as well as a hope for a prosperous and happy coming year. It was also a signal that winter was over.

When the spring rains came, Brenna trudged daily through the muddy slop of the yard to see how Minx was doing. The mare was almost a year old now, tall and strong and perfectly marked. Brenna would watch her for an hour or so, daydreaming about the day when the mud would begin to dry up and she would take her out for a good run.

"Aye, she's needing some exercise," Kevin Ryan agreed, brushing the sleek, dark coat, as Brenna perched on the top of the stall. "The mud's about dried up now, so no need to worry about catching her hoof in a pothole. You might be taking her out tomorrow, if you've a mind."

Brenna nodded in excitement. "Aye, Kevin, I would like that! Poor Minx feels as shut in as I do!" Then she giggled and swung her braids back over her shoulders. "At least she hasn't to endure Father Kinahan's lessons in the morning."

" 'Twill be summer soon and no more lessons for you, lass," he put in, his brown eyes sparkling, for he had missed her gay chatter through the long winter.

At sixteen, Kevin Ryan had begun to fill out. His shoulders were broad and his legs thick, though he would never be a big man. His freckles had begun to fade in the long winter, but with the summer sun, they would be out again, on his arms and hands, and spattered across his cheeks and nose. His dark red hair was long and shaggy, for he hadn't had a haircut in weeks. Brenna playfully reached over to tug on a lock in the unruly thatch. "There now, Kevin, you'll be looking as shaggy as Minx with her winter coat."

He laughed. "Keeps my ears warm in the winter." He reached up to brush her hand away but held it a moment longer instead. His brown eyes widened in embarrassment and he dropped her fingers as though they were red hot

Brenna was thrown into a state of discomfort, aware that something she had done had caused Kevin to forget himself for a moment. She looked away from him, unsure of what had just happened between them.

Kevin turned away and brushed the mare for dear life as he chastised himself for being so stupid. He gave her a few moments to compose herself. "There now, our Minx is as pretty as a picture," he said, deliberately smiling up at Brenna. "I'll have her ready for you the minute you're done with Father Kinahan, tomorrow," he promised.

"Thank you, Kevin! Oh, it will be wonderful to be riding her!" Brenna thrilled, clasping her hands. She jumped down from the stall, careful not to bump into Kevin, who was standing quietly with the brush still in his hand. " 'Til tomorrow then," she laughed nervously.

He could see she wished to be gone from the awkward moment. "Aye," was all he answered as he watched her skip hurriedly out of the barn into the muddy yard outside.

Brenna forgot the encounter when she saw a wagon pulling into the yard, for sitting on top was Bernadette Kavanagh holding a huge basket. Beside her sat one of the Markham lackeys.

"Bernadette!" she called, waving as she tripped through the mud.

"Brenna, I've come with a gift from Sir William. He's just returned last night from London and brought—ah! —so many beautiful presents. Even a length of bright calico for me! He's a good one, he is."

"Aye, but what presents? There in the basket, you say?" Brenna eagerly pressed in closer.

"Now, I'm to be presenting them to your mother,"

Bernadette laughed, climbing down. "Come on and we'll all be seeing what's inside!"

The two girls hurried inside to the kitchen. Nora was cleaning out the pantry. Brenna noticed the flush in her mother's face and felt guilty that she had not been helping; but she swept aside the thought as the precious basket was set on the table.

"Presents, Mama!" she crowed, leaning her elbows on the tablecloth.

Deirdre poked her head in from the sitting room, her gray eyes alight. All four females seated themselves at the table; the day had needed some excitement, and Sir William had certainly provided it!

When Nora parted the cloth cover, she gasped in delight. "Aye, there's fine material for us," she said, "and a letter from Sir William!" She pulled out three lengths of cloth—a fine, soft plum worsted, a vivid green shimmering taffeta, and a soft blue silk, which was as fine as smoke. She unfolded the letter, hesitated a moment, then gave it to Brenna to read.

Brenna took the letter. "Sir William sends his regards with a small token of his esteem. 'So that the ladies of one of my dearest friends can present themselves to me in all their beauty on May Day'," he says. Brenna looked up, her eyes gleaming with excitement. "Oh, he must mean a party then, Mama, for such gowns would be much too fine for—"

"Go on with the letter, Brenna," Nora said, smiling at her daughter.

"Aye, Mama. He says that he's hidden two good bottles of wine in the bottom of the basket for Dermot and Papa. Ah, is he not a thoughtful man?"

"Aye, that he is. And we'll be thanking him for these things properly with letters of our own." She picked up the pile of material and ran her fingers along the edges dreamily. "I think the green for you, Brenna, and the blue for you, Deirdre. The plum shall be for me, for I've some lovely old lace that would trim it perfectly." She glanced over to Bernadette. "I'm sorry, my dear, I had forgotten to greet you properly."

The girl smiled. "I asked Sir William if I could come and bring the basket to you as I—I would like to be seeing Dermot again—if—if he's of a mind to be seeing me." She blushed.

Nora felt the beginnings of motherly anxiety stir in her breast, but she brushed the thoughts aside. "Dermot is outside somewhere," she said, looking to her daughters for more information.

"He left the house with a book under his arm," Deirdre piped up, her eyes agog over the shimmering fabrics. "Oh, Mama, may I have the green—'tis so very shiny! Please, Mama!"

"Deirdre, the blue is much more suitable for your coloring. Now, don't you be telling me that you're quarreling already over someone else's charity! I'll not be hearing it from you, my girl."

Brenna was relieved that Nora had stood by her decision, for she thought the green truly the most lovely fabric she'd ever seen. She touched it lightly. "I think Dermot might have ventured down by the stream," he said.

"The stream? Where is that?" Bernadette asked.

"Come on then," Brenna said, taking her hand, "I'll be showing you, if you're that certain you want to see the likes of my brother."

Bernadette blushed again as she bid good-day to Nora and hurried after Brenna.

"I've not got to be back for an hour or two," Bernadette said when they reached the edge of the forest. "Sir William told me to be back by suppertime, and the footman will wait for me. I've—I've been thinking of your brother a lot, Brenna. He's a fine young man."

"Is he?" Brenna asked absently. Tiny droplets of moisture from last night's rain showered down as she pushed aside the newly budding tree limbs. "Aye, I suppose he is that, Bernadette. He's mostly quiet, though, and he likes reading."

"Aye, he is quiet, but a nice quiet," Bernadette agreed.

They followed the muddy path to the stream and saw Dermot on the far side, seated on a big boulder, his nose in the book he had brought with him. Next to him lay paper and pencil.

"Dermot!" Brenna called, waving to him wildly.

The boy looked up, saw who was with his sister, and nearly fell off the boulder in his haste to stand up. "Hello! Is—is there something the matter?"

"No, silly, but Bernadette wanted—"

"Hush!" Bernadette warned her, putting a hand on her arm. Her eyes pleaded with Brenna not to reveal her boldness to Dermot.

Brenna, only half understanding, shrugged and turned back to her brother. "I thought you might be wanting to see Bernadette, as she just arrived with some gifts from Sir William. Can we come over?"

"Aye, there's a path of rocks in the stream. You can step on them."

"Can you be helping us now?" Brenna asked in irritation as she eyed the slippery rocks.

Dermot, realizing he had forgotten his manners, hurried to the stream to meet Bernadette halfway as she jumped nimbly from rock to rock. As their hands met, he turned beet red, and Bernadette blushed too. Brenna wished she could laugh at how silly they looked making calf eyes at each other.

" 'Tis a mite chilly," Dermot said lightly to Bernadette.

"I've forgotten my shawl in the kitchen," she said. They both looked towards Brenna.

"I'll—go back and get it," she offered, aware that she had been targeted as a nuisance. She had almost determined to stay, if only to irritate her brother—he did look so funny, staring at Bernadette that way—but she realized there would be little conversation directed her way, so she shrugged and trudged back to the house.

Her mother instantly made her sit down to write a thank you note to Sir William, so that Bernadette could take it back with her on her return journey. By the time she had finished and helped Deirdre with her note, she had been gone for almost half an hour. Remembering her mission, she snatched Bernadette's shawl off the peg by the door.

"Where are you off to?" Nora asked, her head once more inside the pantry.

"To the stream—to give Bernadette her shawl," Brenna answered.

"Bernadette's at the stream?" Nora looked out at her daughter, her eyes sharp. "What is she doing there?"

"I'm thinking she's kissing our Dermot by now," Deirdre giggled.

"Kissing! Well, I . . ."

Deirdre looked penitent as Nora eyed her youngest severely. "And where, Deirdre Kildare, have you been getting such thoughts?" she demanded.

"Nowhere, Mama. I was just repeating what Lucy Gallagher told me."

"Go on."

"She saw Dermot and Bernadette kissing off the road once last week, near Sir William's estate. She was on her way to . . ."

"That's enough, missy. I'll not have you talking of your brother and his affairs as though he's some cavalier we can be all gossiping about! I'm sure that he—that he—"

Brenna was surprised to see her mother's hand trembling as she wiped it across her brow. What was she so nervous about? The idea of kissing was not so repugnant; although Brenna had never been kissed by a strange boy, she couldn't imagine that it would hurt anything. Did Mama not like Bernadette Kavanagh? Or was she afraid that Dermot might run away again?

"Mama, I've got to be taking Bernadette's shawl to her," she reminded Nora softly.

"Aye, and I'm thinking that it's time the girl went back to her own business," Nora said in exasperation. "You'll be telling her that we're ready for her to take our thanks back to Sir William."

"Aye, Mama," Brenna said and slipped out the door. Her mother's uncertain attitude disturbed her. She hurried back to the stream. She found the two of them sitting on the boulder, their arms entwined about one another as they quietly talked. Dermot moved his face forward and Bernadette tilted her chin up.

105

"Dermot, Bernadette!" Brenna called out quickly, thinking that perhaps she ought to make herself known.

The two sprang apart guiltily.

"Mama says 'tis time you were going," Brenna called to Bernadette, holding the shawl tightly. "We've written our thank-yous."

"Aye, I'm coming now," Bernadette replied. She gave Dermot a tender glance, started to put out her hand, then blushed in confusion.

The two girls made their way back, leaving Dermot to his book.

"Is it that you're liking my brother as more than just a friend?" Brenna asked curiously.

Bernadette ducked her head. "Aye."

"You—you would've kissed him then?"

"Aye." Bernadette smiled sweetly.

Brenna mulled this over for a moment. "Will you be marrying him then?" she finally asked, coming to the only logical conclusion she could think of.

Bernadette started, glancing nervously at her companion. " 'Tis not for me to think about marrying yet, Brenna," she answered in a low voice.

"When you're older?" Brenna guessed.

Bernadette was hurrying now, for she could see Nora Kildare waiting on the porch with a disapproving frown on her face. Their good-byes were stilted, and Nora couldn't help giving a sigh of relief when the Markham's wagon turned onto the main road.

"I'm not sure I can be trusting that girl," she said to herself, wiping her hands on her apron. "I'm not at all sure she'll not be getting our Dermot in trouble again."

"You mean he might run away again?" Brenna wondered, setting the table for supper.

" 'Tis a different sort of trouble, I'm thinking," Nora said.

Chapter Nine

"AND who are these fair lasses?" Tyrone Kildare teased, smiling broadly and opening his arms to his two daughters. "Such beauties—and right here under my very nose!"

"Papa, don't tease!" Brenna laughed as she kissed him on the cheek.

Deirdre stood back, turning slowly in a circle so that her father could see her new dress. "Of course we're beauties, Papa," she said, impatiently. "But look, here comes Mama!"

Nora, wearing her new plum-colored gown, stepped regally down the stairs. She had trimmed the hem with the ecru lace and had cut the bodice low, flaring the skirt as much as she could with only three petticoats underneath.

"Ah, now, the prettiest of the lot, I'll be bound," Kildare said proudly. He bussed his wife heartily. " 'Tis that proud of you all I am," he smiled. "And I'm to be keeping a wary eye on all of you today, for all the lads will be wanting to flirt with you." He gave his wife a mock frown. "No flirting for you, my lady, for I've a mind to take you with me under one of the willow trees!"

Nora laughed, and the color rose in her cheeks. "Tyrone Kildare, I'm most proud to be with the handsomest man in the county!" He did indeed look very fine in his summer dove gray broadcloth suit.

"Shall we be going then?" he asked, giving her his arm. The family walked out into the May sunshine. "Oh, my," Nora said, and everyone gasped! There, next to the coach block, was the smartest little carriage they had ever seen. It was an open carriage, sleek and shiny black with real velvet seat covers.

Nora, speechless, turned to her husband.

"Now don't be asking me where I got it, wife. I bought it some weeks ago, and it only arrived last night. I had a deuce of a time hiding it from your eyes until this moment. Now you'll be thanking me proper for it later on!" He raised his eyebrows conspiratorially, causing Nora's color to deepen even more.

"But, Papa, 'tis the most lovely thing I've ever seen!" Deirdre squealed, climbing in and spreading her smokey-blue silk skirts on the rich velvet. "Ahh, 'tis heavenly soft." She gave her sister a wink. "So much better than that old hard wagon!"

Brenna climbed in next, her emerald green taffeta skirts rustling in the summer air. "Aye, I can't disagree with you there, Deirdre, though I might think my Minx just a snit better seat if I didn't have this gown on!"

"You and your horse, Brenna!" Deirdre said.

"Hush now, girls. Dermot, get a move on there, lad," Kildare called to his son. "You'll be wanting to see your light-o'-love, won't you now?"

"Tyrone!" Nora objected, but her husband gently pushed her restraining hand off his arm.

"In you go, sweetheart." He leaned towards her. "Leave the lad go with his little serving wench. 'Tis more than time for him to be enjoying himself!"

Nora sighed in exasperation, but she was quiet as Dermot climbed into the carriage, dressed in a handsome suit that fit him snugly. He had gained his weight back, and though he would never be as big as his father, he was a tall lad and firmly built.

There would be no English guests at Sir William's estate this time, for this was a special invitation to the farmers of the district to enjoy a picnic on the house grounds. May Day was a day to celebrate spring and the coming summer, a day for merrymaking and relaxing in the warm sunshine.

All along the road, trees burst with green leaves, flowers poked their blue, yellow, and purple faces towards the sky, bees buzzed above the tall grass, and birds sang lustily in the branches.

Kildare drove his family proudly up the grand drive to Sir William's estate, Markham Hall. The pink bricks of the three-story house could be seen between the curving arches of oaks and maples. The wide green lawns were planted with long rows of shrubbery.

The Kildares drove around the front of the house to the side gardens where servants were already busy setting out picnic hampers and laying blankets on the ground.

Many people had already arrived. There was noise, laughter, and singing as the Kildares climbed from their carriage. Sir William stood beneath a tall, old oak, peacefully watching his farmers as they played games and traded tales among the sedate trees and around the splashing fountain in the center of the courtyard. It didn't matter that he was the English overlord, symbol of the hated tyranny of Victoria's government, and that they were the yoked Irish, who sent oats and wheat, cattle and pigs down the Shannon River for export while their own people existed on a diet of potatoes and milk. Today was May Day, and for a little time, they could forget.

"Kildare! Good Lord, you've a handsome family, man!" Sir William said sincerely, shaking the man's hand. "I see you've put the material I sent to excellent use, madam," he said to Nora, who curtseyed grandly.

Sir William's eyes flickered with admiration over the daughters. "Yes, I think you might be hard put to keep those young ladies around much longer," he said. "I think some young man might come along and snap up a good thing when he sees it!" He nodded to Nora. "Begging your pardon, madam." He put his arm around Kildare's shoulder. "Did I tell you that I'd received a new contract from Quigley in London? He tells me that horse prices have risen fantastically."

The two men walked companionably away, leaving Nora to mingle with the other wives. Dermot searched the grounds a moment, spied Bernadette setting out a basket, and after a quick glance at his mother, he walked over to talk with her.

"Come along, Deirdre!" Brenna called to her sister. "I see there's a game of tag down by the fountain!"

"Not for me, thank you," Deirdre replied primly. "I've a mind not to be spoiling my new gown." She seated herself properly on a blanket and arranged her silk skirts with calculated informality. "Let all my friends come and see me so they can envy me my new gown," she said wickedly. She waved a hand. "Ah, there's Lucy Gallagher—she'll be positively green!"

Brenna frowned at her sister, then shrugged and ran down the gently rolling slope, calling a greeting to Maureen Derry, who looked quite pretty in a new pink gown.

"Lord, but you do look comely today!" Maureen said archly, hands on her hips. "Wherever did you get such a dress, Brenna?"

"Mama made it for me," she answered ambiguously. "Do you like it?"

"Aye, I'll be borrowing it for my wedding day!" her friend laughed. "It's that grand!"

They joined in the game of tag, although Brenna tried to keep her skirts from becoming grass stained. The day quickly became hot and it was time for some cool drinks and cold chicken and ham. Brenna and Maureen walked up the slope and flopped down on a blanket next to Deirdre, who was holding court with two or three of her friends.

"I see Benjamin Markham and Rory Adair staring at us," Maureen whispered to Brenna, between bites of chicken. "Do you think they recognize us in all our finery?"

"Oh, bother Rory Adair!" Brenna whispered back. "And as for Benjamin Markham, I'm thinking he might be a bit too fast for you, Maureen Derry!"

"Really? Oh, tell me! What did you see?"

Deirdre told her the story of Christmas day and the coy beauty from Dublin, much to the other girl's delight. "So he's really much too—too experienced for you, Maureen." Deirdre added in her best imitation of an English dame, "The lad cares only for the shallowest young ladies."

The girls laughed and sipped their cold drinks.

"A bevy of beauties—lovely little flowers ripe for the picking," Benjamin Markham remarked to Rory Adair as they descended on the colorful little group. He turned back to wave to Steven Cruz who had just appeared from the doorway. "Come on, Steven! We are the perfect gallants for these young ladies!"

Brenna glanced at the three young men coming towards them and poked Maureen in the ribs. "Your admirers are on their way," she whispered.

Deirdre looked up. "Oh, the gentlemen have decided to be gracing us with their presence!" she trilled delightedly.

"Gentlemen? You mean, boys, don't you?" Brenna laughed, and glanced sideways from beneath long, black lashes.

"Good day, my pretty colleens," Rory Adair said, bowing elegantly from the waist. "My friends and I couldn't help but notice how fair you all look today."

"Why, Rory!" Maureen laughed, dimpling. "I think you've been learning something under Sir William's influence."

"Aye—manners," Brenna put in.

Rory scowled, but he wasn't put out enough to keep from noticing how pretty she looked in her new gown and with her midnight-black hair coiled about her ears. He bent down and picked a sprig of myrtle, then reached to tuck it in her hair.

Brenna was at a loss and flushed deeply. She wasn't used to such gallantries from her old tormentor.

"So, what games shall we play today, colleens?" Benjamin Markham asked, leaning down to pick a curl from another girl's shoulder. The girl made a move at him and giggled affectedly.

"Oh, do let's play blind man's buff!" Deirdre put in excitedly. " 'Tis a fitting game for the maying time."

"Aye, that it is!" Rory agreed, eyeing Brenna's pink-tinted flesh. "And when you're caught by the blind man, you'll be getting a kiss!"

The females in the group tittered deliciously at such a naughty rule, but they were all young and innocent, and they were not alarmed at the idea of being kissed by these handsome older men. They stood up, shaking their skirts and whispering among themselves, as the young men went to recruit more players.

The adults, seated on the ground, conversed leisurely, as they indulgently watched their youngsters.

"Down here, below the fountain where the land is flat!" Rory called out, waving to the rest of the participants.

A bevy of multicolored skirts and gay ribbons floated down the green lawn after the young men. There were about ten players in all. They drew straws to see who would be "it" first. Deirdre, much to her delight, lost.

"A handkerchief!" she yelled.

"You may use mine, senorita," Steven Cruz offered, pulling out one of the embroidered ones that she and Brenna had given him for Christmas. Brenna glanced at him but shyly lowered her eyes when he returned her stare. Deirdre stood still while Maureen Derry tied the handkerchief tightly around her eyes, then whirled her around three times.

"Don't go too far!" Deirdre squealed. "Oh, do give me a chance, you mean boys!" she laughed, walking carefully with her hands held out in front of her. She nearly stumbled over someone's feet, righted herself and grabbed the back of Terence Gallagher's coat. "Got you!" Tearing off the handkerchief, Deirdre tried not to look too disappointed when she discovered whom she had selected, and she quickly bestowed a peck on his cheek. Everyone shrieked at her aplomb.

After Terence was blindfolded and whirled around, he quickly caught Maureen Derry by her pink sash and kissed her laughingly on the lips, causing her to blush brighter than the cherry red of her flounce.

Brenna ran behind a bush to catch her breath, brushing away beads of perspiration from her brow. As she wiped her hands on the back of her skirt and started to leave her shelter, she was caught by the arm. Thinking she had been tagged, she turned with a smile to encounter Rory Adair laughing at her with twinkling blue eyes.

"Have you caught me?" she asked uncertainly. He wasn't holding the handkerchief.

"Aye, it does look that way," he smiled.

"Well, then, let's be getting back, or they'll be wondering . . ."

Rory chuckled. "Now then, little blackbird, let me look at you, for I've been thinking you're beginning to grow up a mite." He whistled. "Aye. Another year or two, and you'll be filling out just right."

"Rory!" Brenna pulled her arm from his grasp and ran out into the playing area. He came right behind her, intent on catching her again, when he was tagged by Maureen's groping arms. She giggled self-consciously and kissed him on the cheek.

"All right now. Benji, come over here and tie this thing on me," Rory yelled, laughing good-naturedly. "Not too tight now, lad, for I've a mind to be catching someone in particular!"

Benjamin whirled him around, and let him loose. The girls shrieked as he lunged for each of them, picking up their skirts and sprinting away like young foals. Brenna laughed too, ducking when he would have captured her, but coming up quickly to find herself inside his arms.

"I've got one!" Rory crowed in triumph and tore off the handkerchief. "Why 'tis young Brenna Kildare!" he mocked and crushed the breath from her as he squeezed her hard and kissed her mouth.

Brenna felt her heart pounding in her head as Rory's mouth came away from hers. She stood still a moment longer, stunned by his forcefulness.

"I'm 'it'," she laughed shakily, reaching out to take the handkerchief from him as he winked at her triumphantly. He tied it tightly about her head, disorienting her so that for a moment she felt completely alone in the vast emptiness of the clearing, hearing only the sound of his breathing until he stepped away from her.

She was uncertain which way to go and couldn't establish her balance. "Someone, talk to me," she yelled out breathlessly. "You're all hiding from me!" she laughed. " 'Tis not fair!" She groped around in the darkness, then stood still and listened for the swish of silk. There! She whirled and felt air brush her fingers as she missed, but with cunning, she knifed quickly in the opposite direction and caught her hand in the front of a silk waistcoat.

"Aha!" she sang out, lifting the handkerchief. She looked up into Steven Cruz's laughing dark eyes and hesitated only a moment before reaching up on tiptoe to brush his cheek with her lips. Quickly she stepped back, handing him the handkerchief.

"Will you tie it on me, Brenna?" he asked, turning his back to her.

Her fingers fumbled clumsily as she tried to tie the knot tightly. Well, it would have to do! She put her hands about his waist and turned him around so that he staggered for a moment before regaining his balance.

Feminine giggles led him to a covey of girls who split apart as he tried to catch them. Brenna stayed well out of his way, backing hurriedly to the side when his waving hands nearly brushed her hair. He stopped to listen again, then moved forward, stalking an unsuspecting girl. Her squeal smote the air as his brown hand tangled in her skirts.

"Oh, Mr. Cruz, you've got me now!" cried the girl as he pushed up his blindfold.

Brenna saw him glance surreptitiously over towards her, then bend to press his mouth to the girl's. The colleen reddened and giggled again, then waited eagerly for him to tie the handkerchief around her head.

The game went on for some time, the young men becoming bolder as the light faded in the western sky. Dusk began to settle, and Sir William ordered torches lit so that his guests might stay a little longer. Brenna and Maureen retreated to their place beneath a tree to sip some lemonade.

The air was filled with the sawing of crickets and the buzz of June bugs. The grass was still warm from the day's sun and Brenna leaned back on her elbows, her eyes making out the dim shapes of the gamesters who had moved off, away from the bright lights. The younger children had all quit, but the older ones were still playing, stealing kisses even when it wasn't their turn. She wondered idly what Rory Adair might be up to, and she recalled how velvety soft Steven Cruz's hair had felt against her hands.

"Rory Adair kissed you today, Brenna," Maureen was saying.

"Aye, that he did—the game called for it," she defended quickly. The enveloping twilight hid her distress.

"He wanted to kiss you, I think," Maureen went on, sipping from her cup. "Perhaps he would have been doing more than that if you'd let him."

"Well, I wouldn't let him—not in a thousand years!" Brenna stated hotly and stood up.

"Well, of course you wouldn't," Maureen agreed, "but someday—" Her voice trailed off thoughtfully. "He is a handsome lad, isn't he?" she said a few moments later.

"Aye, *he* thinks he is, with his devilish smile and twinkling blue eyes," Brenna asserted.

"No, I was meaning the other one—Steven Cruz. I think he might be liking you a bit too, Brenna." A thin sliver of jealousy wedged its way into Maureen's voice. "I noticed how those black eyes watched you when you weren't looking, aye, that I did."

"Don't be silly, Maureen. He knows I'm disliking him!" Brenna said, genuinely surprised, although she had to admit that she didn't dislike his touch as much as she might have thought. Oh, such talk—she'd get away from that moony Maureen and take a walk through the gardens.

"Where are you off to?"

"Just to take a walk, Maureen," she answered, then couldn't resist adding, "to meet my lover!" She giggled at Maureen's look of shock and skipped away towards the fountain. The formal English garden was planted with roses and high shrubs through which ran narrow gravel pits leading to strategically placed iron benches. She could hear murmuring whispers and giggles now and then in the enveloping brush. She wondered if the wee folk might be hiding somewhere about, casting spells and laughing at these young people so intent upon romance.

She bumped into Benjamin Markham, who was talking animatedly with Steven Cruz about some "appointment." Both young men were laughing and Brenna started to excuse herself quickly.

"Wait, Brenna, let me walk you a way," Steven said, nodding to Benjamin, who winked back conspiratorially.

She didn't like the intrusion into her privacy, but couldn't think of any way to politely tell him so so she suffered his presence in silence. Maureen's words still smarted in her ears, and she was building up a fair ire towards the young man, when he spoke, startling her.

"Have you enjoyed the picnic today?"

"Aye, 'twas grand of Sir William," she answered.

"I missed being here during the winter. I expect the countryside is lovely with snow on the ground." He stopped and gestured to a bench. "Would you like to sit down?"

"No, I should be hurrying on now," she said swiftly. Her brisk step caused him to chuckle.

"There's no need for you to be afraid of me, Brenna Kildare. You're only a little girl."

She stopped in midstep and turned to him abruptly. "A little girl? A little girl!"

"How old are you? Ten? Eleven?"

She was blind to his deliberate baiting. "I was thirteen in February," she said, trying to stand taller. " 'Tis not so very little!"

"Ah, forgive me," he said, with only a hint of a rueful smile. "You see, in my country, when a girl reaches the age of a young woman, she begins to act like one. At twelve or thirteen, her parents betroth her. Then she is allowed, on special occasions, to dress up and stay up late with her *novio*, her betrothed—always well-chaperoned, of course: her *duenna* accompanies the girl and her betrothed even to the theater and the park."

"I hardly care to be hearing about your heathen customs," she said spitefully.

"Por Dios! Heathen customs! We are as Catholic a country as your own," he said, laughing outright.

"Well, then how can you go promising a poor girl to someone she hardly knows?"

"No, you have misunderstood. The girl has usually

grown up with the boy, and their parents are very good friends, so the two have had ample time to be with each other as children. These arrangements often turn out very well." He stopped and considered for a moment. "If we will speak of heathenish customs, we cannot ignore the tradition of abducting women in your country." He chuckled. "Now wouldn't you think that some young girl, kidnapped from her parents' home in the dead of night by some brigand she doesn't know, might be worse off than the young women in my country?"

"I hardly know what you're talking about," she burst out. "You've been sputtering about kidnapping and such —why, I've never heard of anyone being abducted around here. That's how much you'll be knowing of our ways."

He sobered. "All right then, since I know so very little —teach me some of your ways."

She shrugged her shoulders. "I would be guessing you'd learn much more from Rory Adair or Benjamin Markham."

Steven's mouth tightened and his mind flew back to the previous winter at Cambridge when Benjamin had introduced him to his first "doxy." It was his first time with a woman, and he had been clumsy and nervous. The generous flagons of hot rum he had downed with Benjamin in the tavern below had not helped him at all.

Later, he had gone back, curious to see if he might enjoy himself more when sober and not so nervous—and he had. The woman was coarse, overblown, and smelled of cheap perfume, but once he had proved himself with her, he felt confident to test his mettle with more appetizing creatures, all of whom were supplied by Benjamin, an accomplished libertine. Of course, there were "good" women, those he had learned to spot with Benjamin's help, who were interested in nothing more than a drive in the park. Naturally, these were the ladies one married —it was the same in Argentina.

He realized that he had been walking silently beside the Kildare girl for quite a few minutes. He wondered curiously what her feelings were for Rory Adair. The lad certainly thought her a fair catch, but he wasn't quite sure how she felt. *Dios!* What did it matter to him? He had tried to be friendly to the child, but that was as far as he would go. If she didn't respond, then he would not make a fool of himself to gain her attention. Despite the loveliness of her face and the gracefulness of her walk she was still a child—really not worth bothering with.

He stopped and bowed stiffly. "Excuse me, senorita, but I'm sure your parents will be wondering where you are. It grows late, and they are, no doubt, preparing to leave."

"Aye," Brenna agreed, baffled by the change in his mood. "Then I'll be thanking you for the walk—Steven."

Was it the first time she had spoken his name aloud? She turned quickly and hurried out to the clearing, feeling an overwhelming need to escape from the foreign boy and the strange feelings she felt in his presence.

Chapter Ten

As the long, lazy days of summer passed, Brenna began to change—subtly at first, so that only her mother noticed it. Without quite realizing it, Brenna grew away from the boyish ways of her childhood. She no longer tried to emulate her father, but rather took example from her mother; and she found that the change brought with it complicated emotions and a torrent of worry.

When these feelings seemed to overwhelm her, she would ask Kevin to saddle Minx, and she would ride on and on, for hours through the vast fields, over the emerald green slopes, and down the winding roads until her worries were blotted from her mind. Only then would she turn her mare home again.

In July Brenna's father started a repair project on the barn, which enabled him to hire a few of the itinerant workers who wandered about the countryside in the summer months. One of Brenna's duties was to bring down the midday meal to these men—most of whom were poorly nourished and lonely for their families; she would listen compassionately to stories of their homes, some of which were as far away as Cork and Tipperary.

Since Steven had extra time on his hands after the foaling season, he helped Kildare to supervise the men about their jobs. He was a competent instructor, Brenna admitted grudgingly, and he was quite patient with less knowledgeable men.

One hot day in August, his skin glistening with sweat, Steven directed the placement of stones around the base of the barn's foundation. He unbuttoned his soaked shirt just as Brenna came outside. Watching him from the porch, she felt a curious shiver pass through her body. Surreptitiously, she tried to tuck stray hairs back into her braids and smoothed the middle part with her hands. She was no longer sure just how she felt about Steven

Castaneda de la Cruz. Sometimes, she grew angry and resentful just because he was always so calm and composed and sure of himself. But there were other times when she found herself assessing him, and, yes, admitting to herself that he was a handsome lad. Why couldn't she make up her mind about him? she wondered.

He turned around to grab a handkerchief from where he had placed it on a fence post, and began to wipe his face when he saw the slight figure on the porch, staring at him with her head slightly cocked in concentration. He grinned, which infuriated her. She stomped furiously back into the house.

Nora looked up from finishing the lunch trays. "Ah, there you are, Brenna," she smiled, her face a bit flushed from the heat of the baking oven. "I've just finished some good, sweet loaves for the workers. There's apple jelly and plum preserves—" She stopped aware that her daughter was hardly listening. "Is there something the matter, sweetheart?"

Brenna shook her head absently, then eyed her mother, as though trying to make a decision. " 'Tis hot in here," she finally sighed noncommitally.

"Aye, because I've been baking," Nora responded. "Is it the heat that's troubling you, lass?"

"Aye," Brenna replied. She looked at the trays. "I'll be needing Deirdre to help me with those."

"I've sent her on an errand to the Gallagher's," Nora put in, setting mugs on another tray. "Take the food out first and then come back for the tea."

"Why must we be feeding those men when Papa's already paying them wages for their work?" she wondered sulkily. " 'Tis a decent wage, isn't it, Mama?"

Nora nodded. "Aye, your father is quite generous, but the work is hard and a man can't be expected to go on without food, now can he? Most of those men are many miles from home, and they've no one else to be feeding them."

"What about the pub or the inn?"

"Good heavens, they'd spend all their money if your father let them go off to the pub," Nora laughed. She looked at her daughter. "What's the matter, Brenna? Surely you're not resenting those men taking food from us? 'Twould be most uncharitable of you, daughter, and I'd be asking you to see Father Kinahan about such thoughts."

" 'Tis not that I resent them, Mama, only . . ." Brenna stopped and sighed. "I'm sorry," she ended abruptly. "I suppose 'twas just the heat that made me pop off."

"Aye, then, you'll be taking the tray out to them, and I'll be pouring the tea," Nora said, smiling again.

Brenna balanced the tray in her hands and went back outside, treading carefully so as not to trip on some obstacle and send the men's lunches into the dirt. She set the tray on a long table, which was set up beside the fence.

The six men immediately stopped their work to gaze hungrily at the food, like well-trained dogs awaiting their master's orders. Brenna felt guilty as she hurried back to fetch the tea. Steven was telling the men to help themselves. She was certain that he was staring at her, for she thought she could feel his eyes drilling twin holes into her back. She brought out the tea, then hurried back to the safety of the house.

She wished, with sudden intensity, that Steven were gone back to his own country. She could imagine such a country with tall, dark-eyed men and somber-faced young girls, who sat inside all day, only to be let out in the evening in the company of strict duennas. She had found the country in a book of maps and studied the odd configuration for nearly an hour imagining what it was like to live there: there was Buenos Aires, crude and new and uncivilized; behind the city stretched endless miles of grasslands, deserts, and mountains—wild places, where villains and brigands could hide out. There would not be the gentle sloping greenness of her own country, the squares of fertile fields, the cozy feeling of small villages, or the warm, friendly people.

She was certain that Steven had acquired only the surface polish of a gentleman during his extensive travels on the Continent and in England. No doubt, when he returned home, he would revert back to a rough, half-barbaric state of being. A shiver of excited dread passed through her. Aye, she would surely be careful of him, she thought coolly.

"Deirdre Kildare, you're daft!" Brenna laughed good-naturedly. "Do you really think we could simply walk up on the grounds of Markham Hall, bold as you please, look in at the windows, then leave?"

"And why not?" the other demanded, sitting up straighter.

"Well, for one thing, Papa would never let us be leaving the house so late at night."

" 'Twouldn't be so very late," Deirdre pouted. "I heard Bernadette telling our Dermot that Sir William was planning an end-of-summer party tomorrow eve, and 'twould be starting at dusk."

"And how do you propose to be slipping out at dusk without telling Mama?"

Deirdre shrugged airily "You'll be thinking of a way, Brenna, I'm sure of it," she said confidently.

Brenna laughed. "Well, I'm glad you've such confidence in me, but I'll not be promising you anything."

It surprised Brenna that she would even allow herself to consider going along with her sister's harebrained scheme. She was even more surprised when her parents told her they would be going off to the Adairs the following evening.

It was hard for Brenna and Deirdre to contain their excitement as they bid their parents good-bye. "I'll be charging you with watching the two girls while we're gone," Kildare said to Dermot. "We'll not be very late, but I'm still not liking to leave you alone now."

" 'Twill be all right," Dermot put in hastily at the door. "You take care."

The children watched as their parents drove off. When the carriage was safely out of sight, Dermot turned to the girls with urgency.

"Now then, I've got to be going up to Sir William's," he said quickly. "I've been promising Bernadette I'd be meeting her and this is as good a time as any. I've no wish to alarm Mama, so you won't be saying anything about it?"

Brenna quickly grasped her chance. "Not be saying anything? Dermot! We just heard Papa telling you to be staying with us—protecting us, you know."

"Ach, now, you know I can leave without worrying about you. Kevin's here, and the rest of the grooms. There'll be no trouble." He was impatient to be off.

"But Papa charged you with our safety—and you promised!" Deirdre chimed in, seeing her sister's ploy.

Dermot gave a hearty sigh. " 'Twill just be for an hour or two," he said. "I've got to be seeing Bernadette. She's expecting me now."

"All right," Brenna cut in, "then you'll just have to be taking us with you."

"What!"

"Aye, you'll have to let us come too, or—or we'll be telling Papa on you," Deirdre added defiantly.

"You can't be coming! Papa'd switch my hide if he were to learn I took you out at dark. Now, please, girls, can't you be seeing my side?" he wheedled.

They both stood obstinately, shaking their heads.

"We'll be coming along, Dermot, or you'll not be going either."

"Brenna, be serious. Why would you be wanting to tail me when I'm going to see Bernadette?"

"Sir William's having a grand party!" Deirdre explained eagerly.

"So?"

"So, we want to see," she told him.

He laughed. "And how do you propose to be doing that?" he inquired sarcastically. "Peep through the windows then?"

The girls nodded.

"Good Christ! You're both daft! You'll be caught for sure!"

"Oh, Dermot, we'll be ever so careful, you'll see," Brenna pressed. "Just this once—and we promise not to get into trouble. We could meet you somewhere after an hour, and then come right back home with no one the wiser." Brenna waited hopefully for her brother's answer.

Finally, he shrugged his shoulders. His desire to see his love was greater than his fear of the consequences. "But mind you," he warned, "if you get into trouble because of this, 'twill be your own fault. And I'll be blaming *you* if I get a switching from Papa."

They rode swiftly, reaching Sir William's just as the sun was tipping behind the horizon, ending the last glow of twilight.

"Now, I'm going 'round the back to the kitchens. Meet me there within the hour!" he charged them.

They whispered their promise, then hurried to the side of the house that opened onto the magnificent gardens. The riot of summer flowers filled the air with the heavenly scent of roses, honeysuckle, and gardenia. The balcony doors were open to allow fresh air into the house, so Brenna and her sister quickly angled themselves behind a screen of shrubbery, where they would not be seen.

"Oh, I can't be spying anything!" Deirdre wailed. "We must get closer."

" 'Twould be foolish," Brenna hissed back.

" 'Twas foolish to come if we can't see anything," Deirdre returned obstinately.

"All right then, but wait until the sun is gone," Brenna instructed, concerned over Deirdre's bright yellow gown. 'Twould be easy to see it, even in the dark. And she would die of embarrassment if they were caught peeping through the windows, never mind what her father would do to them.

In another ten minutes, when dark had settled, they crept slowly toward the house. Their eyes fastened on the doors that led out into the gardens as they softly slid around the balcony and climbed. With some difficulty, they reached a stone ledge, which jutted out enough to allow them a foothold while they hung onto a conveniently placed trellis and strained their necks to see through a window. After a few minutes, Brenna thought her neck would break, but she was determined to stay a little longer, her eyes glued to the beautiful gowns and coiffures of the few young ladies inside.

The salon was breathtaking with its gleaming oak floor and the marble columns that soared flamboyantly the height of the two-storied walls that were painted a cool mint green. There were two large fireplaces, decorated with gilt fans, above which hung giant mirrors. Dainty benches done in pink satin stood against the walls. The windows in the higher part of the wall were shaped into arches and trimmed with wrought-iron work across their faces. Huge chandeliers hung by ornate chains from the very top of the room and glimmered softly on the young people below.

"Look," Deirdre directed in a whisper. "Ooh, that Benjamin must think he's just too fine for the likes of me now!"

Brenna could see the object of her sister's attention, strutting importantly about the room, dressed in a suit of periwinkle blue with a brocade waistcoat. He alternated among three or four young women, who watched him appreciatively as he bowed and talked and allowed his hand to grace theirs. Obviously, Brenna concluded, Benjamin was an experienced flirt—if that was the right word to apply to a man.

Her eyes flitted about the room and found Rory Adair, who looked unusually fine in a well-made suit, conversing in good humor with a shy young girl, who continually passed her fan in front of her face as though trying to hide from him. Then Brenna caught a glimpse of Steven Castaneda de la Cruz, leaning negligently against the wall on the far side, his black eyes languorous as a young woman engaged him in small talk. His arms were folded in front of him, and his head was cocked a little to one side, as though deeply considering what the young debutante was saying to him, although Brenna was sure she could detect a fleeting air of boredom in his face. For that she despised him even more. How dare he be bored at a party for him! He was certainly an ungrateful wretch. Who did he think he was?

"I've seen enough," she whispered to her sister.

"Oh, just a minute more," Deirdre whispered. She

leaned in closer to the window, avidly keeping an eye on Benjamin as he announced that the dancing was about to begin.

"Oh, the dancing now!" Deirdre breathed. She leaned forward, using her hands to pull herself up.

Then Brenna reached over to support her from one side, for she was sure that her sister was about to fall backwards any moment, and her own grasp loosened from the trellis. As she shifted her weight to the opposite foot, some of the old granite suddenly gave way beneath her. With a muffled cry, Brenna clutched for the trellis, caught it, then heard the wood crack and splinter, and felt a sharp pain in her hand. She fell backwards with a flurry of skirts and landed ignominiously on her backside.

For a moment, she was too dazed to see her sister jump down with a frightened look. "Oh, lordy, Brenna, I—I do think someone saw us when the trellis broke. Get up!"

Brenna got to her feet. She would be black and blue in the morning for sure! Her left hand felt numb and tingling, and she discovered a long gash on the edge of her hand from her little finger to her wrist. The blood was already staining her sleeve, and Deirdre let out a stifled cry.

"You've split your hand," she said. "Oh, God, I'd better be finding Dermot."

"No, I can come with you. Do you have a handkerchief I can use to bind it up?"

Deirdre shook her head and looked even more scared as the blood continued to seep out slowly, dripping onto the grass in bright, crimson splotches.

"Well, I just have to be holding it with my other hand then," Brenna said bravely. " 'Tis nothing more than a scratch—looks worse than it is, I'm sure," she said to alleviate Deirdre's concern. She started to walk behind her sister, but reeled in a wave of dizziness. "I'd better sit down, just a moment," she said.

"I'll be getting Dermot, then," Deirdre said quickly. "You stay right here."

"But, I . . ."

Deirdre was already hurrying through the darkness. Oh, what a mess this was!

To make matters worse, she saw a figure standing at the side of the balcony, leaning over the stone railing and staring with eyes, which she knew were as black as the dark night. The shadows made it difficult to see the lower half of his face, but—was that a slight smile she discerned on his mouth?

His voice came out of the darkness, liquid and warm, with a hint of mockery. "Can it possibly be Senorita Kildare?"

Brenna was silent, hating him for patronizing her, determined that he should not have the satisfaction of seeing her humiliation. With renewed purpose, she turned toward the graveled pathway.

"Miss Kildare—Brenna, don't go away," she heard him say. "Come up and attend the party with me. After all, isn't that why you came?"

"No!" she exploded, and was angrier at herself for breaking her vow of silence.

With horror, she heard the gravel crunching beneath his shoes as he caught up with her. If she hadn't cut her hand, she was sure she could have outrun him, but now she was obliged to suffer his company.

"Young girls should never find themselves walking alone outside," Steven was saying conversationally. "I'm sure your esteemed father would not take kindly to that."

Brenna remained silent.

"I am equally sure that he has no idea that you are here tonight," he went on smoothly. "I wonder just how you managed it?"

"My brother and sister are with me," she declared, unable to remain silent any longer. "So you needn't concern yourself about me, but please return to your friends."

"My stubborn little girl, I am determined to see you safely home or to your brother. I am, after all, a gentleman." He grinned again and started to take her hand, then withdrew quickly at her cry of pain. "What . . ."

"Oh, get away!" Brenna shouted at him, wanting him to leave quickly before he could see her tears.

"*Por Dios!* You've hurt yourself!" he exclaimed, catching her arm to look at her hand in the light from the window.

"Aye, and what of it! I'll be taking care of it as soon as you let me find my brother and sister."

"Such fire even when wounded." He spoke gently now. "It is commendable, but expected in the Irish, I suppose." He clasped her arm firmly, brought her around to the front of the house, and forced her inside, despite her anguished protests.

"You'll have all the servants coming to investigate," he warned her sardonically, "if you don't stop that howling."

"I am not howling!" she whispered back furiously.

"Then be quiet." He steered her through the dining room towards the kitchens.

Brenna breathed easier, for she was sure that now she would be able to fetch Dermot to take her home and away from this odious boy who insisted on behaving with her as though she were hardly more than a babe.

They entered the kitchens, and Mrs. Longstreet, who was trading anecdotes with one of the footmen over a portion of ale, leaped to her feet. Dermot and Bernadette were nowhere in sight. They had surely gone back to the spot where Deirdre had left her. Blast this arrogant boy who seemed so determined to take charge!

"Dermot and Deirdre must have gone back."

Steven turned to the footman. "Find them," he succinctly ordered, and the young man hurried out. The cook stood with her hands on her hips, as though challenging Steven to address her in the same commanding tone. "Mrs. Longstreet, I'm afraid our little friend here has cut her hand badly outside. Might you have something to put on it to ease the pain?"

At the subtle deference in his voice, Mrs. Longstreet relaxed. "Aww, now, the poor chick is bleeding on her skirt there. Bring her over here, sir, and I'll have a look at it now." She inspected the wound. "I've a salve to put on it. Here now, we'll just fill this bowl with water and you lay your hand in it, duckling, until I come back." She left the room to rummage through the pantry.

Brenna tensed at the burning pain as she lowered her hand into the water. Gritting her teeth, she forced herself to keep it submerged until Mrs. Longstreet returned.

She felt Steven watching her. Finally, she could stand it no longer, and she hissed angrily, "I think you're dreadful!"

"And I think you're a spoiled child!" he laughed.

"Child, am I?" she said, challenging with her snapping blue eyes. He noticed, for the first time, the deeper purplish blue around the iris. She was about to give him a good talking to, but Mrs. Longstreet's appearance closed her mouth. For a moment, Brenna dearly felt like sticking out her tongue at the offender—then caught herself sharply, realizing how childish she would look.

Mrs. Longstreet wiped the injured hand gently in a towel, then applied salve to the cut as Steven watched, bracing one foot on a low stool and leaning his arm on his knee. He gazed at the arched, slender column of neck turned so obstinately away from him and found himself wanting to chuckle at the girl's stubbornness. It was too bad, he thought arrogantly, that she was only a child of thirteen, and he was sixteen—very nearly a man.

A moment later, Dermot and a white-faced Deirdre rushed into the kitchen, looking guiltily from Brenna to Steven.

"What happened?" Dermot demanded.

"I'll be telling you on the way home," Brenna said, standing up after Mrs. Longstreet had finished bandaging the hand. "We'd best be leaving, or Papa will be home before we are."

"Aye, let's do hurry!" Deirdre said anxiously.

Dermot nodded and gazed curiously at Steven. "You'll —you'll not be saying anything to our father now, will you?" he asked in a strained voice.

Steven shrugged lazily. "It's none of my business." He bowed to the two girls. "Good night, everyone. I'm afraid people will begin to wonder where I've gone if I don't return to the festivities soon. We wouldn't want anyone to suspect I'd been with the young lady." He smiled pointedly at Brenna's burning face, then left the room.

"Arrogant pup!" she hissed under her breath, in her best imitation of Tyrone Kildare.

"What will you tell Mama and Papa when they see your hand?" Deirdre asked.

Brenna thought for a moment. "I'll tell them I cut it washing a piece of broken crockery."

"But we've no broken pots at home."

"Then we'll have to break one, won't we now?"

Chapter Eleven

ON the eve of Michaelmas, which marked the end of summer in September, Dermot made an announcement to the family. Everyone had noticed how well he had been looking of late, how his cheeks had turned ruddy and his body had filled out. He had diligently attacked his lessons, working on them even in summer. He seemed to have completely recovered from his ordeal of the previous winter.

"Everyone!" he announced at dinner, "I have news of some import." He laughed easily. "At least it is important to me—and I hope you will all share my view."

Brenna, who was helping her sister with the supper dishes, looked up and saw excitement on Dermot's face. Nora's hands stilled, and her face tightened in dread, for she had some idea of what this announcement might be. God help me, she thought, for I cannot let him know my true feelings. He is his own man now and no longer needs a mother to be telling him what to do.

"Well, and what is it then?" Tyrone asked, still seated at the table going over the letters they had received from the post that morning.

"Well, actually there are two announcements—one as important as the other. First, Papa, you have often said you wondered what would become of me as I could never take an interest in horseflesh. Now I will tell you."

Dermot joyfully continued in an explosion of words. No one had ever heard so much come out of him at one time. "You see, when I was in prison, I met someone. Aye, now I can see it on your faces. What kind of man could one meet in prison, eh, Well, the man was in the prison, but he wasn't a prisoner. He's a lawyer, and a very fine one. His name is Isaac Butt, and he is the leading defense counselor for the Fenian prisoners. As he and I took to each other so well, he promised to work for my release

131

—but, of course, when Sir William intervened, there was no need for Isaac to stand on my behalf. No, no, I can see your mouth opening to ask about his credentials. He attended Trinity College and is an Irish Protestant. Mama, I forbid you to look so anguished." He was almost chuckling at the astonishment on all their faces.

"Isaac and I became good friends—don't ask me how. He saw to it that I was not put in cells with hardened criminals, the kind that attack young boys and use them in bestial ways." His face grew hard as he remembered. He saw the terror on his mother's face. "Aye, Mama, 'twas not a pretty place, nor will it ever be as long as it takes the wheels of justice so long to turn. No, Papa, I've not become a rabble-rouser. What I want is to have some say in helping fellow countrymen who spend a good deal of their lives in those stinking holes for minor crimes.

"For the last few months, I've been studying hard, reading books that Isaac sent me—and—and I've been thinking. I've come to a decision. I want to be trained as an attorney, Papa. Aye, and Isaac is willing to help me. It'll mean traveling back to Dublin and going to college, but Isaac says I can work in his offices as an assistant, and he would pay my way through school! 'Tis a dream I've been working toward—something fine and shining to do for my country. Papa, I want your approval, but I'll go without it if I must. Isaac's already found a place for me to live—it's small, he says, but big enough to start a family in."

"A—family?" Nora said quietly.

"Aye, Mother," and Dermot fairly beamed at her. "That's the other thing I wanted to tell you: Bernadette and I would like to be married."

"But you're only sixteen!" Nora sat down abruptly, her face white.

He shrugged off her protest. "I'll be seventeen in six months, and we'd like to be married then."

Tyrone, who had remained silent throughout the whole outpouring, stood up at the table. Brenna could see how his hands trembled. "Dermot, are you sure—very sure—that this is what you want to do with your life? You've got to be honest with yourself, lad. You may be throwing your life away."

Tyrone was struggling with his surprise and outrage. Despite what he knew of his son, he had still held a faint hope that Dermot would, after all, take over the horse farm someday. Now that hope was snuffed out completely. Dermot away in Dublin; he could hardly grasp the notion. His dark blue eyes filled with moisture from his impotent rage.

"Papa, I'm not making a mistake. I've thought often and very hard about this decision, and it's what I want to do. Believe me, I'll never regret it."

"You can say that now. You're young, a boy. And you want to get married soon! Ach, 'tis hard for a man to swallow, his son's being so different from himself!" Tyrone shook his head and ran a distracted hand through his thick hair. "How can you do this to yourself—to me!" he finally ended, his voice bitter.

"I'm doing what I want to do, Father, just as you did," Dermot said quietly. "I'm going to marry the girl that I love. I've loved her, aye, ever since I saw her that first time. Please be happy for me, Father, for everyone has the right to make his own choice. You have known for a long time that I could never be what you wanted me to be, but maybe I can become a great lawyer. You'll not be ashamed of me."

"I don't even know this man, this lawyer, you're speaking of," Tyrone continued, after a moment. His voice was stronger. "How do you know that his words are the truth? What proof do you have that he will take you in and give you a job? And you say you'll be going to school at Trinity, despite all these years of priestly tutoring. Aye, you know what good Catholics think of those godless schools."

"Nevertheless, Father, it is a good school to learn about the vocation I have chosen," Dermot said firmly.

"Would to God you'd have become a priest—anything but this!" Nora said, covering her face with her hands.

"Mother, how can you be saying that?" Dermot asked her. Gentleness warmed his voice. "You say 'anything but

133

this', as though I have chosen some nefarious occupation of which I should be ashamed. My God, any mother would be proud to see her son doing something for the good of the Irish people. Most of those unfortunates in the Dublin jails would see the hangman's noose if it weren't for the goodness of Mr. Butt!" His words grew more impassioned. "He cares about the populace, and he knows that I have the same feeling, the same desire to do something for my people!" Dermot looked at his parents, then at his sisters, his eyes bright and hopeful.

Brenna spoke up softly. "I think Bernadette will make a wonderful wife for you, Dermot."

"Aye, I suppose," Deirdre put in. "And, of course, you must let us come to visit you in your new lodgings, Dermot."

"Bless you, of course, you will come and visit," Dermot answered. "I love you all very much!"

For a moment, all were silent; then Nora wiped her eyes with her apron and looked long at her son. "It may take a while for me to get used to your going away, Dermot, and I shall try not to be the interfering mother," she began. "But if this is truly what you want, I shall not try to persuade you to anything else."

It was left for Tyrone to break the little bit of tension remaining in the air. "Son, you've been honest with me all along, but I suppose, like many a father I had woven my own dreams for you—selfish dreams, I admit now. I'm dearly ashamed of myself, Dermot. Naturally, I cannot help my misgivings about a man I have never met, but you and I will go to Dublin together, and I shall see for myself what manner of man this Isaac Butt is and whether or not his offerings are, indeed, sincere." The bleakness in his eyes was beginning to disappear. "God, I suppose I should be mightily proud to have my son aspire to such things, after all. Aye, and I would have thought you'd have amounted to nothing more than a poet, a dreamer."

"Aye, Father, I still am that," Dermot said softly and smiled.

"Well, then, we'd best be making arrangements for

you and I to be off. I want no time wasted if you're so determined. When does this Mr. Butt want you up there?"

"No later than the first of the year, father, so that I'll enter Trinity in time for the second semester. Of course, the wedding will be nothing elaborate, for Bernadette and I will have to rush back for work and school." He was beaming. "I was the one who wanted to get married before I left, but she, the darling, insisted on waiting 'til my seventeenth birthday."

Both father and son, by mutual silent consent, walked out the door and into the yard to discuss arrangements, leaving the females in the sitting room, staring at each other in silence.

Suddenly, Deirdre burst into chuckles. "Imagine our Dermot, a husband. A husband, indeed!"

"Aye, I'm admitting that 'tis hard for me to imagine it," Nora agreed thoughtfully. "Mayhap I was as guilty as your father of wishing him to other things. Parents are selfish creatures when it comes to their children."

"And what is it you wished for me then?" Deirdre wanted to know.

Nora smiled indulgently at the girl. "Oh, I suppose I often wished that you'd become a princess and live in a grand castle with a multitude of servants to attend to your every wish."

"Aye, that sounds lovely," Deirdre mused. "And what of Brenna?"

"There's no use in wishing for me," Brenna said. "I've all I want right here. The horses and the farm are enough for me."

As September gave way to October, the neat squares of carefully cultivated fields turned ripe with their gifts from the earth: golden oats, wheat, corn, potatoes. Although Kildare used his land mainly for horses' pasture and grazing, he still kept up the tradition of growing his own staples, and so there was plenty of work for everyone to do in reaping the harvest. Brenna and Deirdre were given many varied tasks to do since Dermot was no longer there to do his share. They drove the small cart to the miller's to have him grind the wheat and oats into flour; they helped to dig up the potatoes and took turns at the butter churn. It was a busy, happy time of year.

In November, when all the harvest had been gathered, the hunting season got under way. Brenna always looked forward to the hunt, for she and her family had traditionally been allowed to ride with Sir William's hunting party during his annual fox hunt in the first week of November.

Guests would arrive at the manor house, and, usually, Sir William would give a small party for those from out of town. The next morning, everyone would congregate in front of the house, and Sir William would appoint a master of the hunt—usually his son, Benjamin, home on holiday. The huntsman, who controlled the hounds, was always the senior servant Larrimer, who had been in Sir William's employ for nearly twenty years. Whippers-in were next in importance, and it was considered an honor to be appointed to the task.

On the morning of this year's hunt, Brenna awoke with a feeling of excitement. She hurried to the window to gaze out into the cool, clear morning and sent a prayer of thanksgiving to Our Lady for the good weather.

" 'Tis time," she called to her sister.

Deirdre hated the hunt and went along only to be near Benjamin. She was a poor horsewoman, and usually kept well to the rear, for the dead fox made her sick.

Brenna washed and brushed her hair, coiling the thick, shining blackness into a simple bun at the back of her head; then she dressed herself in her riding costume: a black, divided skirt, and a white blouse with a snowy stock to wrap snugly around her throat. Deirdre helped her with her riding boots and pinned the black bowler onto her head.

"Oh, 'tis a glorious day!" Brenna said enthusiastically as she pulled on her black jacket and gloves. She wished, with a stab of envy, that she might wear the beautiful scarlet coat, but such an honor was reserved for the master of the hunt, the huntsman, whippers-in, and followers of sufficient prestige. At least she could be proud that her father was allowed to wear it. Ah, and how handsome he would look, always at the front of the hunters! Even Nora would come along, but she, like Deirdre, would stay well back from the kill.

At breakfast, Brenna saw the sparkle in her father's eyes, and she felt as though her own reflected the same excitement. She and her father ate heartily of the buttered farls of hard bread, and the warm tea spread a glow of warmth throughout her body. A light breakfast was a part of the ritual, as everyone knew that a heavy breakfast made for poor riding.

"Seems to be a pleasant enough day outside," Nora commented with a trace of sleep in her voice.

"Aye, a fine day!" Kildare replied, grinning widely. His handsome face was aglow with eagerness. "Couldn't have asked for a better one, eh, Brenna?"

Brenna nodded happily. "I'm just hoping we find a fox without too much trouble." She winked at her sister, who made a face.

"Oh, you and your old hunts and foxes and killing!" she cried pettishly. "I just can't help feeling sorry for the fox—and I don't care one whit if you and Papa are disappointed today."

Kildare laughed. "You just stay to the rear, darling, and you'll not be seeing anything unpleasant."

"Aye, except when I bring home the tail as a trophy!" Brenna loved seeing her sister wince.

They rose from the table and hurried outside; Kevin and another groom were already holding their horses. Nora and Deirdre took two gentle, older mares, which would be content to stay behind, while Kildare was given his best hunter, a deep-breasted chestnut that pranced impatiently at the reins. Brenna had chosen to ride Minx, for although the mare had never ridden to the hunt before, Brenna was sure she could handle her sufficiently, and her father agreed. The four of them rode off at a leisurely trot.

They arrived at the Markham house just as the first few guests were trailing out from breakfast. Benjamin was already mounted, dressed splendidly in his scarlet coat and white breeches, his black velvet cap cocked jauntily over his hair. He was conversing with Jonas Larrimer, the huntsman. Two whippers-in had already been appointed to assist Larrimer with the hounds.

Brenna could not help gazing scornfully at some of the guests assembling slowly on the lawns. She could see Sir William dressed in scarlet with a splendid, shiny black top hat atop his silver-white hair, talking with an enormously fat woman whose coat looked as though it might burst at its seams at any moment. Two other women in scarlet coats waited and shivered in the chilly morning air.

"Good morning to you, Brenna Kildare."

Brenna turned in her saddle to see Rory Adair smiling cockily up at her as he laid a careless hand on her mount's flank. He was dressed like herself, except that he wore a top hat instead of a bowler—and Brenna thought he looked a bit comical.

"Hello, Rory," she answered him. "Are you to be riding in front today?"

He shook his head. "Sir William's named me a terrier man today—though God knows I hate the little yippers." His lip curled with disgust. His duty would be to bring, on foot, a group of fox terriers, which would be needed to dislodge the fox should it escape into an underground den. "I'm only hoping the earth-stoppers did their duty and closed up all the dens this morning." He winked at her. "That'll give me time to flirt with some of the young ladies."

"Well, then, Rory, I'm afraid I'll not be seeing you, for I'm determined to stay with the front," Brenna said tartly and moved her mount away from him.

As she directed Minx towards a small group which included her father, she was dismayed to see Steven Castaneda de la Cruz among the men, looking alarmingly handsome in a superbly cut, scarlet wool coat with the creamy stock at his throat contrasting the deeper tan of his skin. His white breeches followed the curve of his thigh muscles, and his shiny, black boots looked as though they had been custom-made for him. His top hat completed the picture of the elegant, young gentleman. Brenna felt envious and sulky.

Sensing her antagonism, Steven barely gave her a glance before fixing his attention flatteringly on a young lady from Bristol, who had come down on the same boat from England with him and Benjamin.

"Well, are we all assembled, father?" Benjamin asked, leading his horse to the group.

Sir William made a perfunctory scan about the lawn and nodded. "If they haven't gotten out here by now, they're welcome to their beds," he snorted impatiently. "I'm one to get to an early start, if we're all agreed."

The hounds were brought out, about fifteen matched pairs, sleek and nervous, all controlled by Larrimer and his whippers-in. Larrimer was able to control the hounds by voice and by blowing a horn, which blew two penetrating notes.

At Benjamin's command, the hounds began to move off to join the riders at a preordained place, called the 'meet'. The prestigious guests from England followed a few paces behind the master, and the others came discreetly a little farther back, with lesser functionaries—grooms, second horsemen, and terrier men—behind. Brenna was at the head of the second group, her eyes ahead on her father's proud, straight back. She turned once to see her mother and sister trailing slowly behind the grooms. She chuckled to herself and turned ahead. Her gaze by chance, fell on Steven, who was talking to a young lady Brenna did not know. Brenna's blue eyes narrowed, and she concentrated on keeping her horse composed in the throng. Minx was stepping nervously, and Brenna reached down to pat her neck, sure that the horse would calm down once they were allowed to begin the hunt and stretch out.

The meet had been selected near a patch of woodland, which thinned out to wide fields dotted by areas of gorse. The riders controlled their mounts while Benjamin sent the hounds to search the covert. A slight murmur rose among the group as they waited for first sight of the fox.

Suddenly, the din of the hounds pierced the frosty air,

sending a ripple of expectant tension through the ranks of the hunters. Two strident notes of Larrimer's horn and Benjamin's voice calling, "Tally-ho!" set riders and steeds bounding after the barking hounds.

Thrills of excitement tingled through Brenna as she felt the surge of Minx's powerful muscles beneath her. She maneuvered to the outside of the group so that when the fox was viewed, she would be able to keep away from the usual clog in the middle. She was obliged to keep a few paces back from the scarlet-coated guests, but once the fox was seen, she could ride as hard as she wished.

Suddenly, Benjamin uttered a high-pitched 'holloa,' which meant that he had seen the fox, and at the same moment, Brenna saw a flash of crimson dart away from her to the left. With her own excited cry, she urged Minx forward, following the white-tipped bushy tail. She could hear the cries of others as they, too, sighted the quarry. The fox darted toward a copse of trees, and Brenna followed. The other hunters fanned out to flank it.

"Come on, Minx," she cried, leaning forward and squeezing with her knees. "We've got him, girl!" She was aware of Benjamin slightly ahead of her and to her left, but she kept her attention on the pack of hounds, barking and yipping, as they drove the fox from the cover of the dead underbrush to the other side of the trees and into the open fields. Brenna nearly lost her hat to a low-hanging branch, but held on to it as Minx's strong hind legs sprang them over a low fence on the other side of the woods.

Cool air rushed past her face, burning her cheeks bright pink and drying her lips. She heard horses trotting on her right, and she veered a little to the left, stretching Minx into a gallop. She glanced to the left to see her father matching her pace, his big chestnut tearing at the turf with his hoofs. And a little behind, she thought she saw Steven Cruz.

The fields spread out before her now, dry and brown, providing little cover for the fox. She watched its red flash weave in and out in front of the slavering hounds, who were being kept in a tight pack by Larrimer and his helpers. The hunters spread out in a wide fan, with Brenna, her father, and Benjamin farthest forward.

The wind picked up and smarted Brenna's eyes into tears. She quickly wiped at them with the back of her glove and collected herself just in time to take a small ditch that opened up in front of her. The jump was sloppy, and Brenna could feel the jar in her bones when Minx landed. It caused her to lose the lead; she looked up to see her father and Benjamin pulling smoothly away. She fought to control her frustration as she tried to bring her horse back into a gallop. Another rider appeared behind her, and they nearly collided.

"Watch where you're going now!" she cried furiously.

The rider was Steven. "Control your horse, little girl, or stay in back with the others!" he yelled back.

"Damn you!" Brenna hissed, without thinking. She finally brought Minx under control, but the fox was out of sight. Then the hounds' barking grew strong again, and Brenna set Minx in the right direction.

Minx's powerful legs were striding to a full gallop, and Brenna was so intent on passing Steven that she was not watching carefully enough as she entered a patch of gorse at the top of a low rise. Loose earth flew away from Minx's hoofs and caused her to lose her balance and nearly fall. Brenna sawed at the reins and drew her horse sharply to the left, bumping her into Steven's mount which had cleared the gorse. Both horses faltered, and their riders were obliged to pull up or risk laming them.

Brenna was breathing rapidly, her blue eyes flashing fire as they met Steven's snapping black ones. She realized that he was not going to act the part of the polite gentleman this time.

"Senorita, if you don't know how to ride a horse," he said harshly, "for God's sake, stay out of my way!" He patted his mount's neck to calm it.

"If *I* don't know—" she retorted in shocked incredulity. "I know perfectly well how to ride a horse, sir, but *you* seem to be having some difficulty!"

"Just stay out of my way," he said, beginning to walk his horse, then cursing under his breath as the animal faltered. "Damn, I think he's pulled a muscle." He leaped down, losing his hat which didn't seem to matter to him, and began to inspect the trembling animal.

Brenna watched him, amused. "Do you really think *you* can tell what's wrong with him?" she inquired. "My goodness, 'tis quite an expert you've become since working with my father."

He didn't trust himself to answer her, but continued to run his hands over the horse's legs, gently prodding. Brenna realized that sounds of the hunt were growing farther away. Even the grooms and terrier men had passed her on the other side. It was probably too late to be catching up with the others, she told herself, but she'd be much happier trying than staying here with this arrogant, ill-mannered bore.

"Well, I'll be leaving your fascinating company," she said waspishly. "Shall I send someone back to be fetching you home?"

He looked up at her with a glare in those black eyes that made her stop smiling. "I don't need your help, senorita—but I think you could use some manners!"

"I'm thinking you could do with some instruction of your own," she returned impudently, pulling at the reins.

"Why, you little Irish brat!" he snapped back and reached up as though to draw her down from her horse.

With a dart of fear and trembling anger, Brenna jerked the reins, pulling Minx's head sharply to the right and throwing the already nervous mare into a worse state. The horse, confused and frightened, reared up, nearly unseating Brenna, who instinctively grabbed a handful of the silky, dark mane. The frightened mare reared again—and this time, her left front hoof caught Steven on the side of his head.

Brenna tugged mercilessly at the reins, sawing at the bridle. She had never hurt a horse before, but she had seen Steven fall heavily to the ground, and she was frantic to get Minx away from his unprotected body. Finally, Minx was calm enough to stand, trembling, while Brenna slipped off and ran to Steven.

His eyes were closed, his breathing shallow, and an ominous dark stain pooled on the grass behind his ear. Brenna gulped for air; she could hardly see through the tears of horror in her eyes.

Dear God! She must get help! She looked around wildly but saw no one.

Quickly, she took off her jacket, folded it into a pillow, and slipped it under Steven's head. His face was so pale beneath the usual dark tan of his skin that for an agonized moment, she thought she might have killed him. But he was breathing. She hated to leave him alone, but there was no time to lose.

After she tied his horse well away from him, Brenna remounted Minx, patting her steadily on the neck and whispering into her ear to calm her down. Then, Brenna urged her into a gallop.

Brenna was lucky enough to catch up with some of the stragglers in a few minutes, and with streaming eyes and breathless phrases, she explained what had happened. Two young gentlemen from London whistled sharply to one of the grooms, and together, they rode back to the spot where Steven lay.

Brenna watched in anguish as they picked up the young man and cradled him gently in the groom's arms. If he dies, she thought, it will be my fault!

Chapter Twelve

STEVEN was taken to Sir William's house, where he was carried gently upstairs and laid in his bed. Mrs. Longstreet, who had been summoned to take temporary charge, clucked her sympathy over Brenna's white, guilty face as much as Steven's wound.

"Where's the others?" the cook asked quickly.

"They—they don't know," Brenna said in a small voice. "I suppose they'll still be hunting—" Her eyes grew rounder as Mrs. Longstreet turned Steven's head to the side to look more closely at the wound. "Has he—has he lost very much blood?" she asked nervously, hovering as close as she dared.

"I can't be telling yet, sweeting," Mrs. Longstreet answered calmly. "Why don't you go downstairs and ask one of the maids to give you some linens. I'll also need a pan of water and my sewing basket."

Brenna hurried to do as asked, asking directions of one of the footmen. Her head was pounding with self-accusation. How could this have happened? It was all her fault! If only she hadn't been so stupid and stubborn. If only she hadn't been determined to put Steven at fault. Was she so mean-tempered that she could not even show kindness anymore?

She ran back up the stairs minutes later, the linen folded over one arm, the bucket of water hanging from the other, and Mrs. Longstreet's sewing basket held under her chin. When she arrived in Steven's room, the cook had already stripped Steven of his clothing and covered him lightly with a sheet. He was groaning and turning in the narrow bed, his face as gray as ash.

"Here are the things you wanted, Mrs. Longstreet," she whispered.

Mrs. Longstreet wiped the blood away from the evil cut on Steven's brow. It started just above the hairline and receded into his black hair. It still oozed slightly.

At the sight of Brenna's horrified look, the cook laid a fond hand on the girl's shoulder. "Don't you be worrying about the lad, Brenna. He'll pull through with a little nursing and your prayers." She hesitated. "Umm, how did this happen, child?"

"I—it all happened so fast that I—I'm not sure," Brenna said nervously. "We were riding with the hunt and our mounts collided and we fell behind the others. Then I—then I misjudged a jump and—" She gulped and tears formed in her eyes. "When Steven got down to check his horse, we—we started to quarrel and my horse reared up—"

"I see. No need to go on, child," Mrs. Longstreet soothed. She was a curious woman by nature, but she could see the torture the child was going through. It was best to drop the matter for now. "I'm going to wash him now," she said gently. " 'Tis not for you to be seeing him like this."

"Then let me wind the bandages, please, Mrs. Longstreet!"

"All right, then. Has someone gone off to take word to Sir William?" When Brenna nodded, she went on, "I just want to sponge the lad off for I can feel the fever setting in from his wound. Why don't you go over to the chest there and tear those linens into strips so that we can bind the wound after cleansing it?"

As Mrs. Longstreet pulled aside the sheet and sponged down the muscular young body, she found her own withered cheeks blushing. When she finished, she covered the boy again with a sheet and a blanket. "It will sweat the fever from him," she told Brenna.

"Now, let's be looking at this frightful cut." She gently pulled away the hair from the sides of the wound and looked at the gash. "It's still oozing a mite. I'll have to sew it up."

Brenna gulped audibly. The older woman gave her a sympathetic look. "One of the other maids can help me, child. It's not for you to feel you have to do it."

"Aye, I *do* have to help!" Brenna returned fiercely.
" 'Tis my fault!"

"All right, then, you be a brave girl, and we'll have
him fixed up before the others even get back." She took
out needle and thread and began talking conversationally
to soothe the girl's nervousness. "Now, don't you remember the day I stitched up your knee, child? Ah, you were
nine or ten, I think, and had come up with your father.
As usual, you ran out to the stables and were playing
about, and down you went in a pile of rock and dried
hay, cutting a great gash just above your knee. Your dear
mama nearly fainted at the blood, I daresay, and you—
why, you were crying loud enough to wake the banshees.
Afterward you slept like a baby on the way home, and
your mother told me you had only a little stiffness." She
laughed to herself. "I'm guessing I did a pretty fair job if
you didn't remember all of that."

She was beginning to stitch together the two lips of the
gash. Steven's groans seemed to shoot through Brenna's
head, and she flinched once when he gave a loud curse.
Mrs. Longstreet finished quickly and asked Brenna to
give her the linen to wrap about his head so that
he couldn't touch the wound in his sleep.

Brenna couldn't keep her eyes off Steven's hands,
which were picking feebly at the blanket. She handed the
cook the strips of linen, one by one, and Mrs. Longstreet
wrapped his head, leaving a fringe of dark hair sticking
out in back.

Satisfied, the cook stood and looked down at the restless boy. "The wound will heal quickly, for he is young
and strong. The only thing we'll be worrying about is the
fever, and for tonight, one of the servants will stay with
him to sponge him off. We'll see how he is in the morning then."

"Oh, Mrs. Longstreet, please let me stay with him tonight!" Brenna begged. " 'Tis my fault that he's this way.
I should be the one to be staying up, losing sleep."

"Hush now, child. Why, Sir William would be scandal-
ized to hear you talk that way! You know well enough,
he'd not allow it. Now, you just tell yourself that you've

done everything you could, and let it be. Don't fret yourself about an accident."

"But . . ."

"No." Mrs. Longstreet could be quite firm when she wanted to be, and Brenna knew that her word was final.

"All right, then, but I'll be waiting until Sir William gets back. He might want to ask me how it happened," she said lifelessly.

"You come on down to the kitchens with me, child, and I'll give you a pot of strong tea. You're tensed up like a spring, and I don't want you fainting away on me!"

Mrs. Longstreet instructed one of the servants to sit in Steven's room until Sir William returned. They hadn't long to wait before the entire hunting party was spilling into the house, demanding to know what had happened.

Sir William looked nearly as white as the patient, for he was quite aware of the consequences, should something happen to the boy under his care. Señor Castaneda de la Cruz would not take it kindly. He strode upstairs to Steven's room, and began to bellow downstairs for Mrs. Longstreet.

"There now, we'll straighten everything out, and you'll be going home with your family," Mrs. Longstreet promised, urging the girl to finish her tea. Just then, her father burst through the kitchen door, looking for his daughter.

"What the hell has happened?" he demanded.

The cook made a quick exit to face the other bellower, leaving Brenna to gaze shamefacedly at her father while she attempted to explain the accident. She had gotten only half-way through when her father interrupted.

"Brenna Kildare, I'm surprised at you, letting your pride make you forget common courtesy." But despite his words, there was a curiously proud look in his eyes when he heard of his daughter's determination to be at the head of the hunt. " 'Twas not Steven's fault that his horse rammed yours."

"Aye, Papa, I know that, but I was angry."

"Lass, you were foolish!"

Brenna could barely hold back the tears of guilt now, and her father saw them trembling on her long lashes. He realized then that she was still under a strain, and that his interrogation of her only made it worse. Quickly, he put his arms around her trembling shoulders.

"Ah, now, lass, I'm that sorry to be causing you more pain, but, my God, if something happens to that boy—" He left the sentence unfinished and shook his head. "There, there, darlin'," he soothed. "He will be all right, I'm sure of it. You're not to be taking all the blame on yourself now."

"Oh, Papa, I can still see him reaching up and the horse hitting his head. It was awful, the blood and him lying there so white."

"Hush, Brenna," Kildare continued, feeling awkward now in the face of his daughter's anguish. "Let's be getting you back to your mother and sister. They're waiting for us at home."

"Aye, Papa, but what if Sir William . . ."

"We'll straighten it all out later," he promised. "It's enough you've been through for now."

He left a message of explanation for Sir William with one of the servants, then hurried his daughter away from the gossiping Londoners and the other curious participants of the hunt who wondered why the young girl was weeping.

Brenna was thankful to be getting home to the comfort of her mother's arms, but she couldn't shake the horrid picture of Steven lying so helplessly on the ground. She had thought she loathed him, but that picture, etched sharply in her mind, haunted her conscience and made her deeply penitent that she had been the cause of it. Nora ushered her daughter up to her room to rest, but Deirdre was too curious to allow her sister a moment alone.

"How is he?" Deirdre asked. She had already dressed in a clean frock.

"Mrs. Longstreet had to sew up his wound," Brenna answered slowly. "I—I begged her to let me stay with him to watch for the fever, but she wouldn't let me. Oh, Deirdre, how can I just be sitting here like this, when I keep seeing Minx striking out at him with her hoof and him falling to the ground with blood on his face?"

"He'll be all right, if Mrs. Longstreet said so," Deirdre comforted her. "Now don't be worrying about him like that."

"I can't help it!"

Deirdre looked exasperated. "Why is it that you're so worried about him? Is it that you're liking him then, Brenna?"

"Why I—I just feel so terrible—I mean I was so bestial to him—"

"Ach, you were that," Deirdre agreed. "But then, he's been bestial to you—"

"No, no," Brenna cried. "He knew I didn't like him and . . ."

"I'm remembering a time when you couldn't wait for him to leave," Deirdre reminded her.

"Aye, but that was different then."

" 'Twas no different," Deirdre replied firmly. "He'll get better, and you'll be spitting at him again, no doubt."

Because she had been certain she wouldn't be able to sleep, Brenna was surprised when she awoke to the dawn. Her cheeks felt raw with the salt of her tears, and her eyes stung. She arose immediately and went to the basin to pour water from the pitcher. Deirdre mumbled in her sleep, turned over and began to snore gently.

Brenna dressed quickly in a simple, cotton frock and brushed her hair into a tight knot at the base of her neck, securing it with pins from Deirdre's vanity box. She tiptoed downstairs. Her mother and father were already up and conversing quietly at the table.

"What are you doing up so early?" Nora asked her gently.

"You should be getting yourself right back to bed," Kildare added.

"I—I only wondered if we might get word of how Steven is doing," Brenna meekly replied.

"Well, you'll be knowing as soon as I get back, for I'm on my way to check on the lad myself."

"Oh, Papa, could I go with you?" Brenna pleaded. "They may need someone to sit with him."

Kildare started to protest, then thought better of it. "All right, lass, you can come along, but you'll be sticking close by me—"

"Aye, Papa—and thank you," Brenna said.

Brenna managed to gulp down a cup of tea and a bit of toast before setting off with her father. They arrived at Markham's house an hour later.

"I shouldn't have let Minx ride the hunt," she said to herself.

" 'Twas not your fault!" Kildare said sharply. "You couldn't know the horse would be so easily spooked."

"She was nervous at the meet. I should have taken her out then," Brenna continued. "But I was so determined to show off. I truly thought I could win the tail if I tried hard enough."

" 'Tis over now," Kildare put in. "And no one won the tail. The damned fox outsmarted us. We thought we had it treed, but the cunning thing . . ." He glanced at his daughter and realized she wasn't listening.

Sir William met them at the door, very nearly bumping into them as he hurried down the carved steps. "Ah, Kildare, haven't time for you now," Sir William said quickly. "The lad's a sight worse than yesterday, and I'm off to the stables to have my best man fetch a physician from Waterford. Damn, what a time for Dr. Mahoney to be away." He looked tired and in no mood for conversation, so Kildare stepped aside to let him pass, and gave his daughter a stern look.

Brenna ignored her father's orders for the first time in her life. She stepped up behind Sir William to touch his arm. He turned around impatiently. "Sir William, excuse me, sir, but there's a woman skilled in herbal remedies who lives hardly half an hour's hard ride away. I visited her last year. She lives down by the beaches. Her name is Siobhan, I think—aye, that's it. She's the *pishogue* of the district, the wise woman. It'd be much faster to bring her back, sir, if you're that worried."

Sir William looked at the girl thoughtfully. "The

woman is known to be skilled?" he demanded. "She's not just some fanatic who thinks she's the reincarnation of a druid or something?"

"She is reknowned for her medicinal skills," she replied forcefully.

Sir William thought for a moment. "All right, then, take one of my servants and fetch the woman, but I'll still send someone to Waterford. I don't want anything to happen to that boy!"

"I'll ride to Waterford, Sir William," Kildare broke in. "I feel partially responsible for the lad's accident since . . ."

"All right, all right," Sir William interrupted impatiently. "And I thank you, Kildare." He hesitated, "Though there's no need for you to feel responsible."

Kildare spoke a few quiet words to his daughter, who was mounting her own horse, then he said a silent prayer to God to watch over the lad upstairs. Waterford was a hard day's riding, he thought grimly. He only hoped that this wise woman of his daughter's acquaintance truly would know what to do.

Fortunately, Brenna and the servant had had no trouble locating the wise woman, Siobhan. She had not yet gone out on her daily rounds and was sipping a cup of tea when the pair arrived. They poured out the tale and urged her to hurry, but she remained calm, and her quiet soothed Brenna's troubled soul. Together all three started back to Markham Hall.

Siobhan had efficiently tied everything she would need in a neat bundle and, holding tightly to her medicine bag, rode behind the footman. Brenna reached the house first, jumping off Minx and handing the reins to the groom. She helped Siobhan down and assisted her up the stairs where the majordomo waited with the door open and Sir William standing anxiously in the hall behind him.

Brenna quickly introduced the woman to Sir William. "I'm relieved to see you, Siobhan," the Englishman said, gesturing up the staircase. "Shall we hurry up to the boy? My cook, Mrs. Longstreet, has been tending to him since the accident. She sewed up the gash yesterday, but now she tells me the wound seems not to be healing properly, and I can see how the fever still wracks him with pain."

"Aye, there must be some evil still in the wound," Siobhan said in her quiet voice. "She has cleaned it thoroughly?"

"Aye," Brenna interrupted distractedly, "and sewed it up tight, and bound it with clean cloth." They entered the bedroom of the sick young man."

"Perhaps not all of the dead flesh was cleaned out," Siobhan remarked thoughtfully, setting her bundle on the bed at the boy's feet. "You did not think of cauterizing?" she asked the cook, who was seated, white-lipped, in a chair beside the bed.

Mrs. Longstreet shook her head, her eyes glancing fearfully at Sir William's gruff face. "I thought to spare him that pain," she answered, knowing the answer was inadequate as the other woman looked at her with eloquent, dark eyes. Although Mrs. Longstreet was older than Siobhan, she felt at a loss beside the quiet purposefulness of the *pishogue*.

" 'Tis a simple matter to cut the stitches. First let me see the wound, then we will decide."

Sir William cleared his throat, as though to clarify his own wishes in the matter. "This boy is a guest of mine," he said to Siobhan as she began to unroll the bandages. "Nothing serious must be allowed to happen to him. Do you understand? He must receive only the best of care, until the physician arrives from Waterford." He could see that the woman was listening with only half an ear, and he thought to himself that she certainly looked competent and level-headed, but who really knew about some of these so-called 'wise women'? He was sure she would be expecting a generous sum for looking after the boy. Perhaps that would be enough to insure that she did her best by him. She was, after all, his best hope. Sweet Jesus, she was his only hope, he amended as Steven let out a long moan of pain.

He noticed the young girl, Brenna, standing at the foot of the bed, anxiety written clearly on her face. He felt for her a fatherly sympathy, for he knew she must be torturing herself with guilt, but—dammit! It was, after all, partly her fault that the lad was lying in this state. Sir William laid a hand on her shoulder.

"Come now, girl, we'd best leave this to the others. Why don't you go on home now, and I'll have one of the servants bring you word."

"Oh, no, Sir William, do let me stay!" Brenna protested, her blue eyes pleading with unshed tears. "I—I can help and . . ."

"Let her be staying, Sir William," Siobhan ordered quietly.

He blustered, not at all sure he liked taking orders from a woman—and a stranger at that. But after a moment, he nodded. Maybe he was getting soft in his old age, but what the hell. The lass couldn't do any harm, and it might help assuage some of her guilt if she stayed. He realized that some of his guests would think it highly improper to allow an Irish farm girl the run of his house, let alone to remain in one of his guest's bedroom, but he really didn't care about them. He would serve them a good lunch and plenty of wine, and, he thought sarcastically, they wouldn't bother themselves with the idea.

"All right, then, you may stay, Brenna," he finally answered, and then to Siobhan he said, "I've got to tend to my other guests, but I will be back up to check on his progress."

Mrs. Longstreet also excused herself, for she had to tend to her kitchen duties, but she promised to send up a maid to assist Siobhan.

" 'Tis not necessary, Mrs. Longstreet," Siobhan said kindly. "Brenna can be helping me, and if I need water or such, I'll send her down to you."

Mrs. Longstreet nodded, resisting a strong urge to curtsey. Really, she thought to herself, where did the woman come off being so damned regal! She muttered as she left the room, and took the servants' stairs down to the kitchens.

As Siobhan unwound the linen from Steven's head, she asked how the accident had happened. Brenna answered clearly and to the point as she took the discarded linen from the older woman. Yellowish fluid had seeped through the layers of the cloth.

"Ah, you see the flesh is putrid," Siobhan pointed out. She pressed the flesh gently; Steven screamed, and his body jerked on the bed. "You'll have to go down and ask Mrs. Longstreet to heat an iron. Bring a razor to shave his head. And have one of the maids tell Sir William what I am going to do. I'll need two strong lads to hold him down."

Brenna, looking as though she might be sick, started down the main staircase. She caught a glimpse of two young ladies coming straight toward her. At sight of the Irish girl, the two Londoners put their perfectly coiffed heads together and began to whisper animatedly. Mortified, Brenna turned around on her heel and found the way to the servants' stairs, which led directly to the kitchens.

As soon as Brenna had brought the needed materials, Siobhan lathered the area on either side of the gash.

"I'll be shaving the hair around the wound while it is still sewn up," she explained. " 'Twill keep the fallen hair from entering the wound." She was deft with the blade, shaving a neat, half-moon on Steven's head. "And now, I'll be cutting open the stitches. Bring me my scissors, there, in the bag." Brenna obeyed. "See, the wound has puffed up. The stitches probably would have popped beneath the bandage. 'Twould have left the boy with a bad scar—and he is a handsome lad, now, isn't he?" she asked easily, watching, for an instant, the reaction on Brenna's face.

The wound gaped open as the scissors cut, exposing the pus and blood that had collected inside. Brenna steeled herself not to be sick, but it was horrible knowing that, with a little more force, Minx could have fractured Steven's skull. She felt close to fainting.

Siobhan continued talking, knowing her even, quiet speech helped to calm her assistant's fears. "Brenna, I'll be cleansing his wound now with a mixture of herbs I've brought with me. Bring me more heated water, and tell Mrs. Longstreet I'll be needing the iron in a moment."

Brenna was glad to leave the room, but it seemed only short minutes before she was trudging upstairs again with more water. She poured some into a bowl, and Siobhan added her herbal remedies. Another portion went into a teapot for a special brew that could steep while the wound was tended to and then be given to Steven to strengthen him when he awoke.

Sir William knocked and entered the room with two strong, young grooms who shuffled about nervously, feeling uncomfortable on the rich carpet.

"You have to cauterize the wound?" Sir William asked bleakly.

Siobhan did not look up. " 'Tis the only thing to do to seal it from infection."

Markham nodded, although he was frowning slightly, wishing he had a second opinion. After a brief hesitation, he ordered the two grooms to hold down the patient while Siobhan began to clean the wound. He watched Siobhan's quick, darting hands, which barely seemed to touch the wound. Yet Steven yelled and cried out and would surely have thrown his body from the bed, had not the two grooms held him down. Sir William tightened his lips together as he watched the woman go about the painfully thorough operation until the wound was cleansed to her satisfaction.

Once, Steven's eyes opened, and he looked in terror about the room; then they rolled back and closed again. This frightened Brenna more than anything else.

"Why does he not stay awake?" she asked Siobhan.

"Because the pain is so great that the body is defending itself by keeping him asleep, so to speak." Siobhan leaned forward to examine the wound a last time before instructing Brenna to get the iron.

Sir William stopped her at the door. "I'll see to it," he said, his face looking green.

Soon, Mrs. Longstreet knocked on the door and gingerly handed the iron to Siobhan, who took the cloth-wrapped handle with a firm grip. She glanced kindly at Brenna's sick face. "Please take the used linen outside," she said, "and then come back up."

"Aye," Brenna said quickly, hurrying from the room as though her life depended on her speed. She nearly knocked into Sir William in the hall. She explained her mission and Sir William released her, but he looked as though he would like to go with her.

A few moments later, she heard a horrible, high-pitched scream, which seemed to go on and on. She knew that everyone in the house could hear that awful scream. She imagined she could smell the odor of burning flesh and hair. Choking, she ran outside to the kitchen yard and was violently sick. She doubled over, retching, then stood up shakily and wiped her mouth with a handkerchief. When she walked toward the gardens to take in some fresh air, she encountered a group of young ladies and gentlemen.

"Good God, what are they doing to that poor young man?" one of the ladies asked sympathetically.

"Yes, what are they doing? God knows what manner of woman is that crone who Sir William allows to attend him!" exclaimed another young lady with a hint of malice in her velvet voice.

"I daresay, we shouldn't be troubling you, miss," a young man interrupted pleasantly enough. "Let's go find Benjamin, shall we?" he suggested to the others. "Perhaps we can go slumming in one of the local villages tonight." He laughed haughtily, and Brenna hurried back into the house. She was angry that Sir William would allow such shallow, heartless people into his house.

They didn't give a fig for Steven Castaneda de la Cruz, Brenna thought as she mounted the backstairs. As long as he was healthy and entertaining, 'twas all right to call him friend and carry on with him, but now, when he needed their sympathy, they could only think about their own fun and games. It was disgusting—and she suddenly wondered if Steven were like that too.

As she entered the room, she saw Mrs. Longstreet, looking exhausted, preparing to leave with the iron. Following her were the two lads, whose faces were white and strained. Sir William, over by the bed, inspected the angry, red puckered flesh around Steven's wound. Steven's face looked blanched, although Brenna could see drops of blood around his mouth where he must have bitten his lip.

"This—this will be all that's needed?" Sir William was asking. He looked to Siobhan hopefully.

She nodded. "Why don't you be going downstairs, Sir William, and get yourself a glass of wine," she suggested kindly. "I'll just be wrapping his head up to protect it, and then I'll be finished."

Sir William escaped the room gladly, leaving Siobhan with a little half-smile on her face. She bandaged the wound with amazing speed. "Now," she said to Brenna, "let's see if he awakens enough to get some tea down him. You and I can use a cup ourselves," she went on.

"Will he be all right?" Brenna asked in a cracking voice.

Siobhan nodded. "Aye, 'twill be a few days before he's well enough to get out of bed, but I should say within two or three weeks he will be well enough to be getting about." She laughed softly. "Oh, he'll have a little bald spot, of course, but his hair is thick and will grow back swiftly. 'Twill not mar his looks, lass, truly."

"I wasn't worried about his looks," Brenna replied tersely.

She poured the tea and sat on a chair, watching Steven thoughtfully while she sipped. Sweat seemed to be beading all over his face now; she knew that this was because of the fever.

"Aye, he sweats and 'tis good," Siobhan said as though she read the girl's thoughts. "The fever shouldn't last through the next day, but he'll need a sponging every hour to make sure. I'll be leaving instructions with Sir William so that he can have one of the servants tend to it."

"'Tis I who should be doing it," Brenna said soberly. "'Twas my fault."

Siobhan held a finger to her lips. "Hush, 'twas no one's fault, only an accident. What would you be doing? You cannot go on punishing yourself for something you hadn't intended. Except for a thin scar that no one will ever see, the lad will be none the worse for the experience."

"Oh, Siobhan, thank you!" Brenna said sincerely.

"Hush now, hush now," Siobhan replied, seeing that the girl was very close to tears. "Why don't you be staying here with the lad while I go to find Sir William."

"You—you must feel wonderful, being able to heal people and soothe their suffering," Brenna said. "I should like to be able to do that."

"If ever you have the time, my dear, I'm thinking I'd welcome an extra pair of hands to aid me." She shrugged. "In any case, I am glad to have helped."

The woman went out the door, limping a little from the twisted foot. Brenna looked back at Steven. How weak he looked, weak as a kitten. Was this the same young man who had teased her and behaved so arrogantly? Where was the haughty demeanor, the condescension that made her feel like such a child? Now, *he* seemed more like a child, lying there so vulnerable. She found herself almost looking forward to his convalescence —would he be grateful that she had brought Siobhan to aid him?

She shook her head and got up from her chair to put the teacup on the chest. Absently, she gazed out the window, realizing self-consciously for the first time that she was actually inside Sir William's house, inside Steven's bedroom. She could imagine him looking from this window over the front lawns and the gravel drive with its graceful arch of trees. The trees were bare now, nude from the swirling November winds, which made great piles of dry, crackling leaves. Still, it was a lovely sight.

A sudden sound from the bed brought her out of her reverie, and she turned to see that Steven had pushed the blankets off, tangling his legs in the covers while one arm dangled off the bed.

Without time for thought, Brenna ran over and lifted the arm gently, placing it at his side, then pushed him by the shoulder back towards the middle of the bed. And then she looked down his length—and felt the heat in her own body. She had known, of course, that he was naked beneath the covers, but never had she considered what he might look like disrobed.

Like a tiny child who has just raided the cupboard, she looked quickly at the closed door, expecting to be caught. Then, slowly, unwillingly, her eyes went back to the young, male body before her. They traveled shyly over the broad, flat chest with a hint of dark, curly hair in the middle of it; the strong shoulders, which would grow broader with age; the long, muscular arms, used to holding a bucking horse or lifting a heavy saddle; the fine-boned, long-fingered hands that were clenching and unclenching in his fever.

Now, with curiosity and excitement, Brenna let her eyes roam over the tightly muscled belly below the rib-cage; then lower, where the dark, curly hair—very like that on his chest—grew in a straight line down his abdomen and branched out around his groin. She blushed, remembering how she had noticed this very same thing on herself. Then, she saw the part of him that made men so different from women—a strange looking assortment, indeed, she thought, wondering how it was that they kept it all hidden inside their trousers. She looked lower, at the long legs covered with hair, and she saw the shape of an old scar on one thigh. She wondered briefly how he had come by it.

Steven moaned suddenly, causing her to jump. She was frightened he might wake up and find her looking at him. Quickly, she reached down, disentangled his legs from the bedding, and pulled the cover back over him. But before she had even had time to seat herself, he tossed it back down again. In exasperation, she reached to pull it up; his hands, surprisingly strong in his delirium, pushed it back to his legs again. For a few minutes, they continued this push-pull routine, which made Brenna feel more and more ridiculous.

"Steven, now you be stopping that!" she finally cried out.

There was a soft knock on the door, and a young lady came in, dressed beautifully in blue watered-silk with yards and yards of snow-white lace edging the wide hemline. It was the blonde young lady with whom Steven had been talking at the hunt yesterday. Involuntarily, Brenna's eyes dropped to the blanket that she was holding tightly against Steven's hands, and she reddened.

The blonde girl laughed indulgently. "It's naughty to peek at the poor boy like that," she trilled delightedly. "I'm sure he's in no state to do your curiosity any justice."

Brenna dropped the blanket as though she had been scalded, and Steven pushed it down, but thankfully, only to his waist.

"How is he?" the girl went on, her eyes playing with a silky curl that lay over her shoulder.

When Brenna tried to speak, she squeaked instead, cleared her throat, and only then was able to answer, "Well enough now, though he'll have to be watched for fever."

"The poor dear. How long will he be laid up?"

"Two or three weeks." Brenna wished she could tell the girl to get out, but she was painfully aware of the thin right she, herself, had to be there.

"Such a shame," the girl responded to herself. "Such a dashing, entertaining fellow he was. I'm afraid I shall be gone before he's able to . . ." She stopped and smiled wickedly. "Ah, well, so much the worse for me." She let her cool stare pass lazily over the Irish girl. "Had you ought to be here with him—alone? I mean in England, it would be considered most compromising for a young lady to be found in a man's bedroom." She sighed in self-mockery. "Ah, but then I suppose you are still a child."

Brenna was gathering herself to spring at the other girl when Siobhan and Sir William entered. The elderly gentleman dismissed the blonde girl with a brief look; the girl dimpled for his benefit, then smiled dazzlingly. His look softened and he patted her on the shoulder.

"Out we go, my dear," he said in an agreeable voice. "The lad needs his rest, you know."

"Oh yes, Sir William, I was just looking in on him," the girl replied sweetly and let herself out.

Brenna, grinding her teeth with suppressed fury, stared after her. What an actress the girl was. Was that the kind of girl her sister wanted to emulate? Heaven forbid that an Irish girl would ever sink so low, she thought, with a sneer.

Chapter Thirteen

ALTHOUGH Sir William had generously invited Brenna to come as often as she wished to visit Steven while he was convalescing, Brenna told herself that she would be too embarrassed to face him after seeing him naked.

Brenna's father often proclaimed his disappointment in her, for he had expected her to make a formal apology as soon as the lad was conscious, but Brenna procrastinated until her father finally dropped the subject.

She knew well enough that it was her duty to make an apology and assured herself that she would when the time was right—when her feelings weren't so mixed up.

November plodded on, gray and dismal. In the last week of the month, Benjamin Markham rode over to the farm for a visit. Brenna and Dierdre were in the kitchen, eating some of Nora's delicious creamed potato soup.

"Well, well, it looks as though I'm in luck, catching these two young lovelies alone," Benjamin joked gallantly as he walked into the kitchen. He seated himself on a chair. "Where are your parents?"

"Papa's over at the Adairs helping out with a sick mare, and Mama's upstairs," Brenna answered quickly. It was odd, she thought, for Benjamin to be here at this time of year. "Why aren't you back at school?"

Benjamin chuckled. "Good Lord, you sound like a mother! For your information, ducks, I'm home until Christmas. Father thought, since Steven was laid up, that we'd just sit this month out and wait 'til after the Christmas holidays to go back. I must say I like the idea myself." He laughed again. "I would say, Rory's happy enough to be here too, seeing as how he's more interested in pursuing a plump, little hen tonight than tackling scholastic studies."

"Rory, interested in chickens?" Brenna asked in confusion.

Benjamin laughed. "Yes, this one's a plump little bird with reddish-brown feathers and hazel eyes. Just the one to get our poor Rory into some trouble, if he's not careful." He winked conspiratorially at the two girls.

"Maureen Derry!" Brenna guessed with amazement.

Benjamin grinned and leaned closer. "Now, how did you become so shrewd, Brenna Kildare?" he asked. "Rory will have my head if he knows I've told you about it." But there wasn't a hint of worry in his blue eyes.

"Well, we'll not be telling him," Deirdre said primly, her eyes suddenly modest. "I'm certainly not so childish as to be tattling on anyone like that."

Benjamin glanced from her soft chestnut hair to the gentle swell of her bosom, modestly understated by her becoming frock. "Why, it's true, Deirdre, you aren't a child anymore," he laughed with a mocking glint in his eyes. "I daresay, I shall have to be wary of you before too long."

"How's that?" she demanded, pleased at his comment despite herself.

"Why, all the girls go after me sooner or later," he told her with an ironic arch of his brow. "I'm just so damned charming, you know."

Deirdre pinkened. "You're conceited and arrogant, Benjamin Markham. More's the pity, too, for you might— and I said, *might*—just have suited my fancy in a couple of years, although, I'm thinking you'll be old and married by the time I'm in my prime."

Brenna was pleased at the dull flush that darkened Benjamin's face.

"Old and married! Why, I'm not that much older than you," he protested.

Deirdre appeared to calculate. "I'm thinking you're seventeen, and I'm but twelve, sir. When I'm your age, you'll be twenty-two and long since packaged off to some doleful, sourpuss of an English wife, who will have given you one child already and be big with another!"

"Deirdre!" Brenna cried, aghast at her sister's boldness.

But Benjamin was roaring with laughter. "Such impertinence!" he finally got out, his eyes streaming with tears of mirth. "Why, just for that, Miss Deirdre Kildare, I suppose I shall have to wait until you're grown up. I promise I'll not marry before then."

He was jesting of course, but Deirdre flushed in triumph.

Having heard the laughter, Nora came downstairs, greeted Benjamin, and asked him about Steven's progress.

"Oh, he's doing well enough—chomping at the bit, you can imagine, for he hates being cooped up in his room all day. Insists he's well enough to ride, but Father is not about to let him sit a horse until that wise woman, what's her name, gives the okay. So, Steven roars about his room and promises revenge on the little one who laid him up." He stopped and looked pointedly at Brenna, who flushed crimson. "Oh, I'm just teasing you, duck." He laughed at her anxious look.

"I do feel badly about it," Brenna said defensively. "You—you may tell him so."

Benjamin shook his head. "Afraid to face the lion in his den?" He winked. "Don't blame you. He's so sour, he's even lit into me once or twice."

Brenna tried to bring back into focus, the weak, naked, feverish young man that she had likened to a kitten only weeks before. Somehow, the memory evaded her. Instead, she could only picture flashing, angry black eyes and a mouth with its corners turned down in a frown. She could see him pacing back and forth in his room and gazing out the window over the brown lawns and the denuded branches of the trees.

Benjamin was talking again. "Well, I should be on my way, ladies. Father charged me with taking payment to Siobhan. I think Father finally has begun to believe in the power of the *pishogues*." He laughed. "That stodgy physician who came up from Waterford would probably have stood over Steven with burning incense applying leeches and mumbling mumbo jumbo." He stood up from the table and tipped his hat. "Please give my regards to Mr. Kildare. Ladies."

"Such a handsome young man," Deirdre sighed to herself, watching him go with a dreamy look. "I do think he finally was noticing me, Mama."

"Don't you be worrying about that, Deirdre," Nora said absently. "Benjamin Markham's had enough practice with the young girls."

Brenna was sitting silently at the table, her eyes downcast, and a slight blush still pinkening her cheeks.

"Lass," Nora said, "the boy was right; you should have given your apologies long before now."

Brenna shrugged, but could not feel as nonchalant as she tried to appear. "Well, I would have, Mama, but I— I just didn't feel right about it."

"Lord and St. Patrick! What kind of thing is it you're saying?" Nora wanted to know impatiently. "The lad was hurt and you had a part in it—an accident, I know, but nevertheless, you should have done the right thing."

"But—"

"I'm speaking to your father about it tonight. Tis time you apologized yourself. I'll not be ashamed of my own daughter, and I'll not have Sir William's looking down on us because we haven't done our duty."

"Ah, good afternoon, dear senorita." Steven pushed himself up from a chair as Brenna entered the small downstairs sitting room. Then, with a look of boredom, he flopped back down. "What an unexpected pleasure." His dark eyes watched her approach and noted, with a faint flash of humor, the trembling of her hands in the folds of her skirt.

"Don't be nasty, Steven," Benjamin smiled, coming in behind her. "It took all of the little one's courage to come up today and make her apology to you." He bowed to Brenna. "I'm afraid I'll be leaving you two alone; I've promised Rory and my father a game of bulls-eye."

Brenna stood stiffly, her eyes on the floor, acutely embarrassed at the situation. "I hope you're feeling well enough," she got out in a weak voice.

Steven yawned and looked out the window. "I can assure you that I feel wonderful. I am as fit as I ever was, and am most anxious to get out of this house and onto the back of a horse again."

"How long will you be . . .

"I can't set a foot out of this house until your friend, the healer, gives her permission," he interrupted, anticipating her question.

Brenna looked up. "Siobhan is very wise in these things. You should be listening to her advice."

"God, I am sick to death of being in this house!" he burst out in exasperation and pushed at the bandage that was tilted rakishly over one eye.

"I'm truly sorry, Steven," Brenna began.

He looked at her curiously. "An apology from the proud Brenna Kildare? I am nearly speechless—please, go on," he said.

Brenna pinkened. "Aye, I've come to tell you how truly sorry I am that my stubbornness caused all this to happen. It was foolish of me to behave the way I did."

"Not foolish," he corrected, "childish."

A flash of temper lit in her eyes. "All right then, if you wish, it was childish, but no more childish than you are behaving right now."

He shrugged. "Don't lecture me, Brenna. I'm afraid that I'm too old to heed your advice."

"Makes no difference to me whether you heed or not," Brenna went on in a huff. "Go on out and ruin yourself if you're wanting to—I don't care. I've said my apology, and now I don't need to be worrying about your welfare any longer."

"Bravo! You have made an apology which sounds like a condemnation," Steven retorted. "I should have known you hadn't developed into the young lady you should be by now!"

"Oh! 'Tis not up to you to be judging me now!" Brenna responded heatedly. "I've seen the kind of lady that you fancy: that blonde witch with claws for fingernails. I want no part of your kind of lady, thank you!"

Steven laughed. "What has she to do with any of this? I doubt that there would have been an accident had I bumped into her during the hunt!" He stood up from his chair and paced stiffly toward the long windows; but after a long moment, his attitude seemed to soften and he turned back to her. She was breathing rapidly, and her face had turned crimson with the effort to keep her temper from spilling out.

"I accept your apology, Brenna," he said in a quieter voice. "Now, I hope that your conscience has been sufficiently cleared for you to leave me in peace."

"Most assuredly," Brenna snapped back and started to leave.

"Wait," he said softly. She turned. "Don't leave so angrily—I wouldn't be able to forgive myself if you had an accident on the way home." He smiled wryly. "I am not at all certain I would be brave enough to face you with an apology, should you fall."

Brenna watched him distrustfully as he patted a chair beside his own.

"Here, sit down and talk to me for a few minutes before you leave. Truth to tell, Sir William's not the best of company unless one likes to play chess until three in the morning. And unfortunately, Benjamin would rather be roistering about with Rory than tending to an invalid—I can hardly blame him." He smiled, and his Latin charm seemed to light the air around him so that Brenna was, for a moment, dazzled by his physical attractiveness.

"Well, I only came to make an apology—"

"And I've accepted it. Now let me play host for a few minutes—at least keep me company until dinner." His eyes lazily regarded her, and he patted the chair again.

Finally, Brenna sat next to him. Steven admiringly watched the graceful way she moved the trim neat figure she presented in her blue-sprigged frock, which he wryly guessed had been picked with special care for this interview. Her midnight-black hair was coiled behind her ears, and he had to admit she looked fetching—so much so that he had to remind himself she was a child of only thirteen. He told himself that he had, indeed, been cooped up in the house too long if he was starting to look with interest at a mere baby.

168

"Well," she was saying, "what would you care to talk about?"

He shrugged as she sat down, leaning forward a little and enjoying her discomfiture. "Anything you like."

She seemed suddenly shy. "Would you tell me something of your country? I—I did look it up in a book of maps that belongs to Father Kinahan. Argentina looks so big."

He glanced at her curiously. "Argentina is a volatile, ever-changing country. She is continuously making war with others or with herself. My father says that conflict helps to strengthen her, but I cannot agree with him, unreservedly. It is true, that the country, as a whole, seems to unify during a crisis from without, but we also lose so many of our finest young men."

"I remember Rory Adair telling me that you have people like the Fenians who constantly stir up trouble."

"Yes, things are almost always, as you say, 'stirred up' there. While I have been away, Argentina has been at war with Paraguay, our neighbor to the north. Father wrote to me about it."

Brenna could see the reverie and homesickness in his eyes. She felt an odd stirring in her. "I suppose it is a most beautiful country?"

He nodded. "We have a wide, fertile plain, called the Pampas, where horses grow strong and beautiful, and cows graze and grow fat, and the soil is rich and black— as black as your hair, Brenna. These wide grazing lands and cultivated fields are divided into *estancias,* great estates which are owned by the great patrician *hidalgo* families. They are mostly descendants of nobles, governors, or viceroys, and they are very rich." He smiled.

"Are you a—patrician *hida . . . hidal . . .*"

"*Hidalgo*. Yes, my family is very patrician, Brenna," and he laughed again, enjoying the wonder in her eyes.

"So, then you and your family would be like Sir William is here in Ireland?"

He nodded again.

"I see." She gave him a sober look. "So, I'm thinking

your parents wouldn't take in a kindly way your talking to me like this, would they?"

He hesitated, thinking of his father—tall, dark, strong, and handsome, much like Brenna's own father. No, she was right; his father wouldn't like it. But he shook his head at her frown. "It is the way of the people, Brenna. They always look with suspicion upon strangers, foreigners," he ended with slight mockery.

She blushed. "I do understand," she said in a small voice.

"Let me tell you something else about my country," he continued. "Can you imagine celebrating Christmas in midsummer, or Easter in the beginning of a cold, rainy autumn?"

She shook her head suspiciously, looking for some trap.

"It is so, in my country. You see, our seasons are backwards from your own. Our summer comes in the months of December, January, and February, and our winter comes from June through August."

"How very odd!" she said, interested despite herself.

He laughed. "Actually, I thought that Europe's seasons were strange. You see, it is all in one's viewpoint."

"Aye, I suppose you're right," she conceded.

"Now, tell me something I've been longing to know about since I arrived in Ireland," he began, noting how pliant and relaxed she had become.

"What is that?"

"Tell me about your 'little people.' I've heard Rory talk of them often."

"Oh, aye, the little people are—well, fairies and the like," Brenna answered.

"What do they look like?"

"Well, I've not seen one myself, mind you," she said, almost whispering as her blue eyes darted about the room, nervously. "I've heard, though, that they are but a few inches high and dress in white, though their bodies are said to be airy, transparent-like. They sometimes dress in shimmery, silvery garments which can be seen in the woods at night. Fairies love to dance and play music. Have you never heard them then?"

"I don't think so, but I'm not sure—"

"Oh, their music would be very gay and spritely. You know, we Irish are great lovers of music." She paused. "Oh, and there are the leprechauns, the fairy shoemakers." She glanced around again and leaned forward to whisper, "They are the real troublemakers, don't you know. They can be the very devil if they've a mind to spite you for something."

Steven nodded slowly, intoxicated with her soft, fresh scent and the way her perfect lips moved as she talked. "Tell me more about these little evildoers," he said lazily.

But Brenna reared back, imagining she heard mockery in his voice. "Well, I suppose you've been hearing enough," she said sharply. "It should be close to dinner, I imagine." She stood abruptly and he came up beside her, close enough to touch her with his hand.

For a moment, they were both still, and Brenna felt that strange sensation in her chest like an iron band constricting her breathing.

"Well," she said softly, " 'tis glad I am that we did talk—"

"You've brought sunshine into my day," he answered her, his black eyes boring intently into hers as the corners of his mouth lifted into the merest suggestion of a smile.

"I should be going then." She turned away from him and looked about her distractedly as though searching for something.

He laughed gently. "Suddenly, you seem to be turning into the young lady you claim to be." He folded his arms and cocked his head at her. "Before you know it, you'll be needing a guardian—a *duenna*—to accompany you on your visits, just as the young women do in my country."

"Aye," she said in a low voice, recalling how he had taunted her before with the words about how all the young girls were betrothed at an early age and matured into women much more quickly. "I'm sure you'll be having a *novia* waiting for you at home—won't you?"

His laugh turned uneasy. "Oh, I can recall my father meddling into that, but I'm not . . ."

"Are you meaning to tell me you're engaged?" she

cried in sudden alarm. "All this time, and I didn't realize! I shouldn't—I really shouldn't even be here alone with you, unchaperoned, should I? Forgive me for being so inconsiderate."

"Don't be silly!" he told her, catching her hand, but she tore it from his grip.

"I'm not being silly," she insisted. "You've reminded me of the impropriety of our being together alone like this."

"Back to the child again," he sneered, as he watched her hurry out the door, but he was really saying the words to convince himself.

Chapter Fourteen

A few days later, Brenna looked out the window of her room to see Steven riding at a gallop toward the farm. She ducked her head away and hurried automatically to the mirror to check her appearance. Then, realizing what she was doing, she drew back in scorn at her silliness. Was she a child or a young lady? Steven had, almost in the same breath, called her both. Was it possible to be grown up at times and childish at others? The answers seemed confusing and impossible to sort out.

It was all Steven's fault, she told herself. Somehow, subtly, without her realizing it, he had affected her in a way that seemed to be changing her little by little. One minute, she loathed him, the next, she was worried about how she looked in his presence. Would she be glad when he was gone? she wondered as she descended the steps.

She found her mother and Siobhan in the kitchen, talking. Since Steven's accident, Siobhan had come to the farm often to inquire about Brenna and to bring along herbal remedies for a cold that had been plaguing Nora. The two older women had become, if not fast friends, at least agreeable acquaintances; and the lonely Siobhan looked forward to hot tea with Nora Kildare.

"Where will you be off to now?" Nora asked as Brenna rushed past her with a hurried kiss.

"To the stables," she called back, snatching a sweater from the peg on the wall. "Good morning to you, Siobhan."

Her mother and Siobhan watched Brenna run out into the chilly, gray morning. Nora sighed to herself and offered Siobhan more tea.

"Thank you, Nora, I'd be liking that," Siobhan answered. Then she added, "You are worried about your daughter?"

Nora was surprised at the woman's shrewdness. "Aye, I

have a mother's worries about both my daughters, but Brenna is the elder, and I suppose she's more on my mind than Deirdre, at the moment."

"Both your daughters are of an age when they will begin to look upon themselves as young women," Siobhan said quietly. "But, like you, I have more concern for Brenna. She has the capacity to be hurt more easily, whereas your youngest child seems, despite her youth, more able to cope with the harshness in the world." Siobhan folded her hands and gazed at the woman. "You must be forgiving me for speaking so bluntly, Nora, but I like Brenna very much. I have grown fonder of her than even I should have thought possible on such short acquaintance."

Nora nodded. "I couldn't help but be noticing. Is it that you see the nursing in her?"

Siobhan shook her head. "No, 'tis not that, although Brenna was most helpful when Steven was hurt." She wondered to herself if the lass would have been quite so patient and thorough with anyone else but Steven.

Nora was wondering the same thing.

"Hello, Papa."

"Why, Brenna, my dear, I thought you were inside helping your mother," Kildare boomed heartily. He was in a jovial mood, for a sickly colt was beginning to show signs of renewed vigor.

"Oh, I just thought I'd come out to see how the colt was doing," she replied. She could see Steven striding towards them, and her eyes quickly shied away from his dark gaze.

"Steven, have you had a moment to look at that colt?" Kildare asked, his attention turning to the young man. "He looks much better, doesn't he? Aye, I'm thinking he'll start growing faster now, if we keep a sharp eye on him. Not nearly so puny as a few weeks ago."

"Much better," Steven agreed, "like myself, I hope." He laughed.

"Aye, I must say I'm breathing easier to see you chipper again," Kildare admitted.

" 'Tis nice to see you about, Steven," Brenna added, looking brazenly at him.

He grinned almost impudently at her. "Many thanks to you, senorita. After our afternoon conversation, I seemed to make a remarkable recovery. Your Siobhan proclaimed me a healthy young scoundrel and set me on my way."

"I'm glad of it."

Just then, one of the stable grooms called Kildare back to one of the stalls, leaving Brenna and Steven together. They walked together out of the barn into the hazy day.

" 'Twill be winter soon," Brenna said lightly.

"Yes, Christmas is coming, and then I shall be going back to Cambridge. Next spring I shall be back for my last foaling season," he reminded her thoughtfully.

"Aye," she said quietly. "Then you'll be gone for good. Just as I was getting used to having you around," she laughed self-derisively.

They were silent, following the line of the corral fence. Then Steven said, "I'm sure I'll be back in Ireland one day—to make business transactions with your father and Sir William. We'll see each other again, Brenna."

Was that a promise? she wondered. "Twould be nice, Steven. I should like to think of you coming back for a visit now and then."

"Of course," he said with a trace of sarcasm, "you'll probably be married to someone in a few years, and I will find it difficult to get your husband's permission to visit."

"Oh, no! I'll not be marrying, Steven!" she protested and saw that he was teasing.

"But a girl like you, Brenna," he went on with a grin, "would make such a nice, temperamental little wife for some brave, young man who would be willing to risk his life trying to tame you!" He immediately saw she had not liked that.

"I really don't see the need to be marrying at all," she said. "You see, I've already promised Papa that I'd be taking over the horses when he gets too old for the business."

He could see the pride in her face, but at the same time, couldn't believe her plans would come true. "I see," was all he said.

She laughed a trifle shrilly. "And what of yourself? I can imagine you'll not be wasting away for lack of females hovering about just waiting for a marriage proposal!"

He shrugged. "My father would say that marriage is a man's duty—the begetting of heirs, the prolongation of the family name; all this he expects of me as his only son."

Brenna nodded stiffly. "Aye, all fathers are like that, I suppose."

"Yes, whereas the mothers hope their sons will all be priests," Steven put in sardonically.

Brenna was quiet for a moment, then couldn't help her curiosity. "Tell me about the *novia,* your betrothed."

His black eyes were amused, but wary. "I can't even recall what she looks like," he answered her. "She was only a child when I left on my travels. I believe she's about your age. Hah! I remember that old crow of an aunt of hers more than I remember the girl! No doubt Tia Hortensia will guard the girl's virtue better than her own father!"

Brenna colored at the reference. "Aye, that's the way of it," she murmured to cover her embarassment. She sighed. "What is your father truly like, Steven? I'm sure he's been missing you all this time."

He answered slowly. "Miguel Castaneda de la Cruz is a man very much like your own father, Brenna."

"Oh, then I should be liking him," she said quickly.

He smiled disarmingly. "Ah, but he can be a bear at times. He is tall and lean and dark with the fiercest eyes I have ever seen."

"Your eyes can be like that," Brenna said, then blushed furiously.

Steven threw her an interested glance. "He would be glad to hear your observation. But he can be gentle too. He and my mother, Consuelo, were so happy the day my sister was born. I can remember the rejoicing on their faces and, for the first time, my father cried with joy. I was almost seven and there had been many miscarriages, so everyone thought her birth a miracle. My father didn't even care that it was a girl, and not another son.

"I recall him saying that I was strong enough and would surely live to manhood so that the line would be assured. There is such importance placed on heirs, you see. But Rosaria, my sister, is like an angel. He would never have let me come to Europe had they not had Rosaria to comfort them in my absence." ·

"I'm sure you're anxious to be seeing her again."

"Yes, she is the sweetest child on earth. I suppose she would be about ten now."

"Does she look like you?"

He shook his head. "Rosaria looks like my mother. Her hair is dark, but her eyes are lighter than mine, and her skin is as pale as ivory. My father will have to worry about the young *caballeros* nosing about the hacienda when Rosaria is a little older." He laughed to himself. "Her older brother shall probably have to defend her constantly."

It was easy to see that Steven loved his family. She couldn't fathom why he had left them for so long.

"It sounds as though you have a wonderful family," she said. She turned to him and smiled with unconscious charm. "I'm glad that you are fully recovered from your accident. Your father would never have forgiven me if something had happened to his fierce-eyed heir."

Chapter Fifteen

THE late autumn days grew shorter and colder, and Brenna began to chafe at the tedious daily routine. She tried to be a good student for Father Kinahan, but excelled only in languages, prompted largely by a desire to make herself appear more worldly to Steven.

Deirdre was an even worse pupil than Brenna, now that Nora had bowed to the girl's wishes to be sent three times a week to Mrs. O'Hara's. Jenny O'Hara taught deportment to the wealthier girls of the district. A widow with no children, she had a great deal of time on her hands to indulge her favorite pupils, of which Deirdre was certainly one.

"Oh, Brenna, I do so love learning how to be a lady!" Deirdre said enthusiastically. "Mrs. O'Hara is so very proper and correct, such a perfect model for me. I know you all think I'm daft for wanting to be learning such things, but—I can't help it. I want to be a proper lady and marry—" she hesitated and looked down.

"Aye, go on?" Brenna prodded with a teasing note in her voice. "Whom do you wish to marry, little sister?"

"I'm not telling."

"Oh, come now. Isn't it someone I might be knowing?" Brenna's eyes were fairly twinkling.

Deirdre's chin came up pertly. " 'Tis none of your business!"

"Deirdre Kildare, you're easier to read than a book," Brenna laughed. "Why I swear you're mooning after that arrogant English boy, Benjamin Markham!"

Deirdre flushed but stood her ground. "Aye, and what if I am? 'Tis hurting no one!"

"Is that why you've been taking lessons with Mrs. O'Hara? Is it that you're wanting to show yourself worthy of marrying a Markham?"

Deirdre wouldn't answer.

"Oh, Deirdre, if Mama knew the reason you're taking those lessons, she'd be stopping them right away. You say you're hurting no one, but what about yourself? Benjamin won't be impressed by good manners and polite talk. You know the kind of girl he likes."

"Aye, well I can be like that too," Deirdre declared fiercely.

Brenna was silent as she studied her sister. It was true, she thought. Deirdre was growing up, maturing faster in some ways than she, herself, was. Her breasts were big for her age, and she certainly knew more about flirting than most young girls. Deirdre wasn't afraid of anything.

"You won't be telling Mama, will you, Brenna?"

"No, I won't tell her," Brenna sighed, hoping she had made the right decision.

"Oh, thank you for keeping my secret," Deirdre whispered gratefully.

Brenna smiled. It wouldn't hurt Deirdre to learn deportment, for she certainly didn't possess the patience or the interest for learning anything else. Besides, nothing would ever come of her infatuation with Benjamin Markham. For Deirdre to marry an English aristocrat was as laughable as it would be for her, Brenna, to marry a footman.

Christmas was full of excitement that year. Nora was determined to make it the best of all holidays since Dermot would be returning to school in Dublin after the New Year. She had taken out a few seams in the lovely gowns that her daughters had worn at the May Day celebration so that they could use them again for the Christmas festivities. She, too, had been noticing the changes in their silhouettes.

Deirdre had practiced and practiced holding a cup of tea while maintaining her posture, and walking gracefully —all to impress Benjamin, whom they would see on Christmas Day. Dermot, who had been studying very hard all during these last weeks, took time away from his books during the holiday, for he was looking forward to being with Bernadette the entire day.

With her bright-faced and laughing-eyed family all around her, Nora couldn't help but feel a chill in her bones. How long would such happiness last? she wondered. With the superstitious nature of the Irish, she was sure that some ill fate would befall them to bring into balance the happiness of this day.

Christmas Day was cold, but there was no snow on the ground. Everyone was red-cheeked and sparkling when they arrived at Markham's estate. Mrs. Longstreet had prepared the usual hot cocoa and buttered rum.

They had not been there long, when Benjamin Markham burst through the door. "Father heard your coach and told me to bring you all straight away to the front parlor," he explained.

Mrs. Longstreet looked sour when she learned she wouldn't be having an audience to hear the latest gossip; but Kildare gave her a friendly, Christmas kiss on the cheek and everyone laughed to see her blushing.

"Would your cheeks be doing that if someone kissed you?" Benjamin whispered to Deirdre as they walked down the hallway, and was pleased to see her blush.

In the front sitting room, Sir William was already playing host to his brother, Theodore, and his sister-in-law, Mary.

"Ah, there you are! Come in, come in!" Sir William commanded, standing up at the arrival of his friends. "Teddy, you remember Tyrone Kildare, his wife, Nora, and their three children?"

"Yes, of course!" Theodore stood up and shook hands equitably with the Irishman. Mary Markham nodded graciously and invited Nora to sit next to her.

The younger set withdrew from their elders, settling in chairs and on stools around the Christmas tree. Deirdre's quick, gray eyes caught Benjamin's, and she smiled an invitation, for she had deliberately pushed her stool beneath a sprig of mistletoe.

Dermot, after greeting everyone, stole off with Bernadette—presumably, he did not need mistletoe. Brenna sighed as she watched the pair of them walk close together down the hall. She would never have dreamed her own brother could be so romantic.

Steven, who had just come into the room, saw the direction of her gaze and wondered, briefly, what Brenna's rosy lips would taste like if he stole a kiss from her under the mistletoe. How sweet she looked, sitting so demurely with her hands folded in the shimmering green taffeta of her skirt.

"Steven, come on in," Benjamin gestured, his eyes merry.

Steven smiled indolently and sauntered into the room. His black eyes studied how Brenna's dress seemed to reflect the light of the Christmas candles a thousand times over. Her coiffure which lent her a disturbing maturity, was done in thick, gleaming curls pinned high at the back of her head and allowed to escape tidily towards her bare nape.

"Merry Christmas, everyone," he said, bowing to all, then took a chair near Brenna.

"Merry Christmas, Steven," she said with a rush of breathlessness which made her voice sound husky.

He laughed richly. "You look quite lovely, señorita."

Brenna smiled proudly. "I'm thanking you for the compliment," she replied, trying her best to sound prim.

Steven smiled to himself. She was, after all, beginning to grow up. He felt a vague twinge of frustration that he would not be here to see the full transformation.

"It's too bad there's no snow outside," Benjamin said.

" 'Twould have been nice to have snow on Christmas," Deirdre agreed. Although the neckline of her blue silk was cut high, Benjamin was a little disconcerted to see the roundness of the girl's bosom. He decided, with a wry grin, to move a little closer and get a better view.

Brenna noticed the movement and tightened her lips, but Deirdre was oblivious to anyone else as she gazed with rapt attention at her idol.

Benjamin was quite pleased to be the subject of her adoration. In a few years, he thought, he wouldn't mind biting off a piece of this luscious little pastry. It wouldn't do any harm to cultivate good feelings now.

"Don't frown so; it spoils the line of your mouth," Steven said to Brenna.

"Was I frowning?" she asked, her blue eyes darkening with poorly concealed irritation.

"Yes, you were," he smiled roguishly. "And certainly without good cause," he added.

She had the grace to look chastised. "I forgot. Both of you are, after all, gentlemen." There was a trace of sarcasm to her tone.

"Don't let that famous Irish temper ruin an otherwise perfect Christmas," he continued lazily. His eyes narrowed a little as he leaned back.

"I am sorry, then, for I'm not wanting to spoil the day for you, certainly!" she retorted flippantly.

Steven moved his chair closer until his long leg brushed the side of her skirt. "To the contrary, you make the day complete for me," he teased her. He could see her visibly calming her ruffled feathers at the compliment. "Ah, now I know the way to tame you:" he said in an undertone, "pay you pretty compliments, and bend my knee to you like a *caballero*."

She looked at him sharply, wondering if he was laughing at her. His black eyes flashed with an emotion she couldn't quite identify. She chose to think that he was trying to placate her, and she relaxed a little, but she decided that she really must turn the conversation away from this dangerous ground.

"I've been studying languages quite extensively these past months," she informed him, determined to be polite. "I've learned quite a bit of Spanish and French."

"What have you learned for me, Brenna?" he asked silkily.

She jerked her head up and fired him a look from eyes of freezing blue. " 'Twas not just for you that I learned it," she defended herself quickly.

He ignored the remark. "I'm proud of you."

She flustered at this abrupt turnabout. "Aye, I'm proud of myself, make no mistake on that!" she hurried on. The look in his eyes seemed suddenly intense, and he leaned closer. Was he thinking of kissing her? She edged a little away from him on the chair.

"Speak to me in French," he said.

"Bon jour," she said, and Steven tried hard not to let his amusement show. "French is not really so hard for me," she went on importantly, "as my mother speaks it sometimes. She was born in France, you know, although my grandmother was Irish."

"So you are a quarter French," he surmised, grinning with some secret delight.

"Aye, but I'd just as soon be all Irish," she added defensively. "I'm proud of this heritage, you see."

"Of course," Steven rejoined. "Don't worry, Brenna, I do think you really are more Irish than French—more's the pity."

"Oh!" Thoroughly confused, she looked up at him.

"And you've learned Spanish too," he continued smoothly, enjoying her discomposure. He said something rapidly in his native language.

Brenna could not catch any of it. Her eyes slid hopefully toward her sister, who was too engrossed with Benjamin's attention to notice.

"Well?" he asked pleasantly as though waiting for an answer.

"I—I didn't quite catch it—" Brenna answered miserably.

Steven let out an exaggerated explosion of breath and looked relieved. "Lucky for me you didn't understand it," he teased her.

"Why? What were you asking me?" she demanded.

He smiled. "You should have been listening more closely, senorita," he mocked.

" 'Tis time to be opening the presents!" Deirdre announced, clapping her hands.

Brenna was relieved at her sister's interruption, for she felt as though she were adrift in a raft on a high sea.

As the wrappings were torn off the gifts, Brenna nervously watched Steven open the gift from her and Deirdre. She half-expected some sarcastic comment, but she was pleased when he thanked her graciously for the small, leather tome of poetry. She then opened her present from him and cried out in surprise.

Inside the box was a small alabaster figurine of a white dove perched on a brown and green enamel twig. The eyes of the dove were tiny blue sapphires, and the whole figure was attached to a small, round box, which, when wound, played a short piece by Mozart. She was speechless as she looked at Steven.

"You should have seen him, hunting up and down Dublin for just that piece," Benjamin put in, winking at his friend.

Steven smiled. His black eyes gleamed like embers as he assessed Brenna's reaction.

"Oh, but 'tis much too expensive a gift." Brenna began, looking nervously at her parents.

Kildare smiled broadly at his daughter and shrugged. He saw nothing peculiar in the matter—nor in anything else, for by now he had consumed four glasses of claret. Nora bit her lip with a worried look, but remained silent.

"We all know how the children favor each other," Sir William boomed in good spirits. "And Steven will be leaving us soon to return home."

"Aye, that you will," Brenna said as though to remind herself. " 'Twill be a keepsake for me, Steven, and I do thank you for it."

"A keepsake, Brenna?" he asked with one black brow cocked expressively. "To remember all our happy times together?"

He was mocking her now, as though to deliberately undermine the importance of his gift, but Brenna refrained from comment. Instead, she voiced her admiration for the pair of gloves Steven had given to Deirdre.

As Deirdre tried them on, she chattered gaily about how she would wear them everywhere, and how grateful she was to Steven. She was disappointed in the box of sweetmeats that Benjamin had selected; obviously he still thought of her as a child.

Benjamin looked with proper admiration at the painfully stitched scarf into which Deirdre had put all her loving devotion. Brenna had embroidered the motif on the two ends. "Thank you both," Benjamin said, but looked longest at Deirdre's upturned face as he reached over to pat her hand.

"All right then," Kildare said a little tipsily. "What say we have a go at a jig, my dear?" He stood and bowed to his wife.

Sir William clapped appreciatively and signaled to a group of three servants to bring out their flutes and Nora smiled indulgently and took her husband's hand. Benjamin held out his arm to Deirdre, who took it and hopped about with more verve than skill. Even Theodore and Mary joined in gaily.

Brenna watched, clapping enthusiastically, aware that Steven was clapping too, though his eyes were on her. She wondered why he didn't ask her to dance, but rationalized that he probably didn't know the Irish dances. Her father was flinging her mother about as though she were nothing more than a sheaf of wheat. It tickled Brenna to see him so merry, and for a moment, she forgot about Steven.

"A little more wine?" Steven touched her elbow lightly.

She shook her head. "No, thank you," she laughed. "I'm thinking one of the family with too much liquor in him is quite enough!"

"Oh, I'm sure your father can hold his own," Steven said.

But Kildare was quickly out of breath and reaching for the nearest chair, pulling his wife along beside him. "Ah, I'm not so young as I was supposing," he admitted.

"Ach, now don't you be telling me that, Tyrone Kildare!" Nora reproved, and lovingly touched the tiny thread of gray at his temple.

Benjamin brought Deirdre back to her seat and lounged back casually opposite Steven. "Whew! That brought the blood back!" he laughed. "You should have tried it, old fellow—would've taken some of the spunk out of you, it would!" He reached for his glass and refilled it with wine.

"It was more pleasant watching you," Steven replied enjoying Benjamin Markham's worn-out look.

Benjamin leaned toward his friend with a snide whisper, "Watch me keep it up all night, old boy, if I can get the little Kildare to drag me under the mistletoe!"

"I don't think that it will be necessary to drag her," Steven answered.

"Hmmm, you think so, eh? What about yourself—the older one didn't seem to take to your gift as I thought she would," Benjamin hurried on between gulps.

Steven shrugged. "She's but a child," he said airily.

"Well, perhaps she doesn't realize how hard you looked for the damned thing!" Benjamin rejoined. His voice grew louder to include the young ladies. "Do you realize, Brenna, lass, that this poor lad spent several days trying to find the perfect gift for you? Going without food, without sleep—yes, even without drink!—to find the right present to give to you as fond remembrance of his days spent on the horse farm." He chuckled to himself. "The poor, misguided boy—was he trying to soften that hard, Irish heart of yours? Ah, but how could he know that your heart was already taken!" He sighed dramatically.

Brenna lowered her eyes uncomfortably at Benjamin's jesting. "Whatever are you talking about?"

"Those horses, girl, the horses! Isn't it true that you're married to your beloved horse farm?"

Brenna reddened.

"Ben, old boy, I think you're getting a little sotted," Steven put in, aware of Brenna's discomfort. "In another minute, we'll catch you snoring in midsentence."

Deirdre's giggle brought Benjamin's attention back to her. "Laughing, are you!" he sighed. "Ah, here I was trying to do my best for my friend here—putting in a good word for him, you know—and I get laughed at!"

"Thanks for the 'good word'," Steven remarked ironically. "I'll do my best for you some time."

Brenna was glad that the bantering of the two young men had taken the attention off her. Her feelings concerning Steven seemed so mixed up tonight. First, he had teased her and acted like a young gallant flirting with a desirable maiden; then he had given her a beautiful Christmas gift which he had tried to make light of, now, just looking at him, she felt her heart hammering against her ribs and her face blushing. She ducked her head and played nervously with the ribbon in her lap. If he tried to kiss her under the mistletoe, she thought, she wouldn't stop him—then she was surprised because she found that she had hoped he would.

At last Nora decided it was time to go. Tyrone was beginning to sing in his rich, deep voice along with the music and, even though Sir William and his brother were delighted with the Irishman's good humor, Nora thought it best to be leaving before any rowdiness began.

"Oh, but, Mama, must we be going now?" sighed Deirdre.

"Aye, miss, or your father'll be singing from the rooftop before long!" Nora answered.

"Now that's something I'd like to see!" Benjamin laughed.

Brenna got up from her chair and rustled through a pile of wrappings.

"Let one of the servants do that," Sir William said amiably, ringing for a sturdy footman, who gathered everything together and took it outside to their coach.

Glancing at the young men nervously, Brenna and Deirdre wrapped themselves in their cloaks. Brenna hesitated, wondering if she might not just slip under the knot of mistletoe fastened on the doorpost. Then her mother called to her to fetch Dermot. Disappointed, Brenna hurried to find her brother.

"Come on," she called when she saw him and Bernadette embracing cozily in a corner of the dust closet. "We're to be going now."

Bernadette smiled and leaned over to put her arms about her. "Merry Christmas, Brenna! I'm so happy that this time next year I'll truly be your sister!"

"Merry Christmas, Bernadette," Brenna responded warmly. "Aye, 'twill be fun planning the wedding, won't it?"

"Aye, and I'll be expecting you to help a great deal

since—" she looked to Dermot for approval "—since I'm asking you to stand up as my maid of honor."

Brenna gasped in delight. "Oh, aye, 'twill be even more fun than I thought!" she laughed. "Come along then, Dermot, give her another kiss, and then Mama wants us to be leaving. Papa's had a mite too many nips at the wine bottle."

As everyone made their farewells, Steven stood by the fireplace, leaning his left arm negligently against the mantelpiece. Brenna's hopes rapidly diminished as she hesitated a moment longer than necessary beneath the doorpost, and Steven made no move toward her.

"Merry Christmas, Steven!" she called.

"Merry Christmas, Brenna," he answered, smiling that half-smile that was a mixture of sincerity and mockery. He remained where he was, looking at her.

"Come along, Brenna." Her mother called.

With a sigh of frustration and a darting look back at Steven, Brenna walked out after her family.

Chapter Sixteen

IT was February 1, St. Bridget's Feastday, before they received a letter from Dermot, who had left for Dublin the day after the New Year. After the customary cloth was left outside the door that night—put there to acquire healing powers according to tradition—everyone gathered about the peat fire to listen to Kildare read his son's letter.

> Dear ones,
>
> Everything has finally settled down here, and I am actually beginning to like it. Mr. Butt has been the soul of patience with my initial ignorance and has helped me more than I could ever repay. I've dined often with him, and his family, and those meals have served to keep the flesh on my bones, as I would much rather learn than eat. The university is a totally new experience for me, but I have already made one or two good friends, which I'm sure you will all agree, is something new for me. I must close now and do wish you all could be with me, but until April, I must keep my nose in the books! Give my love to Bernadette.
>
> Your devoted son,
> Dermot Kildare

Nora sighed contentedly. "It would seem, Tyrone, that we've done the right thing by the boy, wouldn't it?"

"Aye," her husband agreed. He turned to his daughters. "You'd best be riding over to Markham Hall tomorrow and giving Bernadette your brother's message," he said with a wink.

Brenna laughed. "I know I can't do it justice!"

If only Benjamin were there, Deirdre thought with a

stifled sigh, 'twould be easy enough for me to do it justice.

The morning of the wedding, the last Friday in April,
dawned fair and clear, and everyone breathed a superstitious sigh of relief, for good weather meant a lucky
marriage. At Sir William's insistence the wedding would
take place on the lawns of his estate—a generous gesture
that appealed to the humbler folk who would attend.

The nanty-maker, who had cut and sewn the wedding
gown, delivered it promptly at nine o'clock in the morning, two hours before the wedding was to begin. Brenna
smoothed the fine white silk with reverent fingers.

Bernadette smiled nervously. She was sitting on a stool
while Nora worked with her long, corn-colored hair,
brushing it until it shone like sunshine. Today the bride
was allowed to wear her hair long and unbound with a
circlet of flowers about her head.

Finally, it was time to dress, and Nora, who had already donned her gown of dark blue silk, pulled the wedding gown around Bernadette's trembling shoulders and
straightened it about her waist. Brenna slipped into her
lavender gown, and Deirdre patted down the skirt of her
own yellow dimity. Everyone wore white gloves and new
shoes, and carried a ready supply of clean handkerchiefs
tucked inside their bodices for the ready flow of tears that
would follow the ceremony.

"I hear the fiddlers!" Deirdre called, leaning out the
window.

Five fiddlers had been hired for the occasion. They had
slept, as was the custom, at the house of the groom the
night before, along with ten of the groom's relatives, some
of whom had come from as far away as Dublin and Cork.

When it was close to the time of the wedding, the fiddlers would mount horses and ride ahead of the groom's
party—women mounted on pillions led by men afoot.
When the bride heard the horses of the fiddlers, she knew
that it was time for her to go downstairs to greet her fiancé.

"Oh, do I look all right?" Bernadette wondered, biting her lips.

"Lovely," Nora said sincerely, and the two women hugged each other affectionately. It was good, Nora thought, to be able to give up her son now without the jealousies and hesitation she had once felt towards this girl. She was confident that Bernadette would make Dermot the perfect wife.

Brenna, leaning out the window with her sister, picked out the fine, lean figure of Steven Cruz riding close beside her brother. As single men, they were not required to carry women on their horses, and Steven cut a handsome figure today in his black, broadcloth tail coat and stiffly starched white shirt.

" 'Tis time." Nora bustled all three girls downstairs into the small conservatory. Kildare strode in, took his future daughter-in-law's hand, and led her out to the lawn where Dermot awaited her.

Bride and groom were given a plate of oatmeal and salt, from which each took three mouthfuls as a protection against the power of the evil eye. Then the wedding guests gathered around the table, which extended the full length of a barn and was adorned with fresh flowers and a snowy white tablecloth.

When everyone had finished eating, the table was cleared, and Father Kinahan rose to begin the ceremony. His pleasant tenor carried lightly with the breeze over the assembled guests. Brenna, watching from her place next to the bride, felt tears trembling on her lashes and blinked rapidly to clear them away. The ceremony ended when Father Kinahan instructed the groom to give his wife the 'kiss of peace.' Dermot was so nervous that he caught her on the chin, but Bernadette quickly adjusted and the marriage was sealed.

After each guest had received a slice of wedding cake and placed a donation for the priest on the table in front of him, wine and punch were passed around amidst cries of *"Slainte,"* a toast was proposed by Kildare to the health and good fortune of the couple, and the dancing began.

Brenna was whirled around by several partners before she saw Steven making his way towards her. "May I have the honor?" he asked.

She took his hand cautiously and was surprised as he twirled her into the set of an Irish jig. "Steven, you've been practicing!" she laughed, tossing her curls and stepping high as he moved her through the turns and twists.

"Yes, I always wondered what it was the Irish saw in such wild, stomping dances," he returned, laughing too, "and now I know!"

She arched her brows questioningly.

"The exuberance!"

She laughed and nodded, as she felt his hands around her waist, swinging her effortlessly. She wished they could go on like this forever, but soon someone else claimed her hand, and she regretfully let Steven go.

The fiddlers played until they were nearly exhausted, for the music was nonstop and everyone was entitled to dance with the bride. Then the singing began; this needed no music, for everyone was roaring at the top of his lungs. Only Dermot could not sing at his own wedding, for it was considered unlucky.

"Look! Look!" Maureen Derry squeaked, pointing to a group just arriving. " 'Tis the strawboys!"

Disguised in old clothes, their faces blackened with burnt cork, the strawboys were all sons of neighboring farmers. Brenna could discern Rory Adair and Terence Gallagher, and she was surprised to see Kevin Ryan among them. Kevin was held in high esteem by her father, and would someday hold the position of head groom for the Kildare farm when old Carruthers got too aged to handle the job.

Rory, as the leader of the strawboys, headed straight for the bride and demanded the next dance, while the rest found other partners. Brenna saw Kevin coming toward her and smiled as he took her hands to lead her out with the others. One last lively tune was struck, and the strawboys, with their captured partners, danced the rousing steps of the reel with enthusiastic skill.

The fiddlers played as fast as they could so that the

dancers were breathing hard and the women's hair was fast tumbling down from pins and braids. Finally the musicians stopped, and the strawboys, after bowing to their partners, hurried away, carrying food and drink with them as a token of good luck from the wedding party. Father Kinahan made his farewell promptly.

Then, two festively adorned horses drew Kildare's carriage away with the bridal couple inside, and all the guests waved merrily. Sir William, who had discreetly stayed inside during the ceremony, had generously allowed the use of his summer cottage at the far edge of his estate for the use of the couple until Sunday. This would be their only honeymoon, since Dermot would then be taking his wife back to Dublin with him.

It was nearly dusk and everyone was anxious to return to their accommodations. Most of Kildare's relatives and friends would be staying the night—the men in the barn and the women sharing the bedrooms in the house. In the morning, they would all be leaving, but Nora would still have plenty of work to do preparing for the Bride's Sunday, when the wedding couple would bring their closest friends and relatives to her house for the traditional dinner.

"I'll be returning with your father to sort out the sleeping quarters," Nora said to her daughters with a touch of weariness. It had been a full day for her, and she was relieved that everything had turned out so beautifully. "You'll be coming along?"

"Aye, Mama," Brenna nodded.

"I should be happy to escort your daughter home, Mrs. Kildare," Steven spoke up, surprising both of them.

"Well—'twouldn't hurt, I suppose," Nora said slowly. "But mind you, I'm not in the mood for you coming in late tonight, Brenna. You've got to help me tomorrow."

"Aye, Mama."

Her mother, dragging a protesting Deirdre, climbed into the wagon beside Tyrone to return home.

"And how are you proposing to get me home?" she asked Steven, who was standing quite close to her in the fading twilight.

He laughed and his teeth flashed white. "Didn't you notice whom I was riding on the way here? It was Minx."

"Minx let you ride her?"

He nodded nonchalantly. "I think she's sorry for the scar she gave me."

"Very well, but she'll not be liking the two of us on her back, I'm certain," Brenna warned.

"You're little enough weight, and she knows a master when she feels his hands on her reins."

Somehow, Brenna felt disconcerted by his answer.

They walked together to the tethered horses. Minx neighed softly in greeting, and Brenna, anxious for something to do, rubbed the animal's velvety nose and whispered soothingly. She was acutely aware of Steven beside her, and she had that funny tingling feeling in her chest that she had experienced another time with him. Her knees and her elbows seemed to weaken, and her breathing quickened; she heard it, swift and shallow, in her own ears.

"Brenna—" Steven seemed to loom before her, taller than she remembered, his handsome, dark face nearly invisible in the fading light. She felt his hands on her shoulders, his strong fingers digging in almost painfully.

Her heart hammered in her chest, drowning out the small night noises around her as Steven pulled her towards him and bent his head. Reflexively, she closed her eyes, screwing them tightly shut, as she held her breath. His mouth, firm and warm, touched her lips, lightly at first, then pressed deeply, fully, until her mouth opened and yielded to him. The aftershock hit Brenna like a strong, fierce wave, and she put up her stiffened arms to push him away, but realized she hadn't the strength to do more than hold onto him like a drowning person. His mouth moved on hers, feeling the softness of her lips; his hands moved from her shoulders to slip possessively around her back, so that her small, perfect breasts, in their nest of silk, pressed tantalizingly against the front of his shirt.

He was murmuring in Spanish against her mouth, then his lips moved lightly over her cheeks, her closed eyes,

and her temples, while his hands pressed upwards, feeling
the smooth silk against her narrow back and shoulder
blades. Brenna could feel his touch warm and sure, come
around her ribcage and brush so lightly against the sides
of her breasts that she couldn't be positive that he had
actually dared.

She was beginning to think that they would go on forever like this, locked together like the intertwined figures
of a statue, when a cool, faintly bitter voice startled them.

"Touching, very touching," Rory Adair said from the
darkness. He had come back after eating and drinking
with his fellows to see if he might find Maureen Derry
awaiting him for a giggling tryst. The sight of Brenna and
Steven locked closely in a kiss had, at first, caused in him
a feeling of derision, then of sardonic amusement—and
finally, of a bitter, surprised jealousy as the urge to punch
the damned foreigner in the mouth built up.

As he watched the pair spring apart, and saw the
guilt-stricken look on Brenna's face, coupled with the
freshly bruised air of her mouth, he felt mad enough to
kill; and the liquor in him seemed to set his blood afire.

With a bellow of rage, Rory sprang at Steven, knocking
him to the ground with the suddenness of his attack. They
scuffled dangerously close to the horses' hoofs, while
Brenna watched in terror.

"Damn you, foreigner!" Rory spat. He tried to grab
hold of the other boy's neck to squeeze the breath out
of him. "Here I come back to find you patting and maul-
ing and handling when you thought there was no one
else here to be defending her. God damn you to hell!"

They grappled, Rory sitting on Steven's chest, while
Steven held onto his grasping hands and tried to push
him off. With a tremendous heave, Steven threw Rory off
and jumped to his feet. Rory sprang up, swiping at him
with clenched fists, a string of abuses issuing from his
mouth, and Steven was forced to defend himself.

Brenna watched holding her hands at her mouth while
tears streamed down her face. She could hear the horrible thudding of fists against stomachs and cheeks, and

she was frantic to make them stop, but she could see no way to do so.

She needed help. Sir William would still be inside the house, so without giving herself time to think, she picked up her skirts and ran to the manor, calling frantically at the top of her voice for Sir William. She met Benjamin on the porch, sipping whiskey while he fondled a red-faced serving wench on his knee.

"Benjamin, call your father, for God's sake! They're killing each other!"

Benjamin stood up swiftly, dropping both the drink and the maid to the porch. "What the hell—?"

"Rory and Steven—they're fighting!" she screamed at him.

He started to grin with amusement, but the look of contempt that she bestowed on him turned his smile to a frown. "All right, let me come with you." He gestured to the maid who had righted herself hurriedly. "Bridget, run in and fetch my father."

"They're down by where the horses were tethered. Near the stables!" Brenna supplied quickly.

Benjamin grabbed her hand, and together they ran back to the scene of the fight. Brenna covered her mouth to keep from screaming in fright, for both boys were bleeding from gashes and cuts to their faces, and their clothing was in tatters. Benjamin wisely saw that there was no use in trying to step between them, for he would only get punched for his trouble.

He shouted for them to come to their senses, but it was useless. Not until Sir William came running with one of the servants were they able to separate the hotheads. Benjamin held a protesting Rory, while the footman kept Steven in tow.

"You bastard! I should kill you for what you tried to do!" Rory yelled at Steven and tried to kick at Benjamin's legs to force him to let him go.

"You hot-tempered fool! What was I doing?" Steven yelled back, his face more angry than Brenna had ever seen it.

"You bloody son-of-a-bitch!" Rory spat. "If I hadn't

198

come up when I did, where would you be sticking it to her now, eh? Always acting the gentleman, sniffing around her with your fine words and gifts—damn you, I had a feeling you'd try to raise her skirts 'fore you left here!"

Brenna had gone white. She could have wept at the way Rory was turning the whole incident sordid and dirty, dragging it through muck that made her feel cheap and sullied. She couldn't bear to look at any of them, and turned her back, feeling horribly ashamed. Giving both young men a disgusted look, Sir William went to her and patted her awkwardly on the shoulders.

"All right now, you've managed to make the young lady feel suitably ashamed of herself," he said to Rory contemptuously. "And as for you," he continued, looking at Steven. "I cannot believe you would betray my trust or the trust of her father with whom you have been so close."

"I swear we did nothing more than kiss!" Steven returned, seeing Brenna's shaking shoulders and cursing at Rory beneath his breath.

"Oh, aye, and I could see your hands ready at her breasts!" Rory yelled back.

"Quiet!" Sir William said, but he could see by Steven's guilt-stricken face that the words were true. He shook his head. "Both of you, get out of here. Steven, you will retire to your room, and Rory, I think you would be wise to return to your own home for a time."

"Aye, that I will, but not before I see Brenna safely home—"

"You'll not be seeing her home!" Sir William said sharply. Sir William put a hand to his head in the gesture of a man suddenly old and weary. "Lord help us, but you hotheads never rest, do you? Oh, yes, Steven, I know of your little dolly who keeps house for you in Cambridge —Benjamin, don't look so smug, for we both know of your own falls from grace. And Rory—you with your little wench from one of the farms! It makes me sick when I think that among the three of you rest the future of your countries!" he mocked them with a sneer to his lips.

"But now, we've subjected this young lady to enough I think, and I shall see her home myself."

He walked away, his arm protectively around Brenna's shoulders as he called for one of the grooms to bring 'round his coach.

The others, silent in their shame, watched the old man and the young girl go. Benjamin released Rory's arms and the footman did the same for his hostage. The two combatants glared at each other, with no room for forgiveness.

"I'm warning you, foreigner, should I be seeing you sniffing about Brenna Kildare again, I'll have another go at you," Rory promised. "And this time, there'll be no one to stop me!"

"You just watch yourself, Adair," Steven replied tightly.

For the first time, Rory allowed himself a small, triumphant smile. "Aye, I'll be watching myself—and her —long after you've been gone, Cruz. Remember that."

Steven felt a black and bitter hatred well up within. He forced himself not to lunge for the other lad's throat.

Chapter Seventeen

How cruel fate was, Brenna thought as she looked bleakly out her bedroom window, to make the day of Steven's departure dawn rosy and fair. It was only four days after Dermot's wedding. Steven had stayed to see the bridal couple off to Dublin. Brenna had stood stiffly at her mother's side, refusing to speak to Steven or Rory, both of whom had taken positions at opposite ends of the group of friends and family. Steven had a fine cut on his lower lip, and Rory sported a black eye.

Miraculously, Nora had not questioned Sir William too closely about the altercation between the two boys, nor about the reason her daughter's eyes were red and puffy from weeping. Nora had accepted the explanation that the two boys had gotten into a drunken brawl over some trivial matter and poor Brenna had been an involuntary witness.

The day after Dermot's departure, Steven had come by to inform Kildare that, as he'd just received a letter from his father urging him to come home, he would be leaving the following day. Kildare had accepted the lie, for he had no reason to doubt the lad. The foaling was over and there was nothing more for Steven to learn. The contracts had all been signed for a shipment of horses to the Paloma estate in Argentina, and though Kildare hated to see the boy leave, he could understand the boy's own father wanting him back home. The lad was seventeen now—old enough to assist his father in the management of their estate. Kildare had felt, for a brief instant, a twinge of jealousy that he had no strong, young son to help him run his farm, but he shrugged the idea aside. Dermot was far happier and more productive where he was.

And so the morning dawned when the Kildares would be saying their farewells to Steven Castaneda de la Cruz.

Brenna brushed her black hair 'til it shone like the glossy feathers of a raven's wing. She asked her sister to help her dress her hair into the smooth, soft coiffure that she had worn at the wedding. Then she slipped on the lavender silk gown.

"Why are you dressing up so?" Deirdre asked with amusement.

Brenna shrugged. " 'There be no law against it."

"Aye, and I suppose you'd be wanting to look nice—for Steven," Deirdre giggled.

Brenna looked in the mirror. Her eyes did not see her own image reflected there, but the look on Steven's face when he had bent to kiss her. Then Rory's cruel words echoed in her ears. "I had a feeling you'd try to raise her skirts 'fore you left here!" She pushed her face into her hands to blot out the memory, but it came back, slipping into her conscience, and Sir William's words, "Oh, yes, Steven, I know of your little dolly who keeps house for you in Cambridge . . ." It had been obvious, even to Brenna, what he had meant.

With a sudden fierceness, she nearly tore off the lavender gown and threw it on the bed. Deirdre looked up curiously, but remained silent, for even she could see the pain on her sister's face. She watched covertly as Brenna pulled at the pins in her hair, shaking the fine, gleaming length down her back, then determinedly braiding it as tightly as she could into two long tails. She went through her wardrobe and picked out a simple white blouse and skirt. When she was finished, she looked at her reflection again and was satisfied.

"You look twelve years old!" Deirdre observed scornfully.

"Aye," Brenna said shortly, tossing her braids smartly over her shoulders.

"But you're not twelve anymore," her sister insisted. At that, Brenna burst into sudden, raging tears. "Oh, I'm sorry!" Deirdre said hurriedly, rushing over to comfort the other girl.

Brenna cried wrenching sobs over Steven, and his leaving, and her first real kiss, and her growing up. Deirdre hastened her to a stool and picked up a handkerchief, holding it at the ready when her sister finally raised her face from her hands. She offered the square of linen silently.

"Do you feel better?"

Brenna nodded, blew her nose on the handkerchief, and took a fresh one to wipe her eyes. "I must be l—looking a fright," she supposed with a shaky laugh.

Deirdre wet a wash cloth and pressed it lightly against her sister's cheeks. " 'Twill go away in another moment, that is, if you don't go on again," she warned. Then in a softer voice: "I'm sorry you're taking it so hard—Steven's leaving, I mean—'twas—'twas cruel of me to taunt you so."

Brenna sighed. "Truly, I don't know what's the matter with me. So weepy and—and sad this morning, when I mustn't let Steven think—I mustn't let him know—" She pushed her face into the handkerchief quickly to ward off another attack of tears.

"Now, now, 'tis natural to be crying about a friend's leaving," Deirdre soothed. She was astonished by her sister's tears and troubled by the shadowy reasons behind them. Goodness knew, she would never carry on like this about Benjamin Markham. With a mature cunning for one of only thirteen years, she knew that Benjamin was not the kind of lad to put up with a woman's crying for long—perhaps, Steven was the same way. Well, no matter. It would shortly be time to be saying good-bye to Steven and Brenna had better pull herself together, or she would be making one fine fool of herself!

Nora knocked on their door and called in that Sir William had just driven up in his coach and was waiting for everyone to come down. From here he would continue on to Cork, where Steven would embark on a ship bound for Cádiz in Spain. There he would stay for a few days with relatives of his mother before continuing on from Cádiz to Buenos Aires in Argentina.

Quickly, Brenna adjusted her dress, wiped away the last traces of tears, and hurried downstairs; but she slowed a little when she reached the doorway to the yard, holding her head high and proud, determined that his last remembrance of her would not be one of embarrassment or humiliation.

Steven was shaking her father's hand and smiling easily as he talked earnestly—probably about the horses, she thought sourly. Her own bitterness surprised her. What had she expected? That he be sorry and glum and dispirited because of what happened a few nights ago? She remembered that he had obviously known at least one other girl to whom he probably hadn't even bothered to say good-bye. Brenna stiffened her spine.

"Brenna, I'm glad to see you, child," Sir William was saying with an underlying question in his voice as his thick, graying eyebrows arched upwards.

"Thank you, Sir William. I didn't want to miss saying good-bye to our visitor." She let herself look coolly at Steven, who was watching her now with some of the easiness in his smile gone.

Kildare stepped away. "You know how the females are," he said gruffly, winking at the lad.

But Brenna could not move forward to embrace him. She stood as though rooted to the spot, her eyes fluttering up to his face and then back down to the ground. She could hear, as she had heard before when he had kissed her, that slow, hard thundering of her heart inside her breast and the roar of blood inside her head. She thought, surely, everyone else could hear the sound as well.

Nora, sensing that the moment had become awkward, stepped forward and gave Steven a motherly hug, then ushered Deirdre forward, who gave him a chaste kiss on the cheek.

"Well now—well now," blustered Sir William, trying to appear tactful. "I think, Mrs. Kildare, if you don't mind, I will take you up on a cup of hot coffee before we continue on to Cork. Kildare, have a cup with me, won't you? I—ah—I may be in Cork a few extra days on business."

Deirdre followed her parents into the kitchen at her mother's request. The two young people stood there a moment longer, silent, Brenna looking everywhere but at Steven's face.

She heard Steven move a little closer. "Brenna, I'm

sorry that we have to part like this." His voice was hard, harsh—not really sorry, she thought.

Her eyes, that dark blue ringed with purple, stared at him as she tried to keep her voice from faltering. "Oh, Steven! Why did you—?" She stopped, for the sob in her throat threatened to render her speechless. She couldn't make a fool of herself now.

Steven took another step close to her, as if to comfort her as her head dropped forward; then he stopped and let his arms fall to his sides. "Brenna, please believe me," he said slowly, "I would never have hurt you."

She shook her head fiercely. "But Rory said—"

"Rory's a hot-tempered fool."

Brenna glanced at him. Aye, Rory was hot-tempered—but not you, Steven, no, never you. Cool and calm as icy water—never treacherous until one began to trust and took too many steps out—

"Aye, Rory has a temper," she said.

They stood another moment until Brenna took all of her courage and looked into Steven's eyes. Their blackness gleamed with hidden fires of longing, which would have spoken volumes to an experienced woman—but Brenna had no experience. Steven saw nothing in her face that could change his first impression of her—still a child waiting to grow up. Once again, he felt an odd frustration that he would not be there to see the child become a woman.

"I hope your trip is a good one," Brenna said, knowing how banal it sounded.

"Thank you, senorita," he answered her, his smile flashing now, as though he were once more sure of himself and of her. "You will take good care of the dove, won't you? Think of me at Paloma when you look at it."

Brenna nodded, recalling that *paloma* was the Spanish word for dove. "Of course," she promised.

Sir William came out of the kitchen then, saying his farewells to her parents. Soon Steven would be gone . . .

"Well, then, 'tis good-bye I'll be saying," she said briskly, stepping forward to kiss him on the cheek, then stepping back quickly as she felt his hands tighten on her waist.

"Time to go, Steven," Sir William said pleasantly. He signaled to the driver, who had been lounging by the corral, talking to some of the grooms. Tactfully, he climbed into the coach, to allow Steven a last moment with the Irish maiden.

"Good-bye, Brenna," he said, bowing rakishly before stepping into the coach. "Someday, perhaps, I will come back to see you." He grinned and closed the door.

The driver started the horses forward, and Steven stuck his head out the window to wave to her. Then he abruptly disappeared back inside the coach. "*Adiós, mi paloma,*" he said thoughtfully to himself.

Brenna stood in the yard, waving back until her arm ached. She felt on the verge of crying again, and her entire body trembled with her battle not to surrender to tears. Frustration and sadness welled up within her, and she felt like throwing something viciously; yet, at the same time, she felt that if she moved, she would weep hysterically. Everything had gone so unsatisfactorily, everything had been so incomplete. She had wanted to say more to Steven, but there had been no time—and she did not know the right words.

She could hear someone walking up behind her as she stood in the yard. Her hands clenched at her sides, and every line of her body pulled taut. She thought she would scream if anyone touched her.

"Brenna?" It was Kevin, his voice soft and gentle, the tone he used with a skittish colt. "Would you like for me to be saddling up Minx for you?"

Slowly, Brenna turned toward him, taking deep breaths to calm her frazzled nerves. She saw the warm, deep concern in his brown eyes below the unruly waves of red hair, and very slowly, her body began to unwind.

"Oh, Kevin, that would be good of you," she said.

"I'll go do it now, Brenna," he said sympathetically.

"Aye."

Nora and Tyrone watched their daughter walk slowly into the barn. "I'm glad the lad is gone," Nora said matter-of-factly. She sipped at her strong coffee and watched her husband's reaction over the rim of her cup.

"Why, Nora, the lad was the greatest of help to me! He was a good one, he was!"

"Aye, good for the horses, but not so good for your daughter," she replied stoutly.

"What is it that you're getting at?"

"I'm just saying that our Brenna is growing up. She was becoming attached to the lad. Overly fond I should say. It is better that he's gone."

"Nora, the lass is but fourteen!" Kildare remarked with a chuckle. "Good Lord, you'll not have me believing she'll be the next to be going after Dermot! Not that one! No, Brenna'll be staying with us, I know it! 'Tis enough for her that she loves us and the farm and the horses. I'm telling you, there's no room for romancing in that girl's life."

Nora looked at her husband, but said nothing. No use in destroying his dreams, she thought to herself. Let him go on thinking his Brenna would be the image of himself if it made him happy.

In the stables, Brenna pulled on a pair of old riding gloves she kept stored with the harness and bridle. She was so deeply immersed in her own thoughts that she hardly even realized Kevin was speaking to her.

"You're looking better already," he remarked in a pleased voice.

"I'm feeling better, thanks to you, Kevin," she replied gratefully.

" 'Tis glad I am that I could be of some help," he returned. He finished tightening the saddle and led the mare outside into the warm sunlight. "Let me give you a leg up," he offered, cupping his hands to receive her booted foot.

He thought to himself that she was as light as a feather and watched with admiration while she settled in the saddle. He found he wanted desperately to touch her again before she rode off and no longer needed him, for he knew that after this ride, the vulnerability he had seen in her face would be hidden again. His pity and fondness were rapidly growing into deeper feelings, perhaps because she had accepted his help and been grateful to him.

"I think—ah, let me see here," he said, trying to keep

his voice steady. "Aye, the strap is a bit loose. If you will allow me?" He reached down to fuss with the strap and let his shoulder brush against her leg. He felt her flinch, and he hurried his task, wishing not to offend her.

"Thank you, Kevin. I'll be off to Siobhan's for a visit." Brenna caught the reins in her hands.

"Aye, miss, 'twould be a nice ride for you," Kevin agreed and watched after her longingly, until someone called him.

Brenna walked her horse along the stark gray cliffs that rose above the sandy beaches of the coastal plain. She looked down musingly into the Irish Sea and thought of all that had happened to her since Steven had come to the farm. Was it he who had caused all these changes in her? Or had he come at a time when changes would have come about anyway? Well, he was gone now, and doubtless, although he had mentioned coming back someday, she would not be seeing him again.

She urged Minx into a trot and rode back away from the cliffs toward the peat bottoms. In a few minutes, she had tethered Minx and was knocking on Siobhan's door.

"Brenna, come in!" Siobhan said, glad to see the girl.

Brenna sat down and took off her hat and riding gloves. Siobhan hobbled across the room with the aid of a cane. Brenna offered to help, but Siobhan replied that she was neither too old, nor too feeble to get a guest some tea.

"How have things been with your parents and family?" Siobhan asked when she had seated herself at the table opposite the girl.

"Dermot's wedding was lovely," Brenna said. "He and Bernadette left for Dublin Monday morning. 'Twill seem different at the house without him. I can't say I will miss him, since Dermot was never one to add to the family closeness—you know what I mean, always going off to be alone to read and all, but still, 'twill seem different without him. Mama's already talking of giving Dermot's room to me, so my sister and I will each have our own room."

"You don't seem pleased with your present arrangement," Siobhan said.

Brenna shrugged. "Deirdre doesn't bother me, certainly, but she does have so many fripperies and gewgaws—and getting more all the time from Mrs. O'Hara." She laughed to herself. "She needs a lot of room for them all."

"Who is Mrs. O'Hara?"

"Jenny O'Hara. She lives in Enniscorthy and teaches deportment to young ladies of the district. Deirdre begged Mama to let her go—and she got her wish, of course."

"You don't approve?" Siobhan went on, studying the girl with her expressive eyes.

"Oh, 'tis not that I approve or disapprove really. I suppose I don't care what Deirdre does with her life, although setting her sights on someone like Benjamin Markham is a bit unrealistic. Don't you think so?" Brenna gazed steadfastly at the older woman, and Siobhan began to see where the conversation was leading.

"Setting her sights, as you say, on someone like Benjamin Markham is not as unrealistic as you might think, Brenna. After all, she has many chances to see him in the summer months, and your families are quite close. Your sister seems a very determined young lady. Of course, as she grows older, she may find that Benjamin is not for her."

"Does growing older do that to a person,"

Siobhan successfully hid her smile behind her teacup. "Aye, growing older helps a person see people more realistically, I suppose—though sometimes not."

"But in Deirdre's case, you think it might?" Brenna persisted.

"I cannot say, truly, Brenna." Her face was kind, though her eyes had sharpened perceptibly. "Tell me, now, what has Deirdre's choice of a husband to do with why you came here today to see me? I want the truth now, Brenna, for I can see that you are troubled."

Brenna gathered her courage to speak. "Steven left today."

"Aye, you knew he'd be leaving soon enough," Siobhan interjected.

"I knew it, but—it seemed far away when he spoke of it. And now, he is gone." She bit her lip and hesitated.

"You are saddened by his leaving, aren't you, Brenna?" Siobhan said softly, setting her teacup on the table.

"Aye, but more than just saddened, Siobhan. I feel strange, as though I'd lost someone very dear. Yet I'm angry and frustrated too, as though—as though something were left unfinished." There, she had gotten it out at last, and now she dared to look up and hope Siobhan could assuage her pain.

"Do you think it is possible that you loved Steven a little?" Siobhan asked gently.

Brenna shook her head and frowned. "No, I couldn't have loved Steven, for I know how fruitless it would have been. No, I'm sure I didn't."

"Love is seldom wise enough to be deterred by hopelessness," Siobhan returned. "Please understand me, Brenna; I'm not trying to suggest you loved Steven the way you might one day love your husband, but, perhaps because of his accident and those many days that you spent caring for him, the two of you came closer together. You did like him, didn't you?"

"I thought I did, but then, when Dermot was married, Steven—" she stopped, flushing with embarrassment. "Steven kissed me, and then Rory came along and—and they fought, and Rory said some horrible things."

Siobhan thought she understood. "How can you be sure the things Rory said were true, Brenna?"

"I—I don't know that they were, but Sir William said that—that Steven—had—a girl in Cambridge . . ." She stopped, her face a mask of misery.

"That is something you have no control over, Brenna. As long as Steven treated you with respect, you should consider him a gentleman. Most men have weaknesses where a certain kind of woman is concerned. Steven is not the first to fall from grace." She reached over and patted her hand.

"Do you think I could be jealous then?"

"Aye, I'm thinking you were—and maybe hurt because you hadn't thought Steven was 'that kind of lad.' What you have yet to learn is that all men are like that." Siobhan laughed with faint derision. "Men seem to need that kind of—interaction—more than we do."

"But I still feel as though something were left undone," Brenna sighed.

Siobhan was aware that she was treading on dangerous ground here. After all, Brenna was not her own daughter, and though she longed to help the girl to realize her own growing sensuality, she was not sure that Nora would approve of her intervention.

So, all she said was, "Perhaps you felt as though you had misjudged Steven, after all, and wanted to make it up to him in some way."

"Aye, I suppose that must be it," Brenna responded eagerly. She reflected for a moment. "I did like the kissing part," she owned with a girlish laugh.

Siobhan laughed too. "Well, then 'twas not a total loss, was it?"

Brenna shook her head. "It made me feel all tingling and melting," she continued dreamily, then caught herself abruptly and blushed again. "Pardon me, I was forgetting for a moment where I was."

"No need for apologies, Brenna. You're growing up, child. Aye, you're growing up." There was the smallest note of sadness in Siobhan's voice.

They sat companionably for a few more minutes, sipping tea, when the sound of horses' hoofs caught their ears. Siobhan immediately reached for her cane and went to the door to see who the visitor was.

A young man, hat in hand, stood at the door. It was obvious that he had come to the cabin at a fast pace, for he was still catching his breath. "Oh, Siobhan, wise woman, for the love of heaven, you must come fast!" he cried, his hands wringing the cloth of his hat. " 'Tis Beth —she's having her pains already, and I'm thinking the babe's about to come!"

"Is that it now?" Siobhan said calmly, beginning to

pack some things. "The due date is some six weeks away, is it not, Padraic?"

"Aye, ma'am, and poor Beth is fair worried about the babe's being too small as yet."

"Well, now, mayhap we miscalculated, don't you think? Can you ride me on the back of your horse?"

"Aye." The young man started to help the woman out, when he saw Brenna and bowed swiftly to her.

Brenna recalled him: Padraic MacMahon, one of the rood farmers who lived on the other side of the Adairs. He had always seemed a friendly sort; and his wife, Beth, was sweet and quiet, not one to draw much attention. This must be their first baby.

"Will you need any help?" Brenna asked Siobhan, as MacMahon helped the woman onto his horse. "I should like to be coming with you, if you don't mind."

Siobhan stared at her in surprise, then nodded. "All right then, you may come along. I may need you for God knows men are of no help in these situations!" She glanced at Padraic with faint apology. "Hurry now, for time is pressing."

Brenna mounted Minx with a leg up from the young man and kept easy pace with the other horse until they reached MacMahon's small cottage. She couldn't explain why she wanted to come with Siobhan on this call of mercy, but it somehow helped to have something to do besides brooding over Steven's leaving.

Padraic rushed inside to his wife's bedside. Her white, strained face relaxed visibly when she saw Siobhan behind him.

Curiously, Brenna let her glance take in the small area, which was compartmented into two rooms by a folding screen. The larger room was their living and eating quarters, and the smaller area, windowless, contained only a narrow bed and a low table with a burning candle on it.

How dark and lonely to be having a baby in there, Brenna thought to herself. Siobhan obviously thought so too, for she ordered Padraic to unfold the screen so that light from the windows in the living quarters could come into the bedroom.

"Now, Beth, you don't look to be agonizing," Siobhan soothed, catching the young woman's hand. She looked no more than eighteeen, Brenna thought. "Tell me exactly what you've been feeling."

"A little pain," Beth said hesitantly, "mostly in my back and hips, but some aching too, as though I'd been bending over all day."

"Have you been working too hard then?"

Beth shook her head, her eyes flying to her husband's for assurance. "I—I didn't do anything out of the usual, ma'am." She thought a moment. "I did do some laundry for the Adairs. Mrs. Adair was feeling poorly and—and we needed the extra coin, ma'am. So I thought—" She faltered at the stern look on Siobhan's face.

" 'Twas not for you to be doing someone else's laundry, Beth," Siobhan lectured her with a sigh. "Haven't I been telling you all along to do nothing but the cooking and such? Child, you may have pushed the baby down."

Brenna had been standing by the door. Now, as Siobhan gestured to her, she came forward with the medicines. Beth, upon seeing her visitor, gasped audibly and struggled to sit up.

"Ma'am! Miss Kildare, you—you shouldn't be here!" she said hurriedly.

"Brenna is assisting me today," Siobhan told her calmly. "She wanted to come."

"But—but she's yet a maiden. Should she be seeing a babe coming into the world?" Beth asked timidly, lying back down and bringing the cover up to her chin as though to hide the huge mound of belly beneath it.

"Don't you be worrying about anyone except your child," Siobhan intervenêd.

Beth suddenly let out a tortured groan and flinched as though something had smote her on the back. Her hands grabbed at her belly, holding its swollen bulk protectively.

"Aye, that was another pain," Beth gasped. Her breathing was becoming more rapid. She winced again and squeezed her eyes shut.

"Padraic, if you will be taking yourself outside," Siobhan ordered the young man, "I'll be better able to help your wife bring that baby into the family. I don't need you hovering about nervously behind me."

"You're sure?" Padraic asked anxiously.

"Aye, now go—and don't be coming back until I've called you."

Siobhan turned her attention to Beth, who was beginning a long groaning chant that made the hair on Brenna's neck rise. She leaned down close to Siobhan.

"Should I be doing something?" she asked.

"Aye, I'll be examining her now. You'd best set out the charms needed to keep the spirits away."

Brenna knew what she meant. It was said that the little folk, the fairies, would exchange their own offspring for that of a mortal woman. To keep these "changelings" from their homes, the mothers would set up protective spells to keep the wee folk from sneaking in. She glanced at the doorpost: the required horseshoe was hanging over it. Beneath the pillow, Beth would have put her prayer-book, and, if she were very diligent, she might have already cut a notch in a black cat's tail.

Brenna took salt from the kitchen cupboard, poured some onto a plate, and crossed it three times. It would have been better to peel seven roods of hazel, but she could see none about.

To make herself useful, Brenna thought she might make a light broth. She rummaged through the cupboard and found an onion, some lentils, and a large potato, all of which she diced and poured into a large pot. She called Padraic in to light a fire in the hearth, which he did with the air of a dazed man. He could not accustom himself to seeing the daughter of Tyrone Kildare making herself at home in his humble cottage.

Brenna shooshed him back outside and started the water to boil. After half an hour, a delicious smell began to permeate the room. Siobhan turned to see Brenna bending over the cauldron, and smiled a small, secret smile before turning back to her patient.

The pains were closer and harder by now; the baby was not going to wait much longer. Siobhan asked Brenna to

heat some water and tear up a few strips of linen with
which to bind the mother after the baby was delivered.

"And then light that large taper on the table and place
it close beside me," she said. "For upon first opening its
eyes, the child must look upon a blaze of candlelight to
signify a preference for light deeds rather than dark."

As Brenna bustled about, she was acutely aware of
Beth's suffering—the small panting breaths, the bitten-
back groans, the screams. 'Twas even more painful than
the birthing of a foal, Brenna thought.

"The baby is coming now," Siobhan's quiet voice cut
through the other sounds. "Push harder now, aye, that's
my girl. Push again! Again!" Siobhan guided the mother
with soft commands until, in a short time, a tiny wail
added its confusion to the mother's sobs and Siobhan's
delighted laugh.

" 'Tis a boy! A mite small, but otherwise perfect. Aye,
he'll fatten up in no time!" Siobhan said, wiping the baby's
face with a square of linen. "Look at your son, Beth."
She laid the baby in his mother's arms. "Now the after-
birth, Beth. I'll need another push from you."

Brenna watched with amazement as Beth pressed a
kiss to the moist downiness of the baby's head and let
her hands find each toe and finger of her son. The baby
was quiet, his eyes open and staring at nothing. It was
disconcerting how that unwavering stare seemed to meet
Brenna's eyes.

"You may call Padraic in now, Brenna," Siobhan said
proudly.

Brenna obeyed, then set out bowls for the soup. Siobhan had told her that Beth should eat something to help
her produce enough milk for the child to suckle. And,
no doubt, Padraic had been too nervous to eat anything.

"Padraic, I want you to see that Beth eats some soup.
Then I think she deserves a rest before it comes time to
feed the child. She is not to be getting out of bed for at
least three days. Do you understand me?"

"Aye, ma'am, I'll not let her feet touch the ground,"
Padraic promised.

"All right then. I shall want you to come by at the end

of the week for me, and I shall return to check on Beth and the boy. Have you thought of a name for him?"

"Aye, ma'am. 'Tis my father's name—Steven."

Brenna couldn't stop the gasp that escaped her lips, and the young man turned to her with a worried frown. "You're not liking the name then?"

Brenna stared at him as though she hadn't heard the question, then collected herself abruptly and shook her head. "'Tis a very good name," she said quickly. "'Tis a name most dear to me."

The young man grinned broadly. "Ach, then it means all the luck! I'm thanking you for your help today, Miss Kildare," he said.

Brenna nodded silently, wishing that she hadn't come today.

Siobhan gathered her things together briskly, gave instructions to Beth, and reiterated her orders to Padraic. Then Siobhan went outside to where Brenna was bringing 'round her mare.

Brenna's silence hung like a fog all during the ride back to the cottage.

"It was an easy birth," Siobhan commented.

"Was it?" Brenna asked with little interest.

"Aye, the time went quickly. Beth was lucky."

"Lucky?" Brenna gasped. "Did you see where she was obliged to sleep? Did you see the state of their larder? I felt sorry for her, having to do someone's laundry to make money and still having nothing to eat in that place."

Siobhan shrugged. "Padraic will find work, and they have a garden outside. He's just had too much on his mind lately to think about bringing in food."

"But his wife needs food to provide milk for the baby."

"Aye, but 'twill work out fine." Siobhan frowned to herself. "Are you so upset at the way they live then, Brenna?"

Brenna pursed her lips reflectively. "I should hate to be like Beth," she finally said with bitter determination in her voice.

"You have much to be thankful for, Brenna," Siobhan answered. "You need never live like Beth. Your father is fair wealthy, and you live in a big house with always enough food. There is no reason for you ever to know suffering."

"Aye," Brenna said thoughtfully. "I suppose I am as selfish as Deirdre when it comes to such comforts. Does that make me wicked, Siobhan?"

The older woman laughed comfortingly. "No, lass. It only makes you human."

Chapter Eighteen

"DARN! This needle must be getting dull," Deirdre complained, looking ruefully at a torn thread in her embroidery work. "I shall have to ask Mama for money to buy a new one in Enniscorthy tomorrow."

"I think I'll ride in with you," Brenna said thoughtfully. "I'm feeling a little bored, and it might be fun to watch you go through your measures at Mrs. O'Hara's." She laughed teasingly.

Deirdre frowned primly. " 'Twouldn't do you ill to take a few lessons in deportment yourself, Brenna Kildare," she said piously. "You know, you are sixteen and goodness knows who you'll find to marry you the way your manners are."

"What do you mean, Deirdre? What law is it that says a female has to get married by age sixteen?"

"No law," Deirdre conceded, "but look at all your friends! Maureen will be married in April and the O'Casey girl in June. Lucy Gallagher is betrothed already."

"Well, don't you be worrying about me!" Brenna flung at her, rising from her chair. "I'll be getting married when it suits me, and not before!"

Deirdre wisely kept her silence as her sister flounced out the door.

Brenna gazed back at the closed door of the parlor, wondering if, as her sister implied, she was going to be what the matrons delicately called a spinster. The name conjured up a picture of Siobhan, and Brenna caught herself up in the thought that someday she would take over the wise woman's place as the *pishogue* of the district, tending to the sick and the pregnant. Ach, now! She shook her head. Though she was fond of Siobhan and still visited her, she rarely went out with her on her calls. Brenna had determined that she would not get involved with that sort of work. 'Twas all well and good for some, she told herself but she neither had the skill nor the inclination to go about doing good deeds for everyone.

She wandered about in the kitchen for a few minutes. Her mother would soon be home from the Derry's, where she had gone to advise Mrs. Derry on the preparations for the wedding. Maureen's mother was in a fair twit about her daughter's marriage, as Maureen was her eldest and the first to leave home. Nora had offered to help her in any way she could, and naturally Mrs. Derry, like a drowning person clutching a life raft, had latched on to her offer. Could Nora do her the favor of looking over the materials the nanty-maker had selected for the gown? Could she suggest favorable colors for the bridesmaids (one of whom was to be Brenna)? Could she give ideas on suitable flower arrangements, and did she know of another priest besides that dour Father Quinn who looked as though he hardly favored marriages at all? Oh, if only Father Kinahan had not gone traipsing off to Africa to do missionary work. He had done so well with Dermot's wedding! And on and on.

Well, Brenna thought charitably, 'twould do her mother good to be in the middle of a little excitement, for Nora seemed to find more and more time on her hands since Tyrone had hired the plump and cheerful cook, Mrs. Sullivan from Waterford, with the extra revenue from the sale of horses. She was most likeable, and her cooking beyond reproach, but Brenna could not feel close to her; she missed those mother-daughter talks in the kitchen when Nora was preparing a meal.

She talked pleasantly with Mrs. Sullivan until she heard sleigh bells in the yard. Her mother was home. She hurried to the door and saw, to her dismay, Nora bringing Mrs. Derry and Maureen in with her.

"What's the matter, lass?" Nora asked worriedly, gazing at her daughter's face. "You don't look well. Is that cough still bothering you?"

"No, Mama, 'tis not the cough," Brenna replied sulkily.

"Well, then don't make such a face, my dear, but take Mrs. Derry's coat and welcome her in," Nora chided. "Maureen's here too. We thought we'd bring some of the material here, as you and Deirdre have an eye for colors."

"Deirdre has the eye for colors, Mama," Brenna said, petulantly.

Nora cast her a sharp look, but only said, "Well, then, will you be calling your sister in? No, let's go into the parlor, for I don't want to get in cook's way." She smiled at Mrs. Sullivan and ushered her guests into the new wing.

Deirdre sprang up in excitement when she saw the swatches of cloth that were laid out before her on the low table. "Oh, Mama, such lovely, lovely materials! Maureen, who is doing your gown?" she wanted to know eagerly.

"The nanty-maker from Wexford," Maureen said smugly. "She has to come farther than Mrs. Shea in Enniscorthy, but her selections are so much better since she has all her materials shipped down from Dublin."

"Oh, aye, I can see that," Deirdre said wistfully, fingering the samples.

Finally, they all decided on the white organdy for Maureen. That the bride wear white seemed more and more the modern thing to do, and Maureen wanted to be considered a sophisticate in her choice of gown. Her younger sister would wear a frosty pink; and it was decided that the jewel-bright sapphire silk would complement Brenna's coloring stunningly.

Then Mrs. Derry relaxed with a cup of hot tea and proceeded to tell Nora how wealthy the Byrnes were and how they had insisted that no expense be spared. She even admitted that they had been willing to lessen the amount of the dowry, as they realized that there was considerable expense in the new gowns and the cost of the food and drink.

"Your mother seems as excited as you," Deirdre observed as the three girls sat together by the fire. Mrs. Sullivan had brought them hot chocolate and the tiny oat cakes that were her specialty.

"Aye, mayhap, even more," Maureen said thoughtfully, her eyes on the fire.

"Did you hear?" Deirdre went on with a giggle of delight, "Benjamin Markham and Rory Adair are to be coming home in June. Isn't that wonderful, Oh, I for one, shall be glad to see them again! Rory has been made a corporal, and Benjamin a second lieutenant."

Maureen seemed to whiten around the lips, but her eyes gave away nothing as she shrugged noncommitally. "Aye, I've heard it—but I'll be believing it when I see them home."

"It has been a long time, hasn't it?" Brenna said, remembering with a small pang one of the last times she'd seen Rory two years before, when he had been bruised and cut from his fisticuffs with Steven Castaneda de la Cruz. Steven. How fondly she thought of him now, though oddly, she found it difficult to recall his features distinctly. Maureen watched the dreaminess in Brenna's eyes, and her own eyes narrowed speculatively. "Aye, and with me married, I suppose you'll be having free rein with my Rory," she said with a twist of bitterness.

Brenna looked genuinely surprised. "I have no intention of doing anything with Rory Adair," she said earnestly. "I'm surprised that you'd be speaking of it, Maureen, especially with your wedding date so close."

Maureen shrugged. "My feelings for Rory were no secret. I just got tired of waiting for him."

Brenna fell silent, feeling slightly uncomfortable.

"What is Sean like?" Deirdre asked to ease the tension.

"Sean?" Maureen seemed at first not to recognize the name. Then, with a light reddening of her cheeks, she laughed merrily. "Sean is everything that Rory Adair was not," she said, her voice warming. "He is loyal and kind and treats me like a duchess. I remember, when we first met last summer, how he complimented me on this or that, held my hand at the least provocation, and spent all his time in my company as if he couldn't bear to let me out of his sight. I suppose he was smitten," she sighed romantically. "But it wasn't until last Christmas, when his family came to visit again, that he declared his intentions. He wanted to run away and get married! Imagine! He said he couldn't wait much longer to be truly my husband —in every way." Maureen allowed herself a lascivious sigh, which excited Brenna and Deirdre into goosebumps.

"How did you persuade him to wait?" Deirdre demanded.

Maureen laughed. " 'Twas the hardest thing I ever had to do, for Sean was hot that night—" She stopped and put a hand to her mouth. "Oh! I—I—" She blushed and looked away from the two shockingly eager faces of her audience.

"Oh, Maureen, you mean you let him kiss you, right there?" Deirdre asked.

Maureen stared at the girl and barely kept herself from bursting into laughter. "Oh, aye, I did let him kiss me, a wee bit," she admitted.

"How utterly romantic," Deirdre sighed.

"Where will you be living?" Brenna asked, brushing aside the distant memory of Steven Cruz's kiss almost two years before.

Maureen frowned to herself. "We'll be living with my parents for the first three or four months. 'Tis not what I would have liked, but Sean hasn't been able to find himself a good piece of land, he says. I'm thinking that he'll not take to the farming so easily."

"What does he do then?" Brenna asked.

"He raises fighting cocks," Maureen said with a defensive note in her voice. "He trains them, and when he thinks he has a winner, he sells it to the highest bidder. His father taught him the business, and Sean is quite good at it; but now that he's getting married, his father thinks he should settle down on a farm. More's the pity," she said, almost to herself. "I think 'twould be wonderful to travel the country."

"Well, there's no shame in raising gaming birds," Brenna put in.

Maureen glared at her as though looking for hidden sympathy. "I'll be having no pity from you, Brenna," she said quickly. "You'll be remembering the saying, 'Always a bridesmaid, never a bride'."

Brenna flushed hotly, but kept her temper in check. "I meant nothing unkind, Maureen," she said. "I was just meaning that if Sean would rather do other work than farming, perhaps, it would be better to let him."

"Aye, he might just do that," Maureen declared, still stiffly defensive.

Fortunately, Mrs. Derry interrupted to call Maureen to leave. She gathered all the materials together and promised Nora that she would let her know the minute the plans for the gown were drawn up. Maureen, after saying a cool farewell to the Kildare sisters, hurried after her mother.

"Well!" Deirdre breathed. "I'm wondering what that was all about."

Brenna nodded. "How silly of her to get upset."

"Aye, why did she choose you as her bridesmaid, when it's obvious she's got something against you."

Brenna shrugged. But Maureen's voice rang in her ears: "Always a bridesmaid, never a bride."

Chapter Nineteen

"HELLO!" Brenna called amiably, trotting Minx up to stand next to Maureen's mount. "Where is your husband this fine day?"

Maureen shrugged. "He's involved in business."

"Has he found some farming land then?"

Maureen shook her head. "No, he's of a mind to start raising the roosters again—to give him something to do, you understand. He is finding it hard to keep himself busy about the farm. I'm thinking—I'm thinking he's become a little unhappy." Maureen took a deep breath as though it had strained her to make such an admission.

Brenna felt a surge of pity, but out of consideration for Maureen's pride, she kept her voice neutral. "And what does your father think of his raising the fowls?"

"Good Lord, Brenna! Sean is a grown man; he can do as he wishes!"

"Of course," Brenna answered. "Well, then, I'll be wishing the both of you good luck," she said swiftly wanting to be gone.

Maureen held her arm a moment longer. "Have you—have you heard anything more about when Rory and Benjamin will be coming home?"

Brenna shook her head. "Still in June sometime. Sir William thinks they're wanting to surprise him, for they didn't give him a specific day. Maybe they don't know themselves. I suppose the army can be quite confusing."

"Aye, I suppose." Maureen seemed to go into deep thought for a moment, and Brenna took the opportunity to gather the reins.

"Well, I'll be going now. Say hello to everyone!" She hurried the horse forward, fearing that Maureen would detain her again.

After that, she tried to avoid the girl, for her questions about Rory Adair were an embarrassment. Brenna could not understand what was wrong with the Byrne's marriage, but she knew that Maureen had a knack for getting her into trouble by pulling her into her problems, and she wanted no part of this one. She took to riding her horse away from the direction of the Derry farm.

In the first week of June, Sir William's carriage drove up to the Kildare house, and the old gentleman got out to wave a piece of paper in front of Tyrone's nose.

"Just got word, Kildare! Castaneda has increased his orders. He wants four dozen head on the next shipment. Of course, it is too late for that, but think of it, man! He's willing to take all you can supply, and at the most extraordinary prices! You'll be growing richer, my friend, thanks to our mutual acquaintance."

"Aye, that's Steven's doing I'm sure," Kildare rejoined heartily. "The lad knows fine horse-stock when he sees it, and the foals have been especially good this season."

Brenna, listening idly at the window, felt her heart lurch in her breast at the mention of Steven's name. For a moment, it seemed she could hear nothing, and she thought she might faint; but the moment passed quickly. How silly of her to react this way to a distant memory. Steven was a part of her childhood, a part of her past. Resolutely, she stood up from her chair. She would have gone to the stables to get Minx, but she didn't want to walk past her father and Sir William; she had no intention of getting embroiled in a discussion of Steven Castaneda de la Cruz and his superior horse sense.

Quickly, she took the back door outside and walked towards the stream in the woods. She ambled along aimlessly, trying to keep her mind off her memories. So unaware was she, that when someone stepped suddenly into her path, she shied back in surprise.

"Brenna Kildare! It is Brenna, isn't it?" The voice sounded oddly familiar, but her eyes couldn't quite focus on the tall, young man who looked down at her with an infuriating arrogant grin. "Come now, blackbird, you don't remember me?"

With a start, Brenna realized that she had bumped into Rory Adair. Speechless, she let her eyes travel from the top of his wavy, brown hair, over his deeply tanned face with those twinkling blue eyes, and over the shiny, gold buttons and braid of his military uniform to the dusty black kneeboots that encased his muscular legs.

"Well?" he asked, still with amused mockery in his voice. "Do you like what you see?"

"Rory Adair!" Brenna finally managed, her blue eyes locking with his, then shying away.

He laughed. "Is that all you can say after such a long time?" He took a step nearer, and Brenna automatically stepped backward.

"How is life in the army?" she asked stiffly. It was difficult for her to reconcile the man before her with the violent and abusive young bully who had made her feel so ashamed when Steven had kissed her.

He laughed and gave her a long, cool, speculative look. His eyes seemed to take in everything about her with a languid sweep: the childish braids wrapped about her head, the face beneath them with those magnificent blue eyes, circled in violet, behind the long sweep of black lashes, her translucent skin, faintly golden now from the sun, her straight nose with its delicately etched nostrils, and the finely drawn mouth, which curved at the corners and looked so perfect for kissing. He felt an urge to kiss her then and took another step forward.

"Shouldn't you be welcoming me home properly now?" he asked in a husky voice, reaching out to catch her slender arms in his strong hands.

Her eyes opened wide in frightened innocence and they jumped away from his tightened expression. He released her abruptly and was surprised at his own reaction. He had never before let innocence stand in the way of his wants.

They stood, breathing shallowly, looking at each other for a long moment before Brenna, with an inarticulate cry, turned on her heel and ran back the way she had come. Rory caught a glimpse of her blue skirt flitting among the trees, but he suppressed the urge to follow her. It was not for him to be running after some skittish female, God knew, when most women were willing to listen to any offer he might make. It hurt his pride to think that Brenna Kildare had rejected him, but he'd be damned if he'd let her know it.

Brenna couldn't begin to understand her reaction to Rory Adair—this somehow different Rory Adair—who had looked at her as though she wore no clothing, who seemed so easy and sure and conceited. Aye, conceited! she thought, building up her wrath. He had looked at her as though she were a prize horse who needed to be broken in. How dare he!

She walked slowly, still stewing in anger, as she came to the edge of the wood. As though she should be welcoming him home with open arms, she thought. She had never liked him, and she still didn't! It didn't matter to her how handsome he looked in his red jacket and gold buttons; she didn't care how many medals he might have won or how knowledgeable he had become in the military. Fie on him! She'd not give him the satisfaction of thinking she'd been impressed in the least.

Nearing the yard, she could see that Sir William had already gone. She wondered why Rory had been in the woods instead of at Markham Hall to greet Sir William, then realized that he had probably been on his way to see his parents.

But—oh—she didn't want to be thinking of Rory Adair now. She had other things on her mind. Mama had asked her to pick strawberries for dinner, and she had forgotten about it when she had heard Sir William's news.

She hurried inside to fetch a basket, calling to Mrs. Sullivan that she would be gone an hour or two. She debated whether or not to take Minx with her and decided against it. She felt like walking. So she started out down the road that led to Sir William's house. She certainly didn't want to run into Rory again.

The road was dusty and Brenna could feel perspiration breaking out on her face as she trudged along, trying to keep her skirts out of the thistle bushes that grew wild alongside the road. Wild daisies and sunflowers poked their bright heads up from between the weeds and trailing rose vines creeped over the stone fences that separated the fields. A traveler or two passed by and greeted her with a smile.

"Miss Brenna!"

Brenna turned to look up at a horseman bearing down on her with an easy gait. For a terrified moment, she thought she had inadvertently come across Rory again, but when the traveler took off his hat, a shock of red hair sprang free, and she relaxed. 'Twas only Kevin Ryan. She waved in greeting and waited for him to come along beside her.

"Hello, Brenna," Kevin said, jumping down from his mount to walk with her as he held the reins in one hand. "Where are you off to?"

She shrugged. "Picking strawberries for dinner. There's a whole haven of plants just the other side of the road there, beyond that copse of trees."

"Aye. But why didn't you have me saddle Minx for you?"

"Oh, I felt like walking," she said briefly, wishing that she had brought a shade hat to keep the sun off her face.

" 'Tis a hot day for that," he went on absently.

"Well, and what of it?" she asked with irritation. "I can be walking where I please, can't I?"

Kevin flushed and nodded. "Aye, of course, you can," he admitted. He looked around at his own horse as though suddenly remembering an errand. "I'm off to post a letter for your father. I—I suppose I'd best be off."

"Aye, you'd best," she agreed tersely.

But as he stopped to gather the reins and remount, she caught his arm and stayed him for a moment. "Oh, Kevin, I'm sorry about my temper. 'Tis not your fault that 'tis hot and dusty, and that I've been stupid for not bringing Minx along. Please excuse me for being so nasty to you. I suppose I've been out of sorts for a few days now."

Aye, thought Kevin to himself. He had noticed the change in her, the restlessness with her usual routine, the mindless riding that would bring her back very late at times. He wondered if she was upset because no young man had asked for her hand yet—her being all of sixteen now. With his usual despair, he thought how honored he would be if she would only consider a proposal from him; but he squelched the thought. It was a fool's dream. Even if no one asked for Brenna Kildare to marry him—and he couldn't conceive of her growing old alone—she would never, never be allowed to become his wife. Despite Kildare's trust and liking, Kevin had long ago realized his place. No groomsman married the daughter of someone as wealthy as Tyrone Kildare.

" 'Tis not your fault," he assured her, realizing the girl was waiting for him to absolve her. "This heat is bothersome to everyone."

" 'Tis not just the heat," she murmured, almost to herself.

"Aye," he said shortly. Kevin Ryan was, after all, a young man of nineteen now and subject to the needs and urges of any young man of his age. That he was still a virgin was more a matter of choice than of necessity, for there were enough serving wenches who would be quite willing to charm the red-haired lad out of his doldrums. The little laundress whom Kildare had recently hired, Cathy Ferguson, was not beyond waving her bottom at him as she took out the baskets of laundry to dry on the line. She would sometimes hitch her skirt up along her waistband to keep it out of her way, affording Kevin a most delectable view of her unstockinged legs, and there were times when he had been ready to throw his principles away for a quick roll in the loft hay.

He thought now what a shame it was that Brenna couldn't release her pent-up urges in the same way. What law was it that required a woman to be a virgin in her marriage bed? he wondered idly. Poor Brenna, he thought, how I should like to comfort you and give you something to ponder besides the heat and the dust and the horses.

"Well, then, I'm hating to leave you like this, lass, but your father'll be wanting me back soon," he said aloud.

"Aye." She looked at him. "You really are indispensable to him, Kevin."

He nodded, not trusting himself to speak, and remounted quickly. He urged the horse into a trot, fighting the image of her forlorn face watching him from beneath those absurd long braids. As though they could hide her curving figure, he thought, as though they could change the high, perfect breasts, or the waist as slender as a sapling, or the long, graceful legs that he could imagine beneath her skirt.

Brenna watched him go, puzzled by his abrupt leave-taking.

Ah, well, she couldn't blame him for wanting to be rid of her quickly; she was such a shrew lately. Could Maureen have been right? Was she upset because she had not been asked for marriage by anyone? She shook her head. The idea was ridiculous—there was no one in the county whom she cared enough about to want to marry. She was not so foolish, she told herself, that she would accept just anyone!

Chapter Twenty

BRENNA stood nervously in the doorway of the grand ball-room of Markham Hall, looking for someone she knew. Young men, many wearing military uniforms, escorted flirtatious young ladies past her under the archway. The splendid silks and satins of fancy dresses rustled, gleamed, and floated about the parquet floor.

She wished that her parents were with her, but the invitation to Benjamin Markham's party had named Brenna and Deirdre only. Sir William, of course, had promised the Kildares there would be chaperones. Rory Adair would also be there as a guest of honor, and Brenna found herself searching for him, despite her dislike of him.

Standing coyly beside her, Deirdre fluttered a fan covered with the same green silk from which her gown, cut low at the neck to bare her shoulders, had been made. The front of her skirt draped becomingly to meet the flounced bustle in back.

Brenna was dressed in the sapphire blue gown that she had worn at Maureen's wedding. It also was cut to border the top of her breasts and bare her shoulders, though its bustle wasn't as elegant as Deirdre's. Bowing to Deirdre's explicit instructions, first received from Mrs. O'Hara, Brenna had also worn long, white gloves to her elbow. The most striking change in Brenna Kildare's appearance, however, was her hairstyle: shining, black tresses were piled in large curls at the back of her head, a few carelessly left to graze her shoulder, and held there with gleaming blue-enameled hairpins. The effect had struck Brenna with awe as she looked in the mirror; she no longer looked like a child, but like a young woman.

For this very reason, she felt so odd as she stood in the arched doorway and scanned the room. She was aware of several young men staring at her, and her cheeks blushed becomingly. One particularly bold young man took three steps up to her and bowed.

"May I introduce myself to two lovely young ladies?" he asked, smiling with unaffected good humor. "Godfrey Talbot, at your service."

Deirdre dimpled and curtseyed, giving her sister a slight push to do the same. "Good evening, Mr. Talbot. I am Deirdre Kildare, and this is my sister Brenna."

"Charmed," he replied. "If I may, I should like to introduce you to some of my friends." He took Brenna's hand in his with the ease of long practice, making it impossible for her to release herself.

Reluctantly, she allowed him to lead her down the steps and onto the floor where he maneuvered her into a small group of young people. Dierdre had been captured by another young man, and Brenna saw her disappear into the crowd. Though some of the guests were from Dublin, it appeared to Brenna that most of them were Londoners. The talk among the military men was of Russia and India; the young ladies were interested in the latest plays on the London stage and the newest work of poetry that had quite melted their hearts. Brenna felt totally out of her element; she nodded occasionally, but said nothing.

It was in this state that she felt a light touch on her arm and turned to see Rory Adair grinning delightedly at her. With relief, she clung to him. His was the first friendly face she had seen, and Rory taking advantage of the situation, steered her away from the group and out onto the dance floor.

Brenna was surprised at his mastery of the dance, a slow waltz, which helped to relax her rapidly beating heart. "I see you've learned more than just military maneuvers," she commented, keeping her tone as light as she could.

He noted with a smile the slight catch in her breath as his right hand pressed tightly against her waist while his left tightened its hold on hers. "Aye, it wasn't all work," he acknowledged with a self-derisive grin.

Brenna was not quite sure what he meant, but decided not to ask him to enlighten her. She was not quite sure of herself around this new Rory Adair. She had hoped that she would not be required to stay too long at the dance, but now, with Rory's strong arms around her, guiding her through the steps, she did not feel quite so uncomfortable as she had.

Rory passed a leisurely inspection of her as they danced. She had fine, high cheekbones, and her eyebrows arched above her eyes like two black wings. Her lips were parted a little with her breathing, and the edge of her teeth, white and even, caught at the tip of her tongue as she mused. The smooth column of her neck curved gracefully into her shoulders, bared and gleaming just a little with a fine mist of perspiration. He let his eyes delve dangerously along the neckline of her bodice to the separation of her breasts, which sloped deliciously into the froth of lace that cupped them.

He could feel the narrow span of her waist, and he visualized the long, slender legs beneath the drape of her skirt. He felt himself becoming aroused by that exquisite profile and wished to God he could lure her to the lawns outside, where he might wheedle a kiss from her. His square jaw clenched unconsciously as the thought of it brought back that long-ago memory of Brenna on the lawn with that foreign boy—Steven was his name—kissing in the darkening twilight.

When the music stopped, everyone applauded the orchestra appreciatively, then walked to the refreshment table for punch. Rory brought back a glass for Brenna and one for himself, then directed her to a velvet-covered bench along the wall where other couples had seated themselves to wait for the next dance.

"Ah, that's quite good," Brenna commented, sipping the fruity punch. Even though all the windows were open to the June air, the air had grown close from the dancing. Young ladies wielded their fans more for comfort than flirtation.

"Would you like more?" Rory asked solicitously.

Brenna shook her head. "No, I think—if I just stay still for a moment, 'twill take some of the heat away."

Rory took her glass and put it next to his on a side

table. "Perhaps you'd be liking to take a stroll about the park outside?" His blue eyes took on that peculiar gleam that made her feel so uneasy.

"I think not now," she answered, turning to look for her sister. She spied Deirdre among a group of young ladies, who were listening with wide eyes and breathless expressions to Benjamin Markham relating his military exploits. Poor Deirdre looked quite miserable, Brenna thought, with a twinge of sympathy. Apparently, Benjamin had not noticed her new dress or how well she fit into it.

The orchestra was about to begin another tune, and Godfrey Talbot asked Brenna to dance. "I believe that Miss Lawrence said you'd taken the next dance on her card, old fellow," he said to Rory and nodded toward a tall, winsome blonde who was watching them covertly.

Brenna laughed awkwardly. "I'm afraid I've set my card down in the hall, Mr. Talbot, so I don't have anyone signed on it. Is—is that proper?"

Talbot grinned with delight. "No matter, Miss Kildare, but let us hope no quarrels will ensue for your hand."

"Perhaps it would be better if I retrieved it then?"

He shook his head. "Certainly not now, miss. Come, the dance is already starting, and I've laid my claim to you for this one."

With a glance at Rory, who was bowing before the blonde girl, Brenna gave herself up to young Talbot. He was an energetic dancer; by the time they were finished, Brenna's cheeks were flushed, and tendrils of hair were loosened from her coiffure. Talbot begged for the next dance, but Brenna declined breathlessly. She found her sister and retired for a few moments to the ladies' drawing room to rearrange herself.

"Ach, that Benjamin hasn't paid one whit of attention to me," Deirdre mourned as she pinned up the escaped tendrils in her sister's hair.

"He has so many paying attention to *him*," Brenna said.

"Aye, the braggart has good cause to think himself the most sought-after lad in the house," Deirdre went on.

"I'm thinking 'twould serve him right if I just gave up and let one of those shallow-souled dolls have him."

Brenna laughed. "Oh, Deirdre, you mustn't do that!"

Her sister gave her a sour look. " 'Twould seem you've chased your doldrums away."

Brenna blushed. "I'm enjoying myself," she admitted with a quick look at Deirdre's repair work.

"Would it have anything to do with Rory Adair, then?"

"Heavens, no! I mean—oh, aye, I suppose he is part of it. At least he's not the horrible, nasty bully he once was," she said defensively.

Deirdre snorted. "Hah! I'm thinking that deep down Rory Adair can still bully with the best of them. Perhaps he's learned to hide his uncouth ways beneath a handsome uniform and elegant manners!" She gave her sister a severe look. "You be watching out for him, Brenna, for I remember the tales Lucy used to tell me about him."

Brenna stood up. "For goodness sake, Deirdre, you don't need to be lecturing me about Rory Adair. I know him as well as you do, and I'm not about to let him step around me so easily." She patted her sister's hand placatingly. "Why don't you go over to Benjamin and lure him into a conversation? You don't have to worry about my affairs."

As Brenna entered the ballroom, she saw several uniformed young men at the refreshment table, surreptitiously pouring liquid out of a flask into punch glasses. They were joking and laughing, and she had no doubt that they were sweetening the taste of the fruit punch with some hard Irish whiskey. If Sir William found out about the smuggled liquor, Benjamin would be in for a severe scolding, and the dance would be stopped. Well, Brenna decided, she wouldn't be the one to carry tales, but she fervently hoped that none of the young men would get too drunk to carry themselves like gentlemen.

She took a seat along the wall by the windows, where she could catch some of the breeze that had begun to blow lightly outside. Across the room, Deirdre had finally engaged Benjamin's attention, and as she spoke with him, her face lit up with animation. She looked very pretty tonight, Brenna thought and wondered if Benjamin appreciated how mature her sister had become.

During a break in the music, a young man sat next to Brenna and conversed with her. Out of the corner of her eye, she could see Rory in serious conversation with two other young men, and she wondered briefly why he was not trying his wiles on another of the young ladies. Perhaps she and her sister had judged Rory too hastily—it pleased her to think so.

The party wore on until just after midnight, when Brenna felt the first onslaught of weariness assail her. She wriggled her toes inside her new slippers; her feet were beginning to hurt, and she hoped no one else would ask her to dance. Even the chaperones were beginning to yawn sleepily; one man was actually snoring as he leaned against the back of his chair. She supposed that the party would soon be ending, and she wondered what time it was. A few couples had sneaked out the long French doors to the lawns outside—to indulge in some stolen kisses, Brenna thought, feeling remarkably indulgent herself.

"Brenna, I've hardly had a word with you all evening." Rory bowed to her and seated himself close beside her. "Where have you been hiding yourself?" he asked with a careless smile.

"I've not been hiding, Rory," she replied. "I've just been well attended."

He smiled at her flippancy. "Come, let me get you a glass of punch. You look a trifle warm."

She shrugged. "There's a nice breeze blowing through now. I really don't feel thirsty, but thank you."

He sat down again and abruptly captured her gloved hand in his. "I've been thinking how unfriendly you've been with me," he began, his voice soft.

Brenna looked at him, her blue eyes widening. "Unfriendly? Why, Rory, I am sorry if you think so, but I assure you, it was unintended."

"What a nice little speech," he mocked her, squeezing

238

her hand tightly. "Of course, I don't believe a word of it. You've been avoiding me since I came home. Why?"

"I'm sure I don't know what you mean," she insisted. He was bending close to her, and she could feel his breath rolling over her shoulder. She could also smell the faint odor of whiskey, but she was not repulsed: she had always liked the sharp smell of good liquor.

"You don't?" he asked in a lower voice, leaning even closer so that his lips were barely touching her ear. "Then, tell me why I haven't seen you lately?"

Closing her eyes a moment, Brenna luxuriated in the tingling sensation that started in her ear and worked its way down her neck to her breasts. Without realizing it, she turned her body toward his. "Rory, you've been home but a few days," she began breathlessly.

Rory, well-acquainted with acquiescent young females, was encouraged enough to touch her ear with his lips and blow softly. Her hand had gone quite limp in his, and he cursed his luck that this should happen with so many people about. In a few moments, Sir William would probably notice his maneuvers and tactfully impose himself.

Brenna was floating giddily. All her attention was focused on Rory's mouth teasing her ear with soft whisperings, which turned her slowly into melting butter.

"Rory, you Irish rogue!" came a simpering female's voice with an English accent. "So there you are."

Brenna tried to ignore the intrusion, but Rory moved away from her, and she found it impossible to create the exquisite sensation without him. She opened her eyes crossly and stared at the blonde Miss Lawrence with unconcealed dislike.

The English girl, who knew exactly what she had been about, allowed herself a smile as she touched Rory's arm.

"Rory, I daresay I've come only just in time to rescue this young maiden from your devilish wiles, haven't I?"

"Gemma, you do have a keen sense of timing," Rory tightly replied as he recovered his manners enough to stand and bow. "I don't believe you've been introduced to Miss Kildare. Gemma Lawrence, Brenna Kildare."

"How do you do, I'm sure," Gemma said with a trill of laughter.

Brenna nodded and made to leave them. "I should be finding Deirdre," she said to excuse herself. " 'Tis late and we should be going."

Rory hesitated, as though he would have dissuaded her, but then he smiled and bowed. "Then, good night, Brenna, and thank you for coming."

Brenna watched him take the young woman's arm, hating Gemma for her small, secret smile of victory. A pox on all these smiling, glittering foreigners, Brenna thought despairingly. Because they were English, they thought they could treat the native Irish like children. She stamped her foot and strode out the French doors.

"Miss Kildare, may I help you?" It was Godfrey Talbot.

Brenna gave him a short smile. "I was looking for my sister, Mr. Talbot. I can't imagine—"

"The pretty little thing with the green dress who came in with you? Why, I believe I saw her with Benjamin Markham, ma'am, taking a turn about the park."

"Oh, then I suppose I'd best look for them, for 'tis time for us to be going."

"Would you care for some company?" Talbot asked hopefully, but Brenna shook her head impatiently.

"No, thank you, sir. If you will excuse me?"

Brenna hurried down the steps of the balcony, nearly stumbling over a young man who was sound asleep at the foot of the last step. Small lanterns lit up the lawn, but shrubs and trees prevented her from seeing anything in the farther recesses of the park. A faint whispering came to her from the garden, just a few feet away, and she followed the sound to a young couple, who straightened their clothing at her approach. She mumbled an apology, hurriedly excusing herself in her embarrassment.

She found herself in the shrubbery maze, following the path in the semidarkness. She thought she heard the scrape of a boot on the gravel path. She stopped—nothing. As she continued on, she was sure she heard a low laugh. Finally, she turned a corner and came upon a secluded little arbor, where she found her sister and Benjamin Markham sitting on a wrought iron bench and holding each other in close embrace.

For a stunned moment, Brenna could only stare. Deirdre was kissing Benjamin's face with soft, pleasurable little kisses, while he accepted her homage, even as his hands slipped upward from her waist to cup the young girl's breasts. Anger washed over Brenna, and she launched herself at the two of them.

"Jesus!" Benjamin cried. "It's one of your banshees, Deirdre, I swear!" He jumped up from the bench, leaving Deirdre sprawled awkwardly in order to face this unknown assailant, who attacked him with rending claws.

At that moment, Brenna wished she could think of a suitable oath, but all she could do was continue her wild onslaught, kicking him, clawing at his face. How dare he bring her little sister out here and try to maul her? She would see him pay for that. "You villain! You—you stinking coward!" she screamed, satisfied to see the long furrow she'd ripped in his cheek.

"Damnation! Get off of me, wench!" Benjamin snapped, thinking that some jealous girl had spied his amorous advances with Deirdre and was paying him back.

They fought a moment longer before Benjamin finally caught hold of her arms. He shook her hard and danced nimbly to avoid her kicking feet. His eyes had adjusted well enough now so that he could see who it was, and a low, surprised whistle escaped him.

"Brenna Kildare!"

"Aye, you disgusting, slimy toad!" she flung at him. "You sicken me! How dare you bring my sister out here and try to—to . . ."

By now, Deirdre had gathered her wits about her and was dashing toward them, her face a mask of fury. "Brenna, what have you done?" she cried with embarrassment as she saw the bleeding gash on Benjamin's cheek.

"I was defending you, goose!" Brenna said, hurt by her sister's anger.

Benjamin began to laugh. "I was only kissing her, Brenna. Whatever were you thinking, girl?"

Now it was Brenna's turn to feel embarrassment. As she stood facing the two of them, she wished the earth would swallow her up. "I—I thought—I came around the corner and saw you. . . ." She could not bring herself to look at her sister's furious face.

"Brenna!" Deirdre choked. "How could you!"

The two sisters gazed distrustfully at each other. Then, to bring a quick ending to the situation, Benjamin took both girls by the arm and began to lead them out of the maze.

"Perhaps, it's time for you to go home, Deirdre," he said.

"Aye," Brenna mumbled. " 'Tis late."

So great was Deirdre's humiliation and anger that she kept her silence. Finally she had gotten Benjamin Markham where she wanted him, and then her headstrong sister had to barge in like St. Patrick into a den of pagans! The idea caused a muffled giggle to escape her throat. How funny Brenna had been, really, she thought and laughed louder. Benjamin caught her humor and joined in with a chuckle.

"Oh, Benjamin, I am sorry," Brenna finally said.

He smiled charmingly, trying not to wince with the sting of his cut cheek. "It's all right, Brenna," he said cheerfully as he bundled them into their father's carriage. "The next time I'll make sure you can't find us."

As the carriage got underway, the two sisters moved to opposite ends of the seat. Brenna risked a glance at her sister and saw tears flowing from her closed eyes. With a humble apology, Brenna leaned over and put her arm around Deirdre's shoulders.

"Oh, stay away!" Deirdre wailed, as though her heart would break. She pressed a gloved hand to her eyes. "Oh, how could you, how could you! 'Twas cruel of you, Brenna. I don't know how I was able to look poor Benjamin in the face!"

"He didn't seem very upset," Brenna commented

dryly, settling back in her seat. "And despite all his pretty words, don't you realize what he was trying to do?"

"He was trying to kiss me, goose!"

"And succeeding quite well from the look of it," Brenna went on. "If I hadn't come up—" She stopped. A curious feeling of *déjà vu* washed over her, as though she had watched this scene played out before with different characters. Then it struck her: she and Steven kissing in the dark and Rory coming upon them. She recalled how angry she had been at him for his untimely appearance, and with a sense of shame, she realized suddenly how Deirdre must feel now.

Why, I *am* the stupid one, she thought miserably to herself. Certainly Deirdre wouldn't have allowed Benjamin more than a kiss, and there I was, making her feel ashamed for it. Somehow, despite his reputation, Brenna was suddenly sure that Benjamin would not have taken advantage of her sister.

She rode the rest of the way home wondering why she had made such a fool of herself.

Chapter Twenty-One

BRENNA rode with her father to survey the fields and grazing lands of the Kildare farm. Hardly a trace of a breeze stirred the warm afternoon air, and Brenna felt perspiration dotting her forehead and neck, and trickling down the back of her blouse. She took off her riding hat and wiped at her face with a handkerchief.

As they came to a small depression in the valley, Kildare turned to his daughter with a sheepish grin on his handsome face. "Now, lass, I'm not wanting your mother to know about this, but I thought to trot over to the Three Corner Inn today and do a little gaming." He winked roguishly. "I've been hearing a bit about young Byrne and his game cocks."

"Sean Byrne?" she asked in some surprise. "Papa, I didn't know you were a betting man."

He shrugged. "Lass, every good Irishman keeps a little of the gambler inside him for special occasions. Now, let's be going; and not a word to your mother!"

"I'm not sure I'm wanting to go, Papa," Brenna said perversely, holding tightly the reins of her mount.

Kildare gave her a severe look. "Now, is that my Brenna speaking up, whom I trust more than any other soul in the world? You don't think I'd be trusting Deirdre like this, do you? 'Tis such a little thing, but if your mother sees you riding home alone, she'll be wondering where I've gotten to!"

Brenna sighed. "All right, Papa."

They turned their horses in the direction of Three Corners, and she could see how pleased her father was that she had given in. Ordinarily, she would not have acquiesced so easily, but she had to admit she was curious about exactly what went into the cock fights. She had heard so much from Maureen Byrne. When they drove up to the inn, an old building in poor repair, they could hear the lusty shouting coming from the rear. Back in the yard, four poles had been affixed to the ground with a canvas sheet stretched over them to shade the gamesters. Underneath, a pit had been shallowed out in the earth and crudely fenced in with stones to keep in the birds. All around the pit were cheering, dusty-faced men.

Brenna felt sick in the dusty heat. The smell of sweat and blood, which saturated the air, clogged her throat. She could see a few women, sitting to the side, patiently fanning themselves as their men, lusty and steaming in the close air, bet on the cocks.

Maureen caught Brenna's eye and waved, then stood up to walk over.

"What brings you here?" Maureen asked abruptly. She had evidently been sitting in the heat for some hours, for her hair was plastered to her face in long, soaked strands, which had fallen from the hastily knotted coiffure on top of her head.

Brenna tried to laugh, but the sound stuck in her throat. "Papa has proven himself as greedy as any true Irishman. He's come to try his luck." She nodded to her father, elbowing his way in among the other participants.

"Oh, aye, I see him now," Maureen said absently.

"They've already taken bets for the first round of the 'main'—that's the match, you see. There's eight pairs of birds to fight today, and the first round pits all of them until only eight are left. Then those eight will be paired into four until only four are left, then those four paired into two pairs and the winners of that round will fight each other."

Brenna shivered with anxiety as the birds were put into the pit. The cocks had oily, bright plumage and scarlet combs; artificial spurs had been attached to their natural spurs. These were made out of bone or metal, and were usually cut one or two inches longer than the natural spurs.

"Are all of those birds Sean's?" she asked.

Maureen laughed. "Lord, no, Brenna! 'Twould take too much money to raise and train them all, but he's got three in—and if they win, he'll sell them to the highest bidders. 'Tis how he makes his money."

"Oh. And if they lose?"

"Ach, then they're all dead and of no more use anyway. He'll have to begin training some others."

Brenna swallowed hard. The cruelty of the sport disgusted her.

At the front of the inn, a commotion had started between two burly fellows and a young man in the red coat of a British soldier. Suddenly, Maureen's eyes widened to twice their size.

"Why, 'tis Rory Adair!" she shouted.

Hurriedly, she lifted her skirts and ran into the dusty yard. Brenna was amazed to see Maureen deliver a rapid rebuke to the two men, who released their ungentle holds from Rory's arm and neck. They still gazed at him suspiciously, but Maureen persuaded them to go back to the pit. She took Rory's arm cozily and leaned against him as they walked back to Brenna.

Rory flashed a white smile, his left brow cocked in the usual arrogant way, despite his near-besting by the two bullies. "Why, 'tis Mistress Kildare!" he said, and made an elaborate deferential bow to her. "The avenging angel lowers herself to attend a cockfight?" The brow arched even higher.

Brenna's temper began to rise, but she forced herself to remain calm in the face of Maureen's avid interest. "Aye, I've come with my father," she said shortly. "I'm hoping we won't be staying long."

"Aye, especially if the law hears of this," he continued, winking conspiratorially at Maureen. " 'Twouldn't do to have such an esteemed name as Kildare wind up in the slammey, now would it?"

"Whatever are you talking about?" Brenna said in surprise.

He laughed. "My poor innocent, the courts have outlawed cockfighting since 1849. Anyone caught playing this game gets a hefty fine and a free stay in jail for a few days."

"Then what are you doing here?" she asked pointedly.

He sighed. "Why, only to watch and risk a little conversation with my light-o'-love here." He snickered melodramatically, and touched Maureen's arm. The young woman giggled.

"So that's why those two men were trying to bash your teeth in?" Brenna conjectured. "They thought you were nosing around for the bailiff. Aye, you're lucky Maureen was able to save your face for you."

Rory gave Brenna a cool stare. "Methinks the lass is put out with me," he said to himself.

"Oh, Rory, don't be worrying about Brenna." Maureen's voice was petulant. She locked her arm with his and hurried him away, leaving Brenna to watch them angrily.

The thought of her own father breaking the law frightened her, and despite her dislike of the pit, she moved nearer to see if she could catch his eye and persuade him to leave. She saw Rory push his way in next to her father, greet him with a friendly handshake and then bring out a wad of notes, obviously to do some betting of his own.

Then Brenna's eyes were drawn, unwillingly, to the commotion in the pit. What she saw sickened her. Two of the birds were already dead, and the men were trying to retrieve the carcasses, but the rest of the furious birds were fighting too violently, so no one could get his hands in. Another cock had lost an eye, and still another was bleeding from a wound to the head. Brenna compressed her lips and turned away. She walked slowly to the shade of an oak tree that grew next to a makeshift smithy's tent in the yard. The attending blacksmith was in the crowd, betting.

She put a handkerchief to her face to wipe off the perspiration. She wished the heat were not so bad. She waited there until the final round, when only two birds were left, both of them, miraculously, free of wounds. One of the birds was obviously Sean's for she could see him stroking it softly and whispering to it, checking its spurs before loosing it in the ring again. She watched her father bring out some coins and leave them with the "judge", the man who would decide the fight if neither of the birds died of inflicted wounds. She could also see

Rory; Maureen's bosom was pressed, innocently enough it seemed, against his arm.

"Hey, there! Whoa!"

Brenna turned her attention to the yard. A shiny, brown-lacquered coach had pulled up, sporting a pair of matched bays that pranced with high-strung spirits as the driver descended to the ground. A portly gentleman inside the carriage looked out curiously at the goings on, then opened the door of the coach. At the same time, a stable boy bobbed up in front of the horses to take the reins while the gentlemen refreshed themselves.

"That one needs a new shoeing," the driver pointed to one of the bays.

"Aye, sir, 'twill not take long," the boy promised, leading the horses to the smithy. He left them here for only a moment, while he went among the crowd in search of the blacksmith.

What happened next seemed like a nightmare to Brenna. She was sitting in the shade of the tree, fanning herself with her hat. The team of horses, not ten yards away, waited nervously with the coach. Suddenly, a live coal from the smithy's forge emitted a spark which hit one of the bays. Its eyes bulging, the bay reared high, causing the other to do the same. One of the hoofs of the second bay struck the first, which then shied away, toward the smithy, hitting one of the tent poles. The canvas awning fell to the ground and was immediately set afire from the live coals scattered beneath it.

In a few seconds the awning blazed up, frightening the horses anew and sending them rearing and bucking to get out of their frames. The coach was on fire now, its new coat of lacquer sucking up the flames and feeding them. The old oak, dry and splintery from the heat, caught one of the flames and was soon engulfed.

As though struck witless, the gamesters around the cockpit could only stare speechlessly at the havoc. Brenna was numb for a moment and looked curiously up into the fiery limbs of the burning tree as though she were far removed from its reality.

Suddenly, everyone seemed to move at once, shocked

out of immobility. One man shouted for water, another ran to get the innkeeper, still another ran to the horses and started unrigging them from the flaming coach. Someone swept by Brenna and caught her off balance, swinging her up into his arms and running with her to safety beyond the blazing inferno.

Brenna found herself plopped unceremoniously on the ground and looked up into the blue eyes of Rory Adair blazing as brightly as the flames of the fire.

"You little fool! You could have been killed. Sweet Christ, in another moment one of those branches would have fallen down on you!"

As though to punctuate his words, several limbs came crashing down, emitting sparks and catching up scattered dry timber that lay about the ground. By now, chaos reigned in the stable yard, and people were running about screaming and yelling and trying to organize a water line. The harried innkeeper ran to and fro before the fire as though he could worry it away from his inn. Brenna saw her father taking the horses from another man and leading them to the opposite end of the yard.

Rory was already running back to the others, yelling at the top of his lungs, trying to help with the organization.

Several of the inn's lodgers and staff ran about outside the building, trying to decide whether they should help with the fire or retrieve their belongings from the inn. One woman began screaming for no apparent reason, calling for her smelling salts and hysterically tearing at her hair. Brenna, watching her, felt an absurd urge to laugh, but stifled it quickly.

What had started out as nothing more than a burned horse, was now turning into a full-scale conflagration. Flames had burned over the boardwalk around the inn and were beginning to lap at the walls of the old building.

More people poured out of the inn, women screaming and children yelling in mingled delight and dread. The men couldn't find enough buckets to carry water from the trough, so they made do with hats, bowls, and even small trunks. Some people carried barrels down to the river, but the process was agonizingly slow, and Brenna could see that the edge of the inn's roof was already afire. Through the smokey air she spied her father, directing women and children out of the yard and down to the river. It would be the safest place, she knew, so she picked herself up from the ground to follow.

"Brenna!"

She turned. Maureen was shouting and waving her back to the cockpit. Brenna hesitated, then ran toward the pit tucking the hem of her riding skirt inside her waistband to keep from tripping.

"Maureen, come on! You've got to get out of here!" Brenna yelled, trying to force the other girl to follow her by catching at her sleeve.

"Oh, that damn bird," Maureen choked. She was on the verge of tears.

"What?" Brenna looked at the girl in frustrated confusion.

"That bird!" Maureen pointed to where the animal had perched itself on one of the rafters that supported the eave of the inn's roof. Brenna could see Sean Byrne crouching on the wooden steps that led up the side of the inn to the second floor. He was obviously trying, without success, to shoo the stupid bird down. To her horror, Brenna could see that the bottom step was already in flames. If Sean did not retreat now, he would be caught on the second floor with no way to escape.

"Good God and Saint Patrick!" Brenna cried aghast. "Maureen, you've got to call your husband down!"

"He won't come. He says the bird's too valuable!" Maureen cried harder.

"He'll be killed!"

Maureen wept into the skirt of her dress. Frantic, Brenna looked about the yard for help, but most of the men were working on the water line, while several were helping the women and children to the river. A few were leading horses out of the stables, and one or two others were stealthily picking over trunks and packets that had been thrown out of windows in an attempt to save personal goods.

"Maureen!" She shook her friend's shoulder. "Go on with that man over there, and follow him to the river. I'll find someone to get Sean down." She pushed the girl, still sobbing, towards a group of women.

Her eyes tried to pick out Rory through the thickening gray smoke. She coughed and shielded her eyes. By now, Sean, who had comprehended his danger, was calling down for help and screaming curses at the bird, which had flown down from the roof to peck in the short grass outside the yard.

"Rory! Rory!" Brenna called frantically through the smoke.

Sean was edging toward the open door leading into the second story of the inn, and Brenna waved her arms frantically to stop him. "No, no, Sean! Don't go in there, you'll be trapped!"

For a moment he hesitated on the landing of the steps, but his look told her that there was nowhere else to go. The flames were steadily climbing the stairs, and within a few minutes, would reach him. Already, the steps had weakened and were beginning to lean in toward the building. If they crashed sideways, he would be thrown into the blazing inferno.

Suddenly, miraculously, Rory was at her side. His face was angry as he started to lift her up to take her out of the danger. "In God's name, I thought I'd already rescued you once!" he snapped.

"Rory, 'tis Sean! He's caught up there!" She pointed and Rory released her to look up at the young man who was standing perilously close to the edge of the landing.

"Jesus, he'll be fried in another minute!" Rory called to another man, who raced over.

"He'll have to jump. It's his only chance!" the man said quickly.

"Good God, he'll break his neck!" Rory said.

The man thought quickly, then whistled for another to come over. "Take off your coat, young sir. And you," he pointed to the new man. "And you," he nodded toward Brenna, who promptly removed the riding jacket. "Tie the sleeves together, and we'll spread apart and have him try for it."

"It won't work!" Brenna agonized, even as she obeyed him.

" 'Tis the only chance he's got. He's better off with a broken leg than a broken neck. Now hurry, come over here!"

They had no time to check the knots in the sleeves for strength. Brenna and the other three each took an edge and stood as far apart as possible to stretch the makeshift catch-net.

"Jump, Sean!" Brenna yelled, coughing in the acrid smoke.

Sean looked as though he thought they were all crazy. Behind him the raging fire mercilessly devoured the old wood. He raised his eyes heavenward, as though in prayer, then closed them and leaped.

Brenna thought her arms would be wrenched from their sockets as Sean's weight hit. One of her riding jacket sleeves tore out of her grasp, and Sean's body sagged to the ground, hitting with a dull thud. His momentum had been slowed enough by the coats so that, even though he was writhing with pain on the dusty ground, he was alive. She almost wept with relief.

The man who had come up with the idea bent over Sean and gently picked him up. "I'll carry him to the river with the others. He'll need to be looked after. Maybe one of the women can ride for the nearest doctor. It appears he's broken one of his legs, maybe his collarbone too." He looked at Brenna in sympathy. "Lass, you'll be wanting to come with your husband?"

She shook her head. "He's not my husband, sir. His wife is Maureen Byrne; she's down with the others."

The man ducked his head and hurried away, leaving Rory and Brenna staring at each other in relief. Brenna began to cough again, and her eyes smarted and teared from the stinging smoke.

"I'm getting you out of here!" Rory said quickly. "To hell with this scrap of wood!"

He picked her up in his arms, for the smoke was beginning to overwhelm her, and he hurried with her out of the yard, through the grass, and down to the bank of the river where the others had collected. She could hear Maureen's dry sobbing as the man told her what had happened to Sean, who had apparently lost consciousness. Someone shouted that a doctor was needed, and Brenna thought she heard her father volunteering to ride for one.

"Brenna!"

"She's all right, sir. Just overcome by the smoke." That was Rory's voice. It was calm and strangely soothing to Brenna's ears.

"Good God, I didn't know. I—I thought she'd followed me out. I didn't even think to . . ."

"No harm done to her, sir," Rory said reassuringly.

"I leave her to your care, Adair, until I get back with a physician." There was a strained sound in her father's voice as though he didn't quite like the idea of leaving his daughter in the hands of such a reprobate, but he had no choice.

Brenna lay on the soft grass, her eyes closed to ease the terrible stinging. She breathed in shallow gasps so that her chest wouldn't ache so from the smoke she had inhaled. She was content, listening to the sounds around her, knowing that Rory was close by if she should need him.

It seemed hours before her father returned with a doctor. By now, Brenna was able to open her eyes. The physician, a black-coated man, strode to Sean's still form. Maureen was kneeling silently beside him.

"Broken leg, hmmm," the doctor was saying. "No fracture here, perhaps some bruised ribs. . . ."

Rory, who had been sitting beside Brenna and watching the fire consume the Three Corners Inn, felt her stir in the grass as she tried to sit up.

"Hey, there, don't you be trying that," he admonished. "Not until the doctor checks you out."

"I'm all right, Rory, truly," she protested when his

hands pressed her shoulders down into the grass. She looked up at him and suppressed a cough.

He grinned. "Brenna Kildare, would you kindly put aside your stubborn ways, lass, and do as I say, for once?"

She smiled back. "I'm sorry, Rory. You are right. I—I just feel so silly lying here like an invalid when there's really nothing . . ."

"Hush. The doctor'll be the judge of that, lass. Besides, I like the look of you lying there, completely in my power!" He was teasing, but there was a tiny flame in his blue eyes that confused her.

He put down a gentle hand and stroked her cheek. "You've soot on your face, lass."

"You, too," she said. "And you've lost your coat. Oh, Rory, will you be getting into trouble for that?"

He laughed. "No, Brenna. 'Twas all in the call of duty —although my superiors might frown a bit if they knew I'd been to the cockfights."

She was quiet for a moment. "Thank you for helping Sean and for getting me out of there," she said seriously. "I don't know what I'd have done if you hadn't."

"I said to hush," he repeated, laying a finger against her lips. "You didn't think I'd be leaving you behind now, did you?" His finger lingered against her mouth, then glanced away to the side of her face.

For a swift moment, Brenna felt that funny tingling in her chest again and looked away from Rory's eyes. Suddenly, she was intensely aware of his arm close to her shoulder.

"Ah, Brenna, hold on, lass. The doctor'll be here in a moment," Tyrone Kildare said from somewhere close by.

"Oh, Papa, I'd forgotten . . ."

"Are you feeling better, lass?" There was deep concern and love in Kildare's voice as he knelt beside his daughter and looked into her face.

"Aye, much better, Papa."

"Thank you for seeing to my daughter, Adair," he said shortly. "I'll be taking care of her now."

"Aye, sir. I'll see what I can do to help over there," Rory answered.

Brenna looked after him. The summer sun highlighted the sheen in Rory's chestnut hair. Brenna felt a stirring inside of her at the sight of his broad, young back with the soot stains on his shirt.

Chapter Twenty-Two

RORY and Benjamin had only a six-week furlough from their military training. It was three days after the burning of Three Corners Inn that they were scheduled to leave for Dublin, and from there to embark for Bristol.

Brenna had been ordered by the doctor to rest for the whole next day after the fire, so she had little chance to see Rory. Nora couldn't understand the girl's black doldrums, and became accustomed to seeing Brenna in tears for no apparent reason. She called on Siobhan, who prescribed a soothing posset that would calm the lass down. Brenna was afraid Siobhan might be able to see what was beyond the tears, so she pretended to be asleep when the wise woman called.

Her feelings were in a turmoil after the day she had spent with Rory Adair. She feared that she might be coming to like the scoundrel, even though she knew he had no such feelings for her. She was relieved when Maureen visited and told her that Rory had left on the train to Dublin. Sean was laid up with his broken leg, a sprained collarbone, and several bruised ribs, but his time in bed was not being wasted, for he was already planning his next business step, Maureen said proudly. He wanted to move to Dublin, where, he said, all the gentry swarmed. 'Twould be an excellent place to begin the cockfighting again.

"When is it then, that you'll be leaving?" Brenna asked listlessly.

"Oh, as soon as Sean is well enough to travel," Maureen answered. "He's that excited about his newest venture. And despite my father's disapproval, I know he'll be making good. Sean's got a nose for profits, and he's promised me a big house in town and a real fur cape. I'm holding him to it, too. Don't you think I won't!"

"Aye, you'll be liking it in Dublin, I've no doubt," Brenna said.

Maureen was not sure she liked the tone of Brenna's voice. God knew what a stick that Brenna Kildare had become! Maureen had only continued to visit, as she told Lucy Gallagher, for want of something better to do. Goodness, it was plain as day that the lass wanted a husband, but no one, it seemed, was good enough for her.

By October of that year, 1869, Sean Byrne was well enough to make the trip to Dublin. He and his wife boarded the train and waved good-bye to all their friends and family. Maureen kissed Brenna on the cheek, promised her she would write often, then promptly forgot all about her as her thoughts centered on the riches she and Sean would have dropped in their laps in bustling, exciting Dublin.

Brenna, watching the departing train, felt that bits and pieces of her childhood were leaving one by one. There was a melancholy inside of her, a sad sense that everyone seemed to be changing and growing, everyone except her. Even Deirdre was receiving an occasional letter from Benjamin Markham, much to the family's surprise.

It was during Christmas that Nora, alarmed at her older daughter's obvious discontent, decided to write her Aunt Charlotte and Uncle Claude who lived in Paris to ask if her two daughters might come for an extended visit.

At first, Brenna had rebelled against the idea, insisting that she would much rather remain here with her parents and the horses than go to some foreign city, which she knew nothing about, to visit people she had never met. Of course, Deirdre had been in heaven at the prospect. She managed to browbeat her sister into going, for it was understood that she could not go alone. Brenna was forced to give in most ungraciously. That didn't spoil Deirdre's excitement as she drove to Wexford with Nora and her sister to select materials for new gowns that would be made for the trip.

On a wet, rainy day in early March, just after Brenna's seventeenth birthday, Kildare put his two daughters on the train to Cork. From there they would sail to the French port of Brest, where they would be met by relatives, who would take them by coach to Paris.

"Just think of it!" Deirdre breathed, clasping her gloved hands together as the train jounced them over the southern counties of Ireland. "The courts of Paris! Oh Brenna. The newest fashions, the latest gossip, perfume, everything!"

"Aye," Brenna said quietly, feeling a tug of homesickness already. She was recalling the look on Kevin Ryan's face as he helped her into the carriage. Had there really been tears in the corners of his eyes? Was that why he had turned away so abruptly, almost brusquely after a solitary good-bye?

Brenna bit her lip and wondered at the change in Kevin Ryan. He was nearing twenty and was certainly more than ready to take charge of the stables. He was strong, although not overly tall, and he was gentle with the horses. To the rest of the grooms he was kind and as a horseman had earned their respect. She wondered idly why he had never married, for he cut a fine figure with his warm, brown eyes and his unruly thatch of red hair.

The sea voyage passed pleasantly with only an occasional bout of seasickness for either of the two girls when the waves grew a bit too choppy.

When they arrived in Brest, they were welcomed by Aunt Charlotte and Uncle Claude and their small army of children—there were nine in all—ranging in age from six to twenty. Their cousin Claudine, who was the oldest, was a bright-eyed, laughing girl who had just announced her engagement to a rising young diplomatic courier. The wedding was scheduled for September of that year and she insisted that her cousins stay at least that long to wish her good luck.

To Brenna the time spent in Paris passed with the blurred vagueness of a dream. When she and her sister were introduced at the court of Louis-Napoleon, they dressed in ball gowns more beautiful than either of them had ever seen, for Aunt Charlotte had graciously insisted on having her own seamstress make gowns for them, tactfully informing them that their dresses from Ireland were not quite the fashion in Paris that year. There were numerous parties and soirees and trips to the country. Both girls felt as if they were being blown hither and yon in a giant whirlwind to be shown off, admired, talked about, questioned, invited, and received.

They learned too. Aunt Charlotte would simply not tolerate their speaking any language but French, so they were both obliged to polish up their grammar and to lose the brogue, although several young gentlemen thought their accent adorable. Brenna learned to say *oui* and never *aye,* although in moments of distress, the word would slip of its own accord, and much to Aunt Charlotte's consternation, would cause a fit of giggles from her children.

Serious suitors were turned away, but male companions, in the company of a number of other young people, were invited to picnics and parties. While Deirdre thrived and learned to flirt with the best of them, Brenna grew shy and reticent among the bold laughter of the Frenchmen. They thought her reticence adorable, however, and she was never without an eager partner at a dance or party.

The girls enjoyed their stay with their cousins as spring rapidly turned into summer. Letters from Nora were filled with news of home, and although they had bouts of homesickness, the girls were in no hurry to leave.

The end of the idyll came abruptly. The wily fox, Bismarck, had aroused German opinion against the French and had finally goaded Napoleon into declaring war in July of 1870. For their own safety, Aunt Charlotte insisted the girls be returned to their homeland. Uncle Claude was already making preparations to take his own family to his country home in Bordeaux. Preparations for the Kildare's trip home were hurried.

At the end of July, tearfully bidding farewells to everyone, Brenna and Deirdre took the coach to Cherbourg and from there took ship to Dublin. There they met their brother, Dermot, and his wife, and were immediately pressed into staying a few days before returning to Wexford.

Sitting in the small but comfortable apartment, Brenna expressed her feeling that their stay in Paris had been much like a dream. Certainly as she looked about her at the three-room flat with its hand-me-down furniture and worn carpets, the lovely townhouse in Paris seemed far away. She and Deirdre were sitting with Bernadette, drinking tea while Dermot was away at his practice.

"Aye, sometimes I can't believe Dermot and I have been married over three years," Bernadette said thoughtfully.

"Time goes by so fast," Brenna agreed. "I just hope dear Aunt Charlotte and Uncle Claude are safe enough in Bordeaux. If one is to believe the newspapers in Paris, Bismarck is a most odious sort of gentleman. I should hate to see France lose a war to him."

"Poor Claudine," Deirdre put in. "I suppose she and her nice young man will have to wait until after the war to marry. Claudine is the sweetest thing, but she is twenty, after all."

Deirdre had acquired, while in Paris, the manners and speech of a seasoned courtier, and Brenna sometimes wondered in awe at how well her sister fit the role. Why, 'twas as though she'd been born to it, this young colleen off the horse farm in County Wexford, Ireland.

Brenna realized that her own emotions had matured in Paris. She had enjoyed her stay, and the city had been good for her. But she had missed the farm and Ireland and her parents and would never have been happy to stay there for the rest of her life as Deirdre certainly would have.

Although their stay with their brother and Bernadette was congenial, Deirdre soon began to complain to Brenna that she found all these lawyer friends of their brother too dull to endure.

So by mid-September, the girls announced that it was time to be going back home, for they'd been away for nearly seven months now. Even Deirdre, despite her worldly airs, missed her parents. Bernadette hugged them both and watched with Dermot as they left the train station.

"They're so much in love," Brenna said softly, seeing her brother's protective arm around his wife.

"Yes," Dierdre agreed absently. She toyed with her lavender gloves for a moment. "Bernadette told me she'd miscarried again. Isn't that terrible?"

Brenna nodded. "I wondered why there were no children yet. She seemed to have a hard time with it."

"Mama will be disappointed when we tell her. She so wants grandchildren," Deirdre said thoughtfully. "I suppose 'tis up to us, Brenna, to provide her with them." There was a scampish twinkle in her gray eyes.

Brenna laughed. "Someday," she affirmed, although the idea of marriage was still distant to her. She knew, at seventeen, that she should be thinking seriously about it, but she preferred to put such matters off for the time being. Neither her father nor her mother had pressed her on the subject, and if they weren't concerned, why should she bother herself?

Besides, she thought, there was no one whom she'd much like to marry.

Chapter Twenty-Three

"So now, you're a well-traveled woman of the world, eh?" Siobhan asked Brenna, her eyes smiling at the girl.

"Oh, yes, quite the woman of the world, Siobhan!" Brenna returned pertly. "I daresay you hardly recognized me, did you?"

Siobhan shook her head, thinking privately that it really wasn't the same Brenna speaking with such self-assurance and sitting with such composure. The girl had grown even more beautiful than before, and Siobhan was honestly surprised that Brenna had not been snapped up yet by one of the local boys. Perhaps they were a little in awe of her beauty, or feared the power of her father, who could claim the Earl of Wexford as a close friend.

"What are you thinking of, my friend?" Brenna teased her, leaning forward in her chair. She was wearing a new riding habit which she'd had made in Paris. The royal-blue cloth made her eyes sparkle with startling clarity, and put blue highlights in her midnight hair. The snowy jabot beneath her chin was more severe than the ones made in Wexford, Siobhan thought, but it looked proper on the girl, as did the pert, blue felt hat she wore tilted forward on her head.

"I'm thinking what a beautiful young woman you've become," Siobhan answered seriously. "I'm thinking of what a wonderful wife you'd make some nice young man."

Brenna flushed. "Oh, don't talk of marriage please," she begged, and for a fleeting moment, her self-assurance crumbled. "That's all Dierdre ever talks about these days: drumming into my head that I simply must become engaged before she does, or I shall be the laughingstock of all Wexford County. She's gotten the notion that Benjamin Markham will seize his opportunity and grab her up at the first opportunity. Ever since he and Rory Adair returned on furlough from military training, she's been sure

Benjamin will find some excuse to get her alone and go on his knee to her. I feel sorry for her when I see Benjamin riding about with his cronies, visiting the taverns and betting on cockfights and the like. He doesn't seem to have a serious bone in his body."

Siobhan shrugged. "Your sister has a way of getting what she wants. I'm thinking young Markham won't know what's hit him one of these days and find himself bound to Deirdre for good or ill." Siobhan laughed.

"Well, I'll be one of the first to congratulate them," Brenna said defensively.

"Naturally, I don't believe in that notion of you having to get married before your sister does," Siobhan went on quickly. "But you'll be eighteen next February, and here it is the middle of October. . . ."

"And what if it is!" Brenna snapped, rising from her chair to pace about the room, her riding boots digging out divots from the dirt floor. "I'm not about to throw myself at anyone. Papa says I can live with him and Mama as long as I wish."

"Of course, of course," Siobhan soothed. "Now would you like another cup of tea, lass?"

Her abrupt change in tactics brought Brenna up short. She looked at Siobhan bleakly, then quickly changed her expression and shook her head.

"No more tea now, thank you, Siobhan. I'll be going."

"Come back whenever you like," Siobhan said hurriedly, fearing she had offended the girl by pressing her too hard. "You know I can always be using you to help me whenever you've the time."

"Yes, I'll remember that," Brenna said. She stopped at the door and looked back fondly at the older woman. "You and Mama and Deirdre—" she said in a mock-derision "—all of you trying to marry me off. Well, if you find the perfect young man who loves horses, is kind and considerate, and will treat me like the best of wives—I may consider him."

Siobhan, waving her off, thought how closely Brenna had just described Kevin Ryan, the head groom at the Kildare farm. It was no secret to Siobhan, who had been escorted home by young Ryan on several of her trips to the Kildare farm, that he was in love with Brenna. It showed obviously in his face when he looked at the girl, though he tried so hard to mask it in front of others. That, Siobhan thought was because everyone took for granted that no groom or servant would ever have the courage to love anyone above his station. She sighed, saddened by the hopeless situation. Brenna should find someone to love, and Kevin should have a woman to wed.

Brenna turned Minx toward home, racing for a few miles across the boggy marshland to the line of trees along the boundary of the sloping grassland. She settled Minx into a comfortable trot and daydreamed of what it might be like to be married someday. What would she do with all of her free time, she wondered. Of course she would have a cook and a laundress, just as her mother did, so there would be little for her to do in the way of house-keeping. Would she be able to saddle Minx and ride to her heart's content? Or would there be hidden rules and obligations which would prohibit this?

"Oh, bother marriage!" she said aloud and determined to keep her mind off the subject.

"I agree with your sentiments!"

Smiling merrily, Rory Adair galloped alongside her on his horse. He was not wearing his uniform, but was dressed simply in shirtsleeves, trousers, and riding boots.

Brenna, embarrassed, tried not to blush. "I didn't see you," she said.

"I know," he answered cheerfully. "I was afraid you might send Minx into a gallop like you did the last time I caught you alone on the road. If I didn't know better, Brenna Kildare, I'd be thinking you're trying to avoid me altogether." He was at his most charming. "Now, what have I done to deserve such heartless treatment."

Brenna couldn't help the blush that suffused her face. "I've not been trying to avoid you, Rory," she said without meeting his gaze.

"Aye, you have!" he chortled. "I can see the lie in your eyes."

"Rory, I—" She hesitated. "I don't see the need of discussing it now."

He shrugged. "As you wish, Mistress Kildare, but I'm not letting you off all that easy. Now that I've finally caught you, I'm bound to stick to you until you agree to sit a moment with me by the river."

"I can't, Rory I'm on my way home now."

"Another lie?" he asked her with a mocking note in his voice.

"I am!" she said stoutly, but had to admit it was childish to keep avoiding Rory Adair simply because she was afraid she might come to like him. Surely there was nothing wrong in sitting by the river with him for a few minutes. She made up her mind. "All right, then," she said. "The day is lovely."

"I'll try not to ruin it for you," he added sardonically.

They turned their mounts toward the Slaney River, which flowed along the valley all the way to the sea. Here, the river was not too wide and rippled along exposed sand bars and rocks. Lovely chestnut, maple, and willow trees formed shady areas along the grassy banks.

Brenna brought her horse up under an old willow, which leaned out over the river. Rory slipped off his horse and tied it to a limb, then helped Brenna off her mount. Accustomed to jumping from the saddle herself, Brenna had already swung her leg over to slide down, when Rory stepped up and caught her beneath her arms. For a moment, he held her like that, her chin level with his eyes, then he set her down and held her against him, his hands slipping from her arms to the small of her back.

"Ah!" he sighed, his eyes still wry, yet dreamy. " 'Tis a good feeling, is it not?"

Brenna couldn't deny it, but she was somehow a little frightened, as though she didn't expect Rory to keep a leash on his emotions. She tried to push herself free of him. Rory hesitated a fraction of a second, obviously displeased, then let her go.

"You've not changed as much as I'd thought, for all your travels abroad," he said roughly.

"What changes were you expecting?" Brenna asked briskly, trying to compose herself.

"I'm not sure now. Maybe I thought you'd be more a woman than when you left." He eyed her with the old cockiness. "I thought you wouldn't be afraid of me anymore."

"Afraid!" Brenna gave him a suspicious look. "I'm no more afraid of you than I am with—with my own brother." She was standing now, arms akimbo, her head held proudly. "What is there to be afraid of?"

"Exactly," he said gravely, although he was amused at her temperamental display, for he guessed it covered those fearful feelings he had just touched upon. "So, now that's taken care of, why don't we sit down here where the grass is soft and dry." He lowered himself to the ground, sitting Indian-fashion with his hands lying innocently on his thighs. He patted the ground beside him suggestively, and Brenna, after a moment, sat down beside him. She stretched out her slender legs in front of her as she leaned back on her hands.

Rory picked a blade of long grass and chewed on it absently. "Those are nice duds you're wearing," he said presently.

Brenna turned to him, her womanly instincts flattered. "Thank you. I brought it from Paris."

"It suits you—brings out the color of your eyes," he complimented.

She colored. "Tell me about your military camp. Was it very hard?"

He considered a moment. "No. I like the military. Once you get used to some of the bas . . . I mean officers who think they're as good as God Almighty, you settle in right enough. I've had a few fistfights, but I've done my Irish blood proud in all of them. I'll crack the head of anyone who says I'm a coward."

"I'm sure no one would say that."

He chuckled. "Some fools would. Aye, I like the military, and I'm thinking 'tis the best course for me. With luck, I'll be promoted to sergeant when I'm attached to my permanent regiment. I'm hoping for India, for I've heard a fellow who uses his wits can get rich and have a mighty lazy time if he's smart enough."

Brenna's brow puckered. "I don't understand. How can you get rich in the army? Don't you have to live in the barracks with the other soldiers? And the pay . . . ?"

"The pay is a pittance, 'tis true, but there's money to be made, no doubt about that." He stopped, unwilling to elaborate. He turned to her and threw the blade of grass away. "If I go to India, will you be missing me, Brenna?" he asked softly.

Startled by the question, she looked at him then turned toward the river. "Yes, I'll miss you, Rory," she answered.

He laughed. "As you'd miss your own brother, I suppose?"

She drew her legs up and settled her chin on her knees. "Yes," she said stubbornly, and Rory's mouth drew down in a little frown.

He reached over, grabbed her by the shoulders, and pulled her roughly towards him. "Goddammit! I'll warrant no brother would be kissing you like this!" he growled and pressed his mouth to hers while he lowered her to the grass.

Brenna felt his mouth on her lips with a certain curiosity at first. His lips were warm and very soft and moved gently against hers. The hands on her shoulders moved to her waist as he settled himself on her with his chest against hers and one leg holding her down. His mouth, demanding and sure, brought the tingling sensation into being, causing it to spread from her bosom to her waist, then everywhere that he touched her. His lips molded and shaped hers until they opened. She started at the alien touch of his tongue on hers.

Her heart seemed to expand and explode in her chest, and she wanted to cry in newfound joy at the pleasure she felt in this kiss. Worries seemed to fall away from her, replaced by a curious childlike wonderment at this miracle. She relaxed in his arms and kissed him back, her own hands clasping at the nape of his neck.

Time stood still or seemed to go on forever, she was not sure which. All she knew was that she would be sad when this moment ended, for there could never be another like it. When he would have taken his mouth away, she held him there with all the strength in her hands. Finally, though, she could feel him withdrawing, pulling away from her, and she murmured a desperate cry at the loss of that one precious moment.

Rory did not go far, though, for she opened her eyes to see his face above hers, his blue eyes cloudy with desire, his handsome face slightly flushed with passion. His hands were still at her waist, but now they moved up to unbutton her riding jacket and pulled at the stock that wound about her throat.

Brenna was mesmerized. She could only look in his eyes and see the reflection of her own face; she wished he would kiss her again. But her senses came sharply back when she felt his hands finish unbuttoning her blouse and start to untie the ribbon of her camisole. Her breasts would be bare in another moment, and suddenly she reached down with both hands to cover his. She couldn't let him—she couldn't. Years of Catholic training and her own mother's teaching gave her hands a surprising strength as Rory tried to brush them aside.

"Let me," he whispered, and the words, so bold and straightforward, caused a delicious shiver to run up her back.

He still held the two ends of ribbon in his fingers. Only one more tug . . . Rory felt frustration bubbling inside of him and he knew his strength would eventually win out. Still, as he looked into her face, he saw the fear in her eyes.

"For God's sake, Brenna!" he cried out. "Just for a moment let me touch them, let me kiss them. 'Twould make you happy, lass."

"Rory," she whispered, "I can't. Please, don't ruin this moment for me."

Rory tore his eyes from her face and cursed mightily to himself. God in heaven, why did this particular wench have to be the one that he'd always wanted—and now, when he'd thought he'd had her at last . . . He groaned, pulled his hands away, and sat up to turn his back on her. He could hear her soft, rustling movements, telling him that, despite his hopes, she was putting her clothing back in order.

"Are you finished?" he asked, his teeth clenched.

"Yes," she answered unhappily.

Rory cursed himself for a self-serving bastard, for the sadness in her had smitten him like a blow. Sweet Christ, hadn't the lass ever been kissed before? Memory came back of that night when he had seen her kiss Steven Cruz, and that memory brought back a forgotten bitter jealousy. He turned to her, catching her once again by the shoulders.

"How many men have kissed you?" he demanded in a hard voice.

Brenna stared guilelessly up at him, and he saw the truth in her eyes. He released her and drew a hand across his forehead.

" 'Twould seem I've taken up with a poor innocent," he said with a shaky laugh, trying to make light of the situation. "You're not knowing the rules, lass."

Brenna flushed and tried to keep back her welling tears. "No, I—I've never played before," she said with an effort.

He laughed again, more cocky now, in control of his emotions. "Well, then, it seems we'll have to be teaching you, Brenna Kildare."

Chapter Twenty-Four

THE following day Brenna was besieged with flowers sent with a note from Rory thanking her in a most formal way for allowing him to escort her home. Nora, seeing the note, the flowers, and Brenna's radiant face, put things together very quickly; but she couldn't decide whether she was upset or happy about the turn of events. Tyrone Kildare kissed his daughter and wagged his finger at her, telling her that she'd best be careful with young Adair. Deirdre squealed with delight, assuming that her sister's fate was virtually sealed and that she could now go on with the business of pursuing Benjamin Markham with a clear conscience.

For her part, during those first few weeks of gentlemanly visits in the parlor with tea and homemade cakes from Mrs. Sullivan, Brenna never once considered marriage with Rory. Rory talked with polite interest, telling her all about the military and asking her questions about Paris and the Continent. Once in a while, she could discern a wicked gleam in his eyes, and several times he waited until her mother and sister were out of the room, then stalked over to her chair, picked her up in his arms, and smothered her with kisses. He was playful about it, but Brenna could feel the leashed-up passion in his body, which caused it to tense every time she accidentally touched him.

The winter that year was relatively mild and Brenna enjoyed riding with Rory. He had become an excellent horseman—a skill learned while he was in the military, no doubt, for she couldn't remember him ever being so adept before. By now, Kildare had given his grudging consent to Brenna's seeing Rory, though he couldn't understand what his daughter saw in the lad, as he took pains to say; and the couple took every opportunity to be together.

For Brenna, this was a time of inexpressible joy, of happiness in every sweet moment she shared with Rory, of breathless excitement whenever he kissed her or held her in his strong arms. She learned the male smell of him, the mole that he had on the inside of his right elbow, the way his hair curled at the back of his ears. She was proud of his tall handsomeness, his charming air, and his ready wit. Whether she was falling in love with him, she didn't know, for she was, as yet, too inexperienced.

Only one thing shadowed her joy: Kevin Ryan's hostility to Rory. Sometimes, when she and Rory went into the stable and asked to have Minx saddled, Kevin would turn his back and walk pointedly away, calling on one of the other grooms to do the work. Brenna was puzzled by his behavior, but decided that he must still remember those days when she and Rory had been at odds and Kevin had always stood up to him as her champion. Somehow, it hurt her to think that Kevin still did not trust Rory, for she liked Kevin and went to him now and then for advice on practical matters.

One day, after she and Rory had come back from a long ride, she took Minx into the stable alone, for Rory had had to rush back to Sir William's to meet friends, who were coming for a late supper. She spied Kevin, squatting over a saddle, polishing it with furious strokes. He was oblivious to her light step as she came up behind him.

"Good evening, Kevin," she said.

Kevin started, then jumped to his feet, looking over her shoulder as though expecting to see Rory behind her. "Hello, Brenna," he said when he was satisfied that she was alone. He took the reins from her hand and led Minx into her stall.

"Kevin?"

"Aye?"

"Why don't you like Rory?"

Kevin hesitated, then uncinched the saddle and took the riding gear away. When he returned, he was surprised to see that Brenna was still where he had left her.

She was obviously not going to move until he gave her an answer.

"Well?" she asked. Her dark blue eyes, ringed with purple, looked at him with an almost childish anger. "Why don't you like him, Kevin?"

He shrugged. "Did I ever say I wasn't liking him?" he challenged her.

She shook her head. "Not in so many words, but by your actions. You—you make me feel unwelcome in here when Rory is with me."

"I remember a time," he said slowly, "when you would have thanked me for such."

She looked down at her riding boots. "I know," she said, at last, "but things are different now. We—we all have grown up and—and things change when you grow up."

His heart ached for her, but he couldn't betray his own emotions. God, if only for a moment he could put his arms around her and tell her that he hated Rory because she loved him. Aye, they had all grown up, and things did change—aye, and some of the changes were damned painful. He wished suddenly that he didn't love her—that he could lose himself in another's soft flesh and forget about Brenna's blue eyes, midnight hair, and the proud tilt of her chin.

"Well?" She stamped her foot in the straw petulantly. "Tell me why you don't like him!" To his surprise, angry tears sparkled in her eyes now.

"All right," he answered, his temper rising. "I'll tell you why I'm not one to like Rory Adair—'tis because I don't trust him not to hurt you! I've seen the likes of him before, and his kind go after a woman for one thing only. After he's gotten it, 'twill be the last you ever see of him."

"Oh!" He heard the quick intake of her breath and in the next instant, felt the cold, hard leather of her riding glove, still on her hand, strike him on the cheek. The blow stung him for a moment, and he caught her wrist in his hand and held her.

"Let go of me, Kevin Ryan!" she demanded, though there was a look of shame in her eyes for striking him.

"Aye, I'll let you go," he said, wishing he could let go with his heart. He released her wrist, and she rubbed it for a moment.

"I'm—I'm sorry for hitting you," she apologized. She looked up at him in an agony of indecision. "You—you did provoke me, Kevin, but I am sorry for it. Can we forget it happened?"

The pain in her face made him relent. "Aye," he said bitterly, " 'tis already forgotten."

She started to go, then turned. "Kevin? I wish you liked Rory. I wish you could believe that he's changed for the better. You've always been a friend to me, Kevin, more than you know, and I'd like you to be happy for me." She waited, hoping he might say something, but he remained silent.

Kevin stood where he was for a long time, thinking about what she had said.

For Brenna's eighteenth birthday, Kildare threw a huge party, inviting everyone he knew from fifty miles around, and Mrs. Sullivan baked the biggest cake anyone could ever remember seeing.

Brenna laughed and cried and kissed everyone and thoroughly enjoyed herself. The festivities lasted well into the evening, and it was not until quite late that Brenna found an opportunity to sneak away with Rory.

They walked along the lane that led to the main road, and sat down beneath the stars in a field of clover, which had not yet been plowed under for the spring crops. Rory kissed her briefly, then took her hand and stared up at the sky.

"It was a lovely party," Brenna sighed, snuggling against Rory's shoulder. She had forgotten her shawl, and the late-February air was chilly.

"Aye," he said, but she could tell he wasn't thinking of the party.

Brenna was content with his silence for the moment; there was an old Irish proverb: "He who stares into the middle of the fire, does be heavily in love." Rory stared into the sky so intensely that she wondered if perhaps it was not only the fire that a young man, smitten by love's arrow, might stare into. She was still not sure that she wanted Rory's love, although she was certain, from asides and whispers she had heard at the party, that many of the women there were convinced she had it. When they had sneaked off together into the darkness, she had heard one older woman whisper that he was getting her off like that to give her an engagement ring. Brenna looked up at Rory's set face dubiously, for she had a feeling that was not his intention.

"Did you enjoy yourself?" she asked, shivering in the cold wind.

He looked down at her for the first time, and his arm came up to tighten about her shoulders. "You're cold?" he asked, feeling her tremble.

"Just a little."

"Let's be going back then."

"Oh, not back to the house already!" she said. What did he want? Surely he hadn't brought her out here in the starlit darkness only to sit for a brief moment of silence.

"All right, then, but back to the barn at least, for I'll not be having you catch a chill," he said solicitously, standing up and bringing her up with him.

"The barn?" She didn't want to go there, for Kevin slept above the stables and might hear them.

"Aye, let's go to the loft," he said, as though he were able to read her thoughts. " 'Twill be warm enough there."

Brenna bit back her protests, for she didn't want to spoil an otherwise perfect day. She let him lead her into the barn, lit inside by lanterns.

Taking her hand, he climbed up the ladder that led to the loft where fodder hay was stored. He moved a pitch fork out of the way, then pulled Brenna up and pushed her back, with a light laugh, into the fresh, sweet straw. Brenna laughed too, thinking they were still playing a game, as they always had until now. But the pressure of Rory's hands was stronger, holding her arms down in the straw as he half-lay on top of her, bringing his face close in order to kiss her. He hadn't done this since the first day some months ago at the river and Brenna struggled a little in his embrace to let him know she didn't like it any more now than she did then.

Rory seemed oblivious to her desires tonight, and he continued to hold her down, kissing her slowly and expertly, finally gaining the desired reaction as she relaxed beneath him and began to return his kiss. His knee was wedged painfully against her hip, and she could feel it even beneath the layer of silk and lace of her party gown and petticoat. She started to stir against his mouth to tell him to move his knee a little, when he released her lips and let his mouth travel down her jawline to her throat, planting moist, soft kisses against the flesh revealed by the décolleté of her gown.

Brenna trembled as his lips brushed the tops of her breasts, for this had been, until now, forbidden territory; but she told herself he could not be held responsible when they were exposed so openly by the cut of the gown. Smothering the warning in her brain, she allowed him to go on, while she tried to control her trembling and the waves of heat rippling over her body.

Silently, the two young bodies lay in the straw, both beginning to feel their passion building. Rory drew away from her to free the buttons at the back of her bodice. Brenna felt his hot fingers on her back, and knew she should resist him, knew she should make him stop while they could both back out gracefully and with some measure of dignity. Her head pounded with the words she knew she should be saying, but somehow, the words never passed her lips. She was seeking this new experience as breathlessly and excitedly as she had sought his first kisses.

Rory hurried with the buttons, pulling one off with the force of his passion, until they were undone to her waist. He settled her back in the hay and looked into her eyes, barely able to make out their expression in the semi-darkness. Then, with a quick decision, he caught the sleeves of the gown and pulled them down, bringing the bodice with it.

He muttered a strangled oath as her breasts were revealed, high and firm, pale as moonlight; and she closed her eyes tightly when she saw his hand reaching to touch them. Rory's hand was warm and gentle as he cupped each breast in turn, caressing the soft flesh and brushing the pointed tips lightly with his fingers. Nothing prepared Brenna, however, for the icy shock that washed over her when she suddenly felt his mouth, hot and moist, close over one turgid point.

"Rory! No!" she cried, trying to push him away.

But she had waited too long this time, and Rory, finally close to the object of his desires, would not be denied. He firmly held her arms, not hurting her, but effectively keeping her hands from pushing his face away. Brenna's face burned and her eyes teared with shame at this—this—thing—that Rory seemed determined to do to her. Was she a cow to be suckled like this? She had never questioned the function of her breasts in the rearing of children, but to have a grown man, kissing and sucking on her like an infant—'twas shameful indeed!

Then, as he continued, she began to wonder if this, then, was what men were always running after loose women for. Brenna thought she had seen the worst of it. Loyally, for she did believe she loved Rory, she began to think that, perhaps, after a time, she could come to like such treatment. She tried, for Rory's sake, to relax and derive some enjoyment from it, but was so nervous that she could feel nothing.

Rory, mistaking her silence for acquiescence, let one hand leave her arm and stray to the hem of her gown. Thank God she had no corset on, he thought. God knew what beasts those monstrosities of whalebone were. How many men had been denied ultimate satisfaction because of this last bulwark of defense. His hand caught the flounce of her gown and brought it up to her knees, then to mid-thigh.

"Rory? Rory, what are you doing?" she said in alarm.

She felt the coolness on her skin through the silk of her stockings.

"Hush, sweetheart," he whispered soothingly, though it was hellish trying to keep his voice from breaking, so great was his excitement. "I only want to see all of you, my darling," he whispered as he pushed her skirt and petticoat even higher.

This was too much! "No! Rory, I want to leave now. 'Tis enough you've done already."

"Darling, darling," he cooed. "Let me see all of you. 'Twill not hurt you," he said, and was glad that she could not see his face in the darkness. "Please, Brenna, we've come so far and—and I may be leaving soon. You can't let me be leaving without—some parting gift, some giving of yourself."

"You're to be leaving soon?" Instead of bringing soft tears and an abandoned passion as Rory had hoped, Brenna was struggling to sit up, demanding to know where he was going and when. He cursed himself for his stupidity.

"Love, 'tis not for a time yet, but . . ."

"You never told me, Rory!" she cried. "Were you thinking of waiting 'til the last minute?"

"Aye, Brenna," he lied convincingly, "for I couldn't bear to be seeing your sweet face saddened by the news. We only received word last week, and it's been on my mind for that long now."

"Oh, Rory!" She was openly sobbing now and Rory's hopes rose. "You'll be going away. *When* will I be seeing you again?"

"Now, now, darling," he soothed her, rubbing her back and shoulders as she flung herself into his arms. The pressure of her naked breasts against the front of his shirt was driving him mad with longing, but he forced himself to be calm. "We still have a little time together, and I'm thinking we should be sharing of each other while we may."

Brenna's tears dampened his shoulder. All the newly found joy, the heady, carefree days would be gone when Rory left. If he should be stationed in India, who knew when she would be seeing him again? She fiercely wished that she could be going with him. Then a dull thought struck her: perhaps Rory had not even meant to tell her. Perhaps, he had decided to slip away, preferring to leave with no emotional entanglements.

But what was she thinking? After all, he *had* told her. Did he then love her? Was all this leading up to a marriage proposal? Brenna was not vain enough to think that all she had to do was succumb to his lovemaking to make him ask for her hand.

"When is it that you're to be leaving?" she asked steadily.

What a delectable picture she made to her lover in the half-light, with her hair tumbling out of its curls and her bodice pooling around her waist. Rory swallowed and tore his eyes from the sight of her breasts. "In—in the spring," he answered. " 'Twill be the first of April."

"So soon?" Brenna cried, nearly beginning to cry again. "But that's barely four weeks away."

"Aye, they do things that way in the military," he said quickly. "Hurts less when 'tis done abruptly without drawing out the time of good-byes."

"I—see." She spoke in a small, low voice, and she bowed her head to hide the tears she could not stop.

"At least we still have four weeks, Brenna," Rory quickly pointed out. "We can love each other for a time yet."

Love. He had spoken the magic word. Gathering her courage, she faced him with a question. "Do you love me, Rory?"

"Aye, of course I love you, Brenna," he said quickly, almost cheerfully; that was the way she wanted to hear it, he thought cynically to himself. She could not morally give in to his sexual desires until she was sure that he loved her. 'Twould surely erase whatever sin was involved.

He leaned over her and pushed her gently back into the hay, noting the softening in her eyes, the relaxing of her muscles. His hopes renewed, he congratulated himself on holding his trump card until the last moment. He'd received his assignment orders, all right, but he was glad he had obeyed his instincts not to tell Brenna when he'd first heard. Now, it had paid off; she was wiling to give herself to him without reservation. He was going away soon and had told her he loved her—the two most important things to a woman.

A twinge of guilt assailed Rory momentarily as he looked down at the perfect, young body laid out beneath him. She was so damned trusting, he thought. She really believed him. He had not been quite sure that Brenna would fall for the usual schemes, but he reminded himself that she was the most naive girl he had ever pursued in his love-games. For they were just that to Rory—games to be played again and again. Oh, sometimes for different girls the rules had to be changed, or the strategy reworked, but the results were always the same—Rory had never lost since he had taken his first serving wench at fourteen and he was not about to see his record tarnished.

Carefully, so as not to alarm her, he hooked his thumbs into the material of her gown and began to pull the dress down from her waist. He wanted to see all of her now. His excitement was already keen, and he knew that it could be honed to fever-pitch if he took his time with the girl and allowed her a moment of passion too.

A full, drunken giggle, followed by a high-pitched cry of surprise nearly caused both of the lovers to die of fright. Both Brenna and Rory moved at the same time—Brenna to cover her bosom with her dress, and Rory, frantic not to lose her, to stand up and move in front to shield her from the unwelcome eyes of strangers.

"Oh, Miss Brenna, 'tis so sorry I am!" It was Cathy Ferguson, putting her hand to her mouth as she stared at the two culprits. Behind her, one of the guests from the party was trying to keep from falling off the ladder, while at the same time craning his neck to see what was going on in the loft.

Rory felt a fierce wave of anger run through him. He wanted to strike at the drunken girl whose blouse was falling off one shoulder. He could smell the liquor fumes on her breath from where he stood. "Get off with you, lass!" he said tightly. "You've interrupted private business."

"No! No!" Brenna had gotten to her feet after pulling up her gown and had fastened enough of the back buttons to keep her bodice from falling down. "We—we should be going, Rory." She seemed distracted, embarrassed, and disgusted with herself, all at once. Rory knew it would be useless to try to calm her down enough to continue their lovemaking.

"All right," he said in a strained voice, for the ache in his groin made it difficult to remain composed in front of the two strangers.

Cathy and her paramour obliged them by backing down from the ladder. Brenna could not bring herself to look in the girl's face, and hurried away from the barn without waiting for Rory. He called after her, then shrugged his shoulders as he saw her dash behind the house; he stalked back grumbling to the corral where he had tethered his horse.

Chapter Twenty-Five

FOR several days, Brenna refused to appear when Rory called. So great was her embarrassment that she feared she would never be able to face him again. When she thought of how she had lain beneath him, allowing him to fondle her! And she would have let him go further, she was sure!

Nora worried about her daughter's change in mood, but she was not unhappy that Brenna was refusing to see Rory. Nora had divined, with a mother's sixth sense, that Rory had no intention of marrying her daughter—oh, he might love Brenna a little, and he was certainly fond of her, but once the challenge was gone, he would not find it hard to leave her. She hoped that the day he was scheduled to return to his regiment would come swiftly.

Brenna, in her room, sketched disspiritedly when she heard a knock. "Come in." She turned to find Deirdre watching her nervously.

"Brenna, you'll not be mad at me, I hope," her sister began unwillingly. "I was with Benjamin at the gardens at Markham Hall, when Rory happened to come by. He —asked me to deliver a message to you and I said I would."

"Well, there's no need to deliver it to me."

"Oh, Brenna, the poor lad is suffering from your rude behavior!" Deirdre said with a touch of anger. She would never treat Benjamin the way her sister had been treating Rory. "He wants to see you before he leaves."

"He *is* leaving?"

"Yes. He's been called up to leave for India with his regiment the day after tomorrow. Benjamin's been stationed in England."

Brenna wasn't listening now. She had stood up, her face paling. "So soon? But, but he has weeks left."

Deirdre shook her head. "It's all been changed. He—

he requested to be placed immediately. I suppose after you refused to see him, there was no reason for him to stay."

"No!"

"He said he'd be waiting for you today at Casey's Gully, if you have a change of heart about him."

Brenna didn't bother to change from her morning gown, but hurried out to the stables, calling to her mother that she would be back as soon as she could. Nora, watching her go, thought of calling Tyrone in from the fields to follow her daughter, but changed her mind; Brenna would have to sort this problem out for herself. Nora had enough faith in her daughter to believe Brenna would do nothing rash as far as Rory Adair was concerned.

All the way to her destination, Brenna called herself a stupid, self-important goose and berated herself for the way she had treated Rory. But how could she have known that hard-headed Rory would take such an action simply because she had refused to see him. Oh, it was all her fault, she knew that, but she had never expected this! She urged Minx harder, leaning down over the mare's neck as the March winds tore at her hair and face.

As she neared Casey's Gully, she could see the tall, handsome figure of her love, dressed smartly in his scarlet coat. She dashed away the tears on her cheeks and sprang off her horse before he could move to help her.

"Oh, Rory!" she cried, flinging herself in his arms.

As Rory held the sobbing girl closer, waves of emotion washed over him: protectiveness, guilt, tenderness—aye, tenderness, for to his amazement, he found he really did love this lass a little. But he already knew that he would not ask her to marry him. Adventure, excitement, new places, new people—the pull of wanderlust already had him halfway on the road to India. He would be a little sorry to go, but the sorrow would be gone soon enough.

"Brenna, hush!" he said after a while, and her sobs lessened. "There's no need for you to be crying that way."

"But you'll be going. Deirdre told me."

"Aye, but you've always known 'twould be so."

"No, no, no!" she cried, as though by denying his words,

she could make them untrue. "You'll not be leaving like this, Rory. You can't!"

"I must, Brenna; 'tis part of soldiering. I must go."

"No!" she insisted, but when she looked into his eyes, she knew she could not make him stay. Though his arms were strong and warm around her, his eyes already held that faraway look that told her he would not be sad to be going. "How can you leave me?" she asked in a broken voice.

He frowned. "I've already told you, Brenna. I have to go. I'm a soldier in the British Army."

"You're doing this to hurt *me!*" she wailed, moving away from him. "You—you try to make me think it's all for honor and glory, but it's because of what happened in the loft, isn't it?"

He shook his head. "Brenna, Brenna . . ."

"Don't try to soothe me!" she said harshly, anger beginning to wash over her.

"Brenna, 'tis not just because of that night," he said, spreading his arms wide and stepping forward as though to take her into his embrace.

But she stepped back out of his reach. "Liar!" she shouted. "Liar!"

His brows drew down, but he held his impatience in check. "I'm sorry, Brenna, but I never led you to believe that I would do anything but as the army wishes. 'Tis my life."

"With no room for anyone else!" she challenged him.

"What would you have from me?" he demanded angrily. His arms dropped to his sides. "I've given you pleasant times, joy and laughter—and you have given the same to me in a hundred ways."

"Pleasant times!" she repeated, her cheeks streaked with tears. "Is that how you describe them? *Merely* pleasant?" She clenched her fists and pushed them into her eyes, like a child who tries not to let his parents see his tears of frustration.

"Aye, they were pleasant, Brenna. We enjoyed each other."

"Rory, I love you!" she cried brokenly, her chest rising and falling with the passion of her statement.

He was silent. Once, he would have taken advantage of the situation and demanded her submission as proof of her love, but not now. He couldn't do that to her, he thought. She had in some way changed him. Now, he could only look at her bleakly, his face filled with pity and kindness and love.

"Brenna, I'm sorry," he said gently. "It can't be any other way. I'm the way I am, and you're the way you are." With humility he added, "I'm not good enough for you, Brenna."

Brenna, not hearing his words or even trying to understand, was still crying. She could only blame herself, she thought, for she had refused him. If she had given in to him, perhaps he would not now be leaving her so abruptly. She looked up at him through her tears.

"I'll make you take me with you!" she cried. She came closer to him, stood on tiptoe, and reaching up to clasp his neck, pressed her mouth against his. It warmed under hers, and he reached around to hold her at the waist.

"Brenna—"

"Just kiss me, please, Rory," she whispered.

He hesitated, then picked her up and laid her on the grass, his arms holding her tightly as he kissed her with growing ardor. Their limbs entangled and their passion ignited. Brenna gave him her mouth, allowed him to open her bodice and to take her breasts.

I can't let him go, she thought with despair. He's all I have left.

"Brenna," Rory whispered huskily, "we can still pledge our love to one another. We can still share of each other before I leave. Brenna, I do love you, darling, I do love you." His words were forced from the passion that raged through his body.

"And you'll take me with you?" she said eagerly, even as she kissed his face with trembling lips. "Oh, Rory, you will marry me and take me with you, won't you?"

Her words brought his senses back, and he lay on her quietly for a moment, fighting against the urge to lie for what he wanted from her. Then he kissed her breasts softly and began to rebutton the front of her dress. She lay there, tears forming again in her eyes. She knew she had lost him.

"Brenna, I'll not be taking you with me," he said steadily, putting out his hand to help her to her feet.

She spurned his help and stood up by herself, shaking her skirts to free the dust and grass from the folds. She now knew, she thought, why Maureen had married Sean Byrne, and she flushed with shame: Maureen had thrown herself at Rory and been rejected in the same way as she, herself, had.

"You don't love me, Rory," Brenna said, wiping at her eyes with her hands. "You don't love me any more than you loved Maureen Derry or anyone else that you—you set your sights on. You're incapable of loving any woman!"

Rory stared at her. "What are you saying, Brenna? Of course, I love you!"

"You're lying—and we both know it," she continued calmly. "You love only the bloody army because it makes you feel like a more important man than you are. If Benjamin and Sir William hadn't sponsored you, do you think you would have come as far as you have? You would have been a farmer without the help of Sir William."

"Damn you!" He caught her shoulders and shook her so hard her head snapped back. "I was good enough to go chasing after, wasn't I, Brenna Kildare! I only had to say 'I love you' and you would have lifted those skirts quick enough. Aye, it makes my poor, ignorant head swim to think how quickly I would have gotten between those legs if . . ."

Brenna stung him hard with her open palm across his cheek. She could feel the burn in her hand and saw its imprint on his skin—that brought her little satisfaction.

"I hate you, Rory Adair!" she screamed at him. "Let me go!"

"Aye, 'twill be my pleasure!" he yelled back at her.

"I hate you! I hate you!" she repeated, standing alone

now. Her head drooping as she tried to hide her tears of hurt and rage from him. She heard him mount his horse and gallop away, leaving her to lean, sobbing, against the tree, her heart broken.

It seemed a long time that she stood there. The March breeze cooled her cheeks. She felt as though all her tears had been shed, as though everything inside her had been used up. What a fool she'd been. What an ignorant fool.

Like a sleepwalker, she went and mounted her horse, clinging to the saddle like a child: Minx, aware of her mistress's moods, took off at a slow walk, neighing gently as though commiserating with her. Brenna could only rest her face on the stiff, coarse mane and allow the mare to carry her home.

"Brenna! For God's sake, what's happened!"

Brenna lifted her face from the mare's neck with an effort and tried to focus her eyes ahead of her. Two strong arms lifted her out of the saddle and enveloped her in a protective cocoon. She laid her head against his shoulder and allowed herself to be led to a bale of straw. She slowly realized that Minx had brought her back to the stables, and that Kevin Ryan was holding her. She looked up at him in dazed, stupefied amazement as he held her and patted her back and helped her to sit. She appreciated his attentions, for she didn't think her rubbery legs could have supported her much longer.

"Oh, Kevin," she whispered wearily. "My life is ruined."

Kevin misunderstood her meaning, and his brown eyes grew fierce. "Damn that Rory Adair!" he muttered beneath his breath as he stomped off to find a cool bucket of clean water and drew a handkerchief from his shirt pocket. "He should be horsewhipped for what he's done to you!"

She accepted his ministrations, watching him through curious eyes as he dipped the handkerchief in the water and dabbed at her tear-chafed face. The water stung at first and she cried out. Immediately, Kevin held her again, soothing her, allowing her to nestle her face against his warm, strong, neck.

"Brenna, Brenna, I would give my life to change everything for you," he whispered. "If only I could protect you from men like Rory Adair. You'd never be seeing a sad day in your life, I vow it!"

"Oh, Kevin," she sighed, "if only you could."

Kevin pushed her away gently, so that he might look at her face more closely. "Brenna, only give me leave to take care of you—and I will," he said with such intensity that the cold shell around her began to dissolve. "Brenna, you'll not be regretting it, if you choose me. I swear I'd treat you like a queen."

In her confused state, Brenna was not sure what Kevin meant by "taking care of her," but how soothing the words sounded after the harshness between Rory and her. Rory —she thought she might start to cry again, as she recalled she might never see him again. He was off to his dreams of gold and heroic adventure. She hated Rory, she told herself. And here was Kevin, so gentle, so soft and sincere. She clung to the young man and wept on his shoulder.

"Don't leave me, Kevin," she said tearfully. She couldn't bear to be left alone again.

"I won't be leaving you ever, Brenna," he said earnestly. "Only say the word, my dearest, and I will be with you always."

"Yes, yes, Kevin, don't leave me," she said, wanting only to be held and comforted until the dull ache in her heart went away.

Kevin felt his spirit rise, and he longed to hug and kiss the trembling girl he held in his arms. He couldn't believe that he was actually holding her perfect, exquisite body so close. God and Saint Patrick, could miracles actually happen? This had to be one. He still couldn't believe it! Brenna Kildare—could it be possible that she would marry him? He felt himself trembling with love and devotion. Nothing else mattered—not her father, or Rory Adair, or her money! He would have her, the woman he had always wanted and loved. He was afraid to release her for fear she would evaporate like a dream.

"Brenna, darling Brenna, let me take you up to your

room," he said quietly. "Let me take you to the house so that I might speak to your father."

"Yes," she answered dreamily, "please take me home, Kevin. I want to go home now."

"Aye, you'll be wanting to rest, darling. My sweet, sweet darling." He soothed, holding her a moment longer.

"What!" Tyrone Kildare roared. He stared at the young man, his blue eyes storming with rage. "What are you saying?"

"I said, sir, that I'd like to have your daughter in marriage." Kevin stood stiffly in the parlor.

Kildare stared at him another moment, then an incredulous look crossed his face, followed by one of outright amusement. "Lad, you've been drinking!" he said gruffly, relaxing once more in his chair.

Kevin reddened, but shook his head firmly. "No, sir, I've had nothing to drink. You know well enough I'm not a drinking man, sir."

"Aye, well," Kildare cleared his throat. "Then you'd best explain this nonsense you're spouting before I have you thrown out of my house."

"Sir, my intentions are serious. I'm willing to be marrying your daughter, Brenna."

Kildare controlled his indignation for a moment; he knew he must find out the reason for this groom's boldness. What had that foolish girl been up to?

"What does my daughter have to say about this?" he asked.

"She agrees, sir. She—she told me in her very words that her life was ruined."

"Ruined, eh? I'm sure it would be—if she were to marry you, Ryan," Kildare said coldly.

Kevin flushed, but he kept his clenched fists behind his back for fear he would throw a punch at his employer. "You know of her dealings with Rory Adair," he said stiffly.

"Aye?"

"Well, she mounted her horse this morning and rode out to meet the scoundrel. I know because young Tim-

othy told me when I got in from the corral. He said that
Brenna was in a state and looked wild-eyed. I didn't think
any more about it, sir, until she returned this afternoon,
crying and behaving as though she hardly knew her own
name. She would only say that Adair had ruined her life."
He paused delicately. "I'm only thinking of Brenna's protection."

"What! You mean you're actually thinking that my
daughter would disgrace herself with Rory Adair!" Kildare's face was bright red, and his heavy breathing
sounded like the snorting of an angry bull. "And you have
offered to marry her, I suppose, to keep her from scandal."

"I want to marry her because I love her," Kevin said
seriously.

Kildare looked as though he couldn't trust himself to
speak. He sprang from his chair and paced the room
like a caged lion. The afternoon sun slanted in on his
cold, glittering eyes, and Kevin actually took a step backwards, to get out of his way.

"How dare you tell me that you love my daughter?
My daughter! By God, I've an itch to lay you flat, Ryan!
How could you possibly conceive such a notion! My
daughter would never lower herself to consort with the
liveried men."

Kevin, smarting under his words, shouted back. "Aye,
but you let her consort with a common soldier! Everyone
knows Rory Adair's no better than a farmer, for all his
ties with Benjamin Markham. He's the biggest skirtchaser
in the county, and you allowed your own daughter to ride
with him unchaperoned." He was breathing hard now,
not caring that Kildare, fists clenched, had taken two steps
towards him. "I offer her marriage and a decent life. What
would you leave her with? The ruins of her self-respect—
maybe a bastard child?"

Kildare's face went suddenly white and he stopped
in his tracks. "I'll find Adair myself and shoot him if
what you say is true!" he finally said in a deadly voice.

"Adair is off for India," Kevin replied, regaining his

own composure. "What good would it do to kill him anyway?"

"By God, I'll not have my daughter treated like some common serving wench." Kildare spoke between clenched teeth. "Where is the hussy? Damn! I'll get to the bottom of this manure pile, if I have to shake the truth out of her." He strode to the door and yelled up for Brenna to come down immediately.

The two men looked warily at each other, as though each was gauging the other's strengths. Finally, there was a knock on the door, and Brenna and Nora came in. The girl looked wan, her eyes red and puffy. Kildare signaled his wife to wait outside, and when she started to protest, he swore vilely. The poor woman retreated in stupefaction. In bewilderment, Brenna faced her father. She seemed hardly able to stand, and Kevin went to her quickly to help her to a chair. She looked at him gratefully.

"Brenna Katherine Kildare! You'll be telling me the truth, lass," Kildare began. "Ryan, here, has asked for your hand. Can you tell me what gives him leave to do this?"

Brenna raised her eyes to her father's face in surprise. Then she looked at Kevin. "Kevin, you—want to marry me?"

"Aye," he said softly. "I told you I'd protect you from now on, Brenna, if you'd but give me leave."

"But, Kevin I—"

"I'm waiting for an explanation, lass!" Kildare cut in. "Have you been doing things I should be ashamed of?"

Brenna flushed and she seemed to grow stronger under her father's scrutiny. "How could you even think that I would?"

"Damn it, don't you tell me what to think, girl!" Kildare roared, nearly beside himself. "I've trusted you every day of your life, Brenna. I've catered to you, spoiled you, aye, I'm admitting it, but I never thought you'd see fit to pay me back by disgracing me like this!"

"Papa, I'd never disgrace you—or myself!" she declared, jumping to her feet and boiling anger brought her back to life.

"Then why did you tell Ryan that your life was ruined? What did Rory Adair have to do with that, I'm asking you?"

"Rory—he led me on, 'tis true, but I never . . ." She tried not to think of the time in the loft when she had been about to let him have his way with her, and today when she had thrown herself at him like a common strumpet. The guilt showed on her face, and her father saw it as clear as day.

"Get out of my sight!" he roared. "You'll go up to your room and stay there until I tell you to come out!" He stepped towards her as though he would strike her, but his daughter faced him resolutely.

"I'll not go to my room. I'll—I'll marry Kevin, if he'll have me!" she declared. "I'll not stay under the same roof with a father who would think such things of me."

Kevin moved towards her as though to shield her with his body, but she didn't glance at him, intent on her battle of wills with her own father.

"You'll stay here as long as I'm your father!" Kildare ranted. "To your room, I'm telling you!" He turned to Kevin. "And you. I'm not wanting to see your face around here again, or I'll not be responsible for what I'll be doing to you."

"I'll not be leaving without Brenna!"

"You'll be leaving or I'll—I'll—" His words were cut off by a choking cry as Kildare crumbled suddenly backwards into his chair. He seemed to be having trouble breathing for a moment.

Kevin grabbed Brenna's hand. "Go up to your room and pack a few things," he whispered urgently. "I'll be waiting for you at the back of the house."

"But, Papa—"

"Hurry!" he commanded. "I'll be waiting."

Brenna looked at her father for one last moment, then followed Kevin out the door. When she heard her mother's cry as she went to tend to her husband, Brenna closed the door of her room.

"Pack a few things," Kevin had told her. Why? What was he going to do? Take her away from here, from everything she held dear? How could she go with him and leave her parents, this house, the horses? She couldn't do it! But, a small voice insisted. Her father no longer wanted her here. She had disgraced him; he was ashamed of her! She had no choice but to leave.

Oh, God, her head ached. She didn't want to think. She only wanted to be alone, to be the Brenna she once was—but she could never be that Brenna again. She swallowed her sobs and pulled a small trunk out from beneath her bed. Yes, she would pack her trunk—'twould give her something to do to keep her mind off her father's harsh words.

She went about automatically packing toilet articles and a few pieces of clothing. It helped to soothe her jumbled nerves. She felt as though she were moving through a thick, dense fog that insulated her against the pain of the world. She remembered, with dumbfounded amazement, that Kevin was waiting for her outside. Automatically, she carried the small trunk downstairs to the kitchen. There were sounds coming from the parlor, her mother's soothing voice, her father's short bursts of oaths. She did not want to see either of them.

"Brenna, here!" It was Kevin calling to her from the doorway.

Mrs. Sullivan appeared from the pantry and looked curiously at Brenna. She was silent as the girl went through the doorway with Kevin Ryan, telling herself 'twas none of her business what the young folk did. She went back to cleaning the pantry.

PART TWO

Marriage

Chapter Twenty-Six

TWILIGHT was settling as Brenna and Kevin came out of the tiny church at New Ross on the Barrow River. They had pleaded with the elderly priest to marry them without benefit of banns or other preparation rituals of the Catholic Church, so the priest had insisted on saying at least a complete Mass, and the ceremony had been delayed while people straggled in to attend. Mostly old people came, two of whom were picked by the priest to stand as witnesses to the ceremony.

Brenna had gone through the ritual mindlessly. She remembered little details—running to the stables with Kevin carrying her trunk, saddling Minx and riding behind Kevin, for he would take no horse but that which belonged to her outright. Then had come the exhausting journey west to the little church in New Ross for the ceremony. For a wedding band, they had used the gold ring, set with pearls, that Brenna had always worn on her right ring finger since her sixteenth birthday. She had cried when Kevin placed it on her left hand. It had been a gift from her parents.

Now, they stood hesitantly in the dusty road of the town. Kevin turned to his new bride, but she didn't want to see the exultant look on his face. It would break the cocoon around her. She looked down at the ground, and he mistook her action for shyness. He pressed her hand to reassure her.

"Come, Brenna, we'd best find someplace to stay the night. I've enough money to see us through for a few days, but I'll be looking for work in the morning." Kevin was brisk, practical, taking the responsibility of marriage as he took everything else.

"Yes, Kevin, I—am tired," she said.

They mounted Minx once again, although Brenna protested that she would rather walk, for the mare was tired after a day of travel. Kevin dissuaded her, assuring her that he had seen an inn only a mile or two up the road where they could stay for the night.

The inn was a forlorn, dilapidated building that looked nearly full with travelers, Brenna swallowed hard to keep herself from crying as Kevin took Minx around to the stableyard. He flipped a coin to the livery boy to make sure Minx got a good rubdown and an extra measure of feed. Brenna had the distinct impression that his orders would not be carried out, but she felt too lethargic to protest. She followed her husband meekly into the dining room. At least the food smelled good.

"Aye, how can I be helping you two?" The innkeeper was a slender, sallow fellow with a shock of red hair almost as bright as Kevin's.

"I'm needing a room for the night," Kevin said, "and a meal for myself and my wife."

"Your wife, eh?" the innkeeper said with obvious disbelief. He seemed to size them up for a moment.

"We're full up," he finally said.

Kevin banged his fist down angrily on the table. "My wife is nearly asleep on her feet, sir. We've been traveling all day from near Enniscorthy. She must have a bed and some food!"

The innkeeper scratched his head. "Tell you what, young man: I'll give you a bed, but you'll not be alone in the room." He held up his hand as Kevin started to protest. "We've got a drunk who couldn't be aroused by a fire bell, but he's paid up 'til Wednesday, so I can't turn him out. I'll put him on the floor, and you . . ."

"No!" Brenna said, her voice filled with loathing. "I couldn't sleep with another man in the room, Kevin."

"Aye, I can't believe you'd offer such a thing to a new bride," Kevin said angrily.

"Bride, you say?" The innkeeper smiled apologetically. "Why, then, I guess I could give you the 'bridal suite.' " He laughed lightly. "I'd been saving it for another couple from Wexford, but being as they're not here by this late hour, I suppose they won't be coming." He turned and drew a key from a pigeon hole. "Here now, 'tis number twenty-five at the top of those stairs."

"We'll be wanting supper," Kevin reminded him.

"Aye, 'twill be brought up in a twinkling," the innkeeper promised. He hesitated. "Might I be seeing your coin, lad, for I'm not partial to being plucked. I gave one of my best rooms to a couple of filchers last night, only to find them gone early the next morning. Two bottles of my finest wine they'd had too."

Kevin, brought out a small leather pouch and jingled it suggestively so that the man could hear the chink of coins.

"Aye, 'tis the sweetest of sounds," the innkeeper said with a smile and bow.

"Your supper'll be brought up before you've time to unpack, sir."

Kevin took Brenna's trunk and his own small knapsack, and helped his wife up the stairs. She seemed so small and fragile to him that he couldn't imagine himself lying in bed with her. The thought brought a light flush to his cheeks, and he fumbled with the key in the door lock.

Despite Brenna's earlier reservations, the room was quite respectable. The bedspread was old but clean, and most of the holes had been patched neatly with heavy thread. There was one window and a small nightstand with a bowl and pitcher sitting on top. A worn, braided rug covered part of the wooden floor where a table and three chairs were set up. The table was scarred and nicked, but it, too, seemed clean enough. In her bewilderment, Brenna sat down abruptly on one of the chairs and leaned over the table, her head in her hands.

"Tired, my sweetheart?" Kevin asked sympathetically, laying a comforting hand on her back.

She nodded, waiting for him to take his hand from her back. He lifted away her shawl from her shoulders and took her hat. Quietly, he put them on the third chair, then opened her trunk.

"Will you be wanting to comb your hair?" he asked nervously.

She shook her head. "I'm hungry."

"Of course."

In a few moments, a maid came in with a platter of steaming food. She set dishes and utensils out, then served portions of roast duck with gravy, hot bread, and garden peas. The inevitable potato and salted milk completed the meal. Kevin whispered something to the girl. She curtseyed and left, but was soon back with a bottle of wine and two tumblers. When she was gone, Kevin went to the door and locked it from the inside.

"Dinner smells wonderful!" he commented, enthusiastically clasping his hands together. "God, Brenna, I'm hungry enough to eat it all myself."

Despite her hunger, Brenna found she was nearly too tired to lift her spoon. She ate a few morsels and played with the food on her plate.

Kevin wolfed down his food but drank the wine sparingly. When both had finished, Brenna was nearly asleep in her chair from the combination of fatigue and wine. Kevin stood up, stretched nervously, then strode to the bed and pulled back the covers to reveal clean, muslin sheets and downy, goose-feather pillows.

"Hadn't you ought to ready yourself for bed, Brenna?" he asked, seeing her eyelids drooping as she sat in her chair.

"Oh, yes," she said sleepily and stood up. "Where? . . ."

"Here's your trunk, sweetheart," he said tenderly. "Shall I help you?"

She shook her head, realizing vaguely that very soon her cocoon would be shattered. The fog was beginning to lift from her mind, and she was beginning to realize just what she had done—and what was about to happen. She could see Kevin—dear Kevin, she told herself—sitting on the bed, unlacing his shoes, carefully keeping his eyes averted, for there was nowhere else to undress.

With trembling hands, she unbuttoned the front of her dress, the same buttons that Rory had undone—had it been only this morning? She shook her head. It seemed like years ago, she thought. When her bodice was undone, she pushed her dress down to the floor quickly, stepping out of it and picking it up to lay across the chair. She stood in her petticoats and camisole for a moment, risking a look at Kevin who was busy with his britches. She quickly looked away and turned her back as she took off her two lace petticoats.

"Kevin," she began.

"Aye?" He was beside her suddenly, and she knew that he was naked.

"Could you—please—turn out the light?"

"Aye, of course, sweetheart," he said with understanding. He blew out the candles so that only the moonlight through the window lit up the interior of the room. She could hear footsteps and voices and drunken snores and the chink of coins on the other side of the door. It unnerved her that people in the hallway might hear Kevin and her in the room.

"Kevin?"

"Aye?"

"I—am—tired," she managed with a little squeak in her voice.

"Aye, and so am I," he answered.

She thought he understood her meaning.

"I forgot to pack a nightgown," she continued, feeling at ease now. "Do you mind if I sleep in my undergarments?"

He was silent for a long time, and she thought, for a moment, he had actually fallen asleep. "Aye," he finally said. "Take off the rest of your clothes, Brenna, and come to bed."

She gulped and fought back her tears. She nearly tore the ribbon of her camisole as she untied it and brought the fragile fabric over her head.

She was naked. Her face burned. All thought of sleep had left her. She had to exert every ounce of her will-power to make herself turn around and walk calmly toward the bed. When she realized Kevin was watching her, with a little cry she bent forward to shield herself from his eyes.

"Come, Brenna, don't be afraid," he comforted, pulling her body down beside him. He could feel her shaking and knowing how nervous she was helped to take away his own uncertainty. "Are you all right?"

She nodded, afraid her teeth would chatter if she opened her mouth. She had never been so frightened in her life. She knew nothing about what Kevin would do to her, for her mother had not had the time to prepare her for this part of marriage. Ordinarily, Nora would have had a long talk with her the night before the wedding, but . . .

"Brenna, I love you," Kevin said gently and put his hands on her breasts.

Brenna wanted to jump away from him, but she forced herself not to move. He brushed her nipples gently and stroked the firm flesh of her bosom. He was doing what Rory had done to her, she thought. Was this all men wanted? Suddenly, outrageously, she felt like laughing, and she wondered if she was going crazy.

"Brenna, I want to kiss you," Kevin said and leaned over to press his lips against hers. He was, she thought, with that abstract part of her, not as good at kissing as Rory had been. But perhaps he was tired and in a hurry to be done with it so he could go to sleep. She suffered his lips on hers and parted them when she thought he wanted her to.

They lay there awhile, kissing, with his hands on her breasts and her legs drawn tightly together. Then she felt Kevin's hand move from her breast over her waist to her hip and thigh. She stiffened and took her mouth from his.

"Sssh," Kevin whispered when she would have protested. "You're my wife now, Brenna."

His wife? The word stunned her for a moment. How could she be Kevin's wife? When had all this happened? What—what was he going to do now? She felt him stroking her thighs and kissing her again.

He took his mouth from hers and lowered it to her bosom—like Rory had done, she thought again. Was everything going to be the same? She waited for the delightful tingling to begin, but it did not. Perhaps she was too tired or too nervous, she told herself, for all she could feel was a curious numbness as though none of this was really happening to her.

"Kevin, what—" she began hesitantly.

"Brenna," he said, taking his mouth from her breasts. "I know that you're tired, but I—want to make you mine now—tonight. I can't wait until tomorrow night or even the morning. Now, Brenna. I can't stand the thought that Rory . . ."

"Rory?"

Kevin clenched his teeth, sorry he had spoken the name. After a moment, he kissed her mouth again, then drew away from her only to kneel over her and put his hands between her thighs to pull them apart. She let him do as he wished, for at the mention of Rory's name, she had begun to pull the protective fog back around her. It hurt too much to think of Rory—especially now.

She lay quietly as Kevin hovered above her, holding her thighs with his hands; then, suddenly, he pushed himself between her legs. Brenna gasped and held her breath. She looked up at Kevin, able to see the intense look on his face by the light of the moon. He pushed again and she bit back a cry of discomfort.

"Kevin?" she said fearfully, trying to pull away from him.

"Brenna," he whispered back, and there was a joyful thrill in his voice, as though he were glad she felt pain at his entry. "Brenna, you—you're still a virgin!"

She blushed in the darkness. How had he known that? she wondered. Then she forgot about wondering and gasped again as a rending pain squealed up her backbone, only to descend into a throbbing ache a moment later as he sighed on top of her. For a moment, he was supine against her chest. She waited for him to roll over and go to sleep, but it was not over yet. In another moment, he was moving back and forth between her legs, holding his weight off her by leaning on his elbow. She hurt and she wanted it to stop, but she could see the excitement on his face and felt ashamed that she should not be willing to perform this small duty for him. She set her teeth and watched his face, feeling the ache and the movement and the pressure inside of her.

Then, slowly, she became aware that the tingling had started. "Oh!" she said in amazement. Yes, yes, there it was! She moved a little to accommodate her husband, and he, smiling down into her face, bent to kiss her mouth.

"Brenna, Brenna, I love you, my darling," he whispered before stroking furiously, then collapsing on top of her.

Brenna fought to keep that tingling inside of her, but it receded quickly as Kevin lay breathing rapidly against her breast. She felt disappointment and anger that he should be so unfeeling now, just when she had been about to—to do *something*.

Kevin kissed her gently, then rolled off her and lay beside her on the bed. Possessively, his arm went across her breasts, bringing her into the curve of his belly. Brenna lay there for a long time, listening to her husband's regular breathing.

Chapter Twenty-Seven

BRENNA wakened at dawn the next morning, bone-weary from their long ride to New Ross, and a trifle sore and tender in her loins. She looked over at her sleeping husband and felt like weeping. What, she wondered morosely, had she done to herself? The light of day showed the inn's "bridal suite" to be even shabbier than she had thought the night before. She realized, that they would have to find someplace permanent to live, and her heart sank at the thought of living so far from her home.

Beside her, Kevin stirred, stretched, opened his eyes, and blinked rapidly when he saw his new bride staring down at him. He smiled shyly. "Good morning, my love," he said reaching up to pull her down against him. He wanted to kiss her, but Brenna suffered only a token peck, for her mouth tasted stale.

"Good morning, Kevin," she said soberly, and rolled away to sit up on the edge of the bed.

Kevin frowned, then shrugged and got out from under the covers, striding over to the nightstand for his clothing. Brenna kept her eyes averted while he dressed.

"You'd best be getting dressed, too, Brenna," he said matter-of-factly. "We'll go down to the dining room together and breakfast, then I'll be off to the town to look for work."

"Will we—will we be staying here again tonight?" Brenna asked, licking her dry lips.

"We'll probably have to." He gave his wife a kindly look. "Why don't you rest awhile after we've eaten. I'll be back before supper, and we'll discuss our plans."

She nodded miserably. "If you'll just turn your back, Kevin?" she murmured. When he turned around, she stood up from the bed and padded over to the chair to dress herself. "I'm ready now."

Kevin turned and gazed tenderly at this young woman, who was now his wife, legally bound to him by the Church. "You'll be wanting to wash and comb your hair," he reminded her gently. In that moment, she seemed to him like a child, who had to be told what to do.

Brenna obediently poured water into the bowl, splashed her face and neck, then took her comb out of her trunk and fashioned her hair into braids, which she twined about her head.

"You have beautiful hair, Brenna. Must you wear it like that? I'm liking it better the way you fixed it yesterday; 'twas prettier."

"I—I thought you were in a hurry to eat and go into the town," she said apologetically. "If you're wanting me to . . ."

He shook his head. "You're right. Let's go down now, then."

They ate hurriedly in the dining room, and then Brenna walked with Kevin to the stable to get Minx. He promised to make sure the mare was well taken care of. Brenna leaned her cheek against Minx's velvety nose and stroked the animal's face. The mare whinnied forlornly. Brenna was sure the stable lad had done nothing but put the animal in a stall for the night without a feeding, but nothing could be done now; Kevin was in a hurry to be off. He kissed her, squeezed her shoulder, and cantered off toward the small town.

Brenna watched him for a time, then trudged back upstairs to her room, making sure to lock the door behind her as Kevin had advised. She looked at the bed, rumpled and stained from the previous night, and shuddered. She smoothed the covers and tidied the bed, wondering if she would be given new sheets to replace the stained ones. The platter had not been taken away. The sight of the congealed gravy and the smell of the cold leavings nauseated her, so she piled the dishes on the platter and covered them with a cloth. Then she crossed the room and put her trunk on the bed, to sort through the contents. She was amazed that she had forgotten to pack so many essentials. She had forgotten nightgowns, an extra pair of shoes and stockings, and a mirror. At least she had remembered clean underwear and a change of dress.

Her hand came upon something smooth and hard in the trunk, and she brought it out. Her eyes widened when she saw what it was. Carefully, she set the alabaster dove music box on the bed, looking at its bright, sapphire eyes. A storm of weeping shook her when she wound the spring and sweet music tinkled in the room. She threw herself on the bed, cradling the music box in her arm, and wept miserably.

"I—can't let Kevin—see me like this," she said to herself, wiping at her eyes with the wet washcloth. "I can't hurt him like that. 'Tis not his fault."

Resolutely, she packed the music box away with her other things and set the trunk under the bed. Then she went to the window to open it and let in fresh air, but the jamb was stuck and, try as she might, she could not budge the window even an inch. She looked about the room for something to force it open, but there was nothing to use.

She was sitting on one of the chairs, wondering what to do, when a small, diffident knock sounded on the door.

"Who is it?"

"The maid, miss, come to make the bed," a squeaky voice said.

Brenna went to unlock the door and allowed the young, skinny girl to come in. The girl sighed when she saw that the bed had already been done up. "You'll not be needing me then?"

Brenna hated to explain the necessity of clean sheets, but did so quickly and with a reddening face. The maid nodded in understanding, disappeared, and returned with clean linens. She was about to take the soiled ones away with the pile of dirty dishes, when Brenna stopped her.

"Do you have some way of opening this window? 'Tis so airless in here."

The maid thought a moment. "Aye, I'll be sending my brother up to open it for you. 'Twill be but a moment, mistress." She hurried into the hall with her load.

A few minutes later, a tall, gaunt lad appeared. "What's your wish, mistress?" he inquired.

Brenna didn't like the way his eyes slipped over her figure, and she quickly pointed to the window. "Just open it, if you would, please."

"Aye." He walked to the window and worked and jiggled it for a few minutes before it finally opened. Then he turned; a greedy light burned in his eyes. "That'll be costing you, mistress," he said cockily.

Brenna's face fell in dismay. "I've no money with me. My—my husband has it all with him. He'll not be back 'til suppertime."

"Suppertime, you say?" He licked his lips. "Aye, then we've time to pay the debt twice over." He rasped a laugh and came toward her.

Before Brenna knew his intentions, he put his arms around her and tried to kiss her mouth. She squirmed against him, exciting him further. She couldn't believe this lad could be thinking of doing the same thing to her that Kevin had done last night. Why—why, he couldn't be more than sixteen.

Furiously, Brenna pushed the lad away from her. Her bosom heaved and her blue eyes sparkled wrathfully, very like her father's did. She pointed a shaking finger at the boy. "Get out of here—before I call the innkeeper! I swear, if you come one step nearer to me, I'll scream so loud, everyone will be in this room within a minute!"

The boy hesitated, grinning sourly. "Ah, now, you wouldn't mind just a wee bit of fun, would you?"

"Get out!" she yelled at him.

With a snarl, the lad stalked out of the room, slamming the door behind him. Brenna hurried to turn and lock it, and leaned against the door, forcing herself not to fall to the floor in hysteria. Kevin had promised to protect her, but where had he been when she needed him? Oh, God, what had she done? What had she done?

By late afternoon, Brenna was numb with boredom. She had sat at the window for a few hours, watching the travelers come and go; and when that little diversion had palled, she had taken to pacing back and forth about the room. There was nothing to do but wait, for she couldn't go out of the room. She'd had enough trouble with the serving lad that morning; she wasn't about to go looking for more trouble downstairs. She had learned her lesson well. No longer would her father's name and wealth protect her from lewd advances. She could only rely on Kevin's fists when he was with her, and her own wits when he was not.

A knock on the door brought her head up sharply. "Who is it?" she asked warily.

Silence for a full minute. Then, in a gruff—humble voice, "Brenna? 'Tis me, your father."

Brenna gasped in a moment of stunned shock. How had her father found her? Did he have Kevin with him? She glanced hurriedly about the room. How could she let her father see her in this room? She wished she had a mirror to check her hair, her gown—good Lord she had not even changed out of it yet!

"Brenna? I'm asking you to open the door, lass."

Brenna wanted to weep. She wished she could refuse, but finally, slowly, she unlocked the door and opened it. Her father stood in the hall—her tall, strong, handsome father, his blue eyes as fierce as ever, his jaw just as strongly set. It was all she could do to keep from throwing herself into his arms. God, how heavenly 'twould be to sob on his shoulder as she always had when she was a child.

"Papa, what—what are you doing here?" she asked, her voice shaking.

Kildare glanced about the room. "Ryan's not here?" he asked.

She shook her head. "Kevin's looking for work, Papa. He—he'll be back soon."

"He left you alone, lass?" Her father's gruff voice was struggling to hold back the outrage and sadness and bitterness inside of him.

"He—he had to, Papa. He had to make money so that we can find someplace permanent to live."

"You *have* a home, lass," her father went on, more gently now. "I've come to tell you that I—I lost my temper yesterday. I went out of my head." He stepped into the room and turned to face her "God, you're my little girl, my prized daughter, on whom I centered all my dreams. I suppose when Ryan first came to me, I couldn't bring myself to believe him, and then as things went on, I found my stupid temper talking for me. I've had people looking for you all night. One of them spotted Minx in the back of this inn and rode back to tell me. I've ridden all afternoon to tell you—to apologize for everything I said." He bowed his head, and she guessed his admitting that he had been wrong had been the hardest thing he had ever done.

Oh, yes, Papa! Oh, yes! She wanted to say. She longed to throw herself into his welcoming arms, to go back with him. God, how the words burned on her lips. But she couldn't say them, couldn't let him know how miserable she was. Pride and loyalty to Kevin kept her from saying them. After all, hadn't Kevin risked everything to take care of her, to make her his wife?

"Papa, I—I'm Kevin's wife now," she said slowly, dully.

His head shot up and his blue eyes were sharp and agonized. "You—you and Ryan are married? In name only, then." His last hope was that they had not yet consummated the union, for he would move heaven and earth to get an annulment.

But he could see the truth in her eyes. For a moment she said nothing. The silence in the room bore down on them.

Kildare's voice sounded old and weary as he said, "Then I'll be offering Ryan his job back. He'll take it, won't he, Brenna? He's got to be supporting you, lass."

Brenna clutched at the offered straw, seeing her life come back to her. But, oh God, Kevin would never take charity from her father; she knew it. She shook her head. "I don't know, Papa. I can talk to him when he returns."

"Aye." As he sat down heavily in a chair his breathing became labored, just the way it had the previous day.

"Papa, Papa, are you all right?" She cried as she hurried to his side. "You had some trouble yesterday, I remember. Did the doctor . . ."

He shook his head. "Too much excitement and heat," he assured her. "Just lost my breath for a moment, nothing more." He waved her to a chair.

"But, Papa, you've ridden all this way," she said doubtfully. "Are you sure you don't want to lie down?"

He nodded. "I'll just sit here and wait for your husband," he said.

"I'll have some wine brought up," she said, patting his arm.

After a while, Kildare began to relax, but when Kevin opened the door, he tensed again. A black frown immediately crossed the young man's face, and his voice began to shake.

"Get out of here, Kildare. Brenna's my wife, and there's nothing you can do about it now."

Kildare came to his feet, but, with an effort, he controlled his anger. "Ryan, I came to apologize for my unkind words of yesterday. I want to bring Brenna back to her family."

"*I'm* her family now," Kevin declared.

Kildare flushed, but calmly stood his ground. "Aye, and so I'm offering you your job back as head groom on the farm." He looked at the lad pleadingly. "You cannot take Brenna away from me and her mother," he said softly.

Kevin winced. "You've dealt with us harshly," he said. "She's my wife now, and 'tis up to me to make a living for her."

"Then you've found a new job?" Kildare challenged him.

Kevin's anger cooled, and he couldn't meet the older man's eyes. "No," he admitted. "But 'tis only my first day looking. I'm sure I'll be finding work soon enough."

"You've not got that much money, Ryan," Kildare said

confidently. "You can't allow Brenna to live in conditions like this." He gestured around the room. "She's not the kind to be boarded up in a room all day, only seeing you at night. If you truly loved her, you'd want what's best for her!"

"Aye, and she'll have the best," Kevin said, his voice rising to a shrill pitch. "As soon as I'm on my feet again, I'll be making sure she has the best. 'Twill just take a little time, that's all."

Brenna laid a hand on her father's arm. "Papa, would you please wait downstairs. I'd like to talk to Kevin alone for a few minutes. We'll be giving you our decision then."

Kildare gazed at his daughter, then nodded. Brenna waited until she heard her father's footsteps on the stairs, then she turned to her husband.

"Kevin, I'm asking you to accept his offer," she said steadily.

Kevin whitened. "Why? That life is behind you now."

"I can't live this way, waiting all day in a room while you're about looking for work. At least, if you took my father's offer, we could set up housekeeping in one of the grooms' cottages. Carruthers and his wife have gone back to Cork to live with their daughter. His cottage is empty." She looked at Kevin with tears in her eyes. "Oh, Kevin, please, please do this for me. You promised you'd be taking care of me!"

"Aye," he said slowly. He seemed to consider for a long moment. Finally, he reached out to hold her arms. "Brenna, look at me," he ordered.

Brenna obeyed him. He looked into the dark blue of her eyes, which were ringed so intriguingly with purple. He saw the pale oval of her face and the finely drawn mouth.

"Brenna, are you sorry that you married me?" he asked her.

Brenna fought to keep her expression steady and her lips from quivering. "I'm not sorry, Kevin," she whispered.

He looked at her a moment longer and seemed satisfied. "Then we'll be going back with your father." He sighed as though a great weight had been lifted from his shoulders.

Brenna breathed in sharply and reached up to throw her arms about Kevin's neck. "Oh, Kevin, you'll not regret this," she said joyfully. "Oh, you'll see what a wonderful wife I'll be making you."

Chapter Twenty-Eight

"BRENNA, I'll not have you helping in the stables," Kevin said patiently. " 'Tis not seemly for a grown married woman to be doing such work."

Brenna's face colored with anger as she turned to her husband. "Don't be talking to me of what's seemly and what isn't," she declared. " 'Tis because of what my father said, isn't it?"

Still patient, he shook his head. "No, 'tis nothing your father said. 'Twas my own decision, Brenna. I have enough stable lads and groomsmen to help me with the horses. There's no need for you to be making a spectacle of yourself."

"A spectacle!" She clenched her fists. "What is that supposed to mean?"

"Nothing, Brenna," Kevin said, his calm beginning to disintegrate. "But, well, you know my meaning."

"Yes, I think I do," she said, turning away from him pertly. "I'm to stay put in this cottage, go nowhere, and do nothing. I'm not even allowed to help you at the work I love best!"

Defeated, Kevin stood silently, denying nothing she said.

She looked over her shoulder at him and softened. 'Twas not his fault, she thought. He was caught between her father and herself, and there was no easy way out for him. She was aware that her father had made mention of the fact that Brenna had been spending a lot of time in the barn, polishing tackle and currying horses, instead of doing chores more appropriate to a married woman. Tyrone had made it seem a question of Kevin's virility. Dear Kevin! He tried so to please her, but when his manhood was threatened, like all men, he forgot about his woman's feelings.

"All right, Kevin," she said at last. "I'll not be doing any more work in the stables, if you don't want me to."

He sighed with relief and went to hug her, kissing her tenderly, gratefully, on her nape. "You need something to be keeping you busy," he whispered in her ear. "Something like a baby."

Brenna blushed and smiled. "Perhaps we're not trying hard enough," she suggested boldly.

He laughed, delighted with her. "Aye, perhaps not," he mused, "but 'twill not be hard after the spring foaling is over. Then we'll be seeing . . ." He kissed her again on the mouth, and gave her an affectionate pat on her bottom before leaving for the stables.

Brenna watched him through the small window of their two-room cottage. To think, she'd been married to him for all of two months. May was bursting into flower, and spring seemed to make the blood flow strong in her veins. Despite all the extra work she was required to do now—for she had no mother or cook or laundress to be helping her—she found she had extra time on her hands and sometimes grew restless in the small, stuffy cottage.

She recalled, vividly, the day her father had brought her home. At the sight of her daughter, Nora had thrown her arms around Brenna and sobbed uncharacteristically, so that Brenna, after a moment, had broken down too. Even Deirdre had been struck speechless by her sister's return. The moment had been extremely awkward when Kildare had put his arm about his daughter's shoulders and started to lead her inside the house, only to be stopped abruptly when Kevin put out his arm to catch his wife's hand.

"We'd like your permission to be taking over old Carruthers' cottage," Kevin had said quietly.

Kildare had started in surprise, as though realizing for the first time that this marriage was real and that his daughter belonged to another man. But he had gathered his wits quickly, and graciously made the cottage a gift to them. "That is," he added meaningfully, "if that is what Brenna wants." He had turned to his daughter. "You know you'll always have a home with us, lass."

The deliberate exclusion of her husband had strengthened Brenna's determination to make Kevin a good wife. They had gone to the cottage together, appalled by its uncleanliness. But Brenna, young, strong, and determined, had not taken long to tidy up the cottage into a livable home.

The first few days, she had concentrated on cleaning thick grime and dust from the two windowsills, the floor, and the walls. The cottage was divided by a partition into a kitchen-living area and a bedroom. Each room had one window that faced out the front of the cabin. A fireplace had been built in the partition to allow heat into both rooms.

Much to Kevin's displeasure, Kildare had donated furniture, but Brenna assured her husband that they would buy their own as soon as they could afford to. Dermot's old bed and stout black oak wardrobe went into the bedroom. Their kitchen table and chairs were brought down from the attic of the big house, pieces that had come from France with Nora, and looked out of place in the tiny cottage. Brenna had surprised herself by doing a fair job of sewing curtains for the two windows—bright calico to liven up the interior.

As wedding presents, Nora had given her a set of the blue-willow-pattern dishes, crystal, and silverware she had been saving for her daughters' dowries. Deirdre embroidered a footstool and Kevin's fellow workers built the newlyweds a cupboard for the kitchen corner. Siobhan, her eyes curiously indifferent, had presented them with bed linens and towels.

" 'Twill do," Brenna had told herself, when at the end of the first month she surveyed the changes in their home.

But now, as she watched her husband's figure disappear down the path that led to the barn, Brenna had to admit that things just wouldn't "do" as they were, for she was bored. She could go to see her mother and eat there if she wished, but she had done that three times already this week. She hated to make a habit of it, for she knew that Nora, although always happy to see her, had much to do now with community work, teas, and luncheons. Brenna was proud that her mother had taken a place in local society, and she certainly had no wish to keep her from it. Brenna was a grown woman and married, as Kevin said, and she should begin making friends among the wives of the other married groomsmen.

Brenna had tried a few friendly overtures, but the other wives were wary of the young woman, who was, after all, still the daughter of their husbands' employer; so Brenna's overtures had been met with cautious indifference at best, and with outright suspicion at worst.

When she had begun to work in the stables, she was sure she would enjoy herself and take the boredom out of her free hours, but now, even that avenue was closed to her.

"I know your plan, Papa," she said to herself. "You want me to be like Mama, to entertain and be gracious—take my rightful place in society. But, Papa, no one wants to be entertained by the wife of your head groom. That's hardly the top of the social ladder." She giggled, then grew sober again at the thought of the empty day stretching ahead of her.

Suddenly she smiled again, took off her apron, and searched for her riding boots and gloves. She would take a ride to visit Siobhan! 'Twould be the perfect thing! Why, the wise woman might even have an elixir to help Brenna get pregnant, and then all her problems would be solved.

"A baby, Brenna!" Siobhan looked steadily at the girl. "Are you quite sure that that is what you're wanting? Could Kevin support two hungry mouths now?"

"Oh, yes! He—he told me he wanted a baby!" Brenna assured her.

Siobhan bit her lip. "Brenna, 'tis not up to me to be giving you advice in such matters, but I have the feeling that you're not wanting to seek help from your mother. So, my advice is to wait for a few months. 'Twill be best to leave it up to God and nature, don't you think?"

Brenna's face fell, for she had anticipated that the *pishogue* would say something like this, "Oh, but, Siobhan, you don't understand how—how bored I've been.

'Tis terrible going from morning 'til night with not a soul to talk with."

"What about your mother and sister?"

"I can't be going to them all the time. I'm afraid Mama or Deirdre would go telling Papa, and then he would think that I—that I—was unhappy." She looked away from the other woman.

"Oh, Brenna," was all Siobhan said, but she thought, are you unhappy? Do you truly love Kevin? What has Rory Adair's leaving to do with all of this? She shook her head. It wasn't her place, she told herself, to be prying into the girl's life.

"I'm sorry, Siobhan," Brenna said briskly, getting up from the table. "I suppose I shouldn't have bothered you about my problems. I just wish I had something to do!"

Siobhan thought a moment. Then she stood up and touched the girl's shoulder with maternal gentleness. "I've plenty of work to keep you busy and still fill my own time as well," she said. "If you'd be willing to learn, I'd be happy to teach you the skills and the knowledge of medicine—enough for you to be helping me with those who come to me for aid."

Brenna turned towards her. "I remember the time I helped you with the girl who had the baby."

"Aye, and you did very well," Siobhan added encouragingly. "Think of it, Brenna. You would have something to do helping those less fortunate than yourself! You would be doing me a service as well for you know 'tis getting harder for me to get around, especially when the cold months come and my foot pains me."

Brenna knew it had taken a lot for Siobhan to admit to such a thing. She must need her help very much. "What would I have to do?" she asked.

"I'd teach you about the medicines I use in my possets and poultices. 'Twould not be hard for a bright girl like you, Brenna, to be learning everything quickly."

Brenna nodded, her face serious. " 'Twould be something that Kevin couldn't dissuade me on," she said, at length. "After all, he's gone all day at the barn, and he knows I've been restless and bored at the cottage. He'd be happy to see me doing something worthwhile." She looked at Siobhan. "I do want him to be proud of me, Siobhan."

Siobhan smiled, her dark, bright eyes were misty, with affection for this young girl. "Aye, my dear, Kevin would be most proud of you."

"All right then, 'tis settled. When do I start?"

Siobhan laughed. "Why, you can start right now by helping me hem these bandages." She looked at Brenna's startled face and winked. "Why, did I not tell you that there's more to being a *pishogue* than tending the sick?" She laughed cheerily and poured more tea.

When she arrived home late that day, she was surprised to see Kevin waiting for her outside the cottage. She slipped off Minx and tied her to a holly bush, then ran lightly to Kevin.

Kevin received her hug, but his kiss was perfunctory. "You've been out?" he asked, straining to be nonchalant.

"Yes, I've been with Siobhan all day, Kevin, and never have I seen the time fly so fast," Brenna said brightly, in spite of Kevin's coolness.

He relaxed a little. "Well, I suppose 'tis good for you to visit the woman since she is all alone. But you'll not be making a habit of it, will you?"

Brenna stopped mid-stride and looked at her husband. "Why, Kevin, why should you be saying that? I've—I've told her that I'd be helping her with her work. I promised her I would."

"Helping her?" Kevin was stunned. "And why should you be doing that, Brenna?"

"Because I want to!" she blurted out bluntly.

"But you've got work to do here at home," he argued. "And you should be making new friends among the other wives—women who are more your own age. If you're taking up all your time with that wise woman, you'll have no time left to be doing the things you should."

"And what things are those, Kevin?" Brenna asked him temperamentally. "I've tried to befriend those women, but they look at me as though I—as though I don't belong."

Kevin reddened. "Aye," he said tightly, "you don't belong, because you don't *want* to belong! You're not trying hard enough."

"I have tried, Kevin. I'm sorry if I'm not the wife you expected. I don't even know what you did expect, but I can't become a quiet, serious little cottage wife with no interests of my own. I'll go crazy if I don't find something to do—and Siobhan's provided me with something worthwhile."

Kevin took a deep breath. "Let's go inside, Brenna," he said quietly. "I've no wish to be airing our arguments in public."

She gave him a stabbing look, but followed him in the door. Once inside, she faced him warily; the despair on Kevin's face smote her heart.

"Kevin, Kevin!" she said, going up to grab his arm. "Please don't look so hurt. I—I can't help the way I am. You married me, knowing that I liked my independence."

"But I never thought . . ." he began, then stopped. "I suppose I just thought you would be fitting in after a time."

Fitting in! Brenna thought with anguish. I can't fit into this kind of life. I can't! To her husband, she said simply, "Perhaps in time, Kevin, but for now this is what I need to make me happy."

"God knows I want you to be happy, Brenna," Kevin said sincerely. " 'Tis sure I'm the one that's wrong."

"Kevin, don't you worry. I'll be leaving after you've gone to do your work, and I'll be back in time to fix you dinner."

"You were late today," he pointed out.

"I took the long way home," she said quickly. "I didn't realize the time."

Kevin let his shoulders slump as he looked at his wife. "All right, then, I'll be letting you try this—for a time." He straightened up again. "But, there's to be no interfering with your work as my wife and housekeeper," he said sternly.

Brenna balked for a moment at his high-handed tone, then bowed her head meekly. It seemed they would both have to make sacrifices. "Yes, Kevin, I'll be making sure that nothing interferes."

"Good. And Brenna . . ." He caught her hand as she turned away to start their supper ". . . I do wish you'd try a little harder to be friendly toward the other wives."

Brenna sighed, then nodded. "Yes, Kevin, I'll—try."

Chapter Twenty-Nine

BRENNA renewed her interest in life as she began to learn Siobhan's craft. She became acquainted with the remedies for headaches, backaches, and ingrown toenails. A certain posset could do wonders for a sore belly, while it could do nothing for a broken bone. A special powder of certain roots mixed in tea might help to calm an anxious father down, while another mixture might be used to lessen the labor pain involved in bringing a new child into the world.

Siobhan allowed Brenna to watch the birthings and the mendings of sick bodies. Once she had seen Siobhan snap a man's leg to bring the bone back into place after he had broken it while plowing his fields. Brenna stitched countless split lips and heads and even helped a young lad to walk on a new wooden leg. Brenna seemed to gobble everything up eagerly, and she provided a constant delight to Siobhan who saw more of her now than Nora did.

When Nora found out about her daughter's new avocation, she made no comment to her husband. He had been furious to learn that his own daughter was tramping about the countryside watching birthings and soothing young men her own age when she treated them for gashes and cuts acquired during drunken brawls. But when he growled that he would be telling that young Ryan exactly what he thought of a husband who would allow his bride to do such things, Nora told him, in succinct terms, to mind his own business. Of course, Kildare had raved and stamped, but, in the end, Nora had won out.

Kevin, himself, had ceased to object to Brenna's work, for even he could see that it made her happier, more sociable and certainly more loving.

So Brenna Ryan became well-known in the district as someone dependable and helpful in times of sickness and distress. Summer turned to autumn and then to winter. Kevin and Brenna celebrated Christmas in the parlor of her parents' home, where the engagement of Benjamin Markham and Deirdre Kildare was announced. They would be married the following spring. The announcement brought astonishment, joy, gaiety, and happiness to the Kildares.

Brenna went to her sister and hugged her. "I should never have doubted you that night so long ago when you told me that you'd be having Benjamin someday," she said. "I should have known that you'd make it all come true."

Deirdre nodded, proudly gazing up at Benjamin's face. "Yes, it's been a long time coming, but I finally convinced him I was the only woman in the world who would put up with his shenanigans and love him at the same time."

"Whew! and what an argument she gave me!" Benjamin chided, looking down with tenderness at his love's glowing face.

"Well, I'm happy for both of you!" Brenna said enthusiastically.

"Oh, thank you, Brenna—and I know I'll make Benjamin as good a wife as you've made Kevin," Dierdre said with sincerity. She kissed her sister again—and missed the bleak look that passed over Brenna's face that was replaced quickly as she turned to call a "Merry Christmas" to Sir William, who could not quite get over the fact that his wandering son had finally chosen to settle down and to marry someone so emminently suitable.

It was easy to read the pride in her father's face as Brenna reached up to kiss him on the cheek. But when Kildare looked at his oldest daughter, there was still that mixture of despair, loss, and irony that his youngest child would be the one to inherit the horse farm that he had always dreamed would go to Brenna. He could not bring himself to give all that he worked for to a common groomsman. So the family land would go to Deirdre and Benjamin now. He tried to ease his conscience by telling himself that Brenna was no longer interested in the running of the farm—and that he was sure Benjamin would allow Kevin to manage the horses.

All he could think about now was that one of his children—thank God—had had the good sense to marry well. Aye, for love it might be, but wealth only made a good marriage better, and the Lord knew the Markhams had quite enough money to keep the farm expanding for many, many years. He had been a little surprised that old William hadn't made any objections to the surprise announcement; Tyrone guessed that his old friend had probably known for a long time now that his son and Kildare's daughter were eager to tie the knot. It only increased Kildare's respect and liking for Markham that he was genuinely happy, despite the fact that his son was an English nobleman, and Deirdre was the daughter of an Irish tenant. Kildare could only pray that Deirdre would not find it hard to adjust to the new world she would enter when she became young Markham's wife.

Although Brenna was happy for her sister, she couldn't help but compare her own life to the future that awaited Deirdre, and such thoughts only weakened her resolve to be a good wife to Kevin. She quickly replaced her doubts with joy for Dermot and Bernadette, who everyone had just learned, would become parents in March.

Nora scolded her daughter-in-law about not telling her sooner, but Bernadette sighed happily, placed a gentle hand on her belly, and explained to Nora that they had been afraid this pregnancy would end in miscarriage like the others. Not until the critical first months had passed had they felt safe in revealing their news, big belly and all, at Christmastime.

Through all the celebration, Kevin had grown uneasy. When, according to tradition, the Kildares set off the next day for Sir William's, Brenna had declined to go, telling her parents that she and Kevin wanted to spend some quiet time together on Christmas Day. The real reason was that Kevin had declared he would not go where he was so obviously out of place. It was the only real argument they had ever had, ending in Brenna's tears as she shouted they were both "out of place" with each other.

She could not fit into his world, and he could not fit into hers. But the suffering on Kevin's face made her relent once again and she promised she would try harder.

It was one mild day in early April, when everyone was getting ready for Deirdre's wedding and Nora had gone to Dublin to help Bernadette with her new son, Patrick Dermot, that Brenna came home from a weary day spent helping Siobhan and saw a strange carriage at the house. At first she thought that her mother had rented a carriage to bring her back earlier than expected from Dublin, but upon closer inspection, she discovered that she didn't recognize any of the luggage on top. Curious, she dismounted and walked Minx closer to the vehicle. After a quick look, she shrugged and told herself it must belong to one of her father's clients.

Intent on finding Kevin, she walked Minx to the stables when she heard men talking inside. Kevin's voice was among them. As she came closer, her eyes automatically looked over the assembled men. Suddenly, she felt her heart skip a beat, then pound in her chest.

From behind a pile of blocked hay, she stared at the profile of one particular young man. Her unease was communicated to Minx, who snorted nervously and stamped. Brenna automatically reached around to stroke the mare's nose, then turned back to look at the same dark-haired young man. It couldn't be! she thought in anguish. It couldn't be.

Her eyes took in his tall stance, his black hair, as dark and shining as her own, the straight arrogance of his patrician nose, and the sensual fullness of a mouth she had known only once. She wanted to laugh and to cry and to beat her hands against herself in helpless frustration.

Steven, she thought. The name washed over her and brought a lump to her throat. She could only stand there and stare in bemused wonder—stare at the wide shoulders clothed in expensive, black broadcloth, stare at the tan of his cheek against the whiteness of his shirt collar, at the long, muscular legs, bent at the knee where shiny, black boots hugged smooth and tight down to his feet.

Suddenly, like a swift punch, the thought hit her that she might very well make a fool of herself if he saw her, and she moved farther behind the hay, her mind awhirl with memories rolling over her and mercilessly stabbing at her heart. She was no longer the same Brenna Kildare she had been five years before. She was nineteen, a young woman, and married. She bit her lip savagely to keep from wailing in misery. Only a few yards away stood Steven Castâneda de la Cruz, and next to him, talking easily and knowledgeably, was her husband Kevin Ryan. She was Brenna *Ryan* now.

A desolate feeling swooped over her, leaving her stunned by its intensity. She couldn't let Steven see her like this. He would expect to see her in a blue riding outfit, a hat with a perky feather on her head, a gold-crested riding crop in her gloved hand. She looked down at the riding habit she had been wearing all day; it was covered with spatters of blood, mud, dust, and sweat. She felt, with a new awareness, her hair falling down from beneath the felt hat she had put carelessly on her head that morning. And her riding gloves had long since seen the last of their use. She had been too proud to go to her father or to Kevin for new ones, and now her hands were reddened and chafed, blistered and calloused in the palms. She wanted to weep.

And she wanted to escape before Kevin or her father saw her and beckoned her over. Oh, God, she thought with a sudden, terrible anxiety, don't let them see me now. Please, don't let them see me! She backed away, and Minx neighed gently as Brenna pulled at her bridle. The sound seemed as loud as a shout to Brenna's anxious ears; in a panic she wrapped Minx's reins about her hand and pulled almost viciously.

Minx followed without protest, and Brenna quickly tied her to one of the posts outside. Kevin would find the horse later. Dear God, Brenna thought she must hurry to the cottage! Her feet flew over the muddy earth path that led to the cottages.

She was aware of two women watching her headlong progress down the path—two of the groomsmen's wives, but she didn't care that they might wonder at the tears streaming down her cheeks. She hated those women. She opened the door, bolted it swiftly, then threw herself on the bed, sobbing as though her heart were broken. The cottage where she lived had never looked like such a hovel to her. Embarrassment and misery flooded her as she thought of what Steven would think if he saw her here. God! No! No! With impotent fury at the cruel joke destiny had played upon her, she pounded her fists into the pillow and pushed her face deep into the comforter.

It was nearly an hour later, when she realized that Kevin would be home soon and expecting dinner to be ready. Panic welled up within her again, for she was determined that Kevin would not know that anything was wrong. Quickly, she got up and smoothed down the bedcovers, feeling an unexpected surge of distaste at the thought of sleeping there with Kevin. She tried to ignore it, and she went to wash her face in the sink and to brush her hair. She did not dare to look at her reflection in a mirror, but started to prepare dinner, washing the potatoes to steam then in the kish, and heating milk to be put into bowls and salted. She had already made oaten cakes and had only to add honey and milk to them before placing them on the table. There would be no soup tonight, for she had no time to set it to bubbling. As quickly as she could, she set the table, put more peat bricks on the fire, and went back into the bedroom to change out of her riding habit.

Just as she buttoned her last button, she heard Kevin rattling the door latch. She had forgotten that she bolted it from the inside. She dashed over to let him in.

"Kevin!" she said brightly, reaching up to hug him.

"Ah, smells good," he said hugging her back and shutting the door.

He gave her a kiss and seated himself at the table, for he had washed already at the barrel outside the door. Brenna sat beside him, testing the kish to see how the potatoes fared. They were not quite done.

"I saw Minx tied outside the barn," he said casually. Brenna studied him anxiously, wondering if he had guessed at her distress, but no—he seemed only to be curious. "Yes, I left her there because I—I was a little late today, and I didn't want you to get angry with me," she lied.

"Brenna, I wouldn't have gotten angry," he protested, reaching over to pat her hand as he chewed on a piece of dippity bread.

Brenna waited impatiently for him to speak of their visitor. She knew that she couldn't bring the subject up herself.

"Were you very busy today?" she finally asked, when Kevin continued to eat with unconcern.

He shrugged. "The usual. And you, my charitable little wife? How are all your patients faring?"

"All the same, except for Mr. Cavendish, who was able to get out of bed today and walk around with a cane. I was quite proud of him."

"Oh? And who is Mr. Cavendish?"

"Oh, Kevin, don't you ever listen to me? I've told you before. Mr. Cavendish is nearly seventy, and a sweeter old man I've never seen. He was plowing his fields when the plow rope broke from the horse. The plow kicked back and hit him in the leg."

"If he needs help plowing his fields, perhaps I can be helping him on Saturday," Kevin offered.

Brenna's heart softened at her husband's kindness, and she leaned over to give him a kiss on the cheek. "You're a dear, Kevin, but I think one of his neighbors will be able to help him."

"Your father had a visitor today," Kevin went on, tweaking her playfully on the nose. "Sir William called with that boy—that foreigner—you remember him? Steven Cruz from—somewhere." He scratched his head while Brenna's heart skippd a beat at the mention of the name.

"Yes, I think I remember him," she managed to say.

Kevin laughed. "I couldn't believe 'twas the same lad that stayed here for almost two years, although I suppose I was looking different to him too. We've all changed since then."

"Yes," Brenna murmured. She hadn't touched any of the food on her plate.

Kevin was silent then, content to finish his eating, until Brenna prodded him.

"How long is Steven Cruz going to be staying? Did he say?"

Kevin shrugged. "Not long, I'm thinking. He drove up with Sir William and I thought your father was going to have apoplexy. The old boy looked quite happy to see him." There was an unmistakable tug of bitterness in Kevin's voice as he mentioned the father-in-law who would never make him feel totally comfortable in the Kildare family. "He kept going on about how he wished your mother and Dermot could come down from Dublin to see him. Deirdre, too, since she'd been visiting your cousin in Cork for the past few days. And you, of course."

"Me?"

"Aye, he—the foreign lad—said he was anxious to be seeing you again after all these years."

"Oh, did he now?" Brenna forced herself to remain calm and her dark blue eyes met Kevin's gaze steadily.

Kevin shrugged. "I told him that you were my wife now. I don't think he'll be bothering you, sweetheart." He looked at her. " 'Twouldn't be seemly."

Brenna nodded like an automaton.

"Anyway, he said he wouldn't be staying long. He's been somewhere doing business for his father and will be at Sir William's for a few days before going back home."

"I see." Brenna toyed with the food on her plate disinterestedly. "I suppose he only stopped to see my father about new contacts for the horses."

"Aye, something like that."

She suffered through dinner, trying to appear calm and poised. She was glad for the relief when it came time to clear the table and wash the dishes. Kevin sat down in one of the chairs and watched her, waiting until she was finished before nodding toward the bedroom. His brown eyes sparkled.

"Oh, Kevin, I'd hoped to get you to go 'round to the

back and see if you could be bagging that troublesome rabbit that's been eating all my lettuce leaves," Brenna objected, her whole body chilled at the thought of making love to Kevin when her heart had just been rent by the sight of Steven Cruz.

He shrugged. "Time enough for that. You'd best be setting a few traps first. Why don't you ask some of the other wives to help you?" he suggested. " 'Twould be a good way to get to know them better."

"All right," she said in defeat.

Kevin blew out the kitchen candles leaving only the glow of the fireplace to light the dark corners. He took his wife's hand and led her through the doorway into their bedroom. It had been a while since he had last made love to her, for as always in the spring, he had been especially busy with the new foals of late. But tonight, by God and Saint Patrick, she looked so lovely with those beautiful eyes and all that fine, lush hair about her face.

"Take your hair down, darlin'," he murmured as he began to undress.

Brenna obliged his whim and took the pins from her hair. She brushed out the tangles and let her long locks swirl about her shoulders instead of braiding them into tails. As usual, she turned away from him modestly, as she undressed and slipped into her nightgown. When she turned back, he was already in bed waiting for her. Biting her lip, Brenna walked to the bed and slipped in beside her husband. By now she was accustomed to the way he smelled and felt. She settled next to him, and he arched against her, putting his arms about her to pull her closer.

"Brenna, my Brenna," he whispered coaxingly.

He began to kiss her cheek and the curve of her jaw as his fingers worked busily on the fastenings of her gown. Brenna closed her eyes, flinching only a bit when his hands grasped and gently caressed her breasts. After a year of marriage, she had become accustomed to this, and no longer likened it to milking a cow. In fact, sometimes, when Kevin buried his face against her bosom and kissed her there, she felt pleasant sensations, but tonight her head was too filled with memories and her heart too filled with pain.

Kevin began to notice her lack of participation. "What's the matter, Brenna?" he asked anxiously, halting in the act of sliding her nightgown up above her hips.

"I—I'm sorry, Kevin, but I'm so tired, I just can't."

He kissed her gently on the lips. " 'Tis all right then, darlin'," he said quickly. "I'm a selfish husband to be wanting you like this, but I can't help myself when you're so beautiful." He kissed her again. "You just lie still then, and let me do all the work," he teased her. The firelight played across his grin.

"But, Kevin . . ."

He shook his head. "I love you, Brenna," he whispered softly.

Brenna wanted to answer, but the words stuck in her throat. "Yes, Kevin," she said relieved that he did not press her.

Chapter Thirty

WITH determination and luck, Brenna managed to stay out of sight whenever Steven Castaneda de la Cruz was at the farm during the first days of his stay in County Wexford. Her father had already invited Steven to dinner, and Brenna was in a quandary as to how to get out of going. It would never do to give her father the slightest suspicion that she was ashamed to present herself to Steven. Finally, feeling like a child, she told Kevin that she had terrible pains in her belly and would have to be excused from accepting the invitation, but that he should go alone. After some grumbling, he agreed.

That evening, when Kevin returned from the big house, Brenna wanted desperately to question him about Steven, but he seemed silent and taciturn, so she refrained from pressing him. If she knew her father, he had probably set poor Kevin off to bad advantage by talking about all of Steven's accomplishments.

She had a difficult time getting to sleep, tossing restlessly about in the bed, dreaming of how Steven had made her feel with one kiss—a feeling she had never had with Kevin. The following morning Kevin ordered her to stay home from her usual routine with Siobhan, thinking that she was still sick. Brenna would have rebelled, knowing it would be better for her to keep busy, but Kevin might have questioned her too closely.

She stayed inside until she thought she would go mad with the inactivity. She set about collecting the laundry, telling herself it would be a good day to wash and hang the clothes out to dry in the fresh, spring air.

Kevin and the other men had built a small laundry shed where a large wooden tub and soap were kept, as well as a small burner to heat water in. Brenna took her woven basket to the shed, greeting there, with a small, mechanical smile, another woman, who was just leaving.

"Good morning to you, Brenna," the woman said.

"Good morning," Brenna answered shortly. She pushed open the door and set her laundry on the wooden table. She fetched water from the stream, heated it, then added soap to make a heavy lather. Strenuously, she rubbed the clothes against the washboard, slapping soap and water on herself.

By the time she finished washing and rinsing her arms were aching, but she felt glad of the ache, as if it were a penance. As she set the clean clothes back in the basket, humming a little ditty to herself, another young woman came to use the laundry room.

"You're finished?" Bridget Simmons asked politely, her freckled face serious as she addressed the wet, soapy young woman next ot her.

"Yes, 'tis just time," Brenna began, when out of the corner of her eye she could see two horsemen trotting across the field opposite the stables. With a shiver of dread, she watched the riders, recognizing her father's proud, erect bearing instantly. And beside him . . .

"Is there something amiss?" Bridget asked, seeing the other girl's face suddenly blanch.

"Oh—nothing!" Brenna said, ducking her head and hurrying away with her basket.

Her shoes, still soapy and wet, slipped on the grass and she nearly fell; her basket tottered to the side allowing a few things to fall to the ground. Bridget ran to help her, but Brenna snatched up the articles quickly. The riders were passing almost parallel to her now.

"Ach, you forgot this!" Bridget called, holding up one of Kevin's shirts.

"Then give it to me!" Brenna snarled, snapping at the cloth and stuffing it into the basket.

"Well!" Bridget sniffed, revising her kind opinion a few notches. She sniffed again at the girl's back, then went to retrieve her own bundle of clothes.

Meanwhile Brenna was nearly running back to her cottage. She kept her face averted and was almost faint with relief when she heard the horses moving farther away. Perhaps they hadn't seen her—surely, Steven wouldn't have recognized the untidy girl with the overflowing clothes basket. She was trembling as she shut the door to her cabin and leaned thankfully against it.

A few minutes passed before her heart slowed its hammering beat, then she took a deep breath and looked down ruefully at the basket of clothes. She would have to put them out to dry sooner or later; it might as well be now. Picking up the heavy load, she opened the door and checked carefully to be sure her father and Steven had not decided to come back this way. When she saw no one about, Brenna took the clothes out to hang them on the line.

The routine work soothed her frantic thoughts, and she felt much calmer by the time she had finished. A light, warm breeze bent the line and fluttered the clothes as Brenna turned to pick up the empty basket.

It was just as she was going inside that she heard a horse trotting toward her. For a moment, the sound held no meaning for her, and she continued through the door. Only when she turned to close it behind her did she see the rider bearing straight for the cottage. Her blood seemed to freeze in her veins.

"No!" The single word escaped in a rush of air.

She would have scurried inside and slammed the door in his face, but realized she would only be making a fool of herself. Like a criminal grimly awaiting the death sentence, Brenna stood at the door of her cottage.

She saw Steven, sitting astride one of her father's finest geldings, looking tall and agonizingly handsome in beige riding breeches and a white shirt, which was open at the throat. His long black hair brushed the collar of his shirt, and she saw for the first time the thin, black moustache that made him even more romantic, more alluring. A Panama hat shaded his face, so that she could not make out the expression in his black eyes.

She was all too aware of her own face, sunburned from

her travels with Siobhan, and her hair, unwashed and bound haphazardly with a kerchief. Miserably, she watched as he reined up his horse and sat silently looking at her.

"Well?" she finally challenged him, anger tingeing her tone.

He laughed shortly. "Brenna, how good to see you," he said lazily, swinging down off his horse and tying it to the post. He pushed his hat back on his head as though to get a better look at her, and she felt herself growing red under his gaze.

"I'm afraid I've got some work to be doing," she began as an excuse to escape him.

"You mean you don't have time for an old friend?" he asked her softly. His eyes narrowed.

"No, I really am quite busy. I'll—I'll be seeing you before you leave," she said hurriedly. She turned to go into the house and bumped into the basket. Grumbling under her breath, she righted it, then turned on her foot and twisted her ankle a little too sharply. "Ouch!"

"Brenna, you should be more careful," he said soberly, barely hiding the grin that tugged at his mouth. "Let me see that ankle."

"No!" Brenna looked about in alarm. "What do you think my neighbors will be saying if they see you and I—I mean they'll be thinking the worst if . . ."

"Then let's go inside—and keep them guessing." He winked and ushered her inside before she could protest further.

"Steven, you shouldn't be here!" Brenna wailed as he scanned the cottage interior.

"*You* shouldn't be here," he said in an undertone. His gaze was startling in its intensity. "Now, may I take a look at your ankle?"

" 'Tis nothing, really. I just twisted it a bit. You remember how clumsy I can be." This new, grown-up Steven made her uneasy. At 22, he was a magnetic, handsome young man, who knew the effect his dark, glowing eyes had on her. Beside him, she still felt as though she were only 14, that the past five years had taught her nothing.

"May I sit down for a moment?" he asked.

She nodded, and he took one of the kitchen chairs. She sat across the table from him.

"I've been hoping to see you," he began smoothly. "Don't ask me why, but I had the feeling that you've been avoiding me—silly notion, isn't it?" He was watching her like a cat with a mouse. "When your father and I rode by, he mentioned that this was where you lived now, and I decided to pay you a visit. Fortunately, Tyrone had pressing duties elsewhere. I managed to elude him and came back to find you, my dear, little Brenna."

She wasn't sure whether or not he was mocking her. "I'm sorry I wasn't able to come to the dinner last night. I wanted to."

"Ah, yes, your husband told us you were sick." He looked her up and down. "Remarkable recovery," he commented dryly.

"Yes, well you've seen me now, and I suppose you've other things to be doing," she cut in quickly.

His smile made her feel foolish. "You know, Brenna, when I came back to Ireland, I thought to myself, 'It will be interesting to see her again, to see how she's grown up and changed over the years.'" He shook his head. "Now I see I haven't missed a thing. You are still a child."

She colored. "I am a nineteen-year-old woman—a *married* woman!"

"So? Just because you are married, do you think that automatically makes you a woman?" He leaned forward. "I'm not talking about bedroom antics."

"Oh!" She stood up in confusion and embarrassment. How dare he talk to her so intimately! "I think you'd better be leaving right now! My husband won't be liking it when I tell him . . ."

"Brenna, you won't tell your husband anything," he broke in confidently. "What have I done? Paid you a social call—we're old acquaintants after all. Does he keep such tight lock and key on you that he doesn't even let you receive calls?"

Brenna flushed at his intimations. "Of course not! Kevin is—is a most understanding husband. He respects me."

"In that case, he should trust you enough to know that you wouldn't have a strange man in your house who would entertain the notion of going to bed with you." He leaned back with a relaxed air in his chair, though his eyes were avid.

"You—you shouldn't be saying such things to me," she accused him and added a distrustful look. "It isn't proper —me, being a married woman and all."

"You once told me you would never be a married woman," he reminded her.

Brenna flushed and wondered how he had remembered something said so long ago. "That was nonsense. I was a child and things were different then," she murmured, looking into her lap. She lifted her head after a moment. "Did you marry that young woman you told me about?"

"No."

The single word and the look in his eyes made her heart contract. He almost looked, she thought, as though she had betrayed him in some significant way by marrying. She wished he would go.

"Are you happy, Brenna?"

It took her a moment to stiffen her face into a well-composed mask. "Yes." It cost her dearly to say the word and to look at him directly without bursting into unexplainable tears. She could feel her breath quickening, her chest and face flush with heat, and her hands tremble on her knees. Although she tried valiantly to remain composed, she wanted, more than anything, to lay her head on his shoulder and tell him how hard it had been for her to adjust to this marriage, how she had tried so often and always seemed to fail. How good it would be, she thought with surprise, if, just for a moment, he would hold me and comfort me. But nothing about his demeanor led her to believe that he would.

"Then I am happy for you," he was saying lightly. "Kevin is a decent sort, a bit of a magician, I suppose, in being able to get you to marry him at all." He laughed to himself. "Ah, Brenna, I wonder what you two find to talk about at night. Does he entertain you with tales of adventure or witty remarks? Do you tell each other all the exciting things that happened to you during your day—your experience with the dirty laundry, his dealings with the horse manure?" His teeth gleamed in a wicked smile.

"Stop it!" Brenna was red with anger now. "Stop it! You came here only to mock me, to ridicule my life with Kevin. How can you be so mean! You—you're worse than my father—worse than anyone! Get out of my house! Get out!" Her angry screams abruptly turned into harsh sobbing. "Get out," she uttered forlornly.

She missed the brief look of pain that crossed his face. He could see that she wanted him gone—had told him so in harsh words. He sighed to himself and stood up from his chair, watching her shoulders shaking as she kept her face averted from him.

"I will go then, Brenna," he said softly.

"Yes, go!" Her scream was muffled through her hands. "I—hope I never, never have to see you again!"

"Good-bye," he replied shaking off his feeling of pity for her. His mouth turned down in bitter mockery. "I wish you every happiness."

Brenna waited until she heard the door slam and the sound of his horse going off in the distance. Then the dam suddenly burst; she sat down at the table and buried her face in her arms, to weep harsh, racking tears that shook her entire body. She wept for her lost innocence and her lost childhood and her dismal future. The pain in her heart burned more sharply than any physical agony. Dear God, she pined, what had she done to herself? Why—why— why had Steven come back?

She cried until her eyes hurt and her throat hurt and her head ached with sobbing. 'Twas her own fault that she had married Kevin. She shouldn't have married. 'Twas true that she hadn't loved Kevin when she told him that she would marry him, but it was done now, and couldn't be undone. She would have to live with herself and try to be fair to Kevin. If only Steven hadn't come back and said those horrible things to her.

Steven Castaneda de la Cruz—he was gone now, back to her past, and she would not see him ever again. She knew that he would not again come back to Ireland. She wondered, miserably, why he had come back at all.

Chapter Thirty-One

BRENNA never told Kevin that she had met Steven—she was afraid that her guilt would show too clearly in her face. Desperately, she tried to will herself to love her husband more, all the while hoping that she could conceive a child who would cement the bond between herself and Kevin.

But by the time of Deirdre's wedding, it was evident that Brenna was not pregnant, and she began to wonder if she and Kevin would ever be able to have children. She was not allowed to participate in the wedding; as a married woman, she had to take her place with the other matrons, serving food and beverages at the reception.

The days passed swiftly after that. All through the summer, she received amusing and entertaining letters from her sister in Europe, where she and Benjamin were taking an extended honeymoon. Summer also brought visits from Bernadette, Dermot, and little Patrick, who was so adorable that Brenna monopolized all his time during their stay. She cuddled and petted and loved the child, who, at six months, already looked to be the image of his mother: light and fair haired, with cornflower blue eyes that continually crinkled with delighted chuckles, especially when his Aunt Brenna came to hold him.

Toward the end of August, she received a letter from Maureen Byrne. It was postmarked Bristol, England. Brenna was curious to learn why the Byrnes had moved from Ireland, but Maureen was noncommital, merely alluding to the fact that Sean had had some bad dealings with the law in Dublin, so they had gone to England where, they hoped, his luck would come back. She still didn't have a fur cape or a townhouse, but she had a darling little girl who looked just like her father, in fact, Maureen was due again in November. She doubted that they would get back to Wexford by Christmas because of the expected birth, but she hoped that Brenna would think of her now and then, and she promised to visit as soon as she could.

As she read the letter, Brenna was struck by the maturity that came through Maureen's writing. Since she had left Wexford, she had evidently decided to make her marriage work with Sean and had chosen to have children as proof of her commitment. Brenna felt ashamed of her childish fancies and forlorn longings for a life with Steven that she couldn't have, and she resolved not to think of herself and her own problems so much. 'Twould do no good to mope. Like Maureen, she had a man who would provide for her and love her honestly.

Resolutely, Brenna took the alabaster dove music box and put it away in her cedar chest, carefully cradling it in a soft blanket. She sighed as she touched the sapphire eyes and the beautifully carved head—then quickly covered it up and put it away for good. Perhaps someday, when she had her own little daughter, Brenna would give it to her for a present.

All her energies now went into making Kevin a good wife and Siobhan a conscientious helper. Gradually, the wives of the other groomsmen had begun to accept her, and now they waved and called cheerily to her when they saw her on the path.

"I'm proud of you, darlin'," Kevin said one night after Colin and Bridget Simmons had gone home after a hearty supper. "Your cooking was marvelous, and I could bet those two haven't been so entertained since their wedding night." He laughed lovingly and reached out to bring her into his lap, stroking her breast with a light caress.

"I've been trying to make you proud of me, Kevin," Brenna answered and, gave him a kiss on his nose.

"Sweetheart, a man couldn't have a better wife—I'm more proud of you than you'll ever know."

"I'm so glad, Kevin. There was a time when I—when I wasn't sure if I could make this marriage work, but now I'm certain that we can do it together."

"Aye. There'll still be some bad times ahead, Brenna,

but we love each other enough to sustain us through them." He played with a wandering curl. "And God knows how much I'm loving you, lass," he added.

"And I you, Kevin," Brenna answered dutifully, wishing she could make it more heartfelt, but Kevin seemed satisfied, and she was grateful for that.

"I was talking with your father today," Kevin said, his eyes narrowing as he recalled the moment. "Seems he has a mind to ship the biggest cargo of horses to Argentina he's ever sent. He's hoping to have almost a hundred foals in the spring and to be shipping the whole of them to Paloma."

Brenna's heart contracted at the name, but she quickly composed herself. "Is that unusual?" she asked lightly.

Kevin shrugged. " 'Tis for your father, darlin'. He's a shrewd, tough Irishman and doesn't like to be selling himself short that way, but he's been telling me he has a promise of fifty new brood mares and three excellent stallions, all Arabian, from one of Sir William's business associates in Liverpool. I'm hoping it works out for him."

"Yes, he's always been cautious in his investments, but, from what Mama's told me, he made quite a bit of money off last year's spring holdovers at the Harvest Fair last week." She tapped Kevin playfully on the cheek. "I'm thinking he's getting cocky."

"Aye, that he is," Kevin agreed, then sobered again. "The thing I was wanting to tell you, Brenna, is that your father was talking of sending someone over with the cargo, one of his own men, since he's not quite trusting of the cargo men with that many head of horses."

"Oh?"

He nodded. " 'Twould be good pay," he said thoughtfully.

Brenna stiffened in her husband's lap. "Why, Kevin, you're not thinking . . ."

"Aye," he said, his chin jutting defensively.

"But—but you'd be gone for—months! What would I be doing without you?"

He hugged her possessively. "Ah, my darlin' love, what would *I* be doing without *you?*"

"Kevin, I—I can't let you go. Please!" she pleaded, holding his head between her hands.

"Ach, lass, you'll not be needing me. You've got your work to do, and . . ."

"But I *will* need you!" she said, slipping off his lap to stand in front of him. "You can't just leave me like that!"

Kevin was startled by her ferocity. "Darlin', 'tis only a thought," he soothed. "I didn't say 'aye' on it, yet."

She breathed easier at that. "And you won't, Kevin, until we can talk more about it?"

He nodded. "Of course, sweetheart. Now, let's be off to bed, eh? We must get you with child soon, so you'll be too busy to be thinking of me so much!" He grabbed her around the waist and carried her into their bedroom.

Kevin's talk of leaving worried Brenna, but as the weeks went by without his mentioning it again, she began to relax.

Deirdre and Benjamin were expected to come home from London for a week around the first of February. Deirdre had already written her mother with the news that she was pregnant and due in July.

"Oh, Mama, 'tis wonderful news!" Brenna said excitedly, thinking that now she would have another little niece or nephew to cuddle and hold. Then the thought came to her, bleak and unwelcome, that perhaps she would spend the rest of her life holding other people's babies and not her own.

The look passing in Brenna's eyes aroused Nora's sympathy. "Sweetheart, don't be bitter," she counseled. "Your time will come, I'm sure of it."

"Oh, but Mama, I'm letting Kevin down. I know how proud he'd be to become a father, and I'd like a child to pamper and love, but—I suppose there must be something wrong with me." Her mouth turned down.

"Now, now, that's just nonsense," Nora replied. "Perhaps the fault lies with your husband. He works so hard . . ."

"Mama, please," Brenna whispered, flushing.

"I'm sorry, Brenna. I just hate to see you so dis-spirited. Maybe, if you ask Siobhan about it?"

"Yes, Mama, I will," Brenna promised, she couldn't admit to her mother that she had already spoken with the wise woman several times, but no tonic or elixir had seemed to help. Could it be that the fault did lay with Kevin? she wondered. She quickly put aside the disloyal thought. They would just have to keep trying.

Chapter Thirty-Two

"DEIRDRE and Benjamin will be home in a week," Brenna said. It was a cold, snowy day. "Sir William has already made arrangements for a welcome-home party. We're invited, of course." She was smiling with anticipation.

Kevin's eyes narrowed, as they had a habit of doing when he was on the defensive. "Well, we'll not be going," he said firmly.

Brenna looked bewildered. "But we have to go—she's my sister!"

"Aye, that she is, but she's married to an Englishman —a member of the ton."

"And what if she is?" Brenna challenged him.

"I don't belong with the ton, Brenna. And you're my wife."

"What does that mean? That we can't go to a welcome-home party for my own kin? Kevin, don't be so foolish. I'll not hear of it."

" 'Tis you who are being foolish, Brenna," he said. "You keep forgetting you're the wife of a groomsman—a servant, for God's sake. Brenna, don't you realize, they'd all be laughing at us?"

Brenna flushed. "They would do no such thing, Kevin Ryan. Why, I've not been raised decently and tutored and sent to Paris to be laughed at by the likes of anyone!"

Kevin looked at her grimly. "You married me, Brenna, and all that changed."

"No! Just because I'm your wife, doesn't mean . . ."

He gave her a look that spoke volumes. "Aye, you can see it now, can't you?"

Brenna bit her lip. Why was Kevin so stubborn about such things? Why did he have to be so sensitive? "But

345

you can't be thinking that I wouldn't welcome my own sister?" she challenged him.

"Of course not," he soothed her. "We'll be welcoming her—in our own way, not like Markham with a bunch of hoighty-toighty young sparks and painted women."

Brenna's face fell. But I *am* one of them, she thought despairingly. And so are my sister and my mother. According to Kevin, she had given up all rights to a glittering, gay life when she had promised to make him a good wife. A good wife meant pleasing him, keeping the house reasonably clean, being friends with the wives of his friends. Brenna felt like screaming at him, but clenched her fists and kept her tongue. Quarreling did no good, she thought wearily.

"All right, Kevin, I suppose you're right. Deirdre will understand, I'm sure," she finally said.

Kevin smiled and drew her into his arms. "You're a wonder, woman. I'm the luckiest man in the world to have you for a wife."

The next morning, after Kevin had left, Brenna dressed herself warmly and rode Minx to Siobhan's cottage. The snow had stopped falling, and all around was a clean, cold blanket of white, which soothed her troubled emotions as she allowed Minx a leisurely trot down the road, between the high-piled snowdrifts. She tried not to think of Kevin's refusal to go to Markham Hall, or the way he constantly frustrated her attempts to be anything but what he felt was suitable.

She sometimes wondered if Kevin might not be consciously manipulating her. She knew that he was aware of her restlessness. Perhaps he also suspected her unhappiness. Did he resent her for her feelings? Was he bitter now, thinking that she was not really trying? He must know, after being married to her for almost two years, that it pained her to see him hurt. Was that why he put on that sad, thoughtful look when she was about to burst with her frustrations and boredom? She bit her lips, licking at their dryness. No, she couldn't blame Kevin. He tried hard to please her, and he had swallowed his pride to work for her father. Perhaps that was what irritated him most.

Well, she thought briskly, there was nothing to be done about that. She had made friends with some of the other women, even though they drove her crazy with their silly chatter. She tolerated them and saw the satisfaction in their eyes when they could run home and brag to their husbands that they'd had tea with the employer's daughter.

As Brenna neared Siobhan's cottage, she noticed someone had thoughtfully shoveled a path to the door.

Siobhan had a lot of friends, Brenna thought, and she certainly wasn't gentry. Perhaps, as one got older, wealth and prestige didn't matter so much. She hoped it was so for Kevin's sake.

"Siobhan, how are you this morning?" Brenna asked. The woman was sitting in a chair close to the fire with a quilt tucked about her legs.

" 'Tis my bones bothering me again," she replied. "This cold weather seems to have an effect on them, and I can't find any remedy that relieves the pain satisfactorily." She shrugged. "I suppose I'm getting older."

Brenna smiled. "You have never told me how old you really are."

" 'Tis a dark and dismal secret," Siobhan replied. "Now don't you be pressing me about that, lass. How are you?"

"Well enough. 'Tis awfully bitter outside." Brenna took off her outer garments and stood rubbing her hands together by the fire. "Ach, I'm beginning to hate the winter!"

"Well, spring's not far away," Siobhan remarked. " 'Twill be no time at all and the grass'll be greening up and the birds will come out and sing to make the angels dance."

"Ah, seems like 'twill never happen when I look out and see that white." Brenna picked up the kettle and poured two cups of steaming tea. "Here. This will warm us up."

They were drinking companionably when someone knocked on the door. Brenna opened it to reveal a middle-aged man wearing a felt hat pulled low about his ears to keep out the cold, and a thick, woolen scarf wound about his throat so that she could barely make out his features. He was dressed in a shabby coat and looked surprised to see Brenna standing there. She did not know the man, so she held the door cautiously.

"I come to speak to the old woman," he said roughly. "I heard from someone as how she can be healing sick and such."

"Yes, she is here," Brenna said. She hesitated, then swung the door wide. "Come in, out of the cold."

The man took a stool close to the fire, his eyes shifting from Brenna to Siobhan.

"Are you in trouble?" the older woman asked him. She was watching him alertly, noting that he did not take off his hat.

His face seemed to pinch together, then sharpen. "Not me," he answered her. " 'Tis a friend of mine."

"I see; and—where is he?"

"He couldn't be coming with me. He can't be traveling himself, for he's been hurt—shot in the leg—while poaching, ma'am." The man took off his hat now, revealing shaggy brown hair badly in need of a cutting. He punched at his hat absently. "Awful painful 'tis, mistress, and the poor man's been wailing something fierce. I near went out of me wits searching down someone to take out the ball, but no one could help, 'cept they told me about how good you are with the medicinals."

"Shot in the leg?" Siobhan questioned. "How long ago was this?"

"Early this morning, mistress. We were walking close to the road and saw a fenceful of clucking chickens near a farmhouse. We didn't think the owner would mind helping two poor, starving fellows, so Timmy—that's my friend—and me, we went right ahead and grabbed one of those birds. But the owner—seems he wasn't too keen on losing any poultry, so he up and shot us as we were running off. Got Timmy clean through the muscle, I'm thinking."

Siobhan threw off the blanket. "Where is your friend?"

"I put him up in a little shack about four miles into

the woods. 'Tisn't far, mistress, except with this snow, it makes traveling a mite difficult through the trees. Do you have a horse, ma'am?"

"Aye, we can take Minx," Brenna said, standing up to put on her coat and scarf.

The man looked doubtful. "We'll not be taking the lass, will we?"

Siobhan gave him a long look. "The lass knows nearly as much as I do about healing the sick, Mr? . . ."

"Liam Donahue, ma'am."

"Well, then, Mr. Donahue, Mrs. Ryan is my assistant. If I'm to take a shot from a man's leg, it may prove a dangerous operation, and I'll be needing help. Do you have blankets with you?"

He shook his head.

Siobhan quickly told Brenna what to pack. Ten minutes later, the girl and the old woman were sitting on Minx's back, while the man walked ahead of them, leading the way.

"The poor man doesn't even have a horse," Brenna whispered sympathetically. "Do you think he's been telling us the whole truth?"

Siobhan shook her head. "I'm not knowing what to believe, lass, but if someone's hurt, 'tis our duty to try and do our best by him. Let's hope Mr. Donahue had the foresight to light a fire before he came to fetch us." Siobhan shivered in the saddle, and Brenna knew her leg must be paining her.

It took the better part of an hour to locate the small shed among a copse of denuded trees. There was no smoke coming from the chimney, and Brenna could hear Siobhan mumbling discontentedly beneath her breath. They dismounted and tied Minx to a sapling.

"You'd best make yourself useful, Mr. Donahue, and find some dry sticks for a fire. I daresay your friend will more likely freeze to death than meet his end from a farmer's bullet." Siobhan said sharply.

After a moment's indecision, the man went off to do as she asked.

"I'm not sure I'm trusting that man," Brenna said in a

low voice as they entered the shed; but her distrust was forgotten as she looked in horror at the poor soul laid out on the broken floor of the building. He was shivering violently and mumbling disjointed phrases. His boots were wet and freezing in the cold air, and down one leg of his breeches the material had darkened and stiffened from congealed blood.

Brenna hurried to bring in the blankets she had brought along. "Blessed Mary, this poor man looks as though he's half-dead already!" Brenna said worriedly. With Siobhan's help, she set about rolling the man onto a blanket close to the fireplace, which they would soon have burning brightly, if Mr. Donahue would hurry up. They tucked another blanket tightly about his chest and throat, and Brenna opened the heavy burlap bag which contained Siobhan's herbs and powders.

"I've got to be using a knife to get this boot off. 'Tis frozen onto his foot here," Siobhan said. "Hold his leg above the knee there so that I can get some balance on it."

Siobhan worked with the knife, slowly and painfully, against the frozen leather. By the time they had the boot off, Donahue was back with a stack of wood, which he threw into the fireplace and lit into a meager fire. The warmth helped Siobhan to work the boot free. She cut the material of his trousers straight up the leg to mid-thigh and spread the two halves. The wound was in the calf muscle.

"Lucky he is that the ball didn't shatter his shinbone," Siobhan said with some satisfaction. "I'm thinking it shouldn't be too difficult to get the ball out, but the poor lad looks nearly dead from exhaustion and starvation." She looked up at Donahue questioningly. "How long have you been traveling in the open?"

"Week—ten days. I'm not that sure anymore."

"What's the lad's name?" Brenna asked, pulling his hat from his head and rubbing the hair back with gentle hands.

"Timmy O'Brien, ma'am. He and I, we've been to-gether a good while now. I'm fond of the boy."

"Well, we'll be doing our best, Mr. Donahue, but you should be keeping him indoors where 'tis warm for a while. Do you have no friends who could be putting you up?" Siobhan asked.

He shook his head. "We've been trying to make our way to Cork, ma'am, hoping to catch a ship bound for America. We're that sick of Ireland and wanting to make a new life for ourselves."

"I see." Siobhan turned to Brenna and gestured toward a shallow basin. "Please fill this with snow, and put it near the fire so it will melt," she ordered. "I'll be needing warm water."

Brenna hurried outside, gathering the clean, white snow in a huge mound, which filled the basin. In the cold, crisp air, she thought she heard the distant barking of hounds. A foolish time to be hunting for foxes, she thought, and scurried back into the warm shed.

Siobhan probed and found the gunshot with little trouble, although the wound started to bleed afresh. She removed the small piece of iron and flung it to one of the walls. Brenna had to apply wet strips of linen to cleanse the wound while Siobhan mixed a few herbs with water to make a poultice.

The young man groaned and turned his head feverishly, opening his eyes now and then and looking without recognition about the room. Anxiously watching the young man's face, Donahue had taken his hand and was patting it awkwardly. Senseless words and phrases passed the boy's lips, as Siobhan applied the poultice and dressed the wound with clean bandages.

"Liam . . . damned bastards, can't shake them . . . how much longer?" Words tumbled slowly from O'Brien in his delirium.

"There now," Siobhan, drawing the dirty trouser leg down over the covered wound, said with satisfaction. "His leg'll be mending fine now, but I'm still worried about your friend getting enough food to sustain him while he's healing."

"No need to worry," Donahue said swiftly. He stood up and shuffled over to the fire, standing silently.

Brenna pressed a cool cloth to the young man's hot forehead. "Well, you can't be staying here," she began. "He's got to have food and warmth—and a decent bed to sleep in."

"Perhaps old Mr. Cavendish would have a room to spare," Siobhan suggested. "Aye, I'd think he'd be glad of the company for a few days. At least that would give the lad time to rest."

Donahue seemed interested now. "Where is this place?"

"Mr. Cavendish lives about six miles from here. We'll need another horse to take the lad."

"We've got a horse," Donahue growled in a low, menacing voice.

Brenna started back in alarm. "But that's my horse, Mr. Donahue. Siobhan and I can go back and bring another with us for you and your friend."

"All right, ladies." The man seemed to straighten up for the first time. His eyes shifted between the two of them, settling finally on Siobhan with a warning look. "We can dispense with all this fine, genteel conversation now. You've fixed the lad's leg, and now we'll have to be going."

"But how . . ."

"Shut up, lass! We'll be taking your strong horse out there. She'll lead us to this Mr. Cavendish for food and shelter. I'm sure you ladies can make your way back to your cottage with no trouble."

Brenna was more puzzled than alarmed. "What do you mean? Why won't you let us go and get help?"

He smiled for the first time—it was not a pleasant smile. "You ladies have fine hearts for healing, but a mite too stupid and trusting," he said. "Aye, you swallowed that story easier than oysters," he laughed.

"You mean it wasn't a farmer who shot . . ." Brenna began.

"No farmer carries shot that big, lass," the man interrupted. "No, tis the British patrol that are after us, ladies." He seemed to enjoy their frightened looks. "Aye, I thought that'd change things around."

"Why—why is the patrol after you?"

"Lass, you're a mite too nosy for your own good." Donahue pointed to one of the walls. "Now you two ladies just sit together over there against the wall, and I'll be tying you up. Wouldn't want you to be running loose and maybe meet that patrol. You might have a notion to tell them all about me and O'Brien here." As the two women moved obediently against the wall, Donahue took some rope, which had been looped around his waist, and hunkered down beside them to tie their hands and feet. "Shame I don't have time to be getting a little fun out of you," he chuckled, taking a moment to chuck Brenna under the chin. "Jesus, 'tis been a long time since I've had me a nice roll." He looked at her regretfully.

"But—you can't just be leaving us!" Siobhan said. "We helped you!"

He shook his head. "'Tis a heaving shame, I know, ma'am, but there's nothing for it, you see." He sighed with regret and took out a dirty handkerchief, ripping it up the middle to make two gags.

When Brenna protested, she received a quick swipe against the side of her head, which effectively silenced her. Donahue finished quickly and stood back to examine his handiwork with a strangely pleased air. "You look like two trussed chickens." He shook his head once more. "'Tis a real shame, it is."

Brenna slumped against the wall, willing the horrible man to be gone. How could he leave them here without even the means to free themselves. She glanced at the fire. It would not burn much longer with the little wood remaining. Soon the cold would begin to seep in again. Brenna felt a shiver of fear creep down her back.

"Good-bye, ladies. Sorry to leave you, but I've got to be thinking about my own skin." Donahue picked up the younger man, tucking the blankets about him with absurd gentleness, and strode out the door, leaving it open to the cold wind.

Tears of frustration and fear squeezed from Brenna's eyes and trickled cold and burning over her reddened cheeks. She turned her head and saw Siobhan's dark, understanding eyes. Brenna leaned against the wall to wait—but for what? she agonized. No one would find them; no one would even miss them until Kevin came home that evening. She guessed it was now close to noon, but she couldn't be sure. That left at least six hours before Kevin would miss her, plus another hour before he got worried enough to investigate. Of course, he would go first to Siobhan's cottage, but it would be dark by then and difficult for him to follow their tracks. Brenna's head drooped forward in hopelessness. If they weren't found today, they would freeze to death. She looked worriedly to Siobhan; the woman would be stiff with pain in another hour or two.

Brenna strained against the rope that was tied around her ankles, moving her feet forward, back, and sideways to see if there was any give. Nothing. Her wrists were bound behind her back, and she couldn't budge them an inch. But strangely, it was the gag which bothered her most for she felt like retching from the sweaty taste of dirt in her mouth. Like two trussed chickens, she thought, remembering Donahue's words, and cursed him in her mind.

The door banged on its hinges as a sudden gust of chilling wind swirled about the room, bringing in a drift of snow which sprayed the fire and caused it to smoke. If it got too bad, they would begin to cough, and that thought, coupled with the gag in her mouth, made her even more nervous.

With frustration tensing every muscle, Brenna made herself lean back against the wall and close her eyes, following Siobhan's example. It seemed like hours passed before the faint sound of barking reached her ears; she recalled having heard it before. She stiffened and sat up straight. Could a hunting party possibly be coming this way? Excitement tingled through her and she leaned sideways to nudge Siobhan. Siobhan listened, then nodded her head vigorously.

The barking seemed to grow stronger, then, just as suddenly, veered away and started to become fainter.

Desperately; Brenna pulled at her bonds. They mustn't go the other way!

Beside her Siobhan was struggling too, but to no avail. Exhausted, they both panicked against the gags and fought for breath. The gag in Brenna's mouth frightened her enough to keep her still, for it was triply hard to catch a breath when she was active. She could hear Siobhan gasping beside her.

Suddenly, the barking seemed to increase in volume and tempo, as though the frenzied hounds were quite close. Once more, they listened and this time they could tell the dogs were coming their way. Tears spilled down Brenna's cheeks. Oh God, they would be found after all!

Before they knew it, a half-dozen hounds were leaping through the open door, growling viciously as they circled their captive prizes. Brenna gazed fearfully at the slavering jaws and the bright eyes, thinking for one dreadful moment that they would tear her to pieces. One of the hounds stepped forward and nosed her ankles, barking excitedly when he smelled at the rope.

That was it! The hounds must be with the British patrol, Brenna thought. They were smelling Donahue's scent. She forced herself to relax. If either she or Siobhan made an untoward move, the hounds might leap at them.

Fortunately, they hadn't long to wait before they heard horses pulling up outside the house.

"Come out, Donahue!" a voice yelled.

The hounds bayed in a frenzy at their masters' voices, and one dog ran to the door, barking and wagging its tail. Brenna could hear the cautious crunch of snow as boots made their way to the shack. The muzzle of a gun slipped around the door jamb, and Brenna froze once again in terror. Then a man in a scarlet coat stepped in. The features of his round, ruddy visage seemed to freeze in a comical expression of surprise when he saw what the hounds had found.

"What the bloody hell! Lieutenant Coleman! It's a pair of blooming women, sir! They're tied up, sir!"

A short, puffing officer followed him in, then two other soldiers. "By God," the lieutenant said, "you're right,

Lark. It is a pair of women—but what the deuce—" He signaled to his men and they hurried to untie them.

"Oh, thank you, sir. You don't know—you can't imagine how—" Brenna babbled incoherently.

"Who did this?" the officer cut in.

"A man named Liam Donahue," Siobhan answered, her voice breaking. "They call me Siobhan, and this is Mrs. Ryan. We look after the sick people in this district. Mr. Donahue came to the door this morning, begging that we come help his friend—a young lad named Timmy O'Brien, who'd been shot in the leg for poaching."

"Poaching, eh? And you believed him?"

Siobhan looked surprised. "Of course. No one has ever lied to us before."

The lieutenant shook his head, as though amazed at their stupidity.

Brenna felt her anger beginning to flare. "How could we know he was some sort of fugitive? He was Irish and poorly dressed, like most of us around here." Her last words were uttered with a sarcastic note.

The lieutenant looked her up and down. "Mrs. Ryan, isn't it? Well, Mrs. Ryan, might I remind you that your poor Irishman brought you here under false circumstances and, I presume after you'd helped him, he tied you up without giving a damn if you were rescued or not!"

Brenna reddened. "I wasn't meaning to defend the man, sir."

"Well, you bloody well sounded like it!" the officer continued. He turned and ordered one of his men to bring the horses around. "Now, ladies, my men and I will escort you to your homes. On the way, I would appreciate you giving us any information which might aid us in our search for them."

"Did they escape from jail?" Brenna asked curiously.

The officer nodded as he swung her up behind him on his horse.

"But—what did they do? That young man, O'Brien, looked as gentle as a calf, and—"

"That gentle calf is a Fenian, Mrs. Ryan. He has killed

356

two British officers and robbed a small shop in Dublin—took nearly a hundred pounds, though I don't know what in hell they've done with it." He looked around at Brenna's blanched face. "Liam Donahue was in prison for killing the shopkeeper and raping his daughter. He wounded three men during their escape."

"God and Saint Patrick!" Brenna whispered in awe. She realized they were lucky to have come out of it with their lives.

"Yes, so you see, Mrs. Ryan, you should be a little more careful before you go running off to help a stranger."

She hurriedly told the lieutenant that the two men had gone in the direction of Mr. Cavendish's cabin. She described the cabin and her horse, worried lest something might happen to the kind old man or to Minx.

"How long ago did they leave you?"

"I'm not sure—it seemed like hours before you arrived, but I suppose it couldn't have been much more than an hour—two at the most. We took a ball out of O'Brien's leg; he was feverish and still unconscious when Donahue took him on my horse. I cannot imagine them getting far like that."

"Hmmm. Donahue probably was hoping you'd not be found for a few hours, giving him time to hole up at this Cavendish's cabin and to get some food and rest. Then where was he going—did he say?"

Brenna thought a moment.

"Cork!" Siobhan broke in. "Aye, he said he was on his way to Cork to gain passage on a ship to America."

"Ah, and that's what they're going to do with that money!" The lieutenant seemed suddenly pleased. "Well, now you two have helped us a great deal today, and I thank you."

"Thank you for rescuing us," Siobhan said.

Although she would have stayed with Siobhan at the cottage, the lieutenant insisted on taking Brenna safely home. They rode into the Kildare farm, and Brenna's heart sank when she saw Kevin outside the stables. She had hoped to avoid long explanations, but resigned herself to an afternoon of questioning. It made the situation no better when her father stepped out onto the porch and, seeing his daughter in the company of British soldiers, rushed out to meet them. Brenna felt her father's arms lifting her off the horse, and she took a deep breath before facing him. Behind her, she could hear Kevin running up, calling her name.

"Brenna, Holy Virgin, what has happened!"

"Everything is all right, Kevin," she answered as he came up to put his arms protectively around her. "The lieutenant can explain better than I."

Chapter Thirty-Three

"DAMMIT, you could have been killed today. All because
you have to go and help that old woman with her charity
cases. No more of it, do you hear? I'll not have you waltz-
ing about the countryside inviting danger. Nor will I listen
to your father badgering me about the liberties I give
you!" Kildare had already accused Kevin of not keeping
a tight enough rein on his own wife and nearly getting her
killed because of it; Kevin had retaliated with bitter words
of his own which could easily have gotten him fired if
Brenna hadn't intervened.

"Kevin, you can't do that to me!" Brenna protested.
"I—know that today things got out of hand, but I'll be
promising that it wouldn't happen again! I . . ."

"Aye, 'twon't happen again, because you'll not be going
anywhere with Siobhan again!" Kevin reiterated, pacing
up and down the room, his brow deeply furrowed. "I'll
not have your father throwing this up to me again!"

Brenna was flushed and breathless from her anger.
"No, Kevin, I can't agree! What will I do, if you won't
let me continue helping Siobhan?"

Kevin looked for a moment as though he might lash
out at her, but instead took a deep breath and calmed
himself. "Brenna, be a wife to me," he said in a pleading
tone. "Give us a child."

She whitened at this unexpected attack. "Kevin, you're
not being fair," she accused him. "I'd love to be giving
you a child, you know that. But I can't help it that I'm
not yet pregnant."

Kevin opened his mouth, then closed it, as though he
were afraid to say more. "Let's not be talking about it,"
he said. "I'm sorry I mentioned it. But I'll still not be
having you go back with Siobhan. Your father . . ."

"My father shouldn't be able to control our lives!"
Brenna fought back. "Why do you let him make you an-

gry? You and I are husband and wife—he can't be changing that."

"Aye, but he'd like to," Kevin said darkly. "If it were in his power, he'd call on the Holy Father himself to get you a divorce!"

"Kevin!" Brenna was aghast at the depth of his bitterness.

"Aye, 'tis true enough, Brenna. It sticks in your father's gullet that you married me."

"Stop it! Stop it!" Brenna interrupted angrily. "I'm sick of it, do you hear? Why, I'm thinking you enjoy making us miserable by harping about him so often. Kevin, you've got to be a man."

"Like Tyrone Kildare? I'm telling you, he'd do anything to separate us. In the matter of your sister coming home—don't I know he came here to tell you himself about the party? Aye, he wanted you to go and not me. I'm not stupid, Brenna."

"Oh, Kevin, 'tis blind you are if you can't see that I'm not doing things for my father, but for you."

" 'Tis not for me that you wanted to work with Siobhan."

She flushed. "I—I—"

"Aye, now you're seeing the truth of the matter. 'Tis not for me or your father, but for yourself, Brenna," he snapped.

"If I were doing for myself, I would surely be going to the party for my sister," she replied angrily.

He looked at her grimly. "I'd thought we'd settled this, Brenna."

" 'Tis not settled, Kevin. You won't let it be settled."

"We did decide . . ."

"*You* decided!" she declared.

"Oh?"

"Yes, *you* decided that I shouldn't be going because *you* wouldn't fit in!" she blurted out. Instantly, she wished she hadn't said the words.

The red in Kevin's face blotted out his freckles. "And so you're wanting to go now, is it?" He walked to the door and opened it. "Well, you'll not be going, Brenna."

"I'll go if I want to," she said hotly.

"Then go, damn you! Go and simper and be coy and flirt with all the gallants! Aye, that's your place, isn't it? Isn't it!" He slammed out.

Quickly, she opened the door and saw him hurrying up the path. "You and my father!" she yelled after him, uncaring that she sounded like some harping old hoyden. "You'd like to tear me into little pieces and divvy me up between the two of you! It's hateful and mean and wicked of you—and I won't be having it, Kevin Ryan!"

Her words seemed to spur him to a swifter pace toward the haven of the stables. Brenna kicked at the doorpost in her frustration. She couldn't have cared less that Bridget Simmons, just returning from the outhouse, avidly watched the display of marital spatting to glean information for use at the next tea.

Brenna hated her husband at that moment. Why did he force her into this position—making her choose between her family and him? God, why did he do that to her?

After a few minutes, the cold and her own exhaustion began to take hold of her. Wearily, she closed the door and went in to sit at the kitchen table. She supposed she could swallow her pride and ask his forgiveness when he returned home later in the day, but dammit, she wanted to go to that party. It was such a small thing to ask really —one night of gaiety in exchange for his forbidding her to work with Siobhan. Why must she give up everything without getting something in return?

"I will go, Kevin Ryan," she said aloud to the empty room. "I've been a good wife—I've tried to do everything your way, but I will go to that party. I will!"

The next few days were miserable for Brenna. There were many times she almost gave in to her husband, but then she would strengthen her resolve: Kevin was not going to make her feel guilty this time. He seldom spoke to her, except at meals, and at night they slept on separate sides of the bed. It was worse that Brenna had nothing to occupy her time during the day. She had managed to send a note to Siobhan, explaining, without too much

361

detail, that she would not be coming to see her for a while. She refused to think that Kevin would keep to his word forever.

Nora noticed her daughter's sullen expression when Brenna came up to the house to help alter a gown for the party, but wisely refrained from asking questions. Unlike her husband, she thought it prudent to stay out of her children's marital problems. She could only pray that sometime soon, Brenna and Kevin would be blessed with a child.

On the evening of the party, her parents came to pick up Brenna at the cottage. Tyrone Kildare was elegantly dressed in a black frock coat and trousers, his snow-white, pleated shirtfront shown off to best advantage by the wide, navy silk cravat, pierced by his diamond stickpin. As Brenna opened the door at his knock, she thought she had never seen her father looking so handsome. Fearing that an argument between Kevin and her father might spoil the evening, Brenna quickly snatched her silver gauze shawl and hurried her good-bye.

"Good night, Kevin," she said softly, feeling a pang of guilt.

"Good night," he answered woodenly, staring into the fire.

"I won't be late."

He didn't answer.

With a small sigh, Brenna took her father's arm. As she climbed into the coach, her mother was talking animatedly about seeing Dierdre again and how well she looked for her first pregnancy. Nora, herself, looked very well, Brenna thought fondly. Her mother was wearing a deep mauve gown of shot silk, smartly tailored to her still-handsome figure. Brenna looked down at her own gown of light-blue satin, its billowing yards of skirt material falling softly to touch the toes of her high-heeled, satin slippers.

Soon Brenna forgot about her guilt and became confident that the rift with Kevin could be mended. And oh! she so wanted to go to a real party! She and Kevin had his friends over occasionally for dinner, but this was going to be a grand celebration attended by gorgeously dressed women wearing French perfumes and by men who wouldn't constantly try to remind her of her place as the wife of a groomsman. For the first time in years, she felt elegant and beautiful with her hair done so elaborately. God help her, but she felt alive and thrilled at the sound of music and laughter.

As they entered the house and went up to be announced, Deirdre hurried to greet them, her face pink. It was true that pregnancy suited her. She kissed her parents and took Brenna's hands, pulling her into the middle of the room to introduce her to friends. The room was alive with brilliant pinks, blues, greens, rich laughter, vivid perfumes, all of which Brenna tried determinedly to retain for later memories. She thought of Kevin sitting at home, and felt another twinge of guilt, but it had been his own choice not to come.

"Oh, I'm so glad you were able to attend, Brenna!" Deirdre said happily, squeezing her sister's hand. "I am sorry that Kevin couldn't come—I mean I suppose I understand his feelings about coming here." She tried to keep the look of pity out of her eyes. "And we'll be seeing him soon, for Mama's invited me down for tea tomorrow, and I'll waddle over to the stables." She laughed at her deliberate reference to her pregnancy.

"You know Kevin," Brenna said lamely. "But he—he wanted me to come, of course." She hoped Dierdre couldn't discern the lie.

Names and faces filed past her, hands grabbed hers, lips kissed her wrists. Brenna smiled and laughed and talked—though never about her own way of life—and she never once let herself admit it was because she was ashamed.

She danced and drank punch. Once she caught her father looking at her and smiling with triumphant pride, but she was too happy to worry about her father and Kevin's silly feud. Let her father think he'd scored a triumph tonight—tomorrow she would be Brenna Ryan again, loving wife to her husband. But that was tomorrow and she didn't want tonight to stop yet. Not yet.

Then, as she was sipping a third glass of champagne and toasting the happy couple, her gaze moved casually about the room and was captured by laughing, devilish blue eyes that seemed to mesmerize her across the length of the floor. As she started in recognition, a few drops of champagne spilled out of her glass.

She watched helplessly as Benjamin went up to Rory Adair and patted him on the back in friendly fashion. They shook hands and Benjamin brought him into the room to introduce him to those he didn't know.

"You weren't at the wedding to kiss the blushing bride, old man," Benjamin said jokingly as he led Rory to his wife. "So now you'd best do your duty."

Rory smiled and kissed Deirdre, congratulating her; she twinkled at the attention. Brenna watched him, so tall and handsome—and alive—that everyone else in the room seemed to pale into insignificance. In his uniform, with high, spit-polished, black boots and a dress sword at his hip, he looked like a fairy-tale prince in a storybook. All the unmarried women's eyes fastened on the fascinating tall Irishman with the charming laugh.

Brenna heard one such young lady beside her whispering about how brave young Adair had proven himself in India. Some citation or medal . . .

Brenna pressed a hand to her temple and tore her eyes away from the handsome figure that brought back too many memories. It seemed only like yesterday that she had stood in this same room and watched Rory Adair flirting with all the young ladies. How long ago was that—had she really been sixteen?

Benjamin led Rory about the room, presenting him to giggling girls and jovial young officers. Brenna knew that very soon they would come around to her. Putting the champagne glass down on a nearby table, she willed her hands not to tremble. She must get through this without making a fool of herself.

"Ah, and here is our own Brenna," Benjamin said with a fondly teasing note to his voice. "You see, Rory, I married her sister with an eye out for this beauty, in case the other one didn't suit me." He kissed her lightly. "You see what privileges a brother-in-law has!"

"I claim the same privilege," Rory laughed and bent to kiss her softly.

Brenna felt the heat in her cheeks and pushed him away lightly. "Why, Rory Adair," she said with an engaging smile, " 'tis so good to see you again." She tried to ignore the racing pulse in her throat.

His admiration for her poise showed in his eyes. "Aye, you've finally grown up, Brenna."

"Thank you—but you have hardly changed at all," she said quietly after Benjamin had gone to speak with someone.

"And just what is that supposed to mean?" Rory asked, his eyes twinkling as they looked into hers.

"You're the same Rory, flirting with the women, drinking with the men, boasting of brave deeds of honor."

Rory laughed. "You have accurately stripped away all my disguises," he claimed, and then in a huskier voice, "God, 'tis so good to see you, Brenna. You know you're still the most beautiful woman I've ever seen—and I've seen a good many." He took a breath. "Aye, many's the time I looked at another woman and thought what a poor second she would come up to Brenna Kildare."

"Brenna Ryan," she corrected, keeping her tone light, although her heart seemed to constrict in her chest.

His mouth tightened, and his eyes hardened. "Aye, so I've heard." His gaze raked her face. "You didn't wait long, did you, Brenna?"

Her pulse raced, her face grew hotter, and her eyes began sliding away from his, as though he had accused her of a wrong. "No," she finally managed to say steadily.

"Of all the men you could have had, Brenna . . ." Rory began, then stopped, suddenly aware of her distress. "Come and dance with me?" he asked.

She nodded, for she was aware of several pairs of eyes fastened on them in frank curiosity. With relief, she allowed Rory to masterfully lead her through a waltz.

When the music stopped, Rory led her to a window

seat. "May I get you a glass of champagne?" he asked. "You look a trifle flushed, dear heart."

The endearment caressed and pained her, and she wondered, in panic, where her parents were, or her sister, or even a new partner for the next dance. She couldn't be left alone with Rory for long. She looked hopelessly for help. When Rory returned with the champagne, he sat down confidently beside her, his leg brushing her skirt.

"Hadn't you ought to be circulating?" she asked him quickly. "I mean, I feel rather silly monopolizing all your time when there are so many young ladies who . . ."

"I don't give a damn about them. I told you, I know I'm with the most beautiful woman right here, and Rory Adair is interested only in the best." He smiled again and let his eyes drop to her bosom in a caressing gaze.

"Well, I am flattered," she began, taking a nervous sip from her glass. After a moment she continued. "Tell me about your exploits in the military." She was too aware of his stare sliding over her neck and throat, delving into the low neckline of her bodice.

He shrugged. "The usual."

"Not from what I've heard," she said, forcing the subject. "Your bravery has been spoken of by many of the young ladies, and . . ."

He leaned forward, and his breath touched her neck, in that old way he had of arousing her senses. "Let's not be talking of me, darlin'," he whispered. "I want to hear about you."

"Me?" Brenna could feel her skin tingle in response to his warm breath on her shoulder. Even the tips of her breasts had hardened as her bosom rose and fell under his deliberate scrutiny. "There is not much to be telling," she got out.

He stood up, obviously aware of her discomposure and the reason for it. "Come with me, Brenna," he commanded in a low tone.

"No, I shouldn't, Rory."

"Just for a moment," he urged. "I have something for you—a present."

" 'Tis too cold to walk outside," she said, balking when she realized he was leading her toward the archway out of the ballroom.

"Just for a moment," he repeated.

Brenna looked back at the glittering throng, expecting everyone to be watching them with knowledgeable looks, but no one seemed to notice their departure. Even her father was deep in conversation with Sir William. She looked back to Rory, who was pulling her along gently toward the library.

Once in the library, with its old, carved paneling and huge, blazing fire, he pushed the door closed with his foot and reached down to pick up her cloak.

"You see, I had this all planned." He was laughing at her, but there was a tender, aroused look in his eyes. He put the cloak about her shoulders and led her through the double doors to the outdoors, where the chill made vaporous clouds of their breath.

"What are you doing?" she asked nervously. "Abducting me?"

He laughed again. "You wound me, Brenna. Do you really distrust me so?" Then, he pulled her around a design of shrubbery to where a servant was holding a horse, which stamped on the ground and neighed as she came into view.

"Minx!" Brenna exclaimed in wonder. "Minx—but how . . ."

"Lieutenant Coleman and I ran into each other when I came off the ship at Cork. He—ah—told me about your dangerous little episode. He snatched the two bastards on the docks and found your Minx tied in front of a tavern. Naturally, I took the opportunity to take her off Coleman's hands. It saved him a trip, and I didn't have to rent a horse to ride up here."

"Minx!" Brenna rubbed the soft nose and kissed it happily. "My poor dear, I'd forgotten all about you—how could I?" The horse whinnied gently.

"The boy had best be taking her back where it's warm," Rory suggested. Reluctantly Brenna allowed the servant to take the horse to the stables.

"Oh, Rory!" Brenna reached up to hug him in her joy and gratitude.

But Rory caught her waist and pressed her hard against him, bringing his mouth down to hers. His lips artfully molded and twisted hers until they parted under the pressure and his tongue invaded her mouth. The feeling filled her down to her toes, and she clung to him for one selfish moment, letting her hands steal softly up to his hair. The hard length of his body pressed against hers and she shivered as much from excitement as from the cold. Then he released her regretfully and led her back into the library.

With diamond-bright tears on her lashes, Brenna swept quickly towards the closed door; but he caught her hand and turned her around, pressing her wrists against the door.

"Rory . . ."

"Don't say anything, Brenna," he whispered and kissed her again. "Brenna, Brenna," he murmured, his lips traveling from her mouth to her throat.

Brenna arched her head back against the door, offering the paleness of her throat to his loving mouth. Her breasts heaved and her thighs trembled against his. Rory, she thought, oh Rory! But it was the last cry of her senses, the last, desperate selfish cry, before cold reason swept over her. How could she, a married woman, permit this sort of behavior. Horror, shame, and self-loathing filled her as she began to pummel at his chest.

"Get away!"

Through his own sensual trance, Rory heard the change in her voice, and he took his mouth away, but still he held her against the door.

"Please, Rory, don't."

A jaunty eyebrow cocked over one eye, and a wheedling smile spread across his face. "Brenna, darlin', I'm not doing anything you don't want—that you weren't asking me for!"

"No, Rory, I'm married."

"Not much of a marriage," Rory said confidently, "when your eyes could invite me like they did. If your own husband can't satisfy that beautiful, sensual wildness in you, Brenna, then I can!"

"Rory, I'll hear no such sinful talk!" Brenna exclaimed.

"Dammit, how can it be sinful, Brenna, when we both want it so badly!" Rory countered. "I'm a soldier, remember? And sometimes the rules just don't apply."

"But here they do!" she said in agony. "There's Kevin to consider."

"Kevin be damned!" Rory cursed in growing frustration. "He can't give you what I can, Brenna. Do your eyes sparkle so when he caresses you?"

"Please, Rory, don't force me to—"

"—to look at yourself, Brenna? To see the truth?"

She shook her head. "You don't understand. Kevin loves me. He was willing to marry me when you left."

"Willing to marry you! God and Saint Patrick, any man in his right mind would be willing to marry you. You didn't have to marry a damned servant."

Stunned, Brenna stared at him. "He's not a servant! And he did marry me when you weren't interested."

"Brenna, I'm not a marrying man. I'm a soldier, an adventurer—you could never have been happy with me."

"You never asked me." She stopped, realizing the argument was pointless.

"Brenna, for the Lord's sake, do you honestly know your own feelings? Listen—if you loved me, you wouldn't have gone and married Kevin the way you did, now would you? You and I have a different kind of attraction."

Brenna knew what he meant and flushed. "All right, I don't love you, Rory Adair—'twas just a childish infatuation."

"And you don't love your husband either."

" 'Tis none of your business," she said. Then she shivered and looked away, trembling all over now. She felt confused and jumbled, knowing only that she must get away from Rory and back to Kevin—Kevin, who loved her honestly, Kevin, her husband.

"Rory, please," she whispered, her defiance gone.

369

"Brenna, why make yourself so miserable?" he questioned as he bent over to kiss her.

"No, Rory, I can't," she said quietly.

But Rory didn't want to listen; he was kissing her again. She twisted out of his arms and backed away from the door toward the center of the room. She must keep some distance between them.

"Rory, let me go," she whispered, and then, gently pleading, "Let me go."

Her head bowed, and her shoulders shook with her sobs. Instantly, Rory went to her, this time to comfort her, bringing her head against his chest.

"Poor little girl," he whispered, surprising her with the sudden softness in his tone. "I'm sorry, Brenna, truly sorry."

Neither of them heard the door to the library opening, nor, for a moment, did they realize that another young couple saw them standing there in an embrace.

Chapter Thirty-Four

THE rest of the evening was nightmarish for Brenna. The two guests had rushed back to the ballroom immediately, tittering with delicious gossip about the compromising tête-á-tête they had just witnessed. The next thing she had seen was her parents' faces, looking at her in stunned disbelief and disappointment.

"Mr. Kildare, please allow me to explain," Rory began, but Kildare gave him no time. He pushed the young man rudely aside and took his daughter's hand. Without a word, he ushered her behind her mother into their carriage after making their excuses to Sir William.

On the way home, her father roared about the blow to his pride. "To think that my own daughter could behave this way. It wasn't bad enough that you had to run off and marry that—that underling. God Almighty, did you have to go and make a spectacle of yourself with that womanizer, Rory Adair? Lass, you don't have any sense."

Brenna stared stonily out the window. "I did nothing wrong with Rory. He had brought Minx back to me."

"*Nothing wrong!* Why, you should never have been alone in the library with Rory Adair. Whatever possessed you?"

"Papa, please, I told you he brought me my horse."

"And that's why he was holding you in the library?"

Brenna could not meet her father's eyes. "No, he—he wanted to know why I married Kevin, and . . ."

"Well at least the lad knew the right question, though God knows, I've been wondering about the answer myself!"

"Tyrone, please, can't you see that Brenna feels terrible enough?" Nora put in softly. "Between you and Kevin—she doesn't know where to turn. Leave her alone. She's been through enough humiliation tonight." Nora

371

patted his shoulder. "Besides, you'll only be bringing on another attack if you're not careful."

At that, Kildare settled back reluctantly in his seat, though the anger was still plain on his face. His little outbursts continued sporadically until the coach pulled up to Brenna's cottage.

"Will you be telling your husband what happened?" her father demanded. "Or will you be leaving that to me?"

"Tyrone, you've no right."

"I'll tell him, Papa," Brenna said quietly. "I've nothing to hide, after all."

Her father grunted without conviction as she left the carriage. "That lass," he said to himself, "God knows why she's done all this. I would never have thought my Brenna would end up this way." Nora was surprised to hear tears in her husband's voice. "My little Brenna," he murmured, "my poor little girl."

Meanwhile, Brenna locked the door, took off her cloak and mittens, and took a deep breath as she walked into the bedroom. She found Kevin sitting up in bed waiting for her. The light from the fireplace threw his face into shadows. Well, she thought, no use in lying, for gossip like this would soon find its way home. Better that she let him know that nothing really happened.

"Kevin?"

"Aye, you're home earlier than I thought." He sounded pleased.

"Yes, there was a bit of a—commotion—at the party. I—oh, 'tis so silly really," she said, trying to sound matter-of-fact as she began to undress.

"What happened?"

"Well, 'twas such a nice party really. I had the nicest surprise, you see. Rory Adair was there and he—he told me that he'd found my horse. The lieutenant had captured the two fugitives near Cork where Rory was getting off ship from London, and—oh I suppose they started talking—and he rode Minx back up here for Benjamin's party. Wasn't that awfully nice of him?"

Kevin yawned. "Aye, I suppose so, though it doesn't sound like the Adair I know!"

Brenna bit her lip and hung her gown in the wardrobe, making a fuss of smoothing out the wrinkles. She slipped into her nightgown and went to the bed, wishing she knew what Kevin was thinking. He didn't seem disturbed. In fact, he seemed quite pleasant after their last days of quarreling. She could only hope he would understand.

"Well, the funniest thing happened, you see. After Rory and I came in from seeing Minx, he took me through the library, and the door was closed, so we—we stayed a moment talking a little—you know."

Kevin was tensing beside her, giving her his full attention now. "You and Adair were alone in the library?"

She nodded. "Only a moment before two other guests came in and saw us together and—oh, jumped to conclusions. They went about spreading some stupid gossip, and my father got angry and brought me home early."

"What sort of conclusions?" he asked suspiciously.

"How should I know? I suppose they thought we were trysting or something of the sort. Some people just naturally assume . . ."

"Brenna, tell me why they would assume you were trysting?" he demanded, gazing at her with a hard sternness that made her heart beat frantically.

"Well, I—"

"Brenna?" Kevin reached over to hold her by the shoulders, forcing her to look at him. "You're hiding something from me. Is it you're too ashamed to tell me?"

"No," she said with a little laugh, trying to put him at ease. "I suppose they thought we were—kissing, I mean to say he *was* holding me a little because I hugged him when I thanked him for bringing me my horse . . ."

"They thought you were kissing, Brenna? Were you kissing him?"

"No!" She was starting to cry and tried to wriggle away from him. "That's all that happened. Kevin, you must believe me!"

"Brenna, you're lying!" he accused, and shook her a little. "You're lying to me," he repeated incredulously.

"All right. All right!" she screamed at him. "Yes, yes,

he did kiss me! But it meant nothing to me. He was only glad to see me. He . . ."

Her head snapped back as Kevin slapped her hard across the cheek. Stunned, she blinked at him through her tears, unbelieving that her husband, gentle Kevin, could possibly have struck her.

"You let that bastard touch you!" he raged, shaking her again. "You've humiliated me, Brenna. I'll be the laughingstock of the district when everyone hears how Rory Adair tried to cuckold me."

"You're humiliated, Kevin?" she said with mingled anger and surprise. "You don't care about me. You and my father are two peas in a pod. Those were his sentiments too. Do you feel better, knowing that you are, after all, so like my father, Kevin?"

"I'll feel better when I find that bastard and give him the thrashing he deserves for daring to touch my wife." Kevin jumped out of bed, pulled on his trousers, coat, and a pair of boots, and without another word to his wife, flew out the door.

She waited up, sleepless, all through the night, fearful at what Kevin might try to do. All her tears were shed, and she vowed to God that she would be the meekest of wives, if only He would bring Kevin home safely. She could never forgive herself if he was hurt because of what she had done.

The next morning, as dawn's gray light crept over the darkness, Kevin returned, stinking of Irish whiskey. His face was battered, cut, and bruised, all sustained, he told her drunkenly, in his fight with Rory Adair. He was too drunk to get into bed properly and would have fallen to the floor if Brenna hadn't caught him and dragged him into the bedroom. She wrestled him onto the bed, took off his boots and bathed his face and hands with a wet cloth. His lip was swelling grotesquely, and one eye was bruised; but he assured her that Rory had gotten the worst of it.

"Beat hell out of the bastard," he crowed. "Told him if he ever came sniffing about my wife again, I'd shoot him! I will, Brenna! Don't ever want to see him around here again!"

"No, he won't be around here anymore, Kevin," Brenna soothed applying ointment to the worst cuts.

"Brenna, Brenna, how could you do it?" he asked her drunkenly, crying in his maudlin state. "Don't you love me at all? Did we make such a terrible mistake in marrying? I wanted to be the best of husbands—wanted to give you everything—told you I'd be making you a queen." He laughed sorrowfully.

"Hush, darling," she said softly. "Just believe me when I say I'm not caring a fig for Rory Adair. I'm your wife —and that's what I'll always be!" She stroked his head as she would have a child's. "Now go to sleep."

Rory Adair left the next day. Brenna learned the news a week later from Deirdre, who told her when she came to visit. Deirdre was sympathetic and had defended her sister stoutly against gossip, but she was relieved that Rory was gone.

"You and Rory," she said idly, drinking tea, "there was always something between you two, wasn't there?"

Brenna shrugged. "For a little while, but I married Kevin, and that was the end of Rory Adair in my life. What happened at Sir William's . . ."

"You don't have to explain to me, Brenna," Deirdre assured her, patting her hand in sisterly fashion. "I know how charming he can be. Good heavens, you should be excused for having a little fun once in a while, the way Kevin keeps you here in this cottage all day." She bit her lip, knowing she had said too much.

"I keep busy," Brenna said quickly. "You know, since the party, Kevin and I have had some long talks, and I'm thinking that everything will be turning out for the good now. We've both been too stubborn."

"I always knew that," Deirdre laughed. She rose from the table slowly. "Well, I suppose I'd best be getting back to Mama—she wants me to go with her to Enniscorthy to buy some yarn for the baby's clothing." She glanced at her sister. "Would you like to be joining us, Brenna?"

"Another time, if you don't mind, Deirdre. I've a few chores to finish."

"Of course," Deirdre said, "but don't become a stranger now. I expect frequent visits from you when I get too big to come in here."

Brenna smiled, kissed her on the cheek, and watched her walk down the path back to the farm. She really should have gone with her mother and sister, but she hated to be gone when Kevin returned from work. He expected her to be there, smiling and happy, with supper on the table when he walked in the door. She told herself that she wouldn't be blaming him for that. Things would sort out, she was certain.

She was just setting the dishes on the table, when she heard Kevin at the door. "You're home early," she said, going over quickly to receive his kiss.

He frowned a little. "I want to talk with you, Brenna."

"Yes?" For some reason, a cold shudder ran through her, and she went to sit down, intuitively preparing herself for terrible news.

"You remember, some time ago, my telling you about your father's idea to ship a huge cargo of horses to Argentina?"

"Yes."

"And—I told you he would be needing someone to oversee the cargo."

"Yes."

He took a deep breath. "I want to, Brenna. I want to be taking that cargo over."

She sat silently for a moment, absently fingering the rim of her plate. "Kevin, are you sure?" she asked him finally.

"Aye, 'tis the chance I've been looking for, Brenna. Don't you see?" His eyes lit up with excitement and his breath came faster as he bent over her and tilted her face up. " 'Tis the best chance for both of us—for our marriage. A chance to start over. You and I—we could be what *you* want, Brenna."

She was confused, seeing the anticipation in his face, but somehow keeping apart from it. "Kevin, I don't understand. A change in our lives? A chance to start over? You—don't want to continue as head groom here?"

He shook his head emphatically. "That's what I'm saying, Brenna. Look, I know you're having a hard time of it here with all the pressure from your father, and even I can see you will never fit in with the other wives." He held up his hand to stop her quick protests. "Aye, 'tis easy to see that you've tried, but you can't be what you're not. There's nothing else for us here. Brenna, this is the chance for us!"

Brenna's thoughts whirled. "What are you asking of me, Kevin?"

"To come with me, Brenna. To come with me and not to be looking back."

"Oh!" The refusal was already in her voice. "Not come back—to my home!"

"Brenna, 'tis not your home any longer. You've been living in a world in-between, fitting in neither place. But think of it—if we go to Argentina together, we can start anew. You and I—without your father or Sir William or memories that might hurt us."

"But, Kevin, you know nothing of . . ."

"Dammit, Brenna! Here, I'll always carry the stigma of a 'lackey,' no matter how good I am with the horses. I can never be anything more. But in Argentina, immigration is encouraged. My knowledge and skill with the horses would be in demand there. Brenna, you know that this situation is intolerable for you. You can't live like this much longer—and neither can I."

"Oh, Kevin, 'tis such a big step. And how do you know you'll be able to find work? 'Tis true we'd be changing where we live, but—we'd still be bringing the same problems with us."

"We've both got courage enough to do this together," he assured her.

"But, 'tis a foreign place, a different country with different customs. I just don't know."

"We'll adapt!" He was smiling, eager and excited as a lad with a new toy.

Brenna sighed. She could see the zealous fire in her

husband's eyes and knew he wanted this more than anything else in his life. He wanted this chance to become important to her—he wanted to prove his own worth to her. She loved him and pitied him for it. And she knew that she couldn't refuse him.

"What could I be doing to help?" she finally asked weakly.

Inexpressible joy was written on his face as he hugged her. "Why, you could teach English or French—oh, darlin', you're smart enough to think of something." He looked at her as though she had just given him back his life.

"Have you already told my father we'd be going?"

"He's sure I'll be taking the job," he answered her, his joy fading a bit. "But he doesn't know anything about you coming along."

" 'Twill go hard on him."

"Aye," Kevin admitted.

"But if you're sure that this is what you're wanting."

"Aye!" he cried enthusiastically. "You'll not be regretting this, sweetheart."

His words seemed to Brenna to echo from promises he had made to her the day they were married. She shook off the superstitious feeling and smiled up at him, trying to keep the corners of her mouth from shaking.

"I know I'll not be regretting it, Kevin. I know we'll be happy."

Chapter Thirty-Five

WHEN Brenna told her father that she would be leaving with Kevin on the ship to Argentina, he stared at her for a long moment, waves of stunned shock passing over his face.

"What are you saying, lass?" he asked in a trembling voice. "You're to be leaving us for good?"

"Yes, Papa." Brenna was sitting quietly in one of the parlor chairs, gazing compassionately at her father as he paced back and forth. Finally he walked to the windows to look out into the May afternoon.

His bearing was proud and handsome: the thick shock of black hair, graying at the temples, the strong, tanned hands locked together behind his back. She hoped he would not press her too hard about her decision, for it had taken all of her courage to come here and tell him. She had told her mother the week before, but had extracted her promise not to say a word to her father.

Kildare swung around suddenly and faced her. His blue eyes carefully controlling disappointment tinged with anger. "How did you come about making this decision, Brenna?"

She was taken aback by the fierceness in his expression. "Why, Kevin and I decided 'twould be best if we went together."

"Kevin, is it!" He shook his head and his hands clenched. "I should have known he'd be finding some way to take you away from me, lass." He gazed at her, his expression softening a little. "Ah, girl, don't you see what it is he's trying to do? He knows he'll always be ashamed of his background, of his work—he knows you're ashamed to be called his wife. With your mother and me here to take you in, he knows you've got someone to turn to. But in Argentina . . ."

"Papa, Kevin and I have discussed all this. He ad-

mitted that he wanted something better than he has here
—for both of us," she added defensively.

"Aye, and what else did he say? Did he promise you
riches and high position and a palace when you get to
Argentina? Aye, I'll wager he did—but how could you
believe him, Brenna? You, with the smartest head on
your shoulders of the lot." He rubbed his face with his
hands in a childlike gesture. "What has happened to you,
my proud and lovely daughter?" he asked himself. "What
twist of destiny has brought everything down to this? Is it
that fate wants to be having a belly-laugh at my expense?"

"Papa, please, you must try to understand," Brenna put
in. "I'm going to Argentina because I am Kevin's wife—
and where he goes, I must also go."

He looked at her with sly craftiness, as though to trap
her. "Aye, you're married—but do you love him, lass?
Can you honestly look your father in the face and tell
me you love him?" He sat down in the chair next to hers,
leaning towards her with urgency, as though by the sheer
strength of his will, he could make her see the truth, and
admit her foolishness. "Ach, don't you think I'm knowing
how he got you to marry him? I'm not a blind beggar,
daughter-o'mine. You no more loved him than you loved
that pompous jay, Rory Adair. But you married Kevin,
because . . ."

"Enough, Papa, please," Brenna pleaded. "You've no
right to be questioning me like this."

He was silent for a moment, rubbing his eyes and then
his chin. "Don't you see, lass, that I love you?" he began
in a more even tone. "I'm your father, and I'm wanting
only the best for you. Ever since you were small, you
knew I loved you more than the others. Aye, I know 'tis
not right to be admitting it to you—but you were my
joy, my hope, the one of my offspring that was most like
me. I'd always hoped you would be taking over the farm
when I got too old for it."

"But you've told Deirdre and Benjamin that it would
be theirs," she reminded him without bitterness.

"Only because of that damned husband of yours," he

answered, his voice beginning to rise. "It sticks in my craw to give everything I've worked for, everything my family has owned for two hundred years, to that damned stablehand."

"If you dislike him so much, you should be glad we are going away."

"*Him,* Brenna, him. Not you. Why do you think I offered him the job on the ship? I did it for you, lass!"

Brenna looked at her father, puzzled. "For me, Papa? You were going to send my husband away for *me?*"

"Aye." He put his face in his hands again. "I know 'twas wrong of me, perhaps, but I wanted Kevin to go away so that your mother and I could persuade you to come back here with us—to live with us and be our daughter again, the way you always should have."

"Kevin would have come back, Papa," she reminded him gently.

"Aye, but I hoped that by that time you would have tried to persuade him to let you stay in the house with us." He sighed heavily. "I would have even allowed him to stay in my house, if it came to that."

"Oh, Papa!" Brenna said, her eyes filling with compassionate tears. "I know you love me, and I love you too. I don't want to be hurting you like this—but I must go with Kevin. 'Tis his only chance to prove himself."

" 'Tis Kevin talking now," Kildare said bitterly.

"Papa, I want to go," she said quietly.

Kildare sat like a stone statue in the chair for several seconds, his face in his hands, before Brenna realized that her father was crying. She saw, with surprise, his wide shoulders shaking, and she wished for one desperate moment that she could somehow take this pain away from him. But she must go with Kevin—he was her husband, and he loved her too.

"Papa?" She reached out tentatively to lay her hand on his shoulder. "Papa, I'll be back to visit—I promise you."

He pulled his head out of his hands, and she thought her heart would break at the tear stains on his cheeks.

"You'll not be changing your mind, lass?" he asked hopefully.

She shook her head slowly. "I have to go, Papa. 'Tis done."

"Does your mother know then? And your brother and sister?"

"I've told Mama, and I've written to Dermot. I'm hoping he and Bernadette can come down with Patrick before 'tis time for us to be leaving. I'll be telling Deirdre tomorrow."

"You won't be here when your sister has her baby," he reminded her dully.

"I am sorry about that, but there's nothing for it. Deirdre will understand."

"You know that I've scheduled the cargo to be taken down to Cork in mid-July. I could postpone the departure until August, after Deirdre's baby is born." Ashamed of losing control in front of her, he straightened his shoulders and wiped the last trace of tears from his face.

"No, Papa, I know that you've picked the best time to send the horses. I don't want to be interfering with that."

His blue eyes met with hers. "You've made up your mind with no regrets, then. Stubborn as I am, aren't you, daughter?" He sighed and stood up, turning idly toward the window. "What a son you would have made, lass," he murmured quietly to himself.

Brenna rose also and touched him lightly on the arm. "I'll be going now, Papa. I've got to be telling Siobhan too."

He was silent, waving her on without words. Brenna left him quietly, shutting the door and escaping from the room with a mixture of relief and regret.

She found it nearly as hard to tell Siobhan that she would be leaving, although the woman was more adept than her father at hiding her feelings. She only questioned Brenna about the reason for going, her dark eyes watching the girl's face as though searching for a lie.

"So, you go because your husband wishes you to go," she said after Brenna had tried to explain Kevin's feelings.

"Siobhan, you're not being fair," Brenna put in. "You and my father . . ."

"One is never fair when he sees the thing he loves most going away from him," Siobhan said quietly. "Aye, Brenna, you have been like a daughter to me for a long time, at least in my mind. I've watched you grow up from a child playing about the bog banks who came one day and knocked on my door, to the young woman and wife who has proved so wonderful in helping me with my work. I've been with you through difficult times; I've advised you and watched fearfully as you ran toward your future with arms opened wide and both eyes closed." She smiled. "I have cared for you and loved you and now—it hurts to think that I won't ever see you again."

"That's nonsense, Siobhan," Brenna said quickly to hide her own emotion. "I promise to come back."

"Aye," Siobhan said wearily.

"I *will* come back!" Brenna said with renewed strength. Why was it that Siobhan suddenly looked so much older and frailer? It made her nervous to think that she would not be there to help Siobhan in the winter time when her foot pained her so. "You—you will have to get another girl, brighter than I am certainly," she laughed, trying to be light. "You can train her, just as you did me."

It was easy to see there was no spirit in Siobhan's smile. "Let's not talk of my troubles," she put in. "I want to know . . ." she stopped as though debating whether or not to put Brenna through more discomforting questions. She shrugged her shoulders. "Ah, it doesn't matter, my dear. Just—be careful and be happy."

"I will, Siobhan," Brenna replied fervently. "I know that I'm doing the right thing. I'll write you letters—and tell you all about Argentina!"

"Aye, that would be nice," Siobhan said absently, gazing at a space on the floor in front of her as though mesmerized.

"You must write me also—and tell me about Mr. Cavendish and Betsy's new baby and all of them."

"You shouldn't be troubling yourself about them, lass. You'll have enough to keep you busy in a new land."

Siobhan thoughtfully sipped the last of her tea. "Dear God, I will be missing you, my dearest child," she murmured softly, putting the cup down.

Eyes glistening with tears, Brenna stood up and hugged the older woman. Siobhan held her tightly for a few moments, then let her go, her own eyes bright with moisture.

Quickly, so as not to break down completely, Brenna grabbed her riding gloves from the table and walked towards the door. "Good-bye, Siobhan," she said, her throat aching painfully as she held in her sobs. The older woman murmured something, then Brenna quickly strode out the door, shutting it tightly behind her.

Summer rains had rutted the dirt road from Wexford to Cork, and the ride was jolting; it hardly helped that the public conveyance needed new springs. Kevin had insisted that they refuse her father's offer to drive them to the docks, figuring it would be easier on everyone if they said their good-byes at the farm. He had bought tickets on the post chaise, and had sent all their furniture down in a rented wagon the day before. It would already be in the ship's hold by now.

Brenna sat wedged between Kevin and a middle-aged merchant who slept through most of the journey. She was thinking wistfully of her farewells to the family. Her father had been quiet, grim as he kissed her on the cheek and shook hands with Kevin, wishing them both luck. Nora, of course, had been tearful, making Brenna promise to write often and come back to visit as soon as she could manage. Deirdre, misty-eyed, hugged her as best she could with her enormous stomach. "Any time now, I'm sure," she had said, patting it and gazing at her sister as though the knowledge might somehow dissuade her from going. Dermot had been more sedate, although Bernadette and Patrick had cried to see her go.

The last thing Brenna had seen from the coach was her family waving to her, all their faces filled with hope for her future—all except her father, who had turned away to hide his bitterness from the rest. Perhaps he couldn't bear to actually see his daughter leaving him. In that moment, the whole of his figure had looked as though it was carved from granite.

She mustn't let herself think of her father, she told herself, for she and Kevin were about to begin an adventure, a new step which held promise as well as peril for them. They had set some money aside, but that would not hold them for long, once they arrived in Argentina. Kevin would be forced to find a job among total strangers, and Brenna, not for the first time, found herself wondering if he really knew what he was getting into.

But they had to make it work. She could never return to her family, especially her father, if they failed in this new venture, for Kevin, she knew, would never return with his head down. If it killed him, she thought, he would stick this out.

The coach arrived in Cork late in the afternoon. It was the usual busy seaport, crawling with sailors off duty after months out at sea, prowling after painted prostitutes whose garish dresses brightened the otherwise somber wharf. Kevin helped Brenna out of the coach and shouldered their trunk, leading the way to the docks where their ship, the *Suzanna*, was anchored.

They presented their papers with the receipted bill for the trip at the shipyard office and were told which pier to go to. Kevin hurried along, making Brenna run to keep up with him, weighted down as she was with two small valises. She could see the eagerness in his step, the excitement in every line of his body, and she hoped desperately that his dreams would be realized.

On board ship, they were introduced to Captain Porter, out of Southampton. He seemed very kind, and after showing them to their small cabin, he and Kevin went back on deck to discuss the loading of the horses, which were being temporarily kept in a warehouse.

Brenna found herself alone in the cramped cabin, trying to sort clothing into a chest, which was nailed to the floor. There was only one porthole, and she quickly worked up a fine sweat in the heat, so she sat down on the narrow bunk for a few minutes, fanning herself distractedly with one of her slippers.

At dinner that evening, when the horses had all been brought aboard and put below decks without mishap, Kevin and Brenna dined with the captain in his quarters.

"Have you sailed this route often, Captain?" asked one of the other passengers at the table.

"Yes, many times, Mr. Grayson," Captain Porter answered amiably. "There's some seven thousand miles of ocean that separate the English Channel from the port of Buenos Aires, and I've been sailing the route for almost twenty years—about the time steamships first took over the run." He sipped his wine and went on expansively. "It used to take near to two months to sail the route in the days of regular packet service forty years ago. My father used to sail the other clippers—ah, some of the tales he'd tell me about squalls at the equator." He stopped with a discreet cough as one passenger's wife became round-eyed at the mention of storms. "Of course, no need to worry about storms in a steamship," he said hurriedly. "Besides being sturdier, they've cut the trip to just under forty days—about thirty-five we've been running the last two trips."

"Only a month to get to Argentina?" Brenna asked, surprised. "I always thought it—well, it just seemed so far away."

"The steamship has certainly made the world smaller," an elderly gentleman from Bristol put in.

The captain nodded. "The French have had regular service from Bordeaux to Buenos Aires since '60, and our Liverpool to Rio de Janeiro line extended its operation to that city about seven years ago. It's becoming a popular place for British investments."

Kevin gave Brenna a look of excitement. He could hardly wait to finish the meal and politely say good night to the others before he was rambling on eagerly to Brenna about this new country, which seemed so attractive to so many people.

"You see, darlin'," he said in their cabin as they prepared for bed. "I told you we'd made the right decision.

British investors! That means there'll be people like us already there who might be able to help us."

"He didn't say Irish investors," Brenna pointed out.

Kevin ran a careless hand through his red hair. "Dammit, we *are* British subjects. They're sure to help one of their own kind!"

"I suppose so, though I wouldn't get your hopes up too high."

"Brenna! Don't be telling me you're turning sour on this already?" There was an edge of disgust in his voice, which made Brenna turn to him, quickly catching his hand and pressing it reassuringly with her own.

"No, Kevin, I'm not turning sour," she protested. " 'Tis just that I'm not wanting you to—to get too excited if things don't turn out quite as you expect."

He smiled and pressed her hand back. "Aw, now, you're not to be worrying. That's my job," he told her. "Didn't I tell you I'd be taking good care of you from now on? Just you wait. It won't be too hard for me to find a grand position once we've arrived."

Brenna nodded, then turned to the bunk, eyeing its narrowness dubiously. "What do you think?" she asked him, with a sparkle in her eye, hoping to turn his mind from other thoughts.

Kevin dismissed it warily. " 'Twill be hard enough *sleeping* on the damned thing," he said, grinning. " 'Twould take an acrobat to do what you have in mind, sweetheart." He kissed her, put on his nightshirt and slipped into the bunk beside her.

Brenna lay awake for nearly an hour, trying to get used to the rocking motion of the ship and calm herself enough to fall into sleep. She wished that Kevin had made love to her earlier, but the thought seemed to be far from his mind. She told herself wearily, that it could be a long thirty-five days before they reached dry land and a comfortably wide bed.

Chapter Thirty-Six

"ARE you feeling ill, sweetheart?" Kevin asked her the next morning as they got underway.

"A little queasy, Kevin, just a little queasy."

He hugged her. "You'll be getting used to it, darlin'. If I know my little wife, she'll have her sea legs before any of the rest of them."

His prediction turned out to be false, much to Brenna's dismay, for she found herself in the cabin for most of her first week at sea, groaning and rushing to the chamberpot at every roll of the ship. To make matters worse, she could hear, through the thin, wooden partition, retching from the cabin next door.

She didn't blame Kevin for escaping the room quickly every morning. It smelled foul from her sickness, and the one, small porthole provided little ventilation. Of course, in the evenings, when she sometimes felt better, Kevin would tell her that the smell in the hold from the horses was powerful enough to knock a man down. She pitied him, working down there with the livestock during the early part of the day, then coming back to a sickroom in the afternoon.

Then, miraculously, the seasickness abruptly left her on the tenth day out from Cork. Brenna dressed carefully, afraid that at any moment she would be obliged to run for the chamberpot again. Grimly, she looked about the room and decided to tidy it up as best she could. She opened the porthole to look out on a calm, dark ocean, and a blast of heat hit her from the slight breeze that blew in. They must be nearing the equator, she thought. It was hard to believe that they were almost a third of the way through the trip.

When she had tidied the cabin as well as she was able, she went up on deck, for the first time since they left port, in fresh, clean clothing with the scent of lavender touched to her throat and ears.

"Ah, Mrs. Ryan, so good to see you're up and about finally," the captain called to her on his way up deck. "I think you're one of the last ones to come up."

"Thank you, Captain Porter. It does feel good to get on deck and out of that cabin. Do you happen to know if my husband is down in the hold?"

"I believe I saw him with one of the other passengers at the railing earlier," the captain said.

Brenna thanked him and went in search of her husband, following the railing around the ship until she found Kevin talking with another young man whom she vaguely remembered meeting at dinner the first night on board.

"Brenna, darlin', you're up!" Kevin put an affectionate arm about her and pulled her beside him. "I'd like you to meet Mr. Lawrence from London."

"How do you do?" Brenna said politely, wondering what on earth her husband was doing conversing with this posh young fellow. He certainly looked like society to her, and she couldn't imagine why he would be talking with an Irishman.

"Very pleased to meet you, Mrs. Ryan. Your husband was telling me how bravely you've endured the wretched seasickness all these days. I do hope you've recovered." His round, shiny face seemed genuinely concerned, and Brenna assured him that she was feeling quite well now. "I'm so glad to hear it. Kevin has also been telling me about the cargo of horses on board that you're taking to Buenos Aires. I must admit I'm interested."

"Mr. Lawrence is with the railroads down there," Kevin explained quickly. "His father is one of the biggest investors with the Western Railroad line."

"Oh, I see." Brenna really didn't see, but she tried to look polite. She wasn't sure she liked the touch of smugness on Kevin's freckled face. She noticed a small rent near one of the buttonholes on his jacket and hoped Mr. Lawrence wasn't as keen sighted.

"Yes, railroads will certainly be the thing in the next

five or ten years," Mr. Lawrence said. "My father worked with William Wheelwright, himself, on the track from Rosario to Córdoba." He gave a deprecating smile. "Excuse me, I'm sure you don't know what I'm talking about." He cleared his throat. "Anyway, your husband's been telling me about these horses below decks—nearly eighty you said?—on consignment to Miguel Castaneda. I must admit my interest has been piqued. Those tough, rangy animals that grow wild on the pampas are no match for a genuine Irish thoroughbred."

Brenna beamed proudly. "My father raises only the best."

"Brenna, I was telling Mr. Lawrence how your father turned the raising of the horses over to me since his—er —illness," Kevin put in quickly.

Brenna raised her brows in a puzzled expression. "But, Kevin . . ."

"Will you excuse us, Mr. Lawrence?" he was saying, catching Brenna's arm and leading her away from the Englishman.

"Kevin, what in the world . . ."

"Brenna, you'll forgive me for putting a bit of the blarney on Mr. Lawrence, won't you, darlin'?" Kevin said as he steered her toward the hold. "You see I told him that I was in complete charge of the horses."

"But, Kevin, why would you do that?" Brenna wondered.

He looked shame-faced and reddened boyishly. "I was only doing it to—to get my foot in the door, so to speak. I was hoping he would help me to get a job in Buenos Aires. It doesn't hurt to be cultivating the proper acquaintances, if you get my meaning."

"Oh, Kevin, I'm not sure this is right, what you're doing," Brenna said worriedly.

"It doesn't matter whether 'tis right or not," Kevin replied stoutly. " 'Tis the means to an end, Brenna, and a future that will be brighter for both of us."

"I hope so," Brenna said softly.

They were at the door of the hold and she looked down curiously. She could detect, even from on deck, the smell of horse, wet straw, and manure. "How are the animals faring?" she asked, to change the subject.

Kevin shrugged. "Well enough, considering the cramped quarters they're in. I suppose we might be losing ten or fifteen percent of them before the voyage is over."

"Why?" Brenna was astounded. "'Tis a short journey for them, is it not?"

"First of all, I think your father made a mistake in shipping so many together. There's not enough room for all of them to be comfortable. Secondly, there's not enough straw to change their stalls more than once or twice during the trip, and those conditions breed disease. I'm thinking it would have been smarter to ship two separate cargoes. As it is, your father may end up losing some money."

"What a calamity," Brenna mused. "I'm sure you're not very sad about it!"

Kevin put his arms around her playfully. "Aw, now don't be looking so sour, love. Just think, we don't have to be worried about your father's money anymore. We'll be making enough of our own, just you wait."

"You're sounding awfully cocky," Brenna remarked grumpily, despite his show of affection. "I suppose you'll be oiling up young Mr. Lawrence for the rest of the trip?"

"Aye," he laughed, hugging her harder.

They were a week out of Buenos Aires when they hit a small, tropical storm that soon grew into a full-blown gale. Brenna went down into the hold with her husband daily to help with the horses. The dark, humid place was sometimes more uncomfortable than she could stand, but she pitied the animals and steeled herself not to be sick.

The horses were boxed in in large bins made of wooden slats, ten animals to a bin. Daily, Brenna took a cube of sugar to Minx, who always seemed glad to see her mistress after a long night in the confines of the hold. Brenna looked at the younger horses and wondered how many would last through the week. Although Kevin did his best to see to their welfare, they had lost three of the smallest already, and now, with a storm buffeting them about, many more would be injured.

Brenna hoped the storm wouldn't last much longer. All day the waves had lashed the ship, and the wind and rain pounded unceasingly. The horses had to be tied down securely, or the ship's rolling would throw them about like toys.

Captain Porter had spared two of his men to help with the horses, a kindness for which Kevin was most grateful: it gave him some relief and allowed him to get a few hours of sleep now and then. Brenna was proud of him for keeping his patience and calm around the animals. As she followed him into the hold, her eyes took a few moments to adjust to the darkness, for some of the lanterns had been snuffed out by the wind howling down when they had opened the door. She could hear the horses' nervous nickering, their impatient stamping and snorting, and Kevin's voice calling to one of the sailors to relight the lanterns.

"Oh, Kevin, the poor things," she murmured when she discovered two colts lying stiffly on the floor of one of the bins.

Kevin looked at the dead animals grimly. "We'll have to get them up on deck as soon as the winds die down. No use in keeping them below. They'll only spook the others."

Brenna nodded and made her way to the bin where Minx was kept, reaching up to stroke her nose, murmuring reassurance but Brenna's heart was hardly in it. The other horses neighed and stamped, moving about nervously in their small groups as the ship continued to pitch.

Brenna, herself, was nearly thrown to the floor as the ship lurched and she held on tightly to the wooden slats in the bin. She could hear Kevin talking with the two sailors as they began hammering nails into some of the slats to strengthen them in case the horses were slammed against them.

"Look out, Mr. Ryan!" One of the sailors yelled out, then Brenna heard a sharp cry from her husband. Her heart seemed to stop beating for a moment as she listened for sounds above the wind and the water outside.

"Kevin!" she finally called fearfully. "Kevin, are you all right?"

"Aye, I'm—all right, Brenna," she finally heard him answer. "Just got kicked by one of those—damned—animals!" She could hear the pain in his voice, and she groped her way towards him in the semi-dark.

Kevin was sitting on the floor, held upright by one of the other men. Brenna could see the pallor of his face and the sweat on his brow in the dim lantern light.

"You're bleeding!" Brenna cried and went to her knees as she saw the darkness creeping down his shirtsleeve from his chest. Frantically, she looked into his face. "Kevin, what happened?"

"Damned thing—just reared up—and slammed me in the chest," he said, rasping and coughing as though trying to catch his breath.

Brenna looked at the other men. "We've got to get him on deck and back to our cabin. I've got to be looking at his wound."

"Aye, ma'am, if you'll just hold the lantern, me and Tom'll carry him up," one of the sailors said quickly.

It was slow going up the steps and across the deck with the winds rising and the ocean still bubbling and tossing the ship. Tears of relief blurred Brenna's eyes when they reached the cabin and deposited Kevin on the bunk. His face looked ghastly white and his eyes were closed; his breath came in starting gasps.

"Get the doctor, please," Brenna ordered. She hoped the ship's physician was a competent man, for her skills with Siobhan's patients had not prepared her to take care of her own husband. She ripped open Kevin's shirt, noting the purplish imprint of the horse's hoof just a little above his right breast. All around the mark, the skin was bruising with alarming rapidity and there was still a thin trickle of blood escaping from where the skin had been punctured.

"Mrs. Ryan?"

It was the doctor. Brenna hurried him in, hovering around him worriedly as he examined the wound.

"I don't think the lung's been pierced, ma'am," he pronounced gravely. "Perhaps bruised, but certainly no great damage has been done." He leaned over Kevin again. "Still, I trust he'll be keeping to his bed for the remainder of the voyage. You never know about something like this."

"What do you mean?" Brenna wanted to scream at him, but maintained her calm.

"I mean, ma'am, that he may have done some internal damage that I can't see. Things like this happen—and sometimes it's months before something goes wrong. If he did damage the tissue around his lungs, it could weaken the area, and with another trauma to the chest, it might tear it completely."

"You mean—he—he could die?" Brenna whispered.

The doctor shrugged. "I'm saying that once we arrive in Buenos Aires, I would make sure he didn't overtax himself, Mrs. Ryan. There's no sense in taking unnecessary chances."

"Will he—be all right—now?"

The doctor nodded. "I think so, if he stays in bed and rests. As I said, it's probably just a bad bruise, which will heal in time. He's likely to be as good as new in a few months."

"Months," Brenna repeated forlornly. She and Kevin would be in a strange city, with hardly any money and he unable to work for a long time. She closed her eyes and swallowed her fear and disappointment. After all, it wasn't Kevin's fault that he'd been kicked by one of the horses—who ever would have thought that this would happen?

She sat next to Kevin for the remainder of the day, anxious at each little groan and movement.

In the early evening, Kevin regained consciousness and looked up to discover Brenna watching him anxiously. His smile was tired. "What happened?"

"You were kicked by a horse. The other men and I brought you up here to the cabin," she answered him, licking the dryness from her lips. "The doctor's already been in to see you. He bandaged you up and gave me a little salve for your chest."

When Kevin started to sit up, his wife's eyes became round with terror. "What's the matter, darlin'? Just a little bruise, you know. What's the doctor been telling you?" He reached up and chucked her under the chin. "I'm damned sore, but I've got to be seeing to those horses before . . ."

"No, Kevin!"

The freckles on his face seemed to stand out against the paleness of his skin. His brows drew downward with a touch of ire. "What do you mean? Brenna, we're going to lose even more of the horses if I don't go down and see to them. We've lost five already."

"Oh, Kevin, please don't worry about the horses now," Brenna urged him softly. "I'm more worried about you."

He grinned again. "Well, 'tis hard to believe I've finally come before the horses in your affections."

"Oh, don't tease me now, please," she replied. "You must believe me: you've got to stay in bed for the rest of the trip."

"What!"

She nodded. "Doctor's orders."

"Damn the doctor! Is he going to take care of those horses below for me?"

"'Tis for your own good," Brenna soothed. "He—he said you may have been hurt worse than he can tell, and —you shouldn't be taking any chances. When we get to Argentina, he said you may not be able to do any work for a few weeks." She had wisely changed the "months" to "weeks," for she knew Kevin would never tolerate the thought of being laid up in bed for an extended time. "There," she added, "now you're knowing the whole of it —and you can see why you can't be getting up."

Kevin looked as though he had run up against a stone wall. He waited a full minute before answering, "Brenna, how can I be out of work for weeks once we get to the city? You know how much money we have—'tis impossible."

"We'll get by," she soothed. "I should be able to find some kind of teaching job—remember how we discussed that in Ireland? And, perhaps, your Mr. Lawrence can be setting something aside for you—for when you're better. We'll be all right."

"Brenna, I can't be asking you to work while I lie about in bed all day," he put in with growing frustration. "What if you can't find work as a teacher? What then? Will it come down to whoring at the local bar?"

"Kevin!"

He looked sheepish. " 'Tis sorry I am, Brenna—but I can't help it! We've got enough money to last us a week or two—and that's counting it close!"

"We've got some jewelry that is mine," she cut in quickly. "We can pawn that. Oh, don't look at me like that, Kevin. It's my jewelry, and I can do with it as I wish!"

"Brenna, you're not to be putting your valuables in pawn unless you're telling me first—is that understood? I'll not have my wife . . ."

"Kevin, please lie down and rest," she interrupted, pressing her hand to his forehead to check for fever. "We —we have the rest of the week to discuss all of this while you're recuperating."

"And while we continue to lose the horses," he snorted bitterly.

"Hush, now, Kevin, don't be working yourself up that way. 'Tis done and there's nothing for it, but to make the best of it." She pushed back the red hair from his brow and smiled.

He sighed. "Darlin', I suppose you're right, but—if I'm feeling better when we dock, I'll not be lying about in bed, I'm telling you. I'll—I'll not have your father hearing of this and thinking me too weak to finish up the business I was sent here to complete. I'll not have it!"

"All right, Kevin," Brenna murmured, pitying him.

Chapter Thirty-Seven

"How the hell are we supposed to get ourselves, much less the horses, to the docks?" Kevin demanded aloud in the cool, crisp August air. It had been disconcerting to discover themselves at the end of winter here in Argentina, where the seasons were reversed.

"I'm sure the captain will be instructing everyone shortly," Brenna said, but her words held little conviction as she stared into the muddy waters of the estuary. She couldn't see any sign of a pier and wondered if they had stopped in the river for some other reason. She could still see, if she walked to the other end of the ship, the dark waters of the ocean whence they had just emerged into the mouth of the Río de la Plata.

When all the passengers were on deck and standing anxiously at the railing, the captain explained how they would get to the city. It seemed to Brenna, listening, that the process was ridiculously complex. They would remain anchored here in the open roadstead, some six miles from the town; and launches, which plied between ships and shallow water, would take them farther inland—but still a mile from their destination. From there, high-wheeled carts drawn by horses or oxen would carry them across swampy mudflats to the piers.

"Captain, excuse me, but where are the docks?" Brenna asked with strained courtesy. "Why can't the ships steam right up to the shore's edge and avoid all of this mess?"

"That is a question, Mrs. Ryan, that many captains have been asking since we started this route. Unfortunately, the people of Buenos Aires can't seem to find the money or the initiative to dredge the waterways around the city so that they would be deep enough for ships to go right up to the docks. As it is, four miles is the closest any ocean-going vessel can get; some have to anchor nearly eight miles out." He waved his hand over the many ships all around them. "As you can see, naval traffic is heavy here in the estuary, and it is hectic enough just avoiding an accident in the water."

"But this is ridiculous!" Kevin put in quickly. "How on earth are we going to transport the horses?"

The captain shrugged. "The horses will have to be transported in much the same way, Mr. Ryan, as your selves and the other cargo. They will be put on lighters, or large barges, and taken to the mudflats. They'll probably have to walk from there."

Kevin groaned aloud. He had been given the bad news only that morning that six more horses injured in the storm had died and now this—in their weakened conditions, the animals would be forced to trudge through flooded areas of silt and mud for nearly a mile. Disgust showed on his face, but Brenna patted his arm, telling him that, after all, there was nothing else to be done.

"This must be the way that all the other horses my father sent have been shipped in," she told him practically. "I'll be making sure the sailors keep a keen eye on the weaker ones."

As the captain called out the names of passengers to board the waiting launches, Brenna looked down the side of the ship where a ladder had been hung, and shivered. It would be difficult to get Kevin over the side without hurting his wound. Well, they would just have to take their time and care she thought.

"Mr. and Mrs. Ryan, if you'll kindly step forward?" the ship's mate called out. When they did, he asked, "Are your trunks packed and all possessions out of your cabin?"

"Aye," Kevin said. "They've been left in the passageway." He indicated his chest and the sailor nodded.

"I'll have someone pick them up and get them ready for loading."

"And the horses?" Brenna asked hopefully.

"They'll be the last of the cargo to be taken ashore, ma'am," the sailor said politely. He looked at his list. "I see we're to unload them at pier twelve—if you and your husband will be waiting there, I'm sure it will help things along."

"But we can't control seventy horses by ourselves!"

The mate smiled thinly, obviously annoyed at being detained. "There'll be plenty of dockworkers eager to lend you a hand, ma'am. That's how it's been done in the past. There's corrals along the pier and you can keep the horses there until arrangements are made at the shipyard office. If you will excuse me, ma'am?" He tipped his cap and hurried off to supervise another group of passengers.

"Damn this wound, Brenna!" Kevin said in irritation. "What a time to be sick. I'll be surprised if all the horses make it."

"Nothing can be done about it," Brenna said quickly. "We'll go to pier twelve as soon as we arrive at the docks, and we'll just have to recruit some men to help us. Perhaps one of Castaneda's agents will be there to make the arrangements. The sooner we get the horses off our hands, the happier we'll be." She looked at her husband questioningly. "Did my father give you any instructions as to obtaining money upon delivery?"

Kevin shook his head. "All that's taken care of through Castaneda's bank in London. No money to change hands was the order." He seemed to follow her line of thought. "Too bad, isn't it—I'm sure your papa wouldn't have minded if we borrowed a little to tide us over." His voice was sarcastic.

Brenna made no comment, but took her husband's hand as they neared the railing. "You're sure you can make it without any help?" she asked fearfully.

"For God's sake, Brenna, will you stop treating me like an infant? Of course I can make it without help. There's nothing wrong with my arms and legs."

"All right then, I'll go first and you follow," she said, wanting to avoid an argument.

She was relieved when Kevin was finally seated beside her in the launch, although she noted the effort it must have cost him, for there was a slight sheen of sweat on his face and a look of pain about his eyes and mouth. She wanted to comfort him, but didn't dare to in front of the others; he would surely reprimand her.

The oarsmen plied the boat among large ocean vessels and around other launches, which bobbed about in the water like dozens of tiny corks. The flow of traffic was constant, as empty boats pushed out toward the open sea and full boats rowed back upriver toward the docks. The river was a little choppy, and water lapped at the sides of the launch and onto the passengers, wetting their feet and clothing. Brenna anxiously watched as the bottom of the boat filled with muddy water. She made a mental note to make Kevin take off his shoes and put his feet in a basin of hot water once they were settled in a hotel.

Up ahead, she could see the wide, flat barges the mate had called "lighters," which would take the horses to the docks. Heavy ropes fenced the barges' decks, obviously for the purpose of keeping the cargo from falling into the estuary. She hoped there would be no accidents with the horses.

"Ho!"

The call from one of the oarsmen signaled that they were coming to the one-mile limit, where they would be transferred from the launch to an oxcart. Curiously, Brenna watched the water get muddier and shallower, until the boat could go no farther.

"All right, slowly and carefully, everyone. You'll get into carts here and be taken to the docks. Ladies first, if you please." The man was yelling in English, but it was strangely accented—Italian, she thought, or perhaps Swiss.

She was obliged to make her way forward in the launch and step gingerly into a wide-based cart with enormous wheels, which kept it from becoming stuck in the mud. Six oxen stood patiently in the oozing muck, awaiting the crack of their master's whip.

When everyone had been loaded, the launch turned around to make another trip, and the ox driver whipped up his team. Brenna felt the cart lurch as the oxen strained against the load, and she held tightly to Kevin's arm. She was alarmed to feel him shivering slightly.

"Kevin, you're sopping!" she whispered, realizing that his jacket was nearly soaked through.

"I'm aware of that, darlin'," he replied. "But don't you be worrying about me. I'll be fine once we get to the hotel. Just a few more hours, and we can sleep until dawn tomorrow."

The idea appealed to him; she could see that. "Of course, Kevin. A nice, hot bath and clean clothes . . ."

"Will you look at that!" someone yelled from the cart.

Brenna stopped in mid-sentence to follow the direction of the man's pointing finger. She could see, on the banks below the docks, crowds of colored washerwomen pounding and scrubbing their masters' dirty laundry in the stagnant pools and yellow water of the estuary.

"Well, I never saw the like!" an Englishwoman said.

"Jesus, what kind of people are these?" another person asked.

"Negroes, mulattoes, mestizos—every variation you can think of," the driver chuckled in English. "They come down every morning to do their washing for the wealthy *porteños*. 'Tis a common sight."

Brenna shook her head in wonderment. Washing clothes in this dirty river with all the boats and cargo and animals going through it—it was heathenish! She risked a glance at Kevin and saw him watching the show with curiosity and amusement.

But now, the piers could be seen extending out to the edge of the watery mud, and relief swept over Brenna. Dry land, at last, she thought, feeling silly at the tears in her eyes. Now the adventure had truly begun. She squeezed Kevin's hand and felt the answering pressure.

Soon they found themselves handed ashore and standing with stiff legs on wood that was neither rocking nor moving. All around were piles of goods stacked high, barrels and crates put end to end, awaiting the dockhands to take them to warehouses—and most of all, people. People of every description—black, yellow, brown, white, old, young, all swarming about the docks, doing their business, laboring, waiting for passengers, or waiting for a launch to take them to an outbound vessel. Directions to the shipyard office were called out in Spanish, English, German, French and Italian.

"Looks like a long wait," Brenna said bleakly when they saw the line at the office. "Perhaps one of us should be going down to pier twelve to wait for the horses."

"Brenna, be sensible. I'm not about to be leaving you alone on the docks. This is no place for a single woman, alone. Either we wait here together or we go to the pier together."

"Well?" she questioned him. "Which is it to be then?"

After a moment's hesitation he said, "The pier. Better to take care of the horses now and make sure we don't leave them to the mercy of the dockhands." He grabbed her hand and they walked to the designated pier to wait.

"Ho, there! I say, Ryan? Haven't seen you about for some days!" It was young Mr. Lawrence, looking slightly drenched after his tour in the launch. "I dare say, you'll be waiting for your cargo?"

"Aye," Kevin returned, smiling with renewed buoyancy upon seeing this young man coming towards him. "Although, we'll be lucky to save the last seventy of them."

"Yes, I can imagine what you've been through, worrying about the poor beasts."

"What brings you down here?" Kevin said hopefully.

The man shrugged. "I've got to inventory some charts and railroad engineering equipment due to arrive on this pier. Deuced coincidence, running into you, isn't it?"

Some of Kevin's hope was diminished by the indifferent answer, but he went on, "Aye, although I'd been hoping to see you when we docked."

"You know, Ryan, it was funny, my thinking you owned these horses," Lawrence went on smoothly, brushing at the lapel of his tweed coat. "Can't imagine why I thought you could help me. Captain Porter corrected my assumption at dinner a few nights ago. You know how talk will drift to different subjects over port and cigars." His attention was diverted to a small launch in which three large crates were cradled, making its way toward the pier. "Ah, here's the stuff coming now."

Kevin exchanged a wary glance with Brenna. "I don't suppose I can be counting on your help in securing a position, Mr. Lawrence?" he asked bluntly.

The Englishman gave him an indifferent glance. "A position, Mr. Ryan?"

"Aye, something to do with the horses. You see, I've a lot of experience."

Lawrence laughed rudely. "Mr. Ryan, wool is the product here, not horse flesh. Most Irishmen find themselves tending sheep or working for the railroad—or digging ditches, if you get my meaning?"

Brenna blanched. Digging ditches and working on railroads was not something that Kevin could be doing —at least not for a while, with his injury. And tending sheep? Kevin would view that as demeaning.

The three of them waited in tense silence as the launch was unloaded and the crates taken to a waiting wagon. With a touch to his hat, Mr. Lawrence hurried away.

Kevin looked after him, his freckles disappearing on a face so red that it nearly matched the color of his hair. "Goddamned English bastard!" he growled. "Who does he think he is, talking to me like I wasn't good enough for the likes of him?"

"Kevin, calm yourself," Brenna said. "It couldn't be helped. I'm sure the captain didn't know about your little deception."

"So, you're looking down your nose at me too."

"Of course not. But you did lie to the man."

"Well then, why weren't you telling him that they were your father's horses? Maybe he would have come back to sniff around you if he thought you might have some influence with your father," Kevin said with embarrassed scorn.

Brenna let the remark pass, for she could see he was disappointed. The first barge came toward them, laden with horses all neighing nervously as they stamped around the flat wooden floor. She watched anxiously as the barge anchored, and a wide plank was stretched out from the pier. It took several men to push and pull the frightened horses onto the pier and to a corral.

"I'll have to be paying them their wages if Castaneda's agent doesn't arrive before all the horses are unloaded," he whispered anxiously to Brenna. " 'Twill deplete our money disastrously."

"He'll be here, I'm sure," Brenna said, wishing Kevin had allowed her to wait at the shipyard office. She might have been able to locate the man herself. It occurred to her, with a sudden surprising jolt, that Steven Castaneda himself might act as his father's agent in this matter. For a startled moment, the realization overwhelmed her—that she would be seeing Steven again—why hadn't it occurred to her during the voyage?

"Of course!" she said aloud.

"What is it?"

"Steven will help us. I'm sure of it!"

"Steven? You mean Castaneda de la Cruz? Why should he be helping us?" Kevin asked in an annoyed tone.

"Don't be silly, Kevin. He'll help us because he's my father's friend. I'm sure he'd at least be able to help you find a job and a place for us to stay." Brenna became more animated at each new thought. It was like a revelation to her. Why hadn't she thought of Steven before?

With a touch of guilt, she tried to recall the circumstances of his last visit to Ireland. Had she been unforgivably rude to him? Had she angered him? She couldn't remember what she had said exactly, but it seemed they had parted on less than congenial terms. Still, with a woman's intuition, she was positive that Steven would be interested in her welfare. Nothing disastrous would happen to her or Kevin. Oh, God, he was the answer to everything. Oh, if only he would hurry and come down and find them. He could send them to a good hotel—perhaps even lend them some money until Kevin could work.

Such hopeful thoughts buzzed through Brenna's head while the rest of the horses were unloaded and dispatched to the corrals. She wanted to sing and hug herself and laugh out loud with relief. Whatever silly little arguments they had once had, she was sure that Steven would help her now.

It was not until she found herself alone with Kevin on

the docks, the snorting horses all unloaded, that she realized that there had actually been a passage of time. Dazedly, she looked over to where the six strong dockhands were standing in front of the corrals waiting to be paid. She glanced to Kevin as he took out the pouch of silver and gold coins, all their small horde, and carefully counted out the amount owed to each man. When the last one had left, she saw the look of despair on his face as he pinched the few coins in the sack.

"Nearly wiped us out," he muttered.

"I'm sure the agent will be here soon," Brenna said firmly. "He'll reimburse us—I'm sure of it, Kevin." Thoughts of Steven rescuing them brought an absurd smile to her lips.

Kevin looked up at the sky bleakly. " 'Twill be getting on to evening pretty soon, Brenna. We can't be standing out here all night waiting for him."

For the first time, Brenna could see that Kevin was shaking with the coldness of his wet clothing. She had hardly noticed the chill in the afternoon air. But now, with the realization, she began to shiver too, for her wool suit was wet in several places.

"You're right, Kevin, we'd best be finding ourselves a place to stay. Once that's done, we can rest and—perhaps come back later, or even tomorrow and go to the dock offices." She looked dubiously at the horses. "Will they be all right like this?"

Kevin looked at her as though she were incredibly stupid. "On a public dock at night? Brenna, where's your brain, lass? These are Irish thoroughbreds—why, I wouldn't put it past someone like Lawrence to steal one or two if the timing was right." He shook his head. "No, we've got to wait for the damned agent or risk losing even more of the cargo." He let out a foul oath that caused Brenna to flush, for she had never heard such words come from her husband's mouth.

"Perhaps we should walk back to the office then? He might be waiting for us there. At least, we can leave a message." She could see, once again, the sheen of perspiration on Kevin's face, despite the coldness in the air.

"Come on, Kevin, let's go back—they may have a pot of hot coffee or tea, and there'll be some shelter from the wind," she urged.

Kevin let her lead him back to the office where they waited until nearly dusk before Castaneda's agent arrived. Brenna's disappointment was keen when she saw that it was not Steven, but a thin, dark, Spanish man who seemed pointedly reserved and unsociable. He looked as though he would like to end their business quickly, although he fired several questions at Kevin about the condition of the animals and how many had been lost on the voyage. He seemed satisfied with the answers—and at the same time completely unaware of Kevin's misery. He was about to take his leave of them, when Brenna detained him.

"Senor Maliga, if you will kindly reimburse us for the money spent on the dockhands for their help, we will be happy to wish you good day," she said, hardly able to keep her gaze level with the other man.

"Pardon me, Mrs. Ryan, but I had no instructions to pay out money to anyone. No money to change hands was the order. If you will permit me?" He bowed again.

"No, senor, I will not permit you to leave us to flounder in this city without any money," Brenna said stoutly, aware of the surprise in the man's eyes. "As you can see, my husband is ill, and we are strangers to this city."

"Mrs. Ryan, none of this is my concern. I assume you have return passage on board one of the ship's in the harbor."

"We are immigrants, senor, and intend to stay here," she responded firmly. "We need that money that we spent to unload the horses. You must have some kind of authority in these matters!"

He shook his head. "Senor Castaneda or his son are the only ones who can deal in money, Mrs. Ryan. I am but their employee. If you have no money, you may wish to go to the Immigrants' Hotel in the center of the city. You can secure five days' free room and board there until such time as your husband finds work."

Brenna could see she was losing her battle, but her

temper was fast overrunning her common sense, and she reached out to grab at the man's arm. "My husband is sick, we are both wet and tired, senor. We will need money, for at the end of five days, we will be obliged to look elsewhere for rooms and my husband needs to see a doctor. Need I remind you that my father and Steven Castaneda de la Cruz are very close friends?"

He seemed to see her point, although he had already picked her fingers off his coat. "All right, Mrs. Ryan, I will look into the matter. But, please believe me, I can do nothing for you right now. I do not have that much money on my person. I will send a wire to my employer. Might I suggest a meeting here the day after tomorrow at ten o'clock in the morning? I am sure this matter will be straightened out to your satisfaction by that time." He bowed once more and scuttled away, as though fearful of her hand on his arm again.

Brenna watched him go, hoping that she could trust him to keep to his word. Dejected, she looked down to where Kevin was seated on a bench, his eyes closed with overwhelming weariness. She was tired herself, but she would have to see that they got to the Immigrants' Hotel before nightfall, for she had no wish to be out in a strange city at night.

"Kevin, do you feel better now?" she asked anxiously. "We have to go to the center of town to the Immigrants' Hotel for a room and food. Shall I—shall I hail a diligence to take us?" she asked hopefully. "'Twould be cheaper than a carriage."

He nodded. "Aye, I'm tired, darlin'. I don't mind saying it. A bed sounds first-rate to me now."

She nodded and helped him to his feet. She hailed one of the coaches going back and forth between the docks and the city, and told the driver to take them to the Immigrants' Hotel. As they rode, he lay his head on her shoulder, and she worriedly stroked his brow, which by now had grown hot with fever.

Chapter Thirty-Eight

NOTHING could have prepared Brenna Ryan for the Immigrants' Hotel. In the waning light, she could see a large wooden horsebarn, from which issued the high-pitched wail of a woman enduring the pangs of labor, and the yelping of a dog as it played with two small children outside the doorway. She helped Kevin inside, where they were greeted by filthy, stagnant air, and the constant bustle of people. She swallowed nervously, wishing with all her strength, that she would wake soon and discover that this all had been a nightmare.

Despite the grubby accommodations, however, the smell of food cut through the unmistakable stench of human excrement.

"Can I help you?" The man at the desk appeared unaware of the dismal surroundings and smiled cheerfully, as though he reigned over the best hotel in the city. His round, oily face was covered with black hair, and his toothy grin was the only bright thing about him.

"Yes, we—we've immigrated—" Brenna began.

"Ah, yes, from Ireland, I would guess?" He smiled again, although his eyes narrowed when he saw the pallor of Kevin's face. "No sick ones allowed," he said firmly. "There cannot . . ."

"He doesn't have a disease," Brenna interrupted hastily. "He was injured in the crossing and hasn't fully recovered. He needs food and a bed to sleep in."

The man appeared suspicious, but finally shrugged. "All right, I can give you a bed—one bed—in one of our rooms. You'll have to hurry if you want to eat supper. We can't leave the food out or the animals would eat what's left."

"Where?"

He gave her directions. The kitchens were housed in a large extension of the building. Here, several long tables were set up. Stiff-faced matrons hovered over huge caldrons of steaming food, constantly stirring their brews.

Brenna wearily showed one of them the small ticket that the man at the desk had given her, and she was given two bowls of something that looked like stew. She didn't care what was in it—it smelled good and was the first food she had eaten since breakfast aboard the *Suzanna*. Two pieces of brown, crusty bread and two cups of hot tea were also handed out, and Brenna, feeling as though she were sitting down to a feast, brought the food to where Kevin had seated himself.

They ate silently. Kevin had been coughing in the diligence, and she was relieved not to hear it as he finished the last of his tea.

"And now to bed?" he asked, with a spark of playfulness, obviously much refreshed by the food.

She nodded. "I suppose we're lucky to be on the ground floor. The man at the desk said the upper floors are suffocating even in the winter. I think we're down that hall and to the left." She guided him along until they came to a room with their number on it.

To their surprise, there were ten beds laid out in two rows, all filled except for the one closest to the doorway. Everyone was sleeping in clothing, as the cold and damp seemed to seep in from outside. A few men were playing dice in a corner by the light of a taper, and an infant fussed crankily in another corner as its mother snored gently beside it.

"Welcome to your palace," Kevin said softly. His voice choked and caught on a sob that seemed to well up in his throat.

"Hush," Brenna said, feeling sorry for both of them. She hated to tell Kevin that they would be obliged to stay in this room for at least one more night. Better just to get some sleep now. Wearily, she sank down on the mattress. Kevin lay beside her, still shivering, although he didn't feel quite as hot as before. She decided to go back to the desk to ask the man for an extra blanket. The one they had was pitifully moth-eaten and provided hardly any protection against the chill. Yes, she really should get up—and she would in just a minute—just let her get a moment of rest, and she would get up . . .

Brenna awoke with the dawn, an infant's hungry wail penetrating her dreamless sleep. She sat up slowly, wiping her eyes. The young mother in the opposite corner was putting her baby to her breast. The young woman's eyes met Brenna's in a brief moment of resignation, pity, and hopelessness.

She turned to Kevin as she heard his rasping breath. His ragged little coughs seemed to tear at her own lungs. She remembered that he had gone to sleep with his wet clothing on. She felt his forehead—it was still warm. She knew she should get him up and out to breakfast, for the others were beginning to awaken and the first served would get the best of the meal, but she hadn't the heart to bring him back to reality yet. She kissed him softly on the cheek and sat up, stretching the stiffness out of her joints.

The morning was chilly. Through the one window at the end of the room, she could see frost whitening the glass panes. Hesitantly, she went in search of the outhouse facilities, and then to the kitchen to gobble down a thick, hot mush, bland and gritty. At least it filled her stomach. She went back to their room to find Kevin still asleep. The young woman, who had finished nursing her baby, was eating from a bowl of porridge. She looked sympathetically at Brenna.

"I will watch him for you, if you wish to go out and look for work," she said in Spanish. "My husband has already left, and I will not be going out. I will tell him that you have gone."

"Thank you," Brenna said. Until the other girl had mentioned it, she hadn't even thought of going outside in the frosty air to look for work. She had no idea where to start. "Do you know anyplace I might go to seek employment?"

The girl shook her head. "The man at the desk would know?"

Brenna nodded. She kissed Kevin again, careful not to awaken him as she tucked the blanket around his shoulders, then left the room. Determined, she questioned the clerk at the desk, and she was told that she could go either to the customhouse, or to the employment office, which catered exclusively to immigrants. Brenna debated for a moment and decided to go to the immigration office first. Certainly, it would be necessary to show her papers and explain her situation—and she might be able to obtain some sort of charitable relief, although from her experiences so far, she doubted it.

Feeling better with a full stomach and a night's sleep, she stepped out into the chilly morning. The city which greeted her had a low skyline of predominantly colonial structures, made mostly of mud-brick or adobe. Heavy iron grillwork barred the windows in most places and cumbersome paneled doors seemed to forbid entrance to anyone. Through the center of the street ran a drainage channel, which looked more like an open sewer filled with a steady, slick flow of mud, offal, and other debris.

She walked up on a sidewalk, which raised her a full yard above the debris and mud below. She saw a water cart, being pulled by oxen, up the side of the street, and she called to one of the two drivers.

"Can you tell me the way to the immigration office?" she asked in Spanish.

"Two blocks north, senorita," one of them answered, swiping his hat off his head in a gesture of respect. "It is the only two-story building on that street."

"Then, the whole city looks like this?" Brenna asked, with a shade of disappointment in her voice.

The other young man shook his head and giggled. "Ah, no, senorita. The wealthy *porteños,* they live farther north —there you will find three- and four-story haciendas with beautiful patios and horse-drawn trolley cars to take them wherever they wish to go." He laughed again, as though he were slightly addled.

Brenna thanked them for the information and continued up the sidewalk until it ended abruptly along the next block. There she was forced to gingerly negotiate her way between the mud ruts, stepping on debris and wooden planks, staying as close to the houses as she could, until she found herself in front of the immigration office. With a sigh of relief, she entered the building, but she was made to wait nearly two hours before anyone could see her.

Eventually, a harassed-looking Englishman took her papers and explained her rights to her, including the information that only two years' residence in the city, and a sworn statement before a local justice of the peace, were all that was required for naturalization. He also informed her that all British subjects in Argentina were guaranteed freedom of religion and exemption from military service. Brenna listened patiently, but when she proceeded to ask him about work for herself and to tell him the condition of her husband's illness, he shuffled her back to the waiting area, where she sat for two more hours. Finally, another official called her.

"You say your husband sustained an injury while crossing over from Ireland?" the tired-looking man asked her.

"Yes, a chest wound from a horse's kick, sir. He isn't well, and I fear he will—he should be under a doctor's supervision. I would like arrangements made in one of the hospitals."

"There's only one charitable institution here in Buenos Aires, ma'am, and that is likely to be quite filled. I'm afraid you will have to take your husband to a physician in private practice."

"But that will cost money, and I . . ."

"Your funds are depleted, ma'am, and you've only just arrived?" he looked at her unbelievingly.

As Brenna explained what had happened, she felt no sympathy from the cold man seated across the desk.

"I see. Well, it seems you will have to trust to the honor of this agent. I suggest that you go back to the hotel and remain there until tomorrow at the appointed hour."

"But what about work?" Brenna cut in anxiously. "I wanted to know about something I could be doing to earn money while—while my husband was recovering."

The man shrugged. "Mrs. Ryan, I feel sure you would rather wait and see what this man may tell you tomorrow. I'm afraid there are very few openings in the city for young women of child-bearing age." He disregarded the blush on her cheeks. "Perhaps some type of servant's work, although most of the *porteños* prefer their own household servants or their slaves. Other than that, ma'am, I'm afraid your only other choice would be the brothels." He leaned closer across the desk, and for the first time, Brenna thought she detected a sign of interest.

Angrily, she stood up, her cheeks flaming. "Good day, sir. I'm afraid, as you say, I have no other recourse but to wait and see what will happen tomorrow."

She swept out of the office, feeling as though she had been gravely insulted. As she made her way back to the Immigrants' Hotel, she belatedly realized that she had been gone over six hours, and anxiety welled up within her as she thought of Kevin, perhaps in a fever, waiting for her. She hurried her step, arriving out of breath back at the room.

There was no sign of the Spanish girl. Quickly, she went to Kevin, who was still sleeping fitfully and tossing about with a high fever. Cursing her own stupidity, she felt inside Kevin's coat, but knew before she found the empty coin purse that there would be nothing inside of it. What a fool she had been to trust the girl. Why hadn't she thought to take the money with her? Tears coursed down Brenna's cheeks, and she sat dejectedly on the bed, her head in her hands. Kevin would die—and she had no money even to find a doctor to help him.

"Brenna? Is that you, darlin'?" Kevin's voice came slow and thick.

"Yes, darling, 'tis your Brenna," she answered, quickly wiping the tears from her face. "Have you slept well?"

He nodded. "Thirsty and hot," he said imploringly. "Damned chest hurts like a blasted knife wound."

"I'll just leave you for a moment," Brenna said, frightened at his words. "I'll be getting you a cool drink of water, and—and a doctor to look in on you." She smoothed back his hair, sopping with sweat, and hurried out to the desk.

"Please, you must help me," she pleaded with the oily man. "My husband is very sick. He needs a doctor's care. Is there one nearby?"

The man looked over his grimy lists and nodded suddenly, a smile brightening his dark face. "Yes, yes, a German doctor on the second floor, room sixteen. I don't know if he's in now, but . . ."

Brenna was already up the stairs, searching frantically for the room number, rushing in before several pairs of surprised eyes as she called for the doctor. There seemed to be only women and children and a few old men, in a corner, talking among themselves. One of the old men stood up from his seat and bowed to her, speaking in a language she did not understand.

"I need a doctor, you old fool!" she said desperately. "Do you know where he is?"

A young girl, perhaps fourteen, came up behind her. "He is the doctor. He is my grandfather, Josef Heinsius. I am Eva."

"Oh, I—I am sorry," Brenna got out through her surprise. "Does he not understand any English?"

The girl shook her head. "But I can speak it, *mein Frau*."

"You must ask your grandfather to come with me immediately," Brenna said quickly, glancing with uncertainty at the elderly man who had a snow-white beard and silver hair. He must have been nearly seventy. "My husband is gravely ill, running a high fever . . ." She was leading the two of them back downstairs to her room as the granddaughter translated her words to the physician.

Brenna watched nervously as the German bent over Kevin and examined him. He motioned to the ugly bruise on his chest, and Eva, gleaning the details from Brenna, repeated them in German to her grandfather.

"My grandfather thinks that perhaps the injury to his chest may have damaged the lung and caused infection. The symptoms of headache, fever, and pain would indicate pneumonia." Eva looked at Brenna with sympathy. "He needs to be moved to a warm, dry place."

"But I have no money," Brenna said. Fear and impatience gnawed inside her. "The last of our money was stolen only this morning."

The girl translated rapidly to her grandfather, who shook his head and shrugged and replaced the thin blanket over Kevin's body. He hesitated a moment, then reached into his valise and drew out a small vial of powder. He handed it to Brenna, patted her hand, and nodded to his granddaughter.

"He says to give your husband a little of this powder twice a day," Eva said. "It will help the pain somewhat." She curtseyed. "I am sorry, ma'am," she said and was gone with her grandfather, leaving Brenna alone, clutching the vial in her palm, her face a mask of misery.

So, that was that? Nothing else could be done? It was unbelievable that Kevin was going to die here in this filthy room in a strange country. It was inconceivable that they had come seven thousand miles, only to have all their bright hopes dashed so quickly. Brenna felt like screaming her rage and frustration to God, demanding that he make Kevin well again. She realized she was shaking and sat down on the side of the bed, feeling Kevin's fingers picking at her sleeve.

"Have you brought me a glass of water?" he asked slowly, then went into a fit of coughing that left him drained.

Brenna hurried into the kitchen and came back with a cup of the river water, certainly not clear like the water they used to collect at home in the rainbarrels, but at least it was cold and would slake his thirst. She dissolved a little of the powder in it.

"There now, Kevin, you'll be going to sleep again soon," Brenna soothed using the last of the water to wet a handkerchief and lay it against his forehead.

She would stay with him the rest of the day, lending her own body heat to keep him warm, should the shivering overtake him again. She must wait until tomorrow—if she could just get through today and tomorrow, she was sure something would turn up. With the money she would get from the agent, they could move to a decent hotel with a blazing fire and perhaps obtain the services of a physician who might be able to help Kevin. Keep him warm and dry, she thought determinedly—and surely he would recover. It was just his weakened condition—once she was able to get some decent food down him, he would regain his strength.

Biting her lip to keep from breaking out into sobs of terror and loneliness, she pushed her face into the mattress and waited dully for the supper bell.

Chapter Thirty-Nine

AT precisely ten o'clock the next morning, Brenna was shifting from one foot to the other, awaiting the arrival of Señor Maliga at the dock offices. She stepped beneath the overhang of the roof, trying to keep out of the cool wind that blew in off the river estuary. Around her all kinds of people surged back and forth, some giving her tentative, curious looks.

She waited nearly an hour before she saw the lean dark Spaniard coming toward her. His face was still scowling. Her hopes fell sharply, for surely if he had been able to talk with Steven, he would have looked far more pleasant. She swallowed nervously and nodded when he politely tipped his hat.

"Mrs. Ryan, I am sorry to be late, but other business detained me in another part of town. As the day is chilly, I will come directly to the point. I received an answer from Señor Castaneda's legal counsel early this morning. He advised me to reimburse your money; he also gave me the names of several people who might give you employment here in the city. I regret that neither Miguel nor Steven Castaneda could be here to see you, but they have other duties to perform."

"But, do they know I am here?" Brenna asked. Her relief at getting her money back was blunted a little by the feeling that she had just been summarily discarded.

"I was not able to speak directly with either of them, but I am sure they will contact you when they return from their business trips. Meanwhile, I suggest you present yourself to the Sociedad de Beneficencia, which is the national charitable humanitarian institution here in the city. They will be able to suggest an inexpensive hotel."

"Thank you, señor. I—appreciate your efforts," Brenna said mechanically.

He bowed again and left swiftly. Brenna stood in the

open breezeway, her hand clutching the purse of coins, as she stared uncomprehendingly at the names and addresses on the card he had given her. Shaking her head, as though to clear it, she hailed a diligence and returned to the Immigrants' Hotel.

She was relieved to find Kevin sleeping calmly. She hated to wake him, but the sooner she could get him to a comfortable hotel, where she could have their trunks delivered from the wharf, the sooner she could dress him in warm, dry clothes and think about gaining some employment.

It was only after she and Kevin had been deposited in front of the Sociedad de Beneficencia, that she realized she had forgotten all about Minx. In fact, the agent had probably taken her with the rest of the horses, assuming she was part of the shipment. For a moment, she was tempted to hurry back down to the docks and claim her horse—that would at least provide her transportation in the city and free her from the expense of the diligences, but she couldn't leave Kevin again. Besides, Maliga might have already taken the horses out of the corrals and put them on a railroad car. She would have to do something about it later. She hoped Minx would forgive her mistress for leaving her.

The people at the Sociedad were polite, if distant, and helpful in explaining the directions to the addresses on the card. They suggested an inexpensive hotel only a block away, and offered the services of one of their own physicians at a reasonable rate. Brenna promised to return in the morning for the doctor. She hurried Kevin off to the hotel, which turned out to be shabby, but at least they had a fireplace in their room, and the fee for firewood was included in the rent. Brenna paid for a week in advance and ordered one of the clerks in the lobby to send for their luggage. When at last it arrived, Brenna began to relax. She bathed Kevin in warm water and dressed him in clean, dry clothing.

He seemed more alert now and eyed her soberly as she moved about unpacking trunks and finally changing her own clothes, which had become frightfully dirty in the city streets.

"Ah, that does feel better," she sighed, giving herself a moment to sit in a chair by the roaring fire.

"How much money have we left?" Kevin asked abruptly, his brow furrowing.

Brenna looked at him. "About two pounds, I think," she said softly.

He rubbed his face, then winced at the abrupt movement of his arm. "How long are we paid up in the hotel?"

"A week," she answered. "Long enough for me to find some sort of teaching job."

"Aye, and perhaps I'll be able to get out of this damned bed and back on my own two feet." His voice was still faltering, try as he might to push more strength into it.

Brenna didn't feel like arguing, so she nodded her agreement. Presently, she stood up again and went to the small window to look out onto the muddy streets. "I've been given three names of people who might be able to give me employment," she said thoughtfully. "I'd like to be going now, Kevin."

"Out, again?" he asked fitfully, like a small boy. "Brenna, I'm thinking 'tis not right for you to be going out so much alone in a strange city. You—you could get hurt."

She shrugged. "There's no one else to do it for me, Kevin, and you're much too sick to climb out of bed yet. 'Tis windy outside and you'd only make yourself worse." She looked at the signs of his sickness: white face, trembling lips, two highspots of color on his cheeks. As she remembered the diagnosis of the German doctor, all of her strength threatened to drain out of her. "I've got to be going, Kevin. 'Tis the only way—until you're able to find work."

For a moment, she thought he was going to protest again, but then he fell silent. A look of pain crossed his face, followed by a cast of fear in his eyes that hurt her beyond words. She knew that he was afraid—Kevin, who had never been sick a day in his life until now. Was he regretting his decision to emigrate to this strange and hostile country? She looked away. Even if he did, there was no way to undo it now. They hadn't enough money to obtain passage on another ship.

"Then if you must go," he began heavily, "I suppose you'd best be getting off now while there's some daylight left." He tried to give her a severe look, but he failed utterly. "Don't be coming in after dark, Brenna."

She promised to be back before supper and leaned over to kiss him. "Wish me luck, darling," she said softly, forcing her lips into a tight smile; then she went out. She leaned for a moment against the door, until she heard broken sobs coming from her husband. As though fleeing in terror, she hurried down the hall and out into the familiar muddy concourse.

The house of Juan Valera was the last name on her list. Brenna lifted her hand wearily to grasp the heavy, ornate knocker. It landed with a dull clunk against the paneled door, and she waited for the inevitable butler to open it and give her the usual haughty stare of disapproval. She was tired of overly curious looks from strangers. The name of Castaneda had assisted her in gaining two brief interviews; but, at the first address, they had needed a man to attend to the gardening during the spring and summer months (something Brenna studiously filed away in her mind for future use when Kevin recovered); and the second address needed an upstairs ladies' maid or a kitchen helper, both of which paid only room and board for one.

So there was little hope left in Brenna Ryan as she stood waiting for this door to open. It took as long as she had expected, but instead of being met by a haughty old man, she found herself being inspected by a younger man, whose dark eyes and slick black hair identified him as one of the *creoles* of the city, men who prided themselves on their pure Spanish origins.

"Yes, may I help you?" he asked in English. He obviously knew she wasn't a native.

"Yes, I was given this address and told you were seeking an employee," Brenna began, feeling like a small child trying to explain herself.

"Ah, and who gave you the address, senorita?"

"I am Mrs. Brenna Ryan of County Wexford, Ireland, señor. The address was given to me by a man named Maliga, who works for the Castaneda family, with whom my father is acquainted."

"I, too, am acquainted with the Castanedas, senora." He opened the door wider. "Please, come in."

Brenna stepped up into the foyer, shaking her skirts self-consciously on the rug provided for that purpose. The interior of the house was dark with narrow slits to allow the thin lighting to come in above the door. She stared at the young man who had let her in.

"Might I inquire, are you Juan Valera?"

He smiled politely. "Forgive me, Mrs. Ryan—I am Carlos Valera, a cousin of Juan Valera, and here on sufferance at the moment." His words were tinged with faint resentment.

"Then, can you take me to your cousin? I require employment, sir, and this is the last interview on my list."

"Certainly, Mrs. Ryan—if you will follow me?" He led her down a dark hall and up a narrow staircase to the second floor. They entered a drawing room, which was brighter than the hallway, but filled with dark and somber furniture in the Spanish style.

The family seemed to be in the midst of a discussion involving one of the servants, for Brenna thought the young, dark-haired girl in the uniform couldn't possibly be part of the family. She was standing, head down, as though expecting to be severely rebuked by a middle-aged gentleman with a close-cropped beard and jet black hair. The man looked up, obviously irritated at being interrupted, and the woman beside him scowled like a great, fat cat.

"Cousin, I am sorry to interrupt you," Carlos began without a hint of apology in his tone, "but this young lady is seeking employment with you. She was referred to us by old Miguel himself."

"Castaneda!" the man said reverently. "Come in,

child," he said, a thin smile parting his lips. His wife continued to scowl. "Maria, sit down. I will continue my business with you in a moment," he said to the girl, who looked fifteen or so. She obeyed, casting a grateful eye toward the newcomer.

"You must forgive me for not welcoming you more appropriately," Valera rushed on. "You say you were sent to me from Miguel Castaneda?"

Brenna nodded, taking a seat. "Yes, my father is Tyrone Kildare. He and Miguel Castaneda deal in business together. My father ships horses to him from County Wexford in Ireland."

"Ah, those magnificent horses of his! So that is his secret!"

Brenna smiled proudly. "My father is renowned for his horse raising."

"And where is your father? I should like to make his acquaintance."

"He is still in Ireland, senor. My husband and I came to this country to start a new life, but during the crossing, my husband was injured and is confined to his bed. Therefore, it is my duty to find employment to provide the money for the hotel and a physician." She tried to maintain her proud demeanor, though the scowl on the woman's face seemed to cut even deeper. "I am very knowledgeable in languages, sir—English, Spanish, French . . ."

"Oh, French, Mama!" The girl called Maria clasped her hands together in excitement.

Brenna was disconcerted to discover the girl was not a servant but the daughter of the house. She discreetly eyed the plain, somber gown, imagining the girl better suited to more vivid colors that would bring out the dusky rose of her complexion.

"Your father is an acquaintance of Castaneda's—and yet you are looking for work?" Valera was saying suspiciously. "Why is it that your father did not provide for you?"

"We—were robbed of most of our money at the Immigrants' Hotel," she said, hedging on the truth. "And

426

I'm afraid my father was none too keen on my coming to Argentina—so you see I cannot possibly write to him for aid yet." She hoped he *did* see, although his face was still doubtful.

"Juan, I'm sure the girl is telling the truth," Carlos Valera put in swiftly. "And she seems to be an excellent teacher for the children. Truly, you were in need of a tutor in languages."

"True enough," Juan Valera admitted, then looked to his wife for the final decision. "Isabel?"

Brenna was convinced she was doomed if her fate was left in the hands of that scowling woman, but she was pleasantly surprised when Senora Valera nodded slowly. "She will do well enough, but I will insist that she remain as part of the household staff. She is not to be elevated to a higher position because of some vague acquaintance with Miguel Castaneda." The woman's voice was startlingly tiny for her size. Her small, dark eyes roamed quietly over Brenna's happy expression. "She seems eager enough and more than willing to work—I have come to expect much from my servants, señora," she said to Brenna.

Brenna didn't like being called "servant", but she let it pass, too relieved to have a job to do anything more than smile gratefully. "I will do my very best to please you, Senora Valera," she answered.

"Good. Your wages will be twelve pesos per month—paper currency, of course."

Brenna wasn't certain if this was a good wage, but she knew that the hotel would at least be paid, and there would be enough to buy food. She had never felt so humble in all of her life. "Thank you, oh, thank you, señora."

The woman seemed pleased by her gratitude and allowed a smile to replace the scowl. "You can begin tomorrow then?"

"Yes, yes, of course. I am staying at the Hotel del Sol with my husband. At what time should I be arriving in the morning?"

"Eight o'clock, senora—and you will put in a day's

work, you may be sure. I will provide you with your midday meal." Senora Valera skeptically eyed Brenna's yellow and white muslin dress. "I do hope you have more suitable garments to wear."

Brenna wisely held her tongue, and nodded her head in submission. "How many children are there?" she asked.

"I have five children," Juan Valera said with pride. "Maria is the eldest. She is fifteen. Then there are the twins, Guido and Anna, who are twelve; Eduardo is ten, and Santino is six."

Brenna's spirits were lowered when she heard that she would have to deal with a six- and a ten-year-old. She knew from experience that children of that age would not want to learn anything she might have to teach them. She sighed to herself. Who knew? Possibly with a mother as dour as Isabel Valera and a father as rigid as Juan, the children would be forced into behaving.

"It sounds very interesting," she commented diplomatically. "I will see you at eight o'clock, then."

Chapter Forty

BRENNA showed fortitude in settling into her new job. Kevin showed little. He was irritable and resentful when she, tired from the struggle of keeping five children entertained for ten hours, returned at night. He was, he said, disgusted with himself for staying in bed all day while she went out and slaved for him.

Then, a week after Brenna had taken her job, she got up one morning to find Kevin dressed and washed, looking nearly his old cocky self, except for the extreme pallor of his skin and the slight trembling of his hands when he reached up to brush back his hair.

"Kevin, what are you doing up and about?" she asked in concern, for she already knew what his answer would be.

"I've decided, my darlin', that today is the day. Today, Kevin Ryan will be seeking a decent job in the city, and his wife will be putting in her resignation." He smiled beguilingly. "Aw, lass, don't look so nervous. I'm fit, truly I am—fit as a fiddle and ready to do a man's duty—'tis not meant for a husband to be lying about all day like a sick babe."

"But Kevin, your injury—the pneumonia—"

"Pooh! I tell you I'm fine—a little cough is all that's left of it. Ah, darlin', luck is bound to be on our side by now. I'll go right down to the immigration office. Hah! Just wait until I tell them about all my experience with the horses." He looked at her and his freckles seemed to stand out like drops of blood on his face.

Brenna shuddered and closed her eyes, forcing away the premonition. "Well, I'll stay on with the Valeras until you find employment," she said shakily. "No use quitting too early."

"Aye, you're right there, my love. What a smart little wife I have. Too smart sometimes, I'm thinking," he laughed, then walked over and kissed her on the mouth. "Well, it's off I am—see you this evening." He tossed his cap on and waved merrily while Brenna, with a heavy heart, watched him go.

Her day at the Valeras kept her mind off her husband. Guido and Anna were quarreling, and Santino was just beginning a temper tantrum, when the door of the school-room opened to reveal Carlos Valera.

"Mrs. Ryan, there you are. I see you are having your usual pleasant day!" He smiled, showing his white teeth, then winced at Santino's temperamental screams.

"Hush, Santino. Sit down like a good boy, or you'll not help me to erase the blackboard today," Brenna threatened, trying to keep her temper. Why was Carlos invading her at this, the most trying time of the afternoon, when Santino was becoming tired, and Maria was beginning to look out the window in boredom? "Señor Valera, would you be so kind as to come back a little later? Did you wish to speak to me?"

He smiled again. "Yes, I have a visitor for you, Mrs. Ryan, but if you do not wish . . ."

"A visitor?" she interrupted. She knew a moment of terror at the thought that it might be Kevin, coming to tell her he had found a job and creating a scene to hasten her own resignation; she had no intention of giving up her employment here until she was sure that Kevin could actually hold down a job.

She turned toward the doorway, expecting to see his red hair popping around the frame. Instead she was confronted with a pair of black eyes that seemed to pin her to her chair, a long, aristocratic nose ending in a thin, black moustache above firm lips, and a wealth of midnight-black hair that was not slicked back with oil, as Carlos' was, but allowed to wave indolently around the man's ears and at the back of his collar.

"St-Steven!" she got out in a choked voice.

His smile was courteously polite, almost indifferent, but in his black eyes was a look that was hard to define. Brenna, in her shock, sat down abruptly in her chair. The noise of the children was drowned out by the pounding of her heart as Steven Castaneda de la Cruz walked toward her, his hand extended in welcome. She stared at it for a long moment, until Maria's giggle brought her abruptly back to reality. She took his hand, feeling the warmth of him enfolding her palm.

"Brenna Ryan, how good it is to see you again."

She dared not search his face to find the mockery in his eyes, but kept her eyes on his hand as it slipped easily out of her nerveless fingers. She cleared her throat, risked a glance at Carlos' amused face, then stood up again.

"How did you know . . ."

"I am sorry I was not able to meet you when you first arrived, Brenna, but I was on a business trip to Córdoba and only arrived back in town yesterday. My attorney advised me of the payment he authorized to you, and also informed me that you had been given certain addresses where you might obtain employment." He smiled with a kind of dare. "I must admit I was surprised to hear that you were in Buenos Aires. I had always thought that Ireland would be your home forever."

"Things do change," she said defensively. "Kevin wanted to come. He thought that emigration to Argentina would provide new opportunities for us." Her voice was flat with disillusionment.

"Kevin, of course, how could I forget?"

Why did he sound so maddeningly insolent? Brenna felt heat in her cheeks. "It seems you did forget to tell your agent. His refusal to reimburse our money promptly caused us to be housed at the Immigrants' Hotel for two nights, during which time my husband became ill after suffering an injury on board our steamliner." She hated the way her voice sounded, childish and expectant, as though hoping he would offer to undo all the injustices they had suffered since arriving in this damned country.

"I am sorry for your husband's illness," Steven said sincerely. "If there is anything I can do . . ."

It was on the tip of Brenna's tongue to ask him to give her husband a job—something light and not too strenuous that would help Kevin to feel needed, yet not tax him unduly while he was still recovering—but pride made the

431

words fail her. Instead, she shook her head, then stopped abruptly.

"Yes, my horse, Minx, was taken with the rest of the shipment by your agent. With everything else happening, I inadvertently forgot about her—what I would have done with her, I don't know," she admitted. Then she straightened her shoulders and looked at him, "But she is mine, and I'll be taking her as soon—as soon as I can find someplace to put her up."

He nodded. "Be assured she is in good hands," he said. "You have no idea how many memories that horse holds for me, Brenna—I'll make sure she is well taken care of."

Brenna winced as she thought of the fox hunt of so long ago, when Minx had reared up and kicked him.

The children started to grow restless again. "As you can see, Steven, I am very busy right now," she said, indicating the children, "and I would appreciate it if you would leave and allow me to get on with my work."

He grinned and bowed. "Of course, Brenna, I can imagine what stimulating company this must be for you —much preferable to my own." He saw the anger flare up in her eyes, lighting up the blue like a gas flame. Smiling and chuckling to himself, he took his leave, fearful lest she explode and ruin her reputation in front of the children.

Brenna stared at the closed door for a moment, willing her anger to settle down. The pomposity of the scoundrel! She wished he had never come. He could at least have offered to give Kevin a job—but no, he hardly asked about him. She turned back to her pupils, speaking so sharply to Santino that he promptly began bawling again.

The day seemed longer than usual, and it vexed her to come home to an empty hotel room. She was ravenous, and disgruntled that she had to wait for supper. As there was nothing else she could do until Kevin came home, she started up the fire and warmed herself, refusing to dwell on Steven's visit today.

Nearly an hour after she had arrived, Kevin came into the room, his face a mask of weariness. Quickly, she urged him to a chair. "Have you found work?" she asked.

His laughter was harsh and full of bitter disillusionment. "Aye, I've found work," he answered wearily. "Work fit for a slave."

"You—you found nothing with horses?"

His laughter rose again, cold as brass in the stillness of the room. "Everyone looked at me as though I were a loony. Horses? Here in the city? The only horses were those stabled by the *porteños*, all of whom had their own groomsmen, and those used for the public vehicles. Imagine, I can be a stableboy again! Not a very long journey we've made, after all, Brenna."

"Oh, Kevin, I'm sorry."

"They told me," he said in a strangled voice, "I could be railroaded out onto the open country and dig ditches, or I might help manage sheep. Irishmen, I was told, have an affinity for sheep." He laughed again and tears rolled down his cheeks. "Sheep, Brenna!"

" 'Tis not so bad . . ."

" 'Tis disgusting work for me, Brenna! I'll not have it!"

"So—what work did you get, Kevin?" she asked timidly, afraid of offending him.

He bowed before her. "Your husband is now one of the faceless lads who stride about the docks looking for unloading jobs. Imagine, Kevin Ryan a goddamned stevedore!"

"No, Kevin! The work is much too arduous for you now. And being close to the water all day . . ."

" 'Twas all there was that paid a decent wage," he cut in dully. He slumped in the chair and gazed at the fire. "God, I am tired, darlin'. What say we eat and go to bed, eh?" He sighed. "Maybe tomorrow a miracle will happen."

"Kevin, oh, Kevin," Brenna murmured, laying her head in his lap. "What is to become of us?"

She could feel his shrug. "I'll work all day and—aye —you can be keeping your employment for a while yet. If there's one thing we've got to be thankful for, 'tis that you're barren," he ended bitterly. "At least we will have no little ones to provide for."

Brenna had stiffened at his unkind words, but realized

that he hadn't meant to be cruel. He was just stating the facts. She supposed that she should be glad she was unable to conceive, for she certainly could not work if she were pregnant, nor did she think Isabel Valera would allow her to continue if she brought a child into the house every day.

She got to her feet and looked down at her husband, seeing the dark circles of fatigue around his eyes, the pinched look about his mouth. "I'll have supper sent up," she said softly.

The next morning, Kevin was up and gone before her, for he had to be at the docks by dawn when the ships began unloading their freight. Brenna dressed herself and decided to walk the five blocks to the Valeras' house. A sudden rainshower caught her still two blocks from the house, and she had to run to avoid getting soaked. By the time she arrived at the door, she was muddy up to her ankles, and her hair was in total disarray. Agustín, the majordomo, opened the door, and she swept past him to the warmth of the kitchens at the back of the house. She could hear Agustín's mutterings about the trail of mud and water she was leaving on the floor, but she had no time to apologize. With Kevin already ill, there was no sense having another sickling in the family.

"Oh, Mrs. Ferriday, I am soaked to the skin," she cried out as she entered the kitchen. The cook was an Englishwoman and reminded Brenna a little of Mrs. Longstreet at Markham Hall. "Do you have anything I could be wearing until this gown dries? Señora Valera will be furious if I present myself like this!"

"Well," Mrs. Ferriday looked dubiously at her own ample waistline. "I do keep an extra frock in the back, but 'twill look like a sack on you, my dear."

"I don't care if it looks like a barrel on me, Mrs. Ferriday. At least it will be blessedly dry, and I will be decently covered. She can't complain about that."

Mrs. Ferriday laughed. "I don't know why it is, but one peep at the top of your bosom, and the lady of the house has a fainting fit. I do pity poor Maria, having to wear those schoolgirl uniforms all the time." She shook her head in motherly fashion.

Brenna peeled the wet clothing off her shoulders, and was standing in her vest and petticoat, when an unmistakably male laugh scared the wits out of her. She turned abruptly to discover Steven Casteneda and Carlos Valera opening the door from outside. Both stopped their conversation at the vision before their eyes.

"Why—I do believe it's Mrs. Ryan," Steven spoke first, bowing ostentatiously.

Carlos smiled too, though he was less at ease. "It seems we've interrupted something," he got out, retreating a few steps back into the cold.

"For heaven's sake, do close that door, or I'll be frozen in another moment!" Brenna snapped angrily, hugging her arms around herself more from the cold than from embarrassment. "Don't you know how to knock?" she demanded.

Carlos had already retreated, but Steven still lounged against the doorframe, surveying the picture before him. "Yes, senora, I do know how to knock," he answered leisurely, "but I must admit, I am not accustomed to knocking on the kitchen door." He was laughing.

"Well, perhaps you should accustom yourself to it!" Brenna returned wrathfully. "If I catch a cold, I shall certainly lay the blame on you!"

He put his hand to his heart in a dramatic gesture. "Mrs. Ryan, if you catch cold, I shall nurse you back to health. It would be the least I might do for one who has nursed me in years past." His black eyebrows arched upward like the wings of a bird.

"Laugh if you must," she said waspishly, "but I am warning you . . ."

Mrs. Ferriday returned from her room off the kitchen and stopped short when she saw Brenna, clad only in her underwear, chastising Steven Castaneda. In a flurry, the cook bustled into the room with the dress. Brenna pulled it over her head, dismally aware of the comical picture she was making to Steven as she stood there in a dress which was three sizes too big for her and drooping sadly on the floor. Determined not to show her embarrassment, she picked up her own belt from the table and snapped it tightly around her waist to draw the gown in.

"Good day, Steven," she said, nodding her head and wading out of the room. She suddenly recalled that she had left her shoes behind. Well, at least the dress would cover her feet, and it was better than leaving them in soaked leather all day.

"Bravo, Brenna!" Steven called after her.

Of course, the children were all amused by her costume, and she had to endure their giggles and sly glances all day. She prayed that she would not have to see Señora Valera, and in that, at least, she was spared. At the end of the day, she trudged back to the kitchen and climbed back into her own dress, thanking Mrs. Ferriday for the loan; then she wisely took a cab back to the hotel.

Brenna gasped when she discovered her husband laid out on the bed, still dressed, his face pasty white, his breathing labored, and his whole body raging with fever. With a cry of alarm, she stripped off his clothes and put him to bed. He seemed delirious, for he did not know her and could only moan incoherently. He coughed continuously, and Brenna could see flecks of blood on his lips. She must go back to the Sociedad to get a doctor immediately. Kevin should be taken to the hospital.

She built a fire in the hearth, then tied her cloak about her and hurried out into the gray dusk.

Chapter Forty-One

EARLY the next morning, in the Hospital of Saint Sebastian, Kevin Ryan died. He never recovered consciousness. Brenna stayed with him, holding his fevered hand throughout the long night, willing him to live, begging him to live, praying to God that He spare her husband. She had heard the last shallow breath escape in a clicking, buzzing rasp, and she looked up to see the doctor shaking his head sympathetically.

"I am sorry, Mrs. Ryan. The lung had hemorrhaged —there was nothing to be done. Your husband was in too weak a condition to be out in this weather. I'm afraid it was entirely hopeless." He had forced her up from beside the bed and called a nurse to take her down the hall while the body was covered and taken away.

Brenna sat numbly in a chair, sipping at a cup of coffee, which had been pushed into her hands, until the doctor came and sat down beside her.

"Do you have relatives in the city, Mrs. Ryan?"

She shook her head silently.

The doctor frowned in thought. "It's not safe here for a young woman alone, Mrs. Ryan, especially in a hotel. I suggest that you ask your employer for permanent quarters in his household."

She looked at him helplessly.

"Please, understand me, Mrs. Ryan, I am concerned for your own well-being. Your husband can no longer protect you."

"He has not been able to protect me for a long time," Brenna murmured. "He has been ill since we arrived."

"Circumstances are different now. Please heed my suggestion."

"What about the funeral arrangements?" she asked suddenly. "I don't know where . . ."

He patted her hand. "The hospital will take care of

that. A simple casket and burial in the public cemetery —unless, of course, you would wish to have the body shipped back to Ireland."

"Ireland?" she repeated. Tears came to her eyes at the sound of the name.

He patted her hand again. "I'll make the arrangements with the hospital to have him buried here. It will be easier for you," he coughed, "and less expensive."

"Yes."

The doctor stood up. "Shall I have someone escort you home?"

"Home," Brenna repeated like an automaton. She looked pitifully at the doctor. "You mean, the hotel?"

The doctor hesitated. "Please wait here, Mrs. Ryan, while I send a messenger to the home of the Valeras. You should not be left alone tonight in your present state of mind. I'm sure Senor Valera will see to you." He seemed relieved to have found an answer to his dilemma.

Brenna continued to sit silently in the chair, her only movement the unconscious kneading of her fingers as they picked at the material of her skirt. The hospital seemed quiet and dark now; everything was subdued, as though seen through a veil of fog. Brenna leaned back in her chair and closed her eyes. She wished she would never have to get up from this chair again, wished she could let life swirl around and away from her but never touch her.

The most painful truth for her was knowing that she had never loved Kevin as he had loved her, knowing that now it was too late to make up for all those times she could not find the words to return his vow of love for her. Poor Kevin. He had dreamed of coming to a new and rich land where he could be anything he wanted, where he could make as much money as he would ever need, where he could become a Tyrone Kildare or a Sir William Markham.

The dream had been snuffed out by a shabby hotel, by people who would steal your last coins to buy themselves a morsel of food, by the muddy streets and the cold, rainy weather, which had lent a somber, dismal cast to this city from the very first. His dream had died in a charity hospital, and now he would be buried in foreign soil in a public cemetery. She knew that Kevin would have wanted his body sent back to Ireland for burial, but once again, the absence of capital prevented Brenna from doing what he would have wanted. And somehow—and she hated to admit to herself that this was true—she didn't want her father to know, just yet, that she was without a husband in this new country. No, she couldn't go home like this, defeated, broken, to throw herself on the mercy of her father; she remembered with clarity the image of his stiff, broad back turned to her as she had waved goodbye to the family.

Perhaps in the future when she had proved to herself that she could live without her father's money and husband's protection—and she would prove it! But now, sitting here all alone, with Kevin truly gone, the future, the unknown, frightened her.

"Brenna."

She looked up, her eyes opening slowly, and met the dark gaze of Steven Castaneda de la Cruz. "Steven? What are you doing here?"

"The doctor sent a messenger to the Valeras. As an old friend of the family, I offered to come for you." His tone was sober, without mockery, almost indifferent. "Let me take you away from here, Brenna. The arrangements will be made by the staff for Kevin's burial, and you need your rest."

"Yes—I am—tired," she said almost absently, searching around for her reticule and coat.

He picked them up and helped her into her coat, buttoning the front as he would for a child. He was silent, thoughtful, as they walked together down the staircase and into the hospital lobby. He helped her into his carriage.

"Do you want to go back to the hotel?" he asked.

She shook her head, then smiled bleakly. "But I have nowhere else to go. I suppose I shall be all right for tonight. Tomorrow, I shall have to ask the Valeras for protection." She grimaced, imagining the painful interview with Isabel Valera.

"I wish I could help you, Brenna," Steven said, still in that strange tone of voice that always disconcerted her a little. She wondered why he couldn't help her. "Let me, at least, buy you supper. Have you eaten anything?"

She shook her head. "I'm—not—hungry."

He nodded, understanding. She looked at him curiously, studying his profile in the light of the coach lamps. He seemed angry or upset, but she couldn't imagine why —certainly not because of Kevin's death. What was troubling him? She chided herself—probably some worrying business, or perhaps a social engagement he had broken to come for her. The idea grew in her mind and she leaned against the side of the carriage, willing it to hurry to the hotel. She wanted him gone, suddenly, so that she could think and plan and remember.

Although the rest of the ride passed in silence, Brenna became even more accutely aware of the curious tension in her companion, and more puzzled by it. When they stopped at the hotel, he offered to escort her to her room, a wise precaution in this section of town, he assured her. When they reached her room, she fumbled awkwardly for her key, found it, and let herself in, startled as he came in behind her and closed the door.

"What do you want?" she asked, amazed at the sudden note of fear in her voice. This was Steven, her childhood friend—not some stranger pushing himself into her room. Why did she feel suddenly uncomfortable as she watched him looking at her with that odd expression on his face that lingered somewhere between anger and disappointment.

"I am amazed at you," he spoke suddenly, breaking the heavy silence.

She gave him a questioning look.

"I am amazed at the woman you've become, Brenna Kildare," he continued, moving into a chair, watching her try to put on a semblance of composure as she took off her outer garments and hung them to dry on pegs by the fireplace. "I can still remember you as a child—an honest child who cared about people and somehow managed to make everyone forget her little flaws of pride and stubbornness."

"I am no longer a child," she said stiffly, warming her hands by the glow of the embers. She thought of putting more wood on the fire, but waited for him to finish whatever he had to say.

"Yes, I can see that," he said; and at her slight flush, "I'm not talking about the twenty-year-old body of a woman. No. I'm talking about your character, your spirit, Brenna."

Brenna stared at him, wondering what his point was. "I'm tired, Steven, and I want to go to bed. Tomorrow . . ."

He laughed mockingly. "Afraid of a scene? Or perhaps that my coachman is wondering why I have not yet come down from your room? After all, you are the sorrowing widow, are you not? Not about to entertain thoughts of the next man she will be using to her advantage?"

"Steven, I don't know what you are talking about."

"Forgive me. I thought perhaps it might become obvious to you. I am talking about the callousness, the selfishness of a young woman who hasn't even the decency to cry at her husband's death." He held up his hand to stop her protest. "I admit I was startled at your calmness, your extreme composure in the face of such heartbreaking news," he said mockingly. "But, then I recalled how odd was your relationship with your husband, a man you obviously didn't care for."

"Stop it! Stop it! How dare you tell me such things? What has my life to do with you? What do you know about Kevin and me?" she flustered with humiliation.

"It was not hard to see that you did not love your husband," he answered her calmly, watching the play of the firelight on her face.

"That is none of your business! Kevin and I . . ."

"You married a man you didn't love," he went on, still composed. "For what reason, Brenna? That is what continues to puzzle me. Why did you marry, of all men, a lackey? I wonder that you, at the very least, didn't somehow get the dashing Adair to slip the ring on your finger. He might have been able to match you in spirit."

"Get out of my room!" Brenna cried shrilly. "Get out! I refuse to discuss my life with you."

"But we are old friends," he reminded her smoothly. He shook his head sadly as though at a wayward child. "Ah, Brenna, how your father must have hated seeing his beloved daughter married to a nothing." He could see by the look on her face that he had hit the mark. "Is that why you and Kevin ran away to Argentina? to get away from your father who would have constantly reminded you that you could have had something more? I can imagine Kevin quickly wore down under all that pressure. But then I can imagine you were as eager to see him become rich as he was. Then, when it looked as though he would become nothing more than an invalid, a stone around your neck, he conveniently died."

"How—dare—you!" she cried out, her eyes wide with fury.

"But I still don't understand *why* you married him in the first place," he went on, knowing that in another moment she would probably fling herself at him in a flurry of anger. He wasn't even sure why it was so important to him, but he wanted to know.

"If you don't leave me immediately, I will call out for the night watchman!" Brenna said, her voice shaking. Her entire body was trembling, and she could only hope that he would do as she ordered. "Go! I never want to see you again! Don't think I don't mean it—I never want to see you—"

"I recall words to that effect when last we met in Ireland," he mused.

With a cry of fury, Brenna swept towards him, intending to scratch his eyes out, claw the hair from his head, but she found herself capably held in place by two strong hands at her wrists and an iron body pressed against hers. She glared into his face, hating him, shaking with wounded pride and humiliation, so angry that she felt tears rolling down her cheeks—which made her angrier.

"Who are you crying for now, Brenna?" he asked her.

The question caught her unaware, and, slowly her anger died, leaving her to face the truth of being alone. She bowed her head and began to sob in earnest, wracking sobs, hating that it was Steven who was holding her, rubbing her back, and not Kevin, who had never held her like this. Oh, God! Was everything that Steven had said the truth? Was she selfish and proud? She had been a good wife to Kevin—she had! She must hold on to that fact. She had never, never let him know that his love for her wasn't returned. Steven was right—she had lived a lie with Kevin. But was the sin greater or less because he hadn't known it was a lie?

She felt Steven's arms, strong, and solid around her, a comfortable bulwark against the reality of tomorrow. But this was only a temporary haven, she knew. It would be up to her to pick up her life and make something of it. Yes, she had pride and stubbornness, and they would see her through.

"I'm all right now," she said, lifting her face.

He sighed. "Brenna, I don't expect you to forgive me entirely for my earlier words, but you must understand that I care for you, and I'm worried about your being alone. I was too hard on you—all I can say is that I'm sorry. The truth is not always a pleasant thing." He held her a moment longer. "Ah, my little dove, *'mi paloma,'* perhaps *I* should have been the one to marry you—at least I understand you."

He released her and bowed, then without another word went out, locking the door behind him.

Brenna stared at the door for a long moment after he had gone, perplexed by him and his last words. How could he be so cruel to her one minute, and so tender the next? And what was this talk of marriage? Had he ever really thought of marrying her? It was ridiculous to think of marrying again before poor Kevin was even in the grave. Besides, she had no reason to marry now. Her marriage had been a mistake—and she would not be making that same mistake again.

PART THREE

Argentina

1873–1890

Chapter Forty-Two

THE September equinox brought springtime to Buenos Aires like the sudden raising of a curtain. Almost overnight, the chill and the rainy gray skies were gone, and the warm sun brought warm temperatures. Brenna looked out from her small room in the servants' quarters of the Valeras' home, and breathed in the sweet fragrance of the orange blossoms and honeysuckle that bloomed in the patio gardens. She looked with pleasure at the riot of wisteria with its drooping clusters of showy purple and white flowers and the varicolored blossoms of the japonica shrubs, which reminded her of pretty European camellias. It was as though winter had never been, but the painful memory of Kevin's death still disturbed her dreams.

He had been buried in the public cemetery. By some miracle, Steven had found an Irish priest to say the ritual prayers over the gravesite. Brenna still visited the small, granite headstone and laid flowers on the grave once a week. She had written to her parents, and although she carefully omitted any mention of Kevin's death, she told them of the accident on board the steamship and of Kevin's ill health. She knew it was foolish to lie to them, but the thought of her father taking the next steamer to Buenos Aires to take her back to Ireland with him made her tremble.

No, she wasn't ready for that yet. She had a comfortable room at the Valera home, a good job at a fair wage, and a surprising amount of freedom. Freedom was a luxury she could really appreciate, for she had seen the boundaries of social law which forbade an Argentine woman to do anything unless accompanied by a chaperone or her husband. Being a foreigner, Brenna was not obliged to follow these rules, so she came and went as she pleased—within limits.

On many of her excursions, Carlos Valera came along. He had seemed much more attentive to her since the death of Kevin, and Brenna was not so foolish that she missed the connection. She was, after all, a foreign widow who had known a man physically. This would tantalize a young man like Carlos, bored and frustrated with the social sanctions that kept him from taking advantage of creole women. Like many of his counterparts, he often went to the brothels and whorehouses for some measure of relief.

Nevertheless, he had always been a perfect gentleman when he was alone with Brenna, and she appreciated this. She began to look forward to their outings together. If Señora Valera sometimes greeted her with a scowl when they arrived home, she chose to ignore it, hurrying off to her own room and leaving poor Carlos to bear the brunt of the woman's subtle accusations.

Steven, on his infrequent visits to the Valeras, also took Brenna to see the sights of the city. Like Carlos, Steven was always a gentleman, although Brenna received the impression that he was always holding something back. She was puzzled by his behavior, for although they had known each other a long time, he rarely showed the kind of close friendship she would have expected from such a relationship. He was always very formal and reserved when with her, and she wondered if he regretted baiting her the night of Kevin's death.

446

She actually knew very little about Steven's life, although she had been here more than a month now. She knew, from subtle questions to Carlos, that Steven's family had a three-story villa on Santa Fe Street, two or three blocks away, and a vast *estancia*, Paloma, on the pampas, where herds of cattle and horses were kept. Although Steven was one of the rich, charming, and educated members of the elite class in the city, he retained his friendship with Carlos, whose own fortune was considerably less and who was in disgrace anyway with his father for his questionable political activities.

Carlos openly sympathized with the Federalists, who were considered the rabble, the provincials, the gauchos and mestizos who supported a loose confederation of provinces and opposed the strong, central government of the Unitarians, who wanted Buenos Aires to be the self-styled 'queen city' of the country. The ranks of the Unitarians were made up of the *porteños* of the city and the great patrician *hidalgo* families who held most of the wealth in the country.

Brenna wasn't sure she understood the reasoning behind either theory, but she received an almost daily dose of Carlos' Federalist views, which reflected his strong belief in the righteousness of his cause and the rift between him and his father, who, like Miguel Castaneda and to a lesser extent, Steven Castaneda, believed in the Unitarian cause. Still, there was no friction over politics between Carlos and Steven, for each respected the other's right to his own beliefs.

After Mass and a light breakfast with the Valera family on the last Sunday in September, Brenna dressed in her riding habit. She felt excitement rising up in her, for Steven had promised to take her out to Paloma today to get Minx. Juan Valera had grudgingly given Brenna permission to use his stables for her horse, and she had nearly thrown herself into his arms in her joy. She had missed her horse, for only the mare still linked her strongly to her homeland.

She had been surprised when Steven had casually mentioned it to her last week, and her feelings for him were still ambiguous. Brenna found she could appreciate Steven's knowledge and considerable wit, a wit that was still turned to her disadvantage many times. She thought she liked him, and she brought out his old gift, the dove music box, and remembered the time he had kissed her after Dermot's wedding. Sometimes it amused her to think that she might be able to make Steven fall in love with her if she set her mind to it. After all, she was twenty now, a complete woman, and was, to judge by the looks that men gave her, an attractive female. But should she dare to flirt with Steven Castaneda de la Cruz? Although she freely admitted to herself that she might be taking too big a chance, the thought fired her imagination, and made her heart beat a little harder than usual as she finished her toilet and placed her riding hat on the smooth coils of her demure chignon.

She was waiting impatiently in the lower hall when Steven came to the door. Agustín gave her a disapproving glance as she trotted off, her arm linked with Steven's, into his carriage, but Brenna hardly cared. Today was too beautiful and fresh and lovely to worry about Agustín tattling to Isabel Valera. At least she would have Minx now and a lovely afternoon of riding; let the old woman scowl all she wanted.

"You look beautiful this morning, Brenna," Steven commented as they rode down the streets of Buenos Aires. "A certain excitement about you . . ."

"Oh, I do feel good today," she answered animatedly. "Steven, let's not spar with each other—it's just too lovely out!" She deliberately turned her prettiest smile on him and watched the familiar mockery seep into his black eyes.

"You want something, Brenna Ryan," he guessed, his voice teasing.

"Yes, I want my horse—and I'm willing to be nice to an old tormentor if he will graciously lead me to her," she answered pertly.

"Shall I take advantage of your willingness—to be nice?" he questioned ironically. "After all, it's not often that I have such a cooperative young lady alone with me."

Choosing to ignore his subtle nastiness, she continued to smile. As they drove out of the city, she could see, through the open windows of the carriage, flocks of woolly sheep clustering about the grasslands. She pointed to them curiously, asking her companion how it was that so many of the animals were allowed to graze so close to the city.

"It's become a sheepwalk all around Buenos Aires," Steven said. "Sheep graze better in land that has been trampled down by the cattle, so they let them roam at will."

"Do you have sheep on your *estancia?*"

He shook his head and roared with laughter. "Don't ever talk to my father about sheep, Brenna, if you want to be his friend, for given the chance, he would shoot every one of them. He is a cattle man and a horse lover —and there is a great difference between him and the sheepherders."

"And what about you? Do you also hate the sheep?" she asked pointedly.

He shrugged. "I, too, love the horses—and I am content with raising cattle, although I can also see the raising of sheep. At the moment, I am working with the Sociedad Rural Argentina, trying to bring shorthorn cattle into the country. The Sociedad believes, and I agree, that the stringy beef of our native cattle will never appeal to the Europeans as an export. The shorthorn have tender, fattier beef, which will appeal to the people on the other side of the ocean. Unfortunately, the short-horned animals cannot subsist on range grass, so we must raise alfalfa to feed them." He shrugged again. "It's hard to talk the landowners into raising alfalfa when they would rather keep the countryside as grazing pasture for their cattle. Many of the ranchers are nearly as stubborn as you are, Brenna."

Brenna, who had been dutifully listening to Steven's lengthy explanation, flushed at his accusation. "I thought we weren't going to ruin this lovely day," she said petulantly.

He bowed slightly from his seated position. "Forgive me, loveliest of señoritas, but I had forgotten our bargain."

" 'Twas no bargain," she said, with a puckish light in her dark blue eyes. "I simply asked you, as a rich and well-landed gentleman . . ."

"My dear, how vulgar of you to mention it," he interrupted snidely.

"Then I won't do so again," she countered, concentrating on the tips of her riding gloves. "I will devote myself to appreciating all this lovely scenery." She abruptly leaned away from him toward the window.

"I will show you the lovely scenery at closer range when we arrive at Paloma," he promised, leaning back in his seat to allow himself a full view of her profile.

They rode in silence the rest of the way. The ride was uncomfortably bumpy for the roads leading into the pampas were little more than dusty paths cutting through the high grass. Brenna leaned forward eagerly when Steven informed her that they were coming near to his father's estate. She could see, a little farther away to the left, a small, neat brick home with numerous sheds surrounding it, as well as a garden plot and a small orchard of plum and peach trees, under which four milch cows placidly grazed.

"That is Paloma?" she asked, disappointment filtering through her voice.

She heard the suppressed laughter in his voice. "Poor Brenna, are you so very disappointed then—what did you expect, a palace, perhaps?"

"Well, I only meant—"

"My, my, I'm finally realizing, much to the distress of my pride, that you only stay in my company because you think I am a rich man. Brenna, I never thought you to be so mercenary!" The underlying sarcasm in his words stung her.

"Well!" she demanded hotly. "Why else would I be staying in your company, Steven Castaneda?"

"Why, I had hoped it was because of our special friendship," he returned ironically.

She turned back to the window. "Oh, you do like to twist things around, don't you?" she said truculently. "Anyway, where is my horse? I can't see her yet."

"Oh, just a little way up the road here," he said casually, though his black eyes were fixed steadily and intently on her expression.

Brenna sulked as she waited, noting with absent-minded attention that they had turned up a well-kept drive where the bright green grass was clipped; they were slowly approaching an iron gate, fancifully decorated with scrollwork and filigree. A gateman eyed the carriage from his gatehouse window, then hurried to open up the gates, his huge sombrero brushing the ground as the carriage rolled by. Along the drive were beautifully kept grounds, shaded by groves of eucalyptus trees. A suspicion formed in her brain and she was about to turn to Steven with an accusation when the house came into her sight.

A startled exclamation broke from her lips, for she had truly never seen anything so huge since she had visited the palaces of France. The structure with its rose gardens and shade trees reminded her of a gabled English country house. It was grand and sprawling but somehow not vulgar and ostentatious in this panoramic setting, with the windswept pampas stretching out in every direction.

"Steven, this isn't . . ."

His smile was positively wicked. "Now, I suppose, I can count myself back in your favor?"

She frowned "Don't be nasty, Steven." Then with awe, "I had never imagined anything so—so large! How many rooms has it?"

"I've never counted them all, to be honest—does it matter?"

"But then—that other house down the road."

"Belongs to one of the smaller landowners. His name is Dolenga, and he serves as my father's overseer."

"Then, why did you let me think . . . ?"

"Don't be angry, Brenna. Come, I want you to meet my family." The carriage had pulled up in the circle drive and stopped in front of the steps leading up to a front door made of carved ironwood.

Brenna felt as though she were floating as she felt Steven's firm grasp on her hand, leading her up the steps and into the house. So rich, so very rich was all she could think for a moment—rich enough to have helped her when she arrived with Kevin, rich enough to have procured a good doctor for Kevin, rich enough to have lent her money with which to buy a small apartment until she could pay him back. She felt, deep within her, a bitter resentment at all this wealth.

They were walking through the large main hallway, walled with beautiful marble tiles of blue and white. Brenna discovered that, although the outside resembled an English country house, the inside of Paloma was decorated in the style of the Spanish. One could see the fondness for heavy, dark furniture and for the vivid tones of red and blue and emerald green.

Steven led her through an arched doorway into a large, high-ceilinged room filled with heavy furniture, bright-hued carpets, and sedate portraits. Three tall windows let in the light from the outside, which fell on faces, mirroring expressions of interest, curiosity, distrust, and appreciation, in the group in front of her.

"Brenna Ryan, this is my father, Miguel Castaneda; my mother, Consuelo; my sister, Rosaria," and now a slight hesitation before proceeding, "and my wife, Dolores."

For a moment, Brenna thought she had dreamed the final words. She felt as though she had been turned to stone, or worse, that she was still alive and that she would shortly have to say something to the dark-haired, frail-looking young woman who was staring at her with a hint of distrust in her dark eyes.

Steven—married! But he had said—he had told her in Ireland—that he wasn't married—that he hadn't married the girl . . . Gathering her strength, Brenna made herself smile in response to the polite murmurs of welcome. She nodded her head, feeling like a marionette. But her back-bone stiffened as she thought of the deception that Steven had played upon her. She risked a look of disdain in his direction and saw the fleeting admiration in his own eyes, mixed with the pain of an emotion she did not recognize.

"Senor Castaneda, I am so happy to finally have the pleasure of meeting you face to face," she said, all the while wondering why—*why?*—had Steven not told her he was married. Furthermore, why was it so important to her, and why did it hurt to find that he had deceived her?

"Mrs. Ryan," he responded, using the English term. "I, too, am happy to meet the daughter of a most respected business partner, as well as a great friend of my son. We welcome you to our house."

Brenna thanked the tall, dark man who reminded her so much of Steven, except for the silver hair and the lined face. She wondered how much he really approved of Steven bringing her here, unescorted.

Brenna glanced at the fragile, pale-faced young woman, who seemed the kind of wife a man would cherish and long to protect. Would Steven soften the barbs of his tongue when he spoke to his wife?

"My husband has not told us about you, Mrs. Ryan," Dolores said with shy stiffness in her voice. "I do hope you plan to stay."

Brenna shook her head abruptly. "I came only to get my horse. It was inadvertently taken with the rest of the cargo when my husband and I arrived in Buenos Aires."

"Your husband?" Miguel asked. "But—why hasn't he come with you?"

"He died a few weeks ago," Brenna answered flatly. She wanted to get away from all these people who knew Steven so well, and who stared at her as though she were some kind of freak.

"Please, sit down," Consuelo, Steven's mother, finally said, her handsome face breaking into a dignified smile. She indicated the seat closest to her own. "May I call you Brenna? I remember that is the only name I ever knew you by when Steven used to write us about his time in Ireland." She stopped and flushed a little, looking to her husband. "Dolores, sit next to me also," she said, hoping to make up for her faux pas.

Steven, who had remained silent since making the introductions, seated himself next to his father. Rosaria, his younger sister and obviously the favorite, seated herself on a low stool at her father's knee, while she continued to stare curiously at Brenna.

"I am sorry to hear of your husband's death," Consuelo offered politely. "How have you been managing since then?"

"I am tutoring the children of the Valera family in Buenos Aires. Isabel Valera kindly gave me room and board since I could no longer stay in a hotel alone," Brenna answered.

"Are you able to go out very much?" Rosaria demanded. "The city must be very exciting, and I expect you have no one to answer to should you wish to explore it."

Brenna smiled, seeing herself at sixteen in the young girl. "Frankly, I haven't seen that much of the city except for what Carlos and . . ." she stopped abruptly, almost having said Steven's name.

"Who is Carlos?" Rosaria wanted to know, not noticing the hesitation

"Rosaria, you do talk too much, my child." Consuelo said fondly.

"I don't mind answering her questions, senora," Brenna said, steadfastly refusing to meet the eyes of Steven's wife, although she could feel them, big and doe-like, resting on her. "Carlos is a cousin of Juan Valera, whose children I am tutoring. The eldest is Maria, who is very close to your own age."

"And do her parents allow her to go out with the young men?"

"No. Senora Valera is very strict."

"Like Mama," Rosaria ended forlornly.

Consuelo sighed. "Ah, Brenna, children can be such a trial—and such a comfort. Wait until you have them one day."

With a small cry, Dolores had gotten to her feet, her face as white as snow, her hand at her throat. With another sound very like a moan of pain, she fled from the room. Brenna, startled at her behavior, looked to Consuelo for an explanation, but the woman only looked at the fleeing figure of her daughter-in-law and shook her head.

"Consuelo . . ." Miguel began, then stopped and looked to his son. "Steven, perhaps you should go after her."

"She'll be all right in a few minutes," Steven said matter-of-factly.

Brenna could barely hide her surprise at his callousness. Why did he not follow his wife, who was obviously upset and weeping?

"Perhaps I should go down to see my horse, senor," she put in, rising from her chair, wishing to escape from the personal family scene. "I don't wish to intrude on your hospitality."

Castaneda smiled. "You haven't, Brenna. Forgive my daughter-in-law. She has been ill and is occasionally prone to outbursts. Perhaps another time you will visit longer and we can talk about your father and his horse farm."

"I would like that, senor." Brenna looked at Steven, wondering if he would be escorting her to the stables now.

"Father, I should like to take Brenna to get her horse and then to ride back into town with her. I have unfinished business in the city."

"Oh, but, Steven, you hardly ever stay anymore," Rosaria pouted. "Only on holidays—and it is so boring without you," she added mournfully.

"Then, perhaps, it is time for our parents to bring you into the city," he laughed. "Summer will be here soon . . ."

"And we have plans to go down to Mar del Plata, to the beach house," Miguel interrupted. "You will accompany us, son?"

Steven shrugged. "If I can, father."

"Dolores will want you to come," Consuelo put in softly.

His face tightened. "We will see." He offered his arm to Brenna, and she saw the look in his black eyes, which commanded her to take it.

455

Somehow, Brenna felt that she should never have agreed to come here with Steven. Had she disappointed old Miguel? Would he mention this in a letter to her father? She couldn't imagine his troubling himself but, after all, it did involve his son. And the nagging question still bothered her: why hadn't Steven told her he was married?

She wanted to ask him, but he seemed far away, locked in his own thoughts as he guided her through the double doors that led out into a covered porch and down to a graveled drive that led to the stables. His silence seemed filled with tension. What was wrong, she wondered. Had she acted improperly?

Brenna tried to brush her conflicting thoughts to the back of her mind, as Steven led her into the corral where Minx was whinnying gently at Brenna's scent. Brenna ran and clasped the great, strong neck in her arms, pushing her face against the silky mane.

"Ah, my Minx, how I've missed you," she sighed. The horse was already saddled; joyfully, she stepped up on the mounting block and threw herself into the saddle, grasping the reins with a surge of delight. Without a moment's hesitation, she led the mare through the open gate and out onto the cropped lawns of the *estancia*.

She thought she heard Steven call her name, but she ignored him. What had she to do with him, she thought with a mixture of pride and bitterness. He was married, tied to his family and his estate. She had her horse and the wind in her hair and open ranges to explore. She urged the horse on, down the curving drive, and out the open gate that freed her to the pampas.

On and on she rode, as though she were fleeing. Her hat blew off her head, but she did not stop to retrieve it. Like the mare she rode, she tossed her head and let her mane of black hair stream out behind her in careless abandon. She'd had enough—enough of men and work and frustration and tragedy. She was Brenna Kildare again, free and child-like, reveling in life and breathing it in great gulps.

She passed the great squares of shaggy eucalyptus

trees and tall stately Lombardy poplars that formed the windbreaks around Paloma. Out onto the open plains of the pampas she galloped, where there were only miles and miles of grassy land without stone or gravel. Ah, she could ride forever!

It seemed she had been riding for hours when suddenly, out of nowhere, it seemed, an enormous tree with great, spreading branches and knotted roots protruding like knuckles from the ground, loomed in front of her. Brenna forced her sailing thoughts to calm as she eased her mare from a wild gallop to a slow canter and then to a walk up to the curious sight.

"It is called an ombu," came a voice behind her.

Brenna knew who it would be even before she turned her head. Steven's black eyes gave her back her stare; she was the first to look away.

"I didn't know you were behind me," she said awkwardly.

"You might have lost yourself out on the pampas," he said to her. "There are over four hundred miles of pampas surrounding Buenos Aires."

"Oh." She glanced at him again, her eyes narrowing slightly. "Then I am grateful for your protection, senor."

He smiled lazily. "It has its price."

She was startled at his words. "What do you mean?"

"Now that you have your own horse again, you must promise to let me take you riding often."

Her heart slowed its rapid beating. "I hardly think 'tis proper to be riding alone with a married man," she answered him tartly.

He frowned. "It never seemed to bother you before."

She flushed. "That was because you never told me! Why didn't you tell me, Steven?" she asked suddenly in a softer tone.

"What difference would it have made?" He was watching her so intently that she had to look away from him.

"You are married—you have a wife to ride with."

He snorted sarcastically. "She has a fear of horses."

Brenna looked up, amazed, then shuttered her gaze once again. There was a moment of silence before she said, "You told me you hadn't married your *novia,* your betrothed. You lied to me, Steven."

"When I saw you in Ireland, I hadn't yet married her, Brenna." His smile was ironic. "If you only knew why I had come to Ireland—but it doesn't matter now, does it?" The smile twisted on his face. "Now, I am married, and you are free—the shoe is on the other foot, is it not?"

"When—when were you married?"

"Last March."

"Only six months!" she exclaimed.

"Yes, if only I had waited a little longer—until you arrived," he said softly, "but how could I have known . . ." He stopped.

Brenna watched his face and wished she could understand him. Why did his family seem so indifferent to his wife? Why had he not comforted her when she had fled the room, upset and crying? She said as much to him.

"My dearest, Brenna," he laughed bitterly, "you have chosen not to listen to a word of what I have said."

"I don't understand . . ."

"Yes, I see that you don't. Well, if we must talk about my wife, I will tell you why my family and my father, especially, is so indifferent to her." The mockery in his face seemed more directed at himself now. "I married Dolores to provide an heir for my father, to continue the bloodline, as is the duty of every young man to his family. My grandfather, my father's father, was a descendent of a powerful creole family in Córdoba. He became the *caudillo* of the district—the local strong man, if you will —a titled landowner who held great power both militarily, from his force of gauchos and peon underlings, and politically, in his ability to maneuver the government—in fact, he *was* the government of that province. His power was absolute, and many people sought security within his shadow. He was a great man, and he passed this tradition of greatness and power to my father, who would, in turn pass it on to me. The *caudillo* power ended in the 1860s—of course, my grandfather had already been dead a few years, but my father still held on to the tradition."

"But—what has this to do with . . ."

"Hush, Brenna. Let me finish," he chided her. He dismounted from his horse and tied the reins to a low branch of the ombu tree. Then he walked over to her and casually extended his arms to help her down from her own mount. Brenna slipped to the ground and waited as he tied Minx beside his own horse. He continued to talk as he sat beneath the trunk, cradled between two jutting roots, catching her arm to bring her down beside him.

"My father had everything he wanted, you see—wealth, power, prestige, and a son to carry on the tradition of the family into the next generation." He ran his hand absently through his thick black hair. "All that was left was for me to marry and produce a son of my own. Simple, isn't it?" His black eyes were fierce and strangely impassioned as he spoke.

"So, when you came to Ireland, you told me you weren't married, knowing that you would, in the end, be forced to marry," Brenna deduced hopefully, wanting to believe that he hadn't deliberately lied to her.

He looked at her for a long moment as though amazed at her words, then burst into sudden laughter, which seemed to roll like the lonely cry of a wolf out onto the vast pampas around them. "Ah, Brenna, how priceless you are—and how utterly naive! How is it that you can be so beautiful and yet so stupid?" He glanced at her suspiciously. "Or perhaps this is so because you want it to be."

Brenna felt affronted. "Forgive me for not living up to your expectations, but I'm afraid I cannot read your mind."

"Oh, Brenna, what would you say if I told you that I had delayed the marriage to Dolores and persuaded my father to let me go to Ireland—to ask you to be my wife?"

Brenna was stunned speechless. He was lying, teasing her; he had to be. Yes, he would never admit to such a thing—never! What a cruel joke he was playing on her.

"I would be saying that I'm not about to swallow such nonsense," she got out finally, her dark blue eyes stormy. "I'm not that much a fool, Steven."

He shrugged, but his eyes were laughing at her, which

only confounded her further. "The point is irrelevant at this late date. You were, of course, the bride of Kevin Ryan, much to my chagrin."

Brenna smarted under the underlying taunt in his words. She tossed her head, letting the thick tangle of midnight black wave softly down her back. "Well, you've proven lucky, Steven. You should be glad I was already married." And at his questioning look, "Yes, your father would have been highly disappointed to learn that his daughter-in-law was not only a foreigner, but a barren one at that." It had cost her a lot to say those words, and she blushed even as they came from her mouth, but she wanted to wipe smug indolence from his face.

Indeed, the expression left his face, only to be replaced by a look of dark, angry pain. "Yes, Brenna, it would have been unfortunate—but no more than fate would have it." His black brows met over his nose, and he looked so fierce that Brenna drew back. "For you see, my fragile, frail Dolores, with all the blue blood of landed Argentine families in her veins, cannot bear me children. So, my father has been cheated out of his one dream in all the world. After I die, the family line will die with me."

"Oh, Steven!" Brenna whispered sympathetically, although she felt more pity for the unfortunate Dolores who had to bear the brunt of all this.

"Don't feel sorry for me, Brenna," he said harshly. "I don't give a damn about continuing the line, but the idea consumes Dolores. Each week that goes by, she writes to a different doctor, hoping to get good news . . ." He stopped, as though suddenly chagrined by his own outburst. "It's damned hard for her," he ended abruptly.

"Steven, 'tis hard for you, too," Brenna countered. "I know what it's like to have a father pressuring you. Why is it that parents feel they must force their own hopes and demands on their offspring?"

"Ah, Brenna, are we cowards to blame it on our parents?" he asked. "I suppose it *is* easier—crying at the moon, shaking our fists at fate, but is it really so completely out of our hands to make our own destiny?"

For a moment, they stared at each other silently. Then, very gently, Steven reached his arm around her shoulders and brought her forward. "You know," he said, in a strangely gentle voice, an almost-caressing murmur that seemed to wash over her, "I can still remember the night I kissed you. You were young and untried then; now you are a woman, a widow—but your eyes have that same look of innocence. I wonder. Kiss me now, Brenna," he commanded softly, bringing her closer with his other arm.

Brenna could feel his hands tangling in her hair, could feel the insistent pressure of his touch on the back of her neck. A half-recalled sense of tingling, of excitement suppressed for too long, rose within her. She looked warily into the black eyes that melted into hers, and she tried to think rationally, tried to tell herself that too many years had passed since that engulfing feeling of need and desire had overwhelmed her. But her body refused to submit to the will of her mind—and she felt like a fourteen-year-old child again. Quickly, involuntarily, she closed her eyes, trying to sever the accord between them.

Steven, taking her action for acquiescence, bent down and brought one hand around to tilt her chin upwards. Then he was kissing her, his moustache tickling her a little, kissing her with slow, hot lips that leisurely molded her mouth to his, as his hand dropped from her chin to her waist, then around to her back to press her closer.

Brenna felt his arms tremble as he held her, as though Steven were deliberately holding himself back, fighting against a stronger urge—and that knowledge, coupled with his expertise in kissing her, flooded her even more with the tingling sensation of forbidden desire. He bent her backwards against his arm until her head rested against the bark of the ombu tree; her throat was arched and her back curved so that her body was almost lying against one of the huge roots.

He kissed her more, moving slowly, finally parting her lips—causing a thrill to squeal up her backbone at this new intimacy. Her mind seemed to be swaying, darkening, blotting out the warm, crisp morning and plunging her into a hot, sensual arena that frightened her. Resolutely, she tried to swim upward, back to cold sanity, and she found, to her dismay, that her riding jacket was already unbuttoned, and his slender, brown hands were inside her blouse.

As his mouth left hers to travel down her throat, she spoke. "Steven, let me go," she said in a husky, breathless voice that hardly sounded like her own.

For answer, Steven's mouth came up to hers once more and began to kiss her all over again, first softly, and then with a graduating intensity that silenced the part of her mind that had protested. Brenna again felt the rush of helplessness that should have alarmed her but instead made her anxious for the surge of warmth to envelop her totally. For the first time in her life, she thought she might faint. Yes, she would faint if he didn't stop kissing her, stop holding her—but if he stopped holding her, she knew that she would fall into an abysmal darkness that was the reality of the small room at the Valera home.

Her arms came up and held onto him now, clinging for fear that he would release her abruptly. She was shaking, her limbs and her body, her lips against his, as though whipped by a strong wind, as though she no longer had control of herself.

Once again, his mouth left hers to explore, but this time she could not make herself protest. She felt strangely lethargic, as though to lift her hand would have been too difficult a task. He was sliding her down to the ground, shifting his own position so that he could stretch out beside her as he continued, purposefully, to undo her clothing. His mouth, in a sudden fit of passionate impatience, bit away an offending button that held her blouse together at the throat, so that his hands could pull the fabric away.

Brenna forgot to tense, forgot to think about his hands and his mouth on her breasts, so she felt an odd surge of enjoyment flow up in her. Amazingly, she realized she was smiling—smiling like an idiot! The thought made her laugh aloud with pure, unimpeded joy—and Steven, hearing her joy, was spurred onward to new delights below the waistline of her riding skirt, which he unhurriedly pushed away.

Brenna's laughter stopped when she felt Steven's naked thighs against her own. He had said, "Kiss me," but she knew that he would not have been content with that. He was going to make love to her—out here on the rolling pampas grassland, beneath the shade of the giant ombu tree, among its enormous roots that surrounded them like the sides of a cradle. And she could not stop him.

The familiar movements came back to her naturally; she flexed her knees and arched her back, welcoming his body, holding him tightly now, gasping when he entered her, for it had been a long time since she had been made love to. The sensation felt, at the same time, odd and pleasurable and totally new to her. She opened her eyes wide when he started to move, fighting the urge to cry out in newfound joy and excitement, and she saw his black eyes staring back at her, narrowed with his passion, impatient with an almost frightening determination. She wished he would kiss her again.

"Ah, Steven," she murmured, her voice still husky with her own passion, "I love you, Steven." The words had come out of their own volition; she had not been thinking that she ought to say them—but once spoken, she had no wish to take them back.

He kissed her then, as though he did not want her to say anything more. The long, clinging kiss seemed to explode suddenly with their entwined passions, and Brenna felt weak and shaky, as though she were being buffeted by a strong wind. She heard her own pounding heart answered by his pulse, and her arms seemed no longer able to hold onto him as they slipped weakly to the ground. He did not collapse abruptly on top of her, as had always been her experience with Kevin, but instead he settled softly against her, cradling her shoulders in his arms as he rested most of his weight on one hip.

For a long time, they lay together, silent, each one lost in thoughts and dreams.

"Steven, I . . ."

"Hush," he said softly, placing a finger against her lips. "But, I want to tell you . . ."

"Don't say anything, my sweet," he interrupted again, catching her face between his thumb and fingers and bringing it over to his own so that he could kiss her once more. "My sweet, sweet Brenna," he murmured against her mouth.

He shifted his weight completely off her and reached down to arrange his clothing. She watched his handsome head, turned away from her, and suddenly became aware of her own nudity and the enormity of what she had just done. A quick, burning sensation penetrated her skull and caused tears to form in her eyes so that she blinked rapidly to keep them from coursing down her cheeks. She must not let Steven see her crying, she thought with sudden urgency.

She did not know why he didn't tell her he loved her, nor why he didn't want to hear the words from her own lips. She only knew that he had not said them, and she felt suddenly ashamed of her passion and wary of what he would say to her next. She began to clumsily button her blouse, absurdly regretting that he had bitten off the top button so that now she could not find it. She rearranged her underclothing and fastened her jacket and skirt, absently brushing away the dust as she kept her face averted.

He still had said nothing to reassure her. Would he remain silent forever? It was important to her—his first words after their act of intimacy—their act of love, she amended, and then cowered away from the words.

She felt his hand brush the top of her hair as he stood up; she knew he was looking down at her, but hadn't the strength to turn her eyes up to meet his stare.

"Brenna?" His hand caught hers, and he pulled her up beside him with easy grace.

"Yes, Steven," she whispered, finding the courage to meet his dark gaze. What she saw there filled her with dread, for there was no softening, no tenderness—only bleakness and pain and self-condemnation. When he started to speak again, she placed a hand gently against his mouth.

"No, Steven, there is no need to say anything. I cannot undo what we have done, and neither can you. It—just—happened."

"I wanted it to happen, Brenna. I've dreamed of doing exactly as I did today since the first time I saw you at the Valera home." His voice was tinged with self-mockery. "Call me a blackguard, a vile bastard! Anything! But for God's sake, don't absolve me of my guilt. I do not deserve it."

Her eyes widened at his admissions. What was that quaint old term used in the Bible? "Lusting after her . . ." Had Steven lusted after her? Had he deliberately planned that this would happen—though he had a wife, and at that time, she a husband?

"I must get back to the city," she said faintly.

Steven thought how like a lost and frightened child she looked, and cursed himself for taking her this far. But it was done, he thought soberly, and by God, he wouldn't take it back now if he could. She was wonderful and passionate, a lovely, warm creature that should have a man beside her. He cursed the fates that had decreed it should not be he.

"We'll ride back to Buenos Aires from here," he said gently, knowing she would not want to go back to Paloma today.

"Yes, yes, let's do hurry," she said distractedly, avoiding his gaze as he helped her back into the saddle. She wished desperately to be alone, to throw herself across her own bed and weep her heart out.

Chapter Forty-Three

By October, the warm spring breezes were laden with the heavy perfume of jasmine and the clustered blooms of the *paraíso* trees. Brenna avoided Steven on his visits to the Valera house, afraid that she might see indifference in his eyes, that he would look at her like a common whore who had allowed him to use her body in a moment of passion. The memory of that day still burned in her mind, and her dreams were filled with restless longings and unfulfilled desires, which shamed her in the cold light of retrospection. She found it difficult to sleep at night, and her insomnia soon began to drain her energy.

Lately she had been going out with Carlos more often, although Isabel still disapproved of their keeping company unchaperoned, and he helped her to get through the uncertain days that always led to the restless nights. For his own part, Carlos became very attentive and seemed very happy in her company. He liked to take her on tours of the city, showing her around the Plaza de Mayo in the center of town, which was surrounded by the facades of the Cabildo, the Cathedral, and the Casa Rosada. The Plaza, itself, was divided by an arcade of shops and a street into two separate sections. The shops were a bit sleazy, but they were colorful and served to cheer Brenna up considerably.

Carlos took her for a ride on the horse-drawn trolley, which delighted her, and he acquainted her with the public library, the museum, and the literary salons. Of course, there were meetings where the talk was only of politics and revolution and wild-eyed men threw back their heads and expounded on the power-mad upper-class. They warned of dire depressions and hardships for the masses. Carlos would listen with glowing eyes, nodding his agreement and cheering along with the others, until Brenna thought her head would split with all the noise. Headaches seemed to come so easily to her these days.

Sometimes, he would walk with her through the streets, and once, he took her by the town villa of the Castanedas on Santa Fe Street. Brenna breathed deeply to keep her heart from hammering too loudly as they passed by the imposing three-story structure, which occupied nearly an entire block. Carlos cheerfully explained the general configuration of the edifice, telling her how the house was built with three patios extending back from the street; the first patio, he explained, was for family use, the second was for servants and household needs, and the third was for the garden, well, outhouse, and fruit trees. All very nice, he laughed, if one liked living in a palace.

"You don't share Steven's love of luxury, do you?" she asked him, quickening her step to get past the house before anyone came out.

"I suppose I would," he admitted honestly. "But I shall never go on my knees back to my father and spout all of his political beliefs like some damned parrot, just to be pampered like a prince!"

Brenna shook her head, puzzled. "Then, I can't understand why you and Steven are such good friends. He is wealthy and believes, like his father, in the Unitarians' way of thinking; while you, as you keep assuring me, believe in the Federalists and their fight to bring about a system like that in the United States. How can you remain friends?"

Carlos laughed. "So you have been listening—good for you!" He took her arm and tucked it under his. "Brenna, Steven and I have been friends for a long time. Of course, I have known old men who have been friends for a much longer time to get into squalls about the government issue, but Steven is not one of those diehards who sees only one side of an issue. He is willing to see both sides and consider them equally. I admire that in him." He laughed and winked at her. "Besides, I'll never give up hope of winning him to my side. Just think what the Castaneda money could do for our cause!"

Brenna changed the subject. She did not like Carlos

putting Steven on a pedestal. What would Carlos think, she wondered, if he knew what had happened that day on the pampas? She shuddered at the thought of anyone knowing, and fervently hoped that she, herself, could soon forget it.

But, that was not to be, for as early November golden sunshine brought into view the scintillating sight of smooth, pale blue carpets of flax, Brenna finally realized that she, herself, was blooming—with Steven's child.

She could not have been more shocked if someone had told her she had contracted a dread disease. She refused to believe that the frequent headaches, backaches, restless nights, and morning queasiness were signs of pregnancy until the cook, Mrs. Ferriday, diagnosed her symptoms with a studied nonchalance one bright November morning.

Brenna had run outside to bring up her breakfast in the yard. When she had returned, wiping her mouth with a clean handkerchief and trembling from the force of the attack, Mrs. Ferriday approached her.

"Seems to me, young lady, you'd best be telling Senora Valera about the child that's coming," she had said gently. "It might be a good idea to inform Carlos too." She sighed and shook her head. "I could have seen it coming."

"Inform Carlos?" Brenna had sat down abruptly in a chair, her eyes wide and blank with shock. "Mrs. Ferriday, you're not telling me that I—that I—"

"—that you're going to be a mother," she finished, calmly folding a dish towel.

"But I can't be pregnant," Brenna protested. "I can't be!"

"Lamb, there's lots of young ladies who have said those very same words," she countered wisely, sitting down next to the young woman. "Under the circumstances, I think the sooner you go to Carlos with the news, the better. I'm sure he's gentleman enough to do the right thing by you. He's so fond of you anyway, I would bet he's been leading up to a marriage proposal. Of course, being a bit hasty like he was, things have been solved for him."

"Oh, Mrs. Ferriday!" Brenna cried, striving not to burst into tears. "Carlos has never—never even touched me in that way!"

For a moment, the cook's face reddened a little, then she relaxed again and patted the hand lying so listlessly on the table. "Now, now, then it must have been your late husband, Kevin." She cleared her throat in obvious embarrassment. "It's not the usual thing, but sometimes, even when a man is ill, he can—well, you know what I mean, I'm sure. Of course, it's a bit late to be showing all the signs. I'd say you must be at least into your third month, child."

It was on the tip of Brenna's tongue to tell Mrs. Ferriday that Kevin had never been able to make love to her after his injury, but she quickly hushed the words, her mind working feverishly even as a cold sweat dappled her forehead. She could have laughed at the irony of fate. All along she had thought she was barren, unable to conceive a child—had upbraided and blamed herself for not being able to give Kevin the child he had wanted. And all the time, it had been Kevin who was unable to plant the seed of life. But not Steven, she thought with an inward groan at her own bad luck. No, no, not the tall and handsome, virile young man who had made love to her a single time and had found fertile soil on which to plant his seed. Dear God, why had this happened to her?

For one wild, panic-stricken moment, she looked at Mrs. Ferriday with desperation in her eyes. She must get rid of this growing life in her womb. She must, somehow, cast it from her body before Steven found out. He would know it wasn't Kevin's, for hadn't she told him that she had thought she was barren? He would know it was Kevin, not her, who was unable to produce a child.

Mrs. Ferriday saw the desperation in those dark blue eyes, and fear leaped into her own. "Now, luv, you mustn't even consider what I think you're thinking," she said urgently. "Those things are the devil's work and not fit for young women of God. Now, don't you worry, Brenna—we'll be working this out. You—you should be happy you'll have a child to keep alive the memory of your husband and to keep you from being alone."

Was that suspicion that lurked in Mrs. Ferriday's eyes? Dear God, she did suspect; Brenna was sure of it. Was it just her own frightened mind that saw doubt there, or was her shame written plainly on her face? Brenna bit her lip and felt a surge of hate and resentment for the man who had done this to her. From that moment of passion, she would be the one to suffer. Not Steven—he would not have to carry this burden. She felt like crying hard, striking her hands against the floor, and drumming her heels like a child.

"Oh, Mrs. Ferriday, what will I do? What will happen when the Valeras find out?" she cried.

"Hush, you'll be having that baby, of course. Don't you be worrying about the Valeras—good God, they can't throw you out into the street for bearing your own husband's child!"

"They won't want another mouth to feed," Brenna said dully. "And how will I explain this to the children? Isabel Valera will think it most—indelicate—of me to proceed to the schoolroom with a swollen belly, especially in front of Maria, who is at such an impressionable age. And I might be sick some days—and when it's time for the baby to come . . ." She laid her forehead into her hands wearily. "It isn't fair, Mrs. Ferriday!"

"It's never fair," the woman agreed, "but there it is. You've a child coming, and you must take care of yourself and learn to accept it. There's nothing else for it."

"There's nothing else for it," Brenna repeated to herself, recalling the old adage she used to say when fate stepped in to intervene in her life. Well, fate had stepped in with a vengeance this time!

She got up from the table slowly. "I suppose I'd best be telling Senora Valera now. I might as well get the worst of it over—and see how long I'll be allowed to stay."

Isabel Valera was nearly as stunned as Brenna had been. She looked the girl up and down as though seeking to verify the truth. After a long moment, she asked bluntly, "Is this child Carlos'?"

Brenna flushed and shook her head. "No, senora."

The small eyes squinted even smaller as they tried to figure out if the girl was telling the truth. Then, with a deep breath, she decided to believe her, although she would have Juan question that reprobate Carlos anyway.

"Very well, then. What do you intend to do about it?"

Brenna looked bewildered. "I—I suppose I shall just go on as before—until the baby is born. I—I promise I won't need too many days off—I'm strong enough and . . ."

"This will set a bad example for the children," Isabel went on severely, "not to mention the rest of the household staff. You know my reasons for disliking this sort of thing, Brenna."

This sort of thing, Brenna thought, indignation creeping into her brain. What was the old fool talking about? She was going to have a child, a natural function of a woman. Good Lord, hadn't the woman had enough children herself to understand?

"I'm afraid your reasons aren't clear to me, senora," she said with some spirit.

Isabel Valera scowled heavily. "Let us not mince words, Brenna," she began. "I do not like my household staff to be—free—with their emotions. I have already discharged two other girls for getting into the same situation that you find yourself in. It would not be suitable for the children to see you as you grow larger and wonder about it. Maria will be sixteen soon and has too many notions as it is!"

Brenna wished she could have retorted that this child was her husband's, conceived in holy matrimony, but she couldn't bring herself to lie to this woman who would see through such a falsehood. Brenna remained silent and allowed the woman to continue.

"I'm afraid, Brenna, that you must find yourself another position before you begin to—ah—show. I won't have your condition—encouraging the other servants to be careless in their pursuits."

"And pray, senora, where do you think I shall go? If you, in all of your goodness, will not allow me to stay—what other household will, do you think?" she retorted sarcastically, not caring now if the woman became angrier with her. What did it matter? She was ordered out of the house anyway.

"Mrs. Ryan, you will kindly take yourself out of this room," Isabel Valera ordered imperiously. "I expect you to find another position within the month. Until that time, I shall also expect you to put in a full day every day with the children, with no lapses for some silly sickness. Is that clear?"

"Quite clear," Brenna said bitterly. Striving to maintain her composure she left the room, but gave herself the pleasure of banging the door behind her. She could not face the children just yet, she thought. She must have at least a few moments alone to think, to plan . . .

She had been in her room nearly an hour, doing a lot of thinking, but no planning, when she heard a knock on her door. Expecting that it was one of the servants sent from Isabel Valera, or perhaps the woman herself, she took a moment to smooth her bodice and wipe her face of tears, before opening the door.

"Brenna!" It was Carlos, his face full of concern and an unexpected kindness. "Juan just—told me what has happened! Brenna, did that bitch put you through hell?" His dark eyes snapped with fire. "I'd like to throttle her fat neck sometimes. She actually intimated that you would allow a man to—to use you in that way with your husband hardly laid to rest. The whole family disgusts me!"

"Please, Carlos, this is not your problem," Brenna said quickly, blushing in secret embarrassment because she had indeed allowed a man to use her barely a month after Kevin was laid to rest. "I'll manage myself."

"No, you won't, by God! That woman is a fiend, and I shall not stay under her roof a moment longer than it takes to pack my bags. I'm not penniless, despite what my cousins may have led you to believe. It's true, I was cast out of my father's house, but I have a sum of money in the bank here in the city, upon which I can draw."

"Carlos, please, there is no need for you to fight for me," Brenna said helplessly, and wondered perversely if she was just another cause for him to rally to.

But his next words shocked her. "Brenna, marry me!" He came to her quickly and took her hands in his. "I know you must think I'm a lunatic, but I'm quite serious. Marry me, and I'll give you a home for your child. You'll never again have to work for a pig like Isabel Valera!"

Brenna sat down in the chair, taking her hands from Carlos' grasp. Marry again! Hadn't she told herself, not long ago, that she would never make that mistake again —to marry a man who had no hold on her heart, this time a man whom she hardly knew? Dear God! Fate seemed to her like some evil devil that enjoyed torturing her. But what other future was there for her? Carlos had offered means to support the child. She knew she would not be able to find work anywhere else, especially as her belly grew larger. Who would want to employ a pregnant woman, knowing that with the coming of the child, there would be little time for her to do her duties?

She looked up at Carlos' face, and for a moment, she saw the face of Kevin Ryan staring at her just as eagerly, with that look in his eyes that said he would make everything right, that he would take care of her and protect her. She sighed. How wonderful to have a man truly take care of her, she thought. But would Carlos turn out like Kevin, in need of her strength, drawing on her time after time when his own determination gave out?

She told herself that Carlos was different—that he was from the same class as she herself—that now there would be a child to help the relationship grow. But it wasn't Carlos' child—and when Steven knew . . .

"No, Carlos, I can't expect you to marry me, with the child already growing," she said sadly. " 'Twould be too much for any man to accept. And—and you had no wish to marry me—"

"Yes, I did, Brenna, believe me!" he interrupted quickly. "What's happened has only made it easier for me to press my suit. You understand me, Brenna, you understand what I'm fighting for, what I believe in! You are the only woman who has ever understood me!"

Understand Carlos? Did she? Would he, somehow, be different once they had married, as Kevin had been somehow different? Brenna rubbed her eyes and shook her head.

"No, Carlos, I can't marry you!" she said with more firmness than she felt.

He must have been able to detect her faltering, for he stepped closer and took her hands again. "You will marry me, Brenna," he urged. "You can't expect to find work in your condition! You can't be left alone! You need a man to protect you, a man who would love you and think of your child as his own! Let me be that man, Brenna." And then, with flat practicality, "There is no other way for you."

"Oh, Carlos, how can I? I—I don't love you," she admitted, knowing he might now withdraw his offer of marriage.

"It doesn't matter," he said, seeing her begin to capitulate. "You are fond of me, aren't you?"

She nodded warily.

"Then you will grow to love me, Brenna. I am no man to fall ill and become an invalid like your husband did. I am strong and can protect you. We can laugh together and enjoy each other in bed." His eyes glowed at the prospect.

Brenna felt her heart shrink when he mentioned it. Go to bed—with a stranger! What was happening to her? Was she so unfeeling, so materialistic, that she could comply with all this, just because it was the easy way out? Or was it, truly, the only way out?

"Carlos, please, please give me a little time to think. I must have at least a day or two."

"The sooner you make up your mind, the better," he reminded her. "Do you want to stay with those two one day more than you must? After her vile insinuations?"

"She will think she was right when she finds out you offered to marry me," Brenna pointed out.

"Who gives a damn what she thinks? I certainly don't —in fact, let her think the child is mine, let everyone think it!"

"Oh, Carlos, you are so kind."

He pulled her up from the chair abruptly and caught her in his arms, pressing her against his long, lean body. Without hesitation, he bent down and took her lips with his, kissing her for a moment, willing her to submit to him, until she complied, parting her lips and bringing up her arms to wrap them about his neck. Finally, he released her, his dark brown eyes searching her face.

"I am not kind," he whispered softly. "Do not think it is kindness that made me offer you marriage. I want you, Brenna. I want no other man to have a right to your attentions. You will be my wife, and your child will be my child." He kissed her again, briefly, then bowed and left her room.

Brenna stared at the closed door, trembling, her hand going automatically to her lips. "You will be my wife and your child will be my child," he had said. She supposed, then, that it was settled.

Chapter Forty-Four

AFTER their wedding, performed with small ceremony in the Church of San Ignacio de Loyola, Brenna and Carlos Valera took up residence near one of the Irish *barrios,* or neighborhoods, because Brenna insisted that her child be delivered by someone of her own nationality. Carlos complied, although the *barrio,* itself, was little more than a slum, a local community, which had been built around a church district and sported a corner tavern, which was within walking distance from their apartments.

Brenna didn't care that the section of the city where she lived was barely a notch above the *conventillos,* which were the real slums of the downtown area—it was such a joy to talk to people who had come from her home country, who could speak the old Gaelic, and who observed the holy days with the quaint old customs she nostalgically remembered. She wrote a long letter to her parents, explaining Kevin's death and her own remarriage. She gave them an address to write to, for she was hungry for news of her family, wondering how Dermot and Bernadette and dear Patrick were, and how Deirdre's baby was faring. As she finished the letter, tears filled her eyes, but she wiped them away quickly. She was always so quick to cry these days that Carlos frequently wondered if she regretted her marriage to him. But she would assure him that it was only her condition—and she hoped that was true.

They had barely put their small apartments in order when they received a visit from Steven Castaneda. Brenna had felt a strong urge to run into the bedroom and hide, but with Carlos' arm encircling her shoulders, there was nothing she could do but lift up her chin and paste a welcoming smile on her mouth.

Steven's face looked somber, almost angry, as his gaze roamed over the small living area of the apartment, then rested darkly on Brenna's strained face. "I must say, this is a complete surprise," he began, coming over to shake Carlos' hand in congratulation. "I didn't know that you and Brenna were thinking of marriage." Brenna wished his black eyes wouldn't look at her so accusingly. It was all she could do to smile politely and offer him coffee and cakes.

"It came about rather abruptly," Carlos agreed, taking a moment to pat his wife affectionately on the rump.

Brenna blushed furiously and looked away from Steven's eyes as she disengaged herself from her husband and went to pour the coffee. In the tiny kitchen, she was only separated from the two men by a thin partition, and she could hear every word as they seated themselves.

"I suppose I could accuse you of being the sly dog," Steven said offhandedly. "Marrying the loveliest woman in the city without a moment's notice."

"Yes, she is beautiful," Carlos agreed with a sigh. "I'm the luckiest man alive, Steven, I don't mind telling you."

"But why did you bring her here to live then?" Steven demanded in a stronger tone. "This is barely decent for the immigrants coming in off the ships. To ask a woman like Brenna to live like this . . ."

"She wanted to, Steven! She wanted to live as close to her own people as she could."

"Haven't you enough money to give her a better house?" Steven cut in, barely keeping his anger beneath the surface.

"Look here, it's hardly your business where my wife and I live," Carlos replied with an injured air. "She's happy—I see to that," he added with a lascivious note. "Yes, Steven, the only way to keep her kind purring like a kitten is to lay her flat on her back at night, and . . ."

"For God's sake, Carlos!" There was disgust and pain in Steven's voice, and Brenna's heart ached to hear it.

"Sorry, I almost forgot you're a married man yourself, my friend," Carlos said apologetically.

"It's easier to forget than you might think, my friend," Steven replied grimly. "Treat your wife properly, Carlos.

She's worth more . . ." He stopped abruptly as Brenna came back, balancing the tray on her arm.

It was one of the hardest things Brenna had ever done —to lean over to Steven as he took a steaming cup from the tray. Did his free arm intentionally brush her skirts? She tried to control her trembling, for he would be sure to notice it. Despite what had happened once between them, she must never, never let him suspect that she held more in her heart for him than friendly affection.

"How have you been, Steven?" she asked politely, to fill in the silence.

He shrugged and sipped his coffee. "I have been well," he answered, "although I was just telling Carlos how surprised I was to hear of your marriage."

She said nothing to this, lowering her eyes as she waited for Carlos to change the subject, which he quickly did, going off on one of his tangents about politics. Brenna risked a few furtive glances at Steven, noting how elegant he looked in his clothes, how handsome his moustache looked against the dark tan of his complexion, how his thick hair waved naturally around his ears and down to his collar. She wished that she could talk Carlos into letting his hair fall naturally instead of using tonic to slick it back from his forehead.

Once, Steven caught her looking at him, and he returned the stare with questioning eyes, which unnerved her. As her gaze quickly fell away from his, she heard him stand to leave.

"I hope you'll allow me to persuade Carlos to find you more suitable apartments," Steven said to her. "Somehow, I feel as though I've seen this situation before," he added, to remind her of the time he had come to Ireland and found her in the cottage she had shared with Kevin.

Her shoulders stiffened at the inference, and she looked brazenly at him. "I like being close to my own people, Steven. I am as comfortable here as I could be at Paloma." She watched his expression change and knew she had scored.

"After the baby is born, we will be changing locations,"

Carlos added, not wanting Steven to think that he allowed Brenna to make all the decisions.

Brenna's heart skipped a beat, and she looked fearfully at Steven. His face looked as though it had suddenly turned to granite, all except for his black eyes, which seemed to glow queerly as they traveled slowly up and down her figure. His mouth turned down at the corners, and he took an involuntary step forward, then held himself back.

With a low whistle, he smiled insolently at her. "A child, Brenna?" Then to Carlos, "You do work quickly, amigo," he said.

Carlos had the grace to explain. "The child is not mine, naturally, but her previous husband's. When it is born, though, I *will* be its father."

Once again, Steven's black gaze locked with Brenna's, and she wished more than anything that she could tear her eyes away from that terrible look he gave her. He knew! Her heart was beating again with the litany—he knows, he knows, he knows . . . Her eyes pled with him silently.

"Carlos, my friend," Steven said finally, "you are an honorable man—much more honorable than I, myself." He bowed to both of them and turned to leave, when his eyes noticed, on one of the shelves against the wall, the small music box with the alabaster dove on top. His face changed, grew tender, then he closed his eyes, whispered a sharp good-bye and left them.

"I don't think he's well," Carlos said to himself. "See what having all that money does to a person, my love?"

"Perhaps he has a lot on his mind," Brenna suggested, forcing a light tone into her voice. "After all, running a large estate like Paloma, and doing business . . ."

Carlos laughed and put his arms around her, squeezing her against him. "My darling, how you defend him! I might be jealous—but there is no need when I am the lucky one. He is the jealous one, and rightly so."

Brenna hoped her husband would never know how close to guessing the truth he had come.

As the Argentine summer passed lazily by, Brenna watched her figure change miraculously with the burden she carried. She was not sick anymore, and she took long walks and light exercise as recommended by the middle-aged Irish midwife she had found in the *barrio*. The woman had come from County Cork, and Brenna loved to visit her and talk about the old country. Brenna had received letters from her family and had cried with joy to hear that Deirdre had given birth to a boy, Daniel, and that Bernadette was expecting another child in September. Patrick was walking and running now, and he could say at least ten words, among them *horse,* much to his grand-father's delight. The only dark spot was that her father never wrote to her; but she vowed not to let that dampen her spirits.

She was becoming a well-known figure in the *barrio,* as she always went out in the morning to take her walks, frequently visited the neighbors, and loved to pick up the smaller children and play games with them. She had found a stable in which to keep Minx and enjoyed giving the children rides on her.

One night, Carlos even took her to a fiesta in the open street, where gaily colored ribbons and papers festooned the poles of the porches and a small band of men played on sadly out of tune instruments. He pointed out the *compadrito* of the district, the neighborhood bully, who was a dandy and a sport and who eyed the young women insolently; he had only to stick out his hand in a girl's direction for her to come forward and dance with him. He wore tight-fitting black clothing, highly polished shoes, and a knife with a pearl handle tucked inside his waistband, attesting to his readiness to engage in any escapade or accept any challenge, no matter how dangerous.

Brenna had watched him with the same admiration that the others all gave him as he selected a giggling senorita and whirled her into a strange, exotic step. The blatant sensuality of the dance surprised Brenna, and she was not surprised to hear from Carlos that respectable society had banned the tango for its lasciviousness. He was explaining how the origins of the dance went back to the Negro and the people of the waterfront, when the *compadrito* gestured imperiously to Brenna, who laughed, threw her head back, and hastened forward, despite her thickened waistline. Everyone clapped and whistled as she finished the dance with her partner and stood breathing in short, quick gasps, and with a shining face, she accepted a kiss on her hand.

Even Carlos clapped and told her how proud of her he was. Brenna was happy that night and it was not until nearly dawn that she and Carlos dragged themselves up the steps to their apartment. Brenna fell asleep in her husband's arms with a smile on her lips. That night she did not dream of Steven.

Chapter Forty-Five

In 1874, Nicolas Avellaneda was elected president of Argentina. He was one of the youngest presidents the country had ever had, and upon his election, he faced one of the most serious financial crises the country had ever seen. The breakdown of the European economy the previous year was only now beginning to send its shock waves through Argentina.

Carlos was away much of the time now, meeting with other Federalists, who believed with him that the time had come to put their plans to work and overthrow the weak government based in Buenos Aires.

Unfortunately, nothing came of all their intentions, for they had no means to implement a revolution; and as the recession grew worse and the country could no longer rely on Europe as a source of capital, the country was once again made to feel the consequences of Buenos Aires' financial superiority. Through the power of its bank, the wealthy in Buenos Aires were able to dictate policy to the national authorities. There was a small revolt under the organization of Bartolomé Mitre, a former president, but much to Carlos' disappointment, it was quickly suppressed. The entire fiasco reminded Brenna of her brother's experience with the Fenians and their unsuccessful revolt in Ireland of '65, but she did not tell her husband this.

She was, in truth, busy with her own anxieties. The baby was active within her now, and she could no longer negotiate the wet, muddy streets of the city for fear she might fall and injure herself.

Finally, on one chilly morning in June, Brenna calmly asked Carlos to go for the midwife. Nearly nine hours later, a little girl was born to her.

Brenna, her face shining with sweat and her hair plastered wetly to her head, reached for the infant with tired

483

arms but happy spirits. She had wanted a girl, although she would never have admitted that to Carlos. He had been sure that the first child would be a boy, but no matter. Brenna thought her daughter the most beautiful baby in the world as she held the soft, damp bundle to her breast and looked at the tiny, red face.

Carlos was allowed a brief visit inside the bedroom. When he peeped at the child's face, he smiled with as much pride as though it were a son and his own. "She'll be as beautiful as her mother," he whispered, kissing his wife's cheek. "Look at all that black hair—and I'll bet she has your blue eyes too."

Brenna nodded, although somewhere in the back of her mind, the worry nagged her that someday the child might come to look more like her true father. But she pushed the worry resolutely away. The child was hers and Carlos'—and no one else's.

"I'm going to let you name her, my dear," Carlos continued fondly. "What do you think?"

"Katherine," she said quickly, as that was her own middle name, "and Nora after my mother." She looked to Carlos for approval. "And we'll be calling her Katie."

"Katie," Carlos said, testing the word. "Katie Valera. Yes, I do like it!" he pronounced. He looked down at the infant and stroked the velvety cheek. "Katie Valera, you'll never miss your real father, little one, for I swear to treat you always as though you were my very own."

Brenna looked up at her husband with tear-filled eyes. She would never fear for her daughter's future, never fear that the little girl would not have the love of both a mother and a father. For this alone, her fondness for Carlos gave way to love.

Despite her protests, Carlos soon insisted that they move to more suitable apartments. Tearfully, Brenna said good-bye to all her old friends, promising to bring Katie back often. Many of the young men helped to move the heavier pieces of furniture, placing them in two big ox carts which could plow easily through the mud of the streets.

Their new home, Carlos informed her, would be on

Córdoba Street. Most of the wealthiest families of the city lived around Córdoba and Santa Fe Streets, Brenna knew, and she would have preferred not to live so close to Steven's town villa, but Carlos assured her their own home would have modest proportions compared to the wealthier villas, and it would be a much more suitable place to bring up their child. Brenna wondered how any place could be more suitable than the warm, friendly *barrio*, where children played and laughed together, and where Katie would grow up with some of her mother's heritage; but Brenna kept her silence, for she knew that Carlos was proud of his new home.

When they arrived, Brenna discovered that, indeed, their quarters were more spacious. The adobe two-story building had a pleasant, sunny entrance and a lovely tree-lined patio at the center of the house, into which opened the doors of the bedrooms on the second story and the living and receiving rooms on the first floor. It even had a stable in back, where Minx quickly settled.

"We'll be needing more furniture," she laughed as Carlos led her on a tour, carrying Katie triumphantly in his arms.

"Then we'll buy it," he announced. "I don't like to admit it, my dearest, but my father came around quickly when he learned of Katie's birth. He's so pleased at the birth of his first grandchild that he has decided to receive me once again."

"But what about your political differences?"

He shrugged. "I think he might be a little more lenient," he grinned. "Just so long as I don't try to turn him entirely toward my rabble-rousing views."

"You'll split in two trying to keep silent," she teased him, taking Katie from him when she started to fuss. "Now tell me where we can set up Katie's nursery, for she badly needs a changing and a meal."

The Valeras settled comfortably in their new home. Within a few weeks, visitors began coming, most of whom were political allies of Carlos. The meetings often lasted until midnight, and the strain of it might have exhausted Brenna had she not developed so much enthusiasm for politics. The wealth of activity kept her from thinking about Steven and wondering why he had not come to pay his respects since their move. She knew that Carlos saw him often, but she could not bring herself to ask about him. She hated herself, in a way, for still wondering what Steven thought of her, but she could not help herself: part of her heart still belonged to him.

It was spring, and Katie was nearly six months old, when Carlos casually mentioned that Steven would be dropping by that evening. Brenna tried not to let her excitement show when she asked him if Steven would be staying for dinner.

"I think not," Carlos answered. "He's been busy these past months with his father's businesses. Old Miguel's health isn't what it used to be, so the old man keeps pretty much at Paloma. I think that Steven and his mother are planning a celebration both for his father's sixtieth birthday and his little sister's engagement."

"How nice," Brenna commented absently. She recalled pretty Rosaria, who must be seventeen now. Her thoughts also conjured up the sad-pretty face of Steven's wife, and for no clear reason, Brenna rushed over to Katie, playing happily on the rug, and squeezed her to her breast until the child cried out in protest.

That evening, just as the supper dishes were cleared away by Brenna's new kitchen maid, the brass knocker sounded on the heavy walnut front door. Brenna's heart began to pound, and she tried desperately to still the shaking of her hands as she held Katie in her lap. Brenna had donned one of her most becoming gowns, a present Carlos had given her when her figure regained its shape after Katie's birth. It was made of shiny blue satin, which caught and held the glow of the candles in the folds of its skirt. It had a high bustle, and the bodice was cut across her shoulders, baring just the upper slopes of her breasts, which had seemed to grow rounder and larger after Katie's birth. Her hair was coiled, and the blue of the gown set off the violet blue of her eyes. Around her neck she wore a circle of sapphires, which had been a present from Carlos' father.

Brenna could hear Carlos and Steven talking over the clattering of their shoes on the tiles in the hall as they approached the cozy drawing room, which Brenna had decorated in her favorite colors of blue and cream. She turned her head, tilting it just a little, as Steven came through the arched doorway.

She could not know what passed through his mind as he saw her sitting regally in the cream-colored chair, her blue skirts spread around her, her eyes glowing as blue as the stones against her flesh. He thought that she was even more beautiful than he remembered, that she was somehow riper, more desirable, and he thought that he should never have come. Just seeing her awoke a desire to touch her, and the memory of their one moment of lovemaking brought a sharp, almost physical pain to him. The result of that brief passion was sitting happily in her mother's lap, playing with a bauble, gurgling merrily. He saw the crown of black hair, soft and silky against Katie's fair skin, and knew before he saw them that her eyes were as blue as her mother's. The picture of mother and daughter brought an uncomfortable lump to Steven's throat, which he quickly fought down; this picture was not his to own, but another man's. The thought made his mouth turn down with an insolent twist, and he swept from his mind the brief moment of sentiment.

"My congratulations to the mother and father," he said, bowing formally before Brenna's chair. "The child looks healthy and beautiful—you must be very proud, Senora Valera."

Brenna flushed, wondering at Steven's cold formality. Well, she thought, she could be just as indifferent. "Thank you for your congratulations," she answered coolly, "although they are a trifle late in coming, Senor Castaneda."

"Don't mind her, Steven," Carlos laughed. "She's as proud as a peacock because she knows perfectly well there's not a more beautiful child than hers in the entire city." He smiled at his wife. "Nor a more beautiful mother."

"Indeed," Steven concurred, taking a seat next to Brenna. "Might I inquire," he said in a low voice as Carlos went to bring in wine and glasses, "if there are plans for more,"

Brenna's eyes flashed, and her cheeks pinkened. "Surely, that is hardly your business, sir."

"Who knows?" he whispered back insolently.

If Carlos hadn't been in the room, Brenna would have slapped his face for his rude insinuation, but now her husband was handing her a glass of wine and she smiled up at him deliberately, wanting suddenly to hurt this insolent man beside her.

"So, how are things with your father?" Carlos asked as he gave Steven a glass.

Steven shrugged. "The same. The physician tells me his heart is a little worn with use, but that he has many good years left to him as long as he doesn't tire himself unduly or try to manage the business by himself. I suppose I have been officially handed the reins." He turned to Brenna. "Speaking of which, have you done much riding since the birth of your daughter?" he asked.

She shook her head, searching for some kind of trap. "No, the weather hasn't been good, and up until now, I haven't felt like riding."

He smiled lazily. "Then, surely, you would allow me to suggest that you come out to Paloma some time soon to ride out on the pampas."

"Thank you, no!" Brenna said, moving so abruptly that she spilled the wine and startled the baby into a frightened cry. Flustered, she asked Carlos to get a wet rag from the kitchen so that the wine would not stain, and before she knew what he was about, Steven took Katie and put her on his own lap, where she became absorbed with the shiny gold of his watch chain.

For a stunned moment, Brenna watched Steven stroke the baby's hair and put his finger under the tiny double chin. She could not quite define the look on his face—was it the pride of fatherhood? Oh, no! She turned hurriedly, hoping that Carlos would not come in yet.

Behind her, she heard Steven say in a harsh voice, "She does look like you, Brenna—she's beautiful. How lucky for Carlos to watch her grow up—" He stopped, whispered, "you had better take her now."

She reached to take Katie from him, and their hands grazed; she felt a warm tingling run through her arms. She looked away from him quickly as Carlos came back into the room. While she bent to sop up the worst of the wine spill, she handed the child over to Carlos. She finished hurriedly and took Katie back again, reseating herself.

"I understand," Carlos began refilling Brenna's glass, "that there are plans, to extend the railroad tracks from Córdoba to Tucumán in the interior. It sounds as though Avellaneda would like to expand the agricultural colonies in Santa Fe."

Steven nodded, his eyes still fixed on the charming picture of mother and daughter. "Yes, I think he has a good idea, but," and he shrugged, "who knows how long it will take to implement? I've heard the projected date for completion has already been pushed back to '76."

Carlos shook his head ironically. "Everything is so damned slow because there are too many fingers in the pie," he said. "I admit that anything is better than the ox carts they use in the interior now, but if it takes so long for the railroad, why don't they try to improve the existing roads for other vehicles?"

"Too expensive," Steven said flatly. "In the long run, the railroads will do much more to open up the interior for trade. And that is what you Federales want, isn't it?" He smiled with a touch of sardonic humor.

Carlos laughed ruefully. "I suppose you are right, although if your friendly Unitarios get wind that you are for some of my ideas, they might drum you out of their ranks, my friend."

Brenna let the men's talk of politics go by her as she relaxed in her chair and smiled into her daughter's face. What a lovely child she was, so bright and quick, so filled with laughter. She thought of Steven's shameless question as to whether there would be more children. She knew that Carlos would like more, especially a son—the male's desire to continue the family line, she thought wryly.

She supposed that it might be a good idea for her to become pregnant again soon for Carlos' sake.

Her thoughts were interrupted when Carlos addressed her. "Sweetheart, you're dreaming and Katie's wetting your dress," he said. "Don't you think it's time to put her to bed?"

She nodded. "Of course." She smiled at Steven and hurried away. They had employed a nurse to help take care of Katie, but Brenna still enjoyed breastfeeding the child herself, particularly in the quiet peacefulness that descended in the room when she and her daughter were alone. After tucking Katie in for the night and kissing her warm little cheek, Brenna sponged the wet spot in her dress.

When she arrived back downstairs, she found the men were standing and laughing companionably. She felt a tug of gratitude that Steven could act so completely at ease with her husband. She only hoped that she was as good an actress.

"Katie's all tucked in?" Carlos asked.

"Yes, and snoring too, the little imp," she laughed. "Have I missed anything while I was gone?"

Carlos looked uncomfortably toward Steven whose smile was once more devilish. "Well, darling, as a matter of fact, we've been talking about you."

"Me?" she said with a nervous little laugh. "Come now, gentlemen, you are making me blush."

"She's not going to like it," Carlos said conspiratorially.

Steven shrugged. "She's your wife—order her!" he laughed. The gleam of pure devilment in his eyes disconcerted Brenna.

"All right, darling. I was just telling Steven that I will be going away for a few days for a meeting in Rosario. Since I hate to leave you and Katie alone here in a new house, I thought—well, actually, Steven suggested that I let you stay at Paloma while I'm gone."

Brenna blanched. For a moment, she looked with angry accusation at Steven, whose black eyes snapped back with mockery. "It's out of the question, Carlos!" she said quickly. "There is no good reason on earth why I shouldn't stay here."

"Just you and the kitchen help?" he said. "What if something happened?"

"Your father is nearby."

"He's in Bahia Blanca," Carlos said patiently, putting an affectionate arm around his wife's shoulders. "Darling, it would be good for Katie to get the good, fresh spring air out on the pampas." He laughed in an undertone. "And don't worry about compromising your reputation," he joked, "for there'll be plenty of women out there— Steven's mother and sister and wife . . ."

Brenna shuddered. The women had been out there before, and still . . . "No, Carlos, I really couldn't presume on Steven's hospitality, after all his father is sick."

"We're having a birthday party for him on Saturday," Steven put in. "I know how enjoyable it would be for him if you could be there. He's asked about you—wondered why you have not called on them, especially as he and your father still do business."

How cleverly he had backed her into a corner, Brenna thought, wrathfully. Had she ever really been given a choice? "When shall you be leaving, Carlos?"

"The day after tomorrow," he said, hugging her. "Sweetheart, you don't know what a relief it is to know that you'll have Steven's protection while I'm gone."

Chapter Forty-Six

BRENNA packed enough clothes for herself and Katie to last a week, should Carlos be gone that long, but she hoped he would not be. She insisted on bringing the nurse for the baby with her, for she certainly couldn't presume on Steven's household staff nor on his mother to help her watch Katie. Steven protested, but Brenna stood firm. At least she would have someone on her side in the enemy camp.

Steven came for them at the appointed hour, bringing his carriage, although he himself rode a horse. Brenna hoped that this was his way of telling her that he would not be forcing his presence on her while she was his guest —but she could never be sure with Steven. The only thing she was terribly sure of was that she must never allow him to be alone with her.

They arrived at Paloma in good time and were greeted warmly by his mother and father. Rosaria, they explained, was out riding with her fiancé, a fine young man whom they were anxious for Brenna to meet. Dolores was in her room with a headache.

Brenna was led around the large, cool, splashing fountain in the center of the patio to the guest bedrooms on the other side, which had their own informal patio for relaxation. Teresa was given a room down the hall, in the servants' section, and Brenna's own suite opened up into a smaller room, which would be suitable for Katie.

From the beginning, Consuelo Castaneda made such a fuss over Katie that for a moment Brenna wondered if Steven had told his parents the child's true parentage. But there seemed to be no inkling when they spoke of her and Carlos, and she was relieved. She retired to her room to unpack and to put Katie down for a nap, after feeding her.

"Oh, senora, such a palace this is!" Teresa exclaimed

excitedly as she unpacked. "Truly, such a grand place should belong to a king!"

Brenna smiled. "You would get tired of it soon enough if you had to walk the length and breadth of it everyday in doing your chores."

Teresa nodded her agreement. After she finished unpacking, she took Katie from her mother to put her down in the cradle in the adjoining room. One of the household staff knocked on her door to announce that lunch would be served soon, and Brenna told her she would be out within the half-hour. She quickly sponged off some of the dust and dirt she had picked up during the coach ride, then asked Teresa to help her out of the traveling suit she wore and into a cooler dress made of green-sprigged muslin, which had a squared neckline and short, capped sleeves.

When she was ready for lunch, she tiptoed in and gave the sleeping Katie a swift kiss on her forehead, and then whispered instructions to Teresa, who would sit in a chair next to the cradle for a little afternoon siesta. As she made her way past the small patio and out through the breezeway into the main patio, she momentarily lost her sense of direction.

"You are lost, senora?"

Brenna nearly jumped out of her skin at the soft voice behind her. She turned to discover Dolores Castaneda watching her with her big, soft brown eyes, her face paler than ever.

"Oh, thank goodness it is you," she said with a nervous laugh, and then wondered why she said it. "Yes, I wasn't quite sure which way . . ."

"Follow me then. You are going to lunch?"

"Yes—and please do call me Brenna. After all, we must be about the same age and it is nice to have someone . . ."

"Dolores!" It was Consuelo, welcoming them from the open doors of the informal dining room. "I am so glad your headache has gone away, child. And Brenna, have you two been getting acquainted?"

Brenna nodded, although Dolores seemed to shrink

back a little. Was she afraid of Steven's mother? Surely, there was no need to be. Brenna felt a rush of pity for the girl and resolved to be as kind to her as she could during her stay. It wasn't fair for the family to ostracize her for something she could not help—and who knew? Possibly, someday she would get pregnant. After all, with a husband as virile as Steven . . . But she quickly put those thoughts aside as she saw Steven, himself, coming toward them, looking handsomer than ever in a white shirt, casually opened at the throat, and a pair of tight black pants with a wide leather belt and a huge silver buckle.

"Dolores, you look rested," he commented politely to his wife, bowing at the waist, and then to Brenna, "And you too, Brenna." His black eyes danced between the two young women, as though, Brenna thought, he knew he could have his pick. She stiffened at the idea and nodded haughtily to him as she went to take her place beside his father. Rosaria, breezy looking and pink-cheeked as though she had just come in from her ride, dragged her fiancé in behind her. He was a pleasant-looking young man with flashing white teeth and darkly tanned skin.

"Brenna, how good it is to see you again," Rosaria said. Brenna was intrigued by the maturity the girl had developed in just a year. "This is my fiancé, Diego Garcia. Diego, this is Senora Brenna Valera, whose father is a friend of both my father and my brother."

"How do you do, senora?" Diego asked with a polite bow.

"Very well, thank you," Brenna replied amicably and favored Rosaria with a smile.

"Her husband, Carlos, is away for a few days, and she has most graciously allowed us her company while he is gone," old Miguel said as he nodded to the butler to begin serving the meal. "I don't suppose my surprise birthday party had anything to do with your acceptance of our hospitality, did it, Brenna?" Steven's brows went up with suppressed laughter, and a distraught expression appeared on Consuelo's face. Miguel's devilish grin reminded Brenna of Steven's. "Yes, yes, I'm aware of your plans, my dear," he said fondly to his wife. "But no one can keep the household staff from gossiping, and my hearing is as good as ever." He winked at Brenna.

"Oh, but, Miguel, it was to have been a surprise!" Consuelo reproved him indignantly. "You could have at least closed your ears this one time."

Miguel laughed. "I've always hated surprises, my dear," he said with that fond note still in his voice. "You should have known better."

Consuelo sighed as though to say she had tried. Luncheon was served and Brenna was surprised at the amount of fare presented: roasted beef, thick-gravied stews, corn meal, and a refreshing Paraguayan tea, called *yerbal maté*. Brenna sipped experimentally, and found the flavor of the brew decidedly appetizing. She noticed that the *maté* was the only thing that Dolores even tasted, and wondered why the girl did not eat.

During the meal Brenna kept an animated conversation going with Miguel because she did not want to be called upon to talk with Steven, whose attention, fortunately, was occupied with another *estancia* owner. Sometimes, though, she would let her eyes slide discreetly over to where Steven sat, and once, she caught his eyes studying her with a contemplative look, which unnerved her a little. He smiled when their eyes met, then turned his attention back to Diego.

When the meal was over, Miguel declared it was time for his midday siesta, a habit many of the people of Argentina shared. Consuelo excused herself and followed her husband to make sure he was comfortable. Dolores was about to take her leave, when Brenna reached out and touched her hand in friendly fashion.

"I'm afraid I can't get used to sleeping in the afternoon," she said with an encouraging smile, "and I thought I might go out riding—if you would care to come along. Katie won't awaken for another hour or so."

Dolores smiled back. "I—I find it difficult to ride long distances on horseback," she confessed with a tinge of red in her cheeks as her eyes glanced toward her husband.

"We don't have to go far."

"If you need an escort, Brenna, I will be most happy to go with you," Steven broke in. "Really, Dolores does not care to ride, and it would be unwise for the two of you to go out on the pampas alone. God knows what might happen to you!" He chuckled in masculine superiority. Diego joined in his laughter.

"Oh, please, you must come," Brenna urged, deliberately ignoring Steven as her hand tightened on Dolores'. "Some fresh air would do you good, I'm sure." She stopped, wondering if Dolores might be offended at her implication.

"Well, yes, then," Dolores said shyly. "Yes, I will go!" she said in a stronger tone, smiling happily.

Brenna did not dare to look at Steven's face, although she heard him offer to accompany both of them. Already Rosaria and Diego were excusing themselves and holding hands as they walked down the hall, obviously too much in love to notice any undercurrents among the three at the table.

Fifteen minutes later, all three were riding at a leisurely pace away from the *estancia*. Dolores rode sidesaddle, despite Brenna's assurances that riding astride was not as uncomfortable as it looked. Brenna watched the way Dolores handled the sleek little mare she was given and was surprised to see how well she rode. Surely, she had had some training in riding, for it showed in the elegant way she held her hands and the erect line of her back as it curved down into the length of her moss-green riding skirt, which was draped prettily over the horse's flank. Brenna felt unladylike by contrast in her russet broadcloth skirt, which was divided in the middle to allow her to ride astride.

Steven rode ahead of the women, as though he were a guide, shouting out points of interest as they circled around to the back of the *estancia*. They had been riding at an even trot for several minutes, when Brenna looked out over the rich, black alluvial fields of grass, and shouted excitedly at a funny looking animal scurrying off to the side.

"That was a *mara*," Steven told her, reining in as he

watched the running path of the long-legged, long-eared rodent. "They thrive in the pampas."

"Are there many other wild animals on the pampas?" Brenna asked curiously.

Steven grinned and his black eyebrows went up in sardonic crescents. "No lions or tigers, Brenna, so have no fear," he cautioned mockingly, and then in a more sober tone, "There are the *rheas*, which are similar to the ostrich of Africa, and, of course, smaller birds, like the ovenbird, which gets its name from its globe-shaped nest of mud. You might occasionally see *vizcachas*, another type of burrowing rodent, and the pampas deer, called *guanacos*."

"But—it looks so uninhabited," Brenna wondered, looking over the vast sea of grass where nothing seemed to be moving.

"Some of the animals are small enough to hide in the tall grass. See!" He pointed suddenly to a bunch of slender green stalks, which grew from a thick tussock on the ground. Behind the tussock, Brenna could just make out a patch of brown. "A pampas deer, watch him!"

As they came closer, the animal leaped out of its cover and sped away into the distance. Brenna watched its flight, then looked back toward Steven, who was breaking his horse into a faster trot. Dolores, who kept up easily enough, looked as though she were truly enjoying the outing. Brenna was glad, for no reason she could pinpoint; perhaps it was an easing of the guilt she still felt at having lain with the husband of this mild and delicate woman, who looked as though she could not harm a fly.

"Would you like to see our *saladero?*" Steven asked, turning his head back to question the ladies.

Bewildered, Brenna looked to Dolores for an explanation.

"The *saladero* is the meat salting facility," Dolores told her. "My father owned two of them near Tucumán. He was one of the richest *caudillos* of the district, before they lost all their power." Her eyes shone with pride, and for once Brenna thought she truly looked like the daughter of a rich and powerful man.

For a moment Brenna wondered which was the true Dolores Ruiz Castaneda de la Cruz. Was it the meek and gentle young woman who lived like a shadow on the walls of Paloma? Was it a heartbroken woman who fervently longed to have her husband's child? Or was it this proud and intelligent creature, who spoke of her heritage with an unmistakable air of superiority? What still remained the most intriguing mystery to Brenna was whether or not Dolores was a woman in love. Did she love Steven?—or had it been merely a marriage of convenience, of moneyed titles and mutual wealth, a tying together of a dynasty?

Steven, who had watched the exchange between the two women, saw the thoughtful expression on Brenna's face and smiled to himself as he led them to the *saladero*.

As they topped a small rise, Brenna's nose twitched at the acrid smell in the air. Dolores seemed not to be bothered, and Steven was watching her with an amused smile.

She turned away from him, and her eyes beheld, in a small depression in the valley before them, a menagerie of buildings, sheds, and corrals. Curiously, her eyes roamed over the long stone tables, large vats of brine, barrels of salt, huge caldrons, and crude drying and storage sheds. In nearby corrals, cattle were lowing nervously, as though they knew what fate awaited them.

Brenna blithely followed Steven and Dolores to the assemblage, dismounting with them and tying her horse to a fence post. Almost immediately, two middle-aged men, tanned brown as old walnuts, shuffled forward, their hats pressed to their chests as they bowed low. Their eyes remained fixed on the ground until Steven gave them permission to speak.

"Senor Castaneda, it is a pleasure to find you here today," one of them said eagerly.

"You wish to inspect the *saladero?*" the other asked anxiously, crumbling the brim of his hat.

Steven smiled. "No, but Senora Castaneda and Senora Valera would like to inspect it—briefly, I'm sure," he replied, still with that maddening amusement in his voice.

Brenna eyed him narrowly, suspecting that his amusement would prove to be at her expense, but when the two men led the way toward the corrals, she followed stubbornly, Dolores beside her. As they came close to the rangy, long-horned cattle, Brenna remembered what Steven had told her about wanting to import the short-horn from Europe. She watched curiously as several animals were selected and forced into a small enclosure, where one by one they were lassoed, dragged to a chute, slaughtered with a mallet to the head, then bled from a slash in the neck. This last, made her look away quickly, as the bile rushed to her throat. She realized that the smell in the air was the stench of blood and gore, and for a moment, the ground seemed to spin dizzily before her.

A strong arm snaked around her middle and held her steady as she leaned her head against a portion of the wall. Steven's face was close to hers, and as straight as a poker, he inquired if she were all right.

Still weak, infuriated that he had tricked her this way, she pushed his arm away. "I'm very well," she declared flatly, although she could not look at the chute again. She moved on, behind Dolores, who seemed not to be affected as violently, probably because she was used to this kind of sight. Brenna shook her head in amazement and followed Dolores to another building where the hide of a dead animal was being deftly removed. It would then be taken to a section of the plant where, Steven informed her, it would be salted, dried, and treated with arsenic to preserve it from moths and grubs.

"The meat, which is lean and stringy, will be pulled off in long strips an inch or two thick, soaked in brine for a month, then packed in barrels between layers of salt," he explained. His words made Brenna feel even sicker, and she swore to herself that she would never, never eat roasted meat again.

"Even the remains of the carcass are used efficiently," he went on, guiding her toward an area where huge cal-drons were bubbling. "In these vats of boiling water, the fats are extracted and packed in tubes as grease and tallow. The bones and refuse are fed into the fires as fuel, and the hoofs yield gelatin and oils. Quite an efficient operation, isn't it, senora?"

Brenna could only nod, as she was afraid to open her mouth. Dolores' face bore only a casual interest as they once more found themselves in the open air. Was it her imagination that when Dolores looked from her to Steven, there was a triumphant expression on her face? Was she implying that she had a stronger stomach than the young Irish girl? Brenna could not have cared less if she had failed in the test. No uninitiated person could be expected to look upon that operation and come away unaffected.

Brenna felt the relief pouring through her as they went to their horses. She mounted quickly and waited for Steven, who was talking to the two overseers of the plant. She noticed that Dolores was still standing next to her mare, obviously waiting for her husband to help her into the saddle. Steven finished his discussion and politely cupped his hands to oblige his wife's booted foot, before mounting himself.

"What an experience," Brenna managed to say as they rode away from the *saladero*. "No wonder you keep it so far away from the main house—the stench is enough to make one lose his appetite!"

Steven laughed. "The stench is not so bad now, Brenna. Wait until the height of seasonal activity in the summer. Then, even at the main house you can smell it when the wind is right."

"Ugh, I shall certainly make it a point not to visit in the summer," she said steadily.

They rode on, she and Dolores conversing a little to break the silences. They passed windowless mud and straw ranchos, where the doors were closed by sheepskins. These, Steven said, were the houses of the tenant farmers who, for a fixed rent, were allowed to grow animals and grains on the Castaneda land. Brenna looked at the hovels sympathetically. Some of them were little more than lean-tos.

Steven greeted the men and women alike, for they were his people, part of his wealth. More than ever, Brenna was reminded of Sir William riding along the roads, greeting the farmers of his county seat, a proud and noble personage, who held tight control over the lives of those who served him.

She thought of Katie, suddenly, and felt a tremendous urge to be with her. "Forgive me, Steven, but could we turn toward home now? Katie will be up soon and hungry."

His black eyes slid over the neckline of her jacket as though he could divine the shape and texture of her breasts, making Brenna blush a little at his boldness. Out of the corner of her eye, she could see Dolores staring at her also, but with a mixture of envy and longing that made her uncomfortable.

They began making their way back, riding nearly abreast now. Brenna, her thoughts on Katie, did not register the appearance of the enormous ombu tree until they were quite close to it. Suddenly, she felt again all the passion and excitement of that day when Steven had made love to her beneath its shading limbs, in the curvature of its sprawling roots. Her eyes widened involuntarily, and she willed herself not to look at him. Let it pass, she thought desperately. Try to forget that it ever happened —but how to do that when every day, she looked at her small daughter and knew precisely where she had been conceived? With an effort, she straightened her back and looked straight ahead, falling silent until they reached the *estancia*.

Chapter Forty-Seven

BRENNA checked her appearance in the long mirror in her room, while Teresa stood behind her arranging an errant fold of the gown she had chosen to wear for Miguel Castaneda's birthday party. Everyone had been decorating since early that morning, and the entire house came alive with glowing lanterns, bright paper streamers, lush bouquets of flowers cut from the gardens, and the smell of cooking food from the kitchens where the staff had been laboring since dawn.

Brenna had selected an ivory silk gown, trimmed with pale blue lace at the bustle and hemline. The décolleté bared her shoulders and throat, and she had piled her hair simply towards the back of her head and festooned it with a few white blossoms which Teresa had filched from one of the bouquet baskets. Around her neck she wore the sapphires that Carlos' father had given her, and the sight of them made her think of her husband with longing.

She had successfully eluded Steven during her stay in his home, but it was hard to elude the thoughtful stares that Dolores settled on her sometimes, or to escape the glow of happiness that Consuelo took on when she came to play with Katie, or to ignore the sharp looks that Miguel sometimes fixed on her at the dinner table. Only Rosaria seemed without a care, caught up in her romance with Diego Garcia. Sometimes, Brenna wished she were still that young and naive.

Tonight, Rosaria's engagement to Diego would be formally announced to the assembly, which would include many of the wealthy *patrones* from the neighboring *estancias*. There would also be a fiesta for the tenant farmers and the gauchos on the Castaneda payroll—an obligation of the *estancia* owner, although this party would be separated from the pleasures of the wealthier guests.

"I think you are ready, senora," Teresa said finally, stepping back a little.

"Let me give my little darling a kiss," Brenna smiled, stooping to pick up her daughter, who was playing on the floor with a flower petal. She kissed her and hugged her little body a moment before reluctantly giving her up to Teresa. "Good night, my angel," she whispered, then picked up her gloves and left the room to make her way to the main patio.

Many guests had already arrived and were mingling together with glasses of wine in their hands. The men formed small groups to talk about cattle prices, and some voices were raised in political discussions, then lowered again in deference to Miguel, who had asked everyone to refrain from getting into any full-fledged political debates. The ladies all sat on stone benches to gossip about Paris fashions and to admire each other's gowns, while they listened with half-an-ear to their husbands' discussions.

Brenna felt ill at ease without her husband, knowing no one else. She looked around hopefully for Rosaria or Dolores or Consuelo, but Rosaria was off in a corner, her eyes on her fiancée's face as she drank in his every word, and Consuelo was still busy in the kitchens, seeing to last-minute details. Dolores was nowhere to be found. Brenna was about to go in search of her when Miguel spied her standing forlornly, and beckoned her over with an expansive gesture.

He politely introduced her to his friends and to their wives; for a few minutes, Brenna was the center of interest when she told them she had lived in Europe and had visited France, but the interest waned when Brenna could not adequately answer their eager questions on the latest fashions. She cursed herself for not having paid more attention at the time, and thought, with a rueful smile, that Deirdre would have been perfect at this party.

She saw Steven in the midst of a discussion with a few men of his own age, and then found Dolores standing awkwardly alone at the edge of the patio. Of course, it would be Steven's duty to bring her into the crowd, but he seemed oblivious to her for the moment. Brenna quickly went to greet her. Dolores looked lovely tonight in a pastel shade of pink, and Brenna told her so.

"Thank you," Dolores answered politely, although her eyes continually roamed over toward her husband. She looked displeased that he had not come over to receive her, and, Brenna thought, she looked as though she resented Brenna's precipitous intrusion.

Brenna rushed self-consciously into small talk, and was relieved when Steven finally saw them standing together and excused himself to come to them. She took advantage of Consuelo's entrance to get away from the husband and wife.

"My dear, you look charming tonight," Consuelo said graciously, taking Brenna's hand. "Have you met our guests?"

Brenna nodded, hoping to save herself from being paraded around all these people. If it had not been Miguel's birthday celebration, she would have excused herself from the festivities, using Dolores' usual plea of a headache.

"Good. Now you must enjoy yourself, my dear. The food will be served directly, and the cake—ah, it did turn out beautiful—will be in the place of honor. We've an excellent orchestra from the city . . ."

"It sounds wonderful," Brenna said, hoping Consuelo would not detect her lack of enthusiasm.

Apparently, Consuelo had too much on her mind to worry about Brenna, and after another pat on the hand, floated into the circle of guests, the perfect hostess, smiling and talking, nodding and laughing. Brenna watched her for a moment, fascinated and wishing that she, herself, were so calm and poised. Trying to be as unobtrusive as possible, she backed away from the lighted areas of the patio and tried to merge into the shadows at the back wall.

As she stood there, fanning herself and relishing the exquisite scent coming from the rose garden, she could hear, on the other side of the low wall, sounds of music and revelry coming from the fiesta given for the tenant farmers and the gauchos. It sounded so gay and friendly that she wished she might take a peek at the goings on.

Surely it could not be any worse than this, she thought, and making her mind up, she followed the shadow of the wall until it opened into a doorway, through which she could follow a path lined with rosebushes into another section of the grounds. She told herself she could stay only a moment or two, for she must not miss the lighting of the birthday cake and the toast to Miguel's health. He would expect her, and she did not want to disappoint him.

A warm hand caught her elbow from behind, and Brenna started, fearful that her folly might have gotten her into trouble. She turned her head and could make out a tall, masculine figure in the half-light.

"Steven?" she whispered, her voice trembling a little.

"Who else would follow you through these damned briars?" His hand moved upward from her elbow and clasped her arm, turning her around to face him. "Where are you going, Brenna?"

He was so near that she could smell the faint tang of leather, horse, and soap that clung to him; she could make out the snowy jabot of his shirtfront, could feel and hear his breathing match her own. She felt herself grow soft and melting, yearning to press herself up against him, here in the dark with the heavy scent of roses and no one else . . .

"The perfect setting for a seduction, don't you agree?" he laughed mockingly, as though he could read her mind.

His words dispersed the warmth Brenna had felt and brought her back to her senses. She pulled her arm sharply away from his grasp. "It is none of your business what I'm about," she said quickly. " 'Twould be better for you to concern yourself with what your wife will say when she discovers you've followed me."

He shrugged lazily. "Dolores has been called to the kitchens to help my mother supervise some chore or another."

Brenna decided not to get into an argument about the merits of his wife. After all, she shouldn't be concerning herself with his personal matters.

"Well then, go back and talk to your guests," she hissed. "I promise I'll not tell anyone that you tried to corner me in the rose garden and kiss me," she ended sarcastically.

"I? You are accusing me of trying to kiss you?" He let his voice fill with melodramatic affront. "Why, the thought never entered my mind, Senora Valera. Truly, you wound me with your doubts and distrust. Have I, during all the days of your visit, ever tried to compromise you? My, my, what a salacious mind you have, Brenna."

She knew he was smiling and was glad the darkness hid her furious blush. Before she could think of a fitting retort, he continued, lazily, thoughtfully.

"So, you want my kisses that badly, eh?" he laughed with amusement. "Had you only given me some sign, some hint, I would have been happy to oblige this burning desire within you, my lovely Brenna. Only leave your door open tonight, and I will . . ."

"Enough!" she said, turning abruptly on her heel and marching away from him.

"But where are you going?" he asked softly. "Ah, it seems we are back where we started before all this talk of kissing and seducing and . . ."

"I am on my way to a party, senor," she interrupted quickly.

"That would be most unwise, senora, for most of our tenants do not have wives—only mistresses, and they might try to seduce you more forcefully than I. I suggest you allow me to accompany you, if you insist on doing this."

Brenna hesitated. He was probably right, but she hated to admit it. She nodded coolly. "All right then, but I warn you . . ."

"Come along then," he cut in, taking her hand to lead her down the path as though she were a child and he were only humoring her. "But you may stay only a few moments—or we will both be missed and your reputation tattered."

Brenna struggled to keep herself from replying. He laughed softly, as though aware of her inner struggle. When they came out of the gardens, they entered a small patio where she could see a quartet of men strumming quiet ballads on guitars. Others laughed and talked noisily, some dancing with mestizo and Indian women, some drinking from barrels of wine.

Brenna looked over the scene eagerly; she was glad that she did have Steven's protection, for some of the men looked tough and lawless. One caught sight of Steven, and letting out a whoop of welcome, came over to slap his landlord on the shoulders in friendly fashion.

"Steven, you son of a bitch, I knew you'd slip away and join us." He stopped abruptly, seeing the lady. "Ah, pardon me, senora, it is a great pleasure to finally meet Steven's wife."

"This is Senora Valera," Steven said easily, winking at the other man. "She is my mistress, man. You don't think I'd bring my wife to your drunken revels!"

"I am *not* your mistress!" Brenna cried in horror, embarrassed in front of this stranger.

The man exchanged a sly look with Steven, then bowed clumsily and introduced himself as Guido. He urged the couple toward the wine barrels and dipped mugs for both of them, shoving one into Brenna's hands so that she barely missed being splashed with the bright, ruby liquid. With a high-pitched laugh, a dusty-haired woman descended on Guido and pushed him out to where the others were dancing.

"Who *was* that?" Brenna wanted to know, her amazed helplessness showing on her face as she sipped at the wine automatically.

"That was Guido, one of my father's best gauchos and someone I grew up with—before I was sent away to Europe," Steven answered. "He's a good man, a brave man. I'm proud to call him my friend."

"What is a—gaucho, exactly?" Brenna asked curiously, her eyes following Guido as he clasped the laughing woman closely. He was not very tall, she noted, but strong-looking, with a handsome olive complexion tanned by the elements, and piercing black eyes that reminded her of Steven's. He seemed somehow bent or stoop-shouldered as though he was not comfortable on foot, but needed a horse under him.

"A gaucho is a nomad," Steven answered her thoughtfully. "He's a horseman, who sleeps in the open out on the pampas, sits alone under the stars, or sometimes makes a temporary home with any little *china* who'll have him in her mud hut. They are wild and ignorant, totally lawless and without morals. Most are barbarically independent and shun the towns, but some, like Guido, are loyal to their *patrones* and work hard for them."

"How did your father find him? I mean, how did he come to work for you?"

"He just wandered in off the pampas one day when he was about seven. Didn't know who or where his parents were, didn't know anything except—how to ride a horse like the devil himself." There was fond remembrance in Steven's voice now.

Brenna continued to watch Guido, noticing how different even his clothing was from any she had seen in Buenos Aires. He wore black, baggy pantaloons and boots, which looked like they were made from the hide of a colt's hindleg. He had a jaunty soft, black felt hat, turned up in front like a musketeer, which he threw off as he leaned over to pick the woman up in his arms and whirl her frenziedly around in a circle. His black hair was long, and his moustache was flowing and fierce.

She was unaware of Steven's watching her and taking advantage of her inattention to slip an arm about her waist. If she had looked up at that moment, she might have caught the look of eagerness on his face, the look of wanting mixed with something deeper in his eyes, which he could hardly admit to himself. But the look disappeared quickly, to be replaced by one of amused insolence.

"You must stop staring at Guido, or he will think you want him shamelessly," he whispered indolently in her ear.

Stung, Brenna turned toward him, noted his closeness and pulled away quickly.

"Would you like to dance?" He asked her as though they were back in Ireland in Sir William's ballroom.

Caught off balance, Brenna looked back at the wild,

intricate movements of the gauchos and their partners and shook her head. "I—don't think I could."

"Come now, you must dance the *pericón*, or the gauchos will be insulted," he insisted, bringing out his handkerchief and handing it to her.

Brenna took it, bewildered, then saw that the others were taking out handkerchiefs and manipulating them in time to the strumming guitars. She felt foolish, being forced out with the dancers, but Steven was not about to let her go, so she did her best to copy the movements of the other women, all the time cursing Steven under her breath and resolving to retreat as soon as she had the opportunity. The dance was slow, timed to the beat of the mournful guitar. Brenna dipped and swayed, then circled with the women who were waving their handkerchiefs at the men pacing back and forth in measured steps. The rhythm grew subtly faster until Brenna found herself whirling, her skirts flying, the handkerchief fluttering in her fingers. Abruptly, the music died and the women flung the handkerchiefs toward the waiting men. Steven caught his deftly, his white teeth glinting in an enigmatic smile. After the dance, Guido guided them back to the wine barrels, and Steven made Brenna sit on one of the benches between them.

"The senora is very interested in your exciting life, Guido, my friend," Steven said, intensifying Brenna's embarrassment.

"Ah, beautiful lady, never ask a gaucho to tell a story," Guido warned her, "for he can go on for days and days until he dies of starvation or lack of sleep."

Brenna knew that the two of them were laughing at her, using her as the butt of their jokes, and she would have marched angrily away but for Steven's arm carelessly around her shoulders, tensing with steel firmness when she started to stand.

"Let me go," she said angrily.

"Now, now, you wanted to come to the party," he reminded her lazily, "and I am only doing as you asked."

"But I . . ."

"Please tell your story, Guido," he directed his friend.

"Ah, fair lady, we gauchos are Argentina's greatness," he said in a soothing voice, which helped to calm Brenna's ruffled feathers. "We are the frontiersmen, the horsemen. Once we scorned crop farming and avoided towns; we warred with the Indians and took our women whenever we felt the need." He stopped a moment and let his eyes travel over her figure speculatively, but, at a warning glance from Steven, the gaucho shrugged and continued.

"Our home was a saddle and a poncho, though sometimes an adobe hut with a grass roof, where we would keep a *china*, a woman, to raise our children. We love our freedom above all else, and we had a reputation for courage and lawlessness, for brutality and disregard for life." He stopped, as though to gauge her reaction.

"It has been said that we are Moorish in our fatalism, my lady. We care only to ride better, to throw and tame the wild colt, and to gallop across the roughest ground of the pampas. We favor black cigars and white rum. This is the law of the gaucho: it is a crime to steal a horse, but it is no crime to borrow one without the owner's knowledge, for when it is turned loose, it will go back to its owner, no?"

"It sounds—breathtaking," Brenna said, feeling inadequate. "But why do you speak in the past tense, as though . . ."

"As though the gaucho were no more?" Guido asked sadly. "Because, my lady, civilization has reached out with its fingers and fenced, squared off, and parceled out our land. Most of the gauchos work for a *patrón* now as cattle riders, or else they have been organized by the government into fighting regiments to battle the Indians to the south." He shrugged. "The gaucho will not last much longer."

"I'm sorry. I mean—you sound so sad," Brenna whispered compassionately.

"I *am* sad, my lady," he affirmed.

For a moment, all was silent around them, for some of the others had stopped to listen to Guido's mournful story. Then, suddenly, Guido jumped to his feet and let out a cry. "Where are the dice, my friends? A game of taba, eh, to lighten the spirit?"

"No, no! More stories!" someone shouted. "Don't you know any more?"

"No more stories; they're too sad!" Guido shot back, searching for the person who opposed him. "Sancho, you black bastard, you trying to ruin our fun, eh?" he laughed, but there was a quickening in his face as though he relished a fight with this other man.

Brenna, watching him, was reminded of Rory Adair, who so many times had had just that look on his face just before he picked a fight.

"Steven, shouldn't you be trying to stop it?" she asked worriedly.

He shrugged. "It's their business, Brenna. This sort of thing happens all the time—perhaps you'd best get back to the others now."

"But your friend may be hurt—"

Even as she spoke, someone handed Guido a guitar. "I accept the challenge," he laughed merrily. "I can out-sing and outlast this pompous ass who crows how good a *payador* he is."

Brenna watched in total confusion. What kind of duel was this—a singing contest? "What are they going to do?" she asked Steven.

"They are going to sit and sing stories to the crowd, each one trying to outdo the other. They are called *payadores*, like the troubadors of old, except the contest usually ends when one of them gets tired of singing and gets angry."

Even as Steven was explaining to Brenna, the two gauchos began their stories, improvising witty and some-times ironic couplets, their voices rising higher and higher as they strummed their guitars. Some ten minutes must have passed, and their words were getting more and more heated, when Guido suddenly threw down the guitar, and quicker than Brenna could follow, reached into his boot and drew out a silver-handled knife with a shining double-edged blade, a *facón*, Steven whispered to her.

There followed a vicious duel between the two contestants with their long, sharp *facones,* against which the only shield was a poncho draped around their left arms. Brenna watched in stupefied amazement as Guido, laughing outrageously, carved a tidy niche in the upper arm of the other man. A moment later, Sancho's *facón* curved inward and drew blood across Guido's shoulder. All the time they fought, the two men laughed and traded insults, so that Brenna was not sure whether the fight was serious or in fun.

Finally, after a brief tussle, Guido tripped Sancho onto his back; Guido stood above the fallen man, his booted foot firmly planted on his opponent's throat, and demanded that he proclaim him the best of all the *payadores.* When Sancho remained silent, a wicked, brutal light stole into Guido's eyes, and he bent forward, his dagger held high and gleaming in the air, ready to plunge downward.

With a cry, Brenna sprang up from her seat, but neither of the men moved. Grudgingly, Sancho nodded stiffly and proclaimed Guido the best *payador*—for this time, he added—whereupon Guido let him up, and the music began again. Brenna could only sit back and wonder at the lunacy she had just seen.

"I think it's time to take you back," Steven said in her ear. "Have you had enough for one night?"

She nodded. Then her eyes flew up to meet his in the semi-darkness. "How—how long have we been gone? Oh, Steven, your father—his cake! And Dolores . . . ! They'll be wondering—"

"Such a guilty conscience you have, my dear. Why, anyone would think, just looking at your face, that we were adulterers." He leered at her wickedly.

Brenna reddened and stood up. This time, he did not stop her as she fled back down the path to the wall.

Chapter Forty-Eight

IT was Katie Valera's first birthday, and Brenna had invited nearly everyone she knew to the fiesta. She had decorated the drawing room and ordered an enormous cake. Carlos, ever the indulgent father, had presented Katie with a beautiful dress of white lace, ordering her in serious tones not to smear cake on it. Katie had cooed up at him and thrown her plump little arms out to be picked up. "Papa," she pronounced proudly, to Carolos' delight.

The guests arrived promptly. Diego and Rosaria Garcia, with the glow of their honeymoon still showing, presented Katie with a china doll, an impractical gift, which Brenna wisely stowed away for Katie when she was older. Steven and Dolores came, accompanied by Dolores' newest physician, Dr. Galvéz, who had arrived from Tucumán and who had been staying at Paloma for several weeks, administering treatments to his patient. Even Miguel and Consuelo had shown up, making much of the child and laughing with delight as Katie stroked Miguel's graying goatee with her sticky hands. Other friends of Carlos and their wives crowded into the celebration.

Brenna had to admit she was glad when only the Castanedas were left, relaxing in chairs among the litter of unwrapped packages where Katie was toddling about on shaky legs, stooping now and then to pick up some bright bauble.

"You have a very energetic child, señora," Dr. Galvéz commented, watching as Katie stopped to examine the toe of his shoe. "Very friendly, too."

Dolores laughed nervously. "I think she likes the gentlemen better, Dr. Galvéz, for she does fidget whenever I try to hold her."

"That's because you don't know how to hold her cor-

515

rectly," Consuelo commented frankly. "She senses you're nervous around her."

"Senora Castaneda, please—" Dr. Galvéz put in quietly, as Dolores' lower lip quivered.

"Well, I think it's time for you to go to bed, birthday girl," Carlos said quickly in the intervening silence. He reached down to scoop his daughter up, but Consuelo laughed and reached out her arms to her, begging him to allow the child to stay up a little longer.

"She is such a delight," the older woman said fondly, clasping the toddler so close that she protested. After a few moments, she set her back on the floor. Katie immediately made her way to Steven, who was standing near the fireplace.

Brenna observed him as he watched the progress of the child, his face remaining passive. When Katie came closer and reached out to grab at his trousers for support as she stood up, he laughed out loud and reached down to pick her up.

"Not so close to the fire, little one," he said in mock-serious tones to the attentive child, "or you'll singe your pretty new dress."

He held her for a moment and Brenna couldn't help thinking how different Steven could be from the cool, mocking man she knew. For a swift second, his black eyes became tender as he looked into the child's face, and she thought he might lean down to kiss the top of her head. But, as though remembering his audience, Steven strode away from the fireplace and handed Katie to her mother.

"A wonderful child, indeed," he said with a devilish twinkle in his eye, "but she is wetting my shirtfront, senora."

Brenna took Katie from him, risking a curious glance toward Dolores who had been watching the proceedings with unmistakable envy. Poor Dolores, Brenna thought, so wanting a child—she hoped Dr. Galvéz could so something for her. She stood up to put Katie to bed and was about to leave the room, when Steven stopped her.

"I have a special gift that I—and my wife—would like

to bestow on Katie," he said smoothly, bringing a small jewelry case out of his coat pocket.

Brenna took it curiously, wondering why he had waited until now to present it. She opened it and gasped incredulously, for inside was an exquisite necklace of lustrous, milky pearls. She looked in speechless amazement up at Steven's face.

"I believe that the pearl is her birthstone," Steven said lazily, his black eyes challenging her.

"But—but it is much too expensive," Brenna said, looking helplessly at Carlos, who was watching silently.

"Nothing is too expensive for my—" he stopped at Brenna's indrawn breath of horror, then grinned wickedly, "—for my honorary niece," he finished with a slight bow.

Brenna felt weak in the knees, and with a strangled thanks, hurried off quickly to put Katie to bed. Her heart was pumping very fast, and she stood for a moment, holding Katie close against her breast. Would it always be like this? she wondered desperately. Would she always have to worry about some slip of the tongue, some deliberate challenge that Steven would throw out to her? She didn't think she could stand it. It was bad enough, just knowing how she had to deceive Carlos about Katie's conception. She—she must talk to Steven, implore him to forget that the child was his—but how could she ask him to do that?

"Brenna?"

It was Dolores. Brenna forced herself to attain some composure, fearing that Steven's wife might have sharp enough eyes and some intuitiveness to guess at her disturbance.

"I am sorry to interrupt you like this," Dolores said haltingly. "I know how special this time of day must be to you—when you put your child to bed." She hesitated.

"It's all right," Brenna said, shifting Katie to her other arm as she walked to the dressing table, where she would put the child in her nightclothes. "You can watch, if you want to."

Dolores followed her silently, her dark eyes watching

as Katie cooed and kicked and waved her fists at her mother as she changed her. "You must be so very happy with your daughter," she whispered.

"Yes, she is a joy to me," Brenna confirmed, tickling the child's tummy.

"Someday—perhaps—if God wills it—" Dolores faltered, then went on. "Dr. Galvéz thinks that I might be able to conceive," she confided.

"That would be wonderful," Brenna said, wondering why Dolores was telling her.

"Yes, I know Steven would love to have a child of his own, although he doesn't say as much to me," she continued, blushing a little at the admission. "Still, I can tell—it is there, in his eyes, especially when he looks at your Katie."

Brenna was silent, totally engrossed, as though pinning Katie's diaper to her nightshirt was suddenly the most important thing in the world.

"Of course, the conception itself is not the difficulty," Dolores went on conversationally. "It is the carrying of the unborn child to which I am not particularly suited, Dr. Galvéz thinks. In fact, he has told me that I might have been pregnant before, but aborted the fetus too quickly to have even been aware of it." She blushed at her own use of medical terms. "Something to do with the narrowness of the hips." She shrugged, lightly brushing the top of Katie's blanket as Brenna put the child in her cradle.

"Then, if you do conceive, you must take especially good care of yourself," Brenna commented, simply because she thought that was what Dolores wanted her to say.

After kissing her daughter and speaking briefly with Teresa, Brenna closed the nursery door behind her and joined Dolores in the hallway. "Shall we go back with the others?"

Dolores nodded. "I certainly hope Steven hasn't been teasing poor Dr. Galvéz while I was with you. I think he does it for pure meanness sometimes, because he doesn't believe that the doctor is truly helping me." She laughed sadly. "If only he knew how much his attention means to me, if only he realized that if he gave me one-tenth the attention that Dr. Galvéz does . . ." She stopped abruptly, her face reddening "Excuse me, Brenna, I didn't mean to presume . . ."

Brenna waved her apologies aside. "Please don't bother yourself about it," she said quickly. "I shall forget it was even mentioned."

But Brenna found herself wondering about Dolores' statement. Was Steven inattentive to his wife because she could not give him a child? Or was there some other reason—something to do with Brenna, herself? She could not bear to think that she might, somehow, be coming between Steven and his wife—yet, was that a tiny thrill of fierce joy that had swept through her, thinking that Steven still cared for her so much?

She watched him across the room, trading amusing anecdotes with Carlos at the expense of Dr. Galvéz, and wondered at the man behind the amused facade. Would she ever really know him?

As their guests were leaving and Carlos stood a little behind Brenna at the door, Steven bowed before her, thanked her for the evening, and said in a serious tone of voice, "Please don't bother yourself about the expense of the necklace, Brenna. Believe me, it neither cost me as much, nor was it nearly so hard to select, as a music box that I gave someone else a very long time ago."

Brenna's eyes fell away from his intense gaze, and later she could not even recall what she murmured in answer.

The year of 1875 passed quickly for Brenna. She received few letters from Ireland and wrote even fewer in return, for she found raising her child took most of her time.

On this day, however, Brenna had taken several hours to write to her family, telling them of Katie's progress and of life with Carlos. She was in the midst of her letter to her brother when she heard her husband come in the front door. She hurried to greet him in the front hall.

"Ah, my dear, there you are," Carlos smiled, giving her

a quick embrace. Then he stepped back and brought up a young man, who looked perhaps a year older than Brenna. He was of medium height and build and had a handsome-sad kind of face which spoke of past sufferings. Her interest was piqued immediately. "May I introduce, Senor Hipólito Irigoyen? Hipólito, this is my wife, Brenna."

"How do you do, Senora Valera?" The young man bowed solemnly.

"Please come in," Brenna offered graciously, exchanging a questioning look with her husband. She led the young man into the small drawing room and bade him sit down. "Do you drink tea or coffee, señor?"

He accepted coffee, and Brenna instructed the kitchen maid to bring out coffee service for all three. She seated herself opposite this new friend of her husband, politely awaiting further enlightenment from Carlos.

"I met Hipólito several weeks ago during a political rally, Brenna," Carlos said, lounging comfortably in one of the chairs.

"So you are a proponent of Federalism, senor?" Brenna asked.

He smiled. "Not openly, senora. My uncle, Leandro Além, has some political influence in the present cabinet, and he has been able to obtain an appointment for me as *comisario* of police. Because of this appointment, I cannot be openly critical of the government, senora, if you follow my meaning."

"Of course," Brenna said, her interest even stronger. "How did your uncle obtain such a valuable position for you?" She was aware, from Carlos' explanation, that the office of *comisario* of police was a desirable plum in the government. Many governors, legislators, and cabinet members had begun their political careers as *comisarios*. One of the most popular sayings in Argentina was: "The *comisario*'s horse always wins."

Hipólito had shrugged in answer to her question. "My uncle served admirably in the Paraguayan War. Because of this, he was appointed to a prestigious military command. It seems this is all that was necessary to have me appointed *comisario*." There was an underlying sarcasm in his tone.

"And do you enjoy it, then?"

He laughed outright, something which she would not have believed possible from such a serious-looking young man. "Senora, I study the virtues, the vices, and the secrets of the people in my district. By keeping my eyes and ears open and my mouth shut, I have become, if you will excuse me for saying so, quite adept at political intrigue."

Brenna stared at him, noting how he bore himself like a much older man. He had a soft voice, a courteous manner, and a natural gift for making his authority felt. Somehow, too, she could imagine his being very attractive to women. The thought came to her that this man was a very dangerous friend to have, and she glanced at her husband protectively.

"Ah, the coffee," Carlos was saying, missing his wife's glance. "You must forgive my wife, Hipólito. I think I indulge her too much as far as my political activities go, and she can be very persistent in her questioning." He looked fondly at her. "Although I treasure her all the more for it."

"An admirable quality in a woman, especially a wife," Irigoyen agreed. "So many of them are empty-headed shrews who squawk at their husbands for missing dinner because they are at a political meeting." His dark eyes rested somberly on Brenna who flushed a little and sipped at her coffee.

"You—must be very busy then, with your duties as *comisario*." Brenna wished she could shake off her uncomfortable feeling about this man.

Again, he laughed, although not as loudly as before. "Fairly busy, senora, although I have gotten myself admitted to the law school at the University."

"The law school! How interesting—my brother is a lawyer in Dublin," she continued.

"I doubt that Argentina's law compares easily with Ireland's," Irigoyen put in obliquely. "At any rate, I'm not sure whether or not I shall complete the course. It is dull and full of outdated methods, which hardly have a place in modern society. Polite law is becoming obsolete, señora. The only way of truly improving the lot of the people these days is by breaking the law."

"Dangerous words, Hipólito," Carlos put in, frowning.

"Not when I am among my friends," he answered lightly, but his eyes were still somber as they looked pointedly at Brenna.

"For myself, I have never been one to advocate violence in these matters," Carlos said thoughtfully. "But there are times, my friend, that I consider your viewpoint the most sensible. The people who sit in their offices and look down with contempt at the rabble, as they call it, don't listen to the arguments of law. Ah, but distribute guns among that rabble, and the rich will listen quickly enough."

"I agree," said Irigoyen, warming to the subject. "Look at what the masses have accomplished in other countries. The British in the seventeenth century overthrew their King; and the French in the eighteenth century brought the corrupt Bourbons toppling from their thrones. Even the Americans who rallied against the English at the same time—they resorted to guns and munitions despite all their high-handed doctrines and ideals."

Brenna watched the exchange between this man and her husband worriedly. Violence meant bloodshed and murder, often hurting the innocent most. She listened attentively as Irigoyen continued to expound on his ideals of equality and justice for every man, even if paid for with a few lives.

They toss off a man's life as though it were nothing, she thought sadly, as though he should be honored to die for their causes. What if it were *your* life, Senor Irigoyen, she thought further, her blue eyes darkening angrily, and she said as much to the man.

Irigoyen shrugged eloquently. "If it accomplished something, senora, I would not be unhappy to see my life end in that way. It is much better than to die comfortably in a bed at the age of eighty if one has been untrue to one's beliefs." His dark eyes challenged her.

"But what if not everyone believes the same as you?" Brenna persisted. "What if they don't want to die for someone else's cause? What if they would rather live out their lives with their wives and children?"

"Then they are cowards!" he said in a strong voice. "They are like the sheep, the cows being led to the *saladero*. Look at the peaceful cow, senora, who does nothing but her master's wishes. For all her peacefulness, she is slaughtered for her master's supper."

"But men are not like cows!" Brenna said angrily.

"You are right, senora. Men have brains to direct their own lives. And so I say—use those brains to win freedom and equality!" He gazed at her in triumph.

"My dear, I'm afraid you can't get ahead of Hipólito. He's one of those rabid types who will not listen to a woman's reasoning," Carlos put in quietly, although he smiled at his wife.

"He is one of those who will send others into battle," Brenna said carelessly, "while he sits safely at home and waits to see what the outcome will be." She didn't care that she was being rude. She didn't like him and wished he were not a friend of her husband.

"Brenna, my dear, Hipólito is our guest."

"That is quite all right, Carlos," Irigoyen said with a twist of a smile on his somber face. "Your wife has spirit and fire—she will make you a fitting accomplice when the time is right to strike at those fat cats who sit in government." He looked at her seriously. "Yes, senora, I can see you in the thick of battle, once you are won over to our side. Eh, Carlos?"

Brenna excused herself from the rest of their conversation, telling herself it was ridiculous to be upset about the ravings of a fanatic. Still, she worried that Carlos would be unduly influenced by this Irigoyen, who could, she knew, twist a man's thinking to his own way, for he was eloquent and charismatic. A dangerous man, she repeated to herself as she waited in her bedroom for Carlos to come up after Irigoyen had gone.

"Darling, you were most impolite to Hipólito," Carlos chided her as he closed the bedroom door behind him.

"I'm sorry, Carlos, but I can't help disliking the man," she admitted.

"Well, I don't think he was unduly upset. In fact," and he grinned roguishly, "I think Hipólito truly likes you."

"*Likes* me!" she got out in irritation. "Heaven keep me safe from such an admirer!"

Carlos laughed softly. "If heaven won't, I will, for though Irigoyen is a friend and shares my beliefs, I wouldn't trust him not to seduce my wife when my back was turned. He has, I'm afraid, a reputation with the women."

"He is so sour and somber, I can hardly believe any woman would find him attractive," Brenna said quickly, although she recalled what effect he had had on her the first moment she had met him.

Carlos shrugged. "Nevertheless, he has had innumerable love affairs, according to rumor. In fact, one of his first was with the servant of one of his aunts, which resulted in a daughter. They say he took her into his uncle's family and has always kept her close to him, although he's forgotten about the mother."

"A fine, upstanding citizen," Brenna said sourly.

"Oh, don't be so quick to condemn him, my dear," Carlos said seriously. "He has had a hard life. His grandfather, accused of being a member of the dreaded secret police during Rosa's dictatorship, was shot and his body hung for four hours in one of the plazas in the city. His grandmother was believed to be an illegitimate relative of the hated Rosa family."

"I'm sure many of your contemporaries have grandfathers who might have associated with. Rosa," Brenna began in a huff, not wishing to feel sorry for Irigoyen.

"True, but many of them switched allegiances at the right time and avoided death and disgrace for their families. Irigoyen told me that his mother had been given a good education, but because of the disgrace to her family name, she was forced to marry beneath her, to an illiterate Basque who had been one of Rosa's stable boys."

"Kevin, my first husband, was a stable hand," she interrupted fiercely.

"But you married him because you chose to," Carlos said gently.

Brenna decided not to enlighten him further, but sat down on the bed to take off her shoes and stockings, hoping her husband would drop the subject of Irigoyen. Such was not to be the case.

"I've talked to a few people who knew Irigoyen when he was young, and they've all told me what a sad, moody child he was—forced to suffer ostracism after the public execution and disgrace of his grandfather. As if that weren't enough, when he was five, his mother's eldest sister left home to give birth to the child of a priest."

Brenna let out an exclamation of horror, for that was one of the blackest sins imaginable to a Catholic.

Carlos smiled wryly. "She even had a second child under the same shadow and was alienated from the family for the rest of her life."

Brenna swallowed, hardly believing her ears. No wonder the man seemed strange, having to live with the taint of such a sin all of his life. It was terrible! "But now, I suppose he is close to this uncle he told us about? Surely, being a military hero, he must be someone that Irigoyen can look up to?"

Carlos frowned to himself. "I'm not entirely sure he is. Irigoyen has been under Além's influence for a long time, since before he was twelve years old. They were inseparable companions, despite the fact that Além is ten years older than his nephew. They were outcasts in their neighborhood and learned early in life to keep to themselves and to express their thoughts only to each other—not exactly the best way for a young boy to grow up."

"Oh." Brenna shivered, wishing she didn't feel sorry for her husband's new friend, but unable to stop a rush of compassion. No wonder he had the poise of an older man —so serious and sober. She looked up at Carlos. "You have succeeded in making me feel ashamed of myself," she said softly.

He came to her where she was sitting on the bed and embraced her gently, kissing her on the neck and shoulder. "My good Brenna," he murmured, "what a perfect wife you are for me!"

She sighed. "But I cannot help feeling that that man is dangerous, Carlos," she whispered with concern in her voice. "I—I do hope you don't become close friends."

Chapter Forty-Nine

In mid-1876, Brenna found out that she was pregnant again. She laughed at her husband who stood up in the middle of the room and danced something that resembled an Irish jig.

"Oh, Brenna, I am so happy!" he laughed, coming over to hug her until she cried out for mercy. "You have made me the happiest person in all of Argentina, my love!" he added generously, his eyes glowing with love.

"Then I am the second-happiest person in Argentina," she said, kissing him.

"I must go and announce the news to everyone!" he exclaimed.

"Not yet, Carlos. It is so early," she said demurely. "Let's keep it a secret between ourselves until I start to show a little." She reached out to pull playfully at his ear. "Humor a new mother, darling, and don't tell anyone just yet?"

He looked at her oddly, then smiled. "All right, my dear, if you want to keep it a secret until your belly blossoms out and proclaims the news to everyone, I shall comply with your wishes." He hugged her again.

Brenna felt warm and loved in his embrace, and she told herself that her fears were irrational, but she couldn't help wondering how the arrival of this new child would affect Carlos' feelings toward a child that wasn't truly his. When she had first suspected she was pregnant, she had rushed into Katie's room and held her tightly, afraid suddenly that all the love Carlos had lavished on her during her two years of life would be automatically taken away and given to the new baby, leaving her Katie desolate. Then she had chided herself nervously; Carlos was not like that. He would always love Katie.

She couldn't put her finger on exactly why she didn't want anyone else to know about the new baby yet. Was she afraid of the look in Steven's eyes? Or of aggravating the envy in Dolores'? Even Hipólito Irigoyen, on his frequent visits to their home—would he look at her with that sly, insulting glance that made her blush, as though he had personally witnessed the intimacies between herself and her husband? She just needed a little more time, she told herself.

But by Christmastime, Brenna was nearly six months pregnant and showing hugely, much to Carlos' delight. Everyone knew now, just by looking at her, and Carlos indulged in as many congratulatory toasts as he could. Somehow, Brenna was glad that Steven had not heard yet, though she told herself she was being foolish, for he was bound to learn of it sooner or later. Only his business interests, which had sent him on a long trip to Brazil and northern Argentina, had kept him from visiting them in the city. She wondered, absently, how Dolores could ever hope to conceive if she couldn't even keep her husband close by. Then she flushed and chastised herself for such wicked and unkind thoughts. She just couldn't worry about what Steven thought anymore—after all, he had no cause to worry over her.

Still, on one sultry December day, when she was outside on the patio, trimming the roses, she couldn't help the sudden banging of her heart when she heard Steven calling from one of the drawing rooms, asking if anyone was at home to an old friend.

"Out here, on the patio!" she called, wishing immediately that she had had the presence of mind to say nothing so that he would go away. He rarely visited unless he knew Carlos would be at home.

"Why, Brenna, I . . ." She heard him stop and the swift intake of his breath as she straightened up carefully, showing him her profile. For several seconds, she was aware of his eyes on her, but she lacked the courage to speak.

"Brenna, a new baby?" his voice asked her, slipping back into the old familiar mockery that she detested. "When did it happen?"

"The baby is due in April," she said tensely, squeezing

the flowers in her hands so tightly that the thorns pierced through her gloves. "Ouch!" she exclaimed and let the flowers drop while she examined her hands.

Immediately, Steven retrieved the roses gingerly and put them into a nearby basket. "You should be more careful," he said with one eyebrow raised indolently. "A new mother can't be too cautious, I've heard."

"How would you know?" she snapped, then was immediately sorry for having been so cruel. "Oh, forgive me, Steven, I didn't mean to be so shrewish. It's just the heat and being so fat."

He put his hand out and gently felt the swell of her belly below her breasts. Brenna, shocked at his presumptuousness, stepped back quickly, her gaze sliding around the patio to see if anyone was watching.

"You look beautiful, Brenna," he said soberly. "I suppose I just haven't gotten over the notion that I would be the only one . . ."

"Please, Steven," she interrupted. They had never talked openly of their only tryst, which had resulted in Katie, and she did not want to look back now.

He shrugged. "I am sure the new father is head over heels—shouting it from the rooftops," he said with faint bitterness. "I'm surprised no one told me before now." He looked at her questioningly.

Brenna turned away and walked slowly over to a stone bench. After a moment, Steven seated himself beside her, lounging easily, his elbow on the back of the bench so that his hand dangled just at her shoulder. Brenna could feel it barely brushing the material of her dress.

"Was your business trip a success?" she asked, trying to find neutral ground.

"Yes, much to your husband's disgust, I'm sure. I have closed deals on some favorable contracts involving grain and wine exports. The rich getting richer," he added wryly.

"Oh, you know Carlos," she said lightly, "he is too involved in his own political affairs to be concerned with your business transaction."

Steven shrugged. "I have heard he is involved with

Irigoyen—a dangerous man, Brenna." He gave her a serious look. "He doesn't give a damn about his life or the lives of anyone else. Carlos should be wary, or he'll find himself throwing his life away at Irigoyen's request."

Brenna shook her head. "I can hardly choose Carlos' political allies," she said frankly. "Besides, he told me only last week that Hipólito has been removed from his police post—on the same day that his uncle was removed from his military command. It seems they were both on the losing side of a provincial revolution."

"Perhaps, but the man has a remarkable capacity for politics, and I'm sure he will land on his feet."

"Please, Steven, don't worry yourself about Carlos. I'm sure he's intelligent enough . . ."

"Dammit, do you really think I give a damn about Carlos?" he asked her with swift intensity "The man could jump into the estuary tomorrow, and I would come to you the same day and ask you to be my mistress!"

"Steven, you must be joking," Brenna said without conviction. "You can't mean . . ."

"Listen to me, Brenna." Now his hand caught one of hers and held it tightly. "Despite what I've said in the past, despite how I treat you, I care deeply about you! God knows how many times I've cursed the day I let my father force me into marriage with Dolores."

"Steven, please don't tell me these things," Brenna implored, trying to free herself from his grasp.

He jerked her towards him. "Despite everything else, you have borne my child!" he said, his black eyes blazing at her with a strange wild glow. "Yes, I will say it to your face. Katie is mine. Not Carlos', not your first husband's, but mine!"

"You must forget that!" Brenna said breathlessly. "Please, please, Steven, you mustn't . . ."

"Dammit, I must, and I will! I don't care how many husbands you have, Brenna, or how many children you have—Katie will always be mine, and I will always love her. What gives you the right to keep her from me?"

"The *right!*" Brenna glared back at him furiously. "She's my child too. Every time I look at her, I can't help remembering that day when you—when we—" she could not bring herself to say it. "I love her too, and so does Carlos. He is her father in the eyes of the law and society. Do you think I would risk her future, her happiness, by declaring her a bastard, the product of one moment of foolishness between us? What would that do to her—to Carlos! No, Steven, you cannot possibly ask me what right I have to keep the knowledge of her true father from her. It is her right to have a normal life."

They were both standing; Steven still held her fast and she could see anger and bitterness, pain and coldness in his eyes. She hated to see that look on his face, but she knew she was right—she could never let anyone else know that Katie was Steven's child.

"Senora?"

Steven let go of her hand abruptly, and Brenna swung around to face Teresa, who had timidly come into the patio, her brown arms cuddling Katie against her breast. For a moment, a chill swept through Brenna at the thought of what Teresa might have heard, but the servant seemed neither surprised nor disturbed.

"What is it, Teresa?" she asked.

"Katie has just awakened from her nap, senora, and wishes to come to her mama. Isn't that right, *niña?*"

"Yes, Mama," the child said, eagerly holding out her arms.

Brenna took her and held her close, sitting back down on the bench. She was aware of Steven's watching her as she kissed the shiny, black curls, the pink cheeks, and the heavy lids of Katie's blue eyes, still sleepy from her nap.

"Mama," she said contentedly, cuddling against her a moment before looking up and smiling at Steven. There followed a stream of baby words, followed by an unmistakable demand for Steven to hold her.

Reluctantly, Brenna gave Katie over to Steven, who held her comfortably in his lap, his black eyes amused as he looked at Brenna's face. "My, you are getting to be such a big girl," he said seriously to his little daughter.

"So big!" Katie affirmed, playing with Steven's ascot and the lace of his shirt.

Brenna dismissed Teresa and looked back at Steven, her eyes pleading. "Uncle Steven has to be going, Katie. Tell him good-bye, darling."

Katie looked up mutinously at her mother, then nodded. Steven hesitated a moment before giving the child back. "Tell your mother I love you too much to hurt you," he said, looking at the child intently.

"Love you," Katie repeated obediently, smiling brightly at her mother and Steven. "Love you, love you, love you," she babbled happily.

Brenna held Katie close and watched as Steven made his way toward the drawing room, her heart feeling the same pain that she knew he was feeling. Why, she wondered, was life sometimes so unfair?

Another daughter was born to the Valera household in April of 1877, during a cool, overcast autumn day. This birth had been even easier for Brenna than her first, and soon afterwards, she was sitting up and putting the new baby to her breast, calling for someone to bring Katie to her, afraid that the child might be worried about her mother. At nearly three years, Katie was a sensitive child, and Brenna wanted to reassure her.

"You have a new little sister, Katie," Carlos whispered to her, holding her up on the bed so that she might peep into the tiny face.

"Love you," Katie said woefully, her wide, blue eyes gazing at her mother.

"Mama loves you too, my sweet," Brenna smiled, reaching out to hug her. "That's why Mama brought you a new sister—to play with when she gets a little older. You'll like that, won't you, darling?"

The little girl shook her head. "Mama," she said again, her lower lip quivering.

"We must let Mama sleep now, Katie," Carlos said, lifting her down from the bed. "She is very tired and needs her rest."

Katie looked as though at any moment she might burst into tears at the thought of leaving her mother. Brenna glanced towards Carlos who looked perplexed. Then an idea came to him.

"You know something? We must go out and do some shopping to buy your mama a pretty present for giving us such a nice, new baby. Don't you think so, Katie? You'll have to help me pick out something extra-special now. Do you think you can do that?"

For a moment, Katie looked dubious, her blue eyes still anxious as they traveled from Carlos to her mother to her new sister.

"Oh, that would be such a surprise!" Brenna joined in, looking at Carlos with gratitude. "You must keep it a secret until you help Papa wrap it for me, darling."

A smile finally broke out on the little girl's face, and she nodded happily. "Yes, a pretty present for Mama," she cried out in excitement, scrambling out of Carlos' arms and hurrying out the bedroom door.

"Dress her warmly," Brenna said, receiving a kiss on the lips from Carlos. "And don't let her talk you into buying anything too expensive," she admonished with a playful grin.

He laughed and shook his head. Brenna, smiling, watched him go out. She sighed with relief, telling herself that everything would be all right. She even began to daydream about the future, imagining what beauties their two daughters would be, the belles of every ball. She and Carlos would have to watch out that some handsome, arrogant, young creole wouldn't steal the heart of one of their offspring. She bit her lip. What had she been about to add—and break it, he shook her head. No, not her Katie, nor little Maria either. They would both grow up surrounded by love.

Chapter Fifty

BRENNA was very happy with her two little daughters and affectionate husband. Sometimes she wondered where the time went. Maria was a year old now, a plump, healthy baby—admittedly not as pretty as Katie, but still, with her dark hair and big, brown eyes, everyone made a fuss over her, especially her father who would do anything to get the baby to smile or to crow with laughter.

Brenna told herself not to worry, that it was normal for Carlos to favor his own child a little more, especially since she was the youngest and everyone liked to spoil a baby. But sometimes, seeing the look on Katie's face when Carlos went to the cradle to pick up his daughter, Brenna found it hard to keep from saying anything to her husband.

Oddly enough, it relieved her to see how Steven, on his visits to their house, continued to show interest and give encouragement to Katie. Despite Brenna's protests, he constantly brought her little presents: cookies, pastries, toys, and baubles.

"God knows, it's the least I can do for her," he told her, in an undertone one afternoon, as she was showing him to the door. His look was serious, intense, as though he were questioning their continuing the deception, so Brenna, afraid he might blurt out something in the hallway, hurried him out nervously.

Steven, who could read her like a book when she was agitated, smiled lazily and bowed to her. "Your secret is safe with me, fair lady," he whispered like the villain in a play. With his black moustache and that amused, wicked twinkle in his dark eyes, he could very well have been one, Brenna thought spitefully as she shut the door on him.

She had just gone back to the drawing room, when the brass knocker sounded again. "What does he want now?"

she said to herself angrily and hurried to open the door before their manservant could do so. To her surprise, it was Hipólito Irigoyen, bowing formally and asking if her husband was at home.

"Of course, he is here," she snapped impatiently. "Didn't you see our guest just leaving here?"

He smiled blandly. "I don't presume to understand the intricacies of social custom," he returned, entering the hall. "I have known many ladies who have entertained guests while their husbands were not at home."

Outwardly, it was an innocent remark, but Brenna was sure he had meant it as an innuendo, and she gave him a haughty look. "Perhaps, your acquaintances, Senor Irigoyen, do not come up to my standards."

"Perhaps not," he agreed, looking as though he would have liked to say more.

Just then, Carlos came out of the drawing room, his daughter nestled in the crook of his arm. "Hipólito! How good to see you again! Good Lord, it must be—what?— five or six months since you've honored us with your presence."

Irigoyen shook hands with the other man, smiling thinly. "Yes, it has been a while, my friend, but I have been spending the time usefully. I've been elected to the legislature of the province of Buenos Aires."

"So I have heard. My congratulations!" Carlos exclaimed, slapping the other on the back. "Come in, come in, and have a glass of wine with us. Brenna?" He handed Maria to her and led the way into the drawing room.

They seated themselves to have a drink, while Brenna listened to Katie tell her about the latest present Uncle Steven had brought her. She was interrupted in her enjoyment of her daughter's tale, as Carlos brought her into the men's conversation.

"Brenna, I was just telling Hipólito that he barely missed running into Steven! I'm sure these two would have a most interesting conversation if they could keep themselves from drawing swords," He laughed ruefully.

"Unfortunately, Senor Castaneda and I see the same

situation in two entirely different ways," Irigoyen commented. "I'm afraid we would hardly have anything to say to each other."

Brenna longed to say that she thought them remarkably alike in some ways—they could both be rude and ill-mannered—but she held her sarcasm and only commented, "I'm sure Senor Irigoyen could restrain himself from drawing his sword, Carlos, and Steven as well. After all, they are two civilized gentlemen, who both have their country's welfare at heart. Isn't that so, senor?"

Irigoyen smiled thinly. "As you say, senora, but we do not agree upon the way in which our country may be made to grow and to prosper and to take its place among the world's great countries."

"I would say, senor, that in your new post as deputy, you might have more say in the matter now," Brenna retorted archly.

"Never underestimate the power of money," Irigoyen said smoothly.

"Hold!" Carlos said. "Or you two will be drawing *your* swords in a moment," he laughed. "I should hate to have to bet on the outcome, Hipólito, for my charming wife can be a tigress."

Irigoyen smiled, and his eyes slid easily over the contours of Brenna's bodice. "I am sure of that, Carlos," he said.

Brenna flushed and murmured an excuse about seeing to the children. She hurried out of the room, wishing more than ever that Irigoyen's visits would come to a stop now that he would be busy leading the province. She hated his influence on Carlos. With a few fiery speeches and accusations, Irigoyen could agitate Carlos into attending those long meetings again, which often took him away from the children for days at a time.

In fact, a week after Irigoyen's visit, Carlos announced that he would attend a seminar at the university and that Hipólito had kindly offered the use of his apartments, which were located much closer to the university than their own. Brenna sighed impatiently.

"Why must you go now?" she wondered. "The weather

is so fine and crisp, and I had thought we might do a little traveling around the country, now that Maria is older."

"Darling, it will only be for a few days," Carlos insisted impatiently. "Listen, why don't you stay at Paloma for a while. I'll ride out when I'm finished, and we'll come home together. Then we'll think about a trip, all right? You haven't been out there since before Maria was born. It'll do old Miguel good, and you know how they dote on the children."

The idea appealed to Brenna, as lately she had begun to feel restless. She would send a messenger out to Paloma to give the Castanedas time to prepare, then tomorrow afternoon, she would hire a driver to take her out. She could take Minx with her and ride out onto the pampas. In her delight, she gave Carlos a kiss and told herself she would hardly miss him.

The next afternoon, she and the children arrived at the *estancia* right after siesta. Consuelo met her at the door and exclaimed over the new baby, although she saved her biggest hugs for Katie, who beamed happily at her.

After changing her clothing, Brenna met the family in the main patio, watching with secret pleasure as Katie went boldly up to Miguel and demanded to sit on his knee. The old man derived keen delight from the child, and he told Brenna he was looking forward to the birth of Rosaria's baby, which was due in a few months. Consuelo echoed the words as she rocked Maria contentedly in her arms. Dolores, who was sitting off to the side, watched the scene silently, and once again Brenna felt a rush of pity for her.

"Steven should be back from his ride any minute," Consuelo was saying, and just then Steven, himself, appeared at the front of the patio, his white shirt dusty from his ride. He was wearing the flat-crowned, wide-brimmed hat that the gauchos sometimes wore, and with his wide, leather belt and his knee-high boots, he cut a dashing figure as he sauntered in to the family gathering.

"Uncle Steven!" squealed Katie in delight and wriggled off Miguel's lap to run over to the other man, who picked her up high over his head and demanded a kiss before letting her down again.

"Who brought this little rabbit to my house?" he inquired, his black brows drawing up as he looked into the little girl's face.

"Not a rabbit, Uncle Steven!" Katie replied, her face broadening into a wide smile. "Mama brought me—and Maria, too."

"Oh, I see," he remarked, then said with mock-seriousness, "I suppose I must give Maria a kiss too, don't you think?"

Katie frowned and glanced at her mother. "Well, I suppose so—and Mama, too!" she added, smiling again.

"Katie!" Brenna said in surprise, her eyes flying guiltily to Dolores. "What ever would make you say such a thing?"

"Oh, your papa would be angry if I kissed your mama," Steven interrupted seriously, although his eyes were full of amusement. "Only papas can kiss mamas."

"Oh," Katie replied with a perplexed air. She looked to her mother, who was about to say something, when Steven broke in again.

"Come along, Katie, I want to show you my horse. He's been wanting to meet you for a long time." And, turning on his heel, he carried a happy, squealing Katie in his arms, leaving a bemused expression on Brenna's face.

"He does take to your little girl, Brenna," Consuelo said, smiling gently. "I'm sure he'll be careful with her."

"Of course, he will!" Miguel growled crustily. "He knows how to handle the child better than . . ."

Fortunately, Maria started to wail at that moment; it was time for her feeding. Brenna still breast fed her, even though Katie had been weaned by this age. She took the baby and began to walk off toward her rooms, when behind her, she heard footsteps following.

"Do you mind if I follow, Brenna?" Dolores asked.

"Of course not."

"How lucky you are—to have two such beautiful and

healthy children." Dolores sighed as they reached the room.

"Yes, I am lucky," Brenna admitted, sitting down in a comfortable chair and unbuttoning her bodice.

Dolores sat across from her. "You must be very happy with Carlos."

Brenna stared at the other woman curiously. "Yes," she answered, "very."

"I have been to another doctor since the last time I saw you in the city," Dolores enlightened her. "He feels certain that I am able to conceive, but he isn't sure that I can carry a baby the full term. He thinks my womb may be oddly shaped." She flushed. "Anyway, I know if I can conceive, I will do anything he says to keep the baby growing inside me." She leaned forward, her dark eyes blazed in sudden intensity, and her hands tightened into fists, the knuckles showing white. "I—I *must* have a child!"

Brenna was taken aback by her intensity and hardly knew what to say. "Well, if the doctor thinks it is possible . . ."

"Steven laughs when I tell him," Dolores went on. She stood up from her chair and walked absently to the window, looking out into space. "He thinks I am making this up to get him in my bed." She turned viciously toward Brenna. "What do you think of a wife who has to trick her husband into coming to her bedroom?"

Brenna reddened. This conversation was too private for her comfort. She had no wish to become embroiled in Dolores' problems with Steven. "Dolores, I really can't presume . . ."

"Oh, I know he goes to other women. He must! A man can't hold that inside of him for so long. And he has another child."

Brenna nearly dropped Maria, she was so shocked by this admission. Was it possible that Dolores knew? With hardly a breath, she waited to hear terrible accusations heaped on her.

"Yes, another child. I can see the shocked look on your face, Brenna, but it's true. I saw him with a mestizo woman and her little boy one day when I went out riding; he was out on the pampas in some horrible little hovel with that insolent gaucho, Guido! It—it disgusted me to think my husband could—could go with another woman—and such a lowly creature. Dear God, I could smell her from where I sat my horse."

Brenna's mind whirled as she pictured Steven making love to another woman, and, as Dolores said, a half-Indian woman at that. Pictures of muddy feet, crawling lice—she stopped herself quickly, repeating over and over that it was not her business. But the thought of Steven making love to her—and then going to—to . . .

"Dear God, why is he so cruel to me?" Dolores cried out. "I want to give him a child. I know he wants a legitimate heir."

"Perhaps he doesn't care as much as you think," Brenna suggested, relieved that Dolores did not suspect Katie was Steven's child. "Perhaps if you didn't worry so about it, he . . ."

"But if not for the child—for what other reason would I wish him to come to me?" Dolores inquired with a hint of anger. "Why on earth would I want him to *touch* me after being with—with other women!"

"He is your husband," Brenna quietly reminded her. For the first time she was beginning to see why Steven could never be happy with his wife.

"So, he is my husband. As such, he should provide for me and our children. But if there are no children, there is no reason to behave like a husband and wife, is there? My mother told me, when I was a little girl, that men wanted —'things' from women, and that it was a wife's duty to allow them to—to do as they wished, but only for the sake of having children. If there are to be no offspring, there is no reason to have to be forced into such—such acts!"

Brenna looked at the other woman in horror. How twisted she made it all seem. Was that what Dolores truly believed from the beginning of their marriage, or had she simply become bitter when she found she could not have children? Pity rushed through her for this poor, lonely woman who could not even allow herself to enjoy the feel of a man's arms about her. She knew it would be useless to try to make her see otherwise.

Dolores still stood at the window, but now her expression sharpened; even her nostrils pinched like a hound on the scent. "I can see him, now, out there in the corral. He has your daughter with him—ah, he is sitting her on the horse. No! Don't get up, Brenna, he will not let her fall down. He is as gentle as a dove with her—I can see them both laughing now, and your little girl is leaning down to kiss him." She turned suddenly to stare at Brenna. "He— why, he loves her, doesn't he?" she said softly.

Brenna returned the stare, her own eyes widening as she fought for words. Dolores continued to gaze at her, and Brenna could almost see the notion revolving from a tiny sprig of doubt in the woman's eyes into a full-fledged seedling. A look of hate and envy suddenly twisted the fragile face. Without another word, Dolores ran from the room, leaving Brenna alone, unshed tears gathering in her eyes.

At dinner that evening, everyone at the table was unusually quiet, no doubt because of the stony looks Dolores continuously gave to Brenna. Consuelo was clearly confused by her usually reticent daughter-in-law's open display of animosity for their guest. She even sent an occasional scathing glance to the child, Katie, who sat beside Steven—oblivious to the cold stares—chattering gaily.

Steven, however, was not oblivious and felt his own anger growing, tempered only by his curiosity as to what might have caused this turn of events. The thought of a lengthy discussion with his wife exasperated him, but nevertheless, at the end of the meal, he walked over to her.

"Dolores, I would like to speak with you for a moment."

"No, Steven, I would rather stay here in the drawing room with your parents and our guest," she replied, hardly looking at him.

He considered making a scene, then shrugged and smiled thinly at her. "As you wish, my dear." He poured himself a glass of port and walked over to sit by the fire. He watched her over the rim of the glass.

"Dolores, you really don't look well tonight," Consuelo said worriedly.

"Thank you, Consuelo, but I feel perfectly fine," Dolores answered.

"Well, if you all will excuse me, I must retire," Miguel said, standing up to look at his wife. "The meal doesn't seem to have agreed with me tonight, my dear," he said.

Consuelo nodded, and still glancing worriedly at Dolores, went to assist her husband.

Brenna watched the two older people make their way slowly from the room. Wondering frantically what they would think should Dolores be cruel enough to tell them of her deception, she bit her lip worriedly and automatically reached down to stroke Katie's long, shining black hair.

"Your daughter's hair is beautiful," Dolores said.

"Yes," Brenna answered nervously. "Maria's is the same shade."

"Do you think so? No, no, I would say Katie's is much darker."

"Like mine," Brenna put in quickly.

Dolores seemed to think about it. "Perhaps."

Katie, sitting on the floor, yawned and leaned against her mother's skirts. "I'm tired, Mama," she said. "Uncle Steven let me ride his big horse today."

"Oh, how nice of him," Brenna said, her nervousness increasing. She looked over at Steven, who was watching both women speculatively while pouring himself another glass of port. "Darling, it really is time for you to go to bed. Mama will tuck you in."

"Don't run away yet, Brenna," Dolores said softly.

"The child is overly tired," Brenna got up and without another word, she hurried out of the room as fast as she could with her daughter.

Not until she reached the haven of her room and tucked Katie in did she allow herself a sigh of relief. She would have to leave here tomorrow, she told herself. She would make up some excuse—anything to flee from here.

Perhaps there was still a way to convince Dolores that her suspicions were wrong, but Brenna knew her face would betray her. No, the only way was to leave here and wait for Carlos at home. Carlos! For a moment, Brenna felt cold fear settle icily on her. If Carlos should find out—should hear of this—! She shuddered. He would probably break her neck—or worse, he would shun Katie as the bastard of a friend who had betrayed him.

Nervously, Brenna began to pack her suitcases in preparation for an early departure in the morning. She would create some excuse to give to Miguel and Consuelo—unless, of course, Dolores told them the truth. And poor Steven. Dolores was probably in the drawing room now, accusing him, reviling him. Dear God, how had all this happened? If only Dolores had been able to have children, perhaps none of this would have happened.

Brenna finished packing, then sat down on her bed and put her head in her hands. If Carlos turned her out, where would she go? Certainly he would not send his own daughter away. He loved Maria as much as Steven loved Katie. Perhaps they would live as polite strangers, staying together for Maria's sake. No, she couldn't bear living that way, every day seeing the accusation in his eyes. She would—go back to Ireland! Yes, that was the only way—only an entire ocean could separate her from all this.

Her decision made, Brenna felt more comforted and proceeded to dress for bed. She put on her nightgown, and brushed her hair; the familiar routine helped to calm her jangled nerves. She blew out the light and got into the bed. It would have been nice to bring Katie, to feel the warm little body snuggling comfortably close to her own under the covers, but Brenna didn't want to wake her now. The child had been asleep for two hours already.

Brenna's head hit the pillow, and she closed her eyes, but it was nearly an hour before sleep came to her. Her dreams were troubled, restless, and so, when her bedroom door was abruptly pushed open, it took her only a moment to come awake. A tall, dark figure was outlined by the moonlight from the window.

"Senora Castaneda, if you will pardon me for this intrusion," came Steven's voice into the melting darkness, slurred and fuzzy. "Or—could it be that I have the wrong room?"

He closed the door, and stepped into the shadows of the room. Brenna heard him walk towards the bed, stumble over her suitcases, and curse loudly. He continued to curse softly, almost to himself, as he made his way past the offending luggage and around to her side of the bed. Brenna, frozen beneath the covers, could smell the liquor on his breath, and she drew back.

"Steven, you're drunk," she said desperately. "Your parents might hear you—or someone else—"

"My parents sleep heavily," he said, sitting down on the bed. She scuttled away from him beneath the covers. "Your children are asleep and my wife—" he laughed drunkenly—"my wife ordered a lock put on her bedroom door to keep me out."

Brenna wished she had asked for a lock on her own door to keep him out. "Steven, please go."

"Quiet, dammit," he said, leaning closer and nearly falling over her. "I told you—my wife has locked me out, so I have come to you, my lovely Brenna, to ease my pain."

Brenna sat up, anger beginning to stir. "You come to *me!* Steven, you're too drunk to know what you're doing. Go to your wife—or to your little mestizo girl out on the pampas!"

"Ah, you and Dolores have been conspiring against me," he laughed. "She accused me of the same thing. In fact, she was naming more women than even I could possibly keep satisfied." He hiccoughed and laughed softly again. "This woman and that woman and some poor girl who's in love with Guido and has his child to prove it."

Brenna stiffened. "You mean, the mestizo girl's child is not yours?"

"Christ, Brenna, don't let's go over this again. I've just been through it with my sweet-tempered little wife, who, by last count, has accused me of fathering at least twenty little whelps. God in heaven, my loins must be as fertile

545

as the pampas!" He laughed loudly and Brenna told him to hush.

"Be quiet! And please go. What do you think she will do if she hears you in here?"

"I told you, she is in her room! And she already thinks you are my mistress, dearest Brenna, so why disappoint her?" He slumped closer and reached out to gather her closer to him. "The poor, deluded woman—if she only knew that it only took once to . . ."

"Steven, she knows about Katie. She knows."

"Brenna, she suspected, that's all, but I've taken care of that!"

thing in his present state. She swung her hand out, mean-

"Get out of here!" she whispered furiously, wondering how he could have possibly convinced Dolores of anything to push him away, but instead, the flat of her palm landed on his cheek, making a stinging sound in the stillness of the dark room. For a moment, she could hear only her own loud breathing.

Then, suddenly, both of her hands were caught in his, caught in twin vises that threatened to break her fragile bones. She whimpered in pain and felt him jerk her forward, throwing her neck back.

His voice was no longer fuzzy now, but angry and pained and impassioned. "By God, drunk or not, Brenna, I want you. I want you naked underneath me. Can't you understand that? You're the only woman besides Dolores—and, hell, a few whores in town when the pain got to be too much. But you, Brenna, you're the only woman whose skin is this soft, whose breasts curve high and proud, whose thighs can wrap around a man and make him go crazy!" He brought her forward, pushing his face into her breast.

Brenna could feel his hot lips, warm and wet, against her skin where the nightgown tied at the bodice, evoking sensations that reminded her of another time, another place. She hardly knew when he let go of her hands and reached up to slide the gown off her shoulders. She hardly knew when he laid her gently back in the curve of his arm and began kissing her mouth with slow, hot kisses that melted her soul and made her pliable and warm beneath him. Oh, how the memories flooded back over her and intensified as he pushed the nightgown impatiently down past her hips, leaving her naked on the bed.

Her breath came in a long sigh and she cared for nothing, no one, but him. Surely, this was her heaven, her destiny—for there was no other man to whom her body seemed so perfectly attuned. No one had ever made her feel so complete, so fulfilled as a woman. She groaned with the intense passion that was overwhelming her, and closed her eyes to blot out that other face, that white, fragile face that had become suddenly pinched and bitter.

She was breathing heavily, almost panting, as she felt his lips scalding those secret parts of her flesh. She wanted him terribly—she must have him tonight, she thought fiercely, for tomorrow—who knew when she might see him again?

Then, suddenly, she stiffened and strained to listen in the darkness. What? What was the sound she had heard? She tried to sit up, imagining a horrible scene as Dolores opened the door and barged into the room; the thought brought her back to reality, and she cringed as she looked down at Steven's dark head against her pale flesh. She had forgotten that she was in the house of his parents, that his wife slept only a few yards away, that the children were—good God! The children!

"Steven, Steven," she whispered frantically. "I—I can hear one of the children—please let me up!"

He was not listening, was too drunk on liquor and her flesh to pay heed to her frantic calling. She brought her hands down to grasp at the shoulders of his shirt, tugging at them to gain his attention.

"Mmm," he murmured into her flesh, "so sweet, so sweet . . ."

"Steven, for God's sake, one of the children is awake. I must go to them!" Brenna curled her legs up beneath him, flexing her knees and then shoving at his chest with her feet. He shot backwards in surprise, then let out a low growl of frustration and started to lunge forward again.

"No, Steven, please!" Brenna jumped up from the bed

and hurried to the adjoining door, her hand on the knob.

"No, you don't!" he growled again, low in his throat and he pounced toward her from the bed, his hand sliding ineffectually down her hip as she skipped away and threw open the door.

"Mama, there's too much noise!" Katie protested sleepily between huge yawns. "Maria is waking up."

The sound of the child's voice stopped Steven in his tracks. He stared into the dark room, and then at Brenna, who was still standing in the doorway. For a moment, he waited, quivering, and Brenna could almost smell the brutal animal in him. Fearfully she backed against the door, holding her breath, praying that Katie would go back to sleep.

Suddenly with a foul curse that made Brenna cringe, Steven strode from the room, sending the door rattling on its hinges. Brenna was suddenly afraid that he might do harm to someone else or to himself. She closed the door to the children's room, grabbed her nightgown, and donned it as she ran, pattering in her bare feet, in Steven's wake.

She had no idea what she would do should he stop suddenly and realize that she was behind him. No doubt, he would try to take her again, perhaps out here in the hallway. She called herself twice a fool, but kept doggedly after him until he swerved suddenly and leaned against the wall, as though to catch his breath. As Brenna crouched behind a large potted plant, she saw Steven hesitate visibly, then throw open a door that led into one of the rooms.

"No!" The voice was Dolores', but so thin and high-pitched that Brenna barely recognized it.

"You are my wife!" he commanded in the doorway, swaying as though buffeted by a strong wind.

"No!" the voice came again, stronger this time, expressing unmistakable fear and revulsion. "Get out! Leave me alone and go back to your other women!"

"I have no other women," he said with deadly intensity. "You are my wife," he repeated and strode into the room, slamming the door behind him.

Almost immediately, there was a shrill scream of terror, followed by another lower cry. Brenna stood indecisively in the hall; the cries from the room made her entire body go cold. As she hugged herself for warmth, she realized she was naked beneath the nightgown and had nothing on her feet. Then from the silence in the room, she heard another cry, different this time, a kind of choked-off groan, which abruptly died away. Then, "Steven!" a voice cried out in passionate tones that made Brenna's cold dissolve into liquid warmth.

She suddenly became aware of the inexcusability of her presence outside that closed door. Shame bit deeply through her body, and she turned quickly, breathing hard. Only a few minutes before, Steven had come to her, had wanted *her*—and now he had gone back to his wife. Brenna burned with shame at her own wantonness, and tears burned her cheeks. She was a fool! Running now, holding back choking sobs, she fled to her room and flung herself on the bed.

Chapter Fifty-One

THE next morning, Brenna awoke with a sore throat and a headache; she could hardly get out of bed when she heard Maria's fussing. Groggily, Brenna pattered to the next room and smiled tiredly at her younger child, who gazed back at her with round, brown eyes and a pouting rosebud mouth. Katie was still asleep, and Brenna crept back into her own bed with the baby, cuddling her close as she gave her a nipple. Eventually, Maria fell back asleep, her mouth falling away from Brenna's body; Brenna, too, fell asleep.

Some hours later, a knock on her door awoke her. Maria was still tucked in the stiffened crook of her arm, and Katie, who must have come in a while before, snuggled on the other side of her.

"Yes?" Brenna called, feeling better for the extra hours of sleep.

Katie stirred against her as she heard Consuelo calling. "Brenna, my dear, it is nearly ten o'clock. Would you like coffee brought to you, or perhaps some strong tea?"

No sign of shock on Consuelo's part, Brenna noted in surprise. Could it be that Dolores had made no mention of her suspicions? "Yes, thank you, Consuelo. Please come in."

"Oh, the little dears," Consuelo murmured fondly upon seeing the two children with their mother. "My goodness, have they slept with you all night?"

Brenna was about to tell the truth when the thought struck her that her children could be her best alibi for the night before. "Yes—Katie has. I brought Maria in with me this morning for her feeding."

"Oh, well, just let me take her for you, my dear," Consuelo offered as Brenna sat up, disturbing the infant. "She'll want her bath now—and you too, I suppose. I'll have coffee and tea brought up and some hot water for the tub. Will Katie bathe with you?"

"Yes, we'll both fit—and just bring coffee, please, Consuelo. Thank you." Brenna watched as the older woman took Maria away. How nice it would have been she thought, with a sudden fit of homesickness, to have had her own mother with her while her children were growing up.

She brushed the thought aside as Katie stretched beside her and requested breakfast.

"We'll wash first," Brenna said. "And I'll let you have a sip of Mama's coffee, if you don't splash me too much." She smiled and pinched her daughter's chin gently in her fingers.

Katie eyed the suitcases on her side of the bed curiously. "Are we leaving today, Mama?" she wondered. "I don't want to go home yet! Uncle Steven promised me we would ride in the corral again—perhaps even further!"

When the water was brought in for the bath, Brenna helped her daughter into the tub and settled in opposite her, reaching for the cake of soap and washcloth. "Uncle Steven may not be able to keep his promise, dear," she said evenly. From her recollection of the night before, she was quite sure that Steven would be in no condition to take Katie riding. He was probably nursing a sore head right now—in Dolores' bed. She shoved the thought aside and began scrubbing at herself earnestly.

When they were dressed, Brenna sat in a tufted chair and sipped her cool coffee while Katie nibbled at biscuits and begged for a swallow or two from Brenna's cup.

Consuelo returned, bringing with her Maria, whose plump little body glowed from her bath. "She's as happy as a lark," Consuelo said, smiling and bending down to receive a kiss from Katie. She caught sight of the luggage and gave Brenna a questioning look. "You are leaving, my dear?"

Brenna pinkened. "I—I—" she floundered, wondering what to say.

"Of course, Brenna is not leaving," came a mocking

voice from the doorway. "At least, not until I've taken my most favorite little girl for the ride I promised her."

"Uncle Steven!" Katie cried joyously, running to put her arms about his neck.

"Oww! Oh, your voice sounds ten times too loud this morning, chatterbug," Steven said, wincing.

"Are you sick, Uncle Steven?" Katie wanted to know. "Mama told me you might not be able to keep your promise today."

"Did she now?" He gave her an amused look despite the headache he was obviously feeling. "Why, your mother should know that I always keep my promises!" he said in a confiding voice.

Brenna turned her eyes upward and caught Steven's dark gaze; she noted his eyes were a trifle bloodshot. Her own eyes looked away quickly, and she sipped at her coffee.

"Steven, you look terrible!" Consuelo finally gave vent to her feelings as she had been studying her son throughout his dialogue with Katie. "What—what happened last night?"

He shrugged and gave his mother a warning look. She, too, looked away and said to Brenna, "Why don't you come down to the dining room, my dear, and have some breakfast? It's late, but the cook will fix you something."

"Yes, yes, I will," Brenna said quickly, wanting to stay with Consuelo for protection. Relentlessly, the images of last night sped through her mind—she and Steven on the bed, her nakedness against the darkness of his hair, the sick feeling in her stomach when he had flung open his wife's door and stalked inside to claim his rights . . .

She took Maria from Consuelo and held her closely, feeling Katie's hand fasten itself to her skirts.

"Come on, Uncle Steven!" she chirped. "I'm too hungry to go riding yet!"

He laughed, then winced and followed silently, although Brenna was acutely aware of him behind her, as if he were stalking her . . . stalking her. Why did she keep thinking that? She was glad to enter the dining room and take a seat next to Consuelo. There was no sign of Dolores.

"So, Brenna, tell me—were you thinking of leaving us already?" asked Steven, his voice lazy, yet somehow intimidating.

"Well, I wasn't sure—I felt a little ill last night, and I—" She faded off, looking at him bleakly.

"You felt ill last night?" he prompted her, his black eyes seeming to drill holes in her brain. "The food perhaps?"

She shook her head. "No, it was nothing really. I just didn't feel—well." She looked to Consuelo for help, but the older woman was watching the children.

"I see." His eyes narrowed slightly in amused sympathy. "Well, I'm told women often feel these—er—sicknesses. I hope you feel well enough now to stay a little longer."

"Stop pressing me!" she said in low tones, leaning towards him. "You know what I'm talking about."

He looked stricken. "I? Why, Brenna, I couldn't possibly know about your ailment. I drank a little too much last night and fell asleep quite soon afterward." He dared her to challenge his lie.

Brenna's dark blue eyes sparkled with temper. "You weren't too drunk to—to—" She gasped, remembered Consuelo's presence, and folded her lips together.

"I am anxiously awaiting what it was I wasn't too drunk to do," he prompted her, smiling wickedly, his eyes dancing with insolence.

"Nothing!" she said, standing up abruptly and throwing her napkin on her plate. She turned to Consuelo. "I feel like riding, Consuelo. Do you think one of the stablehands might saddle Minx for me?"

Consuelo, startled by the girl's abruptness, quickly nodded. She watched Brenna leave the room with little Katie trailing behind her, then glanced at her son, noting the wolf-hungry look in his eyes, the yearning look that was quickly veiled when he realized his mother's eyes were on him.

"Will you be riding too, my son?" she asked quietly.

He shook his head. "I've promised another young lady to give her a riding lesson, *mamacita*," he winked and bowed to her, taking his leave.

Brenna rode in the direction of the *saladero*, instinctively remembering the way. She passed herds of cows and a few gauchos. One of the gauchos raised his hand in greeting, then charged off after a straying calf. She watched him curiously for a moment, then realized that it must have been Guido. She recalled what Steven had told her about the mestizo girl and the baby. Or had it been a drunken lie? Her curiosity got the best of her, and she spurred Minx forward to catch up to the gaucho.

After a few minutes she caught his attention, and he brought his horse over to her, smiling in greeting. "Hello, señora. Have you been watching my superior horsemanship?" he asked, grinning widely.

She nodded and her horse fell in beside his as they rode comfortably alongside the herd of cattle. "Guido? Do gauchos, like yourself, often have families?"

He shrugged. "If you mean marriage, senora, not many of us do."

"Oh." She blushed a little. "But—I suppose—you do —I mean—you—"

He looked at her knowingly. "Do we make little gauchos?" His teeth gleamed whitely when he grinned. "Of course, we do." He did not seem curious about her questioning.

"I see—and you, Guido, have a young woman?" she pressed.

He laughed outright, then leaned closer and leered at her. "Many, senora."

"And there are children?"

He gave her a swift, darting look. "What's this? Are you trying to make an honest man of me, senora?" He turned back to his horse and looked out over the herd, whistling to bring a stray into line. Then he turned back to Brenna. "It is, after all the nature of the thing, isn't it, senora?"

"Yes—yes, of course."

He could see that she was embarrassed, and he smiled

again. "I have seen your little one, sitting atop Steven's horse. She will make as fine a horsewoman as her mother in a few more years."

Brenna relaxed "Yes, thank you. She is like me in many ways, I think."

"Certainly, in the fairness of her skin," he said smoothly.

She dimpled at the compliment, then reached down awkwardly to pat Minx's long mane. "I—enjoyed our little talk, Guido."

"As I did, senora, although we talked too long of me. Steven and I . . ."

"Oh!" she looked up at him worriedly. "You mustn't tell Steven we had this discussion. I mean—I don't think it would be—I—" she stopped.

Guido looked into her face and sighed to himself. "As you wish, senora."

She nodded to him and urged Minx away, galloping swiftly in the opposite direction. Guido, watching her, thought to himself that the young woman should teach herself how to hide her expressions—she was as easy to read as the stars over the pampas on a clear, crisp night.

Chapter Fifty-Two

"BRENNA! Steven's here, my dear. Come downstairs—and bring the children! It seems we must offer him our congratulations." Carlos was calling from the bottom of the staircase.

Brenna had just finished dressing the children after their naps. She came down, smiling hesitantly, for she hadn't seen Steven in the two months since Carlos had come to Paloma to take her home.

Carlos gave her a wide grin and winked at her conspiratorially. "Come on, darling. Steven has news of the greatest importance for you."

She looked up at him. "Oh? What is it this time? Has he acquired more land or more stock in the downtown bank?"

Carlos laughed indulgently. "Darling, don't be nasty. Come and I'll let him tell you himself."

They entered the drawing room to find Steven standing at the window, holding a drink absently in his hand. Katie ran over to him, and he picked her up to give her a kiss. As his eyes met Brenna's over the head of the child, she was confused by what she saw in them. With trepidation she sat down in a chair to await his news.

"Brenna, how good to see you again," he said with considerable warmth in his tone, unbalancing her for a moment. Then he put Katie down and took a drink from his glass.

"Good God, man, tell her the news before I burst with it!" Carlos prodded him.

"Dolores is going to have a child, Brenna."

The words seemed to echo in the room. Brenna was hard put to keep her composure. "How wonderful for you," she murmured.

Carlos winked at Steven with an air of camaraderie.

"I suppose you have told everyone. The first time is the greatest, believe me!"

"Yes," Steven said slowly, then, as though regaining his own poise, "My parents are ecstatic with joy, and Dolores' father can hardly contain himself from traveling down for an extended visit." His lip curled down at the corner. "I hope he changes his mind and waits for a few more months."

"When is the birth date?" Carlos asked him, giving his wife a look of consternation.

"In February."

"A summer baby; how very nice," Brenna commented. Mentally, she counted backwards; Dolores must have conceived that night. That night . . . She felt her face growing hot. "I'm sure she must be very happy."

"Yes, she has ordered me to find the finest doctor in the city to attend her during the pregnancy." Steven smiled wryly. "I'm afraid I haven't the faintest idea where to start looking for one."

"Why, Dr. Dolenz is very good," Brenna said. "Or Dr. Juarez—his townhouse is on Córdoba Street, close to yours. Is Dolores coming to town to have the baby?" Brenna began to feel composure return to her spinning mind. She was even able to smile politely at Steven—as though he were nothing more than a social acquaintance. And so he would be, from now on, she told herself firmly.

"I will call on them both," Steven said. "Dolores would like to have the baby at Paloma. Miguel would like her to give birth there, too, but I'm not so sure."

Brenna thought she saw nothing but indifference in his eyes; then for a moment, she glimpsed a disconcerting look of pain in them.

"I am very happy for you, Steven; please convey our best wishes to your wife." She stood up from the chair. "Carlos, I'm going to take the children outside for their afternoon walk."

"Go ahead, dearest. Steven and I have a little politics to talk over anyway." Carlos laughed good-naturedly as he filled his own wine glass again. "Tell me, Steven, I've heard that Julio Roca, Avellaneda's Minister of War, wants to build a permanent line of outposts along the western boundary of Buenos Aires. Do you think it's a waste of money—trying to keep the Indians out that way?"

Steven shrugged. "I've heard tales of the Araucanians burning villages and stealing white women and children. We must do something to civilize the frontier."

"But, good Lord, digging a ditch ten feet wide by six feet deep and two hundred miles long to keep out the Indians!" Carlos whistled and laughed scornfully.

"There's talk of arming the provincial gaucho militias. They would exterminate the Indians completely," Steven put in. "Though I do not agree such a violent solution is necessary."

Brenna listened with half an ear as she dressed the children and placed Maria in her pram, then opened the door and left the two men inside. The air was still bracing and cool, but she hoped they would have an early spring this year. As she walked slowly, so that Katie could keep up on the wooden sidewalk, she let her mind slip back to that night at Paloma, when Steven had come to her bedroom.

The memory brought a swift surge of desire, which she guiltily tried to squelch. She had been right to send him away, she told herself firmly. She had never, never intended that she would be unfaithful to Carlos after their marriage—and she hadn't, physically. But—her honesty surged upward suddenly—God knew how she had wanted Steven to take her again, just for a few minutes, even drunk as he was that night. She hated to face the fact that she felt more for Steven in just those few minutes than she did for Carlos during the many times he had made love to her in their marriage bed.

What was wrong with her that she must continually hurt herself this way, like a moth drawn to the bright but forbidding flame? Oh, stupid moth, would you never learn? She recalled how Steven had once called her a dove—*la paloma*. If only she were a real dove, able to fly away from all this, to fly high in the air and to look down and laugh to see everyone try to catch her. But as she looked at Katie's hooded head and Maria in the pram, she knew that she would never again be so wild and free.

But why? Why, when she was happily married to Carlos, did she still want Steven? The answer came to her, gently as a raindrop kissing her eyelashes or the petal of a rose brushing the hem of her skirt—she loved Steven Castaneda de la Cruz. She loved him. Brenna stopped in the middle of the sidewalk. She felt hot, then cold as the idea grew in her. That was why she had lain with him under the ombu tree; that was why she had wanted him so that night. Had it also been the reason, after all, that she had allowed Kevin to bring her to Argentina?

As always, the real world swooped back on her, and she realized that Katie was tugging at her sleeve and Maria was beginning to fuss at the chill air on her face where the blanket had separated. She had to laugh out loud—at herself, at her emotions. A fine thing! A woman finds out she's in love with a man the very day she learns his wife is going to have his baby! She laughed loud and hard until tears came to her eyes and dripped down her cheeks.

"Mama, Mama! Are you hurt?" Katie inquired worriedly.

Brenna sniffed and shook her head, reaching inside her sleeve for a handkerchief. "No, darling, Mama's not hurt," she replied.

"Then—why are you crying?"

"Oh, I think the wind blew something in my eye, sweeting," she answered, dabbing at it. "Come along, I think we'd better turn around and go back to the house. It's colder than Mama thought, and you and I will both have some hot chocolate."

Katie clapped her hands in wholehearted agreement. She slipped her palm into her mother's and confidently led her back the way they had come. "Papa can have some hot chocolate too, if he likes," she said generously.

"Yes, dear, of course, he can," Brenna replied absently —and felt an absurd desire to burst into tears again.

Dolores Castaneda was moved into town in September, and by October, she was proudly showing her five-months pregnant stomach to visitors. But her visitors only remarked, after they had left her room, that she did not look well.

Brenna saw Dolores several times, obligated by the guilt she felt and by the desire to still Dolores' suspicions that Katie might be Steven's daughter. Brenna also wondered at the pinched look in the woman's face—the way her skin stretched over her cheekbones as though they might poke through at any moment. Her arms had also grown thin.

"Which doctor do you have advising you?" Brenna asked, trying to keep the concern and dismay out of her voice.

"Doctor Diaz—I found out he had delivered two of my cousins," Dolores answered, sipping apathetically at her tea as they sat in the magnificently decorated sitting room of the Castaneda town house. Like the rest of the house the room was high-ceilinged and airy, its multi-paned windows letting in the sunlight to touch the heavy oak wood and subdued browns and golds of the furniture.

Brenna had never before been inside Steven's house, and knowing that he might come in unexpectedly at any moment made her uncomfortable. "Yes, I believe I've heard of Dr. Diaz. He is a most highly esteemed physician," Brenna commented. "Has he—made any comments on your progress?"

Dolores gave her a sharp look. "He tells me I'm doing well—for a first baby. He has assured me that most new mothers lose weight and look—well—rather sickly the first time." Her smile softened her earlier sharpness.

Brenna recalled how she, herself, had steadily gained weight with Katie. She was sure she could never have looked as washed-out as did Dolores. "I suppose you'll start to grow plump pretty soon," she said, although she couldn't help thinking that if Dolores gained any more weight in her belly, it would surely burst. "I—ah—I remember your telling me how one of the doctors was concerned over the width of your hips—"

"Dr. Diaz hasn't discussed it yet with me," Dolores cut in swiftly. She eyed Brenna with such a frightened look that Brenna reached out, but the look was gone as quickly as it had come.

"I'm really so happy that I'm finally able to give Steven a child," she murmured as she looked at her cup. "I—I feel so foolish remembering what I said to you—I thought—" She looked up at Brenna, her tense expression revealing her inner struggle. "I'm sorry for being so mean that day."

That night, Brenna thought, then shook her head to clear it of remembrance. "It's all been forgotten a long time ago," Brenna assured her. She stood up from her chair, "I really must be going now. I've left Carlos alone with the children and there's no telling what predicament they've gotten him into." She smiled.

"Oh, I can hardly wait for my child to grow. What good times Steven will have with him!" Dolores glanced almost shyly at Brenna. "It must be a boy, you see, for I'm not sure that I could—I could go through—" She hesitated; the faint reddening in her cheeks accentuated the pallor of her bloodless lips and neck. There were dark smudges beneath her lovely, tired eyes, which spoke of sleepless nights.

"If there is anything I can do, please do call me," Brenna said, putting her hand out to pat Dolores'. "And take care of yourself."

"Thank you," the other replied, rising carefully from her chair. Immediately, she put a hand to the small of her back and her whole body winced as though from a sudden, sharp pain.

"Are you all right?" Brenna asked with a quick intake of breath.

Dolores nodded. "Oh, it happens now and then—just the baby moving."

"Perhaps, you'd better send a messenger for Dr. Diaz. Or I could go myself."

"No, no, please. I'm fine, really."

Brenna looked dubious. "But don't you think it would be better to let him know?"

"He does know, Brenna. Now, you said you had to get home . . ."

"Yes, if you're sure you'll be all right," Brenna replied, still worried and loathe to leave Dolores alone.

"I'll be fine. Steven should be home very soon."

With one last worried look, Brenna hurried out of the sitting room and downstairs. The butler let her out the front door. She flipped open her parasol, a gift Carlos had bought her only a few days ago, and prepared to walk the short distance home.

"Brenna!"

She turned and saw Steven alighting from his carriage. He came toward her, bowing formally, his eyes assessing her modish yellow silk dress. "It is refreshing to see a young lady with a figure that does not resemble a pumpkin," he grinned.

Brenna frowned, her dark brows slanting inwards over her dark blue eyes. "How can you jest, Steven, when anyone with eyes can see your wife is suffering so. Why must you be so cruel?"

"But she has often told me of late, that her reason for being, her entire reason, as a matter of fact, for being a wife is to have children. I doubt that she is suffering as much as you believe, Brenna."

"Perhaps you should speak with her, Steven," Brenna said. "I do think she's not well, and the doctor . . ."

"Dear Christ, she constantly raves about that doctor. Now don't ask me to have her see someone else, for it would be easier to lead a young bull to the *saladero*." His black eyes traveled lazily over her. "I've missed you, Brenna. You always seem to slip over when I am out on business."

"Have you never thought that I do so deliberately?" she asked archly, starting to walk away from him.

"No, the thought never occurred to me." He fell into step beside her, his hands behind his back. He appeared to be deep in thought. "What is it about me that you so dislike?"

She felt the heat rise in her cheeks, and she commanded herself to maintain her composure. "I don't dislike you," she returned tartly.

"How odd, then, that you try to avoid me," he teased her, and playfully caught one of her hands.

"Steven! It is broad daylight."

"Holy Mother, you sound like one of the staunch matrons I see at those dull charity balls," he laughed, but released her hand. "Tell me, Brenna, how old are you now? Surely, you can't be over forty?"

Despite his laughter, she felt affronted. "Steven Castaneda, you know very well how old I am. I'll be—I'll be twenty-six in February."

"Certainly too young to be talking like a fusty old matron," he laughed again.

"But not too young to tell you your presence is neither wanted nor needed," Brenna said angrily. "Now, just turn around and go home."

"You make me feel like a small boy, dearest Brenna—but when I'm around you, that is certainly not how I would like to feel." Those black eyes danced with mockery and good spirits.

She flushed again. "How disgusting you can be sometimes," she primly replied.

"Not nearly as disgusting as I would like to be," he countered, leaning toward her so that she thought she felt his lips brush her shoulder.

"Steven, you have a wife who is soon to have your baby," Brenna began, using the last and surest weapon she had. "You must go home to her. She needs you—and I have a husband who is waiting for me."

For a moment, she saw the flash of anger in his dark eyes, but it quickly disappeared. "How kind of you to remind me of our separate duties, senora," he said. He bowed to her and turned abruptly on his heel, leaving her alone on the sidewalk, watching him.

Two nights later, as she was retiring for bed, she heard a ferocious knocking downstairs. Grabbing her robe, she walked out into the hallway to peer down the staircase as Carlos ran to open the front door.

"What the devil—"

It was Steven, his face pale, his eyes dark and, for once, without a trace of mockery. "Carlos, please ask Brenna to come with me—it's Dolores!"

"I'm coming!" Brenna called from upstairs, flying back into her room to dress. When she hurried downstairs, Carlos was already informing one of the servants that they would be going out. "What is it?" she asked fearfully.

Steven hardly seemed to see her. "Dolores has miscarried. She's still at home—the doctor doesn't think she can be moved, but she asked that you come. Her father is too far away and my parents . . ." He stopped himself.

"Please, hurry, I promised her that I would come right back to her!"

Carlos and Brenna followed Steven into his carriage, and in a few minutes, they were hurrying into the Castaneda town house and upstairs to Dolores' bedroom. The doctor, standing in the doorway, signaled to Steven that he wanted to speak with him.

"May I go in?" Brenna asked.

The physician nodded, and Brenna stepped into the room. The pungent smell of ointments and medicines hit her first, followed closely by the hot, close smell of blood; she remembered that smell from the births of her own children. She came closer to the bed, thinking that Dolores was resting. On either side of the bed were two servants whose eyes were wide with fright.

"Is she asleep?" Brenna whispered. She could hear the nasal breathing, the struggling for breath—and the shocking thought came to her that Dolores was dying.

Pushing one of the servants out of the way, she leaned over the bed. The woman lying there was not Dolores, she thought in surprise, but some older woman, whose skull-like face and wasted body showed no sign of pregnancy. But then, the eyes opened, and despite their smudged and bruised look, Brenna recognized the round, doe-like eyes of Steven's wife.

"Dolores," Brenna whispered. "Let me help you."

A faint smile touched the lips. "I've—lost the—baby,"

she breathed. "There is no more reason for me to live. I—tried, Brenna, for—Steven's sake—"

"Steven loves you so," Brenna said desperately, "and he's worried about you. He's sorry about the baby, but . . ."

"He doesn't—love—me," Dolores said, shaking her head slightly. "And now—there—won't be anymore—b—babies." Tears were beginning to roll silently down the wasted cheeks.

"Please, don't say that," Brenna pleaded. She took the thin, fragile hand that was outside the coverlet. "Please, don't say that," she repeated softly.

A harsh sound came from between the white lips, and Brenna wasn't sure whether it was a laugh or a sob. "That night—that he came to me—I hated him. I—hated—him so much that I screamed—I'd rather die—than have his child! How—ironic of fate—to have granted my wish."

"You need not tell me this, Dolores."

"I wanted you to come—because—because I must know—I must know—"

"What, Dolores? What is it?" Brenna asked her.

"Your child—your first child—"

Brenna drew back in horror. So, the suspicions had not gone away. They had always been there, lurking, torturing this poor, pathetic woman. Brenna looked away from her, biting her lip, as the guilt and self-recrimination poured through her.

"Tell me—Brenna—that your child—was—not—my husband's."

Brenna felt the hand, which a moment ago had seemed so lifeless, now dig painfully into her own. How could she lie? Yet, how could she tell her the truth now, as she lay on her deathbed?

"Dolores, listen to me. You mustn't think that Katie was Steven's child. It will only hurt you. Carlos is her father in the eyes of the law."

"*Was—it—Steven?*"

For a long moment, Brenna stared into the eyes of the other woman. Then, bowing her head slowly, she said in a low voice, "Steven could not have been Katie's father, for he never—he never touched me in that way."

A long sigh escaped from Dolores' lips, and Brenna saw the dark eyes gazing at her almost in a friendly fashion, as though the two of them shared a secret. As though—as though she knew that Brenna had lied to protect her from pain.

"Senora Valera, you must come away now," the doctor called from the doorway.

"Oh, Dolores, I am sorry. Please, please do try . . ."

"Come, senora." Dr. Diaz was behind her, gently pulling her away from the bed. "Senor Castaneda must come in quickly . . ."

Brenna put her face in her hands, and weeping, allowed the doctor to lead her away. She felt a faint whoosh of air as Steven stepped past her to go to his wife. Suddenly, she knew that she could not stand to remain here any longer—she wanted to go home—home to her own children, who now seemed more precious than ever.

"Carlos, please take me home," she murmured.

"But, my dear, Steven may need us."

"I cannot stay, Carlos. Please take me home."

Reluctantly, he put his arm around her shoulders and led her downstairs. "Did she—is there a chance—?" His voice trembled.

Brenna shook her head fiercely. "Just take me home, Carlos, and hold me."

campaign against the Indians. For the warrior, it was
the last glorious act of bloodshed, that night shooting
and bloodletting, for it was their end as well as the

Chapter Fifty-Three

IN 1879, Julio Roca, the Minister of War under President Avellaneda, led the provincial gaucho militias, which had been amalgamated into a national army, on the last great campaign against the Indians. For the gauchos, it was one last glorious riot of bloodshed, hard riding, shooting, and throat-cutting, for it was their end as well as the Indian's. Army discipline would civilize the pampas gaucho; telegraph lines and Remington rifles would exterminate the Araucanian Indians.

The "Conquest of the Desert" opened up lands for expansion and added the great expanse of Patagonia, to the south, to the national domain. This conquest lasted until 1880 and made Roca a hero. Among the several men who rode with him who were his equals was Steven Castaneda de la Cruz, whom everyone understood had only a few months before lost his wife and unborn child in a tragic miscarriage.

In October of 1879, a year after Dolores' death, Brenna Valera and her two children rode out to Paloma for a visit. Carlos was once more embroiled in politics, now that a new presidential election was coming closer, and he and Hipólito Irigoyen, along with Irigoyen's uncle, were among the leaders of a group of politically active young men who were trying to introduce Federalism into the Argentine government. The elections would take place in 1880, and the Federalists wanted to make sure that their candidate received a majority of votes.

During this hectic period, Brenna felt as lost as a ship in a storm at sea. Following Dolores' death, she had not seen Steven again, except at the funeral, and had heard a few months later that he had joined up with Roca on his war against the Indians. With Steven gone and Carlos so involved in political meetings, she felt a growing restlessness within her.

It was Carlos who suggested she go out to Paloma to visit the Castanedas. With Dolores gone and Steven off to war, there was only Rosaria's visits to keep the elderly couple company. So with only a little persuasion, Carlos convinced his wife to go off to the country for a while.

Spring had come to the pampas again, and Brenna found peace riding Minx through the high grass. The mare was getting older, but she could still gallop with the best of them. Sometimes Brenna was reminded of her days in Ireland when she had ridden off into the emerald hills and flower-covered valleys. Had it really been twelve years ago?

She felt a tug in her heart for the land she hadn't seen for six years. So much had changed since then. Her mother and father were now accepted at Sir William's often as near-equals. Tyrone, whose bitterness had faded with time, even talked of becoming a politician once he got too old to handle the horses. Dermot was an attorney of great renown, and Deirdre had become a society matron, who traveled to Paris for the winter season. Brenna wondered if she could ever find a place in their lives if she went back. Would it be possible for her to turn back time and be Brenna Kildare again? She shook her head sadly. She could never be that girl again. And would it be too hard for her to accept what everyone else had become? What of Siobhan? Dear Siobhan—she had always known what she was thinking—just like . . . But Brenna refused to even think of Steven. Always, Dolores' face would come into focus, haunting her with the knowledge she had seen in those dark, round doe-like eyes—and Brenna would hate herself for even daring to think about Steven.

She became a well-known figure on the pampas. Mestizo women, tending the children of gauchos who had ridden off to war, waved to her as she rode by. She thought of Guido and hoped he would soon come back to his little *china*.

She had been at Paloma for nearly two weeks, when she came in one afternoon from her ride and met Consuelo in the main patio. Steven's mother had aged considerably in the year since Dolores' death and Steven's departure. Her efforts to keep Miguel from overexerting himself were wearing her out faster than her husband. She had suffered from what the doctors had called a slight seizure a few months before, and she now walked with the aid of a cane and frequently dozed off at the dinner table.

"Ah, Brenna, my dear," she said as Brenna came in and gave her a fond kiss on the cheek, a custom that had seemed to grow quite naturally between them. "I'm so glad you're back, dear, for we've just received a letter from Steven. I thought you might like to hear it."

Brenna was surprised at the ease with which she controlled her leaping emotions. "Yes, I would like to hear it, Consuelo."

"I must tell Miguel to come out here. I think he's just awakened from his siesta."

"Where is Katie? Has Teresa dressed her for dinner?"

"Oh, my dear, Katie is outside in the stables playing with the servants' children. I hope you don't mind, but she does enjoy herself with them. Oh, I should tell you that Teresa said Maria had a terrible temper tantrum after you left to go riding."

Brenna immediately felt stricken that she hadn't even asked about her second child. Maria, who was a sturdy two-and-a-half years old was quite a handful for Teresa as well as her mother. She was her father's girl, and missed him terribly when she was away from him.

"I'll go find Maria and see what she's been up to," Brenna said. "I'll be right back." She went off to her rooms and found Maria fast asleep, sucking her thumb; and tiptoeing quietly out of the room, Brenna resolved to give Teresa a present for her help in watching the children, once they returned to the city. As for Maria—Brenna decided to take more time out to be with the little girl.

She went to her room and changed quickly into a light, afternoon dress after washing the dust from her ride off her face and neck. She was just about to go back to the patio when she heard a wail and knew that Maria had awakened. She hurried back to the children's room.

"Mama! Mama! Maria missed you!"

Brenna bent down to pick her little daughter up and comfort her. "Sweetheart, Mama missed you too. Shall we take a little walk to the patio and listen to Consuelo read us a letter?"

"From Papa?"

"Well—I'm not sure, it might be," she fibbed, knowing that if she said no, the child might refuse to go. "Let's go find out."

"Katie?"

"Oh, she's playing outside."

Maria seemed to consider this, and for a moment, Brenna was afraid she might demand to play outside too, but she leaned against her mother and cuddled in her arms, sucking her thumb contentedly. Brenna smiled and kissed the child's dark hair. They walked back to the patio and sat down on one of the benches to read the letter. Miguel was leaning back in a chair and Consuelo was beside him, fitting her glasses over her nose.

"He says he is well," Consuelo began. " 'We are near Patagonia today, and the heat here is unbelievable. It's a desert really, windswept and nearly unoccupied—except for the poor, dumb bastards who continue to fight us with their wooden lances.' " Consuelo looked up apologetically at Brenna, then continued, " 'I don't know, father, if you've ever been to Patagonia. It truly is a hell of a place with its plateaus and granite hills making a chaotic jumble of the terrain. I've heard they rise like that straight to the coastal cliffs at the foot of the Andes. There's a continual haze of dust in the air, which gets in your nose and ears and your mouth; it seems as though you eat and breathe dirt.

"The fighting has slackened a bit today, so I hope to get one of the messengers on the supply route to take this letter back on base with him. I've shot my first puma. I wish I could bring home the skin to you, but the vultures came down too fast. There seems to be an abundance of strange creatures here: armadillos, lizards, poisonous snakes, scorpions, and some disgusting bloodsucking insects, which keep a man from sleeping at night. There must be a thousand varieties of spiders; poor mother, I don't mean to give you gooseflesh.

" 'I don't know when I'll be home, but don't despair. I've tried, God knows, to get killed out here, but luck seems to be with me.' "

Consuelo stopped and cleared her throat, glancing at her husband who was gazing stoically into space. Brenna felt a sudden discomfort at being privy to such a personal message. She wanted to cry out in despair for the wretchedness that Steven must feel. She was grateful when Maria began a restless squirming in her lap, so that she could excuse herself as Consuelo continued reading the letter to her husband.

A few days later, she returned to the city with Carlos, bidding a fond good-bye to the Castanedas and promising to return as soon as she could. Carlos, filled with visions and excitement, talked constantly about plans and ideas that he and Irigoyen had drawn up. Brenna listened absently, her heart was still back at Paloma, on the pampas, riding among the tall grasses and watching the stars twinkling over the hacienda at night.

In 1880, the "Conquest of the Desert" was completed. The Indian menace would never again be a threat to Argentina. Roca returned a hero and enjoyed great popularity among the people. Nearly the entire country was dominated by the National Autonomist Party, composed of *estancia* owners and wealthy businessmen, which supported Roca in his bid for the presidency.

Carlos Tejedor, the governor of the Province of Buenos Aires, however, had wanted the presidency for himself, so he refused to allow the city to become the capital of the entire country and forced the outgoing president, Avellaneda, to leave. The *porteños* seized on this excuse to start a brief revolt which was quickly suppressed by the government. Tejedor resigned as governor of the province, and Congress passed a law that stated the city of Buenos Aires would henceforth be federalized and separate from the province of Buenos Aires. A new capital for the province would have to be selected.

Carlos was not happy with the election of Roca, and because Steven had been appointed to a post in Roca's Cabinet, he had not been invited to visit since the election.

It was a surprise, therefore, when she received a formal card from him, asking permission to visit on the eve of Katie's sixth birthday.

"No! Definitely not," Carlos said in his first rush of anger. "I'll not have that damned conservative in my house."

"Carlos, he only wants to come because it is Katie's birthday."

"So? He didn't bother to call when it was Maria's birthday in April," Carlos said stubbornly. "I won't allow him to come here and try to make it up to me. He thinks he's a great hero—he and Roca—killing off those poor savages who never had a chance. I've always thought Steven was smart enough to see both sides of an issue, but I was wrong. Now he's allied himself to Roca, and I'm not about to be laughed at by my own colleagues." He snorted derisively. "I've no doubt he'll get even richer from his government post!"

"Carlos, how can you say that when you, yourself, live on the proceeds of your father's lands and the cattle he sends to market?"

He looked at her sharply. "Are you ashamed of me—that I'm not more ambitious? Do you not have enough to satisfy you here? Would you want me to turn into one of those grasping, pot-bellied businessmen, who grab at everything they can at the expense of the middle class?"

"Of course not," she replied patiently, cursing herself for forgetting how touchy Carlos was on the subject of his livelihood.

"Then you must understand my position."

"Steven has been your friend for a long time, Carlos," she said simply. "He is godfather to Katie and has a right to see her."

Carlos was about to shake his head, then shrugged.

"All right, woman. I can see you won't stop harassing me about this until I've given in—although why you display such an interest in the fellow is beyond me."

Brenna turned to walk out of the room. "I'll send a card and tell him he may come tomorrow afternoon," she said quietly. Now that she had won over her husband, she wasn't at all sure that she wanted to see Steven, herself. It had been over a year, and she knew he had changed in that time. She thought of his letter to his parents. How bitter and hopeless he had sounded. She shook her head and told herself that, after all, she was only doing it for Katie's sake.

Despite her determination to be calm, Brenna felt nervous to the pit of her stomach as she dressed for Steven's arrival. She had already discarded two gowns as unsuitable, and her maid, Conchita, was patiently buttoning up the third when the brass knocker sounded on the front door. She hastily looked in the mirror, she hated the dress she had on, but it was too late to change now. She had to get downstairs before Steven and Carlos found an excuse to argue and spoil Katie's birthday. They weren't having the party until later this evening, but Carlos had invited too many of his political allies and their families to comfortably include Steven.

She swept downstairs, rounding the corner of the banister in time to see Steven disappear into the drawing room. She hesitated, took a deep breath, and walked in behind him as sedately as she could.

Steven turned and Brenna felt her confidence dissipate at the sight of those black eyes touching her as warmly as loving hands. At thirty, Steven was even handsomer than she remembered. His face was tanned, a little thinner perhaps, his hair long, and his moustache fuller, though not nearly so full as was the fashion from Europe. She noticed a faint scar at his jawline that disappeared beneath his collar, and wondered how it had happened.

"How are you, Brenna?" he asked, and suddenly, as Carlos entered the room, the warmth left Steven's eyes. A constraint came over his features, then with a half-smile, he walked over to the other man and offered his hand. "Carlos," he murmured, "it's been too long."

For a moment, Brenna held her breath, and her eyes pleaded with her husband to be kind.

"You're right, Steven," he said gruffly. "But I hear you've been keeping yourself busy enough."

Steven laughed in the old way, breaking the tension between them. "My friend, I hear reproach in your voice. So you think I'm a turncoat, eh?"

Carlos shrugged. "What am I supposed to think, when I hear you've been appointed to Roca's Cabinet? I thought perhaps you had become too important to remember your friends."

Brenna's eyes narrowed as she glanced at her husband. How quickly Carlos liked to put the blame on Steven—hadn't he been the one who wanted to turn Steven away? How quickly Carlos forgot his own friends, she thought with a tinge of disapproval.

"I thought you might be a little angry when your friend Irigoyen lost his post," Steven said. "I understood that he wants to teach children now." He shook his head and laughed softly. "No doubt he wants to plant the seeds of rebellion in our youth."

Carlos flushed. "Some day, the people will listen to Irigoyen as willingly as his closest friends do now."

"God save us," Steven muttered. "But why do we argue? You have nothing to fear from Roca. He's open to the thoughts of those around him, which, you must admit, is a point in his favor. He wants to develop the meat-packing ideas introduced by the British and phase out the old *saladero*."

"I wouldn't doubt that he finds many friends among the British," Carlos said sourly. "I still think of him as *El Zorro,* the fox, as he was nicknamed when he was a soldier. And despite the fact that he comes from an old creole family, his blue eyes and fair looks make him look like a foreigner."

Brenna blushed, and Carlos cleared his throat uncomfortably for his slip of the tongue.

Steven watched them both with an ironic smile. "Surely

you can't be against his ideas of making Argentina a major power in the Western Hemisphere, my friend?"

Carlos could not think of a suitable answer for a moment, and Brenna quickly broke in. "Please, no more talk of politics, Carlos. It's Katie's birthday, and I know Steven's come to see her."

"Quite right, Brenna," Steven said, meeting her dark blue gaze. "I've brought her a present which will make even her mother green with envy. Where is the little one?"

"She's in the nursery with Maria, I can take you upstairs, if you like," she answered, glancing at Carlos, who was lighting a cigar.

"Go on up and wish her a happy birthday," he said, waving his hand and the cigar smoke with it. "I'll pour us a glass of wine, Steven."

Steven followed Brenna upstairs. When she opened the door to the nursery, the two dark-haired little girls, one six and one three, looked up expectantly at their visitor.

"Uncle Steven?" Katie asked hesitantly, for a child's memory is not as long as an adult's, and she hadn't seen him for over a year.

"Who else would it be?" he demanded, bending down and opening his arms to her. "You didn't think I would forget your birthday, did you, kitten?"

Still, Katie hesitated. "You forgot last year," she accused him solemnly.

Brenna watched anxiously the play of emotions crossing Steven's face, and she silently prayed that Katie would go to him.

Steven looked at the little girl. She was taller than he recalled and more slender, but she still had those wide, blue eyes like her mother's, and the same black hair, curled softly at her shoulders. He cursed the fates for denying his claim to this exquisite little being—his daughter, he thought angrily, and she hardly remembered him.

"Katie, I'm sorry I couldn't come to see you last year, but I was away on a trip," he explained.

"Where did you go?" Maria asked shyly, popping her

thumb out of her mouth just long enough to say the words

Steven looked at the younger girl, whose hair was lighter than Katie's and whose eyes were the deep brown of her father's. "Well," he said, as though taking her question into serious consideration, "I went off to be a soldier. Do you know what a soldier is?"

Maria nodded and Katie put in, "Tomás, next door, plays soldier sometimes and let's me play too." She puffed out her chest importantly. "He won't let Maria play—she's too little."

"Then you must know all about it," Steven said patiently. "I was a soldier and went off to fight the Indians." He watched the look of awed excitement cross Katie's face.

"Did you kill many of them, Uncle Steven?" she inquired breathlessly.

He nodded. "It was hot and dusty and lonesome at night. I missed you while I was away," he added softly.

Katie considered for a moment. Finally, she smiled shyly. "I missed you, too," she admitted.

"Show me how much you missed me," Steven demanded with a smile and was rewarded by a little cannon ball bowling into him, nearly knocking him backwards as two slender arms threatened to strangle him. "Whoah! You really missed me that much?" he asked, laughing.

"Oh, yes, Uncle Steven. You always bring me presents," she confided expectantly.

"Katie!" Brenna reproved.

Steven laughed again. "And this time isn't any different, sweetheart, for I've brought you a birthday present." He looked at Maria, who was still standing anxiously an arm's length away. "And something for you, too," he added, "if I get a kiss first."

Hesitantly, Maria came up and gave him a chaste peck on the cheek. "I must save my big kisses for Papa," she said seriously.

"Well then, here's something for you," he said, bringing out a treat from his pocket. Then he reached behind him, where he had set Katie's package, and handed his present to her. "And this is for the birthday girl."

Katie glanced at her mother, who nodded, and fell to tearing open the paper, revealing an exquisitely wrought little bluebird atop a music box. "Oh, it is beautiful," she breathed, hardly daring to touch it. "Oh, Mama, now I will have my own music box, just like yours," she declared, smiling at Brenna.

"Does your mama have a music box, then?" Steven questioned softly.

"Oh yes! It's not as lovely as mine," Katie said, "but it plays pretty music, and Mama plays it for us in the morning when we come in to wake her up." She grinned impudently at Steven and leaned over to whisper, "She gets so silly! Sometimes she dances around the room and we pretend we're all princesses. And sometimes," she added more seriously, "she cries, and we're all sad to hear the music stop."

Brenna stood rigidly, her cheeks blossoming with color. She felt Steven's eyes on her and didn't dare to meet his gaze.

"Well, I'm glad your mama likes her music box, and you must take care of yours as well as she has," Steven said softly to the child.

"I will, Uncle Steven!" she promised, winding it up to listen delightedly. "Oh, Mama, let us dance right now!" she exclaimed, looking eagerly up at Brenna.

"Not—now—darling; Mama and Uncle Steven have to go back downstairs to talk with your father. You and Maria may dance together." She turned abruptly and headed down the hall, listening as Steven said good-bye to his daughter.

Chapter Fifty-Four

PRESIDENT Julio Roca brought order and tranquility to the country. He accomplished his purposes with reserved quietness and authority. When a provincial governor had too much to say about the president's autonomy and the rights of the provinces that governor somehow always ended up in private life. There was no fanfare, nothing to draw attention to what he was doing, but for those officials who toed the line, there were always subsidies to pay provincial salaries, grants for waterworks and inland ports, and other manifestations of good will.

Steven's visits became as frequent as before—for he could not bring himself to stay away from his daughter, despite the growing chasm between his own beliefs and those of his old friend, Carlos. He was always careful to come only when Carlos was at home, and sometimes Brenna wondered how he knew these things about her life.

Carlos seemed to grow more moody at times, prompted by the ups and downs of his political party. Hipólito Irigoyen had, indeed, been appointed Professor of Philosophy, History, and Civics in one of the provincial normal schools. With that appointment, his interest in political causes seemed to dwindle, causing Carlos more frustration because he could not keep the following together without Irigoyen's zeal and charisma.

Brenna fretted when Carlos stayed out until very late, first missing him, then worrying about him, and finally becoming angry. She once suggested to him that, as the girls were growing older, she might be able to find a part-time tutoring job in one of the nearby schools, but he shook his head determinedly. He would not allow her even this avenue of escape from the tedium of days and evenings without him.

They were surprised one evening by a visit from

Irigoyen. Brenna was intrigued by the changes in the man. He told them that while studying and teaching philosophy, he had come across the works of a German philosopher, Karl Christian Friedrich Krause, who had tried to reconcile the idea of God with the idea of the world.

"I am determined to study harder and to meditate," he said. "For I am seeking to gain communion with my inner consciousness."

Carlos threw up his hands. "What is all this jibberish you're spouting now, Hipólito? What of the cause of Federalism? What of all the changes we wanted to bring about in the government? Have you thrown all our hopes away so that you can sit silently in a chair, in the dark—and think?"

Irigoyen who had grown more somber than ever, shrugged his shoulders. "First I must communicate with my inner soul, my friend. Only then will I gain the knowledge and the pureness of spirit I need to carry out our goals. Have patience, Carlos, all these things will come about."

"When? When!"

"Calm yourself. Perhaps if you tried things my way, you might come to feel as I do," he suggested.

"No!" Brenna interrupted, unable to keep herself from shouting the word. "Carlos, Hipólito can do as he wishes, but you have a family."

"Your wife talks foolishly," Irigoyen said bluntly. "I have a family too, but what I am doing has nothing to do with them. I am seeking self-realization, which will lead, eventually, to the realization of God."

Brenna was bewildered by his talk; she hoped Carlos would never turn into someone like Irigoyen, solemn, somber, without laughter. She was glad when their visitor left, but she could sense her husband's curiosity had been piqued. He needed something to hold onto again, something to put order in his life. Brenna had no answers for him—except one, perhaps . . .

"Darling," she whispered to him after they had gone to bed that night. She knew he was still awake for his body was stiff and unyielding as it always was when he was thinking in bed. "Darling, why don't we have another child?" she asked. "Katie is seven and Maria is four—wouldn't it be nice to give them a baby brother?" She listened, holding her breath for his answer.

"Brenna, another child would only be a drain on our finances," he said. "If we had a son, he would need a father to stay at home and teach him the lessons a father must teach his son. I'm not sure that I will have the time. Without Irigoyen, the responsibility of keeping Federalism alive has fallen on me and my uncle. I just don't know."

"Carlos, for my sake, then," she said. "I would so love another child. Our daughters are growing up so fast and becoming so independent . . ."

He turned toward her suddenly, looking intently into her face. "Are you so restless, my poor Brenna? Have I neglected you so often?"

"Oh, Carlos!" she murmured, putting her arms around his neck. "You would have such a happy wife." She laughed softly. "Besides, isn't that what you Latin men are supposed to do? Make your women pregnant every year? We certainly seem to have fallen behind."

He laughed too, encouraging her, then stopped and frowned, dashing her hopes even before he spoke. "Perhaps next year, darling, when Irigoyen gets all these foolish notions out of his head. Yes, that would be a better time, I think."

"But . . ."

"Just keep counting the days, like the doctor told you," he advised, yawning now that he had resolved the matter. "Next year, I promise you"

Brenna would have argued with his decision, but in his present mood, she was afraid she might start a quarrel. She sighed. If he didn't want a child, she shouldn't bring up the subject again. Funny. She had always thought a man would want at least one son.

By 1882, La Plata was established as the capital of the province of Buenos Aires. Roca was applauded for his wisdom and became even more popular among the people. He had sponsored a national education law and created the National Board of Education, guaranteeing everyone equal chance at schooling. He also organized the courts and drew up the penal and mining codes.

"Good God, man, are you still so stubborn that you cannot at least agree Roca is doing all he can to make this country great?" Steven demanded, during one stormy session with Carlos.

"There are still the poor, the hungry, and those who have no land and no property," Carlos steadfastly insisted.

"If your friend, Irigoyen, was in power, do you think the poor would have any more food or money than they have now?"

"Perhaps! At least his roots are in the lower class, he feels for the people, he . . ."

"He tries to lay every one of those young ladies he teaches in the normal school!" Steven cut in sharply. "Yes, don't look so surprised, I admit that Roca has him watched. And what we find out might change your mind about this man you worship like a saint, the man with such high, moral fiber that he refuses to marry a sixteen-year-old schoolgirl who is pregnant with his child."

"I·don't believe you!" Carlos shouted. "Irigoyen has his faults, like any other man, but he truly believes in his principles." He quieted then, and tried to explain. "Listen, Steven, I've heard Irigoyen speak about this man, Krause, and some of his ideas are very good. Krause thinks that the individual mind is part of the Universal Mind, that the inner self is the source of all knowledge, that the objective of religion is to unite one's life with the life of God and that the ultimate goal of ethics is to do good for good's sake alone. A man who believes in that must be a good man. And he would make this country a good president. A man with compassion ·for the people, a man who believes in absolute justice for all, in the equality of all men and all nations, and in universal peace." Carlos' face nearly glowed with his triumphant words. "And someday, this country will be ready for a man like Irigoyen to take over. I want to be with him then, Steven. Can't you understand?"

Steven cursed impatiently. "Carlos, the man is fooling you. He would have little interest in the so-called equality of men were he to find himself leading them. Do you think he would refuse to live in the president's palace? Would he set up his government in some slum or *barrio*, close to the people, so that he could consult with them?"

"You're twisting the issue, Steven. Ah, you can be clever with words, but not clever enough to talk me into believing as you do. You should see when Hipólito talks to the poorer classes. They leave his presence transformed, their faces glowing."

"For God's sake, Carlos, what has he ever done but talk? What has he tried to accomplish for the people, for those he claims to champion? Look at Roca's record—he has founded the National Mortgage Bank, organized the police force in the city, and signed a contract for construction of a real port in the estuary so ships won't be forced to anchor eight miles away!"

"How you spout off about him, Steven," Carlos said glumly. "What a magnificent politician you would make!"

"You're a fool!" Steven said, losing his patience.

The two men stared at each other for a long moment.

"You had better go," Carlos finally said in deadly earnest. "And I would prefer that you not come here again. There is no need for you to pay social calls to my wife or my children."

Steven would have spoken, but he glimpsed the white face of Brenna in the hallway. He bowed abruptly, took his hat and coat, and left the house.

After he was gone, Brenna ran to her husband, her eyes huge with concern. "Carlos, you haven't—he will come back, won't he?"

"I certainly hope not!" he replied tersely, and reached for a cigar to ease his own agitation.

"But, he's our friend."

"Don't begin again with all of that!" Carlos said sharply. "I don't want the man in our house again, do you understand?"

"No, I don't understand," she answered him.

He took a deep breath. "Brenna, we just cannot reconcile our political beliefs behind polite words anymore. We've grown too far apart. I have no desire to have continuing arguments with him." He glanced at her severely. "I am sick of all his propaganda for that bastard."

Brenna felt her anger surfacing. "And I am sick of all *your* propaganda for that other bastard, Senor Irigoyen!" she shouted at her husband, careless of her words. "Yes, I was listening, and it made me sick when I heard how he tells you one thing, then turns around and does another. Yes, I heard what Steven said about that poor, young girl."

"Lies!" Carlos cut in, putting his cigar down and staring at his wife in disbelief. "You would believe a man like Steven over your own husband?" He shook his head. "God only knows if Roca doesn't have people spying on me—on you and our children. I wouldn't doubt it. No, Brenna, don't defend Steven Castaneda when you have no idea what he's really like."

"I know what he's like," she burst out passionately, and then seeing the hooded look from Carlos. "I mean, I've known him a long time—*we've* known him a long time. Look how close he is to our children."

"Enough!" Carlos roared. "I'll not have you defending him, Brenna! I don't want to talk anymore of it. That man is no longer welcome in our house."

"Carlos—" Brenna began, then stopped, knowing that she could only make matters worse by arguing. But he was being so unfair, she thought angrily.

She turned away from her husband, willing herself not to plead with him. It would only drive him further away—and they were already miles apart. She couldn't even recall how it had happened, how it had all started, but she no longer knew what Carlos was thinking, how he reasoned, what his plans were.

How could he forbid Steven to come? she agonized. God knew it was hellish for her to see him as often as she did, but she could stand it knowing that at least he was seeing Katie. She knew he loved the child, and she knew what could happen if Carlos no longer allowed him to see her. Steven might grow angry enough to tell Carlos the truth. But yet—Oh, she mustn't think of what might happen, she told herself, wearily. No use in trying to out-think either of them.

Several weeks went by. Then Carlos told her that he would be going away for two or three days. Because of his rift with Steven, he did not suggest that she ride out to Paloma with the girls. Brenna ached to think of old Miguel and Consuelo, growing more feeble each year and so happy when she came to visit. It was cruel of Carlos to deny her that, but she knew it was too soon to bring up the subject. Perhaps, in a few more months, when his anger against Steven had cooled.

She watched him leave the house. The girls were becoming so used to their father's leaving that they no longer cried to see him go. The thought nearly made Brenna break into tears, and it was in this mood that Steven found her later that night. She was sitting in the library after the children had been put to sleep.

It was very late, and the rumblings in the sky promised a thunderstorm. Brenna had sent the servants to bed, then decided, for once in her life, to drown all of her sorrows in drink. She would get properly sotted, rolling down drunk, she declared to herself, and she hoped she wouldn't recover until after Carlos returned. Let him think what he liked, she told herself, wincing as the hot taste of brandy burned her throat.

"Ach, how can the men stand the stuff?" she asked the empty room.

She had already put away three stiff drinks, and the walls seemed to be weaving on either side of her, when she heard the front door knocker. She struggled to her feet, wondering who in the world would be visiting in this awful weather. What time was it, anyway? She couldn't make out the face of the clock through the blur. The knocker was sounding again. She hurried to open the door before the servants awakened and witnessed their mistress' unrespectable behavior.

"Who is it?" she asked, peering blearily into the darkness.

A low laugh greeted her. "Can't you see, my darling?"

Then a tall figure came in out of the sudden rain, shaking water on her.

"Steven—is that you?" she wondered stupidly as he took off his outer coat and hat.

He turned to her. She was barefooted, and her silky, black hair was falling past her shoulders onto her nightdress. "Not quite the upright, stiff-boned wife tonight, are you?" he commented with a smile which looked wicked in the half-light.

"Steven, what are you doing here?" she asked, then hiccoughed.

"I have come to save you from drinking yourself into a stupor," he told her, turning her around and marching her upstairs. When she would have gone into her bedroom automatically, he swerved her away. "Not in there! Don't you have a guest room or a sitting room—or something?"

"Are you spending the night?" she inquired in her best imitation of a stolid matron of the city.

He was hard put to contain his laughter. "Darling, you are very drunk. I hope you can stay awake, for you and I have some serious talking to do." He opened a door and saw that it held an unoccupied bed. "Ah, the guest room."

He pushed her inside and closed the door, leaning against it a moment, studying her in the light of the candelabra he had taken from the hallway.

"I shall have the servants make up the bed," she said, trying to sound dignified and wondering what he was doing here. A sudden thought came to her. "Carlos will be angry if he finds out," she said, her eyes widening.

"Carlos is gone," he said quietly, and she wondered how he knew that. She remembered Carlos telling her that he most probably had spies watching them. Well, she supposed he did.

He lit the lamp, and the small room brightened into a warm light. Brenna plopped down in a chair, yawning.

"Oh, no, you don't!" he ordered, pulling her out of the chair by her arms. "I don't want you to sleep yet, Brenna. I want to talk to you—and this may be the only chance

I have." He felt her body slacken as he held her, and he knew that she was beginning to slip down to the floor.

Gruffly, he set her on the bed and slapped her, once, hard.

Her eyes flipped open and putting a hand to her cheek she glared at him.

"That's better," he remarked, ignoring her angry look. "Now listen to me. I'm not sure if you understand just what your husband's getting into. Irigoyen has him—I would say 'in his power,' but that sounds too melodramatic. Anyway, let us say that your husband is becoming a fanatic about political causes."

She sat glaring stonily, still angry at his having slapped her.

"He attends dozens of meetings every month. Irigoyen's uncle, Leandro Além, has persuaded your husband to join in the leadership of a new group of anarchists."

"How do you know all this?" she demanded suddenly.

He sighed impatiently. "The president tries to keep an eye on those groups that oppose him politically."

"Spies!" she shouted.

"For Christ's sake, Brenna, will you keep your voice down! I wouldn't relish having to explain my presence to one of your servants, especially with you looking like that and both of us in the bedroom."

"Or to Carlos," she added with a sulking look.

He grinned mockingly. "Do you think I give a damn if Carlos knows I've been here? I told you once, Brenna, that if Dolores were gone, I'd come to you and ask you to be my mistress."

She eyed him, still half-drunk. "If that is a joke, it is certainly in the poorest taste, Steven."

"I assure you, I did not mean it as a joke," he told her, his black eyes growing bolder. "In fact, seeing you like this reminds me of the last time you were in your nightgown and I came in on you. I believe that time, though, I was the one who had been drinking."

She was silent, distrustful, watching him as he stood against the door. "You really should go."

"How old is Katie now, Brenna? Nine—ten?"

"Ten," she said.

"Ten years," he said almost to himself. "It has been a long time since we—how should I put it?—had our little indiscretion."

She turned away from him, smoothing the counterpane on the bed automatically. He watched her nervous, agitated movements. Cautiously, he drew closer, wanting to touch her. Gently, his hand came down to feel the softness of her shoulder beneath the silk of her nightgown.

"I've never forgotten that moment, Brenna," he said huskily.

She shook her head. "You were a married man then—it was a sin."

"And now you are the married one—would you think it a sin if I should make love to you?"

"No, Steven!" She shrugged off his hand and stood up from the bed, her head clear enough to hear the rising passion in his voice. "You cannot even think it! I *am* married, and I have two children."

"One of whom is mine!"

"And would you have me bring another of yours into the world?" she challenged, her dark brows slanting downward. "Do you care so little for me that you would use me like a brood mare—since you have no one else to do it for you."

He reached out and shook her, yet he was curiously gentle, as though he were holding back the depth of his emotions. "You little fool—why do you think I haven't remarried in these past few years? Do you think it is for lack of eligible women? There isn't an unmarried woman in the city who wouldn't like to get her hands on the Castañeda fortune. It would be a simple matter for me to marry a young and beautiful woman, who could give me all the children I should ever want." He forced her head back when she tried to look away from him. "Listen to me. I don't want children from any of those others— only from you, my Brenna. You and I are so alike—so obviously meant for each other. Don't ask me why fate decided to play her tricks on us, but we are meant to be together!"

"No, please, Steven, don't say such things!" she pleaded, straining away from him. "You're only torturing me."

But he would not let her go. He was still talking, saying words that were like arrows stabbing at her conscience, forcing her to remember what she knew she must not. "Brenna, Brenna, I can still recall that day when we kissed after your brother's wedding." He shrugged self-derisively. "I was young and stupid, and I didn't know that I should have said something then—but you were only fourteen, and I—I had been pledged already to Dolores by my family."

"Steven, please—"

"I told my father when I came home that I would not honor my pledge. I would have bought off her father, but when I came back to Ireland to find you, you weren't the same girl anymore. You had married Kevin Ryan, and I no longer cared who I married."

"Oh, Steven, how could I have known? . . ."

"So I came back home and married Dolores, and I was content, even though I knew we could probably never have children. I wondered how many children you had given to your husband by then.

"Then to hear you were here in Buenos Aires! It was unbelievable. For a moment I forgot we were both married—it didn't matter. You had come to me, and I wanted you, Brenna! But the fact was that we were bound to others, and I almost hated you for coming."

"I shouldn't have come," she said dully. "None of this would have happened. . . ."

"Don't talk foolishly," he chided her as he would have a child. "I would never have known you as I did that day under the ombu tree if you had not come. I would never have had the chance to be proud of my child, as I am of Katie. And I would never have loved another woman as I have you, my dearest Brenna."

She looked up at him, astonishment, surprise, amazement on her face.

"Yes, I have loved you since the last day we saw each other in Ireland when I called you my dove and promised to return. I love you now, Brenna, and I want you more than any other woman I have ever known."

He loves me, she thought happily, triumphantly, he loves me!

"Brenna, let me take care of you," he said. "Bring Katie and come away with me."

She looked at him, puzzled. "But what about Carlos —and Maria?" she asked.

He shrugged them aside. "Do they matter? It's you I want—and my child. Carlos can have his own daughter, but give me mine!"

"But—what are you saying? Carlos—he would never agree to a divorce!"

He shook his head, his black eyes glowing with inner fire. "Then run away. Come away with me, and we can go anywhere you like—to the United States, or back to Ireland, or to Europe. . . ."

"But you can't leave your parents."

"They'll have Rosaria."

"Then I can't leave my own child. Maria is mine too, Steven." She looked up at him in anguish. "You can't ask me to leave her behind."

He was beginning to frown in that old, hateful way, his black brows arching upward in sarcastic crescents. "So, position, security mean more to you than what I'm offering?"

"Please, Steven, you must understand me. I wish I could come with you—but not as your mistress. What about the children—how could I face them? No matter where we went, I would always know that I still had a husband here."

He groaned aloud, and his hands tightened at her shoulders. "Brenna, you said yourself he would never . let you go legally."

She stared up at him, saw the handsome face, the leaping brightness in his dark eyes, the strength in his body—and she knew that she loved him as much, perhaps even more than he loved her; but she could not cheapen herself and that love by accepting his terms.

She could not become mistress to a man and run away from her responsibility. She shook her head in despair.

"No, Steven, I can't go with you."

The hopeful light was snuffed out of his eyes, leaving only the banked fires of desire leaping up as he looked at her. Almost involuntarily, his hands went to the neckline of her gown, grabbed at the material, and ripped it away.

For a moment, Brenna didn't understand what he was doing, but when she looked up into his face and saw the bedeviled torment that masked it, she let out a cry of hopelessness.

Ignoring her terror, he pushed her onto the bed, intent on claiming her physically if he could not have her any other way. He pushed her torn nightgown aside and brutally clamped his hand across her mouth to keep her from crying out as he loosened his own clothing and fell on top of her.

Brenna closed her eyes, unable to bear the sight of him behaving like a ravenous wolf devouring her flesh. "I forgive you, I forgive you," she said over and over in her mind. He was not hurting her—how could he when she loved him so much that her body welcomed him despite the opposition of her mind. Never again, she thought. Never again will I see you, Steven, after this night, for she could not face him again after this. Tears crept slowly down her cheeks—not tears of pain, but of a lost love—a love that she could never regain after this night. Oh, Steven, how I've loved you, she sighed.

When it was over and he lay panting, she placed her hand gently on his shoulder. She met his black eyes proudly, boldly. "I shall always love you, Steven," she said softly.

For a moment, his features seemed frozen. Then, quietly, he rose and straightened his clothing, with his back to her and his shoulders trembling, so that she wondered if he was crying. But she said nothing. She wanted him to go now. It was done, and she would never see him again.

She watched him leave from the bed where she still

lay, her nightgown drawn about her in reflexive modesty. That proud, dark head was bowed, and she felt his pain in her own heart, reflected a thousandfold. She listened to his footsteps on the stairs and heard the door slowly open and close. Then there was silence in the house, broken only by the steady pattering of rain at the windows.

Chapter Fifty-Five

BRENNA paced back and forth in her bedroom, her swollen belly cramping with discomfort. She didn't want to go to her bed yet. Why was she so nervous about this baby, she wondered? The entire pregnancy had gone by with very little sickness, but even the physician had admitted that this baby looked as though it would be larger than the first two.

As she continued her pacing, Teresa looked on in concern. Where was Carlos? She bit her lip in agitation. He hadn't really wanted this baby, she thought. She remembered the day she had told him, and he had looked at her with such damning accusation in his eyes.

"I asked you to wait. I told you I wasn't ready for the responsibility of another child," he had said, straining to keep patience with her.

"I'm sorry," she replied with the little dignity she could muster. "Sometimes these things just happen, and there's nothing anyone can do about it."

He sighed. "As you say, there's nothing we can do about it, but you must understand, Brenna, that I can't remain home to humor you during this pregnancy. Irigoyen, Além, and I are trying to sort our constituents into a viable party so that in the next election we'll be able to wield some power. It's very important to me."

"And the baby is not?" she couldn't help asking.

"Of course, the baby is important, but we have over seven months to wait, and there's much for me to do during that time."

She had accepted his answer to appease him, but she really didn't understand why he couldn't share his time with her, as well as with his constituents. The months had dragged by slowly, although she was comforted by Katie's excitement about the new baby. Maria, who was seven, could not understand why it took so long to come out of Mama's stomach.

Brenna glanced at the calendar on her vanity: March 18, 1885. Despite her confidence, despite all the times she had counted and told herself that this was Carlos' baby, her mind lingered uneasily over that night with Steven—the last time she had seen him. He didn't even know she was pregnant, unless, of course, Roca's spies had reported even this fact. She clasped and unclasped her hands, feeling another cramp rip through her abdomen and lose itself somewhere in her lower back. Her legs buckled a little, but still she did not want to lie down. Where was Carlos?

An hour later, the physician was summoned. Brenna had finally agreed to get into her nightgown and under the sheets of her bed. The cramps were still coming at quickly spaced intervals, but there was no sharp pain yet, and she knew that the birthing would not be for a long while. She glanced out the window. Twilight was settling outside.

"Carlos?" she asked as candles were lit and a man came to sit next to the bed.

"No, Brenna, it's Dr. Garcia," the man said, patting her hand comfortingly. "I believe one of your servants has sent a message to your husband. He should be here shortly."

Brenna nodded. She wished the doctor hadn't come so soon. She hated the waiting and knew he must have other patients to attend to. The hours seemed to click by, one by one, with the slowness of a dripping pail of water down a well. The pains were beginning to grow sharper so that Brenna squirmed in the bed.

She thought she heard voices in the room, but now the pain was with her like the drone of a constant chant, which drowned out all other sound or thought. Pain like none she had ever known screamed through her body, and sweat drenched her face. Was that her own voice piercing through the layers of pain? Who was that dreadful woman who was screaming like that?

Something cool patted her face, and she licked at it,

desperate for moisture, but like a tantalizing phantom, it was gone in an instant, leaving her lips parched and dry. Was she having a child? Or was it something else? Never before had the pain engulfed her so completely. Perhaps she was too old to have children—or perhaps there was something wrong this time. She felt an icy finger of fear touch her spine, but it was quickly pushed away by the burning of pain.

Then like an animal, she was beyond thinking. She knew that she was screaming, but she no longer cared. Just get rid of the pain, she thought, just get rid of the pain!

And then, miraculously, she could hear again. She opened her eyes and could see again. There were no longer red and black blotches before her eyes. Instead she saw the doctor's face; he was leaning over her, calling to her. Somewhere, she wasn't sure where, she could hear a baby wailing lustily, its cries rolling over all other sound in the room.

"You have a son, Brenna," the doctor said, his smile as broad as his face. "And quite a son! I'm not sure that he really wanted to come out."

"Oh, a son," Brenna said smiling feebly. "How proud Carlos must be."

"I'm afraid he hasn't arrived yet, my dear," the doctor said gently. "but I trust he will be here soon. No man should have to wait to hear he has another child."

"Oh, yes, he will be so happy," Brenna sighed, watching as Teresa went to the window to open the shutters, letting the afternoon light stream into the room.

"Marcos Carlos Hipólito Valera," the priest intoned solemnly as he sprinkled water over the baby's forehead. Marcos, or Marc, as the parents had decided to call him, squalled discontentedly and screwed his face up into the semblance of a prune.

Brenna, holding him proudly, rocked him in her arms to quiet him at least until the priest had finished the baptism. On either side of her stood the three men for whom the child had been named: Carlos, his father, Marcos, and

Hipólito Irigoyen, whose brows knitted solemnly as though he strongly disapproved of a child's crying in church.

Brenna did not want Irigoyen to stand as the child's godfather, but Carlos had insisted, and she had given in, if only to keep the peace. Although she had been disappointed when Carlos did not show the same loving, fatherly affection with Marc he had with Maria and Katie, she said nothing to him. He would change in time, she told herself—after all, he hadn't really wanted this baby. Yet, her heart contradicted her. Shouldn't a father love his child no matter what, she wondered. She couldn't understand him. Carlos had always been warm and loving toward his children, but then of late, he had been acting so strangely.

After the church service, Brenna went in the carriage with the children, while Carlos saw his father home, then brought Irigoyen to the house to celebrate the child's baptism. Brenna watched the two of them discussing politics, religion, philosophy—everything, in fact, except the little boy whose soul had been pledged to God only this morning.

"Carlos?" she called from the doorway. "Shall we have a toast to your fine, healthy son?" She smiled hesitantly as she came into the room.

Carlos turned to her; his brown eyes were as cold as she had ever seen them. "Brenna, enough of this farce," he said with deadly slowness.

She looked at him in confusion. Irigoyen stared at her with the faintest smile on his lips. "What—what do you mean?" she demanded.

"I mean, dear wife, that I have claimed the child as mine in the eyes of the law and of the church. My father has witnessed it. But now, I want no more trickery between you and me. We both know the child is not mine."

The words hung in the air, and the three of them stood like characters in the frozen tableau of a play. Finally Irigoyen held his hand up to signal peace.

"Please, Carlos, I know how embarrassing this must be for you—as well as for your wife. Allow me to take my leave now."

"No, you may stay," Carlos said, still accusing Brenna with terrible loveless eyes. She couldn't bear to see him like that, and she rushed forward, her hands outstretched pleadingly.

"Carlos, what are you saying? Of course Marc is your son."

"Liar," he said calmly, deliberately. "I know of your treachery."

"My—?"

"Yes, you recall the night I had gone to a meeting some months ago, leaving you alone with the children for a few days?" He watched her as she nodded slowly. "That night you had a visitor—a man—"

Brenna gasped and stepped back with a shudder, her hand going involuntarily to her throat as though she feared violence from her husband.

"Yes, you do recall, I can see that," Carlos said, poisonously. "I was a blind fool not to have seen it before—not to have realized how prettily you pled so that Steven might be allowed to come here—because he was my friend, you said, and he loved the children so!" Carlos' face twisted with his pain and fury. "But I didn't see—didn't see the lust burning between you two. A lust, Brenna, that culminated that night and produced this child!"

"Carlos, please listen to me," Brenna begged.

"I know all I want to know," he said quickly. "I will hear no more of your lies and protestations." He laughed shortly. "I would never have known had not one of Roca's people, who was stationed here to watch the house after I had gone, gotten drunk one night and blurted out the story to one of our political followers. Yes, Brenna, one of Steven's own spies let the whole story slip weeks ago! Ironic, isn't it? I would have thought our dear friend, Steven, would have been more discreet."

"Carlos, Steven did come here, but only to warn me."

"Warn you?" he asked her, his brows upraised.

"He warned me about Irigoyen!" she cried out. "He is the one who has poisoned your mind against everyone, even your wife!"

"Shut up!" Carlos yelled at her, then looked at Irigoyen apologetically. "I don't care to hear anymore."

"You will hear," she cried desperately. "Marc is *your* child, Carlos."

"Are you so very sure, my faithful wife?" he asked her silkily. "Can you be certain that he is mine—or is there some doubt in your mind, some slim notion that perhaps fate would have it otherwise?"

Brenna whitened with guilt. Carlos swore and threw and splintered his glass into a hundred pieces against the wall. "You look as guilty as a thief, Brenna, as guilty as a whore!"

She swayed and her hand went to her forehead, as though to relieve a vise that had tightened there. Finally, she looked up to her husband, "I will leave you if that is what you wish, Carlos. For such a thing as you imply, the Church will grant a separation."

"Separation!" He strode over to her and grabbed her arm, shaking her. "Do you really believe I would be so obliging, my dear? How convenient that would be for you and your paramour. How gloriously free you would be! You and Steven could run off and live happily forever after in a lie—people would never guess you were not husband and wife." His hand tightened like a claw on her flesh so that she barely kept herself from crying out with pain. "I tell you now, Brenna, I will never let you go. No one shall ever know a word of this. The spy who told the story has been disposed of, so the only three who know of your indiscretion are in this room—except, of course, the guilty male, who, alas, is out of my reach. But, I have a feeling that Steven is too noble to tell anyone.

"No, Brenna, you will be my wife until you die, my dear. I will not risk the scandal, the humiliation of a separation. You would, no doubt, rejoice to see my political aspirations ruined, wouldn't you?"

"No, Carlos. Just let me go, and you can do anything you like."

He shook his head and released her. "Never."

"And, should you ever decide to say or do anything

foolish, measures can be taken to see that you never see your children again," Irigoyen put in succinctly.

Brenna's eyes swerved from her husband's blazing face to the dark, somber one of her nemesis. With a wild cry of despair, she ran toward him, her hands outstretched to rake his face, to gouge his eyes, to hurt the man she hated and feared above all others. Irigoyen dodged her hands, but not before she felt his flesh beneath her nails. She felt a sudden pain in her wrist as he caught it, twisting it back, bringing tears to her eyes. She tried to swing with her other hand, but it too was caught.

"How I should like to punish you for daring to raise your hand to me," he said between his teeth, speaking low so that only she could hear. "Be wary, woman, or I shall find a way to put you at my mercy." His eyes glittered and she struggled to get away from him.

"Let her go, Hipólito, we have other things to discuss. I don't think we will have to worry about her now." It was Carlos, standing calmly behind her, watching as the man mauled her.

"You coward!" she cried, directing her words at her husband. "I would warrant that if this man were to seduce me, you would stand by and give your permission. You disgust me! Both of you disgust me!"

Irigoyen released one wrist and cuffed her lightly across the mouth. "I think, senora, that you would do well to silence yourself. Perhaps you should learn to use your time in meditation and communion with your inner soul."

She glared at him silently until he released her. Then, with an apologetic look at Carlos, Irigoyen said softly, "Forgive me for so handling your wife, Carlos. Come now. We have other matters to discuss."

Carlos dismissed Brenna with a nod, and she picked up her skirts so that she could run away, run upstairs to her children, in the haven of her room. As she stood, breathing hard, against the door of the nursery, her eyes leaped between her two astonished daughters to her son in his cradle. She wished fervently that the boy was not Carlos', that he might, after all, be Steven's son.

601

IN the ensuing months, Brenna devoted herself exclusively to her children, taking her joy in Katie's beauty, so like her own at that age; in Maria's seriousness, which could break suddenly and devastatingly into a pure sweetness that melted the heart; and to Marc, whose size at a year was nearly double that of either of his sisters at the same age. He was a curious little boy, getting into everything, frequently driving his sisters to distraction when he got into their ribbons and furbelows, but they were patient with him, as though they sensed his need for all the love they could give him.

Carlos remained indifferent to the boy, and Brenna felt herself pitying her husband, who was missing all the joys of raising a son. If only he would try to love little Marc, she thought sadly, it might change his outlook, but he stubbornly refused to believe that the boy was his own offspring. More and more, he took refuge from his family in his politics. The girls missed the old Carlos—and so did Brenna.

She had promised herself that she would never again talk with Steven or even try to see him. She could not risk Carlos' blind wrath and its effect on the children. Katie was nearly twelve now and going through a difficult period in her young life as she approached young womanhood. She needed a father, and his absence disturbed her more than she would say. Maria, at nine, also missed Carlos and the stories and games he used to play with her. She could not understand why her mother and father no longer came together to the nursery, and it hurt Brenna to see Maria's bewildered look when her father left for long periods of time. Marc seemed not to miss having a father, relying on the abundance of love that he received from the women in his life. But Brenna feared that as he grew older, the absence of a father would, perhaps, be felt most keenly by the boy.

Elections were held for the presidency again in 1886. Despite Carlos' organization and planning, and the support of Irigoyen and Além, the Federalist candidate lost badly to Roca's chosen heir, Miguel Juarez Celman.

One afternoon, after the elections were over, Brenna was in the library selecting a book for Katie to read. She had engaged a tutor to instruct both her daughters, but Carlos had sent him packing after investigating his political leanings. As she looked for an interesting book, she wondered where she would find another tutor, when just then she heard the door open and Carlos enter.

"Good afternoon," she said. Perhaps today he would be friendly.

Carlos looked up and frowned absently. "Good afternoon, Brenna. Expanding your mind, I see."

"It's for Katie."

"Katie?" He seemed puzzled.

"Yes," Brenna said with a touch of impatience, "she reads excellently now, in case you didn't know."

"Brenna?" And when she stopped and turned toward him at the door, "What has happened between us?" he said in a wondering, hollow voice, which unnerved her.

For a moment, she felt joy rising up inside her. "Oh, Carlos, I am always here, ready to help you if you want me. Please—"

He seemed to snap back to attention, and his face composed itself into the indifferent lines she had become used to in the past year. "Excuse me—it's just—I haven't been feeling well—"

"Then let's go on a vacation. Oh, the children would love to go to the beach! Katie and Maria both want to learn how to swim, and I thought, perhaps, you could teach them."

He shook his head. "I'm much too busy to take you to the beach, Brenna."

"But the elections are over. . . ."

"We may not wait for the next election to make a stand," he said, his voice growing with zealous fire. "I'm sick of doing things the civilized way. Where does it get us?"

Brenna said nothing. She had heard these same words often before. She started to leave, but once again his voice stayed her.

"I know what you're thinking," he said sarcastically. "You think all I can do is talk, that my words never lead to action. You wonder sometimes—oh, yes, I know you do—if my interest in politics has blinded me to reality." He came closer to her. "Brenna, if only you would come to one of our meetings," he said with an edge of pleading in his voice. "Irigoyen takes fire when he speaks to us—he makes us believe we can do anything we want. And if what we want is right, then what is to stop us?"

"The government," she said dryly. "You talk of rebellions and riots, Carlos, as though the president will let you walk into the armory and take as many guns as you need. As you've told me many times before, he has spies—an entire network of them—who monitor the activities of people like yourself and Irigoyen. You couldn't make a move against him without his knowing."

He shrugged. "Someday, when the timing is right—"

"Carlos, I don't want anymore of your political speeches thrown at me. I've heard them all—from you, from Irigoyen, and from all the others who come here and eat and drink and talk treachery."

"Treachery is a word you well know the meaning of. I'm surprised you've not asked me how your precious Steven fared during the switch in power." His dark eyes gleamed. "I'm sure you would like to know, wouldn't you, my dear?"

She disciplined herself to remain calm. "I have no interest in what happens to Steven Castaneda, although I'm sure you're determined to tell me."

"How well you do that," he said approvingly. "Sometimes I almost believe you when we are together and disposed toward one another in our bed at night. I think, 'Carlos, you are a fool. She could never have been unfaithful with your best friend—not this woman of such strength and beauty.' Then I think back and remember those odd times when I caught you looking at Steven, or when he sat close by you, then quickly turned away when I entered the room, and I say to myself, 'Carlos, you *are* a fool—to even think that she might have been faithful!' "

"Carlos, must we go over this again?" she asked wearily.

He shook his head. "Well, you can be sure that your lover has landed on his feet very nicely," he said, ignoring her plea. "Before he left Roca's Cabinet, he was given lucrative shares in certain railroad companies, which added another slice of pie to his wealth. It seems President Celman has not yet found a place for him, but have no fear; once Steven has had a taste of political power, he is unlikely to give it up. I'm sure he will turn up again somewhere."

"May I leave now?" she asked bleakly.

He considered her. "Such a shame," he said absently. "Such a waste of all your talents, Brenna. Beauty, knowledge, wit—what a fine wife for a president you would have made. Of course, the day Steven tries for the presidency—" He stopped and looked away. "But, alas, you settled for a man whose wealth is little enough to pay the household expenses."

"That's what it really is, isn't it?" she said softly, her eyes brightening. "It's not the fact that I might have once gone to bed with Steven, or had his child—it has nothing to do with me, does it? It's you, Carlos, and your greed for the things that Steven has. Oh, if only you were appointed to a government post, how quickly you would have changed allegiance. Yes, how different things would have been then. Now I see you clearly. You are jealous of Steven—jealous of his wealth, his position, his power—and for *that* you hate him." She allowed herself the luxury of a small laugh. "What would high-moraled, religious Irigoyen think if he suddenly saw you as I do?"

Carlos' lips tightened ominously, and his hands clenched into fists at his sides. "What a bitch you've turned into, my dear," he said, through his teeth. *"You're* the one who wants Steven and everything he can give you, not I.

How clever, how devilishly clever you have become to twist matters so adroitly."

Brenna laughed at the stupidity of his words. "Don't try to make me believe anything but what I've just said, Carlos. I've pinned you to the wall, and you know it. But it doesn't matter to me. The lust for gold is in everyone, my dear husband—I have no doubts, that Irigoyen himself carries the very same lust."

She gave him a little mock curtsey, and tucking the book under her arm, went upstairs.

The end of that year, in the full bloom of the hot Argentine summer, Brenna was called out to the stable by one of the boys. She hurried, a sense of unease rising up in her throat. She arrived to find Minx lying in the straw, nostrils dilated, breathing in ragged gasps. With a cry, Brenna flung herself down in the straw, her arms going about the animal's neck, tears springing from her eyes.

"Oh, Minx, not you. You're my only true friend," she whispered into the mane, where she had so often put her face before. She felt the horse shudder beneath her, and she looked up tearfully at the head stable groom, who shook his head hopelessly.

"It is her heart, senora," he volunteered. "I've noticed that the last few times you've taken her riding, she has returned more winded than usual."

"Why didn't you tell me?" she demanded in agonized tones. "I wouldn't have taken her out."

"Senora, what will be, will be," he said, punching at his hat nervously.

She looked back at her horse—dear Minx, the last link with her old homeland. Had it been—how long?—over twenty years ago that she had leaned against the corral fence and watched a red-haired, freckle-faced stable lad bring the silky black mare over to her? How long it had been since her father had teased her and told her she could have the little horse for her own.

"Oh, Minx," she said again, forlornly. "Surely you don't have to die now?" she pleaded, her tears running into the mane. "Don't leave me, old friend. If you go, who will bear me across the pampas?"

The horse whinnied gently, nervously, and Brenna became frantic to do something for her. "Is she in pain?" she asked the groomsman. "Is there time to get the doctor?"

"Senora, I have sent a boy for him," the man told her, embarrassed by the intensity of the woman's emotion.

Brenna nodded and began stroking Minx's neck and shoulders, whispering soothing words, singing disjointed phrases she remembered from old Irish songs. As she knelt there, memories assailed her from every direction—she and Minx riding among the emerald hills of County Wexford; riding to the fox hunt and that terrible day when the mare had reared up and struck Steven in the head; the first day Steven had ever kissed her as they stood beside the mare—and the more recent memories of the long rides on the pampas, the delighted laughter when Katie and then Maria had been allowed to ride their mother's horse. Surely, Marc would have his turn, she thought frantically. She continued to stroke the satiny skin as her mind pictured a black-haired girl on a black horse galloping madly along the valleys, through the creeks and up the hills, delighting in life and revelling exuberantly as the wind whipped her hair back away from her face. All of her youth had been shared with Minx. So many years, she thought.

"Senora—"

She looked up, startled out of her reverie. "Yes?"

The man nodded toward the mare. "Senora, she is gone."

Brenna's whole body jerked as she looked downward; her hand still automatically stroked that beloved neck—so still now, so very still, the muzzle quiet, the large, liquid brown eyes unseeing. With a sudden cry, Brenna bent over in pain and bewilderment and loss; racking sobs shook her body. In her grief, she barely heard the voices around her.

"Mama? I wanted to find you—"

Brenna looked up to see her eldest looking down at her worriedly.

"Mother, are you all right?"

"Oh, Katie, I am so sad right now. Minx has died."

Katie looked from her mother to the mare. "I'm sorry, Mother. Here, take my hand, and I will help you back into the house."

In a daze Brenna stood up and felt her daughter's hand fold comfortingly around her own. It did not seem odd to her that Katie was leading her inside, upstairs to her room. Oh, Minx, she thought again, what fun we would have had together; you and I and Katie and her own little mare!

A sudden tinkling of music filled the loneliness of Brenna's soul, and she looked up from where she was sitting. Katie, sitting on the stool at her feet, held the little music box with the dove on it. With a soft smile, Katie handed it to her mother.

"Look, Mother. Remember how you used to give me my music box when I felt sad or lonely? Remember how we would listen to its music and laugh and dance and pretend we were princesses?"

Brenna nodded, staring at the white, alabaster dove with the sapphire eyes.

"Now, you mustn't cry anymore. Listen to the music," Katie said.

"Listen to the music," Brenna repeated softly, and held the music box against her heart.

Chapter Fifty-Seven

DURING the late 1880's Buenos Aires seemed hysterical with the fever of sudden wealth and progress. Everyone was launching into a frenzy of speculation, confident they could pay loan obligations out of future profits. Banks and corporations were organized without capital. Instead of trying to stem this trend, the government, under the direction of Celman and his advisors, encouraged it.

Carlos frequently came home late at night nearly exhausted from meetings, his voice hoarse from delivering fiery speeches. Brenna wondered how he could keep the pace up. For the last two years, these political meetings had become a way of life for him—a life far more important than his own family.

Because Carlos no longer cared what she did, Brenna became involved in charitable organizations, fund-raising events, and the like, trying to fill her empty hours with activities to take her mind off the misery of her private life. It wasn't that Carlos was physically brutal—his indifference hurt more than anything.

"Go ahead," he told her when she would tell him her plans. "Perhaps you will run into Steven."

She had given him a cold eye and taken the children with her. It was spring—a time to grow out of the stagnant life she had endured for so long. Katie was fourteen now: old enough to help decorate booths and attend meetings; even Maria, at eleven, enjoyed helping. Little Marc, who was now a robust three years old, played happily and beamed like a small cherub, quite melting the hearts of the matrons who spoiled him generously. Ordinarily, Brenna might have tried to curb such precocious behavior as Marc was beginning to display, but she hadn't the heart to cancel out the love he got from others when Carlos still refused to warm to the boy.

Oh, sometimes Carlos talked with him, asked him

about his activities. There were even times when he acted like a normal father, but then, when the mood struck him, he would shut the boy out again, leaving Marc bewildered, uncertain, and wondering what he had done to anger his father. At such times, Brenna felt her heart wrung with pity for both the boy and the man.

Now, at the charity bazaar, as she watched Marc toddling between Katie and Maria, she sighed and shook her head. "Keep an eye on your brother, Katie," she called out. "Don't let him put his fingers in the pastries again."

"Yes, Mother," Katie called back, reaching down just in time to prevent a pie from toppling to the floor.

Brenna felt a tentative hand on her shoulder, and she turned around, brushing at a smear of flour across her cheek. A young woman was staring at her.

"Brenna?" she asked finally, tentatively. "Brenna Valera?"

"Yes?" Brenna answered, smiling pleasantly, then her mouth rounded in surprise. "Rosaria!" she cried.

Her visitor smiled with delight. "Brenna, I wasn't sure it was you—it has been a long time, hasn't it?"

"Too long," Brenna agreed, laughing as she reached over and hugged the other woman. "How have you been?"

Rosaria shrugged happily. "Diego and I are wonderfully happy."

"Diego. My goodness it has been a long time," Brenna said. "How time flies! Sometimes I wake up in the morning and think I'm still a young girl instead of a middle-aged matron of thirty-five."

"I'm not far behind you," Rosaria laughed. "With five children, mind you! Three boys and two girls—Diego would love to make it an even half-dozen, with the addition of another girl, of course." She smiled to herself fondly.

"Five! Good Lord, I've only three," Brenna said incredulously. Rosaria was only a sixteen-year-old when Brenna had first come to Argentina. Now she was a thirty-one-year-old woman with five children. "What are you doing here?"

"The same as you, baking pies for the poor," Rosaria chuckled. "Diego would rather I bake them for a cause than eat them myself." She displayed the figure which had blossomed from girlish thinness to rounder proportions. "But you, Brenna, you haven't changed at all. Not even a gray hair yet. It's a crime!"

Brenna smiled. "I suppose I haven't anything to worry about," she commented, then wished she hadn't said it as she saw Rosaria's face become curious.

"I see Steven quite often when he's in town," she said softly.

"Oh?" Brenna replied airily. "How is he? I—I suppose you know that he and Carlos—they—"

"I know. I can't imagine why Carlos has changed so, but then I suppose we all have, haven't we?"

"I suppose," Brenna said hesitantly.

"Brenna—you and Steven—"

"Rosaria, I'll not permit you to concern yourself with my affairs," Brenna said firmly.

"All right. I understand. Did you know that Steven was offered the position of Minister of the Interior by Celman, but he refused it? He said the administration was too full of corruption for him to want any part of it. A big change from Roca, I would say."

"Dear God, I suppose that's why Carlos is so exhausted when he returns from his political meetings. He must be frothing if there's word of corruption in the government— just the sort of thing he and his friends pounce on, you know."

Rosaria nodded thoughtfully. "Steven's been spending most of his time out at Paloma. The shorthorns are doing wonderfully, and we've planted a quarter of the land with alfalfa to raise them. He no longer uses the old *saladero*, of course, no one with any brains does anymore. He's even put up barbed wire around the *estancia* —it's cheaper than wooden fences and keeps out the stray longhorns that some people persist in raising." She shook her head. "I suppose he's lonely out there."

"Lonely?" Brenna asked, telling herself it didn't matter to her. Wasn't she lonely too?

"Yes, he never has remarried, you know."

"No, I didn't know. I—Carlos—" She reddened, then changed the subject. "How are your parents? Consuelo and Miguel are glad, I'm sure, to have their son with them finally."

Rosaria's face fell suddenly and her lip quivered. "My mother died last year, Brenna."

"Oh! Rosaria, I'm so sorry. Believe me, if someone had only told me, I would have come to the funeral." Brenna looked at the other woman sincerely, "I truly liked her, Rosaria."

"She loved you too, Brenna," Rosaria said softly. "Father, ironically enough, is still very much alive, although his health has deteriorated since Mother died. His heart hasn't been strong for a long time, and Steven thinks it only a matter of time."

"I'm sorry."

"I think my father is just biding his time, waiting and hoping that Steven will marry again and give him the heir he's wanted ever since I can remember."

Brenna shook her head. "Odd, how tenaciously we hold onto our dreams, isn't it? I suppose Paloma will go to you and Diego if Steven dies without an heir."

Rosaria nodded. "But you know, Brenna, I'd be happy to give up the *estancia* if father could have the joy of knowing that Steven had a son to carry on the name. Diego's father has plenty of property—half of which will go to Diego, and the other half to his brother. My children will be well provided for, even without Paloma."

"Poor Miguel," Brenna said softly. "How hard it must be for him. Steven should remarry and give him a grandson." Her voice turned hard.

Rosaria shrugged. "I've tried, God knows, to convince my hard-headed brother of that very thing, but he refuses to tie himself to another woman he doesn't love. Odd, I have never thought my brother a romantic. But, after all, he is thirty-eight and old enough to make up his own mind without my help—as he continually tells me."

"You'll simply have to try harder," Brenna said, going back to work on the pie in front of her, hoping to get away from the subject of Steven. She wasn't sure just how much Rosaria knew of their relationship, and she didn't want to tread on dangerous ground where a slip of the tongue could cause her embarrassment.

"It's like trying to talk to a barbed-wire fence," Rosaria put in with a slight chuckle. "Every time I try to get close to him, I wind up getting the worst of it."

Brenna's attention was caught by a slight ruckus to her left, and she looked over, not really surprised to see Marc the center of the distraction. Wiping her hands on her apron, she excused herself from Rosaria and went to retrieve her son from another disaster. She walked back, cuddling him close and chastising him for not being a good boy.

"Mama, I was good!" Marc insisted with a sniff.

"Oh, I suppose I must believe you then," Brenna said with a smile, unable to stay angry at her son for long. She brought his attention 'round to Rosaria. "This is Senora Garcia, Marc, a friend of Mama."

"How do you do, Marc?" Rosaria smiled, patting him maternally. "My, he is a big boy, isn't he? And such a handsome fellow."

"Oh, don't tell him that," Brenna warned. "He already hears it too much, and I believe he's becoming quite vain." She tousled Marc's hair affectionately.

"How old is he?"

"Three."

"My goodness—and your girls are what?"

"Katie is fourteen and Maria is eleven."

Rosaria laughed. "Eight years between your second and your third, Brenna—that's a lot of self-restraint. Now Diego would never have let me get by with anything over—oh—three years!"

Brenna turned away abruptly. "Carlos didn't want so many children," she said softly.

Rosaria reddened at her blunder. For a time, they worked silently, each thinking their separate thoughts. Then Rosaria sighed aloud. "Listen, Brenna, you really

615

must come and visit Diego and me sometime. Bring Carlos with you."

"I—I'm not sure—"

"We're in the town house on Santa Fe Street until the summer; then we'll be out at Paloma for a couple of months before we go down to the seashore. You really must come visit. I want you to meet my children—I'm shamefully proud of them," she laughed. "And I'm sure Steven would like to see you."

"No, I couldn't," Brenna said quickly.

"But—"

"I really couldn't. Ever since Carlos and Steven—well, I just don't think it would be a good idea, Rosaria. But —sometime I'll come and bring the children over to the town house to visit you and Diego."

Rosaria gave her an odd look and seemed about to open her mouth when she caught sight of a man moving toward her. A sly, slow smile crossed her face and she stretched idly, keeping an eye on Steven's progress through the crowd of women. Several of the unattached ones eyed him hopefully, even brazenly as he passed politely by; he was such a handsome figure—mature-looking with a wisp of gray at his temples, his moustache and eyebrows still black and perfectly shaped. His constant riding and working about the *estancia* had hardened him, kept him trim.

Rosaria was not sure what had happened between her brother and Brenna Valera, but she was not above playing a little trick on both of them to see if she could find some answers. She kept a wary eye on Steven, waving to him surreptitiously so that he could find her; then, as he walked purposefully toward her, she glanced at Brenna, who was again giving her son a lecture on the art of behaving oneself in a public place.

"Over here," Rosaria called to her brother. And as he approached, "Look who I've bumped into, Steven."

Brenna straightened and quickly turned at the mention of his name. Her blue eyes widened in surprise as she met his dark gaze. His eyes were unreadable. At that

616

moment she felt Marc tugging at her skirts for attention.

"It's Brenna Valera, Steven."

"Rosaria, I'm quite aware who it is," Steven replied and bowed to Brenna. "Your servant, as always, senora," he murmured.

Brenna felt as though she would strangle if she spoke, and her distress increased as Steven noticed the movement of the small boy at her side.

"Another child, Brenna. My heartiest congratulations," he said absently, although his black eyes were intense as they slid over the young boy.

Marc blinked innocently at this fierce-looking stranger and shrank against his mother. "Mama, I don't like him," he said pointedly.

Brenna shook herself out of her silence, appalled at the boy's reaction. "Marc, darling, don't be silly. This is a friend of your papa and mama. Mama has known him a very long time." She dared not look up at Steven, so she bent to comfort her son.

"I don't like him!" Marc said belligerently in a higher voice.

Brenna looked distressed. "Marc—"

"Come here, boy," Steven said suddenly, hunkering down so that his face was on the same level as the child's. "Come here and introduce yourself."

The boy's belligerence faded rapidly under this direct assault. He gazed up at his mother questioningly, then at her nod, he took a step forward and bowed like a young gentleman. "Your servant," he piped in a trembling voice.

For the first time, Steven smiled. "That is much better. Your father did well to teach you the proper manners," he said approvingly.

Marc looked up. "My papa didn't teach me," he said truthfully. "Mama did, and my sisters."

Steven glanced up at Brenna's frozen face, his left brow arching sardonically, but all he said was, "Then they are to be commended, for every gentleman needs some supervision in the proper way to act."

"Are you a—gentleman, sir?" Marc asked seriously.

Steven stood up and laughed aloud, causing several curious heads to turn in his direction. His black eyes caught and held Brenna's gaze for a moment. "Well, I'm not sure. You would do better to ask your mother about that, boy."

"His name is Marc," Brenna put in breathlessly. She looked down at her son. "This is Senor Castaneda, Marc."

"Steven," the older man cut in, smiling easily at the boy now.

Brenna moved impatiently. "I think we're finished, Marc. Why don't you find your sisters and tell them we'll be going home now." Marc nodded and went in search of them.

Brenna looked around for Rosaria, but she had disappeared. Brenna, now alone with Steven, brushed flour from her apron, wondering what to say. "You're looking well," she finally managed.

He smiled, aware of her turmoil. "So are you, Brenna." He leaned slightly toward her. "It's good to see you again."

She appeared skittish, looking around as though she thought people were watching them. He smiled again to mock her fears. "I don't think this is the kind of rally your husband would attend."

She looked up at him. "Perhaps not, but his friends have wives who might say something."

He frowned suddenly. "What's this? Does Carlos have you watched?"

"Steven, please, it really is not your business."

"For God's sake, Brenna, is it because of me? Is that why you looked like a scared rabbit when you saw me? What on earth is happening to him?"

"Steven, it's not your concern. I can manage him myself. Please . . ."

"Brenna—" He stared at her, knowing she had no idea how he ached to touch her.

"Steven, the children are coming back. I had better go."

"Katie is here? And Maria?"

She nodded miserably. "It would be better if they didn't see you. They have never understood why you and Carlos quarreled, but—"

"Brenna, Katie's my daughter," he said in a hushed voice. "How can you deny me?"

"Think of her feelings. She's fourteen now, practically a young lady. She can't be expected to understand all this." She gazed up at him pleadingly. "I know you love her, Steven, but it all happened such a long time ago, and she's grown up thinking of Carlos as her father, believing her real father died before she was born. You can't change that now. It's too late."

She watched in anguish as his face tightened. "You've grown hard, Brenna. I was wrong to think you hadn't changed. How could you help it—living with that fanatic all this time?"

"Oh, Steven—"

His black eyes snapped around the room, looking for Rosaria. With an abrupt bow, he left Brenna standing hopelessly alone.

Chapter Fifty-Eight

CARLOS' group of dissenters had grown considerably from its humble beginnings. Several distinguished people, who were often in the public eye, had joined their ranks. There were many thinkers and doers, who lent a veneer of respectability to the group. And still, among them all, walked the somber form of Hipólito Irigoyen, who was gradually finding acceptance as their leader; he held them entranced as he spoke of God-given rights and equality of the soul, which were the birthrights of every man.

President Celman and his government officials fueled the cause of the opposition, for graft and incompetence ran riot in the national administration, and the government had begun to print paper money as fast as it could be spent. Earlier in the decade, Roca had established a national currency freely convertible to gold; paper notes had been issued and supported by the Buenos Aires customhouse, but their gold value fluctuated wildly with every revolution, war, depression, and boom. By the mid-1880's, inflation and gold shortages had forced the authorities to declare the paper peso inconvertible and to revert to daily market quotations for the peso's gold value. Now widespread corruption and speculation was beginning to take its devastating toll, further discrediting the oligarchy in power. The people told themselves that, now, any government official could be bought. For Celman and his friends, it was the beginning of the end.

One day early in 1890, Brenna heard Carlos in the library, talking heatedly with friends. She stood in the hallway, reflecting what a farce their marriage had become, how dismal life would be without her three children to love and return that love wholeheartedly. Carlos seemed to have forgotten about their existence. He seldom slept at home, and when he did, he was up late with his business affairs, then went to bed on a cot made

621

up for him in his study. Brenna hated what her life had become, but there was nothing she could do to change it. She had asked Carlos to grant her a civil divorce, but he had only looked at her strangely, almost with triumph at her misery—and he had told her that he would never consider such an action.

She had decided that, despite the wall that had grown between them, it was time that she spoke to him about Katie. The girl would be sixteen in June, only three months away, and they must make some decisions about her future. Brenna had talked with her often of late, and Katie had expressed a desire to see her maternal grandparents, an idea which had taken root in Brenna's mind and had grown until she had all but decided to make the trip with all three children. Marc was five years old now and well able to make the journey.

Brenna waited patiently, sitting on the bottom step of the staircase, watching the hands of the hall clock wind slowly about its face until, finally, Carlos came out of the room and saw her sitting there.

"What are you doing up so late?" he inquired cooly.

She stood up, stretching her cramped muscles. "I wanted to talk with you, Carlos."

He frowned. "If it's about a divorce again—"

She shook her head. "No. It's about our children."

He seemed startled when she mentioned them. "What's the matter? Haven't you enough money for suitable clothing, schools, food? Have the girls had trouble at the academy?"

"No. They're doing quite well at school," she said quietly, surprised that he had even thought to ask. "Specifically, I wanted to speak with you about Katie."

He shrugged. "Brenna, I have people in the library right now. It will have to wait."

She took a step forward urgently. "It can't wait, Carlos. I have already let it wait over long, and now I finally have your attention for a few moments. I don't know when I may have it again."

His frown deepened. "Brenna, for God's sake, I can't talk to you now."

"Katie will be sixteen in June," she interrupted quickly. "and we haven't yet made any provision for her future—school, travel, marriage—"

"Marriage?" He snorted derisively. "I'll advise her against it."

"You know nothing of Katie, Carlos. She slipped through your fingers years ago. You know nothing of her friends, her dreams, her wishes. You've let fatherhood go by without enjoying it. It's almost too late with Maria, too. She's thirteen now, and quite a young lady." She refrained from mentioning her son.

Carlos winced as he thought of all the years of love he had denied his children. For a moment, he looked shamefaced, but the look quickly disappeared. "I'll let you attend to their dreams, Brenna—you are their mother, after all. When it comes time to make betrothal plans, you may have Katie come to me. I won't have you matching her with anyone not of our political persuasion."

"Carlos!" Brenna felt anger tinge her cheeks pink. "Don't you care about your children anymore—at all?"

He started. "What are you talking about? I see that they're fed and clothed. They can be proud of their father's name . . ."

"I'm talking about love—or has that been totally driven out of you?" She stopped and looked at him. "I feel sorry for you. We could have had a wonderful life together—watching our children grow, growing old together, awaiting our grandchildren—"

"What nonsense are you spouting, Brenna?" he said impatiently. "I have six men in there waiting for me."

Brenna drooped with weariness—she had worn herself out against his stubbornness, his indifference. "All right, Carlos. Go back to your friends. I just want to tell you now, that in June or perhaps July, I'm taking the children on a trip to Ireland. Katie would like to see my family, and I don't think it's too much to allow her that. I know you wouldn't want me to leave the other two with you, so I'll take them all with me."

Carlos eyed her thoughtfully now. "You want to leave me?"

She followed his drift of thought. "Just for a trip. I'll not cause any scandal by abandoning you," she assured him.

He scratched at the stubble on his chin. "I've got to get back into the library, Brenna, but I don't want you to make any more plans until we've talked further."

"We are going, Carlos," she said with angry impatience. She turned and started up the stairs.

"I'm warning you, Brenna, don't push me on this," he called after her.

She stopped on the last step and looked down at him over the bannister. "I'm not pushing you, Carlos," she said with deadly quiet. "I've waited almost seventeen years for this—and you're not going to stop me."

"Damn you, woman, make your plans then!" he yelled up at her and returned to his guests.

A few weeks later, one evening in April, Carlos curtly told Brenna that he was going out to meet with some of the leading young men of the city, and that he would be back very late. He slipped out the back door of the house, and Brenna watched him go without curiosity. He often left this way, since it seemed that government surveillance of his activities had intensified lately.

A little while later, as she and the children were sitting in the drawing room, busy with their own activities, the knocker on the front door sounded. A servant appeared a few moments later, followed by three gentlemen dressed in military garb.

"Yes? What is it?" she asked, rising from her chair, thinking that perhaps something had happened to her husband.

One of the men bowed and introduced himself. "Alonzo Gomez, senora. May I speak with your husband?"

Brenna looked at him suspiciously. "My husband isn't here right now, Senor Gomez. Perhaps if you came back tomorrow—"

"I'm afraid I must speak to him now, senora. I have my orders." He produced a sheaf of notes with the presidential seal affixed to one of them.

"Then you will have to search for him, senor, for, as I have told you, he is not here. He left only an hour or so ago for a meeting."

"Precisely, senora, and do you know where this meeting is taking place?"

She shook her head. "I'm afraid, senor, that my husband and I never discuss his political activities—or perhaps you are already aware of that," she added with a sarcastic slur on the constant surveillance put on her.

The man's lips clenched involuntarily, and he noticeably stiffened. "Senora, you cannot expect me to believe that your husband does not inform you of his whereabouts."

"That is precisely what I expect you to believe, senor," she answered him.

The man appeared frustrated and looked to his two companions for help. "Senora, we have orders to take your husband for questioning. I'm afraid that if you refuse to cooperate, we will have to take you in his place."

"That's absurd!" Brenna snapped. "I have no affiliation with my husband's causes. Senor, I think you should leave us now."

Gomez turned to the other two, and after a whispered conversation, turned back to Brenna who was trying to control a sudden attack of trembling. "Senora Valera, I'm afraid I have no choice but to take you back with us for questioning. If you will kindly get your cloak? . . ."

"Senor Gomez, you cannot—surely you cannot be serious."

"Most assuredly, senora. Now, please come quietly." Gomez motioned to the children who were all staring wide eyed, mouths open. "I assure you it is only for questioning."

Brenna could see she had no choice but to obey. Reluctantly, she collected her outer wear, instructed Katie what to tell her father should he return, left the children in Teresa's hands, and followed Gomez to his coach as the other two soldiers formed an armed escort. This was all a mistake, she told herself stoutly. Surely, Carlos couldn't command this kind of attention from Celman.

Inside the government administration building, she was ushered into a small anteroom with a guard posted at the door. She stared about her cold, bleak surroundings, noting the total absence of any decorative touches. Was this some kind of interrogation room? she wondered, her amazement giving way to nervous fearfulness.

She was obliged to wait nearly an hour before Gomez came in with another man who introduced himself as Señor Romero. Romero was a short, fat man with a balding pate—the kind of man you would expect to see behind a shop's counter, she thought.

"Senora Valera, you have been brought here for questioning. I am told by my informants that your husband is plotting treason against the government." Romero squinted as he spoke. "You do know of your husband's activities, don't you, senora?"

"I—I only know that he and his friends meet often and discuss politics," she replied carefully.

"Politics, senora? Like overthrowing the government and supplying arms to revolutionaries?" He leaned over her and she could smell garlic on his breath.

"I don't know what they discuss, specifically," she answered. "I do not attend their meetings."

"But, in the privacy of your chambers, senora, I'm sure you and your husband must discuss something of what goes on."

"My husband and I—do not sleep in the same chambers, senor," she said with some difficulty.

Romero did not appear surprised. "But you live in the same house, don't you?" he pressed. "Surely you see him at dinner time, during the day, when his friends come over?"

"Yes, but we—never discuss his politics."

"Never, senora?"

She nodded. "He knows that I disapprove of—of his friends."

"His friends?" he prompted.

"Irigoyen, Além—"

"Ah, now we are getting somewhere. Do these two men visit your husband often?" Once again Romero was leaning closer, almost nose to nose with her, so that she began to feel hemmed in, strapped to her chair.

"I—I don't know. They usually come when I'm out. I—detest them."

Romero, pleased, smiled at her. "If only your husband shared your good sense." He stroked his chin reflectively. "You told Gomez that your husband went out tonight to attend a meeting. Is that correct?"

She nodded. "But he didn't tell me where he was going —only that he would be home very late."

"He told you nothing of the nature of this meeting?"

She wrinkled her brow as though trying to recall. "No."

"You are certain of this?"

She looked up at him. "Yes, of course. I told you. . . ."

"We have it from certain people that your husband, along with Irigoyen and his uncle, are meeting to organize an opposition front. They have already named it: The Young Men's Civic Union." His eyes turned piercing again. "Have you ever heard that name before?"

"No." She said with conviction.

"This group plans to harm our president in some way," Romero went on. "An open rebellion—or perhaps an assassination."

"Assassination?" Brenna whispered. "My—my husband isn't a murderer, Senor Romero. He—he has a family. . . ."

Romero shrugged. "Don't we all, senora?"

"But he would never agree to anything so violent," she said staunchly. "Carlos is not a violent man."

"We have heard that Irigoyen and his fiery speeches can drive a man to extraordinary deeds. They think of him as a saint." His mouth drew down as though the word tasted sour in his mouth.

Brenna recalled the changes she had seen in her husband since he had come under Irigoyen's influence. Romero, keenly studying her face, watched the understanding dawn in her eyes.

"Ah, senora, so you do know what I mean, don't you?" he asked softly. "Now, tell me what you know, and we can get your husband away from this dangerous man. You must help us, senora."

She looked at him blankly. "I cannot help you, for I do not know where he has gone. Please, senor, you must believe me when I tell you that I have not discussed his political causes with him for many years."

Romero let out his pent-up frustration in a sigh. "You realize, I assume, that your husband could end up in prison should he and his friends try anything foolish."

"Prison?" She felt a sudden coldness assail her at the word as she recalled the day her brother came home from the Dublin jail and told her of the horrors there.

"President Celman will not tolerate sedition," Romero told her.

"But—you have no proof—"

Romero's eyes sparkled dangerously. "We will get the proof we need, senora."

Brenna realized that her husband would have little chance against someone like Romero. Despite everything, Carlos was in essence a man who believed in his own cause, and everything he did was for the good of that cause. This man who stood in front of her now believed only in his own power, a power without a conscience.

"I'm sorry, but I cannot help you, senor."

His eyes continued to hold her gaze. Finally, he moved away from her with a snort of disgust. "Let her go," he commanded abruptly.

Brenna stood up stiffly and hastened to the door. She was about to pass the guard, when Romero's voice stayed her a moment more.

"Remember, senora, you have been warned. It might serve you well to tell your husband of our meeting and of the warning I have given you. Believe me, should he try anything which could be construed as harmful to the president—it will be the end of him."

Chapter Fifty-Nine

BRENNA waited anxiously for Carlos to return home; it
had been weeks now, and she still had received no word
from him. Of course, she assumed he had found out about
her meeting with Romero and had hidden himself with
others of his party members. She could only hope that
he would stay hidden.

Winter came upon the city. Still Brenna could do nothing but wait for Carlos to come to her. She must warn
him, must urge him, plead with him—do anything to convince him that his life was in real danger.

Late one afternoon, a carriage rolled up in front of the
house, and through her window, Brenna watched a tall,
cloaked figure emerge and walk up to the door. Something about his bearing was hauntingly familiar; then she
realized, her heart hammering painfully under her ribs,
that it was Steven Castaneda.

With a glad cry, she opened the door to him, flinging
her arms about his neck, careless of anyone who might be
watching them.

"Oh, Steven! Oh, Steven!" she sobbed. "Oh, I'm so glad
you've come!"

"Hush, dearest. Let me close the door first so that
those bastards outside won't be able to watch." He fla-
vored his warning with a touch of mockery, watching as
she pulled away from him anxiously.

"Are the children here?" he asked, pulling her with
him into the drawing room.

"Katie and Maria are in school. Marc is next door
with a friend. . . ."

"Alone at last," he mocked her, but there was a tender
look in his eyes, a look she was too upset to notice.

"Oh, Steven, don't tease me now, please. I'm so frightened. I don't know where Carlos is. A man named Romero
questioned me about his activities a few weeks ago, and

since then, I haven't seen or heard from my husband. I'm afraid."

"Brenna, Carlos is all right," he said softly.

"How—how do you know?"

He motioned her to a seat, then sat down beside her, taking her hands in his own. "Brenna, I've seen Carlos. No. Listen to me and don't interrupt." He took a breath and his hands tightened on hers. "Celman's government is corrupt—it's blacker than any we've had in the last thirty years. The officials are bribed, the government coffers have been skimmed too many times to count. The paper peso is practically worthless and the entire country is heading for a depression."

"What has this got to do with—"

"Be quiet, my dear, you never could resist interrupting." His black eyes were grave. "Through my own contacts in the business world, as well as in the government, I have found out just how deeply in trouble Celman is. Even a small rebellion could topple him from power. I endorse Carlos' reasons for wanting to oust Celman, but the vice-president, Carlos Pellegrini, is not attached to all this corruption. My constituents feel he is the man to assume the presidency—at least until elections are held again in two years."

"But Pellegrini is a *porteño*," Brenna broke in again, "a citadel of the upper class. I've heard Carlos talk of him—and he doesn't like him anymore than he likes Celman."

"But Irigoyen and his brotherhood can compromise—as long as they get Celman out and get rid of the corruption with him."

"They'll never do it!" Brenna exclaimed. "Pellegrini's parents aren't even of this country—they're both immigrants. I've heard Carlos refer to him as 'The Gringo.' I'm sure—"

With a small frown, Steven held her hands fast and bent closer to close her mouth with his own. For a moment, Brenna forgot to take a breath as she felt Steven's lips on hers. So gentle, so sweet, she thought, feeling a faraway ache inside of her. He released her, but did not move away.

"Just to quiet you for the moment," he said, his black eyes even more intense. "Although, I must admit to my selfishness in choosing my method." He grinned ruefully.

"But you said you have seen Carlos," she prompted him, unwilling to be led from the subject.

He nodded. "I was almost shot for my pains, but I was able to get in to see him. Yes, Brenna, they have arms now—and plans for a full-scale revolution. God knows, we don't want a bloodbath now. Irigoyen can be damnably stubborn, but your husband finally relented enough to speak with me, and I told him what had happened to you."

"What did he say?"

"He told me to stay out of his business. I think he still suspects me, because of my past political affiliations." He shrugged as though to say there was nothing more he could do to convince him.

"So you think they will go ahead with their plans?"

Again he shrugged his shoulders. "With Irigoyen leading the way—from behind the battle lines, I'm sure. I must admit, Brenna, I don't like that man even though I can empathize with his beliefs. It's just the way he wants to go about it that worries me. A rebellion, unfortunately, usually hurts innocent people the most."

"But why are you concerning yourself with all of this?" she wondered.

"Perhaps, in my middle-age, I have finally developed a conscience," he said with wry amusement. "I've looked back on what I've done to you, Brenna, and I realize that I may have contributed to some of your unhappiness. Your children are getting older—they need a father, not a political revolutionary who is never home with them. I thought, perhaps, if I can throw my own support and that of many other *estancia* owners behind Irigoyen's cause, the nation might be able to avert bloodshed and appoint a president to govern until the next election."

Brenna's cheeks flushed a little at his confession, and Steven, lifting her chin with a finger, looked into her eyes. "It amazes me, my dear, that you still look so refreshingly innocent. How can it be that we've known each other as

631

long and as well as we have—and yet we can never be completely at ease with each other?"

"Steven there are too many things between us," she said quietly.

He sighed, and for a moment, his dark eyes were stormy. "Too many things," he repeated. "God, Brenna, when I think of all the wasted years. I couldn't even watch my own daughter growing up."

"You should have married again, Steven," she murmured. "Rosaria told me that your father—"

"Old Miguel won't give up—even now that he's dying. It's been coming on for a long time. I brought him into the city from Paloma, despite his protests. Now he lies upstairs in his bedroom, holding on—holding on. . . ." Steven brushed a careless hand through his hair. "Perhaps you're right, Brenna."

"There can never be anything between us again, Steven. Carlos has refused me a civil divorce, and there are no grounds for an annulment by the Church."

"Ah, I wondered," he said thoughtfully.

"I—I've asked him to let me take the children back to Ireland for an extended visit. Katie wants to see her grandparents."

"Ireland," he said absently. "It seems so far away and long ago, Brenna."

"Yes," she admitted.

"But—you'll be coming back?"

"I've promised Carlos."

They were both quiet for a moment, each thinking of the past, until Steven shook himself out of his reverie. "We must be getting older, Brenna," he laughed sardonically.

She looked at him, frankly assessing the handsome masculinity that he still seemed so careless of, the long, black hair with a hint of gray, the clear, black eyes, the strength and character in his face. Dear God, how handsome he was, she thought with a renewed ache. At forty, he was in his prime—and it was a shameful waste to see him go without a woman. He should get married, she told herself and felt a hurt in her heart at the thought of Steven marrying again—marrying a younger woman who could give him many children.

"I hope you find someone suitable. . . ." she began, then faltered altogether.

"Brenna, you're a hopeless fool if you can't see that I—"

"No, Steven, don't say it, please. I couldn't bear it. I have to stay as I am, as Carlos' wife."

"You haven't been a true wife to him for a long time, Brenna," he reminded her gently.

She shuddered with embarrassment that he knew so much about her life. Well, at least Carlos had not mentioned his suspicions about Marc's parentage. It would be so senseless to bring it up now, she thought wistfully.

Steven stood up silently, walking agilely over to the window. "It seems we've gotten off the track," he said. "I came here only to give you news of your husband."

"I'm grateful," she answered.

He shook his head. "Would you still feel the same gratitude if you knew that I would give anything to have an hour alone with you? A free hour, Brenna, so that I could love you and have you all to myself—and pretend, for a little while, that we had finally found each other." He laughed at himself. "A foolish dream for a grown man. I'm becoming like my father."

"Poor Miguel—I would like to see him," she commented, switching the subject adroitly.

"He would like that."

"I'm sorry about your mother. I told Rosaria that I would have come to the funeral if only someone had told me of her death."

"I know."

Once again there fell an awkward silence. It was interrupted as the door banged open, and her son spilled through. His face was bright, although his left cheek sported a ripening bruise.

"Mama, I've beaten Roberto next door. He said—" He stopped at sight of the visitor.

"Marc, what have you done to yourself?" Brenna cried, hurrying over to him.

"It was just a little fight, Mama, don't fuss," he said proudly, eyeing the stranger, who looked somehow familiar. "Do I know you?" he asked bluntly.

Steven smiled. "I met you two years ago at a charity bazaar."

Marc frowned and winced at the pain in his cheek. "I didn't remember, but I knew I'd seen you before. Are you a friend of my father?"

"No."

"Oh!" Marc looked at his mother. "Why is he here?"

"He came to tell me about where your papa is," Brenna explained, still trying to examine the bruise. "Stay right here and let me get a clean, wet rag to put on that. Don't you move, young man."

Brenna returned a few minutes later to find Steven seated on the sofa with Marc on a stool by his knee, listening to him as he described Paloma and the beauty of the pampas. She hurried over to her son to apply the cold rag.

"Mama, Steven's been telling me about his *estancia*. He's invited us out to visit. Oh, Mama, we can go, can't we? It would be such fun—better than visiting old Ireland!"

Brenna eyed him severely. "Marc, you know how much your sisters and I want to go to Ireland."

"Then you go, and I'll stay with Steven."

"But—you can't stay with Steven." Brenna looked to Steven for help.

But he was not in a mood to give her aid. "Of course, he can stay with me. Marc and I could ride out on the pampas, and Guido could show the boy how to throw a horse and rope a steer."

"Mama, it would be such fun!" Marc crowed enthusiastically. "Better than anything!"

"Well—perhaps—" she said, willing to say anything to get past the awkward moment.

"You promise?"

"Yes, yes, I promise!"

"Hooray! I'll be a—a—what do you call it?" he asked Steven.

"A gaucho."

"Yes, a gaucho! I'll ride horses all day and drink rum and smoke cigars. . . ."

"Hold it! No drinking or smoking until you're at least six," Steven warned with a smile. The boy grinned up at him, and Steven felt himself warming to little Marc instantly. "You've a remarkable son here, Brenna," he said.

"A remarkable son who is getting his dirty shoes all over the carpet," Brenna remarked. "Marc, you go out back and wash at the pumps."

"Oh, Mother!"

"Now!"

Marc gave his mother a rebellious look, then glanced at Steven, who winked at him. "Better do as your mother says," he ordered. "Don't worry—I won't let her forget her promise. I will see you at Paloma."

Marc let out a whoop and ran out of the room in typical headlong flight. Brenna watched him go, then turned back to Steven, catching the thoughtful look on his face. "Carlos must be proud of that boy."

She stood up, agitated. "Steven, you really shouldn't have made me promise. You know Carlos wouldn't like it—"

"To hell with him! The boy needs to be out in the fresh air with a horse underneath him. Too many women surround him here." Steven laughed at her righteous look. "You know I'm right—the boy needs a father who is home more often."

"Steven, Marc is not your concern."

He mumbled inaudibly, then shrugged. "Perhaps we had best return to the reason for my visit." He reached into his pocket and drew forth a small, folded note. "Carlos wrote this and gave it to me to give to you."

"Carlos! And you didn't tell me!" she accused him, snatching the paper from him.

"I have saved the best for last, my dear. Now, I suppose I must leave you to read his loving words in private." His tone was suddenly terse. "Just remember, should you need anything—"

"Thank you, Steven." She watched him walk toward

the doorway. "I'll—I'll try to come and see your father before I sail for Ireland."

"You'd best not wait too long," he said insolently, and bowing again, walked out the door, leaving her with the letter clutched in her hand.

It took her a moment to open it and scan the contents. Carlos had written very little: only that he was in good health, high spirits, and he was hoping events would happen quickly so that he could come home again. She wondered why he even cared to come home. He made no mention of Steven. Brenna gazed at the letter with disappointment. It had told her nothing.

Chapter Sixty

In 1890, the bubble finally burst. A rebellion against Celman was led by the Young Men's Civic Union, which now numbered nearly 15,000 followers. The Civic Union's slogan, spread about the city through pamphlets and brochures, was: "Free elections," condemning the practice of government interference.

On July 26, the rebellion broke out in the streets of Buenos Aires. Brenna was sitting in front of the fire with all three of her children, for schools had been cancelled because of rioting and looting in the city.

"Mother, is Father out in the streets—with the revolutionaries?" Katie wanted to know, her sixteen-year-old form draped anxiously in a chair close to Brenna's.

Trying to maintain calm, Brenna looked evenly at her children. "I'm sure he is. His last letter to me told the rebellion was coming and that he would be in the thick of it." She shook her head, not understanding. "Poor Carlos, I've never even seen him hold a gun, much less shoot one."

"Will Father be all right?" Maria chirped, her brown eyes wide with worry.

"I don't know, Maria. We must all pray for his safe return to us." Brenna bit her lip, wondering at her own hypocrisy. Did it even matter to her anymore whether or not Carlos ever returned to them? She was still planning to leave for Ireland, although her departure now had to be delayed a few days. But even if Carlos did come back before they left, she would not cancel the journey.

"Mama, what if Papa is killed?" Marc demanded, lying on the floor with his head propped on one hand. "What will happen to us?"

She flushed and started at the directness of her son's question. What would happen to them? Would she leave for Ireland—and never come back? She could sell this house—with the money, she could certainly make a fine living for herself and her children without relying on charity from her family. She gazed worriedly at each of her children.

Katie, at sixteen, was on the very threshold of complete womanhood. She reminded Brenna so much of herself at that age, that Brenna would often recall little things from her own girlhood which she had thought she had forgotten. She was glad that Katie loved animals, and planned to give her a horse of her own for her sixteenth birthday, but that had to be postponed until they heard from Carlos. Already, the dark blue eyes and long, curling black hair proclaimed her a beauty, and Katie was going through her first adolescent "crush" on her history professor, something hardly to Brenna's liking as she recalled that Irigoyen had once had that very same job and had gotten a student pregnant during his tenure.

Still, Katie had something of her mother's sense of self-respect and honesty, and Brenna felt sure she would not throw it away on an indecorous incident. But Katie needed her father, Brenna thought. She needed a strong male to act as a model for her in her own selection of a husband.

Maria, at thirteen, was entering that awkward stage of puberty, resentful that she could no longer be considered a child and unwilling to take on the responsibility of a young adult. She too needed her father to listen to her girlish problems and display a loving interest to help her through her hard times. She was truly Carlos' daughter with the same-shaped face and form, the same large, brown eyes. Only her hair was different, lighter than either her father's or mother's, reminding Brenna of her own mother's shade of chestnut.

Marc . . . Brenna sighed as she let her eyes slip lovingly over the small five-year-old. Even more than the two girls, he needed a man around. Steven had been right to say the boy was around too many women. Brenna could tell that he chafed under their constant supervision and concern—he needed to be a wild little heathen once in a while, to release all the pent-up energy of boyhood, and a father could understand that. He needed a father to be both an indulgent friend and a stern judge. If Carlos came back to them, she resolved to speak to him about the boy. He must realize by now that he could just as easily be his own son as Steven's. Marc was black-haired and dark-eyed, tall and sturdy—there was absolutely no way to tell for certain who his father was.

"Well, Mama?" he prompted her now. "You're dreaming again."

"Marc, you'll never have to worry about what will happen to you as long as you have me to protect you," she said confidently. "We must all stay together and try to cooperate with each other—until we hear from your father."

Marc sighed. "I guess this means I can't go out to Paloma?"

Brenna hesitated. "Not now, dear, but perhaps, later. We'll see."

He scowled, then flopped forward onto his stomach, his chin propped on one arm as he stared into the fire.

"Will there be fighting here?" Katie asked, her distress showing clearly.

"I don't know, but I'm sure if there is any danger, someone will come to our aid."

"Uncle Steven will protect us," Maria said confidently. "He loves us, doesn't he, Mother?" She turned wistful in one of those quicksilver moods that marked her age.

"Yes, of course, he loves us."

"If he loved us, Mother, why did he stay away for so long?" Katie wondered.

"He and your father argued about something," Brenna explained patiently.

"But what did they argue about?"

"Well—they both believed differently about the government, and—"

"Will Uncle Steven be fighting too?" Maria cut in.

"Darling, I don't know—"

"Mama, I'm hungry!" Marc proclaimed suddenly. "Can we ask the cook to set the table now?"

Brenna sighed and reached down to ruffle her son's

black hair. "You're always hungry, aren't you, you raga-muffin?"

He grinned and shook his head. "I want to get fat and fatter until I burst!" he crowed, hopping to his feet. With a mischievous look on his face, he reached over to pull a jeweled pin out of Maria's hair. "I've got it!"

"Give me that, you little grasshopper!" she cried out, clutching at her falling curls. "Give me that or I'll catch you and slap you good!"

Marc stuck his tongue out. "Come and get it, then!"

"Mother! Make him give it to me!"

"Now, Marc, give Maria her hairpin, or you will go to bed without dinner," Brenna scolded. "I'll not have you teasing your sister today when we must all keep calm until we hear something—"

"I won't give it to her!" Marc declared belligerently. "Not unless you let me go out to Paloma with Steven!"

"Marc! You'll do as I say."

"No! No!" He skipped about the chairs nimbly, speeding out of Maria's grasp when she reached out to catch at his shirt.

"Marc, do as Mother says," Katie put in, slapping at his hand when he tried to pull out one of her hairpins.

"Catch me!" he challenged and sped away out of the room.

"Mother!" Maria cried, mortified as her hair fell over her face. "Oooh!" And she went racing after her brother, presumably to box his ears in if she caught him. Brenna looked helplessly after her.

"Mother, you really should do something about Marc. He can be such a horrid little urchin," Katie sniffed in an injured tone. "I'm afraid to take him anywhere with me for fear he'll embarrass me in front of my friends."

"Katie, he's your brother," Brenna chided. "And he's the littlest in the family. Don't you think it's hard on him to have no one in the house his age, or even his sex?"

Katie reddened under the rebuff. "But, Mother, we do try to be nice to him."

"He needs more than that," Brenna sighed thoughtfully. "He needs the supervision of a father. He needs—"

She stopped, not wanting to burden her daughter with these problems. "Just try and be patient, dear. Now, please go and find them both before they hurt each other."

Katie nodded and left the room, leaving Brenna alone to sit in front of the fire and wonder where her husband was.

After the explosive violence of July 26, there followed two days of fierce, serious fighting. Both sides claimed victory, with the Civic Union even gaining support from some of the disgruntled government military. But the uncertain division of command in the opposition between the military and the civilians gave the national authority its chance to bring supplies and loyal forces in from garrisons in Rosario and Córdoba. This did not diminish the Civic Union's fervor. The fighting continued with heavy casualties on both sides. The entire city had taken up arms on one side or the other and most women and children were bound to stay indoors during these two days.

Finally, in the interest of protecting these innocents, the revolutionaries laid down their arms. The leaders of the Civic Union were either arrested or, like Hipólito Irigoyen, they fled into exile. His most loyal ally, Carlos Valera, was not so lucky.

On the morning of July 29, Brenna was in her bedroom, pacing nervously, still awaiting word of her husband. She had heard, through rumor, that Carlos had been arrested and imprisoned. She recalled the evil, cold eyes of Senor Romero the day he had questioned her. If Romero had anything to say about it, Carlos would be in prison a long while.

"Brenna?"

She turned swiftly, startled to see Steven Castaneda standing at the doorway to her bedroom. When she saw the serious look he gave her, she immediately realized he had brought bad news. Trembling, Brenna sank to a chair, gazed up at him in trepidation, and folded her hands in her lap.

"It is Carlos? You have word."

Steven nodded, devouring her with his eyes as she sat waiting for him to speak.

"He—he has been imprisoned by Celman?"

"Celman has abdicated, Brenna, in favor of the vice-president, Pellegrini, for even though the rebellion was crushed, the government had been so completely repudiated by the people, that Celman was forced to resign. I think Pellegrini represents a compromise which will work —at least until the elections are held again."

"But Carlos—then—"

"Brenna," he sighed finally, "Carlos is dead."

"Dead." It was not a question, but a repetition of the fact. Brenna, even though she had tried to prepare herself for this, could hardly grasp the reality of it. "Carlos is dead," she said again, as though saying the words might make them clearer. For some reason, she thought of Kevin Ryan, gone almost eighteen years now. Another husband to bury—another husband who had left her. She felt a heavy weight descend on her. The children —she must think of them.

She stood up automatically and went to Steven. Her eyes seemed to look through him. "Thank you for bringing me the news, Steven. At least, I know now what has happened."

"Brenna, I know this is not the time, but—"

"No, I must go tell the children," she said, not hearing him. "They must know."

"Brenna, I know you're in shock over this, but you must think of the future. I'm not sure if there will be any repercussions from Carlos' actions, but you may be involved in more government action, unless I can persuade Pellegrini—"

"The children and I are going back to Ireland," she said, still looking at a point beyond him.

"To Ireland?" His black eyes gazed with growing impatience at her still face. "Don't be foolish, Brenna, you can't make any plans until all this is straightened out."

"I'm going!" she said, the placidness finally leaving her face as she met his gaze. "You can't stop me, Steven. I want to go home."

"Brenna, for Christ's sake, don't talk like a child. The authorities aren't going to permit you to leave Argentina until after they've conducted a thorough investigation and with the turmoil in the government right now, that may take weeks."

Her chin went up stubbornly. "I'm going, Steven." A sudden, scared look crossed her face. "You won't let them stop me, will you, Steven? You do understand, don't you? I—I must go home. . . ."

"Brenna, you can't leave now."

"I'm going!" she cried, her voice rising stridently. "I'm going, Steven, and you mustn't stop me! I'm going home!" She put her hands up as though to strike at him.

He caught them easily and held them without force. He could see the tears welling in her eyes and the weariness in her face. "All right, Brenna, my love, I'll do my best with Pellegrini. But you must promise me something."

She shook her head, like a contrary child.

"Yes, Brenna, you must," he said again, releasing her wrists and tilting her chin up so that he could look into her eyes. "You must promise me that you will come back."

"There is nothing for me here," she said in a faraway voice.

A look of pain crossed his features, followed swiftly by anger. Once again he grasped her hands and forced her to look at him. "Listen to me. Yes, look at me! I won't let you go—do you hear me? I don't know what's gotten into you, but those children need a father. Katie is mine anyway, and I'm not about to lose her to someone else. I've waited too damn long to let her—or you—go now!"

Brenna looked at him like a sleepwalker. Nothing of what he said was sinking in. She was obviously still too deeply in shock to understand what he was saying. With an impatient sigh, he released her hands.

"I'll try to arrange for passage to Ireland," he said slowly. "But they will be round-trip tickets, Brenna."

He bowed and was about to leave, when he suddenly

turned her back, pulled her close against him, and with contained ferocity, bowed his dark head to take her mouth, kissing her masterfully, leisurely, as though he were willing to wait the entire day for her to respond.

Brenna felt strong arms around her for the first time in a very long time, and instinctively, she relaxed against them, letting him hold her, grateful to have someone to lean on. It would have been pleasant if he had just held her without kissing her, she thought in the back of her mind. She really didn't feel like kissing now—there was so much to do. Why didn't he let her go? She had to tell the children, had to pack their luggage, had to close up the house . . . These thoughts all flew through her head like flittering birds trying to find a place to land. But it was hard to continue such thoughts when Steven was kissing her, demanding a response that was suddenly, almost without warning, beginning to grow within her.

His lips were so warm, she thought with bemusement, so warm and soft—unlike any other man's who had ever kissed her. Of course, there hadn't been so very many, she told herself. There had only been—who had there been? It was becoming more and more difficult to think as he engulfed her with his presence, pressed her closer to him, bent her backward, held her head in the crook of his arm.

Slowly, inexorably, warmth spread through her body, growing into pleasurable liquidness that tingled in her flesh. Her hands went around his neck, creeping up from where they had been stilled against his chest. His hair was soft and thick against her fingers, and she pressed against it to bring his mouth ever deeper into hers. Her own mouth moved beneath his, and she returned his passion, forgetting, for the moment, the children, the luggage, the house.

When he finally released her and looked into her face, her eyes were still closed; the vein in her neck pulsed rapidly with the beat of her heart. Steven smiled at this picture of vulnerability. But he was also aware of his own feelings, his own quick breathing and his desire to protect her.

Brenna opened her eyes and smiled into his, her fingers still curled in the hair at the back of his neck. Her breath passed her lips in a sigh.

"Do you still want to go back to Ireland?" he asked her softly—and immediately realized his mistake as the dreamy look left her face and reality once more made it purposeful.

"Yes," she answered with a touch of willfulness. "I must go back."

"Brenna, you don't."

"Steven, please don't tell me what to do," she said extricating herself from his arms. "I've been on my own for a long time, despite the fact that I had a husband. I've learned to take care of myself."

He had to smile at the cocky picture she drew of herself. He longed to hold her again, to show her that he could take care of her from now on. But the look on her face warned him off.

"All right, Brenna. I suppose you know your own mind." He reached out, almost playfully, and tweaked a stray curl against her cheek. "You will come back, though—preferably without a new husband. I'm getting tired of waiting to catch you in-between marriages." He laughed and bowed again, then left her standing there, alone.

Chapter Sixty-One

TRUE to his word, Steven used his influence to obtain a full pardon for Carlos Valera, thereby clearing his name of any wrongdoing. Brenna was now free to go wherever she wanted. She had expected to see Steven again before the date was set for her ship to leave, but to her surprise, and disappointment, he made no more attempts to dissuade her from going. Sulkily, she wondered if he had really meant all his fine words. In the three weeks that had gone by, perhaps he had decided that he wanted someone else—someone younger—

Working herself into a fury, she charged the servants with packing their luggage and placing dust covers on the furniture. On their last night in the city, she and the children checked into a hotel nearer the waterfront so they would be sure to make their ship's sailing time a little after dawn.

It was with some surprise that Brenna received a visit from Rosaria Garcia. Ushering her guest into the drawing room and ordering tea, Brenna glanced at the woman suspiciously, as though expecting some plea on Steven's behalf—sending his sister over to speak for him, she thought disgustedly.

But Rosaria's visit took a different tack. "Steven has told me that you plan to go back to Ireland."

"Yes, we're leaving tomorrow morning. In fact, you caught me as I was about to have the children gather their things together for the overnight stay at the hotel. The carriage will be sent 'round soon."

"Then I am glad I came as soon as Steven told me." Rosaria looked at Brenna seriously. "My father is dying, Brenna. The physician says he may go at any time during the night, or perhaps tomorrow, but—there is no hope of another recovery like the last time."

"Oh, Rosaria, I am so sorry. I wish there was something I could do," Brenna said sympathetically.

"You could come and see him before you go," Rosaria suggested quietly.

Brenna bit her lip. "Oh, but I have so much to do before tomorrow morning. The ship is leaving just after dawn, and I—" She stopped, helplessly watching the swift change of expression on Rosaria's face. It was on the tip of Brenna's tongue to refuse flatly—there was something too painful in going to bid the old man farewell.

"I understand, of course," Rosaria said sadly, and stood up swiftly to take her leave. "My best wishes go with you on your trip, Brenna."

"No, wait," Brenna said with a sigh. "Tell your father that I will come as soon as I can this evening—but, Rosaria, please don't tell Steven. If he happens to be out when I arrive, it's all for the better."

Rosaria nodded. "Thank you, Brenna. I'm sure Papa will rest easier, knowing that you are safe and happy."

Brenna showed her out, wondering if she, herself, truly was safe and happy. Crafty old Miguel—would he notice the sadness and confusion inside her? She didn't know his condition, but she almost hoped he was not lucid enough to ask her any questions. She would rather not go, but she had committed herself. She thought a moment, then decided to take the children. Their presence would be needed to keep a distance between herself and Steven, should he be there.

After their luggage had been taken aboard the ship—only two suitcases put in their hotel room—and dinner had been eaten, Brenna told her family of Miguel's illness, and that they would visit. Katie and Maria, who both remembered Miguel from earlier times, expressed their sorrow and dutifully prepared themselves to go. Marc, on the other hand, never having met or talked with Miguel, grew sulky, as he had already planned to work on a model ship Brenna had purchased for him to keep him busy during the voyage home to Ireland.

"But, Marc, Miguel is a dear friend of mine," she explained patiently. "He knew Katie and Marie when they were little girls, before you were born."

"I don't care!" Marc said. "Why do we have to go?"

"Marc, how can you be so mean?" Katie demanded. "Miguel is Uncle Steven's father, and he was always good to Mother and Marie and me. You should be ashamed of yourself!"

Marc sulked, his lower lip puffing out for a moment. "Why do you call him Uncle Steven?" he wanted to know, changing the subject. "He's not our uncle, is he, Mama?"

"No, he isn't," Brenna admitted, "but he wanted your sisters to call him that as a symbol of affection. He has always taken an interest in all of you."

"Not me," he said with a touch of woefulness. "I wasn't around to share all those good times that Maria and Katie told me about."

"Marc, don't be silly. Steven loves you just as much as he does the girls," Brenna said firmly. "Didn't he promise to take you to Paloma and teach you to ride a horse?"

"Yes," Marc said reluctantly.

"That was a nice thing to promise—and now you must show how much you appreciate that by going with us like a good little boy to see Steven's father."

"Oh, all right, I guess I will then."

Brenna breathed a sigh of relief. "Now come along. I don't want to be out too late. We have an early morning ahead of us."

They arrived at the Castaneda town house just as the street lights were being lit. The interior of the house was dark and hushed, causing Marc to grab a handful of Brenna's skirt for reassurance. Together, they climbed the staircase to Miguel's bedroom where two or three servants huddled together outside his door, weeping silently into their handkerchiefs.

"Mama, I don't want—" Marc began plaintively, but was quickly hushed by his sister.

Brenna, understanding her son's trepidation, told the three children to wait in the hallway while she went in. Inside, Rosaria conversed quietly with the physician, while her father lay in the curtained bed, his eyes closed, his breathing hardly more than a whisper. Unaccountably, Brenna was reminded of the night that Dolores had died in this same house. She shivered at the memory.

"Oh, Brenna, I'm so glad you have finally come," Rosaria whispered, tears streaking her cheeks. "Please come over—I told him you would be here."

Brenna reluctantly walked to the bedside, taking a seat on the stool close to the old man's pillow, looking with shock at the wasted face and the sparse white hair, which barely covered his freckled skull. She tried to remember how he had looked so long ago when she had first come to Argentina, but the memory eluded her and she could only stare numbly at him, feeling a lump forming in her throat.

"S-Steven?" the old man croaked, his eyes still closed.

"No, father, it's Brenna—Brenna Valera. You remember?"

"Where is Steven?" he whispered.

"He has gone out for a few minutes to the apothecary. He'll be back soon, father." Rosaria soothed, stroking the claw-like hand. "But Brenna is here."

"Brenna Kildare," Brenna clarified. The ache in her throat made it hard for her to speak.

"Ahhh," the man sighed, opening his eyes. "Brenna."

He looked at her a long moment. Brenna wasn't sure whether he was having difficulty in focusing, or whether he just wanted to reassure himself that she was truly here at last. Shame burned hotly within her breast, and she remembered those many months before when Rosaria had told her about his illness—she had not even come to see him. Tears gathered in her eyes and burned until she could no longer hold them in. Why had she been so horrible, so wrapped up in her own problems that she could not even spare an hour to visit the man who had helped make her father rich, who had always welcomed her into his home, who was, after all, the grandfather of her daughter—who might even be the grandfather of her son.

Miguel's eyes closed suddenly, as though he were satisfied at having seen her. After a pause, he drew a long breath and whispered, "It's good to see you again, Brenna."

"Oh!" Brenna chewed her lower lip, the tears falling afresh at the simple pleasure she could have brought him months ago with only her presence.

He must have heard the sob that escaped her. "Don't cry for me, my dear. I'm not unhappy to be leaving this life—I've missed Consuelo." He sighed. "Of course—I'll miss my children—and m-my grandchildren . . ." He stopped.

"Yes?"

"I—always wanted a—grandson, you know, from—Steven. Would have liked to see him—"

"I know," she said, swallowing hard and pressing the hand she held.

"Doesn't matter anymore, I guess—damned, stubborn boy—" He sighed again and was still for so long that Brenna looked up, fearful he might have drifted off.

"Paloma," he said softly, almost inaudibly. "Wanted it to go to Steven's son. . . ."

Brenna's heart stood still as she contemplated telling the old man a lie. Was it a lie? It would ease his mind if he thought—no! She couldn't. She patted his hand comfortingly, all the while knowing the best way to ease him on his way would be telling him that Marc . . . No. No! It wouldn't be right. Her soul cringed at the thought and she suddenly looked about the room wildly, as though some grinning devil lurked in the shadows, daring her to speak, but she only saw Rosaria near the door, weeping quietly into her handkerchief, while the physician tried to comfort her.

Listening to the catch in the old man's breathing, as though he were trying to cry, she made up her mind.

"Miguel, listen to me," she said in a low voice, but with an intensity that willed him to listen to her.

He opened his eyes again, watery, dark, sunken eyes, drowsy with death. She hoped he would understand, hoped she could make him understand.

"Miguel, you—you do have a grandson—Steven's son," she whispered, feeling his hand, beneath hers, moving with his sudden agitation. "Miguel, my son, Marc—Steven is—his—father," she got out, closing her eyes and waiting for heaven to strike her a blow.

But the blow was soft, gentle, and she realized that Miguel had put his hand on her head to make her look up at him. She didn't want to look up, didn't want to face those eyes, but the soft tugging at her hair, no more than a child's tug, forced her finally to meet his gaze.

"Brenna, you—and Steven?" he whispered. There was no surprise in his eyes; it was as though he had already guessed and had only needed this confirmation. "And—I have—a—grandson?" Two large tears rolled into the furrows of his face. "Let—me—see—him."

Brenna's heart stood still and fright assailed her. What had she done? What would Miguel say to Marc? How could she ask the boy to come into this room filled with death and listen to this old man? She wanted to refuse him, but could not find the words. Slowly, feeling as old as Miguel, weary with the weight of her own actions, she stood up and walked to the door, opening it and gesturing to her son.

Marc's small face whitened and his dark eyes grew large as he saw the look on his mother's face. For a moment, Brenna thought he might turn and bolt, but he rose from his seat and came toward her, his whole body trembling.

"Mama?"

"Hush, dearest. Miguel would like to meet you," she said softly, holding his hand and leading him into the warm, still room. They walked over and Marc leaned worriedly against the bed, as the old man stared at him intensely.

"Marc," the old man croaked, bringing a hand up feebly.

Marc caught the hand before it could fall again to the covers. He glanced at his mother, who nodded, and he held the old hand in his, still fearful.

"You are a—handsome—child," Miguel said, trying to smile, knowing somehow that the boy was frightened. "As—handsome—as your—father."

"Thank you, sir," Marc mumbled.

Brenna's body tensed as she waited for the fateful words, ready to deny them the minute they were spoken. She had to think of Marc—not an old man who would soon be gone.

"Do you—like—to ride—horses?"

Marc nodded, a little reassured by this commonplace talk. "Yes, sir. That is, I'm sure I will when Steven teaches me. He's—your son, isn't he?"

"Yes."

"He promised to take me to Paloma and teach me to ride a horse and herd the cattle and—and everything else. Mama said I could go," he added defiantly.

"K-keep her to her—promise, Marc." Miguel's lips thinned against his teeth in a weak smile as tears slipped down his face. "You'll—be a fine boy, a fine boy," he murmured to himself. His hand slipped out of Marc's grasp and lay limply on the covers. The look of struggle finally went out of the tired face. He had found his ease at last, and Brenna put her face in her hands to weep, hating herself for not bringing him this triumph long before.

"Mama, should we go?" Marc asked hesitantly.

Brenna nodded, wiping swiftly at her face. She looked back at Miguel, whose eyes were once more closed as his breathing seemed to grow ever more shallow. On impulse, she leaned down and kissed his cheek.

"Good night, Miguel," she said softly.

For a moment, she thought he hadn't heard her. Then his eyes fluttered open once again; the look in them was so very peaceful. "Thank you, Brenna," he whispered.

Brenna and Marc left the room as Rosaria went to sit beside her father, weeping copiously into her handkerchief, having heard none of the exchange.

Out in the hallway, Brenna motioned to her daughters that they would be leaving now. With a few kind words to the servants, they made their way downstairs just as the front door opened to allow Steven in. He looked distractedly at Brenna.

"You've already seen him?"

She nodded, seeing the obvious pain in his eyes.

"Thank heaven. I'm glad you came in time." He gazed upstairs and started to leave them, then stopped and looked back. "Thank you for coming, Brenna."

"Yes," she whispered, and watched him take the steps quickly. She hurried her family out to the waiting carriage and sat silently, lost in her own thoughts, as they went back to the hotel.

Chapter Sixty-Two

BRENNA passed a restless night, and it was with difficulty that she prepared everything for their departure the following morning at dawn. A servant would fetch their baggage for them, and she and the children would be deposited on the docks at the designated pier.

The children were still yawning, half-asleep, as they piled into the carriage and took the short ride to the pier. Spilling out onto the dock, they stood huddled together, waiting for the next oxcart to come to take them out to the john boats a mile from shore. Brenna could see signs of dredging begun in the channel and tried to visualize what the habor would look like when it was completed. Would she be there to see it? she wondered idly.

"There, Mother!" Maria called as she spotted an oxcart, emptying itself of its passengers from one of the incoming ships.

"All right then," Brenna said, searching through her reticule to make sure she had their tickets.

She was stopped in her progress toward the cart by a careening coach that spilled onto the dock, nearly knocking down an unwary stevedore. It came to an abrupt halt in front of her, so that she had to step sideways to go around it. The door was thrown open, and she gasped to see Steven, tall and somehow forbidding, as he jumped out and looked at her with no trace of a smile.

"Steven, what—are you doing—here?" she wondered casting a wary eye at her children, who were already climbing into the cart a few yards away.

"Brenna, why did you lie to my father?" he demanded abruptly.

She blanched and took a step backward. "What—what do you mean?"

"You know damned well what I mean! He told me what you'd said about your son. Yes, just before he died early this morning, he told me how happy he was that he had his grandson, finally." His black eyes were filled with rage. "How could you lie to a dying man?"

"Steven, I—"

"Brenna, I can't believe you would do this. What kind of a woman are you?" He was walking back and forth in front of her, his hands clenched tightly behind his back, as though if he were to let them go, he might try to strangle her.

"I—I only thought 'twould ease him. . . ."

Brenna bit her lip and stood like a guilty child, watching him as he stared back at her. The muscles of his lithe body rippled against his well-tailored clothing, slightly rumpled from his sleepless vigil of the night, as he continued to pace. The sense of his great physical power struck her suddenly as she watched the swell of his shoulders against his coat when he flexed his arms. His body seemed so tough and so hard, she thought—as tough and hard as his mind, and just as relentless.

His black eyes studied her from beneath those perfectly arched brows, and he seemed intent on waiting here all day in order to extract an explanation from her. She glanced worriedly over to the waiting oxcart.

"Steven, I loved your father," she began desperately.

"Like you loved your husbands, no doubt," he said swiftly. "At least if you loved him, you didn't bother to show it all these months he was ill."

"I—I know and I feel terrible enough about that without your throwing it up to me," she said, reddening now. "I've just had so—so much on my mind—"

"I know all about your problems," he reminded her.

His unrelenting anger stirred her own suddenly. "I said I was sorry, Steven. Your father was a sight more forgiving than you are."

"Because you gave him the dream he had always waited for," he told her, standing still and giving her an intense look. "You unlocked the door, you had the key."

"He died happy, Steven."

"He died believing a lie," he accused.

"It wasn't a lie!" she screamed at him.

He suddenly went so still that he frightened her. His black eyes closely studied her face, as though searching out the truth. "Brenna, you can't mean—"

Her anger drained away as she felt the weariness of the past weeks overwhelm her. "Oh, Steven, I don't know, I truly don't know! Yes, Marc could be yours. You remember that one night—when Carlos was gone? You came to me that night." She flushed at the memory and could not meet the flashing brightness of his gaze. "Carlos—he found out about it, and when Marc was born, he thought —he thought—"

"—that the boy was mine?"

She nodded, her eyes looking down at the dock boards.

"My God, Brenna, why didn't you tell me?"

She raised her chin a little. "What good would it have done, Steven? Another bastard? What could you have done about it? Carlos wouldn't let me go."

For a long moment, they were both silent.

"Brenna?" Steven began, taking a step forward. "Can you forgive me?"

She shook her head, bringing her hands up to wipe at the tears on her cheeks. "Crying again," she murmured to herself. "What is the matter with me?"

"Brenna—look at me," he said gently.

Unwillingly, she raised her eyes and met the black gaze. It was warm and melting now, willing her to stay. "Brenna, I love you," he said.

"No."

"Brenna, I love you," he repeated, catching her hands. "I want you to marry me."

"You don't want me," she said, suddenly fierce even through her tears. "You want Marc—you're just like your father."

"Brenna, my dearest love," he said quietly, keeping his gaze locked into hers. "You know I've loved you for a long time—and I've waited for you a long time. I was even willing to wait a little longer, to let you go to Ireland. I thought it would be good for you. You could rest there and think and come to believe that I love you. Then you would come back to me."

"Steven—"

"But now, don't you see? I can't let you go like this. I want my son and my daughter—and yes, Maria, too. I've already missed sixteen years with Katie that should have been mine, and it still hurts to think of everything I've passed up. I won't miss out on Marc too, Brenna. I won't."

"But, I told you, Steven, I can't be sure—"

"The boy has nothing of Carlos in him," he said slowly, confidently. "Paloma belongs to him—and to Katie and to Maria—and to us," he ended passionately.

"Steven, please, I—I can't think."

"I don't want you to think," he said. "My poor darling, you've been without a husband for so long that you still think you need to bear up under everything alone. Let me share some of that responsibility with you." He brought his face closer to hers, and she gazed into the depths of his compelling stare, finding there the raw flame of passion. "I love you, *mi paloma*," he said simply. "I have loved you for a long time, and I will love you for an even longer time."

"But—the children—how will we explain? . . ."

He saw victory within his grasp and allowed himself a small smile. "Gradually, darling, we can tell them the story. I know—I know there may be doubts, recriminations, guilt—but together we can do it!"

"Oh, Steven, I know you're right. But it has been so long a time since I could trust anyone else with my life, that I'm not sure that I can do it now."

"Do you love me, Brenna?" he asked her.

He could read the answer in those startling blue eyes even before she spoke. "I love you, Steven," she said softly.

"My sweet dove," he murmured.

"Oh, but Steven, we can't just get married—just like that—"

"We love each other and we can do anything we want," he said happily. "We'll live in sin a little longer if we have to, but I'll be damned if I'll let you slip away from me now. Come on, let's get the children."

Brenna looked up at him, and suddenly she felt as

though the great weight she had been carrying around for years was slipping away from her: the weight of guilt, of Carlos' indifference, of the pain of watching the years going by—all that was loosened and pulled away as she accepted Steven's strong arm around her.

"I have always loved you," she said as they walked toward the children.

Epilogue

ONCE more, spring had come to the pampas. Senora Brenna Castaneda de la Cruz stood in the large *sala,* the living room of the house that now belonged to her, watching her children outside in the corral with Steven. Gradually, they had come to accept the fact that their mother had remarried, and that they would be living at Paloma now. Steven had cautioned her about telling Katie, too quickly, about her real parentage. She was sixteen, growing into womanhood, and she was shy and awkward around this new man who was so handsome and charming. It would be a shock when she learned that he was, after all, her real father.

Then there was Maria to consider. She too thought Steven was the handsomest man in the world and blushed frequently when he teased her. It would be hard for her when she found out that Steven was Katie's father. It was a delicate situation, and Steven advised patience; the time would come to tell the girls.

Marc, on the other hand, was becoming more and more attached to Steven every day. Steven provided the boy with the love and interest that he had been starved of when he was smaller. Brenna smiled to herself thoughtfully, as she watched Steven helping Marc up onto a pony. Whether or not Steven was Marc's real father, it was clear to see that he would quickly erase the boy's painful memories of Carlos.

It amazed her sometimes to think how long she had waited—half her life—to be with the one man whom she could love as much as he loved her. Who would have thought, she wondered, when she had tripped over that rock at the tender age of twelve and embarrassed herself in front of a fifteen-year-old boy, that they would end up married to each other?

It had certainly surprised her family. She smiled to herself, recalling the letters that had come from her family—and the smile was mixed with tears of happiness, for at long last, she would be reunited with all of them. Steven had promised they would all go to Ireland for a reunion in the near future, for he agreed with her; it was time Nora and Tyrone met their grandchildren.

She wiped the tears out of her eyes to watch as Steven swung Katie into the saddle. As a late-birthday present, Steven had ordered a new riding habit made to fit Katie's lithe form out of dark blue cloth, exactly matching her eyes. He had given her a few lessons, and now she was ready to take one of the horses out by herself. Steven had selected a mare who had not yet bred, a dark, satin-coated horse, which stood patiently while Katie got the feel of the saddle beneath her and adjusted her feet in the stirrups.

Brenna felt a strange excitement rise within her as she watched Steven walk the horse outside the corral and give it a playful tap to send it on its way. Katie's face broadened into an excited smile as she tilted her head back and let the horse spring into a gallop away from the *estancia*.

Hurrying outside onto the low porch, Brenna shaded her eyes against the sun and gazed at her daughter as she rode the black mare down a small knoll and then came up again to level ground.

"Look, Mother!" she called, waving with one hand, as she guided the horse farther away.

Brenna waved back, feeling a wave of emotion wash over her at the sight of that slight, blue figure on the back of the black horse. How many times she herself had taken Minx out to ride just like this into the green hills of her homeland. She sighed with nostalgia.

When Steven saw her standing alone on the porch, he left Marc under Maria's watchful eye and strode over to put an arm about his wife's shoulders; he noticed the tears glistening in her eyes.

"She'll make a fine horsewoman," he commented, watching his daughter fondly. "Almost as fine as her mother."

"Oh, Steven," she half-laughed, ashamed of her tears.

"I guess it's a sign of age to think so much about the past."

He laughed and kissed her briefly on the lips. "We are so lucky to have each other in the present," he said. He kissed her again in a way that promised more later on. Then he walked back to the corral. Brenna sighed again as she went back into the house. Absently, she looked over at a nearby shelf and smiled to see the little alabaster dove music box sitting in its place of honor. She had felt foolish about putting it in the living room, but it was special to her, especially now, and she wanted it where she could see it during the day. She reached over, wound the key, and held it in her hands as she listened to the tinkling music and, through the window, watched her daughter ride the black mare over the blossoming earth, her black hair streaming behind her.

COPING, LOVING and SUCCEEDING

Ballantine has everything to help the modern woman in today's world.

AL-28